C.C. TYLER

TO RISE & REBEL

THE PROPHECY OF SORIN TRILOGY

To Rise & Rebel

Copyright © 2026 by C.C. Tyler

All rights reserved.

No part of this book may be reproduced in any form without written permission from the publisher, owner or author, as permitted by U.S. copyright law, except for use of quotations in articles or book reviews.

Publisher's Note: This is a work of fiction. Unless otherwise indicated, all names, characters, businesses, places, events and incidents in this book are either the product of the author's imagination or used in a fictious manner. Any actual person, living or dead, or actual event is purely coincidental.

Cover design by: Fantastical Ink

Developmental Edits & Manuscript Critique: Mallori Sorensen at Fiction and Fables

Copy Editing and Proofreading: Krista Dapkey at KD Proofreading

Interior Art: Stardust Book Services

Published by Author C.C. Tyler

www.authorcctyler.com

1st ed. January 2026

E-book ISBN: 979-8-9895549-6-6
Paperback ISBN: 979-8-9895549-7-3
Hardback: 979-8-9895549-8-0

Author's Note

Please note this book contains content that might be upsetting to readers, including violence, mature language, death, war, anxiety, hallucinations, and sexual content. It is not intended for anyone under the age of eighteen.

CRYSTAN
THE VOID
THE SAPPHIRE SEA
MORROW
SORIN
NOA CITY OF WITCHES
DRENGR VILLAGE
THE VADON MOUNTAINS WEREWOLF TERRITORY
CIRRILLO
CONNACHT CASTLE
TORREN
CALLUM
DINBERRY
LAKE GLENN
THE GRAY WOOD
KILDARA
N

To Drew. This one's for you.
Thank you for being the best partner.

PART I

*As frost bites trees and ferns, whispers
of Gods and Goddesses travel on the wind.
The banished One reaches from Below,
grasping the hope of a heartbroken mortal.
A bleeding bargain struck, weaved with
trickery, and the tendrils of immortality.*

Chapter One

Evelyn Carson was dying.

A full month had passed since the Blood Moon when she'd ripped her magic from her soul and placed it in the bloodstone. The gem reflected in the window she stood near, glinting more orange than red these days, evidence that her flame remained inside, locked away. They were no closer to getting her magic back than they were three weeks ago when they'd arrived in Nūa, the city of witches.

Autumn decorated her home city in hues of crimson and copper, and yet, winter was at Nūa's doorstep. Despite the ominous chill, leaves clung to the trees lining her sister's neighborhood, holding true. It seemed the city's best season was just as stubborn as its witches.

Evelyn wrapped her sweater tighter, hugging the fuzzy, warm material closer, and exhaled. Her breath fogged the glass ahead, blurring the warm, vibrant colors. The condensation disappeared as quickly as Evelyn's hope.

For her homecoming had been nothing she'd expected.

"Moons."

Paper smacked against the table behind her. She turned and found Kade in his seat, pinching the bridge of his nose. Evelyn sauntered over to him, putting herself between his legs. She cupped his cheek, making him peer up at her. Sun-kissed hair pulled back into a bun, beard recently trimmed and combed, and amber eyes with the power to buckle her knees—even frustrated, Kade Drengr, third born, protector, and Son of the God, was an exceptionally handsome male.

"What did I tell you about reading the papers?" Evelyn asked, raising a brow.

Kade grunted and pulled another one closer. "It's hard not to when they're posted on every inch of the city."

As if to prove Kade's point, outside the kitchen window, papers pinned to lampposts on the street flapped in the wind. Sketches akin to Evelyn's and Kade's likeness sat under egregious headlines inked in bold lettering.

Traitor . . . A disgrace to Sorin . . . A Rebel . . .

Nūa's dripping disappointment prickled across Evelyn's skin. She'd foolishly forgotten what it was like to be the Daughter of the Goddess. A spectacle. Someone others judged and marveled at, now more than ever, with her decision to run years ago. Even though she'd not yet walked the streets of home, locked in Mirella's townhome all to evade arrest.

The Elders, those that ruled over the covens and led the city of witches, had called for both her and Kade's arrest. Guards, the very army Evelyn had been a part of, hunted for them in the streets. The Son of the God and the Daughter of the Goddess, a third-born witch and werewolf prophesied to defeat the darkness in Sorin, had become outlaws overnight.

Because someone had leaked the truth, had wished to create unrest, to distract from the actual conflict at hand.

The Blood Curse.

"The things they say about you are horrible. *Wrong.*"

"It's lies," Evelyn said, pushing the paper back across the table. "This is typical witch gossip and exaggeration."

Mostly, Evelyn internally corrected. She'd ran and never married Kade, but for good reason. Evelyn believed that down to her bones, but the challenge would be convincing the Council. *If* she secured an audience with them.

Evelyn peeked over at the clock atop Mirella's floating shelves stocked with worn and well-used cookbooks. Her heart raced, anticipation creeping at her spine. Mirella had tried to convince the Council to call off Evelyn's arrest. She couldn't get her magic back sitting here doing nothing. Her sister had one final attempt with the Council today, but where was she?

"We should practice your new power," Evelyn said. Perhaps training Kade would pass the time as she waited for Mirella's news.

Kade lowered his hands to her hips, pulled her close. Flustered, Evelyn gripped his shoulder for balance. He'd brought them flush together, nothing separating their lips but a bare inch. His fresh-rain-and-evergreen scent comforted her, as did his kind stare roaming over her.

"Don't think for a second I don't know what you're doing," she whispered.

Kade brushed a thumb over Evelyn's bottom lip, and heat zapped through her. *Fucking flames,* this male.

"We have the house to ourselves. Why not pass the time with something we'd both enjoy rather than waste our time."

Right, because Kade hadn't conjured his power since the Blood Moon. That night haunted them both, and there were still nights Kade woke with a start, crying out Todd's name.

Indecision warred inside Evelyn. Not only had they shared a space with Mirella, her husband, Emmet, and their daughter, her sister was the Carson coven Elder, and visitors came and went often. *Hourly.* All too eager to reunite with her and pride themselves on keeping a secret from Nūa. Her and Kade's alone time usually happened at night when they finally excused themselves for sleep, and yes, of course they'd enjoyed each other, but the walls of their guest room were far too thin for the passion they thrived for.

They could both use a release, a moment to forget what they faced. Yet, Riven still remained a threat. The Blood Curse had its hold over Drystan. Demons and scáths crossed the Void more than ever—some truth in the reports they read in the papers. Even if Evelyn's magic was locked away, she and Kade both had to prepare, once and for all, to defeat the darkness.

"Avoiding your power also won't help it come forth," Evelyn said, taking the seat across from him.

"It's still there," he said. "It's as though I'm not connected to it. Not like my inner wolf."

There was still so much they didn't understand about Kade's power, seeing as other werewolves didn't possess similar traits nor was it similar to another witch's bronntanas. Still, power resided in the soul, no matter its origin or kind.

Evelyn sighed. "If you resent your magic, fear it, hate it even, it won't answer. I know from experience."

Kade flexed and unflexed his hand. "I feel like a right bastard struggling with my power when you're . . ."

Neither of them said the word out loud. What use was there when they both *felt* it? Or the lack of.

Evelyn's ripped soul had begun to fray, and that phenomenon extended to their mating bond. It was there, barely. She'd damaged the thread they'd weaved in the small cottage in Drystan. No mind linking. No sensing the other's emotions. Like an unfurling knot, it was risky to reach for it. The more one touched it, the more it came undone.

"Did Mirella say how long?" Kade whispered.

Evelyn didn't meet his gaze. Didn't have the stomach for it. Goddess, they didn't lie to one another, and Evelyn didn't dare about this. Not when her heart and whatever was left of her soul belonged to him. Too, they were in this together.

"Three weeks."

Kade stiffened. "That's . . ."

"No time at all. I know."

Kade rose, picking Evelyn up out of her seat, and switched places with the chair so she sat in his lap. He held her, nuzzling his face into her hair.

"We'll get your magic back," he said.

"I know," Evelyn whispered, voice cracking as she fought fear, tears, and anger.

At herself. Her city. And the *fucking flames* clock that indicated Mirella was late. Perhaps her meeting hadn't gone well, or she didn't have good news—

A tiny figure dashed into the kitchens.

"Uncle Kade!" Evelyn's niece, just shy of her fifth birthday, sprinted towards him.

Evelyn giggled, wiping tears away. She untangled herself from Kade's lap, giving him the opportunity to stand and squat down to Skye's level, bracing for impact. She leaped into his outstretched arms, and as Kade caught her, he rose to his full height.

"Well, good afternoon, Skye. What have *you* been up to all morning?"

Skye beamed. "Magic!"

Kade mocked surprise. "Is that so? What kind of magic?"

Mirella and Emmet entered the kitchen as their daughter said, "Lavender! And sleep!"

Skye took after her mother and Evelyn with her blue eyes, but her mop of russet curls was from her father.

Emmet sighed. "We learned today that Skye takes after her mother."

He gave his fated a wistful look, and Mirella beamed. They'd been together for almost fifteen years, and yet, Evelyn found their love as infectious as the first time Mirella had brought Emmet home for a coven feast. The two had spent most of the evening stealing glances at the other instead of mingling, the same glances they shared over a decade later.

"Yes, she lulled an entire wing in the infirmary to sleep. It was an eventful morning." Mirella shared a knowing look with Emmet, and Evelyn stiffened.

She braced her arms over the table, attention jumping between her brother-in-law and niece. Had her sister brought them on purpose? It wasn't a mystery that Kade held a soft spot for Skye or that Emmet had a knack for diffusing disputes between the three Carson sisters when discussions got heated. But usually, arguments started when all three were in the same room, yet Evelyn's middle sister was—

A breeze twisted through the kitchen, and Blair, the second-born scholar, stepped through her wispy *danu*. "Has the Council *finally* come to their senses?"

The same question sat on the tip of Evelyn's tongue, but she caught how Blair found the farthest position in the kitchen away from her. She fought the frown forming across her lips.

Evelyn crossed her arms and refocused her attention back onto Mirella. "Please tell me you have good news."

"Somewhat."

"Don't you dare start without us," a voice full of dramatics called.

Two more witches, Evelyn's twin aunts, strutted into the kitchen, both with the signature dark Carson hair.

They were Evelyn's father's sisters. The eldest twin, a scholar; the younger, a protector. Their birth order post wasn't enough to differentiate them from afar. They both sported leathers and Carson crimson, but Ruth, the third born, had an eye patch over her right eye.

"Italog demon," she'd told the Carson sisters as a bedtime story as children.

"We've waited for this all damn day." Ruth pointed at Skye in Kade's arms. "*That* was a good idea."

Emmet winked. "I take full credit."

"Since we've already alluded it's not fantastic news, can we move on with it?" Kade asked, but his tone lost all bite as Skye tugged at his beard.

"*Oof!*" someone grunted. "You've made us late. They've already started."

Evelyn clamped her eyes shut, rallying her breath.

Goddess, give me strength.

"We're right on time," another responded. "The problem is, I'm a cousin and *always* forgotten."

"You're a century old, Rodrick, let it go."

Evelyn's second cousin—if she recalled correctly—Rodrick, who didn't look a day over thirty-five, rounded the corner in tow with another. He pushed his spectacles up the bridge of his nose, swallowing as he caught sight of Kade. Everyone in the Carson coven had warmed up to him, but the senior scholar still hadn't grown used to Kade's tall presence.

Shifting is such a peculiar magic, he'd said.

Evelyn's great-uncle, Artie, jutted his chin towards Emmet and Kade in greeting—the three had created a quick comradery, all fated to a witch in the coven, therefore not Carsons by name.

Artie whistled as he took off his coat and wool cap. "Guards are practically blocking the streets these days. You'd think they hunted a vampyr, not the third borns."

Before anyone could entertain Artie's assessment of the city, Evelyn faced her sister. "Mirella, please, tell us their decision."

"Goddess, I forgot how impatient you are." The Carson Elder rolled her eyes. "I secured you a hearing with the Council in two days' time."

"Two days?" Evelyn asked. "Sorin doesn't have time for us to sit around and wait any longer."

She didn't have time. But she, Kade, and Mirella had all agreed the fewer who know, the better. They'd not told the rest of the Carson coven she was dying, including Blair. Kade hadn't updated Eldrick of it either in their letters to Drengr Village, which meant they were keeping the truth from Tovi and the Gray Fenris, too. Riven had a contact in Nūa, and they couldn't let him learn this setback. If he learned of this, what was to say Riven wouldn't capture her again and allow time to do its job for him?

Or worse, take the bloodstone back, and with it, Evelyn's magic. Sure, the Blood Moon had passed, but Evelyn didn't doubt Ingrid's determination to find another way to allow vampyrs to walk in the sunlight.

Emmet scratched his chin. "The other Elders disagree. Riven hasn't made a move or attacked. They're skeptical of both your claims as is."

"But there are rips in the Void," Evelyn said. "More demons than ever having been crossing into our lands."

"She's right," Ruth said, one eye landing on them all. "Reports came in this morning from the north. The papers are downplaying the danger."

"The *Council* is minimizing it." Evelyn shook her head, planting her hands on her hips. After a breath, she sighed, placing a hand on Mirella's shoulder. "I'm sorry. I didn't mean you."

Her sister grasped her hand, giving it a squeeze. "I'm the only Elder on the Council who still recalls there's a prophecy and a curse. All they're concerned about is their image, their reputation. The Elders are angry, blaming Evelyn for the lies they told their covens."

Kade shook his head. "Is it possible to get the hearing sooner?"

Mirella crossed her arms. "I already tried. This morning's discussion began with demands for your arrest, urging our coven to turn you both over by sundown. They insisted a trial for your 'crimes' against Sorin. I refused. Unless they want to attack the Carsons directly and start an internal war inside the Wall, so be it. Getting them to back down was no easy feat. A hearing was the best I could do."

Josepha, the scholarly twin, snorted. "They're hoping you'll both come out of hiding in those two days."

Mirella nodded. "Precisely. Both of you will need to stay out of sight. They're lifting the call for your arrest only on the day of the hearing."

"Fucking flames," Evelyn cursed. "I didn't miss witch politics and games."

"What's our best way to prepare for this hearing?" Kade set Skye down, and she raced over her to father.

Mirella lips fell into a thin line, and the rest of the witches didn't say a word. Silence swallowed the kitchen.

"Kade, Evelyn will be the only one to speak at the hearing," Mirella said. "You're permitted to *attend* the hearing. That is all. "

"What?" Kade shook his head. "That's unacceptable. It's us, the third borns stated in the prophecy. Evelyn's fight will always be mine."

"And what other choice do you have?" Blair asked, her question cutting through the group. "Leave the city? Evelyn already ran away, and that didn't exactly work out well, did it? She must face the Elders because of that decision, and hopefully they see reason."

Blair's comment didn't sit right with Evelyn. The accusatory tone laced into her words rose the hairs on her arms, and hurt swam in her gut. Why was Blair acting so cold? She'd expected this from Mirella, not her middle sister and once best friend.

Later, she decided. After she survived the Council.

"Kade, it isn't perfect, but this is what we want," Evelyn said.

He jabbed the paper on the table, jaw ticking. "I have a right to defend you. To clear the truth about the Daughter of the Goddess."

"I don't care about my title." The truth shot out of Evelyn before she'd fully thought it through. Yet, she'd considered this for some time now—*believed* it—especially with the fight to come. She stared at her coven members, even Blair who her refused to make eye contact, and then Kade.

His amber stare brimmed with pride and light.

"Daughter of the Goddess, Son of the God," Evelyn started. "Those titles don't define us, our actions do. In the end, it'll be our efforts that truly matter. That is what I'll remind the Council tomorrow. If I tell my story of running away, it opens the discussion to tell the truth of vampyrs, the Blood Goddess, the entire prophecy, *everything* to a room full of witches."

She crossed her arms, and her resilient being tightened. The council could ridicule her decisions all they wanted. In the end, their opinions didn't outweigh the threat Sorin faced. Evelyn didn't have time to care what they thought.

Literally. Her soul pulsed with pain as a reminder.

Yet, she'd triumphed over much these last two years and felt invincible, even without her magic, ready to take on whatever else the darkness threw at her.

Strong yet kind hands fell to her shoulders, and Kade nodded. An understanding passed between them. He was with her, no matter what. He believed in her, loved her, and that only fueled Evelyn's resolve to convince the Council to clear their names.

Then, they'd be one step closer to getting her magic.

Chapter Two

Eldrick

"We no longer accept Aramis Drengr as the Earl of the Vadon Mountains. The decree outlines everything. I'm afraid the decision is unanimous."

In the wake of Alpha Bjorn Johannes's words, silence rang in the grand hall of Lār. The blinding afternoon sun bled from the main window. There wasn't a cloud in the sky for miles. Not even the whistle of a breeze against the glass.

The stillness contradicted the war raging in Eldrick Drengr's blood.

It'd been three weeks since the council meeting when they'd discussed the prophecy, the curse, and the Blood Goddess. Eldrick hadn't considered the other alphas' lingering presence in the village—winter berated the Vadon Mountains with all its might these last weeks, making travel unwise, a reason enough to stay until the snow cleared. Despite being guest in the Drengr Village and recipients of their hospitality, the alphas had plotted right under his father's nose, in *his* territory.

"On what grounds was this decision made?" Eldrick didn't fight the shake in his voice. Let Bjorn hear his ire.

He'd believed the council meeting had made a difference. When Bjorn requested an audience with Eldrick and his father, they'd expected a discussion on strategy, planning how to proceed with the conflict to come, not a decree stripping Aramis of his title, a werewolf who, despite being poisoned by Claus, his own brother, had never yielded or stumbled these past ten years.

Bjorn's scar running from brow to cheek pulsed as he gritted his jaw. Two others flanked the alpha. His son Sam—one of the werewolves they'd set free in Drystan during their mission to save Evelyn—stood on his left, and a female warrior to his right.

If Eldrick recalled, she was the alpha's youngest daughter. Pinched brow, narrowed gaze, unruly dark head of curls like her father and brother, and nose stuck high in the air. Her hand rested on the hilt of the axe strapped to her hip, and Eldrick's inner wolf growled at the audacity she'd even enter the hall with it.

The air bristled with their beastly energy, yet their attire suggested they were readying to travel, not warriors gearing up for a fight. The hilt of Bjorn's sword strapped to his back glinted in the sun, bright against the signature Johannes green of their tunic and trouser. Northern packs customarily made their furs from bear and beaver, braiding chestnut brown tufts.

"We no longer trust your judgment, Aramis," Bjorn said.

A growl vibrated behind Eldrick, and he turned. His father seethed in his seat. He rose to his full height. Silver peppered the alpha's brown hair. His cheeks had filled out, his shoulders tauter. Thanks to Linx's healing remedies, his mate, Nadia, returned, and after almost a full month without wolfsbane, Eldrick's father grew stronger with each day.

Aramis prowled down the steps, joining Eldrick's side, and snatched the decree from Bjorn's hand. "If you're bold enough to set this in motion, you're bold enough to spit out the truth."

Alpha Johannes's daughter wrinkled her nose. "Your mate is a bloodsucker."

"Dalinda, hush." Bjorn sent her a glare. "Excuse my daughter's directness, but she is right. Nadia Drengr is a no longer one of us."

Sam flinched. The young werewolf appeared uncomfortable, standing with his father and sister, eyes focused on the stone floor. But Eldrick recalled Bjorn's anger the last time Sam had intervened, standing up for Tovi during the council meeting when the Johannes Alpha had first declared his mistrust of the vampyr queen. Eldrick's brows pinched as he considered the Johanneses. He and his father agreed on most matters, and he found the divide between Sam and Bjorn foreign. He couldn't imagine disagreeing with his father about something so important.

He grabbed the decree from his father, unfurling the rolled parchment. The opening words shot scorching anger through Eldrick's muscles, but he leaned into the surrounding silence, stilled his racing heart for a moment, and focused on reading the rest. It detailed Bjorn's message and was, indeed, signed by the alphas of the Vadon Mountains. Except for there were six names, six packs—Skau, Johannes, Thorn, Drabek, Aland, and Lindström—not seven. The Drengr's pack name was missing amongst the others that declared the end to a centuries-old practice, one that honored the Son of the God's pack as the ruling one.

"Nadia risked her life to reveal who Claus was!" Aramis's voice rose, his alpha baritone booming against the stone walls.

"Ah, yes, the Lone Wolf. That brings me to my next point." Bjorn surveyed Eldrick, expression hardening. "You killed Claus."

His gaze flicked between Eldrick and the very spot he'd shoved the wolfsbane down his uncle's throat. No blood stained the stone, nor guilt on Eldrick's conscience. Not a moment had gone by where he'd regretted his decision.

"My uncle deserved his end," he said.

"Perhaps, but there are laws amongst werewolves." Bjorn shook his head. "Despite your uncle's crimes, he had a right to a trial, and the alphas of the packs, not a next-in-line alpha, deserved to deliberate and decide his fate. Yet you acted out of impulse."

Eldrick bristled. By technicality, Bjorn *was* right. In the chaos of learning his uncle was the Lone Wolf and threatening Tovi's life, he hadn't thought consequences. With the sight of her in danger, Eldrick had lost all sense. It was no wonder he'd forgotten the customs of his people. Nothing else mattered but protecting her, a wild instinct coursing through his blood.

"Claus was threatening Tovi Verena, our neighbor's queen," he said. "I was simply defending her from an enemy in my home."

Dalinda's nose twitched, and her permanent scowl made her appear like she was always smelling something foul. "Drystan isn't our neighbor, they're our enemy."

"Riven is our enemy." Aramis released an exasperated sigh. "Unless you've all forgotten the council meeting, the true threat is the Blood Goddess and her curse."

"But the vampyr queen suffers from the same affliction, no?" Bjorn said.

"Yet she remains an ally. It's a disgrace to our kind, to those that lost their lives to her people's darkness," Dalinda added.

A sour taste coated Eldrick's tongue. It wasn't long ago when he'd shared Dalinda's similar disgust towards vampyrs. Now, Tovi was an official ally of the werewolves—another decision he'd made without the other alphas. This may have been his home and pack, but the decisions of the Drengrs' reflected all the packs. He and his father shared a quick glance, and Aramis's shoulders fell, like the realization dawned on him, too.

Eldrick had acted brashly.

All for what? Tovi hadn't agreed to his request.

Stay, he'd asked.

Yet, the vampyr queen had left shortly after the meeting to return home and spy on her brother. She'd promised to write if she'd learned anything worth sharing, and yet Eldrick hadn't received a single letter.

Like a fool, he'd envisioned taking her east to the frozen waterfalls, sampling the street fair of the village or tasting her rose-pink lips again, and places he'd yet to explore, kissing every inch of her, earlobe to toes. This wanting had Eldrick strung tight, ready to burst at the seams.

Yet, she wasn't here. A hundred miles away, and she still consumed his thoughts.

"Tovi is a powerful ally against our enemies," Eldrick finally said.

She wasn't just an ally, though, was she? If that were the case, he wouldn't feel her rejection like a punch to the gut, too keenly aware of her absence in the village.

"She's nothing but a whore who's bewitched you," Dalinda hissed.

Eldrick bared his own teeth, a thread of control separating him and his wolf from shifting. "Watch your tongue, or I'll cut it from your head."

Eldrick's promise bounced off the walls like booming thunder.

A strong, grounding hand squeezed his shoulder, and Aramis pulled him back, green eyes darkening like the forest during a summer storm.

His jaw pulsed as he addressed Bjorn. "Vampyr or not, we can't forget what Tovi has done. She led the journey to rescue Evelyn Carson from her brother's clutches and helped free captured werewolves, your son included."

Pride flushed through Eldrick, and he admired how steadfast his father was. This decree robbed Aramis of his title, but he still defended Tovi and Eldrick's agreed alliance.

"You have always been full of hope, Aramis, and I believe that served werewolves for a time, but we've entered a new era. Our own captured and chained, brothers betraying brothers, the Void spreading, and more demons entering our lands. We must elect a new alpha who understands vampyrs *are* the enemy."

Dalinda smirked at her father's words, malice etched into the creases of her eyes. Sam paled.

Aramis growled, shaking his head. "Stars above, Bjorn, see reason. Now isn't the time to divide the packs and leave them without a leader."

"There will be a vote for a new alpha in a month's time," Dalinda said.

Eldrick balked. "But Riven could strike at any moment."

Bjorn readied to leave, drawing his cloak tighter. "Which is why I'm acting alpha during the interim. You'll find that clause detailed in the decree."

With his parting words, Bjorn swiveled on his boots and strode down the center of the grand hall. Dalinda followed soon after, her nose so high it ran vertically to the ceiling.

Sam paused for a moment, bowed his head and said, "Alpha and Magu." And then he, too, left the hall, leaving Eldrick and his father buzzing with the news of the decree.

Once their retreating boots were out of earshot, Aramis turned to him. "We need to find your mother immediately."

Eldrick stilled, every fiber of his being turning rigid. "You think he'll hurt her?"

"*Bjorn* won't, not if he wants to secure the Earl vote, but nothing's stopping those who share his beliefs about vampyrs." Aramis took the decree from Eldrick, rereading it again as if the words might change. He didn't balk, nor reflect any feelings at all, but his reserved silence was telling enough.

"I'm sorry, Father," Eldrick said.

Aramis scoffed. "Don't be. I accepted Tovi, as well as you. Though I was naïve to think werewolves would accept your mother so quickly, the alpha they knew had died long ago."

A sadness seeped into his tone, and Eldrick swallowed. An unsaid tension had brimmed between his parents, and Eldrick wondered if his father resented his mother's decision to stay away for so long or how their mating bond fared after so much time apart. He didn't have the courage to ask, not when his mind wandered to his own matters of the heart.

His feelings for Tovi were costing him. It's not that he didn't trust them, but he feared it led him in the wrong direction—a place that put the future of his people, the werewolves, at risk. Perhaps it was for the best she wasn't in the village.

"I'll find Mother," he said. "What of Bjorn and the other alphas?"

His father scratched his beard. "We do nothing. Allow them to remain as long as they wish before they travel back to their own villages. If we push them out, they'll see us as bitter and feel better about their decision. Besides, I'll meet with the other alphas, see if I can undo the mess of this decree and call off a vote entirely."

Eldrick nodded. He left his father and headed out of Lār, the crisp air a cooling reprieve after such frustrating news.

If werewolves had any chance of beating Riven, they needed an alliance with the rightful Queen of Drystan—that was certain—and ensuring his father won back his title was imperative to keeping that alliance intact. It was only a matter of making the other packs understand they needed Tovi in the fight to come.

Purpose put a spring in Eldrick's step, but as he weaved through streets of his home, he couldn't shake the sense they were in this mess because of him.

CHAPTER THREE

Tovi

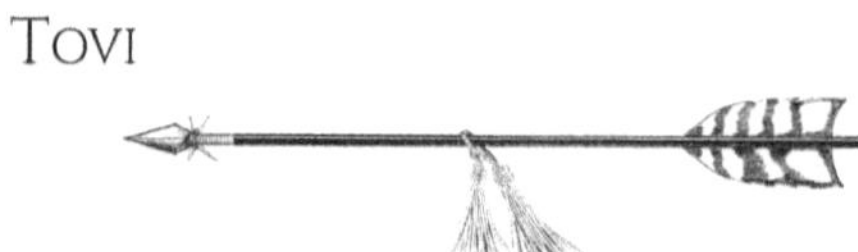

Frigid raindrops slid down the bridge of Tovi Verena's nose, and the hardened cold of her cursed homeland dug bone deep. Yet, she remained still, watchful as she hid in the shadows of an alley inside Drystan Village.

Lightning streaked across the sky, shaking the timber bones of the building she leaned against. The rainstorm didn't deter vampyrs from venturing out, and the flash of light reflected off the sodden satin outfits and leather trench coats of the bodies hanging by the river's dock. Hand-painted signs dangled from their feet, listing their offenses like warnings, as if the dead bodies frozen from the Drystan cold weren't enough to strike fear into the village.

Traitor to Prince Riven.

Princess sympathizer.

Heretic.

Tovi had inspected the faces, searched for friends and contacts she recognized, but all were foreign, each senseless death driven by paranoia. Her gut twisted at the sight—she'd lost her insides the first time she'd witnessed the barbarity. It didn't matter if she didn't know them. Vampyrs were her subjects, those that depended on her.

And she'd failed those dragged to the gallows, let her sister's wretched ways find themselves outside court. Because the bodies swinging in the thunderstorm's gusty wind had Visha written all over them, and it was her name whispered the most in the village streets and establishments. The longer the Blood Curse remained, the crueler Visha grew. How long did Tovi have before it wasn't only her sister, far worse than a demon or scáth, wreaking havoc across Drystan?

A light and balanced gait clattered across the cobblestones. A hooded figure walked up the street and weaved through the vampyrs, headed in Tovi's direction. No one was the wiser as they braced against the rain with heads down, but Tovi spied the shape of Yennifer's bow. Not far behind, another figure trailed her, and Bétar's red beard peeked out from his hood.

Moments later, the mated couple fell into the alleyway with Tovi, and once they were farther out of sight, they dropped their hoods back.

"We're all set," Yen said.

"Lou?" Tovi asked.

"In position," Bétar said.

Tovi nodded, clamping her jaw shut. Cinnamon and sugar wafted off the two werewolves, but not the scents of what they were. Bétar and Yen both wore enchanted necklaces around their necks, and for safe measure, their wrists, too.

"I hope you all didn't start without me."

Tovi couldn't help it, she jumped right alongside Bétar. The Gray Fenris's mage healer appeared beside them, as if she'd conjured from thin air.

"Linx, what in the bloody hel are you doing here?" Tovi hissed. "I thought you were still mending Todd."

The mage healer shrugged. "Belle's taken over that task, more than happily I might add. I also might've snooped in one of Nadia's letters detailing your plan to rescue Sven, Opal, and the littles. I wasn't going to miss out on that."

Tovi had left the Drengr Village weeks ago to spy on her brother, Riven, intent on learning his influence in Drystan, only to discover Sven and his family were prisoners of court. Thanks to spies and tactics of her own, Tovi discovered they were confined to rooms in the west wing. All they had to do was sneak into the castle.

Simple, Tovi lied to herself.

Bétar shook his head, rain falling off him. "Only you could make it through the Void alone."

"It isn't that difficult after Tovi showed us the way," Linx muttered. "What is the plan exactly?"

Tovi set her shoulders back and addressed Linx. "Well, Riven discovered the tunnels after we broke Evelyn out of the castle."

"So, we've decided to hide in plain sight," Yen finished.

Linx blinked. "With you're hair, Tovi? That's not possible. Here." The mage sifted through her traveling sack and retrieved a vile of sparkling purple liquid. "Thank the goddess I arrived in time. *This* concoction should be enough for you and Sven to change your Verena hair."

Tovi inspected the vile then Linx's usual vibrant colored hair. "It won't turn our hair purple, will it? I can't say that's any less inconspicuous."

Linx shrugged. "Hair has a mind of its own. I can't guarantee what it'll be, but it's better than what you have now."

Tovi sighed, agreeing at that point. "Alright, thank you. Now, you'll be most useful at the docks with Bétar. Find a ship called the *Sel* and tell them the dove sent you. No matter what happens, don't, under any circumstance, use an explosive. We're to be discreet. Riven doesn't know I'm here, and I'd like to keep it that way."

"Aye," Bétar nudged Linx. "Did you hear that, mage?"

Linx sighed, rolling her eyes. "Fine."

Tovi drew up her hood, making sure to hide her distinct hair that sheened like the Vadon Mountain's snowfall. As she peered around the corner, she tried to dismiss a certain werewolf's gem eyes from her thoughts.

Stay, Eldrick had asked.

Yet, she'd left. After all, Tovi had a throne to secure and kingdom to save. The dreaded clouds that had blanketed Drystan's sky for centuries had all started because of a Verena poisoned by love. A bargain then a curse, and now, Riven followed in their father's footsteps, seemingly unable to process the grief of losing his wife and child, he was willing to draw darkness all across their world to bring them back.

Tovi released a breath, letting it cloud ahead of her and mingle with the drizzle. She refused to be like either her father or brother, but a queen, one who put her people and their well-being over everything else, even if Eldrick's absence ached like a physical wound in Tovi's chest. Her newfound friend, Yennifer, might as well have shot an arrow in her heart. The wound festered, but Tovi chalked it up to a measly bruise, something that would heal in time, and with so much on the horizon, she'd be too busy to notice it.

Like now, as she readied to release Sven and his family from the imprisonment of Drystan Castle.

A covered wagon hurried down the street, yet another friend's face concealed by their cloak and upturned hood. It slowed as it passed the alley, but at the last second, Tovi launched herself up and over into the wagon.

She shuffled on light feet, drawing farther into the back to give Yennifer room to join her inside. Linx and Bétar darted into the street, disappearing in the throngs of vampyrs as they headed towards the docks.

"How does she just appear?" Tovi whispered to Yen.

The archer shrugged. "Linx? It's a mage thing for all I know. Unnerves Bétar to no end, something I love to tease him about."

Tovi bit back a laugh and shook her head. A cart with an enclosed compartment awaited them. Stacked with pastries and breads and painted Verena purple, they'd borrowed it from the castle kitchens.

Yennifer sighed, peeling off her cloak, bow and arrow, and several other hidden weapons. "I don't suppose we get this part over with."

The werewolf opened the cart's door and wedged herself inside first. Tovi shed her gear, too, hiding it all underneath a spare basket of baguettes. Inside, Yen eyed her with disdain.

"Whose idea was this?" the werewolf grumbled.

"Blame Lou."

Tovi cursed as she tried to push herself inside. It was practically impossible with the both of them, but hunched over and legs entangled and seated across from each other, they made do. They jolted from side to side as the covered wagon began its ascent to the castle.

Time stretched and quickened all at once. The last time Tovi had stepped foot in the castle, she'd broken Evelyn out of it. It wasn't lost on her that, yet again, she was saving those she loved from the clutches of her twin brother.

The clattering of the wheels changed tune, the sound of *thud, thud, thud,* indicated evenly laid brick instead off cobblestone. Voice resided outside, chatter and pleasantries from the front. Tovi's heart raced inside her chest and skipped a beat as the wagon halted.

Soon, unseen, someone pushed the cart out of the wagon and into the castle. The sounds of a kitchen echoed around them. Clanking spoons. Banging pots. Chopping knives. Servant chatter. Next, music played, presumably from the ballroom. Court laugher filtered from afar. Eventually, it was only the squeaking wheels of the cart and Tovi's rattling bones that she heard.

After the sensation of climbing stilled, keys rustled—another "borrowed" item they'd secured—and the cart entered a warmer room with a fire crackling close by.

"Cake!" children's voices screeched, and it took all of Tovi's willpower to not burst from the cart and embrace her niece and nephew.

What if someone they didn't trust sat inside the room, too? What if it wasn't Lou pushing the cart? Tovi held her breath, counting to keep her nerves steady—

The door burst open, and Lou's red-framed glasses came into view. "You two look splendidly comfortable."

Yennifer exhaled. "Moons, I can't believe this worked."

The archer climbed out first, and Tovi caught the distinct exclamation "weeful" from Bryn. As she emerged next, the children ran into her legs, screaming, "Auntie!" All the adults encouraged them to be quiet with a direct, "Shhh," and Juni frowned.

Tovi spied Sven and Opal across the room. "Are you both ready?"

Sven, her younger brother with cropped hair, nodded. "Yes."

Tovi sighed and squatted to Juni and Bryn's level. "Will you play a game with me?"

They nodded, their too-wide eyes studied her with excitement, innocence, and nerves.

Tovi dropped her voice into a playful whisper. "We're going on an adventure, but you both must remain silent."

"The quiet game!" Juni said.

Opal rushed to the children. "Yes, my loves. We're all going to play together, and after, we'll have a slice a cake. How does that sound?"

With mouths clamped shut, Juni and Bryn nodded fervently.

Opal kissed them fiercely and placed them inside the cart. Sven squatted to his haunches and whispered encouraging words before he closed the cart's door, hiding his children inside.

"We need to move," he whispered. "Servants will be here within in the next hour to deliver our scheduled lunch."

Lou pulled Verena purple uniforms out her sack. "We all need to put these on."

"And Sven and Tovi need to drink Linx's tonic." She gestured around her own wheat-colored curls. "To change your hair."

Right. Tovi's stomach swam with apprehension, but Linx had shifted her hair color successfully once before. She popped the vial's cork free and swigged. She winced, sourness stinging her tongue, and passed the vial to Sven next.

Ahead, in an oval mirror decorating the east wall, Tovi's snow-white braid bled auburn, drawing out green in her eyes. Sven's cropped hair shifted to a dark brown, tittering closer to black. It made him paler than usual.

With the first part of their disguises dealt with, the five of them dressed in the servant uniforms.

"No one said anything about wearing a dress," Yennifer growled.

Lou snorted. "You're in Drystan, wolf."

"How in the stars above am I supposed to use my bow in this nightmare?" Yennifer attempted to nock an invisible arrow, but the back seams of her dress groaned in retaliation.

"No weapons, no fighting. We leave the castle without bringing any attention to ourselves," Tovi said.

Each of them grabbed a prop from the cart and exited Sven and Opal's suite. Sven carried a cake. Opal held a basket of baguettes. Yen balanced a tray of macaroons, Tovi led the charge with a stack of towels and Lou resumed pushing the cart, Bryn and Juni silent as ever.

No one traveled through the hallway on the other side, giving them a clear path to the servants' hallway beyond a makeshift hidden door.

Riven had discovered most of the tunnels after their successful mission to save Evelyn, but at least the passageways the servants used remained obscured from Tovi's brother and any lords or ladies who might spy her features past her missing white hair.

Tovi donned a mask of indifference, keeping her eyes straight ahead. Yet, inside, her heart hammered, and her blood turned to ice. A cold breeze tunneled through the passageway, and Tovi was yanked back to the docks, the hanging bodies swinging in the breeze. If they were caught, who would Visha punish? Opal? Sven? Would she return to the Drengr Village without Yen?

Tovi shuddered, dismissing thoughts that only distracted her from their mission: get Sven, Opal and the littles out of the castle.

They crossed paths with a few real servants, but with heads down and their own tasks at hand, no one paid Tovi and company any mind as they marched back to the kitchens. Work continued in the lower levels of the castle, bustling with activity.

Tovi stayed on course and reached the kitchen's back door without a single chef taking notice. Lou followed next—thank the Goddess, the littles were out of those dreaded stone walls—then Sven and Opal, and last, Yen.

"To the wagon," Tovi whispered.

Perhaps fate kept tabs on Tovi that day. The wagon remained in position, its horse munching on weeds growing in the grooves between stones.

"Uniforms off," Lou hissed. "Prepare for a checkpoint."

Sven and Tovi hauled the cart with Bryn and Juni into the back of the wagon. Behind the wagon's fabric covering, they all changed out of their servants uniforms, dressing in extra attire stashed in the wagon—*bloody hel*, Lou had thought of everything.

"The three of you, ride in the back," Tovi whispered to Opal, Sven, and Yen. "Heads down, and Yen, if needed . . ."

The werewolf nodded. "Understood."

In the castle, confrontation was too great a risk, but outside, they were so close to the village, they had the advantage. They'd battle their way down to the docks if needed.

Tovi changed into attire more suited for a commoner than servant or queen. Food stained the weathered wool, and for safe measure, she smudged dirt on her cheeks and the tip of her nose.

Lou pocketed her red-rimmed glasses for rusty, wiry ones. With the others situated in the back, they climbed atop the wagon's bench and set the horse in motion towards the east checkpoint. Less guarded than the front, but a slightly steeper climb down.

It'd have to do.

Guards stepped ahead of their path, blocking the exit with hands held up. Tovi held her breath. To make matters worse, rain quickened, spilling from the gray sky. At least the color shielded their features, and as the rain pelted the guards face, cold brimming in the air, he checked the wagon swiftly, eager to get out of the rain and back into the enclosed post.

Lou urged the horse forward and released a pent-up breath as they left the castle grounds.

Tovi didn't dare to, not until she scented the river over the rain.

The largest ship at the docks creaked as it bobbed side to side, and a familiar set of pink-haired buns stood out amongst the gray and black of Drystan Village. Lou brought the wagon to a screeching halt at the docks, and Tovi jumped down and onto the cobblestone street. Opal and Sven emerged from the back of the wagon, Bryn and Juni in their arms.

"We're almost there," Tovi whispered.

Rain poured, clearing the street and docks as they descended down the pier to last ship tied at the end.

Bétar paced by the ship's ramp. A lantern caught the rusted plaque bolted into the ship's belly, reading *The Sel*.

"Boats and vampyrs don't seem natural," he muttered to Tovi.

A vampyr pirate, Jasp, strode down the ramp and smirked. "We sail at night, wolf."

Bétar bristled, but Tovi stepped between them before the tension escalated.

"Jasp," she said.

He tipped his head, fangs jutting over his bottom lip. "Calling in a lot of favors lately. Smuggling werewolves is one thing, but now were dipping our toes into the royal family. Risky business."

Tovi sighed. "Tell him I appreciate it."

Jasp scoffed. "Tell 'em yourself."

Tovi stiffened, searching the ship for its captain, a male she hadn't seen in decades. "Is he here?"

"No," Jasp said. "In Morrow. He'll expect a visit eventually. Is this them?" His attention landed on Sven and his family, the children whispering about cake while their mother promised them treats would have to wait.

Tovi dropped a pouch filled with coin into Jasp's awaiting hand. "That should cover their passage east."

Jasp weighed the pouch up and down, the gold and gems jingling in his hold. "Aye, it will indeed, but don't think money can keep buying you time. Captain's waited almost a hundred years to speak to ya." He jutted his chin towards Opal and the littles. "Follow me."

Sven ground his teeth, staring off at his wife and children as the boarded the ship. His gaze snapped to Tovi, and brother and sister stared at the other under the spilling rain of Drystan.

"Riven's declared himself king," Sven whispered.

"What?" Tovi hissed. "You're just *now* telling me this."

"I couldn't jeopardize getting Bryn and Juni out of the castle," he said, tone stern.

"I'd never risk them, Sven," she said. "I'm not Mother and Father—"

"I know." He swallowed, jade eyes dimming. "You can never be too sure as a parent."

Tovi sighed, her insides twisting. The words, *I understand*, tickled on her lips, but she hadn't the slightest empathy for what Sven endured with his littles as Riven's prisoners. Yet, she knew what Riven was after, bringing back his wife and child from the dead.

"Besides," Sven said, "I was protecting you, my sister, as well. Riven's at his wit's end, I hardly recognize him. The brother we once had is gone. Visha is worse. Unhinged. If they'd caught you . . ." He shook his head, exhaling. "What you did today, for Opal and me, means far more than you'll ever know."

Tovi dragged her younger brother into a tight hug. "You know where to go?"

He nodded. "Yes."

"Good," she whispered.

He laid his hands onto her shoulders. "You are the rightful queen, Tovi. It's time you assumed the throne."

"At this point, I'd have to—"

"Fight Riven for the claim, yes," Sven said. "And kill him if you must."

Without another word, Sven climbed the ramp, and the *Sel*'s quarterdeck whooshed into a frenzy of activity as the crew prepared to depart.

Tovi turned, heart aching, as she faced north again, Drystan Castle looming over her like some ferocious beast ready to devour her resolve. Her freed family fled on the ship behind her. Her dead subjects swayed in the breeze to the west. Her home village crept with muck, mists, and misery from the curse all around.

Tovi stepped foot onto the cobblestone street again and trudged through a puddle. Her reflection, marred by auburn hair, stared back at her with sharp eyes.

"What's next?" Yen asked at her shoulder.

Tovi's heart raced, her mind reeling with possibilities, but it always came back to the same one, over and over.

"We need to leave Drystan."

"Are you sure?" Bétar asked. "After what Sven told you?"

Fair, Tovi thought. Though she had a team well-equipped to break her family out of the castle, she'd need a much larger force to face Riven and his claims to the throne.

An army.

Tovi nodded. "Once Riven realizes they're gone, he'll tear through the village. It's not safe to remain here."

She glanced one last time at the Drystan Castle and swore the next time she soaked in its mightiness, it'd be *her* throne inside it.

CHAPTER FOUR

LORKAN DRENGR TREADED ON soft feet. The surrounding forest stood silent and still. He inhaled, detecting a cloying stench.

Darkness.

The cloudy night draped the northern territory of the Vadon Mountains in a dusty sage. Shadows clung to the pine trees like sticky, cold veils, and fog snaked over the forest's bulbous roots. Lorkan had never seen so much gray bleeding into his homeland before, even in winter.

A branch snapped. He and his companion both stilled. Inch by inch, they turned, and Lorkan sniffed the air again.

"Bear," his friend, Alvin, whispered.

A breath later, a grizzly shout out of the fog. Tufts of fur stuck out from its chestnut coat. It stared at them with sleepy eyes. Deciding they weren't worth its time, the bear trotted off, shoulders edging through the fog that eventually swallowed it whole.

"That's not the first beast I've seen out of hibernation early," Alvin said.

"Animals get confused with the seasons all the time."

Lorkan tried to dismiss Alvin's worry, but his friend's piercing blue eyes landed on him, the look of an unbending warrior. It'd been years since Alvin had raised a shield as a third-born protector, but he'd never lost his sharpness or axe. He'd shaved the sides of his head, leaving his pale hair longer in the center, braided to his shoulder.

"Let's keep moving," Alvin said.

Up ahead, the fog grew thicker. Death clotted the air, and as the fog parted, a dark ooze dripped like oil over the skeleton of dead trees. Pines stood bare and pale while ferns sat in piles of blackened fronds.

"They're dying," Lorkan breathed.

"It gets worse," Alvin breathed.

Lorkan stilled. The elm tree was stout as it was wide, its branches crooked and bending like roots above the ground. It was too early for its leaves to have bloomed, yet its bark was black. Sickly.

"How many are like this?" Lorkan asked.

"Half."

"Fuck."

Lorkan shook his head, ridding the worry snaking through him like the shadows had penetrated his skin. Other werewolves coveted elm timber for making bows, but otherwise, elms were poisonous if eaten. For werewolves like Lorkan, Alvin, and their secret pack, Fjall Pack, it was a gift.

In springtime, they harvested the flowers to create a tea that subdued their beastly urges. If they didn't have blossoms to harvest, they wouldn't have enough tea to last the coming year. They'd all risk falling too deep into darkness and became the wretched creatures who'd created them.

Alvin handed him a leather flask. Lorkan nodded his thanks and took a swig. The wine laced with blood awakened his baser instinct. Like dunking into an icy lake and emerging, it jolted his muscles and mind. He sniffed, discerning the animal like one did when checking the aromas of wine. Chamomile, cherry, and saline . . .

"Elk," he said, passing it to Alvin.

"Ah, good nose." Alvin drank, silent for a moment. "What do you suppose we do about the elms?"

Lorkan sighed, reaching for the wine again. Alvin obliged, and thanks to the blood, the next swig brushed the edge off of the mess they found themselves in.

"We search for more."

The beads in Alvin's beard gleamed silver. "And then what? The Void is spreading, Lorkan. At this rate, it isn't the elms we need to worry about, but the entire Vadon Mountains."

Lorkan stewed. He didn't want to accept that darkness was spreading, not when that same wretchedness coursed through his blood. What did that mean for him?

But this wasn't about him. It was about Sorin, his family in the Drengr Village, and the pack he led with Alvin, those that needed him. His fingers itched to get his hands on a book, to research how to save Sorin, his scholarly instincts wishing for parchment, ink, and too many cups of tea. But poring over books and working until the sun rose hadn't led him to answers yet. Time was like an ancient text, delicate and risked crumbling at a single misstep.

Lorkan sighed. "I'll write to our contact. Perhaps they can help us find elm trees in the south, farther from the Void—"

A *caw* cut through the forest, and Lorkan flushed with recognition. A raven descended from above, landing on his shoulder. His feathered friend hoped on one foot, the other holding a rolled missive. The Drengr navy seal was vibrant compared to the foggy night.

Alvin stalked closer. "How in the stars above does that bird find you?"

Lorkan shrugged, though he had his theories regarding Rook. But he pushed those back into the corners of his mind and unfurled the missive written in his brother's handwriting.

As Lorkan read the words, shock rooted him in place. He had to read the letter three times to be sure the light of the forest wasn't playing tricks. Lorkan had always considered the darkness inside him a curse, that *he* was cursed. Punished by fate.

Stars above, his brothers had discovered tangible answers.

"Gods, Lorkan, you're paler than usual. What is it?" Alvin asked.

Lorkan passed him the letter. On a good day, he didn't have the energy for words. Tonight, there were too many to sort out. A foreign feeling rose within him, warmth spreading across his chest—he could set his pack free.

The shadows snaked closer towards them, as if they were hungry for the spark of hope Lorkan had found.

Alvin jabbed a finger into the inked lines. "This means there are others like us, vampyrs that aren't like scáths."

Lorkan gritted his teeth. Even though they were out of earshot of anyone for miles, he still hated to hear that word.

Hated *what* he was.

A vampyr. Because they'd never landed on a term to call themselves, were-wolves and witches who'd been bitten by scáths and turned. *Changed.* Along with their original abilities and magic, they endured the same horrors as their makers—no sunlight, thirst for blood, and innate darkness.

Years he'd hunted for answers, a way to undo what they'd become. During his research, Lorkan had discovered the tea from elm tree blossoms. It changed their scent, suppressed their thirst for blood, especially during the full moon when their hunger was at its worst. But now the Void was spreading, killing the trees they needed in its wake.

"What if breaking the curse turns us back?" he asked.

Alvin exhaled, studying the mists. "What if it simply rids us of darkness?"

Curse. Darkness. Vampyrism. Weren't they all the same?

"Eldrick's letter demanded I return home."

Regardless of his brother's request, Lorkan's thirst for knowledge was too great to ignore. Answers. *Moons*, he craved answers.

"And what of me?" Alvin sighed.

"The pack needs you, now more than ever, with the dying elm trees."

His friend snatched the wine back. "I had a feeling you'd say that. *Moons*, you always have all the fun."

Alvin had transitioned eight years ago, two years after Lorkan. While searching for a rare type of moss, he'd discovered Alvin in a cave—pale, covered in blood, confused about how he wasn't dead after being mauled by three scáths. His desperation for answers clashed with Lorkan's in the air.

"I don't know how long my brother needs me for," Lorkan said. "But I'll write and keep you up to date regarding anything I learn."

Rook clacked his beak, as if agreeing with the plan.

"What do I tell the others?" Alvin asked, though he sounded unconvinced of Lorkan's request.

"Everything," Lorkan said.

Alvin's brows pinched. "Are you sure? This kind of news instills hope. Some may try to leave."

"They can't," Lorkan whispered. "But news of the curse and the prophecy will travel north, and eventually, they'll hear about it. It's better that it comes from us, along with the message that this doesn't change our rules. We need to ration the elm tea, too, which means staying out of the sunlight as much as possible."

Glacier-blue eyes drilled into Lorkan, and for a moment, he feared he hadn't gotten through to his friend until—

"Fine, I'll keep an eye out for that damn raven."

"Don't sound too excited."

"That feathered menace has stolen over ten of my best beads."

Lorkan snorted, noticing the lack of silver and gems woven into Alvin's braid. He reached inside his travel pack, retrieving a handful of his friend's stolen things.

"Moons, he brings them to you?" Alvin collected them in his hand, picking one up and inspecting the pearly design.

"I think he does it to prove he's delivered my letters."

Rook stomped his feet into his shoulder.

Alvin grunted. "Annoying, but clever. Hmmm, where do you think he took the other half?"

Eyes as dark as night flashed through Lorkan's mind. Phantom curls threaded through his fingers, and the scent of storm clouds and sage tickled his nose.

He knew exactly where his messenger spent half his time, but he lied and said, "That is something only Rook knows."

Chapter Five

B LAIR CARSON'S RELEASE BARRELED through her, and she cried out to the ceiling above.

Her lover's talented thumb kept drawing rapid circles over her aching nub, and she rocked her hips once, twice, and a final third time as he stilled beneath, his manhood twitching deep inside her as he, too, found release. His other hand gripped her ass tighter, nails digging into her sensitive aroused flesh—and *shit*—another climax crashed down on Blair, and she shot forward, hunching over as her body lost all sense.

With toes curled, panting, and sweet somnolent running through her sedated being, Blair peeled herself off her partner's hips and crashed to the rumbled bedsheets. The two lay side by side, arms barely touching, as they caught their breath.

"Stay for breakfast."

Blair laughed, stomach churning. She peeled herself from the sheets and rushed from the outstretched hand, tempting her with promise. "I've never stayed before, Jace."

Not in any of her few lover's beds after their entanglements. No matter the late hour, she always created a *danu* home, more than eager to climb under her own quilt with the slick sweat of sex still clinging to her skin. Blair knew better than to deviate from her rules and strict ways.

Underneath tousled blond curls, Jace's blue eyes shined with an eagerness she'd never seen before. Jace was a good fuck—okay, an *excellent* fuck and

Blair's favorite—and not only for his wicked thumb or attentive tongue, but also because he wanted nothing more. Not a glass of wine before. Not dinner. Nor to even lie in bed together after. They'd been entangled for years, learning the art of release and flesh and sounds without frills and feelings.

He placed a hand behind his head, flexing his strong biceps. "Why not change it up a bit?"

Blair snorted, searching for her trail of shucked clothes littered around his room. She'd arrived ready and wanting, and Jace hadn't said a word, not even a *good morning* before his fingers had plunged into her slick core. *Ah*, she found her bralette on his work table—they'd started there with Blair bent over, his hands threaded through her curls, as he gave her such a delicious, vigorous pace after such long, tiring weeks.

"Since when have you wanted change?" Blair tugged on her undergarments, raising a brow.

Though both second borns and scholars, they had different areas of study and rarely crossed professional paths. Jace's research pertained to ancient and magical artifacts, spending most of his time at Nūa's museum, the Ealaíona, as well as his coven's shop that sold high-end collectables.

Blair found her sweater hanging from a copper sundial that buzzed with magic, one of the few artifacts Jace had kept for himself.

"I thought perhaps we could discuss what had you so tightly wound earlier." Jace rested his arms on his bent knees. His naked body gleamed with their earlier endeavors, fluttering Blair's insides. Screw breakfast—she was half-tempted to crawl into bed and have him again.

But laying twice in the same day with Jace was dangerous territory. It lead to sharing meals, which turned into conversation, and then feelings, and they was strictly off the table for Blair.

"Work is stressful."

Jace raised a brow. That was a lie. Well, a partial lie. She was working on deciphering the prophecy Evelyn and Kade had discovered, but in terms of her scholarly post at the Nūa Library, well, she'd been sacked months ago for encouraging the Son of the God to leave his position at the Void and search for the Daughter of the Goddess, disobeying direct orders from the Council.

And since Sorin was naïve to the fact that prophesied third borns had never married, she could not explain her dismissal from the city's most prestigious scholarly position during job interviews.

Sourness coated Blair's tongue. With that truth now revealed, the Carson coven faced shame and disgrace at all angles from the city. Blair's scholarly status should've been the last thing on her mind, but it was all Blair had—her research, published journals and anthologies series, and an office in the library with the best view of the city.

Yet, Evelyn's hearing loomed. She'd not told Evelyn she'd lost her position. Dread weighed like the force of a summer storm pressed into Blair's chest. But if she figured out this prophecy, learned it before any other scholar, there's no reason the Council wouldn't reinstate her. Books and research gave Blair's life order, and she needed that stability back in her life.

Blair finally found her green velvet trousers. She searched its back pocket and found a folded piece of paper tucked inside. She sauntered over to the bed, crawled towards Jace and saddled his hips.

"Have you ever seen something like this before?"

She'd sketched the bloodstone necklace onto the parchment. Not a single text detailed the type of stone Evelyn had placed her magic into, and perhaps with Jace's expertise, he'd recognize it.

"I suddenly feel used," he said with a frown.

Blair rolled her eyes. "I came here for the delectable sex. This is just a bonus."

Jace raised a suspicious brow but studied her rendering, regardless. "What color is it?"

"Deep red."

"Hmm. Magic?"

Blair couldn't speak to its magical qualities prior to Evelyn placing her magic into it, but a certain phrase her sister had used stood out. "I think so. I read it's the blood of fallen gods."

Something flashed in Jace's eyes, and he folded the paper back up. "Blair Carson, are you interested in dark magic?"

She snatched the sketch from his hand, hiding her wince at Jace's taunt. "What if I was?"

"I'd say you're lying, but you don't do that either."

Blair exhaled her impatience. "Are you familiar with it or not?"

"I've read about something similar. A god's soul is so grand, it imbeds in the earth as gems after they die. But that's if gods even can die."

Soul. The word nagged in the back of Blair's reeling mind, and she bookmarked it to think about later.

"Which text is this?" she asked.

"One hailing from Torren."

Interesting. "Written by the humans?"

Jace cocked his head and smirked. "Ancient fae."

That had to be some ancient text. Blair brimmed with excitement—nothing beat a good book except a rare, ancient one. Bonus if she had to transcribe a forgotten language. Her fingers twitched to get her hands on it.

"Did the text call it anything?" she asked.

Jace shrugged. "It was translated, but I recall the term *blood*. That's why I asked for the color. It gleamed a deep crimson."

More questions sat on the tip of Blair's tongue, but a small brass clock chimed the half hour. *Bloody hel.* Blair sprang from the bed, yanking her trousers on.

Jace turned on his side, watching her with sleepy eyes. "I heard rumors your sister, the Daughter of the Goddess, had finally returned and has a hearing today with the Council."

Blair scoffed. She had no intention of attending the hearing, not that she was permitted, *technically*. An oily sensation snaked through Blair at the mention of Evelyn, and the feeling awakened a wickedness in her she tried desperately to hide. She'd kept her distance, afraid she'd say the angry words that surged through her like storm winds barreling against the city.

How dare Evelyn just waltz into the city as if she'd never ran? As if she hadn't lied to their homeland. Lied to Blair, her own sister. And Mirella—now so kind and welcoming. As if the last two years hadn't happened and they hadn't dealt with Evelyn's mess.

The Elders had worried over Evelyn like a misplaced weapon, and yet Evelyn was Blair's *sister*. Out of love, Blair had taken matters into her own hands and sought Kade out. Thank the Goddess, he'd found her sister, but what did Blair's efforts have to show for it?

Nothing. No job. No status amongst witches. No *love*. Nothing like Evelyn had. Nothing true and real.

"Bleedin' suns, Blair. Try to at least look happy that your sister is home." Jace handed over her cloak.

Black velvet brushed against Blair's fingers, and she grasped the cloth for comfort. Of course, her heart swelled at the sight of Evelyn home—worry had riddled Blair for so long—but her sister had returned . . . *different.*

In love.

It was nauseating. Every small kiss, every glint of Kade's lingering gaze. It was like an invisible dagger twisting into Blair's belly, reminding her of what she didn't have. She couldn't blame either of them. That was unfair. They didn't know she walked around with a scarred heart, a wound that never truly healed.

Nevertheless, Blair's resentment was a wretched beast, and she didn't have the reins to tame it, not when she had worries of her own.

"Is there any chance you have that fae text?" Blair asked.

Jace nodded. "You're welcome to come by my coven's shop and take a look at it."

"Thank you."

Her lover sighed, running his hands through his blond curls. "You know . . . Making an appearance at the hearing might work in your favor. The Daughter of the Goddess has returned and there's a so-called 'entire prophecy' to research. Why not grasp that opportunity?"

Blair had already started the very endeavor, but in the comfort of her townhome and no official post, there was no status or recognition that came with it. Yet could she sit through Evelyn's hearing and stomach her excuses?

Come to think of it, Blair could sit through anything to get back to her official office, texts, scholarly research, and quiet life.

She sighed. "Perhaps you're right, Jace."

Blair conjured her *danu*. Her magic sang a haunting song and furled her curls. As she stepped through and into her townhome, she prayed the hearing went well, but for entirely selfish reasons.

Chapter Six

Evelyn

Evelyn's voice echoed and carried high throughout the glass atrium, louder and prouder than the anxious chatter of the witches who'd gathered on the side pews. They whispered. They gawked. They glared.

Let them.

Years ago—*Goddess*, dare she say months ago—Evelyn would've cowered and shrank away from the appraising crowd.

But she was no longer that witch.

She didn't give a *fucking flame* what they thought. She cared for the truth swelling within her, the threat they all needed to understand.

Riven. The Blood Goddess. The Blood Curse.

Through the floor-to-ceiling window ahead, the darkening sky above Nūa carried an omen with it, settling shadows across the buildings of a place Evelyn had once called home. The clouds ballooned like ink blooming in water. Dozens of flags depicting the various covens across the city bowed against the coastal winds.

But Evelyn would not bend, not even as the Council listened with hardened expressions. Her hearing was well underway, and yet not a single one had unmasked their indifference.

While Elders lead their covens, and dozens resided in the city, only a select few governed Nūa, one for each of the five districts—Stag, Knot, Harp, Cross, and Ailm. Residents elected their council members for the first four, while the Elder of the same coven as the Daughter of the Goddess oversaw the Ailm, the central and governing district of Nūa. Mirella sat at the center, while Stag and Knot sat to her left and the Harp and Cross sat to her right.

With shoulders back and voice steady, Evelyn admitted she had run and why. She confirmed Kade had left his own post to find her, and that they'd met an ocean away in Callum on the continent of Torren. To the east, the Sapphire Sea was a gray sheet of glass for miles, no signs of the magic she and Kade had experienced together on the horizon. To the west, the lingering storm clouds reminded Evelyn too much of the Drystan sky.

Evelyn ignored the chill in her bones and detailed her time in the land of vampyr as Prince Riven's prisoner. The more she unveiled, the quieter it became, and the wide eyes of the onlooking witches turned to horror.

"Oh, Goddess."

"To the sun."

Witches uttered prayers upward, holding their hands out to the atrium's domed ceiling. A stained-glass circular depiction of the sun stared down at them, it's usual flaming color muted from the outside gray. Her aunts, Ruth and Josepha, sat amongst the crowd, and the third born rolled her eyes while the scholar frowned, wary.

Evelyn's stomach twisted. She hated inciting fear into her own people, it wasn't her intention, but she needed them to understand the threat they faced. She glanced behind her, meeting Kade's kind, amber stare. Leaned up against the back wall, he was a tall, brooding presence amongst the high-nosed witches. Those seated in the pews closest to him had scooted away, giving him a wide berth.

A decorative vase clattered to the ground, severing the tension. Evelyn stumbled over her words, and everyone's attention swiveled to Blair. She froze, wild curls amiss and eyes downcast. Murmurs peppered the air, and Evelyn's instinct buzzed with unease. Her sister, a punctual and studios scholar, had arrived late.

Elder Circe, a witch and scholar Evelyn despised, rose out of her seat. "Blair Carson, you aren't permitted to attend this hearing."

Evelyn straightened. "My sister is a leading scholar in the Nūa Library."

Circe snorted. "Blair was dismissed from her position six months ago and hasn't stepped foot there since."

"What?" Evelyn breathed, searching for her sister.

Onyx collided with Evelyn's gray, and Evelyn was certain it was the first time the sisters had truly looked at one another since they'd reunited. Blair sat amongst the rest of her coven, Emmet, Rodrick, and Artie, their expressions grave at Circe's news. Is that why her sister had acted so cold since her return? But why lie about her dismissal from the library?

Mirella stood. "Blair is a member of the Carson coven, who are permitted to attend in support of Evelyn, Elder Circe. Now, let's proceed with the hearing."

Betrayal seared through Evelyn, but she turned away from Blair, refocusing on the Council. *Fucking flames*, what had she been saying?

Right. The prophecy. The curse. She cleared her throat and said, "I discovered Matilda Moore's journal—"

Someone snickered. Elder Brookes, seated the farthest left, masked his disruption with a cough. His onyx velvet cloak shimmered under the atrium's hanging orbs.

Beside him, Elder Rose leaned over and muttered, "Here I thought this tale couldn't get any more far-fetched—"

"Do you have a question, Elder Rose?" Evelyn raised an expectant brow.

Tension cut through the atrium. Elder Rose squirmed in her seat, a flush rising up her neck. "Do you really expect us to believe that you found Matilda Moore's journal in the vampyr castle? Miss Carson, you must know how ridiculous this all sounds."

The muscles in Evelyn's resilient being tightened. "Are you implying I'm lying?"

There. Call it for what is was—doubt. Evelyn refused to enter the political dance the Elders waltzed. They didn't have time for it. Riven hadn't attacked since the Blood Moon, but sooner or later he would, and Sorin needed to be ready. *Evelyn* needed to be ready.

With her magic.

"I think Elder Rose is merely shocked, like us all," Mirella said, seated at the center of the five Council members. She offered Evelyn a soft smile. "Go on."

Evelyn nodded and continued. The rest of her tale flowed out of her like the words had been engrained on her heart—Kade saving her, the attack on Eldrick, meeting Prince Sven and Opal, the battle of the Blood Moon, and when she'd placed her magic into the bloodstone.

"That is an atrocity!" Elder Burns shot up, wagging his meaty figure at Evelyn. Every bit of him was square-shaped. His head, shoulders, build. Even the edges of his mustache framed his lips in ninety-degree angles. Evelyn had found his demeanor just as rigid. "You willingly cut your soul. It's dark magic—"

"What other choice did I have?" Evelyn challenged. "If Prince Riven had secured my magic, there would be an army of vampyrs waiting outside the Wall, walking in the sunlight."

Elder Burns shook his head, face growing redder. "Nūa would rather face that threat than this disgrace. You were gifted by the Sun Goddess with a power unlike any other. Yet, you so easily sacrificed it."

"Let me make myself very clear, Elder Burns," Evelyn hissed. "I'd live the last two years again to ensure our homeland is safe. *Every bit of it.*"

Shock rippled through crowd. Evelyn spun, locking eyes with whom she could. Ruth nodded for her to go on, Artie, too.

"You haven't seen the devastation the curse has left on Drystan, or the wicked mind games the Blood Goddess has played with Prince Riven. Neither are a threat easily dismissed. I did what I had to do, and I will not stand here and be accused of dark magic or made to regret my decision. What I can offer though, is a beacon of hope." She held up Opal's note. "This is the entire prophecy. All of it."

Evelyn recited it:

As frost bites trees and ferns, whispers
of Gods and Goddesses travel on the wind.
The banished One reaches from Below,
grasping the hope of a heartbroken mortal.
A bleeding bargain struck, weaved with
trickery, and the tendrils of immortality.

But when true love dies,
it'll be the land's demise.
Not until the land is cast in
red, a new dawn will rise.

The age of curse, a crack in the land, the
seep and sorrow of death, darkness, and rot.
Her children cast in night, whilst a
hunger for blood will be their blight.

After a storm between mistaken enemies,
the wolf and dove, the clash of the light and night,
those of these lands will unite.

A sowing of seeds, a journey to the beneath where
Life and death meet. A King and Queen will emerge,
With the seeds sown from elsewhere, life

to rid the shade and make way
for the Prince to walk with Light.

With bones an old friend now set free,
And the blade of the ancients
The truest of unions between the third-borns of
the Sun and Moon will defeat the darkness.

Evelyn clutched the parchment like a shred of evidence, and stressed the different stanzas, making sure it was heard that this was so much more than they'd believed for centuries, that it was more than her and Kade.

Stunned silence rippled through the atrium, and Elder Quinn, a spritely witch with azure hair was the first to speak. "What is it that you're asking, Evelyn? Why agree to this hearing at all?"

"Because I know what Sorin faces," she said. "Yet, I can't defend our homeland or fulfill this prophecy without my magic. I ask that you drop the charges against Kade and I. Work with us, not against us. We are not traitors, but protectors who *need* to focus on getting my magic back. Then, we can learn how to break the curse."

"You mean defeat the darkness?" Elder Quinn leaned forward.

"The darkness and the curse are one in the same," Evelyn said.

"How are you so sure?" Elder Burns asked.

Evelyn shook her head. "From what I've read, learned."

Elder Burns laughed. "That is not your concern. You are a third born, a protector, not a scholar. Leave the prophecy to the others to decipher and focus on fighting, protecting our borders, defending our lands."

Elder Rose humphed her agreement. "Yes, why don't you focus on the very duties you've both been neglecting."

"Well, I can't do that with my magic, now can I?" Evelyn asked.

Elder Rose shot out of her seat, seething. "How dare you speak to me that way—"

Mirella's eyes widened. "You've let spite and fear guide you. Goddess forbid your almighty beliefs are challenged. For once, can you try and not be a pious pricks?"

Evelyn stilled, her heart lodging in her throat. Mirella had never stepped in to defend her before—not when she'd begged her to postpone her wedding to Kade, not when she cried for more time, or when the Elders had berated about what happened to her parents—and by her sister's watery gaze, it'd been festering inside her to do so for some time. A comment rang from the crowd, and Evelyn swore Emmet said, "That's my girl."

Elder Rose sank back into her seat while Elder Burns turned redder than the glass depicting the sun above.

"We cannot accept the ramblings of a seer turned vampyr! Anything found in our enemy's lands is subject to suspicion," he said.

"Not all vampyrs are our enemies," Evelyn said.

Elder Quinn tapped her fingers against the table. "Like Queen Tovi? Why is it that you trust her after she lied to you for years?"

"Like myself, Tovi Verena made difficult choices to protect her people."

Elder Quinn's painted-blue lips spread into a smile, an understanding sheen flashing across her yellow stare. "Valiance isn't always pretty, is it?"

The tension in Evelyn's knotted belly eased. It felt like the first time someone, despite her sister Mirella, had agreed with her about *something*.

"Protect?" Elder Burns laughed and Elder Rose joined. "Is that what you think you've done? You ran away like a frightened bride, and in doing so, lost the very thing that made you worth anything at all. The greatest gift, the Sun Goddess's power, ran through your veins, and where is it? Where is the hope of defeating the darkness in the wake of your selfishness? Can we still call you the Daughter of the Goddess now that's it gone?"

Gone. The word wedged into the gaping hole in Evelyn's chest, but she balled her fists, refusing to back down or feel the aching loss festering inside her. She may have ripped her flame out of her, but defiance scorched through her blood. She refused to admit the full truth that she was dying. It would be a wasted effort, like this damn hearing.

The Council didn't care for *her*—no, they cared only for her magic, like it was some weapon for all witches. How was she supposed to convince them she needed it back when they didn't even believe it belonged to her? That it was *of* her. When they only saw her for a title, not the efforts she'd endured or the truths she discovered, how did she convince them to see reason?

She wouldn't. *Couldn't.* Why bother wasting her time on stubborn, set-in-their-ways witches? Evelyn wished to break the Blood Curse and save Sorin, and they couldn't stop her.

"I'm not asking permission to get my magic back," Evelyn said, tone unbending. Goddess, she was dying, but she still had resolve. "I don't answer to any of you, not anymore."

Elder Burns laughed. Throaty and deep, it echoed off the atrium's glass walls. "What a brave and rebellious little speech you've prepared. Let me make something very clear. The moment you took your first breath, you answered to Nūa, Evelyn Carson. You are nothing but a weapon, albeit broken at the moment, but when we say jump, you ask how fucking high. Do you understand? The Council decides how to proceed after—"

A growl vibrated through the atrium. A beastly energy prickled in the air, and Kade's boots clattering against the marble were like the deafening beat of a gavel. He joined Evelyn's side, and for the first time since she'd stepped into the hearing, he spoke.

"Evelyn is far more than her flame, and you, Elder Burns, have insulted her bravery one last time."

CHAPTER SEVEN

K ADE'S PATIENCE WANED LIKE the moon.

For an hour, he'd remained silent as Evelyn faced her hearing against the Council. He stood by and said *nothing* as the witches around her doubted and judged, despite his wolf demanding to defend his mate. Not because the Elders hadn't permitted him to speak during the hearing, but because he loved Evelyn and believed in her.

She didn't need him to—she'd commanded the floor like a warrior facing their enemy on the battlefield.

Yet, the Council Elders had their heads shoved so far up their politically threaded asses, they'd overlooked her true message.

"Have you not heard anything Evelyn has said?" Kade demanded. "Or are you too blinded by fear to accept the truth?"

An Elder, frail with skin the thinness of paper, who hadn't uttered a word all morning rose from her seat. Beside Kade, Evelyn stiffened. Without their mating bond intact, he wasn't able to ask who the Elder was mind to mind, but by Evelyn's balled fists, straightened shoulders, and *thud, thud, thud* of her racing heart, she had history with this Elder.

Drab, she wore a high-neck dress that reached to her toes and covered her arms with only skeletal hands exposed as well as her face, set in a permanently pinched expression as if something sour sat on her tongue.

"May I remind you, Kade Drengr, that the terms of this hearing agreed you would not interfere," she said.

Elder Burns nodded. "Elder Circe is right. This is a matter between witches."

Kade's wolf, along with another force, wrestled inside him. "I'll not tolerate the blatant disrespect of my mate."

Circe smiled like a cat that caught its prey. "And that"—she threw her arms out and addressed the atrium—"is the biggest lie of them all. You talk of truths? Here is one: witches and werewolves can't be mates, fated, or whatever you fools believe it to be. It is the prophecy guiding you together."

Kade bared his teeth. Evelyn braced a hand on his forearm, but he ignored her. Doubt the prophecy. Hold prejudice against vampyrs. *Fine.* But Kade wouldn't stand for them discrediting their mating bond, the realest and purest part of them. Their *love* for one another.

"How dare you?" he growled.

"Silence!" Circe shouted, shaking from the baritone in her voice. "I have heard enough! We granted this hearing for diplomacy, but I see it has been a waste of our time. I fear"—she addressed the crowd—"that Elder Burns is right in his assessment. The Daughter of the Goddess and the Son of the God have forgotten their place. It's in the best interest of Sorin that we remind them, and for that reason I am calling a Council vote for a formal trial."

"What?" Kade growled, energy building inside his core.

Mirella shot out of her seat, bracing her hand on the panel. "You are in no position to call for a vote on the Council."

Circe snarled. "Are you? You may have the Ailm seat, but you're the Elder that allowed Evelyn to run. I question if you're truly fit to sit on this Council at all."

Mirella seethed, mouth set in a thin line. She glanced over at Kade and Evelyn, a storm brewing in her Carson-blue eyes. They'd anticipated this and discussed it. Mirella had to tread lightly, and despite what was thrown at Kade and Evelyn, she needed to keep her seat on the Council. If the Carson coven had any chance of protecting them, Mirella couldn't risk her seat. Kade nodded once, and with tears gathering at the edge of her eyes, Mirella sat back down.

Circe inhaled, addressing the others. "Now, those in favor of dropping all charges against Evelyn Carson?"

Kade's heart dropped like a stone to his gut. Evelyn sucked in a breath. Mirella and Elder Quinn raised their hands. The others three remained still.

"Those in favor of moving forward with a formal trial?"

They didn't have the decency to look Kade in the eye as Elders Rose, Burn, and Circe raised their hands.

Evelyn charged forward. "Please. See reason. We don't have time for a trial! There is a curse we must break."

Circe waved her hand. "Of course, of course. You're right. The trail can't delay. We will start tomorrow morning. Until a verdict is reached, the blood-stone must be turned over to the Council for safekeeping."

"*What?*"

The outburst was a collective cry from Kade, Evelyn, Mirella, Blair, and every other Carson coven member present. Those in the pews sprang from their seats.

Roderick jabbed a figure in Circe's direction. "To take another's magic from them is an outrage!"

Evelyn stumbled back a step, shaking her head as tears welled in her eyes. Circe tracked each step, and Kade angled his body ahead of Evelyn, protecting her.

"My mate's magic doesn't belong to you!" Kade roared.

"The gift of the Sun Goddess belongs to the people of Sorin, and your mate has proved unworthy of keeping it in her possession. If Riven is such a threat as you all say he is, what's not to say he isn't hunting it down as we speak."

"You want the power for yourself!" Ruth cried, pushing her way through the crowd to meet them on the floor, Josepha in tow behind her.

Mirella rounded the panel, rushing down the steps. Emmet and the others hurried forward. The atrium erupted. Most objected Circe's demands. Some screamed for Evelyn to comply.

This is madness, Kade thought.

"Please, Kade," Evelyn whispered. "Not *her*."

Kade's attention jumped between the Elder and Evelyn, his instinct screaming something was wrong, and he caught the *thud, thud, thud* of her heart again. Moons, she was petrified. He reached for Evelyn's hand, grasping it in his own.

"Evelyn, it'll be alright," he said. "I've got you."

She blinked. "I won't do it . . . " Her next words were aimed at the council. "I'll not hand over my magic!"

Circe flattened her hands against the table, rearing over it like some snake waiting in the underbrush. "Elder Carson?"

Mirella, with Emmet at her side, said, "The Carson coven stands with Evelyn. What you ask was not voted on by the Council."

At her words, Roderick, Artie, and Blair reached the floor, surrounding Kade and Evelyn on all sides. Kade's inner wolf paced, howling with rage. Like the yank of the moon against tides, a tautness brimmed deep inside Kade.

Stars above. He'd mentally prepared for many things these last few weeks—Riven attacking, the curse spreading over the Void, and more demons leaching across Sorin's borders. Yet, he'd never imagined their own turning against them.

"If you will not comply with the best interests of Sorin, we are left with no choice but to take the bloodstone by force." Circe inclined her head at the Guards stationed at the doors. They charged, sights on the bloodstone resting on Evelyn's chest

The energy inside Kade amounted to an uncontrollable force. Weeks' worth of tension tipped over the edge he'd teetered on. The power he'd not conjured since the Blood Moon rose in an untamed wave. Kade had no grasp on it and unleashed.

Kade's power spread out in a circle of immense blue. The witches gathered screamed, and the glass walls burst into shimmering dust. Stunned silence rang in the atrium, and Kade stumbled, an emptiness flushing through him.

"What is this?" Circe roared. "What *are* you?"

Kade blinked and snapped back to the present. The winds of Nūa escaped past the aftermath of his destruction. Witches cowered yards away, pressed into the brass beams of the atrium's frame. Kade spun, finding the council wide-eyed and fearful along with Mirella and Emmet. He searched the crowd, hoping, wishing, praying to all the gods that might listen, that he hadn't hurt anyone and thank the stars above, he found only the Guards on their back sides, struggling to stand.

But Kade's shred of relief was short lived.

"More lies . . . " Elder Burns whispered. "This was certainly left out of your tale, Miss Carson."

"Kade's power is new." Evelyn grabbed his hand, standing with him. "He is still learning it."

"Power?" Circe's eyes narrowed. "It's an abomination. Werewolves do not have magic. Not like that."

"It's darkness," Elder Rose hissed.

"It's not." But Kade couldn't fight the tremor in his voice.

Mirella pushed forward. "Kade is the Son of the God; he isn't just any werewolf."

"The first third-born werewolf, Finton, possessed no such power," Elder Burns said.

"The *truest* unions will defeat the darkness," Blair said. "Kade and Evelyn are mates while Finton and Carena weren't, and there is no stronger bond than souls tied by fate."

Kade balked, caught off guard by Blair standing up for him.

"This is nonsense!" Circe slammed her fist into the table. "Regardless of where or how Kade has come by this power, he is dangerous. Arrest them both! They're a threat to city."

"*No,*" Kade growled.

His mate had already endured enough. Locked away in Drystan Castle. Sacrificed her magic. Kade wouldn't let the witches through her in a cell—

Evelyn hissed in pain, cursing as she snatched her hand from his.

He whirled. "Ev—"

It took every ounce of strength to keep standing.

Evelyn, wide-eyed and panting, clutched her hand to her chest. Blair held her shoulders, dark-as-night eyes tracking Kade like some wild beast. His wolf's sense of smell caught burnt flesh and blood. *No. No. No.* Blisters formed across her palm and fingertips as the dreadful seconds trudged by.

Evelyn stepped forward. "Kade, it's alright—"

He retreated out of her reach, shaking his head as tears stung at the edge of his eyes. His heart cracked. "I fucking hurt *you.*"

"It was an accident. You didn't mean to." Her words turned small, desperate.

Kade's wolf whimpered, and his instincts screamed to protect her. But how could he with this *abomination* coursing through his veins? Perhaps a cell was where he belonged after what he'd done to his mate.

Evelyn strode towards him again, but he flinched. She halted, face falling.

He couldn't bear to look at her and witness the pain she tried to fight, knowing she didn't have her magic to heal the angry red wound on her hand. That she was already dying, and he'd hurt her more. All because this power was too great, too unpredictable for him to master.

Protect her, his wolf howled.

"Arrest me." He averted his attention away from her, locking his gaze on Circe. "I'll comply with your wishes, but leave Evelyn and the bloodstone with her coven."

"*What?*" Evelyn cried from behind him. "*NO!*"

He moved towards the Guards and held out his hands.

"Kade, don't do this!" His strong, beautiful mate's tear-laden words strangled his heart. Commotion resounded behind him. Guards forced him to his knees. He fell with ease, no fight left in him. Evelyn's sobs and her sisters' comforting words echoed in the corners of his wary mind.

But he didn't dare turn and meet Evelyn's steely stare. He tamped down his wolf, and allowed shackles to clamp around his wrists. Unfitting relief washed through him, his power subdued, locked away so he couldn't hurt anyone else.

Circe peered down her nose at him, a sickening smirk playing on her lips. "Our Council vote remains. Evelyn's trial will start in three days' time, but in exchange for your surrender, she is permitted to keep her bloodstone and remain with her coven while you, Kade Drengr, are under arrest—"

"*No!*" Evelyn cried.

"—and Tùir's newest prisoner."

Chapter Eight

Dark, ominous clouds seemed to have followed Tovi all the way from Drystan to the Vadon Mountains. She, Yennifer, and Lou had returned to the Drengr Village late the night before, climbing into bed and waking with the sun for morning training.

As they weaved through the main street, headed back towards the Shield-maiden, Tovi braced against the sneering stares from surrounding werewolves. Merchants stopped mid-sentence, mothers drew their children closer, and the smithy paused his hammering.

Walking through Drengr Village was like pushing through a tangled holly bush—the werewolves' stares pricked every inch of Tovi's exposed skin, all because she was a vampyr. But why did Tovi expect anything less?

It's one of the reasons she'd refused Eldrick's request. How could she remain in a place that hadn't accepted her?

Lou caught up to Tovi's side. "Do you think it's wise to stay at Lucy's tavern?"

"Where else would I stay?" Tovi asked, feigning ignorance.

"Lār," Yennifer called over her shoulder. "As a political guest."

Tovi ground her teeth, her muscles growing taut with the biting cold.

"I agree," Lou said. "It's far safer."

She almost snorted. Eldrick resided in stone fortress to the north, and she considered staying—*sleeping*—beyond the same four walls as the alpha far more dangerous territory than risking a disgruntled werewolf at the Shield-maiden. She could at least fight her way against an unfriendly foe, but the mere thought of Eldrick unraveled her resolve. Tovi wasn't certain she couldn't resist him.

To the left, warriors sat huddled together on a lone wooden table, waxing their shields. The crests etched into their armor glinted various colors—evergreen, violet, midnight blue—indicating they were all from different packs. Yet, they shared the same caustic energy.

Spit landed near Tovi's boot, jarring her to a halt. Shei stepped forward, a hiss vibrating through her chest, but Yen grabbed her wrist, halting her in place.

"It isn't worth it," her friend whispered.

Tovi seethed, but Yen was right. If she reacted, she gave the warriors a reason to attack.

"Let's go," she muttered.

Tovi, Lou, and Yennifer turned the corner, and thankfully onto a busier street brimming with activity.

Red splattered all over Tovi's boot as she trudged through a puddle. The crimson resembled blood, and Tovi had to blink past the haze of her vampyr hunger. She inhaled, scenting metallics. *Paint.* Why in bloody hel was there red pain in the middle of the street? Her senses were honed enough that she caught Yen's gasp. Tovi whipped her head up and stilled.

A single, horrid word was painted across the Shield-maiden's front. The fresh letters dripped down the doorway, the color crimson running with the grooves of the redwood trunks.

Bloodsucker

Winter wind barreled into Tovi, but the cold force was nothing compared to the numbness buzzing in her limbs. This was *her* doing. She'd been staying at the tavern, and her presence had brought unwanted attention.

Closer to the door, Lucy wrung her hands into her apron, moisture glistening in the usual proud and jolly tavern owner's eyes.

"Did you get sights on who did it?" Yen asked, loose wheat curls from her braid whipping in the wind.

Lucy sighed. "No. The Shield-maiden was empty this morning, and I thought maybe the frost had kept everyone away. When I went to check the state of the sky, that's when I found . . . this."

Tovi set her shoulders back, fighting the rage flushing through her centuries-old being. "Lucy, I'm sorry—"

"Don't you dare apologize for something you didn't do." Lucy's tone left no room to argue. "This is someone else's hate, not your own."

Silence ballooned between them, tension brimming in the street air.

Hate.

Tovi swallowed, her sense of foolishness like lodged glass in her throat. Eldrick had declared her an ally, but he was *one* werewolf. Their alliance was up against a deeply woven prejudice. Demons and *caillte*, vampyrs lost completely to the Blood Curse, had crossed the Void and ravaged and slaughtered innocents in Sorin for hundreds of years.

All because of the curse *her* father had set in motion.

Tovi held the weight of the painted word on her shoulders and her father's mistakes. Worse, her brother, Riven, was following in their father's footsteps. Which was the reason she needed the werewolves to ally with her. To break the curse. Undo her family's mistakes. Yet did she really expect relations between vampyrs and werewolves to change in a matter of weeks?

"You're not the only vampyr in the village, Tovi," Nadia's words ceased Tovi's rampant thoughts.

The werewolf-vampyr emerged from an alley, lips down turning at the sight of the paint on the Shield-maiden's front.

Tovi shook her head. "I brought this to your village."

"No." Nadia approached the door, running her fingers through the wet paint and rubbing it between her pale fingers. "I'm partially to blame."

Lucy's brows pinched, and she rested a hand on her hip. "You're our female alpha."

Nadia sighed, the gold in her eyes dimming. "I haven't held that title in a long time."

Tovi's stomach tightened. She'd turned Nadia into a vampyr and honed her into one of the best spies in Drystan. Under the disguise of Tala, she'd had a front-row seat to Riven's council and plans.

With the news that Nadia Drengr wasn't dead but a vampyr, they feared she'd blown her cover as Tala, and so she'd remained in the village, home at last. Tovi's heart had warmed at the sight of her friend returned to her mate, sons, and pack.

Yet it appeared they'd both been naïve.

"There's a chance it wasn't a Drengr, seeing the other packs have remained after the council meeting," Yennifer said.

Nadia sighed. "Whoever it was, they'll answer to Aramis—"

"Filthy bloodsuckers, indeed," a male voice sneered.

Behind them, three male werewolves prowled towards the Shield-maiden. Tovi assessed their weapons and clothes, noting the leader possessed Johannes green on his breastplate. Her stomach dropped as she spotted the other two's Drengr navy cloaks layered under furs.

Though, she didn't spy any evidence of a red paint, not a single drop. They hadn't been the ones to write the word, but they agreed with it.

"Move along." A male growl echoed off the buildings, and Bétar emerged from an alleyway. Todd joined his side, the Gray Fenris weapon's master emerging from the shadows. Orange hair streaked with pink popped into the light next. Linx's catlike eyes focused on the lone wolf. Belle was last, and the air tingled as she flexed her fingers. The tension on the street grew tauter and tauter, like Yen's bow string before she released it.

The Johannes werewolf's gaze narrowed on Tovi, and she fought the instinct to bare her fangs. Any other instance, she'd give the bastard a piece of her mind. Let him feel her anger. But if she reacted, she gave him a reason to attack. She couldn't afford to escalate the tension in the village with a fight, and as much as Tovi hated it, she refused to give him the satisfaction they riled her.

The werewolves grumbled, disappointment bleeding into their expressions as they left without another word.

A collective sigh eased from Tovi and the group, and she averted her attention back to the Sheild maiden's door, ignoring the questioning glances sent her way.

Lou cleared her throat. "Tovi, I really think it's best you stay at Lār. You'll be—"

"*No.*" Tovi flinched at her own tone, clamping her eyes shut.

Despite the danger she faced in the Drengr Village, she feared something else more. *Eldrick.* Tovi didn't trust herself around him, and she'd rather face a unit of Drengr warriors than sleep in the same building as him, battling the temptation to—

Tovi cursed and shook her head. She refused to dwell on such traitorous, wicked thoughts. She was a *queen*, and slipping into bed with an alpha was anything but queenlike. In fact, she was certain any sort of relationship other than allies worsened the relationship between vampyrs and werewolves.

"If I leave, it's a sign of weakness." She paused for a moment. This affected not only her. "But I can understand, Lucy, if you need me to."

"I've made my decision about you, Tovi Verena. No number of slow days at the tavern or paint is going to change that. You're welcome to stay here as long as you like."

Tovi gave her a small smile. "Thank you."

She avoided Yen and Bétar's worried stares, objections pursing on their lips. Todd studied the paint, Belle at his side.

"What do we do next?" the weapons master asked.

Tovi removed her cloak, thrust it to the side, and rolled up her sleeves. "We start by cleaning this off."

"Tovi, you're the vampyr *queen*. Are you sure cleaning up vandalism is your job?" Lou asked, brows creased with concern.

Tovi braced against the winds tunneling through the village street. More snow lay in the air, and she tried to inhale that promise and ignore the battle warring inside her. She'd fought so long for the title of queen, yet she wasn't sure what it meant. How to act. Who she was.

But she knew one thing. "Leaders set the precedent."

"She's right."

Eldrick's commanding tone thrummed up Tovi's spine. She shuddered and fought the urge to run. Instead, she turned to face him. Sharp jaw. Proud shoulders. Assured walk. She blinked past it all, but there was that insatiable tug, the invisible thread that pulled them together.

"We get rid of this word as quickly as we can, and then we move forward." Eldrick addressed everyone, and then his stare landed on Tovi and stayed. A thousand words stirred in his gem eyes, and by the way his jaw ticked, he fought them all.

For they'd not seen one another in weeks.

Tovi severed their intense connection and glared back at the painted door, but she couldn't shake the way her body responded to Eldrick. Tovi had faced challenges, yes, but no enemy or power had thrown her off balance like Eldrick Drengr. His eyes. His touch. His *words*.

Stay.

Eldrick's request after the council meeting played in the back of her mind, but it was different words in another voice that intruded on her thoughts as constantly as the chirping of the nearby songbirds.

The wolf and dove.

Opal, her brother's wife, had whispered that line from the prophecy, and it haunted Tovi's thoughts, following like Drystan mists.

That was why she stayed away. Run to Drystan and let the cursed cold of her homeland nip at her skin and remind her of what was truly at stake. What her people faced.

Yet, the power of fate frightened Tovi. She'd searched for answers on how to break the curse for decades. She'd believed in Evelyn and Kade, the third borns. Tovi never imagined that the prophecy included *her*. When she considered what the words meant, she couldn't breathe. Couldn't *think*.

Because it begged the question, *what* was Eldrick to her?

And why was she so afraid?

Later—

"They're right, you know."

Tovi snapped her attention to the alpha werewolf who'd joined her side, sour ire coating her teeth. "About?"

Eldrick leaned in close, *too* close, his next whisper tickling her ear. "As an ally of the Drengr Pack, you're a formal guest staying at Lār. I'll have servants collect your things, as well as Lou's, from the Shield-maiden—"

"That isn't necessary—"

"This my village, and ensuring your safety protects the rest of my pack, too."

Eldrick didn't give Tovi room to argue and stalked off into the tavern to retrieve cleaning supplies with Lucy, leaving her rooted to the cobblestone.

Hours later, as she scrubbed and washed paint away, Tovi tried to convince herself it didn't matter. Not Eldrick's words. Not Opal's words. Not now. She had to focus on maintaining a relationship with the werewolves, especially with Riven's growing power back home. A *diplomatic* kind. Prove vampyrs weren't all monsters and working together saved Sorin.

But as the paint cleared and her mind wandered, Tovi's stomach tangled into knots. She'd fought relentlessly for her people for centuries, to free them of this curse, to disprove the very word she tried to wipe away, but perhaps the freedom she'd battled to win for herself was slipping through her fingers.

CHAPTER NINE

B LAIR'S YOUNGER SISTER PACED. The dark clouds looming over the city may as well have tunneled into Mirella's kitchen, brewing above the Carsons as they discussed Circe's harrowing move.

She'd locked Kade Drengr—third born, protector, and Son of the God—in Tùir. Nūa's enemies were demons or scáths; they weren't exactly the thrown-in-prison sort. No. Cells in the prison were reserved for the worst witches, those who'd found dark magic. There were fewer and fewer since the Great Burnings, but it didn't overshadow the connotations that came with the prison, nor the stain of those who spent time in it. Circe was making a statement—witches should fear Kade.

Blair fidgeted where she stood, leaning against the kitchen counter. Her own secrets slithered like hissing snakes in her blood. She drove her fingernails deep into her biceps, refocusing on that pain instead of the childhood fears that *she'd* one day end up in that prison. For witches who possessed powers like she did were branded dark and thrown in Tùir.

"Mirella," Evelyn pleaded for the tenth time. "There must be something we can do."

Emmet braced his hands on the Elder's shoulders. "We will do something, Evelyn, but first, we must take a step back. Recoup, rest—"

"*Rest?*" Evelyn hissed. "I know he chose this, but I can't leave him there. I *won't.*"

Blair nibbled her lip, wishing she could agree, but she feared if she spoke out loud, all attention would fall on her, shifting Evelyn's wrath. Rook, her familiar, shot through the open window, gliding over the table and landing straight atop the counter. He dropped a silver bead embedded with moonstone, rolling it towards Blair with his beak.

"Little thief," she whispered, tucking the keepsake into her trousers pocket.

Rook hopped into her awaiting hold, and Blair tucked him into her arms, and ran her hands through his feathers as she thought. Blair remained silent, watchful, her usual tactic since Evelyn had returned home.

Josepha exhaled, thrumming her fingers onto the table. "What do you think Riven will do when he learns Kade is locked away? If he didn't have a reason to attack before, now he does. Kade's absence leaves Sorin vulnerable, as well as Evelyn."

Evelyn bore her stare into the floor tile, the gray shifting back and forth as she considered. "That has to be a reasonable argument to the Council."

Mirella sighed. "There's no changing Circe's mind so quickly."

Ruth clucked her tongue, her eye widening. "Who says we include that spiteful bitch?"

Evelyn nodded. "I agree. At this point, I'll be acting with or without the Council's wishes."

Blair stiffened, and Rook ruffled his feathers.

Artie and Rodrick shared a silent conversation while Josepha said, "What do you suppose we do?"

Evelyn didn't bat an eye, and Blair's insides twisted. For her sister was different. *Changed.* Prouder and surer of herself than ever before, and Blair hated that brumal sensation crawling up her spine.

"We break him out," Evelyn said, tone absolute.

No one said a word. Mirella's brows furrowed, calculative. Was Blair's eldest sister considering it? Ruth's eyes danced with excitement, and the other Carsons' reserved silence screamed agreement. *Goddess,* where had their unwavering support been last year when *she* was sacked?

Blair saw red, the angry wave she held back unleashing. Rook shot out of her arms, retreating to the windowsill to look on from afar.

"You all can't be serious," she hissed. "Go against the Council? Mirella, you sit on it!"

"As far as I'm aware, they went against Kade and I first," Evelyn said. "We aren't players on a chessboard that they can move about whenever they please."

Blair gritted her teeth, and she held out her hands, gesturing them at Evelyn. "You're protectors. It is, in fact, *exactly* what you are."

Read books. Study until the late hours. Thrive off research. Arrive on time yet stay late. Shoulders back, presentable. Speak your mind but think first. And don't, for the love of the Goddess, step out of line. Every time Blair had, fate yanked her back. She'd been born a second, a scholar and a witch. *That* was her place. Why didn't Evelyn, out of all the third borns, not understand that order was in place to keep them safe and on course?

Evelyn's expression shifted to an unsettling indifference. "Alright, how would *you* suggest we proceed, then?"

Blair sighed. All she wanted was to sit in the Nūa library again, surrounded by her books and everything she'd worked towards all these years. The prestige and recognition. But that meant the Carson coven had to remain in Circe's good graces, seeing she was the leading scholar of the city.

"You attend the trial and appease the Council," she said.

"No." Evelyn's nostrils flared, arms tightly folded over her chest.

She scoffed, and the rest of the Carsons looked on, sitting back as the two sisters who'd once been dearest friends fought.

"Is your plan to run again? Need I remind you, it didn't work out well the first time." She jabbed a finger towards the bloodstone.

Hurt flashed across Evelyn's face.

"Blair." Mirella's mouth fell open. "That isn't fair."

"Neither is a trial," Evelyn said through gritted teeth.

"*You ran!*" Blair's voice ricocheted in the kitchen. Shadows crept over the walls, and Blair blinked. No, her mind played tricks. Evening descended across the city. "Whether you like it or not, you're being held accountable for your actions. Give it time—"

"*Fucking flames,* I don't have time, Blair!" Evelyn said. "I'm dying."

The air whooshed out of the room. Cold pricked across Blair's skin like a blanket of mist. "What did you just say?"

Both Mirella and Evelyn clamped their eyes shut.

"Oh my gods, have you both kept this from me?"

The rest of the coven shifted in their seats, mirroring Blair's surprise.

"It's news to all of us," Ruth muttered.

"Does Kade know?" Emmett asked, avoiding Mirella's pleading stare.

Evelyn nodded. "We realized it together, with the mating bond."

All these weeks, Blair'd kept her distance. Two years she'd wished for her sister's return, and in the days of her homecoming, Blair'd warred with herself. Be grateful. Feel relief. Yet, resentment had rooted itself in her, so she'd stayed away, and to what end? She'd wasted time. She was a fool to think her sister's fractured soul didn't have dire consequences, impending ones.

The darkness lying dormant rose now more than ever. Anger was so easy to grasp. Blair pushed off the counter, charging towards her sister. "Why didn't you tell me?"

Evelyn's expression turned tired. Hair amiss, reddened cheeks. "You haven't exactly been around to tell."

Blair scoffed. "I've been busy, researching how to get your magic back."

"Is that so?" Evelyn asked. "Where exactly?"

Blair ground her teeth. "I have my ways." She didn't go into detail about sneaking into the Nūa Library, not when she'd berated Evelyn about her place. *You're a hypocrite,* cruel voices whispered in the back of her mind. Rook clacked his beak, ruffling his feathers as if he'd heard them, too. Or worse, agreed with them.

"I also have an extensive library of my own as well as contacts in the city," Blair said.

Her sister shook her head, snorting. "Were you ever planning to tell me you'd lost your position?"

Mirella cleared her throat. "I'd like to clarify that I thought"—she gave Blair a pointed look—"she'd told you."

Blair laughed, and the darkness lying dormant in her blood rose like thorny vines crawling up a tree.

"Ah, yes." She threw her hands in the air. "Continue to grovel, Mirella. It's such a flattering look for you."

Emmet rose to his full height. "Watch yourself."

"Why are you being cruel?" Evelyn's dark brows pinched, the blue in her eyes dimming to gray.

"Did you forget how horrible Mirella was?" Blair asked. "In the days leading up to your wedding, you begged for time, and she refused, practically using it as a punishment for Mother's and Father's deaths."

Mirella winced, and Evelyn frowned, moisture collecting at the edges of her eyes. Thunder rumbled outside, and lightning flashed across the windows. The streaks of light only darkened the kitchen, sucking the hope out of them all.

"But where were you?" Evelyn asked. "Silent and at Mirella's side. The only one there for me was Tovi."

Blair froze. She didn't want to think of her old friend, someone else who'd left and forgotten her. Who'd lied. Evelyn had found forgiveness, and perhaps her sister was a better witch than her.

"Call it groveling all you like." Mirella stood, planting both hands on the table as she leaned over it. Her proud shoulders, stern expression, and kind eye reminded Blair so much of their mother. "But I was a shit sister when Evelyn needed me most, and I won't make the same mistake again. If that means going against the Council and breaking Kade out of Tùir, so be it."

Blair's boots melted to the tile floor.

With eyes closed and a deep inhale, Evelyn took a moment to calm herself. "It doesn't matter what happened then, it matters more about what we do now—"

"No." Winds howled outside, and the window shot fully open, clattering against the wall. Papers furled atop the table, and the pots and pans hanging above the stove rattled as Blair's wind bronntanas arose with her heightened emotions. "It *does* matter. I fought for you and pushed the Council to keep searching. I knew Kade was the key to finding you, argued that point at this very table with all of you, and *no one listened*. Not even Mirella, who played the obedient firstborn. So, I took matters into my own hands and found Kade myself. He never would've left this damn continent if it weren't for my help, and yet, what do I have to show for it? I lost my job and none of you"—she glared at those seated at the table—"fought for me, but Evelyn waltzed into the city, and it's as if she's done no wrong, like she never even ran. Even worse, you expect all of us to fall in line behind you, Evelyn—"

"That isn't true, and you know it," Evelyn stated. "I know running had consequences, and I've carried guilt with me every day since I walked out of this city, but I can't go back in time, Blair. It was the best decision I could make."

"I don't accept that," Blair said. "You chose to not come to me, *to lie*, as if I, your sister, wasn't good enough."

Evelyn swallowed, moisture collecting in her gray stare. "I'm here now, Blair, asking for your help, and the threat is far worse than when I lost my flame. Will you?"

Six expectant stares landed on her. Rook flew to her shoulder, picking at her curls as she wavered. How could she stand in a room with so many of her coven members and yet feel so alone?

She's your sister. Blair's heart thumped with that truth.

The last time she had tried to help Evelyn, though, she'd ended up with nothing. No title, purpose. Fate had taught her time and time again that her birth order protected her from hurt, and as a scholar, she had no place in helping Evelyn.

Worse, her shadows were harder to snuff down with heightened emotions. Blair couldn't risk something far more fitting for a third born. Especially when the plan hinged on Tùir, a place where witches who had magic like hers were locked away.

"I can't." She stepped back.

"Perhaps it was a good thing I never came to you when I lost my flame," Evelyn whispered.

"What is that supposed to mean?" Blair hissed.

"Only days ago, you said you'd done something wrong as a sister if I couldn't trust you," Evelyn's voice shook. "I believed you, and yet now, you don't have my back."

Blair's chest heaved as she gritted her teeth. "I also recall us promising one another to be honest from here on out. So, here is the truth, Evelyn: You *are* a third born. With that comes the expectation you listen to orders."

"I'll not be caged by my title," Evelyn shouted, her words shaking the walls. "Especially when the Elders are blind against the looming threat of Riven and the curse."

Blair threw up her hands. "You only feel trapped because you haven't accepted the way of things. Our birth order, duties, and titles matter. They keep us in line for a greater purpose. "

Evelyn shook her head. "I used to think you were so brilliant, so apt in your post as a scholar, *jealous* even, and now I see all it does is control you."

Blair seethed, not bothering to draw back her winds as they whirled around her feet. "*Fuck you.*"

With that, she stormed out of Mirella's kitchen, leaving the Carson coven and whatever plan they had to face the incomings storms without her.

Chapter Ten

Evelyn

Evelyn tiptoed her way down Nūa's docks. It felt oddly eerie that the last time she'd had entered the harbor, she'd been readying to flee the city then, too.

Ships bobbed on the choppy water. Clouds remained overhead, more storms rumbling on the horizon. Evelyn's heart hammered in her chest as she eyed the prison tower situated on the isle a mile offshore.

Tùir glared down at her. Small windows ringed the thirty levels, like a thousand eyes narrowed to slits. Evelyn gritted her teeth, a scorching heat flushing through her.

For Kade sat in one of those cells.

Because he'd walked away from her.

Evelyn's shoulders slacked with an imaginary weight. She'd been there, struggling with her flame but everything they'd endured together, did Kade not trust her? Did he not understand that she was with him in this, no matter how immense his power was?

One, two, three.

The planks under feet. The whooshing waves. The salty wind. Evelyn grounded herself and tucked her worries into the back of her mind—she had a meeting point to get to.

Evelyn peered left and right, ensuring the dock was clear, and scurried across. The door atop a fishing boat groaned open, and Evelyn ducked out of sight between two barrels covered in netting, clamping a hand over her mouth to stifle her breathing. Boots clobbered out of sight, and tobacco carried on the wind.

"I'm telling you, these storms aren't natural this time of year," a fisherman said, his voice growing nearer.

Evelyn pressed further into her hiding space. Not Guards, thank the Goddess, but Evelyn didn't want to be seen by a single soul, not when the stretch from here to the tower was long and difficult, and coming across the wrong witch might alert a Guard before she'd even made it to the shores of the Tùir's island.

"Nothing natural of late," another muttered as he huffed. Tobacco grew thicker in the air, tickling the back of Evelyn's throat.

"I suppose you're right." The fishermen grew closer, their worn boots near enough, Evelyn could reach past the nettling and touch them.

She didn't move. Didn't breathe.

"The fish are scarcer while more of those water-like demons are paying us a visit," the fisherman said. "*Spitting squids*, I swear I saw one not too far off the docks. Venturing out of deep waters, I'm telling you."

Fucking flames.

Evelyn glanced towards the sea—dark, murky, and *angry*. Were demons swimming below the choppy waves? Sea demons dwelled farther north, near Morrow, a party town that bordered the Void. Evelyn's stomach churned like the waves trapped under the docks. The darkness *was* spreading. Why hadn't she considered the Sapphire Sea?

"Now who's spouting the ridiculous? You've been smoking too much of that pipe of yours, gotten your magic and sights all in a twist."

"Just trying to take the edge off," the fisherman grumbled.

A resounding smack bounced off the boats. Evelyn fidgeted ever so slightly, catching the two fishermen three feet away. One had grasped the other's shoulder, a soft smile tilting his moustache and lips.

"Well, there's a bit of hope—the Daughter of the Goddess is back," he said.

Evelyn's heart skipped in her chest. The bones of the dock bruised her ass, as she waited for the onslaught of insults she'd read for weeks in the Nūa papers. Or worse, beliefs as strong-willed as her sister's.

Yet, the fisherman sighed, mirroring his friend's smile. A lightness beamed in his eyes. "Indeed, she is. With that other third born, the werewolf, I hear. I suppose you're right."

The two fishermen continued on, their conversation turning jolly as they laughed their way up the docks.

Buzzing with infectious energy, Evelyn peeled from her hiding place and hurried down, running with the shadows of the fisherman's boat. Wind nipped her ankles and bare arms. She searched the end of the docks, Goddess, she wished she had her magic to assess the area.

"*Psst*, Evelyn," a male voice whispered.

She whirled, finding Emmet and Artie waving behind a crate. Evelyn checked her surroundings before she ran to meet them, and together, they hunched out of sight.

"Mirella?" she asked.

Emmett tapped his temple. "She and Ruth made it into the prison."

Evelyn fought a wince, told herself Kade'd not be stuck in a cell for much longer. *If* their plan worked.

"Here's a bag of supplies," Artie said, handing her a satchel. "Enchanted it myself, so nothing will get wet. I suggest you tuck the bloodstone inside there, too."

"Thank you." She studied them both. "And thank you for helping me. I know this must be difficult—"

"The true challenge, Evelyn, is watching you leave again so soon." Emmett offered a sad smile. "Your sisters missed you. Every day. Even Blair, despite her decision."

Her sister's berating words weaved with the wind, as if Blair's bronntanas encircled Nūa. She'd refused to help, and that left Evelyn off-balance, like the uneasy waves stretching between the harbor and Tùir. But was she a fool to have expected such a warm homecoming? That Blair *wouldn't* resent her for losing her scholarly position?

Evelyn sighed, averting her gaze from her brother-in-law. She blinked back tears and assessed the waves. "Any wager there are demons out there?"

"If there are, I bet they're more afraid of you than you are of them." Artie winked.

Evelyn snorted, appreciating her relative's tease.

Emmett shut his eyes, tilting his head. "Mirella just mind-linked. They're on their way to Kade's cell now."

Evelyn nodded and swung the enchanted satchel over her shoulder. She'd donned a simple mock tank top and linen trousers. Light and airy, the attire suited her better than her usual fighting leathers or high-waisted trousers. If she made it across the sea—

No—*when* she reached the island, another set of clothes would be waiting.

Evelyn gritted her teeth as she caught her reflection in the water. Yellow bled from the lanterns behind her, drawing out the determination edging her brow. She squatted down and swung her legs over the edge of the dock. The sea kissed her legs with crisp droplets, and goose bumps prickled up her flesh.

Goddess, please let there be no demons.

She didn't have time to pay the fisherman's story any mind, not when others were counting on her, Kade most important of all. As she eased into the water, Emmett and Artie stared down at her with encouraging smiles.

"Good luck, Evelyn," her uncle said. "We'll keep the Guards distracted while you're swimming across."

"Thank you," she breathed.

With the help of the choppy current and her strong legs, Evelyn kicked her way from the docks. As the boats shrank, the water turned colder, enough that her teeth chattered, but ahead her, the tower grew taller, the distant lanterns surrounding its base like beacons.

The last shred of light from port vanished, and Evelyn reached waters drenched in night. She swallowed, calming her ragged breaths, and began to swim with her arms and legs. Waves barreled into her. Salt stung her eyes and pinched the back of her throat. After twenty-five yards, Evelyn's lungs burned. Exhaustion reached up like the tentacles of some demon and gripped her ankles.

But Evelyn didn't care.

With each kick, stretch of her arms, and pull against the sea, she rallied her might and swam towards her fated. No different than a ratlike demon in Connacht Castle. No different than the Void, Drystan snow, or the vampyr fighting rings. Whatever they faced, whatever separated them—a vast sea, thick iron bars, or lost time—they'd always fight to be together again.

Evelyn didn't have her magic or a weapon, but she did have her mind, body, and will.

As well as her love for Kade.

And she harnessed hope.

It energized her all the way to the rocky shores of the Tùir.

CHAPTER ELEVEN

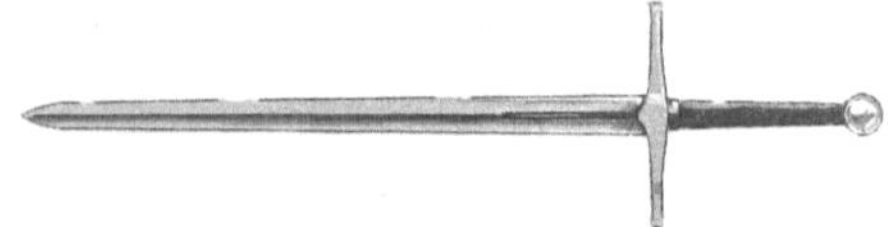

S TARS ABOVE, KADE'D SCREWED up.

What had he been thinking? Evelyn was dying, and he'd abandoned her. *Moons.* He had to get back to her.

Kade clawed at the seams of his cell's metal door until his fingers bled. He'd found no luck with a loose stone in the wall around him. Briny winds crept in from the window, melding with the stench of mildew and piss. He'd already tried to break out that way, but it was far too narrow to fit through.

Thunder shook Tùir, and Kade banged his hands against the door. He hated the power coursing through his blood, the reason he'd fear himself and why he'd retreated from Evelyn.

It's an abomination.

Circe's shrill voice echoed in Kade's mind. He didn't wish to believe it, but the scent of Evelyn's burned flesh roiled his stomach. He'd hurt Todd weeks ago, and now his mate. Who would he harm next? When would his luck run out and he *more* than hurt someone?

"You taste like darkness, so very, very sweet."

Kade snapped his head up, focusing ahead. On the other side of the metal door, someone hummed a jolly tune. But who? He'd not heard or smelled anyone since the witches had deposited him in the cell. He stood and walked towards the door on cautious feet, the absence of his wolf jarring as his instinct sensed *other*.

He peered through the barred slit in the door and fought the urge to rear back as a male's face appeared, and an all milky-white eye roamed over him. It swiveled on its own accord, while the other eye, russet with flecks of crimson, pinned him in place. Chains grated against the stone as he paced the hall, and Kade stilled further.

"Who are you?" he asked. "What are you?"

"Tenebris, witch, and prisoner."

Yet, he wasn't in a cell. *How?*

The witch giggled. "Delighted to discover the darkness has brought a new friend."

Kade's hackles rose. "I'm not a friend."

As pale as bone, Tenebris's face split into a too-wide smile. Teeth, brown and yellow with decay and sharp as needles, pierced his bottom lip and drew blood. "Right, right. Forgive my excitement. I haven't had someone on this floor in over a century, and one becomes lonely when all one's friends die."

A century. Kade's blood turned to ice. Sorin didn't have a hundred years, but he doubted Evelyn, Eldrick, or the Gray Fenris would allow Circe to lock him away that long. Neither would he, despite his own fuckup of landing himself here.

"Why are you here, Tenebris?" he asked.

The witch tilted his head. "Same as you. I'm a witch who used dark magic."

"I'm not a witch," Kade bit out. Nor had he used dark magic.

Doubt snaked through him. Was he certain about that? With a frustrated growl, he shoved his shoulder against the door. The metal rattled with the force, but not enough to budge.

The white eye darted left while the reddish brown one widened. "Ah, that is why your magic tastes so different."

Kade ignored any mention of his power, hating that he couldn't sense it, and yet this witch still felt it. "Why aren't you in a cell? How did you get out?"

"The darkness helped me—could help you, too, if you let it."

"No." Kade gritted his teeth.

"Why not?" Tenebris asked. "Your power rises in darkness, has the force to shine *with* it."

"You're wrong." Kade shook his head. "I am Kade Drengr, Son of the God and third born, prophesied to defeat the darkness."

The witch tilted his head back and cackled with laughter, his bony collarbone pressing out of his tattered clothes. "Why are you so certain which god gave you *that* power, hmm?" He stepped towards Kade's cell. "You could burn the world. *Rule it.*"

Kade's stomach back flipped. With the enchanted walls, no part of his power, new or his inner wolf, answered. It was only his heart racing against the prospect that he *was* darkness. Perhaps that was why he couldn't control it. Maybe that was why more harm than good came from it.

A door groaned down the corridor, and Tenebris squeaked. "I best be going."

"*Wait,*" Kade said.

But the witch ignored him, disappearing into the shadows of the hall, chains and feet eerily silent.

More light bled down the hall on the left. Three sets of boots clattered against the stone, and Kade narrowed his gaze, inspecting their silhouettes and attire. One was cloaked, and two others glinted in the Guard's signature gold-and-black uniforms. They were still too far to make out the colors of their coven, but Kade inhaled, trying to gage their scents.

One was familiar. Medicinal, herby, and—

"Mirella," he breathed, as Evelyn's eldest sister stopped outside his door.

She dropped her hood, revealing her blonde hair slicked back in a low, tidy bun. She smiled. "Good evening, Kade."

"What am I?" Ruth planted her hands on her hips. "Scáth dinner?"

Kade almost smiled, a hundred questions hurrying up his throat, but stopped. Both Mirella and Ruth gave him a pointed look, widening their eyes a fraction that screamed, *Don't.*

For a Guard joined them last. Unlike Ruth, her colors glistened Burns coven green. She kept a wide berth from the cell, eying Kade with disdain.

Ruth shot her a glare with enough power to freeze the desert lands of Cirilo. "Well, are you going to let us in or not?"

"I'm not permitted to open his cell," the Guard said. "Circe's orders—"

"She isn't here, and yet we are," Ruth said, brows raised. "I outrank you, protector. Elder Carson also sits on the Council. Her orders outrank us all."

The Guard gritted her teeth. "You requested to *speak* to the prisoner."

Mirella snorted. "I requested to see Kade. I'm a healer and can't do my job through that door, now can I?"

The Guard's nostrils flared as she debated. Kade remained silent, the tension in the corridor bristling with so many unsaid words. But eventually, the Guard relented. She retrieved a key from her uniform pocket and unlocked the cell.

Silence stretched as Mirella stood there, unblinking. "Break the enchantment."

The Guard stumbled back. "*What?* He could shift into a wolf without that in place."

"How do you expect her to help heal his injuries if she, too, is bound by the enchantment in the cell?" Ruth raised a brow.

Kade, again, remained silent and unmoving. He had no injuries to speak of, but kept his mouth shut.

The Guard swallowed and laid her hand against the metal door. She muttered a few words in Olde Script, and groves cranked as magic bristled.

Kade's wolf reemerged, jumping and howling in his blood. He fisted his hands, relief washing over him at the feel of his inner beast, but another power reared to life. Immense. Tugging like the moon—

"*Finally.*" Mirella entered the cell. She dropped a satchel beside her and started riffling through it. "Ah, here." She handed Kade a waxy, blueberry-colored pellet. "Chew this." Kade followed orders, the Elder's tone unbending, but paused as Mirella slipped a pellet into her mouth, too. "Go on. You'll need it. Trust me."

Kade chewed the pellet, the sour material stinging his tongue. His inner wolf wrestled as he swallowed it, an odd sensation coming over him.

"How's Evelyn?" he asked.

"She's fine." Mirella didn't meet his stare, and it was like a stone dropped in his stomach.

A growl rumbled through his chest. "Mirella—"

"Goddess, she warned me about this. Evelyn is *fine,* albeit a little angry." The eldest Carson sister possessed a tone similar to that of a whip. It was harsh and demanding, and despite Kade's better judgment, his inner wolf sat to attention, no interest in upsetting the witch.

She clucked her tongue, shaking her head at the Guard. "Are you just going to stand there? He doesn't bite."

"Oh, I wouldn't be too sure about that." Ruth winked.

Mirella cursed the gods.

Ruth rolled her eyes. "I'm joking."

The Guard opened and closed her mouth, eyes fleeting over Kade. "Alright."

Magic brimmed in the air as she joined Mirella's side, eyes never leaving Kade. Those in the Vadon Mountains respected him, sure, and balked at his warrior reputation, but his kind didn't *fear* him.

"You know," Mirella went on, rummaging through her satchel again, "It's rude to stare."

The Guard narrowed her gaze. "Werewolves don't have powers like him. It's unnatural."

Ruth snorted outside in the hall. "*Hush.* Are you an expert in all magical things now, third born?"

The Guard opened her mouth—

"That was a rhetorical question." Mirella handed her an open jar and then a second. Lavender wafted from the paste and something else soothing and floral. Kade relaxed, the desire to close his eyes and sleep overcoming and then—*zap*. Magic shot through him, waking him and his inner wolf.

"Here's another," Mirella said, pushing a third jar into the Guard's arms.

She huffed. "I only have two hands!"

Mirella waved her hand. "*Shhh!*"

She stood up, putting her hands on her hips, and just . . . stood there. Seconds ticked by, time crawling up Kade's spine.

He cleared his throat. "Now what?"

"We wait."

"Wait for . . . " The Guard's lashes fluttered, and she slurred her words. She teetered back and forth until her eyes rolled back, and she collapsed to the floor.

Kade stepped forward and halted. Her chest rose and fell, and a small sigh escaped the witch's lips.

"She's . . . asleep." Kade raised a brow, peering up at Mirella.

Ruth poked her head into the cell. "Well done, Mirella."

"If the Goddess is in favor of our mission, she'll remain unconscious for the next eight hours. That's if someone doesn't come looking for her first." She positioned the jars into the corners of the cell. "Sleep seaweed, by the way. Perfect for those with insomnia or in need of a good night's rest or—"

"Knocking out a Guard for a rescue mission," Ruth said.

Mirella hummed, a frighteningly bemused smile playing on her lips. "Precisely."

Kade couldn't contain his anxiety any longer, moments away from bursting at the seams. "What of Evelyn?"

Mirella rolled her eyes—*rolled her eyes*—like Kade was infuriating and a passed-out Guard wasn't lying at her feet. "She's a little busy, and if we want to meet her on time, we've got to move. Here."

She handed him a set of clothes—a Guard's uniform with turquoise detailing, similar to Elder Quinn's hair. Mirella pulled a set of her own out, too.

Kade turned around as he undressed and put on the disguise. *Moons*, by some stars-above miracle, they fit his large stature. "How did you come by these?"

"A friend," Ruth said. "More importantly, an ally to you and Evelyn."

Neither Carson gave him a name, but the Guard below released another sigh, snapping him back into focus.

Get out. Meet Ev.

Dressed in disguise, Ruth led him and Mirella down the hall. With stolen keys in hand, she unlocked the main door, and they began their descent down the spiraling staircase. Without a single window, the only sign the outside world existed was the sea wind howling like some demon.

The descent felt like a mile long, sandstone and salt melding together with the distant whooshing of waves. At the bottom floor, Tùir possessed two large tunnels intersecting like a cross. Sconces flickered, and a few guards mingled by the entrance to the right. The contrast between the night and the darkness of the tunnel was too similar to make out the Sapphire Sea or Nūa in the distance.

At the bottom floor, a few guards mingled in a group. Mirella pointed two fingers to the other side. "Fast feet now."

She darted out into the open, and Kade stuck close, keeping his hood in place. The Guards were none the wiser, too busy with their conversation to notice as he and the Carsons fell into the shadows of the next tunnel. Pressed close to the damp wall, Ruth urged them to the opening. The lights dotting the Wall twinkled across the waves. Kade searched for Evelyn, but no one was in sight, not even a Guard.

"Where is she?" he asked, heart racing inside his chest.

Ruth groaned. "Goddess, Mirella, we best tell him the plan before he bursts blue again."

He stopped, and the eldest Carson sister sent the protector a glare. "Sometimes your brashness—"

"What?" Ruth's one eye jumped between them. "You conjured your power when Evelyn was in danger, no? It also happened last time when Riven attacked during the Blood Moon. It answers when you want to protect. If we tell you Evelyn is a part of the plan, you'll stop worrying."

"Doubtful," Mirella muttered.

Kade fought the urge to growl while his mind warred between Ruth's assessment of his power and Tenebris's chilling words. Perhaps if he hadn't hurt those he loved with it, he'd dismiss the latter.

He sighed, changing the subject. "What is the plan?"

"We're meeting Evelyn at the abandoned docks on the east side of the island," Ruth said.

Mirella nodded. "You're leaving the city tonight."

Guards walked along the beach, and the three of them pressed themselves to the stone, hidden by the shadow of Tùir. The Guards assessed the waves, but they never studied the perimeter of Tùir and disappeared around the bend.

Ruth didn't give them time to relax. She trailed the outskirts of Tùir and stopped near an area littered with supplies. Barrels and abandoned boats lined the beach, and she gestured for them to follow, running from item to item and disappearing behind the darkness cast onto the sand. Tucked behind an overturned boat, the three hunkered down and waited, the waves lapping towards their boots.

Mirella kept her sights on the sea while Ruth peered around the boat, eying Tùir. While he sat between them, the tension of their mission heating the chilly air, it reminded him of the Gray Fenris, anticipating his next move aside Yen or Linx. He'd known his archer and mage healer for years, and though he'd met Mirella a handful of times over the years, neither the Carson Elder nor the protector knew him, and yet here they were, risking themselves to break him out of Tùir. Kade fisted his hands at his sides, jaw ticking.

"Why are you both helping me after what happened?" he whispered.

Mirella turned and studied him. "A lot of reasons. For one, you're my sister's fated, which makes you part of the coven now. Second, Sorin needs you—"

"As well as the blue sparkles," Ruth threw over her shoulder.

"Yes, and your power. Third, Circe is a bitch, and I quite like pissing her off." Mirella shrugged, attention returned to the twinkling waves.

"Listen." Ruth fell closer to his side. "I've trained over a hundred bronntanases. Power is power. The hardest step is accepting it, not mastering it. Don't fear yours, Kade."

As the moon's pearly light bled through the storm clouds, Kade wrestled with the question—was it his power he feared or himself? He was supposed to be the Son the God, a protector. Yet, the only blade he gripped with precision these days was inadequacy. Was he worthy of the titles bestowed upon him? Was he capable of fulfilling the prophecy with Evelyn?

Before Kade had time to answer, movement caught his eyes. Water droplets glistened off a female figure like crystals, illuminating the silver in her stare. Kade's heart raced. A breath whooshed out of him.

For Evelyn emerged from the waves like a Goddess touched by the night, here to save him.

Chapter Twelve

In a hidden cave tucked into the coastline, an ancient dock ran parallel to a stone platform, its posts overrun by barnacles and sea sludge. A lantern buzzed bright with magic, hanging from the rusty bollard at the end of the dock, casting the sudsy sapphire waves and sandstone rock in a golden hue.

Kade shook the off-kilter sensation in his legs, hurrying after Evelyn as she hiked up a set of weathered stairs. They'd had a swift reunion at Tùir, with no time for sweet words before they said their goodbyes to Ruth and Mirella, hurried into a boat, and set off back across the angry bay.

Now, Evelyn's silence roared louder than the crashing waves echoing deep below Nūa.

"How do you know this place?" he asked.

Evelyn faltered a step, then kept walking, not bothering to turn to him. "As a teenager, I used to come here to hide away."

Kade winced at her curt tone, sighing as he stared down at his boots. The witch's creed lined the ancient stone steps, each word carved with precision:

Our eyes to the Sun, and hearts full of fire, minds open, and hands for good.

Whilst pouring over texts back in Callum, the words of the creed had once pushed Kade and Evelyn apart as they fell farther into the murder investigation. It often felt like centuries separated them from that time, not months. Things were different. *They* were different. But some things hadn't changed.

Kade recognized Evelyn's hurt a mile away, and he didn't question if he'd caused it.

"Evelyn, look at me."

His mate stilled two steps above him, shoulders rising and falling as she heaved.

"Ev, *please*."

She turned slowly, lips in a thin line and jaw set. She'd acted against the words of the Council, risked her coven, and swam across the sea.

All for him.

"I'm sorry," he breathed.

Evelyn shook her head, tears welling in her gray eyes. "*No.* You don't get to just say those words and expect it to all be alright."

"I know I fucked up," he said. "I'm aware—"

Evelyn marched down a step. "What are we, Kade?"

He paused, chest tightening. "Mates."

"No." Evelyn shook her. "Before we loved one another, before we tied our souls together, what were we?"

Kade studied his mate's beautiful face etched with hurt. The words below his boots seemed to tickle his feet, and moments in Callum rushed to the forefront of his mind. The time they'd agreed to work together in the Runaway Radish. Fighting side by side inside Connacht Castle. Entering the Gray Wood.

"Partners."

Evelyn nodded, and Kade's heart cracked at the sad smile lining her lips. "Yes. We are partners, and yet you walked away from me."

"I burned you with my power."

Evelyn grabbed his wrist, forcing him to look at her. "Pushing me away hurt more than any wound could."

"Ev . . ."

She swallowed, her expression so adamant Kade had no choice but to stare into the determined gleam in her eyes. "No matter what we face, may it be matters of the heart or an enemy on the battlefield, we face it *together*. I am with you through anything and everything, Kade. I swear it."

Moons, he loved this woman.

His heart swelled, and regardless of their severed mating bond, in a cave, tucked away from the rest of their homeland, her words etched into his soul. Her promise. Her love. Her *partnership*.

Kade leaned his forehead onto hers. "Alright, love."

She released a shaky gasp. "Never again?"

"Never," he whispered. "You were right. I fear my power, and I'd be lying if I said I still didn't, but with you by my side, I can face anything. I'll master it, Evelyn. That is my promise to you."

She lay her hand on his cheek. "I love you."

"I love you, too."

He planted his lips on hers, and it wasn't hungry or sweet, but *just*. Not third borns, protectors, or even mates, but two souls who loved one another enough to fight, rage, and battle whatever threatened their peace. Evelyn kissed him with the same tenderness, hand fisted in his shirt as she held him close.

She pulled away, peering up at him. "Whatever comes next—"

"We'll figure it out—"

"Together."

They said the last word in unison, as one. Kade kept his fingers intertwined into Evelyn's, the simple, barest touch enough to keep them standing amid their racing hearts.

"Where exactly are we?" he asked, studying the cave's curves. Waterlines etched into the rock, edges smoother near the water's edge and the ceiling dotted with sharp stalactites.

Evelyn led them towards the top of the stairs. "Technically, we're underneath the library." She nodded towards the left. "That leads to a direct route to the south entrance of the city where Bleu and Maxie are waiting for us at the stables, while that door"—Evelyn nodded right—"leads straight into Nūa Library through a hidden passage. I have a hunch, but it is a risk."

Kade shrugged. "We're used to risk. What's your hunch?"

"What if Circe is Riven's contact in the city?" she asked.

Kade stilled, his muscles stiffening. He'd forgotten the prince had two spies, one in the Vadon Mountains, his now dead uncle, and another in Nūa.

"She wanted to take my bloodstone and threw you into Tùir. What better way to set Riven up for success if he attacked the city? Perhaps she provided him with Blair's address, and according to Tovi, the prince was informed of our wedding plans. Where and when. She's on the Council, Kade, privy to that information."

"*Moons.*" Kade agreed with Evelyn's assessment. The Elder unnerved him and his wolf. Further, he'd detected a history between Evelyn and Circe. One weaved with fear.

"Do you think she's the sort of witch to fall to darkness?" he asked. "Like Ingrid?"

Evelyn frowned. "Yes. Trust me. Circe isn't a kind witch."

Kade's wolf reared to life. "Did she hurt you?"

"We don't have time for specifics," she said, shaking her head. "We need to be out of this city before sunrise." She glanced at the door on the right. "Circe is a leading scholar with an office in the southern wing. I've seen the letters from whoever wrote to Riven, the symbols, the handwriting. I understand it's a risk. Maybe I'm wrong. But I have this *feeling*."

"Then let's trust it." Kade stepped closer, giving her hand a deliberate squeeze.

Evelyn blinked. "Are you sure?"

"Yes, it's better to rule out the possibility than do nothing." He assessed Evelyn again, wishing he could grasp hold of their mating bond even just a hint, so he knew exactly how she felt. "But are you sure want to leave Nūa? This is your home."

His mate laid a hand on his chest. "I don't think it is anymore."

A flighty sense swarmed Kade's belly. He kissed her again. Soft and slow. Taking his time.

When he broke away, he whispered against her lips, "Let's go, love."

Chapter Thirteen

Tovi

RIVETS OF RED TWISTED down the drain as Tovi scrubbed the paint from her hands. Inside the shower, steam smelling of wildflowers and her thunderous thoughts engulfed her.

With no other choice, Tovi'd retired to Lār as a respected guest.

She lay her hands on the stoned wall, allowing the water to rain over her hair and back. The waterfall drowned out the noise. Her nerves, too. But the scorching temperature was nothing compared to the anger heating her blood.

The closer she came to grasping the title she needed to save her people, the more the freedom she'd fought for slipped from her grasp. Nothing—no move, no decision—was made out of *want* but instead, necessity.

Saving Sven and his family.

Retreating from Drystan.

Allying with the werewolves.

And now, more recently, staying inside Lār.

Of course, Tovi didn't deny the safety of the fortress. She was no use to her people dead because werewolves who hated vampyrs killed her in the village. No—it was the risk within the fortress's walls. The temptation. Her heart ached, an invisible thread yanking her across the fortress as if her body *felt* Eldrick's nearness. It was as if fate leered in the corner, laughing.

Tovi sighed. Her choices lay weaved into a rug, and at any moment, fate threatened to pull it out from under her.

Because not only were her choices not of her own, but it also didn't matter which way she leaned. Pain found her at every front.

With an agitated hiss, Tovi twisted the shower off, tiptoed into the bathroom hall and grasped a warm towel the servants had laid out. Once wrapped, she pattered out into the main room, inhaling the scent of the roaring fireplace. Logs groaned and split, and the dancing flame had her chest aching for Evelyn. What she'd give to open a bottle of wine and discuss the day's events with her best friend.

Luckily, there was wine already poured waiting on the nearest side table. The suite stretched twenty yards. From the sleeping area with a bed covered in a dozen fur blankets, to the lounge with reading chairs and a desk under the largest window. Snow fell in sheets, thousands of flurries shielding the village. Tovi sipped her wine, water dripping from her soaked being, and molded the notes of violet and stone fruit on her tongue.

Tovi considered the suite cozy, a reprieve after a long day cleaning Lucy's tavern, but her skin crawled with the familiarity of her home castle.

Dark stone had walled the darkest versions of herself, and after the curse infected Drystan, she'd ventured out to meet her people, those truly affected by the Blood Goddess's wrath. Outside the castle, she'd discovered herself and those she truly served. Her stomach roiled. Was this what it meant to be a queen, locked away while enjoying finer things?

All for precedent and safety.

Because no matter what corner of the continent Tovi walked, there was an enemy. Vampyrs who served Riven, lords who detested the fact she was a woman, and werewolves who hated vampyrs.

Tovi rubbed her aching chest, kneading the various threads of worry tangled together. If she turned north, they disputed her claim as queen because of what lay between her legs, and here, they snarled at what ran through her blood. *A curse.* She'd helped set Evelyn free of her brother Riven, discovered the entire prophecy from her sister-in-law Opal, and promised to be an ally of the werewolves. A question nagged in the back of her mind—did her efforts matter?

Because it seemed the rest of Sorin cared for her for simply *what* she was and not who.

A knock broke Tovi from her brooding. "Come in."

She ran a brush through her hair, staring into the dancing flames. Boots tapped against the stone and scuffed to a halt.

"*Moons,*" a male voice she knew all too well hissed.

Tovi whirled, finding Eldrick standing steps away. Tension creased the lines of his gem eyes, and his jaw ticked. *Goddess,* she'd stepped into Lār an hour ago, and here they were, already ten feet from one another, alone for the first time since Eldrick had asked her to stay in the Drengr Village.

Shadows wavered on the walls, and fate cackled in the corner.

Eldrick exhaled, nostrils flaring as he moved farther into the space. Tovi's hackles rose, a foreign feeling swirling in her gut. With her fangs and hidden talons, Tovi was the beast amongst others, but in the presence of Eldrick and the heat brimming between them, she stood the prey and he the predator.

Breathtaking, sharp, and with a stare screaming that he was ravenous.

Yet, he strode by her gaze. He deposited something onto the table near the wine and retreated to the fire.

The scent of sweet iron weaved with the burning wood, and the warmth of Tovi's earlier shower dissipated from each of her limbs. She inhaled. Exhaled. Tried to still her racing heart.

"Is that..."

"Blood, yes." Eldrick didn't meet her stare as he barely peered over his shoulder, as if his back was a shield between them both. "I don't know how it works. Didn't know how much you'd need. But I recalled..." He swallowed, finally meeting her stare. "I know you like to lace your wine with blood."

Tovi's insides stretched and tightened. She opened and closed her mouth. There weren't enough words or the right ones but—

"Thank you."

Eldrick's smile was almost a frown, etched with sadness. "How are things in Drystan?"

"Tense," she said. "But we were able to get Sven and his family out of the castle."

"I'm glad to hear it," Eldrick said.

Tovi managed a smile. "What of things here?"

Eldrick ran a hand through his hair. "Tense with news of the decree."

Tovi reached for another glass, readying to pour a glass for Eldrick. "Will you stay?"

Eldrick stiffened, and Tovi winced at her word choice. *Bloody hel.* She didn't bat an eye facing a demon. Didn't balk from the word *bloodsucker* painted in bloodred. Faced her brother with blade in hand. But it was *this* male, showing her kindness, that threw her off.

"For a drink, I mean, to discuss . . ."

Eldrick turned, muscles of his shoulders, back, and arms cording with his controlled movements. His gaze locked onto her, pinning her in place.

"If I stay, it'll be more than a drink, Tovi."

"I know."

Winds howled against the window, snowflakes clinking against the glass. They were specs in their homeland, yet an infinite thread connected them. Too expensive to outrun or ignore. And exhaustion gripped her bones. Tovi'd tried to outrun this for weeks, but wanting him wasn't the choice. Her body and fate had decided that for her. As for the decision plaguing her heart?

She'd leave it for another day.

Eldrick's emerald eyes dropped to her lips, and Tovi's breath whooshed out of her. Images of her sucking, tasting, *kissing* him flashed through her mind. Days, weeks. That's how long she'd gone without sedating her maddening want for him.

Sometimes, the minutes had ticked by. The hours had dragged. Restless nights where no matter the times she'd found released with her own fingers, she'd lay there panting, wishing Eldrick lay beside her.

His boots boomed against the stone floor as he reached her. Silence echoed like the thousands of words neither of them whispered. He brushed his hand over her whitened knuckles, still clutching her towel. Tovi didn't break their stare as he eased each one of her fingers loose.

The towel dropped.

Tovi stood bare before Eldrick, and his darkened gaze drank her in with the same power as a lover's caress.

"You're so gods damn beautiful," he breathed, running his fingers across her bare shoulders and down her arms. She gasped, and that invisible thread Tovi had ignored didn't pull.

It snapped.

Eldrick's lips crashed to hers, answering her plea in an instant. Her cursed being ignited, sustenance finally quelling weeks' worth of starvation. Tovi moaned as Eldrick's lips molded to hers. She couldn't get enough of him. Not his touch, taste, *feel* of him. His hand grasped her neck, and as he tightened his grip, Eldrick spun her around, dragging her body flush against his.

Tovi's chest rose and fell, the movement catching her attention. Ahead, a full-length mirror leaned against the wall near the armoire, reflecting both of their breathless faces back at them. With breasts peaked, her need pooling between her legs, Tovi leaned back into Eldrick's mercy, and the slight smile tugging at the edge of his lips threatened the strength in her knees.

Eldrick nipped her ear, one hand still bracing her throat as the other dipped between her breasts, traveling down her taut abs, and stopping just above her wet sex.

He trailed kisses down her neck, whispering after each one. "Tell me you don't want this."

A kiss to her collarbone next. She hissed. Pink bloomed across her cheeks, and her lips parted, eyes wide as Eldrick's stare didn't break from hers in the mirror.

"Tell me you're not soaking wet from me."

Just as he said it, he glided two fingers through her folds. Tovi's head fell back, but Eldrick tightened his grip, keeping her steady. There was no escaping the sight of them together, witnessing what they were doing—he was making her watch as she unraveled in his arms.

Yet, she couldn't deny how right they looked. Together. Her grasping his arm, naked, whilst he was in control.

"Tell me you haven't dreamed of my fingers here."

Eldrick trailed his digits through her sex again, finding that bundle of nerves like he'd written the roadmap to her pleasure. A whimper broke from her as he drew circles over her clit. Slow, attentive. With little to no pressure at all. *Perfect.*

His gaze darkened even more, a growl rumbling through his chest and vibrating through her. Eldrick's stiffening length pressed against her. And *fuck.*

Pressure built between Tovi's legs, her building need too much. She fidgeted in his hold, but Eldrick held firm, using his knees to widen her stance.

Bloody hel.

"Eldrick please," she panted as he eased his fingers towards her entrance and—

Oh.

He plunged a finger inside her, and she wasn't certain what was more so her undoing, the feel of him pressed against her, the tingling of being stretched, or the sight of him on the brick of unleashing as he coaxed whimper after breathless whimper from her.

"You know," Eldrick whispered into her ear, not breaking the rhythm of his pumping finger. "There are few things I regret in life, but not tasting between your legs that night is one of them."

He pulled his finger out, and Tovi didn't have time to protest as he lifted her into the air. Eldrick carried her to the bed, depositing her on the furs and blankets. His sights fell onto her sex, male intent glinting, but Tovi planted her foot onto his chest and pushed.

"Undress."

Eldrick's jaw ticked, nostrils flaring. Tovi swore she caught a twitch in his pants, and she bit her lip, more heat rushing to her sex, knowing she, too, had the same power over him that he had over her.

The alpha took no time shedding his clothes—throwing off his shirt, discarding his belt, tossing his boots and trousers aside. He stood in all his naked glory, taut muscles glowing in the fire's light. Tovi crawled backward as he joined her on the bed, his length straight and proud, taunting her with a promise she desperately needed to deny.

No.

Her body warred with the notion, and Tovi accepted that there were many things she stood strong against, but with Eldrick, she was weak. Yet, she didn't give a bloody hel as he looked at her like that, emerald eyes so intent, her heart beat with the intensity of the words he didn't say.

He grasped both her ankles and pulled her under him, and his head fell between her legs.

"Gods," she cried out as his tongue licked her back to front, not missing an inch of her.

"*Goddess,*" Eldrick corrected, his words tickling the insides of her thighs. "There is only one goddess here, and I plan to worship her with my tongue."

Stars above, he did. His tongue licked and sucked her clit. The only appropriate word was worship—Eldrick's attention was pure devotion, his exploration alighting every fiber of Tovi's being on fire, hot and burning and alive like the one crackling at the hearth.

She laced her fingers into his hair, twisting through the dark, tousled strands, still damp from his shower. Eldrick dug his fingers into her backside, her skin prickling alive at his touch. Her body buzzed, toes curling into the furs.

"*Eldrick.*" Tovi had one foot dangling off oblivion, and as Eldrick drove two fingers into her, sucking her clit, she fell.

And burst into a thousand pieces.

Her hands tightened in his hair, her legs locking around Eldrick's smiling, triumphant face. She'd never known pleasure to feel like rebirth, like some damn awakening.

Eldrick peppered tender kisses up her legs, such a gentle contrast compared to the destruction of her senses.

The need he'd sedated only drove Tovi's baser instinct into overdrive. Thought and rationale left her completely. It was only the building pressure in her chest, this tug between them. She pushed Eldrick onto his back, climbed atop of him, and straddled his hips.

"Fuck," Eldrick cursed, as his length slid through her folds.

Two shades of green collided. Emerald bore into her jade, and a mixture of disbelief and admiration shined there. *This* would only make things worse, her decisions more complicated.

"This is a terrible idea," she whispered.

"I know, dove," Eldrick breathed, but his hands glided up her thighs and gripped her waist, not stopping Tovi but positioning her. She guided his length towards her entrance.

No. No. No, her mind screamed.

Yes. Yes. Yes, her body chanted.

But Tovi was too tired to think about it any longer, and all she understood was *want*.

Tovi sank.

They both cried out as their bodies joined. Tovi planted her hands onto Eldrick's chest, grounding herself as she found her tempo and *moved*.

Why had she denied herself this? Why had she pretended she didn't need this?

Need *him*.

This differed from the last time they lay together. That had been desperation, build up, yet this was like coming back together. Finding *home*. Breathing in the scent of where one's soul came alive.

The wolf and dove.

Tovi drowned out the whispers of the prophecy as she rode Eldrick's cock, and for the first time in centuries, she chose pleasure over sensibility. As Eldrick sat up and wrapped his powerful arms around her, he held her steady as she shattered again.

When his own release found him, they sat entangled with one another, and he said in a hushed tone, "I could watch you like that for forever."

Tovi used her ragged breath and limp limbs as an excuse to not answer, shutting her eyes. Such beautiful words that pierced her ribs like a blade.

For there was no doubt in Tovi. Fate *had* chosen Eldrick as her forever, yet she was certain neither of them would step foot on that path.

CHAPTER FOURTEEN

ORKAN'S BREATH PLUMED INTO the air like some beast emitting smoke.

It was times like these, with gray sprawling above, snow blanketing the land, and cold nipping at his pale, cursed skin, that his inner wolf howled, *Set me free.*

For Lorkan craved to run and feel his homeland under his paws.

But the Drengr Village sat a mile northbound, the distant puffs of chimney smoke dotting above the tree line. This close, Lorkan couldn't risk a pack member spotting his shifted form, nor did he have the time to defuse another sighting, a cumbersome headache that affected Fjall Pack.

His pack couldn't afford another worry. Their dwindling elm tea supply nipped at Lorkan's heels like a herding dog. He brushed his hand over his satchel, insuring it hadn't vanished during his rushed journey. He had enough elm tea to last two weeks, plenty to visit the Drengr Village, get information from his brother, and return to Vísdómr with more answers about vampyrs.

Snow clung to the pines and evergreens, frosting the branches of oaks and maples. Songbirds pecked at the icy surface, diligently hunting for seeds. The hill sloped to the most northern path leading into the village, and—

Lorkan stilled.

He saw the blood before he scented it. Up ahead, crimson splayed across white, stark against the peaceful forest. Sweet iron traveled on the wind, conjuring his inner beast to the surface. A growl shuddered through him, and his keen hearing caught the faint *thump, thump, thump* of the werewolf slumped against a tree.

Lorkan sensed death like it was the absent twin to his darkness. He quickened his pace but didn't run, sliding down the slope on his boots. If he ran, he risked his hunting instincts snapping into place. He chanted his purpose inside his mind—*help them, help them, help them*—loud enough to drown out the hissing in his mind.

A dead mule with its throat slit lay on the path, its glassy eyes reflecting the snowcapped canopy. Winter root vegetables littered the path, and upturned dirt and leaves showed signs of a struggle. The wounds were fresh, the blood not yet frozen. Lorkan sniffed the air, a dangerous gamble with so much blood, but he had to be sure the assailants weren't near.

Thanks to the stars above, he didn't detect the sharp scent of another vampyr or the anise hint from a demon. No—it was only the tantalizing clot of blood. A hunger-filled haze fell over Lorkan. His sights flashed red like he'd replaced his glasses with red-tinted ones. Each step was a struggle; the temptation to feed was as strong as his need to help the werewolf.

Lorkan had been here before, at the intersection between wanting and losing control. He'd sworn to never let his affliction *win* again. It was wretched and fierce, but he'd not let it ravage his heart.

He reached the werewolf, thoughts of feeding squashed. Red trailed down the werewolf's chin, soaking his wheat-colored beard. Familiarity hit Lorkan like a cane to the back of his knees. He couldn't think straight or remember the werewolf's name, but he was a Drengr pack member and a farmer on the outskirts of the village.

The man blinked, face far too pale. The Otherworld had its grip on him, life fading from his skin by the second.

Drink. Drink. Drink.

Phantom whispers chanted in Lorkan's mind. His gums ached, his fangs begging to be released. He shed his cloak, reaching for the wide cut at the male's neck, only to pause. A gash deep enough to reveal the man's insides stretched from rib to hip.

No amount of pressure would stop that amount of blood.

"Dr . . . Dren . . . you're a Drengr son," the werewolf breathed, each word wet and bubbly.

The truth barreled into Lorkan, knocking him off balance. *Who* he was—as well as his father and brothers—was a reminder to rein in his bloodthirst.

"You're alright—"

"Don't lie to me, boy."

Lorkan grunted, shifting on his haunches. No one had called him a boy since he'd grown taller than his father and brothers.

The farmer laughed, which only quickened the river of blood seeping from his wounds. "You're . . . s-s-supposed to be the smart one."

Lorkan swallowed, a laugh so far out of reach, all he could muster was to say nothing—there was no sense in arguing the truth; the man *was* dying. He draped his cloak over the farmer's body, a measly comfort against the cold.

"How many scáths?" he asked, searching the path for signs. But aside from the bite on the farmer's neck, his other wound and the mule's neck were a singular cut, a swipe not made by talons but a blade.

"Not scáths . . . but the k-king." The farmer's eyes searched above, growing distant.

"*What?*" Lorkan hated how he hissed, how he leaned too close into the dying man's space. Yet, it wasn't the red haze filling his sights but images of his village destroyed. Eldrick, his father, the Gray Fenris . . . His fears flashed before his eyes, his heart pounding in his chest. "Are you sure?"

"It is true . . . he told me he is t-t-the vampyr king . . ." The man slacked against the tree, and the last bit of light extinguished from his gaze.

Lorkan reared back. He'd witnessed death before, far too much for his twenty-eight-year-old heart, but the king had killed this close to the Drengr Village on the path leading to his home.

He rushed to his feet, searching the trees again for any sign of vampyrs. No sharp scent. No crunch of ice under their boots. *Stars above.* He glanced back at the dead werewolf. All the signs were there—he was minutes behind the vampyr king.

Shift, Lorkan's wolf roared inside him, but with the blood behind him, he worried shifting might flip the switch for his hunger. There was too much risk. He'd drank the elm tea in the last day at least, but all his jumbled emotions—fear, anger, and desperation—heightened the curse. He was alone. If he lost control, Alvin and his pack wouldn't be there to help.

Hide what you are.

Lorkan's long-standing rule rippled through him. He couldn't stomach the possibility of his brothers discovering *what* he was. That truth tasted of salt and shame. Lorkan feared rejection above all else.

But did that matter if Lorkan lost them to the vampyr king? His pack *needed* him. Even without shifting, he was the fastest werewolf in the Vadon Mountains.

He couldn't explain his shifted form, but he could outwit discussions regarding his speed. He was no warrior like Kade nor a leader like Eldrick, but he knew these forests, trees, hills, and the best way to the village.

Lorkan ran southeast instead of southwest, where the path ventured. The world blurred around him. Distinct brown and navy became clear up ahead.

The palisade walls of his home, the Drengr flags high and proud.

He growled, he grunted.

Because he couldn't howl. Not like the other werewolves of his pack. To them, he was latent, unable to conjure the call of his people.

Fuck.

Lorkan cursed just as his satchel caught the branch of a dormant rosebush. The cold, stiff material ripped, and half of his elm tea spilled into the snow. Wind picked up the bags, pulling them out of reach. The land was toying with him, fate pulling the strings like he was a puppet for entertainment.

Laughter yanked him back to the present. He hurried behind a tree and stilled his breath.

NO!

Ahead, a tall, lithe man clad in silver and gold marched down the path Lorkan had abandoned. Four others flanked his sides. Magic bristled the air, anise thick on the winter wind. A witch, with hands flared and magic twisting around her feet, led them. Lorkan stepped left and—

Moons, they disappeared from sight. The witch created a mirage, hiding them with magic; no werewolf manning the wall would spot them.

Lorkan whirled his attention back to Drengr Village. He was closer. But barely. If he shifted, he'd be there first, plenty of time to warn his pack. But his werewolf was different, darker. He risked getting killed before he had time to declare who he was, but even then, he'd reveal his darkness.

But they need you!

A thousand voices shouted in Lorkan's whirling mind. What, *in the stars above*, was he going to do?

Think, Lorkan, think.

Ahead, a cluster of evergreens grew together, their intertwining branches creating a wall of needles and snow. A plan clicked into place. *Hide.* Like he had been for the last decade.

With one backward glance towards the king, certain they didn't see him, Lorkan dashed over to the trees and hunkered out of sight.

NOW!
Lorkan shifted and let out a ground-shaking howl.

Chapter Fifteen

Eldrick

Eldrick lay with Tovi in his arms, tracing his fingers over her pale skin and praying to any god that might listen that tonight would last for an eternity. They'd not spoken a word to one another since they'd both calmed after their blissful releases, soaking in the peace of the snowstorm outside, the crackling of the fire, and their gently beating hearts.

An important discussion sat on the tip of his tongue, but he couldn't bring himself to fracture this moment. For there was a difference between want and need. He wanted Tovi, but there was so much more that needed him. His pack, homeland, and duty.

Eldrick envisioned two futures—Tovi staring at him like this for years to come, discussing their worries late into the night. Another, where he lay alone with his thoughts, the warm fire and the promise of a whiskey his only comfort.

The wolf and dove.

Opal's distant words contradicted the latter future, and so did Eldrick's soul. They'd laid together before, but this had been different. His chest ached, a phantom emptiness pulsing. Yet, he didn't dare breach the subject, afraid Tovi might flee from his arms, and he'd lose this night with her.

Tovi peered up at him, resting her chin on his chest. "What will you do about the decree?"

"Stand by my father's side like I always have." Eldrick ran his fingers through her white hair, tucking it behind her ear.

"Does your father need the rest of the alphas?" she asked. "For the alliance between vampyrs and werewolves."

"If we want a united army, yes," he whispered.

Tovi nibbled her lip, brows furrowing. "What happens if someone else wins the title of Earl? Will your father have to listen to their orders? Will *you*?"

Eldrick exhaled. He wasn't one to hold back the truth, no matter how harsh. "By technicality."

The magic weaved into an alpha's blood made them leaders within their packs while the magic within the title of Earl extended power over all werewolves, including alphas. All these years, Aramis hadn't ruled, he'd led, not using the magic within his blood, but seeking council and collaboration with the other alphas. A common purpose had united them, and Eldrick feared new leadership might shatter what Aramis had built.

Tovi shut her eyes and cursed. "As if we didn't have enough stacked against us."

We . . . Us . . .

The words almost made Eldrick smile. "He'll win the vote."

"My presence in the village hurts his chances. Our alliance does, too." She ran circles across his chest, jade eyes churning with thoughts.

Eldrick grasped Tovi's hand and peered down at her. "If he backs down from his promise to you, it makes him look not only weak but disloyal."

"To a vampyr?" Tovi snorted. "I doubt the other alphas will see it that way."

"You're not the only vampyr in the village. My mother's here, and she's my father's mate."

Tovi stiffened in his hold, and her gaze snapped elsewhere.

Eldrick's heart thumped, his soul yearning with truth. Tell her. Ask. *Moons, admit your suspicions.*

He swallowed, gearing up to speak his mind when a distant howl carried on the storm's wind. Tovi's head snapped up, and she turned her ear.

"Did you hear that?" he whispered.

"Yes," she breathed.

Eldrick sat up, carrying Tovi with him. He didn't recognize the howl echoing in the forest, but he knew the kind, felt it in his blood. A warning.

Horns resounded in the village, and Eldrick's hackles rose. Werewolves howled across the wall. He and Tovi shared a silent, knowing look, but before either of them spoke, Tovi's door burst open, and Lou rushed in.

"Tovi—" The vampyr halted, eyes widening at the sight of Eldrick.

The vampyr queen cursed, grasping a fur blanket and pulling it over her naked body. "*Lou.*"

"I . . . *Bloody hel.*" The vampyr struggled to grasp words. "The village is under attack. Your brother has arrived outside the gates."

Eldrick sprang from the bed, and Lou squealed, covering her eyes. His wolf snarled in his blood.

FUCK.

He was here. With Tovi. Nowhere near an axe. Far from the Wall where his pack manned the village. What sort of leader was he? Distracted. Tempted. Selfish.

Tovi reached for him, but he couldn't look at her, couldn't stomach the sight of her jade eyes. "Eldrick, wait—"

"Stay here," he snapped, his alpha baritone bleeding through his words.

"Excuse me?" She followed him as he rummaged the floor for his clothes and boots. "If you think for one second I'm not fighting—"

He whirled. "Goddamn it. I can't think straight when you're near, Tovi."

She reared back. His chest heaved. The room prickled with the fact that whatever was between them was *too much*.

Tovi's beautiful face hardened, and her fangs glinted as she said, "Then I suppose we should keep our distance from one another."

Eldrick growled. "*Fine.*"

He retreated from her suite, throwing on his shirt and sprinting to his room. He gathered his armor and axe, mind reeling as he readied for whatever battle awaited him outside of Lār.

CHAPTER SIXTEEN

Tovi

Eldrick's words slammed into Tovi like the door boomed shut after his retreat.

Her chest rose and fell, and the last hours of bliss evaporated, leaving her skin cold and hardened like the cursed ground of her homeland.

"*Bastard,*" she hissed with fangs released.

Village horns bellowed. *Bloody hel*—she didn't have time to worry about the infuriating, rude, and prideful alpha. Her brother was here. Riven had finally attacked.

But Tovi was queen. The true heir. She refused to stay here like some damsel. This was her war, too, and she'd meet her enemy with a blade in hand.

"Where is my armor?" she asked, tone as cutting as the weapons she hunted for. *Goddess*, back in the Shield-maiden she'd tucked away her things for easy access. Sword by her bedside. Leathers by the door. The suite was too expansive. She rooted for clothes in the armoire. Tunic. Trousers. Boots. Half prepared, she raged against the gods. Where *the fuck* was her leather armor?

"Tovi."

Lou's voice stilled her frantic search. Her friend held her breastplate and bracers, while her sword rested by the reading chair. A thousand questions churned behind Lou's red-rimmed glasses. But Tovi didn't entertain them, grasping her things like one needed air.

"Thank you."

Fully dressed with weapons secured at her belt, Tovi and Lou hurried down the halls of Lār in silence. They descended the steps two at a time, and as they crested the last set, the main hall came into view around the bend; warriors sprinted back and forth, preparing for battle, while Lār's servants ushered children into the stone fortress.

A tentative grasp took hold of Tovi's wrist, stalling her descent down the stairs.

"Tovi—" Lou started.

But she didn't want to talk about the alpha she'd shared her body and bed with. Couldn't stomach the conversation brewing in her friend's stare. Especially when it was *her* brother attacking the village.

"Not now."

"No." Lou's hand tightened on her wrist, tugging her into the shadows. "We've avoided this conversation for too long—"

Tovi hissed, snatching her hand back. "May I remind you, I am your *queen*."

Lou's chest rose and fell. "Then start acting like it."

Tovi snapped straighter. "How dare you?"

"I will." Lou pointed a finger at her. "I've watched you fight for your people for so long, and I refuse to stand by while you risk it all. He jeopardizes *everything*."

Tovi's heart hammered in her chest like it fought to get away from the pain lancing through it.

"You think I don't know that?" she hissed.

It's why she'd avoided him and kept her distance and said those hurtful words moments ago, all to push him away again.

"Then why was he in your bed tonight?" Lou asked.

"It's nothing," she whispered, throat burning.

Lou shook her head. "That's a lie. You know it. *He* knows it. We all do. *Goddess*, I am your friend, and I hate to see how happy he makes you, but our people will never accept him, Tovi. You *must* know that. The lords of Drystan—"

"I'll handle them." Tovi fisted her hands at her sides.

Lou didn't back down. "Your brother has made his move. He wears a new crest, staking his name as king. To unite Drystan under *your* name, you will need the lords of Drystan on your side. Dance their dance. Allow a whisper on the wind of you and Eldrick, and they'll doubt you."

Tovi's gut twisted. Goddess, she knew this. *Had* known it. Breathed the inevitable for weeks. But it still hurt to hear it out loud. To accept it as council from a friend.

Whose mouth opened and closed, hesitating.

"Well, go on," Tovi said. "You haven't held back yet."

Lou exhaled, meeting her stare with a level of severity that rooted Tovi in place. "You must prepare for all options."

Each bone, muscle, and tendon of Tovi's centuries-old being stilled. *Options.* Her mother had used that word. Many, many times. Before balls, scheduled meetings. "Surprise" visits when a suitor arrived to the castle. Yet, her mother's eyes had glistened with promise and greed while Lou's shined with apprehension and torment.

Because what she suggested hurt them both.

"*No.* I'll stroke their egos and learn the dance, but marriage is off the table. That is my line." Tovi's tone was unbending, one of a queen commanded her subject.

"Then don't put yourself in a position where it is the only card you have left," Lou whispered.

The truth stung. For a breath, nothing else had mattered while lying in bed with Eldrick. Not her crown, the curse, her worries, or what was and wasn't *queenly.* It was just *them*, and the inevitable thread thrumming between their souls. Yet, like an ascending fog, she couldn't outrun it. Circumstance overshadowed Tovi's hint of happiness, as if reminding her she wasn't privy to it.

"There you are."

Nadia stepped into the shadows and studied them both. Curiosity etched into her pinch brow, but another set of horns bellowed through the village. *Goddess.* Tovi had almost forgotten the village was under attack.

"This is for you." Nadia handed her a sword. "We had it made by the village smith."

Tovi wrapped her hands around the scabbard, intricate carvings in the wood and leather pressing into her palm. "We?"

"The Gray Fenris and I."

Warmth spread through Tovi's chest, and she blinked away the emotion stinging her eyes. An amethyst stone gleamed at the hilt—a softer shade of purple than the Verena banner. She unsheathed the newly made blade a few inches, the metal singing in the stone hall. Etched letters ran down the center, but Tovi couldn't sort out her thoughts, let alone make sense of the word.

"Thank you," she breathed.

Lou and Nadia had been Tovi's closest allies and spies in Drystan, and though fate tugged her many directions, she didn't dare ignore how they stood here, in this moment, the three of them together. Her hand molded to the hilt of the blade, like she'd held it for decades, not seconds. The weapon anchored her in purpose.

As did her loyal friends.

"Where can I help?"

"With me," Nadia said.

Tovi gave her a curt nod and readied to follow Nadia when Lou grabbed her wrist.

"Wait—"

"I hear what you're saying," Tovi said. "I'm just not ready to accept it."

With that, she tugged free of Lou's grip and sprinted up to the Drengr female alpha. They stormed out of Lār to air that smelled of impending battle.

Chapter Seventeen

Winds weaved with the scent of anise hurtled into the north gate, and snow crunched under Eldrick's boots as he slid through mud. He growled and shoved his shoulder against the quivering wood and braced.

"Hold!" Bétar roared to his left.

Boom.

On the other side, Riven alongside Ingrid, the dark witch, attempted to breach the village. A dozen werewolves, some shifted into their wolf forms, flanked Eldrick and Bétar. Together, they pressed their collective weight against the onslaught of dark magic. The gate trembled, but the Drengr pack held true.

"Any idea whose howl alerted the village?" Eldrick asked through gritted teeth.

"No idea." Flurries collected in Bétar's red beard. "It wasn't a werewolf from our pack."

"A visiting werewolf perhaps," Todd said to his right, breath ragged.

Boom.

The weapons master grimaced. "*Moons*, dark magic smells ghastly, doesn't it?"

Eldrick and Bétar grunted their agreement.

"More vampyrs spotted in the trees!" Yennifer called from an overlook on the wall above them.

"How many?" Bétar asked.

Yen dashed from sight, and then a beat later returned, peering down at them. "At least twenty."

Bétar's pinched brow mirrored the bewilderment flushing through Eldrick.

"That's a small attack party," the Commander breathed.

"They must've traveled through *danu*," Todd said.

"What?" Bétar and Eldrick asked at once.

Sweat traveled down the weapons master's temples, matting his dark hair twisted into a bun. "Belle told me of her sister's wind magic. She can travel with it. Usually—" They heaved as another wave of wind knocked into the gate. The wooden polls anchored into the ground groaned. "A witch can only create a *danu* to a place they have visited, but since Ingrid's magic has touched the dark, she can create a *danu* to wherever she pleases, *but* she's still limited to how many can cross her threshold from place to place."

"They can reach the Vadon Mountains but only with so many." Eldrick's mind reeled. "Does distance matter?"

"Yes," Todd nodded. "The greater the distance, the more magic used."

An idea sparked. "Magic depletes, dark or not. She'd have to reserve her energy if they want a chance of getting home. Let's tire her out and don't let them breach this village. We need to take care of the vampyrs in the forest."

Bétar nodded. "Yen!"

"On it!" she cried. "*ARHCERS!*"

Arrows whistled above, and a slew of grunts, *pops*, and screeches followed. An aggravated growl vibrated beyond the gate, and the onslaught of wind ceased. Unrelenting cold tightened Eldrick's skin, and his wolf paced in his blood.

"Keep steady!" Eldrick cried.

"What are you doing?" a distant voice roared. "Grab a weapon! March to the gate!"

Eldrick whirled, his hackles rising at the tone. Ahead, Alpha Johannes stalked down the village's main street with chest puffed out wide and irritated sneer crinkling his eyes. His knuckles were bone white, an axe in his left, sword in his right. Behind him, Dalinda bared her teeth, disgust dripping off every step as she watched a family hurry towards the fortress.

"Cowards," she spat at their feet.

Eldrick saw red.

"Hold the line," he ordered Bétar and the others.

He didn't think he *moved*, springing from his place at the gate and prowling towards the bastard disrespecting *his* pack.

Bjorn grabbed a farmer by the arm, jerking him close. "Did you not hear me—"

"Unhand him." Eldrick's alpha baritone echoed in the night.

The Johannes pack members lingering near their alpha stilled, along with Alphas Skau, Lindström, and Alland. *Stars above*, they had an audience.

Bjorn's venomous stare snapped to Eldrick. Twice his width. Veins bulging from his arms. Scar ruddy and angry down his cheek. But Eldrick's wolf bared its teeth, begging to be unleashed, not daring to cower in the presence of an older and larger alpha. This was *his* home, lands, and pack.

"I said, *unhand him.*"

Alpha Skau growled while Lindström and Alland stepped back. Bjorn stiffened, eyes widening a fraction at Eldrick's wolfish magic peppering they air. He snarled, shoving the farmer to the ground, and turned his wrath onto Eldrick. The other alphas stood and did nothing.

"Your pack is fleeing," Bjorn roared.

Eldrick ignored him and grasped the farmer's shoulders, helping him rise. "Go. Get your family and head to Lār."

Relief fluttered across the male's face. "Thank you, Magu."

He hurried off, and Eldrick sidestepped, blocking Bjorn. "You don't give orders in this territory. We are under attack—"

"Yet you allow for cowards!" the alpha said.

"He isn't a protector!" Eldrick said. "Each werewolf has their place in our pack, and there are protocols in place."

Bjorn stepped toe to toe with Eldrick. "All Johanneses are warriors. They all know how to pick up an axe, sword, or bow, not run with their tail between their legs."

The hairs on the back of Eldrick's neck rose. *All* Johanneses? Sure, the Drengr pack trained in self-defense, but third borns were warriors and called upon during vampyr and demon attacks. Not that second borns and first-borns didn't have a place—each werewolf had a role, none more important than the other. There was honor in duty, no matter the kind. Why was Bjorn's pack full of warriors? The Johanneses were a sharper and more cutting pack, but to deviate from birth order so strongly . . .

Eldrick fought the confusion gripping him. He remained calm. Collected. Buried his unease. *Not now.*

He entered Bjorn's personal space, smelling his foul breath. "This is the Drengr pack, not the Johannes. Remember your place."

Bjorn grabbed his breastplate, a growl vibrating through him. "You arrogant pup."

Horns blared through the village. Warriors called for aid, commands rippling across the wall, tower to tower.

Eldrick seethed, knocking away Bjorn's hands. "I have more important matters to attend to than to bicker with the likes of you. The vampyr prince stands outside the gate."

"I'm sure he'll leave once he gets what he wants," Dalinda said. "Hand her over."

"Are you mad?" Eldrick asked. "Even if the Daughter of the Goddess was here, we'd never hand Evelyn over to the enemy!"

Dalinda snarled. "Not the witch, the vampyr whore. His *sister*."

Eldrick swallowed his scorching rage. "We might not be a pack full of warriors, but at least we're fucking loyal to our allies."

"You're a fool," Bjorn scoffed.

The other alphas murmured amongst themselves, patronizing looks skating across Eldrick's face. He didn't dare balk under their perusal. Let them think what they wanted.

"I'd rather be a fool with honor than a true coward."

Red bled up Bjorn's face. "Mark my words, if werewolves die today, I'll make sure the entire Vadon Mountains know it is because you chose a bloodsucker over them."

"Unless you plan to stand by the Drengrs and help fight against Riven, back the fuck off." Eldrick peeled away from the alphas, assessing each one of them. He headed towards the gate as his name carried on the wind.

"Eldrick!" a deep, male voice shouted.

He stilled—he recognized that voice but never with such desperation. His usually reserved, studious brother pushed through the werewolves gathered at the gate. Sweat matted his dark hair and tunic. No cloak, pale skin blooming red with exertion. Cracked glasses. He'd *run* here, and fear laced the gold in his widened stare.

"Lorkan! *Moons*, what is it?"

"The north entrance." His brother gulped rasping breaths. "Vampyrs surround the village."

"Shit." Eldrick turned his attention back to the gate. "Bétar—"

"*Scrios!*" A high-pitch screech from the other side of the wall sent shivers up Eldrick's spine.

"Brace!" Yen cried.

But it was no use. The gate burst into a hundred pieces. Eldrick and Lorkan flew back with a dozen warriors. He landed with a harsh thud. Wood and debris fell around him, and his ears rang with a piercing pitch. Eldrick fought conscious. His vision blurred. *Get up! You're a leader!*

He rolled to his side, fighting the shake in his legs and stood. *There.* A few feet away, Lorkan groaned as he cracked his neck side to side, dark hair amiss, glasses gone. Eldrick helped his brother stand, and side by side, they faced the destroyed entrance, dark tendrils of Ingrid's magic snaking around the splintered wood.

Dark winds roiled through, and Riven, clad in armor, marched into the village.

"Where is she?" he roared. "Give us the Daughter of the Goddess, and we will not harm you!"

"Line!" Bétar called, stepping to Eldrick's side.

Bruised and bloody, werewolves flanked him, Bétar, and Lorkan. Beastly energy bristled the air. Above, an arrow soared towards the prince. Riven unsheathed his black blade, and in one swift step, sliced it in half. The severed pieces clattered to the ground.

A stillness entered the village. Like the winds had fled with the vampyr prince's arrival. Eldrick's wolf begged to be unleashed. How *dare* Riven invade his home?

He stepped forth, his axe's hilt groaning under his grip.

Riven's sharp gaze tracked his movements. The dark purple circles under the prince's eyes didn't match his regal armor. Desperation clad in gold. He held the enchanted blade like he couldn't muster the weight, tip dragging through the snow. Ingrid stood at the entrance, black winds circling at her fingertips as she waited for her master's next command, but Eldrick didn't miss the blood dripping from her nose or her frantic sweep over the warriors gathered, as if she might spy her sister, Belle, amongst them.

But the witch was nowhere in sight along with Linx, the Gray Fenris's mage and healer. Nor Eldrick's father and mother, alphas of the Drengr pack, but commotion from the north resounded out of sight, and Eldrick didn't have time to ponder where his family was.

To the right, shielded by his pack mates, Bjorn sneered, lips etched in mirth. He raised a brow that taunted, *Let's see what you're made of, pup.*

Eldrick drew his shoulders back, and engaged the power of his alpha baritone into his next words. "Evelyn isn't here, Prince Riven. Leave these lands."

The Vadon Mountains shifted. Crows shot through the night and cawed their retreat, becoming lost behind the gray snow clouds hovering above the village. The warriors at his back tightened the grip on their weapons and shields. No one breathed or moved.

Riven snickered, flashing a fang. "That is shame. I didn't come all this way to leave empty-handed, wolf. Give me someone else, then. Perhaps my sister? I know she's here, *smell* her on you. Hand Tovi over, and I'll leave your village intact."

Eldrick's blood turned to ice. His fingers twitched with the remembrance of Tovi's flesh. An uncontrollable growl vibrated through his chest. Pain seared through his hand. *Moons*, his claws threatened to emerge. Eldrick reined in his wolf, pulling them back.

"*Never*," he snarled.

"No?" Riven laughed, wet and hollow. "*Hmm*, what about your mother, then? Not my first choice, but she is a spy and traitor to my court. Punishment is due. Surely, you won't choose vampyrs over your pack, will you? Come, come, Tala," Riven cried out over the gathered crowd. "Save your son from embarrassment and show yourself."

"Her true name is Nadia Drengr." Aramis's voice severed the tension as he weaved his way through the warriors. He laid a reassuring hand on Bétar's shoulder, pushing past him and joining Eldrick's side, sword in hand. Green eyes piercing. Muscles taut. Blood soaking his left brow. The pale light of the night caught the silver in his hair, and Eldrick's jaw hardened.

Was his father ready for battle?

"Nadia is the female alpha of the Drengrs and has hence returned home. You, Prince Riven, are not permitted on these lands. Leave now, or you'll face the valor of werewolves."

At those words, the Drengr Pack beat their fists against their shields. Eldrick's wolf paced and snarled, awaiting his father's command.

But then he spied Lorkan, paler than usual. Stone-faced. *Moons*. Eldrick hadn't revealed that truth in his letters for fear of this risk—Prince Riven discovering his mother's identity. Hurt and disbelief marred his brother's face. Eldrick's chest tightened, and he severed their tense stare. *Later*, he swore.

Riven pointed the tip of his blade at Aramis. "I'll give you one last chance. Turn her over, and I'll not burn your village to the ground."

Snow drifted on the wind, and the village fell silent enough to hear the gentle whisper of flurries as they landed. Aramis's jaw ticked, a similar reaction to Eldrick's moments ago when Dalinda had suggested turning over Tovi. His mother was the alpha, but she, too, was a vampyr. His father's choice influenced the Earl vote, and by Bjorn's triumphant stance, the alpha knew it, too.

"No," Aramis said. "Your blood will soak my blade before I allow you to touch her."

Riven snorted. "What a shame."

The prince blurred as he spun, a flurry of white and gold. His cape billowed behind him as he charged. Ingrid followed, her dark winds whipping to the warriors on the right. Fighting ensued. Bétar led werewolves in formation, shields bracing as vampyrs emerged from the shadows of the forest, blades and talons sheathed. Yen's battle cry pierced the air, and arrows fell from the sky with the snow.

Metal clanged as Aramis and Riven clashed. Eldrick sprang forward, fighting by his father's side. Alpha and Magu. *Drengrs.*

The prince struck downward. Eldrick caught his blade under the belly of his axe. He tugged, dragging Riven closer. Vampyr fangs glinted in Eldrick's line of sight. He tore his axe free, and as Riven stumbled back, he planted his boot onto his gaudy armor and thrust.

Aramis charged forward, slicing his sword across Riven's belly. Iron rang against silver. Riven regained his footing. A frustrated roar erupted from him. He swung his enchanted sword. No finesse. No skill. No reason. Aramis matched blow for blow—

Black mists collected in Eldrick's peripherals. Ingrid lingered. Her crooked and gnarled hands appeared broken as she whirled magic at her side. Winds snaked around Aramis and Eldrick's ankles. She hissed. Blood streamed over her lips and chin. Sweet anise rose in the air. *Stars above.* Eldrick sprang forward, knocking his father out of the way.

"Eldrick, no!" Aramis said.

It was too late. Ingrid released her magic. An onyx sphere barreled into him. But unlike the attack at the gates, the witch's power didn't launch him back. No. The tendrils bled into him like ink on parchment. Wretched cold feasted on his magic, acid corroding his insides. Eldrick crumpled to his knees, fighting the urge to wretch. He dug his hands into the soil.

Home.

The Vadon Mountains whispered on the true winds of this land. *Get up!*

His wolf answered the call of his homeland, and Eldrick shifted. Bones snapped. Muscles tore. Tendons stretched. His face pulled, and claws shot out of his morphing hands. The beastly magic running in his blood burned through Ingrid's attack. On all fours, he howled to the heavens.

With canines bared, he prowled towards Riven, the intent to kill coursing through him. His land. His home. His pack.

The prince's jade eyes widened. "I *am* a king!"

"You are nothing, Riven"—Tovi appeared on the wall, perched at the edge; a new blade glinted between her shoulders, secured on her back—"but a king of madness."

The Queen of Drystan leapt.

CHAPTER EIGHTEEN

RIVEN DIVERTED LEFT, RECOILING from where Tovi landed on strong, balanced feet. Behind her, Eldrick and Aramis fought vampyrs rushing from the forest. Chaos held it's thorny grasp on the village.

"Leave, brother." Tovi stalked towards him, holding her sword out wide. "You can't win with such few numbers."

"You're right. I can't." A faint smirk painted Riven's face in amusement. *"Call them forth!"*

Behind them, Ingrid whispered a word Tovi didn't recognize, her tone like a snake's hiss. Screeches reached from above, and *italogs*—demons with leathery wings that shared a likeness to bats—dropped from the snow clouds. The monsters ascended, aiming for werewolves lining the palisade wall. The hairs on the back of Tovi's neck stood, and howls grew louder in the forest.

"Madras!" Yennifer called. "A whole pack of them."

Tovi's skin tightened with cold—*Goddess,* Ingrid had summoned the creatures of darkness. But how?

Riven circled her as the battle shifted. Tovi trailed his footing, positioning her sword ahead of her.

"Mother and Father would be so disappointed in you," he whispered.

"Nothing I'm not used to. They always were," she said with gritted teeth.

Something flashed in Riven's eyes. "Do you really wish to fight?"

Tovi didn't hesitate. "If I must."

"So be it." Riven charged.

In a flurry of silver and white, sister and brother fought. Tovi's new blade felt good. *Right.* Molded to her hand as she twisted, struck, and deflected her brother's attacks. Around them, metal and magic clanged together. Teeth clanked. Talons pierced. Flesh tore. The sound of death and darkness beat against Tovi's focus, and the scent of so much blood—demon, vampyr, and werewolf—perfumed the air.

She locked eyes with her brother, jade connecting with jade. They were far too similar, like Tovi stared into a mirror. But a lost reflection stared back at her. Riven's hands had shifted to talons, shredding his leather gloves. Spidery veins surrounded his eyes, darkening the scar running down his face to an angry red. He teetered closer than ever to a caillte. So far gone, there was no reaching beyond and yanking him back. The winds whistled. The ground trembled. As if the lands of Sorin agreed.

Their blades intersected, and both of them pushed, unrelenting.

"Are you truly willing to destroy this world to bring back Iona and Oli?" Tovi breathed.

"Yes," Riven said without hesitation.

The new crest on his breastplate glared at her. A raven with its wings spread open, facing north as if it soared towards home.

Tovi's mouth turned dry. "There will be no world to bring them back to if you continue down this path."

"I care for *nothing* but holding my son again," he snarled. "To kiss the wife that was taken from me. Love is a poison, dear sister. Us Verenas know that best. It is an infliction we cannot outrun."

Riven flung his enchanted sword up. Tovi sprang back and brought her weapon across her body, deflecting his next strike.

Vampyrs drew closer, flanking her on all sides. *Goddess,* she was surrounded—

Eldrick tackled the closest vampyr to her left, tearing him apart with his werewolf canines. On all fours, he stood at her side, and *united,* they faced the enemy of Sorin.

The winds sang as they whipped across the village. Tovi ignored the whispers of the land. Snuffed the elation trying to course through her. *No.* She was in the heat of battle. She was Queen of Drystan. Nothing else mattered. Eldrick was an ally in this fight.

That was all.

She hissed, channeling her frustration into her next attack on her brother. They fought, blood of the same blood clashing. Two against one, Riven grew tired, leaving himself open. He slowed, allowing Tovi to step too close.

She screamed, her heart tearing as she seized the opportunity and drove a dagger into Riven's thigh. He fell to his knees, shock bleeding across his face. She drew her sword to his neck. Metal pressed into flesh. His racing pulse drummed in her ear.

Do it, reason yelled.

He's your brother, her heart begged.

Tovi bared her fangs, fighting the tears stinging at the edge of her eyes. If she faltered, she showed the werewolves she was weak. She *failed* her people, too. He didn't fight to free them but to cast them into more darkness.

Tovi's hesitation cost her. Riven pulled the dagger free of his leg and stabbed her in the side with it. She cried out in pain, faltering, and Riven escaped her clutches.

Eldrick shifted back to his male form. "Tovi—"

Riven whizzed behind Eldrick and planted the enchanted blade at his neck.

"No!" Tovi screamed, panic rocking through her like a bolt of lightning. She stumbled, not caring that the blade pushed deeper into her side. Warm blood leaked from her wound, but all she could think, see, and feel was for the male she loved before her, his life threatened by her brother.

"Let him go," she seethed.

Riven laughed. "If only you could see yourself, so like Father, more like *me* than you think." Eldrick shook in his hold, but Riven pressed the blade closer to his neck. "You're her downfall, you know? She'll never be queen because of you."

Eldrick and Tovi's green stares connected, and there was no denying the truth in Riven's words.

"Oh, dear sister!"

Tovi stilled. She searched the battle. *There.* Visha marched through the conflict, dragging someone through the front gate. Tovi gasped. Lou struggled in her sister's hold, red-rimmed glasses smashed, nose broken. Bruised and bloody. Her friend had fought. *Hard.*

The fighting continued while Visha stopped ten yards away and whipped Lou ahead of her. She positioned the tips of her black talons against Lou's throat and pressed. One swipe across *that* vein and there'd be no saving her friend.

"Choose," Visha hissed. "The werewolf or the vampyr."

Tovi's blood turned to ice, and her attention jumped between two people she loved.

"Where does your heart truly lie?" Riven whispered. "With your people or this wolf?"

This was what Tovi feared above all else. Tovi stood at the very decision that haunted her nightmares. What was best for her people versus what she wanted. But she more than wanted Eldrick, and that feeling eclipsed rational thought and reason. Lou was her friend. Loyal and dedicated. A subject of Drystan she'd sworn to protect. The gods mocked her as they made her choose.

Eldrick struggled under Riven's hold, a growl vibrating through his chest. "Tovi, look at me—"

"Tick tock, tick tock," Visha sang.

Tovi's body shook. Her heart ripped at the seams. *No. No. No.*

Fighting slowed. No demons survived. Their dusty remnants twirled with the snow, landing on the dead. So, so many. Tovi's gaze jumped between Eldrick and Lou. She couldn't stomach the notion of either of them joining the stiff bodies strewn across the village. Her entire being refused to. *Goddess,* what sort of queen was she?

Tovi gripped her stomach, not because of her wound, but because of the bile working its way up throat. She *knew* who she'd chose, and she met his gem eyes through the snow drifting on the wind.

"Tovi." Eldrick shook with rage. "You don't need to do this."

But he was wrong. So very, very wrong. Riven was right. She was a Verena. Love's poison swam in her veins as thick and wretched as the Blood Curse.

Lou sprang forward. "Never forget what you're fighting for—"

Visha yanked her back by the hair, pressing her talons deeper into her flesh.

Freedom. The word sang on the wind, a reminder that yanked Tovi to the present. She refused to allow her siblings to rob her of choice, and she knew what Riven wanted more than either Lou or Eldrick's death.

She inhaled and set her shoulders back. "Take me. Let them both go, and I'll surrender."

Riven's eyes flashed with greed.

"No," Eldrick growled. "*No!*"

"Fine," Riven said, not breaking their stare.

He lifted the blade from Eldrick's throat and backed away. One. Two. Each step was heavier than the last.

The fighting around them stopped. Silence and stillness bled into the battle's carnage. Tovi inhaled the scent of death and exhaled defeat.

"Now, release Lou," she shouted.

Her sister's lips curled into a smirk. "I'm afraid this turn of events is far too boring for me."

Tovi stepped forward. "Wait—"

"Don't!" Riven roared.

Visha swiped her talons across Lou's neck.

Blood splayed across the snow, and an air-splitting scream ripped from Tovi.

The battle began again. Riven cursed and retreated towards the gates. Tovi charged, but her legs gave out from under her, the dagger still wedged at her side. She yanked it free with a warrior's crying, staggering to standing. Powerful arms wrapped around her, holding her back.

"Stop, Tovi," Eldrick breathed. "She's gone."

"*No!*" Tovi fought. Raged. *Broke.* "I failed her!"

Words, touch, *nothing* undid her heartache. Her last interaction with Lou wouldn't stop playing in her mind. Over and over, it consumed her. There was no *later*. No conversation to undo how they'd left things, how Tovi had *treated* her.

Visha kicked Lou's dying form into the snow. She slunk backward and blew Tovi a kiss.

"I'm going to fucking kill her." Tovi squirmed in Eldrick's hold, but he didn't relent.

"You're not the only one in pain," he whispered.

Werewolves—Yen, Bétar, Todd, and Lucy—advanced towards the gates, vengeance gleaming in the eyes.

Visha grabbed a lit torch and threw it into an oily puddle. Fire roared to life. It devoured the debris and climbed up the wall. Ingrid stepped forth and twisted her hands. Dark, screeching winds carried the fire further.

Tovi pushed one last time in Eldrick's hold, and he released her. She charged towards Visha.

But it was no use.

As she leapt through the air, Ingrid's *danu* closed shut. Her siblings were gone, and Tovi fell to her knees. Hollow. She was too tired to sob, speak, or *think*.

Lou's lifeless eyes stared back at her. Flour stained the baker's clothes. Her red-rimmed glasses lay broken by her stiff fingers. *Gone.* Her friend was gone.

But her last words to Tovi lived, carrying on the wind.

Never forget what you're fighting for.

Chapter Nineteen

Blair

Blair stumbled through her *danu* and into the narrow hall of her townhome, her winds cooling her wine-locked limbs. Tannins still gripped her tongue, but she couldn't discern if it was the remnants of the fifteen-year-old wine she'd drank or her sour mood. The onslaught of a headache formed at the center of her forehead, and Blair let out a stream of curses as she kneaded the pain away.

"Pass the bottle, will you?" a female whispered.

Blair stilled. Had she drank so much she was hearing voices? Was the wine laced with a hallucinogenic tonic? *Goddess,* she *really* needed to read the fine print on those wine-bar menus.

And water. Yes, she needed *to hydrate—*

"Damn, this is good. Think she'll notice it's gone?"

"If you keep drinking it like water, then yes."

Both voices were familiar, and as Blair crept around the corner and into the front wing of her townhome, her aunt and second cousin's faces blurred into focus. Seated on the love seat by the bay window, Josepha and Rodrick smiled at her arrival.

"Good of you to show up. We were getting worried," Rodrick said.

Blair rolled her eyes. "How uncharacteristic of you."

Worried? She almost laughed. Her coven fretted over Evelyn and Mirella while they overlooked *her.*

A dusty collectible bottle resting on the ottoman table whispered its sweet notes, beckoning Blair to have another drink, but her early buzz dwindled thanks to the unexpected company. She sauntered into the kitchen and readied herself a glass of water. Behind her, Rodrick and Josepha discussed in hushed voices.

"How did you both get inside?" She leaned against the counter, sipping her water—*Goddess*, it tasted divine.

Josepha pointed left. Curtains ballooned like some breathing ghost around the kitchen's open window.

"I left that open for Rook, not wine smugglers." Though her familiar was nowhere in sight—the snarky raven had abandoned Blair after she'd stormed out of the coven meeting hours ago. Blair swallowed, unsure sure how to interpret the opinion of the creature tied to her soul.

For what if his absence mirrored the regret she held for hurting Evelyn? No amount of wine numbed that ache.

Rodrick held up a finger. "The bottle was an afterthought."

"He's right." Josepha nodded. "We came to check on you, and when you didn't show up for hours . . ."

"You opened my most expensive and oldest bottle of wine." Blair tilted her head to the side.

"Precisely!" Rodrick said.

"Hmm," Josepha agreed as she sipped her glass.

Pain pulsed through Blair's forehead. "Well, I'm back and fine, so you can both leave now."

Rodrick pushed his spectacles up the bridge of his nose. Josepha's dark stare—much like Blair's father—pinned her in place.

"You Carson sisters are all so stubborn." The scholar set her wineglass down with a loud clank. "We paid you a visit because . . ."

Rodrick leaned in. "Neither of us knew you were feeling so alone, books."

As a child, she'd earned the nickname amongst her coven. *Where there's Blair, there's a book, and where there's a book, there's Blair,* her father and mother had teased. Her parents practically begged her to sleep instead of read while Josepha and Rodrick snuck her new texts like aunts and uncles handed out candy. But it wasn't the nickname that had Blair's insides twisting.

For it was the word *alone*. The fellow Carson coven scholars stared at her expectantly. How did she admit that the sense of otherness had engulfed her as much as the winds she conjured at her fingertips? Yet, they'd noticed a decade too late. When would she have a chance to be seen?

Tiredness washed over Blair, and she lumbered over to the seating area and plopped into her oversize reading chair. *Yes, water, now sleep.* The leather hugged her on all sides, but no amount of comfort eased her wary conscience.

"It's getting late, and I think you should both leave."

Tension bristled through the townhome, and on uneasy feet, the fellow Carson scholars rose and retreated towards the door.

Josepha paused, a frown etched into her expression. "We weren't there for you these last nine months because we didn't think we needed to be. The truth is, we were proud of you when you sought Kade out."

Blair blinked, certain she'd misheard. "But I lost my position—"

Josepha snorted. "We don't care about some fancy title. You're still Blair without it, still our books."

Was she? Blair sank deeper into the chair, unconvinced by Josepha's flippant attitude. Without her position, there was no order, structure, or purpose, leaving Blair stretched too thin and wild.

"Agreed," Roderick said. "The Blair we know wouldn't abandon her sister in a time of need."

The door clicked shut, and they left Blair alone. Her stomach roiled, and burgundy threatened to ruin her decorative rug. She gripped the chair's arms and focused on the floor-to-ceiling bookshelf. She'd built this home, life, *all of it* around being a scholar. What was she without it?

A caw broke Blair from her brooding. Rook shot through the open window and landed on the reading chair's wing. He clacked his beak, staring down at her, as if to say, *Hello, hello.*

Since the earliest tales of witch folklore, ravens, with their dark, glossy feathers and haunting calls, were painted as dangerous omens since the Gods War—singing over the slain, their shadows falling over those who neared death, and bringing mischief wherever they landed.

Blair was partial to believe the latter, but she'd ignored the tales and whispers regarding Rook for over a decade. Nothing compared to the zap of power between a witch and a familiar, not even the superstitions of witches, and Rook was her companion in *otherness.* She was less alone with him on her shoulder. Her chest warmed, and she ran the back of her finger down Rook's neck in greeting.

"I'm glad you're back, little one."

Rook blinked, his deep-black-almost-blue eyes far too knowing. He ruffled his wings and stomped, as if to say, *I'm not little!*

"Anymore," Blair whispered. She'd found Rook as a chick, a mere puffball of black feathers wedged—to no one's surprise—between two books in the small, hidden corner of a werewolf library.

He stomped his feet again in response, and Blair laughed. The sound was forced and jagged in her throat. Here she was, slumped and drunk, pretending her sister wasn't in the middle of breaking Kade out of Tùir. She sighed, absently brushing Rook's dark feathers.

Boots clattered down the street, and a voice called, "The Son of the God has escaped!"

Blair sprinted out of her chair. Two Guards stood outside her townhome, and Blair ducked under the window, holding her breath as she eavesdropped.

"How did he get out?"

"Evelyn Carson. They found a Guard dead in his cell—dark magic."

What?

Blair stilled, slumping against the wall. *No.* That was neither Evelyn nor Kade—they wouldn't kill a witch or touch dark magic. She refused to believe it. Something or someone else was at play.

"Elder Circe has ordered units to surround the Nūa Library. She spotted them inside."

"Goddess, this is madness."

"I'll gather my unit and surround the east exits."

"Good. My unit plans to enter the library and ambush them with Elder Circe. Alert those on the Wall, too. No one gets in or out of the city, per Elder Circe's orders."

Their boots clattered against the sidewalk again, growing distant until only silence and dread sat with Blair. Evelyn and Kade didn't stand a chance with that many Guards. *But they disobeyed orders*, a voice hissed in the back of Blair's mind. She winced. Did her sister deserve to be treated like the enemy? Could *she* stomach her sister getting captured?

Blair's magic surged through her. Not her winds, the *otherness*. Shadows flicked around her boots, snaking like living things. The darkness she kept dormant rose like the mists of the Void—tall, mighty, and *dark*. The truth beat in her heart, as if wickedness weaved into her magic egged her to step out of line.

Rook landed at her feet, tilting his head as if in question—*What are you going to do?*

"Save my little sister," Blair whispered.

CHAPTER TWENTY

EVELYN

THE SHARP EDGES OF the Nūa Library glared at Evelyn and Kade as they slunk around corners, tiptoeing deeper into the rows of bookcases. The soothing sound of fluttering pages echoed as books floated to and from shelves, disappearing around bends in a uniformed line. Evelyn peeked around a marble column and darted out of sight, falling flush with the adjacent wall.

"Scholars?" Kade asked.

Evelyn nodded.

A clock chimed to their left, signaling the time. It was well into the early hours of the next day. Evelyn nibbled her lip. Time was of the essence. They had two hours before sunrise, and if they had any chance of not being seen by the Guards stationed at the Wall, they needed the last minutes of night.

"Alright," Kade whispered. "What do we do next?"

Much like the architecture throughout the city, the library's rotunda-like shape depicted the sun. The building curved in a circle, and on the main floor ahead, a dozen desks lined the center. Five scholars, shrouded in shawls and lost to their studies, sat at desks lit by small lampshades. Above, a glass dome revealed the star-filled night sky peeking through a rip in the clouds.

"The lead scholars' offices are on the third level." Evelyn dropped her voices to mere breath. "There's a set of staircases in each corner but there's no chance of making it to any of them without getting spotted."

"Any other ideas?" Kade asked.

Evelyn pointed behind them. "There's a set of older stairs, but it'll take longer to reach Circe's office."

"Leaving us less time to search."

Evelyn sighed, studying Kade's thoughtful expression. "Something is better than getting caught."

The corners of his lips twitched into a smile. "I suppose you're right. Lead the way, love."

Evelyn grabbed Kade's hand and dragged him down an aisle brimming with books. On the wall to their left, spines with chrome lettering glinted in the light of the sconces, and to the right, bookshelves cast their leering shadows onto the limestone tile. Evelyn paused at each end, and Kade tapped her lower back to single the coast was clear. Without encountering a scholar, they scurried into the abandon staircase lost behind a column.

The sensation of walls closing in around them fell over Evelyn as they climbed higher. Uncomfortable memories skated down her back. Her tutelage under Circe had been painful. Tough. She'd not visited the northern wing of the library in years, let alone the Elder's office.

As she and Kade crested the last step and entered the third level, Evelyn inhaled the fond memories with her tutor Uzoma instead. *Those* had taken place in the east wing and far outshined the brief season of abuse done by Circe's hand.

Thunder rumbled in the distance, and past the library's stone walls, the electricity of an inevitable storm pricked the air. Evelyn fingers ached, injuries long healed awakening as if her bones remembered.

They weaved through columns and bookshelves until they paused in an open seating area. Behind Evelyn, a growl rumbled through Kade's chest.

She whirled, heart racing. "What is it?"

Kade's gaze penetrated the hall across from them. The end was swallowed by darkness, and Evelyn didn't *see* anyone or anything through the shadows, and without her magic, she couldn't sense anyone either.

Kade blinked, brows relaxing as he refocused. "Nothing. I thought . . . I saw someone."

Questions churned in the pit of Evelyn's belly, but more thunder echoed outside, the storm on the bay growing closer to the city. She didn't have time to ask. Besides, they were both wary. Who knew the last time Kade had eaten, and they hadn't discussed what he'd endured in Tùir. She, too, sat on edge.

"Let's keep moving," she whispered.

Evelyn led them up and around the circular floor. Ten feet away, the rounded hall lined with oak doors awaited them. Circe's sat in the center, her title etched into a brass plaque. Evelyn's heart lodged in her throat, and she fisted her hands at her sides, refusing to let the past, her pain, or title stall her efforts.

Black smudge at the bottom of the bookshelf that bled into the floor caught her eye. She paused, running her boot across the scorch marks. Kade's tall frame cast a shadow over it, and his evergreen-and-rain scent calmed Evelyn's nerves.

She nudged his shoulder. "That was *my* doing."

Kade's brows furrowed, and then his golden eyes widened, landing on her. "You burned the Nūa Library?"

"More specifically, I set fire to the entire section dedicated to creatures and myths."

"Stars above, I'm glad you've had a change of heart when it comes to beastly things."

Evelyn pursed her lips, fighting laughter. She nodded her head to the left, and they continued to Circe's door.

"It was an accident, which tends to happen to those still learning their power," she said, giving Kade a pointed look.

"How old were you?" he asked, a small smiling tugging at the edge of his lips.

"Fourteen."

Kade grunted. "I don't know if that makes me feel better or worse."

Evelyn grabbed his hand. "Per the prophecy, we were gifted by the gods with immense power. Yours manifested *weeks* ago."

Her fated sighed, and *Goddess*, Evelyn wished she had access to their bond to sense how he felt, for he said nothing more on the matter. Outside Circe's door, Kade placed his ear against the wood. Eveyln waited, pulse thrumming.

After a few breaths, he said, "I don't hear or smell anyone on the other side, nor sense magic."

He grabbed the handle, and in one mighty turn, the metal cracked, and the door swung open, revealing Circe's office. Orderly. Sterile. *Massive.* At the back, Circe's desk sat ahead of a green chalkboard. To the left, her own personal library spanned twelve shelves while to the right, a set of wrought iron steps spiraled to a lofted area shrouded in night. Above, a slanted skylight twinkled with first few droplets of rain.

"Goddess, where do we start?" Evelyn asked.

Kade dropped to his haunches and laid a hand flush against the maroon carpet. "Wherever Circe spends her time the most."

He closed his eyes, and the hair on Evelyn's arms rose as Kade sent out his tracker magic. He inhaled. Exhaled. Jaw tight, shoulders straight. He'd honed an admirable level of control. As his eyes sprang open, Evelyn swore silver flashed across them.

"She's thoughtful, anxious, and determined at her desk," he said as he stood to his full height.

"That would've been a lovely skill while I searched Drystan Castle," Evelyn muttered.

She sauntered over to Circe's desk, and unlike the time she'd sifted through Riven's, Evelyn rooted through papers with no finesse and threw them to the ground when she found nothing useful. Breaking and entering *was* an offense in Nūa, and this building made it all that much worse, but Evelyn didn't have a care in the world if Circe discovered she'd snooped. *Let her.*

Truthfully, Evelyn was running out of fucks.

"What are you looking for?" Kade asked.

"A flower." Though there were no signs of the tansy flower symbol or the prince's purple seal in any of the Elder's letters. Evelyn inspected the handwriting and found it nothing like the script she'd read in Drystan. There was nothing incriminating on Circe's desk.

A sensation caressed her cheeks, and she peered up to find Kade staring. The amber in his gaze glowed as bright as the sconces lighting the columns surrounding the office.

"What?" she whispered.

He shrugged. "I love that look you get."

She waited.

Kade ran a finger in the creases between her forehead. "When you're focused, your brow pinches, and there's a special sheen in those gray eyes. I've admired it since Callum . . . Pure determination."

Evelyn sighed at his touch. As nice as his words were, it felt like they were leaving the city with nothing. No way to get her magic. No closer to understanding Kade's new power. No research on how to break the Blood Curse.

"I knew I smelled disappointment."

The shrill voice grated up Evelyn's spine, and old memories gripped her mind like sharp talons. Kade shielded her behind him, and a low growl vibrated through his chest.

Circe stood in the doorway, upper lip tugged in a snarl, revealing her sharp, yellow teeth. She splayed her hands at her side, and Evelyn searched for an exit, but Circe had cornered them.

Fucking flames.

"It was always my idea to keep you two apart." Circe prowled closer. "What a fucking headache you've already both caused."

"Why?" Kade hissed, hand flexing towards his sword.

"I feared your bond would grow too strong for us to control."

Evelyn's fingernails dug into her fleshy palms, Circe's final word ricocheting inside her skull. "That's why you requested to be my tutor. You thought of us as things to wield."

"You *are*. Both of you are keys within the prophecy—"

"That may be true, but our fate belongs in our hands, no one else's." Evelyn's adamancy rang in the office—an unbending declaration. She'd never backed down these last few months. Why start now?

Circe shook with rage. "You stupid, naïve girl."

The Elder shot out her hand and reached towards Evelyn. The bloodstone necklace tightened and tugged around her neck, and Evelyn clawed at her throat, struggling to breathe. Her knees buckled, and Kade dropped with her.

"Ev!" he cried.

"I was wrong all those years ago, believing you were nothing without your power. The truth is, you're not worthy of it. Not then and not now," Circe said. "I should've disciplined you harder! Handing you over to that pathetic seer was a mistake."

Kade whirled, unsheathing his sword. Air rushed back into Evelyn's lungs. Her necklace relaxed. Evelyn patted her neck, confusion gripping her. Circe's cruel stare shifted to Kade.

Fucking flames, it'd been a trap.

"Kade, don't!" Evelyn shouted.

But it was too late. He charged ahead to defend her just as Circe had hoped. A triumphant smile split across Circe's face, and her hand snapped towards him. Kade fell to his knees, dropping his sword. Icy panic shot through Evelyn as he gripped his head and unleashed a strangled roar.

CHAPTER TWENTY-ONE

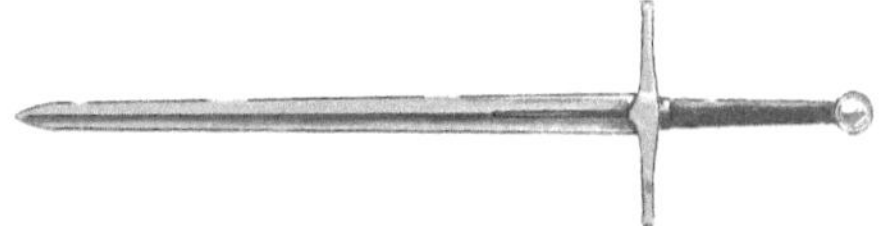

K ADE LANDED WITH A bone-rattling thud. Brutal cold nipped at his skin, and above, snow lollygagged from a fathomless gray sky. The ground beneath his knees scorched through his traveling leathers. Wails joined the chorus of thunder, and Kade's werewolf wrestled with the presence of death lingering in the slinking mists.

He stood in a desolate wasteland, the Nūa Library gone.

As was his mate.

"Evelyn!" Kade righted himself on shaking legs, searching wildly for her.

"Kade!" His name traveled from beyond the blanket of thick clouds.

A sharp pain lanced through his head, like a blade had been wedged into his skull. He gritted his teeth, his wolf raging inside his blood. Circe had entered his mind. But how?

He growled at the scent of licorice filling his nose. Inky. Oozing. Slithering against the crevices of his mind. He stepped forward, charging mentally ahead against Circe's hold. He needed to wake up and get back to Evelyn.

But as he became aware of its presence, the dark magic sank its power deeper.

Bile rose up Kade's throat, and he almost wretched onto the battlefield. Ravens descended out of the mists, landing atop piles of dead bodies. They picked at flesh, feasted on the dead. Arrows protruded from stiff limbs. One raven perched atop a sword's hilt, cawing incessantly at Kade.

Familiarness settled across Kade's skin like morning dew. The wasteland came and went as he blinked, shifting from the vastness of Sorin back to the rolling hills of rot.

Move. Do something.

Yet, no direction Kade traveled mattered. The same bodies lay around him. The mists lingered, trailing him like hungry serpents. And the raven remained ahead, and Kade's wolf couldn't discern if its cries were a taunt or a warning. Kade roared. He was stuck, *caged* in the dark crevices of his own mind.

"Please! Let me out!" a young voice said, thick with tears.

He whirled. Yards away, a terrified girl beat against the hazy walls of a transparent box. Obsidian hair tied in braids. Large gray eyes she'd not yet to grow into.

Evelyn.

Kade's heart cracked. What sick mind game was this?

He rushed to her and beat his fists against the box. Its firmness rivaled stone, yet its transparency mirrored water. "Evelyn, can you hear me?"

"I'll try again! Please!" No older than seven, the child-version of Evelyn sobbed. She clutched one bruised, shaking hand to her chest. Two fingers jutted at crooked angles, and Kade flushed with a level of anger he'd never tasted before.

Stars above, he begged the gods this wasn't real. *Fear.* That's what Kade had endured when he'd burned Evelyn with his power. But *this* . . . This was different. Wilder. Monstrous. His mind battled sense and reason. Was this real? A memory? Or a trick to unravel his sanity?

I should've disciplined you harder, Circe had shouted.

"Let me out!" Evelyn's crying worsened. She was so young and frightened, and Kade sat with her, gutted.

"Look at me, it'll be alright. I'm going to protect you." Always. Forever. Even if this wasn't real, he couldn't deny his innate instinct.

Thunder boomed over his words, as if the wasteland knew how useless they were.

"Kade!" Evelyn's adult voice rang from above. "Push her out! Fight!"

Circe's hold tightened, and Kade's inner beast whimpered. He couldn't leave this version of her behind, not when she was hurt and in pain. It was too *real*. Was he a protector if he didn't do *something*? He leaned into Circe's magic, *gave in*, and—

The mirage ahead of him faded, lifted with the winds and drifted from existence.

"No!" Kade's banged his hands into the scorched earth. The remnants of vanilla and cedar tickled his nose, and the dying moans around him grew louder.

"You, you, you," they chanted.

The pulse of his power threatened to release. The sounds, sights, and pressure was all too much.

Dirt-covered toes appeared ahead of Kade. He peered up and bared his teeth.

"Tenebris."

The dark witch wore a tattered cloak, the hood pulled over his head and casting his stonelike expression in shadow. No chains ringed his ankles or wrists, but instead he held a metal scythe, it's curved metal blade the brightest object for miles.

This isn't real, Kade told himself.

"What if it is?" Tenebris's lips didn't move, but his voice carried across the wasteland like a thousand versions of him said it all at once. "Can you not smell the future in Circe's visions? Can you not taste the *death* you will bring?"

Stars above, Tenebris's words planted seeds of doubt. Kade shut his eyes. Dug his fingers into the earth. He was meant to protect his homeland, not destroy it. This wasn't him. He refused to believe it.

He thought of Evelyn. Envisioned her strength, the look of *pure determination* he loved so fucking much. Her smell, touch, *everything*. He pushed against the notion he was darkness, fought against Circe's hold. The dark witch faltered, and Kade rallied his honor like a blade.

The raven soared across the wasteland and landed on Tenebris's shoulder. It fluttered its wings, restless. Dark, bottomless eyes bore into Kade. Far away, a warrior's roar bellowed, and Kade's wolf howled alongside the likeness, answering the ancient call humming in his blood.

Dark magic fled Kade's mind, and the raven's beak opened unnaturally wide and swallowed him whole.

CHAPTER TWENTY-TWO

S HADOWS DRAPED THE ANCIENT tunnels of the Nūa Library. Blair hurried on quick feet, following Rook's glinting wings as he led them.

Usually, she detested witches' superstitious tendencies, but tonight, she appreciated the passageways the first witches of Sorin had created. After enduring the Great Burnings, they'd carried their fears from Callum across the Sapphire Sea, and the city brimmed with unseen ways to escape it. As well as *through* it. It was how Blair had sneaked into the library these last weeks, researching how to get Evelyn's magic back.

And if the Goddess was on their side, she'd help Evelyn and Kade out of the city using them, too.

Old stone and secrets soothed her roiling stomach. She'd left her townhouse in a rush. Wrinkled clothes. Half-tied cloak. Curly hair frizzed from the damp underground. Goddess, here she was again, stepping out of line. Who did she think she was? She was no third born, no warrior. She had no business being on a rescue mission, but Blair loved Evelyn.

Her knuckles popped as she tightened her hold on her *shillelagh*. Evelyn had her staff. Kade had her sword. She had her enchanted blackthorn walking stick. Not a weapon exactly. The hardy tree stood up to winds no matter their might, and it worked as an excellent anchor when Blair conjured her *danu*. If it could ground her traveling magic, what else could it assist with?

Voices echoed down the next tunnel, and Blair skidded to a halt. Her breath *whooshed* out of her, and Rook didn't hesitate. He shot down the passageway. A werewolf growl shook the library's foundation.

Blair ran. Her fingertips pricked with power. The air in the tunnels shifted with her, like a current carrying her forth. She swore that the shadows in her peripherals snaked along the fractures in the ancient walls.

Blair gritted her teeth. *Not tonight.* She couldn't afford to step *too* far out of line. She feared the inky part of her was too much, and if she unleashed it, how would she draw it back?

"Get out of his mind!" Her sister's desperate words sharpened, but even so, they beat against the stone, beyond the passageway.

Rook cawed up ahead, fluttering his wings and hovering by a hole in the stone walls. Light shot out of it, illuminating his onyx feathers. Blair reached him and peered through it. Although the opening was no larger than her hand, Blair glimpsed her sister's dark hair.

Evelyn spun. Sword in hand. Teeth bared. Blair's sister fought Circe with Kade's sword.

No. *Defended.*

Kade was crouched on his knees, *writhing*.

"Fuck."

Blair had only heard the tales of Elder Circe's mind control, used to invade scáths' minds to learn more about vampyrs and darkness. The air oozed with wrongness, as if the witch's power teetered on the edge of dark magic.

Blair had to get to them. Help Evelyn. Before the reinforcements arrived to assist Circe.

The hole in the stone was far too small to fit through, and Blair searched the Elder's office. *There.* On her tiptoes, Blair spotted the loft above the classroom area.

"Rook."

Her familiar answered her call and landed atop her shoulder. Blair drove her shillelagh into the ground and drew up her bronntanas. Unlike other elements, wind reached far beyond the land. It traveled across the plains, whirled around mountains, and kissed the sea's waves. Blair loved the thrill, enjoying the wind coursing through her veins. Wild, alive. A truer reflection of her caged soul.

She shut her eyes. Memories were the key to jumping place to place. They fluttered past her eyelids—time spent as a university student in the loft, meeting for group projects, and writing research papers. Elder Circe was her least-favorite professor, and the memories were faint and few, but Blair possessed enough to conjure her *danu*.

Air wisps outlined a doorway ahead of her. Blair, with Rook secured on her shoulder, stepped through, and she closed the *danu* with restraint—surprise was an advantage.

Piles of books collected dust, and it appeared some time had passed since other students had used the area, and as Blair tiptoed to the edge of the loft, a stomach-churning cackle resounded from below.

Circe held up Evelyn's bloodstone necklace. *Her sister's magic.* The Elder snickered. "Like I said, you're unworthy of this power—"

Blair didn't think; she *moved*. Rallying her winds in a force fueled by her anger, she used her winds to grasp the books piled in the loft, and drew a mighty wave of them over the edge.

The Elder's stare widened, but her surprise quickly vanished as a hundred texts buried her under spines, covers, and bent pages.

Evelyn stumbled back, confusion pinching her brow. Blair heaved, her breath shallow as her chest rose and fell. She'd stepped *way* out of line. *Blasted books*, she'd harmed an Elder. Blair searched and searched for the ounce of regret blooming inside her.

But found none.

Rook soared through the rafters, his caw snapping her to the present.

Evelyn gasped, gray eyes widening. "*Blair?!*"

She descended the spiral staircase, averting her attention from the emotion shining in her sister's gaze. Was it judgment? Anger? Shock? Blair didn't want to know. She could barely stomach what she'd done. What she was *doing*.

Breathe, damn it. Breathe.

Blair couldn't think straight, and the only comfort she found was in the shadows dancing at the edges of the office. For once, she let them stay, and it gave her the courage to face her siter.

"We don't have time to waste," she said. "Guards are on their way. Get Kade. We need to move."

Evelyn didn't hesitate, rushing to her fated. Movement caught Blair's attention. Circe's hand stuck out from the heap of books, fingers twitching around Evelyn's bloodstone. Blair's earlier rage resurfaced. How dare the witch take another's magic?

She snatched the necklace back—

Heat seared Blair's palm.

She dropped the bloodstone. It clattered to the ground, steam rising from the gem. She peered down at an angry burn blooming across her palm.

What in the Goddess—

"Blair, is everything alright?"

She stilled. Swallowed. Blinked back into focus. Kade and Evelyn waited, wearing expectant expressions. Blair hid her wound and dismissed the stinging pain. Hesitant but inquisitive, she reached for the necklace's chain, *not* the gem. She braced for another burn, but pain never seared her fingertips, proving her theory.

The bloodstone had burned her.

A thousand questions tumbled through Blair as Evelyn draped her magic back around her neck, but they all lodged like shards of glass in her throat.

Later, Blair's unease begged.

"Thank you," Evelyn breathed.

Blair sighed. "Don't thank me yet. We need to get you out of the city."

They abandoned Circe's office, and the Elder with it. Kade used his werewolf strength and positioned a bookshelf against the door, trapping her inside. Commotion ripped through the library's silence.

"Guards," Kade confirmed.

Blair nodded. "Let's go. I know how to get past them."

"Can you create a *danu* straight to the stables?" Evelyn asked. "That's where Maxie and Bleu are waiting."

Blair shook her head. "I have to conserve my energy if you'd like a *danu* straight to the Drengr Village."

"*Moons*," Kade breathed. "You can get us that far?"

"Yes," Blair said. "But we'll have to move on foot across the city."

"I'd prefer to outrun the Guards in the city than in the open plains of Sorin," Kade said.

"Agreed," her sister whispered. "Lead the way, Blair."

She nodded and headed east into the library. Evelyn and Kade followed, keeping with her pace. Rook flew ahead and paused by a niche carved into the wall. Blair pulled back a heavy purple and gold tapestry. For over a mile, they raced through the tunnels. Left, right, and left again. Soon, the passageway transitioned into the pipe system under the city. The streetlight above shone through the drain grates, and ahead, the tunnel ran into a dead end where a ladder climbed up to the street.

"I'll go first and make sure the street is clear," Blair said.

Her boots clanged against the metal rungs, and as she eased the drain gate open, night cold twisted her curls. The street was empty, not a Guard in sight, yet Blair's skin prickled. *Something* lay in the air.

"Blair?" Evelyn whispered.

She nodded for her sister and Kade to follow and scanned the street as they climbed up to join her.

Two blocks over, Blair guided them through the residential neighborhood. Brick townhomes stood mighty in the night, a tranquility reaching beyond the pulled curtains and locked doors. The city still slumbered as they crept through the shadows and headed north.

Kade grabbed Blair's wrist and yanked her back. He held his finger to his lips, signaling to remain quiet. He eased her behind him and peered around the corner. Blair's heart hammered in her chest as she and Evelyn waited.

"Guards are positioned at the end of the street," he said.

"Blasted books," Blair cursed. "We'll have to go around."

The three of them backtracked three blocks, and commands on the wind stilled Blair's gait. She stopped and fell flush against a wall between homes, the street name ahead blaring like a beacon. Her townhome sat on this street.

"What do you hear?" Blair asked Kade.

"More Guards." He inhaled, and his eyes widened. "And I smell licorice."

"*Fucking flames.*" Evelyn shook her head, brows pinched.

"What is that supposed to mean?" Blair jumped her attention between Evelyn and Kade, who shared a grave look.

Evelyn swallowed. "That's the scent of dark magic."

Blair instinctively clenched her fists. Had she unknowingly drawn her dormant power up and revealed it to Evelyn and Kade? The shadows didn't whisper across the cobblestones. The wind didn't sing as it tunneled down the alley.

"Burn it to the ground!" Circe's voice rang down the street. "Show all of Nūa what happens to witches who turn against us!"

Blair's heart dropped like a stone into her gut. *Knowing* flushed through her.

"No," she breathed, rushing forward.

"Blair, wait," Evelyn hissed.

She didn't listen. *Didn't care.* It was too late to stop her. Blair stepped onto the street, revealing them all, and stumbled to a halt. Pain pierced her heart, and the winds surrounding Nūa howled.

Flames engulfed Blair's townhome. Beams groaned and split. Windows burst as flames curled out to scorch the brick. She felt the death of each of her books as if their stories were tied to her soul.

Vermilion climbed and devoured the many years of Blair's work and reduced it to cinder. In a world where she didn't belong, where she was constantly reminded of her *otherness*, those four walls and three levels had been her one place to find solitude.

Hers.

"Blair, we have to move!" Kade hissed, war raging in his eyes.

"That is my life. Everything I've worked for . . . It's gone," she said, words brittle.

Haunted whispers filtered on the wind, like Blair's ancestors, the ones who'd endured the Great Burnings, had awakened at Circe's atrocity.

The Elder stood ahead of her townhome, and the light of Blair's burning life painted the Elder's haunting, sharp face in a fiery glow. Fifteen Guards stood on either side of the street, forcing Blair's neighbors, who had been evacuated from their homes, to move back. Children cried and clung to their parents' legs, shivering in their sleeping gowns.

A tentative hand grasped her wrist. "Blair."

Evelyn's anguished tone ignited her anger. Her sister was the closest to lash out against.

"This is your fault," she bit out.

Her sister flinched. *Believed* her words. "I'm so sorry. I didn't—"

"Get them!" Circe shouted.

"Stars above." Kade's sword cried as he unsheathed it.

Blair whirled, and despite her anger and all the hurtful, sharp-edged words stuck in her throat, she dragged Evelyn close, intent on protecting her sister.

"We need to leave," Kade called over his shoulder. "*Now.*"

"But Maxie and Bleu—"

Rook cawed from above, and the thunderous hooves of a gray beast echoed down the street. Kade's horse sprinted towards them, and the Guards positioned in a line darted out the horse's way. Bleu circled them, huffing and neighing as if agreeing with his owner's assessment of the situation.

A ball of fiery red fur joined them next, Maxie darting between Evelyn's legs.

"Unless you want a cell inside Tùir," Kade growled, "I suggest we fucking leave."

"Blair." Evelyn's gray stare begged.

Apprehension seeped through her. She was a scholar, not a third born on the run, protecting Sorin. *No.* She couldn't leave. Her place was *here.* Her life—

What life? A nasty voice hissed. She had no position in society. No title, books, or *home.*

The rising smoke meeting the clouds taunted her with that truth. Blair had nothing. But if she left, she was running, doing the very thing she'd belittled her sister for. Rook landed on her shoulder, cawing as if to say, *Do we have a choice?*

No, the winds answered for her.

She spun her shillelagh and drove it into the cobblestones. Air spun in a circle. She stretched her power for hundreds of miles, all across Sorin to a werewolf village tucked into the Vadon Mountains, a place she swore she'd never return. She found she didn't have to draw much power.

Because the lands answered.

Winds whirled down the street from the sea and plains, weaving into the *danu* she created. It drowned out Circe's protests, and Blair didn't dare look back. Kade ushered Evelyn through first and followed. Bleu and Maxie went through next. Rook dug his talons into Blair's shoulder, and she counted—*one, two, three.*

And stepped into the western lands of Sorin.

She collapsed into the muddy snow, her *danu* snapping shut. Beside her, Kade wretched from the great distance they'd traveled, and Evelyn sucked in a breath, a small "no" rasping from her.

Blair peered up. Shock rooted her in place. The Drengr Village was ablaze; the aftermath of a battle lay around them. Smoke, death and flurries hung in the air. They'd escaped destruction, only to walk into another.

"Here."

Blair snapped her attention left. The most beautiful witch she'd ever seen—hair as golden as summer, eyes bluer than the Sapphire Sea—outstretched her hand.

"Belle," Evelyn whispered.

Realization dawned on Blair. She recalled the name of the young witch who'd helped Evelyn inside Drystan Castle, and she possessed a water bronntanas, one of the rarest elements witches wielded.

"I need your winds to put the fires out," Belle said. "Can you help?"

Blair swallowed, drawing forth her wind bronntanas to her fingertips. Her shadows answered, too, but she was too tired to care, too spent to worry. She stood on shaky legs and took hold of Belle's dainty fingers. There was a pureness, such light in the witch's magic as it met hers that Blair winced at the contrast.

Water and winds whirled as they called upon their bronntanases. Blair drove everything into her power—sorrow, loss, and *anger.*

Gray churned above. Clouds darkened to a shade of amethyst. Rain poured, and with the push of her winds, Blair guided it over the village until only steam and numbness remained.

Chapter Twenty-Three

Defeat clung to the Drengr Village like frost on pine trees, and Lorkan exhaled the blood-clotted air. It wasn't as sweet, seeping from the dead, but it still conjured his thirst like a demon emerging from the Void. Ravenous, wild. Lorkan weaved past warriors and caught the *thump, thump, thump* of their beating hearts, a hypnotizing tempo drawing him back. He slipped out of the village, away from temptation and in pursuit of finding the elm tea he'd lost.

The morning sun crested the pines, and the clouds parted to reveal the blue sky of the next day. Lorkan slunk from shadow to shadow, wincing when the sun's rays kissed his skin through gaps in the forest's canopy. Shifting into his werewolf form had cost him—the elm tea's effects were dwindling. If he didn't drink a cup soon, others would sense what he was.

But did hiding what he was matter anymore?

There were vampyrs like him, his *mother* one of them. She was alive. Lorkan didn't know how to grapple with that fact. There wasn't a single day in the last ten years when he hadn't thought of his mother. *Missed* her.

Lorkan's thoughts tumbled through him as he searched for his abandoned satchel. A dusting of snow had fallen since he'd alerted his pack, and as Lorkan squatted on the forest floor, he found most of the tea bags wet and ruined.

The color hazel bled into the snow, the tea's properties wasted as they seeped into the ground.

His shoulders slumped as he assessed the rest of the forest. *There.*

Relief shot through him. Up ahead, his satchel sat atop the roots of an ancient oak. He sifted inside it, and *stars above,* he found a week's worth of tea. What the hel was he supposed to do if he remained in the Drengr Village longer?

"Using your howl was a risk," his father said from behind.

Lorkan sighed, breath pluming into the morning air. "Every day is a risk for those like me." He stood, raising an expectant brow at Aramis.

He joined him under the oak tree. "I suppose you're right."

The weight of a thousand stones lifted from Lorkan. After witnessing his father's ailing health up close and working tirelessly to find remedies, he sent a thanks to any gods that would listen. His father had aged *backwards.*

"How?" Lorkan asked.

His father sighed and told him the details of the council meeting, his mother's timely arrival, and revealing Claus as the Lone Wolf.

Aramis's next words came out rushed. "I didn't write to you because I feared it compromised your mother's whereabouts—"

"Father, it's alright," Lorkan said. "I don't need an explanation."

They'd operated on secrets for years, and yet, Lorkan trusted his father above all others. Aramis had held Lorkan's vampyrism close.

After Lorkan had turned, he'd sought his father out. Alone and frightened, he didn't know where else to go. *End it. Please,* he'd begged. But his father had refused to let the curse take another soul he loved away from him. He'd let Lorkan live, *protected* him, and hid what he was from all of Sorin.

But bitterness coated Lorkan's tongue. "I feel like a fool. I should've noticed the effects of wolfsbane."

"There is no one else to blame but Claus." His father's spring-green eyes bore into him. "I had healers attending to me daily, and they didn't even notice. Eldrick spent almost every day with him, too. My brother was more fox than wolf, it seems. He fooled us all."

Still, responsibility nipped at Lorkan's heels. After everything his father had done for him, he'd not protected him in return. He'd assumed it was the severed mating bond from his mother, but to learn it was Aramis's own brother made it all that much worse.

The foundation of everything Lorkan knew shook, and he was certain there was no coming back after today's events. Prince Riven's attack aside, things were different. The definition of darkness had shifted, or so he hoped.

Lorkan sighed, driving his hands into his pockets. "I never liked Claus."

Aramis laughed. "You and Kade both."

At the mention of his brother destined to defeat the darkness, a lingering question came to the forefront of Lorkan's mind.

"What now?" he asked. "I'm sure my secret will come as a shock to Eldrick and Kade but—"

"You can't tell them," Aramis said, tone stern.

Lorkan straightened. "Why? Have they not accepted mother as a vampyr?"

"This goes beyond your brothers." Aramis clamped his eyes shut, sighing as his shoulders sagged.

Lorkan waited, his heart hammering inside his chest. The forest stilled around them. No snow or winds to disrupt the tension between them.

When his father's eyes sprang open, his saddened gaze pinned him in place. "I've seen it firsthand with your mother and Queen Tovi. Sorin still isn't ready for your darkness, Lorkan. We must continue to hide it. There is also a matter of the Earl vote. If the other alphas discover I've withheld Fjall Pack from them for years, it'll jeopardize your brother's chances. Our secrets will tarnish the Drengr name."

The truth of his father's words wrapped around Lorkan's limbs like a set of chains. "I'm tired of lying to my brothers. Our family has had enough secrets. I want to help."

"You can as the second born and scholar. There is an entire prophecy to decipher, and your expertise is best suited for the task. If we reveal what you are, it puts you and your efforts at risk."

Phantom chains tightened at his wrists and ankles, but Lorkan understood Aramis's caution, had for over a decade.

"What of my scent?" Lorkan said. "The Void is spreading, Father, and the elm trees are dying. Our tea stores are dwindling, and I've already lost half the supply I brought with me."

Aramis dropped a ring into his awaiting palm.

Embedded in the gold band, a scarlet gem reflected his hardened expression. Rook cawed his arrival, descending from a nearby tree and landing on Lorkan's shoulder. He tilted his head as he, too, inspected the ring and crimson jewel.

"It is called a bloodstone," his father said. "Made from the blood of fallen gods, or so they say. It allows vampyrs to walk in limited sunlight and conceals their scent. Tovi used it for years among the witches in Nūa, when she befriended Evelyn. While you wear that, no one will detect what you are."

Lorkan turned as rigid as the stone in his palm. He'd learned what his mother was. Glimpsed the vampyr queen in battle. And allowed hope to wiggle its way under his skin like a fool. *Alone.* Before Lorkan had found Alvin and the others, he was the only one of his kind—part werewolf, part vampyr. He'd navigated those first few years clinging to the shadows, desperation his only friend. To know he lived with the same affliction as his mother but couldn't utter a word about it was like a blade piercing his lungs. It was suddenly a likeness Lorkan wished they didn't share—something that should've drawn them together only wedged a larger distance between them.

But his father was right. Too much was at stake, and there was honor in working in the shadows. Lorkan had discovered that with Fjall Pack in the north. With them in mind, he couldn't risk their safety with so much uncertainty, too.

Lorkan clenched his fist, clutching the ring like a lifeline. "What of my hunger?"

Aramis shook his head, frowning. "That, I'm afraid, is up to the elm tea."

His father clasped his hand on his shoulder. "I'm proud of what you did today, Lorkan. Continue to be brave. One day, when the curse is finally lifted, we'll share what you are and reveal the Fjall Pack."

Lorkan nodded, trying to find some hope in his father's words, but like the frost clinging to the winter forest, a sense that Sorin would never be ready for his kind.

Chapter Twenty-Four

"That's an interestingly shaped burn."

Blair blinked through a heavy haze of exhaustion. A pink-haired witch—no, *mage*—inspected the angry red mark left by the bloodstone. Beside them, a fire crackled in the infirmary. Earlier activity had died down, and the warriors who remained lay on the cots lining the wall. Healers hovered nearby, checking in on their patients' wounds. The scent of ointments reminded Blair of Mirella, but that was where the similarities between the werewolf village and home ended.

"It's a perfect circle, with two half crescents on each side," the mage continued.

Blair fought the urge to snatch her hand back, for she'd lied about how she'd gotten the injury. *A mishap with a torch*, she'd said. A mortifying excuse surrounded by warriors who fought demons, but Blair wasn't ready to investigate why the bloodstone had left a mark, let alone admit to others what had happened.

"It's almost like three moons—"

"What did you say your name was again?" Blair asked.

"I didn't." The mage's lips fell into a thin line. "It's Linx, and I'm hurt to learn Kade nor Evelyn mentioned me. My colorful hair usually gives me away."

"You can blame me," Blair said. "I've spent very little time with them."

"I see." Her catlike yellow eyes gleamed. "I guess you're a rebel now. Like the rest of us."

Blair shifted in her seat. It was like Linx saw too much. She swallowed, uncertain she liked what the term *rebel* implied while on the contrary, her shadows hissed with excitement.

Linx sighed. "I'm afraid I don't have reserves of my power to heal the burn completely. Does it hurt?"

Like it was more than a burn. As if venom pulsed in Blair's hand. But did she risk more questions regarding how it happened?

"Only a bit," she lied.

Linx scoffed. "*Right.* Well, I can make you up a salve to ease the *bit* of pain."

"Thank you."

The mage busied herself with a pouch and a mortar and pestle. The silence crept over Blair. She'd fled straight here after putting out the flames with Belle. A reunion had begun with Evelyn and the others, and then she'd spied Tovi. Blair didn't have the stomach, words or rational thought to face her once friend. So, she'd retreated into the village and found herself in the infirmary.

Blair craved a distraction. *Something.* A conversation that took her mind off vast unknowns lying ahead of her.

"Earlier, you mentioned reserves regarding your power," Blair said, trying to deflect her unease. "What does that mean? Is it your magic?"

"*Magik.*" Linx blended herbs, and crushed calendula and lavender perfumed the air. "Mages are connected to the land around them. It's like a doorway to energies, but the more we use it, the doorway closes and then shuts altogether." She shrugged. "Similar to a witch's magic, which I've heard described as a muscle. You keep strong *and* rested."

Blair sighed, her own fatigue washing over her. A *danu* from the eastern coast all the way across Sorin had taken a considerable amount of magic. Her body screamed for sleep, while her mind remained restless.

"Which god gave mages their gift?" she asked.

Linx shook her head, pink buns bobbing from side to side. "Mages aren't gifted like witches and werewolves. We've learned the art of connection to the land. Gods gave you all your power, a seedling inside your souls."

Blair snagged on Linx's last word, and a recent conversation with Jace resurfaced.

A god's soul is so grand, it embeds in the earth as gems after they die. But that's if gods can even die.

But what did the gods have to do with a witch's magic? Of course, Blair knew the tale. Demons came to be, and mortals in Torren prayed to the gods for a means to defend themselves. The Sun Goddess graced them with a single touch over their hearts, granting them her power. *Light.* It transcended generations, running through bloodlines for a millennium. Werewolves had a similar origin story but with the Moon God.

The word *soul* nagged at her, like she was missing a key detail in how to get her sister's lost magic back. The tips of her fingers itched. *Goddess,* she needed to get her hands on some books.

Linx rose with a heavy sigh and handed her a petite tin with freshly made salve. "Use this twice a day—once in the morning and then at night. If the burn blisters, come find me." Linx pointed south outside the infirmary. "Two streets over and on your left, you'll find the library."

Blair gathered her cloak and stood, taking the salve and slipping it into her trousers pocket. "Thank you."

But she didn't mention she knew exactly where to find the Drengr Library.

Blair inhaled the scent of books. The werewolves' library wasn't as grand as Nūa's, but the books invited her all the same—as it had, many, many years ago.

Mahogany shelves spiraled up three stories, round and round, like a serpent with bones made of paper, spines, bindings, and ink. Above, the sun shone through the center skylight, peeking through scattered clouds.

Blair climbed the stairs on determined feet. She swore she smelled soot on her tired, wary limbs, like the smoke of her burning life's work had embedded itself into her pores. She tried to ground herself in the library and breathe in the leather, parchment, and promise. These weren't her books, but they were comforting all the same.

She'd spent the latter half of the morning pouring over texts, an idea coming to life. A dangerous, wicked theory. But if Blair presented this to Evelyn and Kade, she had to be sure. Her hand tightened on the banister of the third level, pausing as she calmed her racing heart. She'd avoided the highest level until now, but she was certain that the book she needed resided in the upper sections.

Rook flew at the center, his onyx wings silent as he climbed alongside her. She passed a few werewolf scholars and sent them warm smiles, or at least, she tried to. *Blasted books*, her skin felt like glass. It might break at any moment if she continued to force a false sense of calm.

So much had begun in this library. Finding her familiar in the rafters. Exploring love. Envisioning her dream home, one with marigold flower beds on a street with mismatched colored doors. A place with dozens of shelves filled with books and trinkets. She'd made the dream a reality in the years after she turned her back on the eastern lands of Sorin.

Now, her townhouse was ash and memories.

A rebel like the rest of us.

Yet, Blair was a scholar, through and through, not a third born. Her insides fluttered to life *here*, in the safety of a library, surrounded by histories and answers.

The section ended, and Blair found herself at the precipice of the Drengr Library's secret—a hidden attic. Curiosity had gripped her a decade ago as fiercely as it did today, and she'd checked beyond the bend. Wedged between the wall and the bookshelf's end, a set of stairs, no larger than a shoulder's width, spiraled out of sight.

Pain and yearning warred within Blair's heart. She planted her foot firmly on the first step and climbed. Step by step, her breath came out hollow. At the top, she discovered the hideout hadn't changed. Not one inch of it.

A lone love seat sat on one side, overlooking the smallest of windows facing east. Lost behind the library's roof, one wasn't able to spot it down below, but that didn't rob the window of the view straight to the snowcapped mountains lining the horizon.

Blair hovered her fingers over the remaining things. The abandoned books. The two dust-filled mugs. Her forefinger caught a splinter near the set of initials carved into the wall, but it didn't compare to the sting of heartache. Loose strands of the neatly folded blanket reached out to her fingers. It smelled of smoke and moss. Of *him*.

A boy who'd broken her heart.

Bittersweetness coated Blair's tongue. She'd lingered too long in a space she no longer belonged, and she returned to the stairs and descended on the balls of her feet.

On the next level, movement caught her eye. A spider, no bigger than her thumbnail, hung from a web glinting like spun silver, scrunched like a crumbled leaf at the end. Blair paused, tilting her head, staring into the beady, globe-like eyes of the tiny beast. Most would run, yet her magic leaned towards the *otherness*.

"Hey there, little one," she whispered.

The spider remained, and she swore the tiniest *hello* sang through the corridor. The creature lingered for a moment and scurried back up its strand of silk. It jumped onto a book's spine and waited, pincers twitching as it stared at Blair. She squinted, reading the worn chrome-lettered title: *Tales of the Otherworld.*

She laughed. It was the exact text she'd been searching for.

"Why thank you," she said.

The spider scurried out of sight as she grabbed the book, dust falling away with it. The spine creaked as she peeled it open. Pages crinkled by time stuck together, as if desperate to hold on to one another to hide their secrets.

The next moments blurred together as Blair simultaneously read and returned to her studying area on the first floor. The Otherworld, according to more scholarly texts, was the realm where the gods oversaw souls once they parted the land of the living. This text was more suited for a child's bedtime stories with its richly painted visuals and fabricated tales of the gods, but it mentioned how those in this realm visited the Otherworld.

With her head down and lost mid-paragraph, she turned the corner based on muscle memory, expecting the table and chair she'd abandoned, but collided into a tall, solid frame. Strong hands gripped Blair's shoulders, holding her steady.

She blinked and peered up. "I'm so sorry—"

Blair stilled, boots melding to the floor. It was *him*. Golden eyes. Hair as black as night. Still towering over her like years ago. But *blasted books,* he was no longer a boy, but a man.

"Lorkan," Blair whispered. "I assumed you'd be at Vísdómr."

Or she'd *hoped*. He was a well-known professor at the university attached to the oldest and largest library on the continent, a place they'd once discussed visiting together. If she'd known the risk of bumping into him, she'd never have wandered into the Drengr Library like a fly to honey.

"Eldrick asked me to return home." He pushed his metal-framed glasses up the bridge of his proud nose. Compared to the beastliness etched into Kade and Eldrick, severity clung to the middle Drengr brother, like he was sharp-edged stone. After all this time, the sight of him still made Blair's stomach flutter.

"I see . . ." She trailed off, catching the paper he held in his hand. It was the entire prophecy, the copy written by Opal and given to Evelyn.

Lorkan drew a hand through his hair, dropping the note back onto the table. "I'm sorry. I came to start my research when I came across this, and I couldn't help myself—"

"It's alright." Actually, Blair was the farthest one could be from "alright," but the lie was a needed filler to push aside her rising emotions. "You and I could never outrun curiosity once it found us."

The edges of Lorkan's lips twitched. "That at least has not changed, I suppose."

Ah, but so much else had. But Blair didn't linger on what, not when her interest drew her to Lorkan's filled-out frame, and especially when the prophecy was *right there* and the fate of their homeland was at risk. The broken heart of a teenager felt rather trivial in comparison, no matter the jagged pieces she'd never truly mended. The heartache she'd endured from Lorkan's rejection had honed her into the dedicated scholar. She'd learned then not to step out of line, to follow the path fate had paved for her.

To be back here with him in the space where she'd dared fall in love with a werewolf felt like fate was a sadistic bitch. Above all else, though, Blair had her pride. They were older. Grown. Established adults, their adolescent years more blurs than memory now.

Liar, Blair's inner voice taunted.

Perhaps, she argued back.

But she refused to reveal her scars.

She swallowed her nerves and sauntered over to the desk and gathered her things. "If you'll excuse me."

"I actually came looking for you," Lorkan said.

"What?" Blair halted.

Lorkan's expression was unreadable. "Eldrick sent me to fetch you. He's called for a meeting."

Confusion rippled through her. She'd not told anyone where she'd headed. Not even Evelyn. "I don't understand. How did you know I was here?"

Lorkan ran his hand through his dark hair. "Wild guess."

Blair swallowed, gripping her book tighter. She fought the shake in her voice. "Why didn't you send someone else?"

"And risk—" Lorkan cursed, sucking his teeth.

Blair scoffed, rolling her eyes. "Go on then. Risk what?"

Lorkan met her stare dead-on, his cheeks and chin etched with a coldness that hadn't been there during their youth. "If I'd objected to coming and finding you, it risked revealing . . ." He clamped his eyes shut as he struggled with words. "That we knew one another."

Blair stumbled back. Words on the tip of her tongue. Angry, loud words she wanted to shout into the silence of the library and disturb it all. And not because it was a lie. Everyone knew that. They'd been the scholars of their families, off with their books. But *knowing* put it so fucking lightly, Blair raged.

She'd cherished his dreams, fought away his fears, recalled how he tasted. That was more than *knowing*. But what good did saying those words out loud do? It edged close to that line that Blair no longer crossed—and how much of her anger was actually fueled by her sense of grief for everything she'd lost?

"Next time," she said, "send someone else to fetch me." She spun on her heel and marched out of the library without a backwards glance.

CHAPTER TWENTY-FIVE

THE WOOD-BURNING STOVE IN Kade's cottage warmed the first floor. The fire's crackle joined the gentle tip-tap beat of snow against the window above the kitchen sink.

Evelyn dug her fingers into the wooden counter, fighting drowsiness, nauseating nerves, and wariness. Maxie weaved under her arms and nuzzled her head and ears into Evelyn's chin. She gave her familiar a gentle brush down her spine, and Maxie continued her exploration of the kitchen.

Clay mugs and plates lined open shelves, and the baskets once filled with vegetables and food lay empty from their time away. Seemingly satisfied with her inspection of the space, Maxie assumed her favorite spot on the windowsill, yellow eyes wide and focused on the songbirds pecking at the frozen ground.

Outside, their chirping grew louder, like an alert through the forest. Kade emerged from the tree line ahead, trekking through the snow with parchment bags and parcels in hand. Bleu trailed behind him, nudging his nose into the largest one. Kade's steed emerged victorious, a meaty, crooked carrot lodged between his square teeth.

Evelyn relaxed at the sight of them.

She and Kade had said little since fleeing Nūa and returning to the Drengr Village. In the aftermath of Riven's attack, the others had encouraged them to stay at Lār. To Evelyn's relief, Kade had respectfully declined, muttering something about the feeling of *home* to Eldrick.

The mismatched seating in the main area. The kitchen with copper and wooden details. Even the room that smelled distinctly of Kade. *He* was her home, but being back here, in his cottage, tucked into the magnificent forest of the Vadon Mountains, Evelyn inhaled where she innately belonged, and exhaled the last shred of grief she had for her failed homecoming. Circe's atrocities aside, Evelyn couldn't shake that *this* was where she belonged. Here, with Kade, snow falling, the fire crackling, and the promise of friends and family coming over for a warm, hearty dinner. Her torn soul beat for it—a promising glimpse of the future they fought for.

The door clicked open as Kade entered the cottage. Maxie darted out the door, joining Bleu in the stable suited for one. The animals played in the snow, their size differences almost comical.

Kade shook flurries from his shoulders and hair, golden eyes widening as he spied Evelyn in the kitchen.

"I thought you'd be resting." He walked into the kitchen, setting the bags onto the counter and planted a kiss on Evelyn's temple.

"I couldn't sleep," she said, inspecting the bags. "Did you go *grocery* shopping?"

Her fated shrugged, scratching the back of his neck. "I thought we could have breakfast for dinner."

Evelyn swallowed, a gentle warmth spreading through her very tried, spent limbs. Goddess, he knew her so well.

"I'd like that."

Kade tucked a strand of her freshly washed hair behind her ear. "Divide and conquer?"

"Of course."

The hint of a smile threatened on Evelyn's lips, but it felt wrong to do so. With Riven's attack. Circe's relentlessness. The Blood Curse. If she thought too much on it all, she grew emptier and emptier, the hole in her soul more pronounced.

Instead, she busied herself first with coffee and found comfort in the fact they'd made it out of Nūa. Kade, thank the Goddess, had grounds stored in his cupboards, and some metal contraption that brewed the coffee and squished the grounds downward for a clean, comforting drink.

The clatter of kitchen utensils, the hissing stove, and clanking bowls took over the cottage. Snow quickened outside, and Evelyn and Kade got lost in the peaceful task of cooking a shared meal. Kade whisked up pancakes, and beside him, Evelyn readied a hot iron skillet for bacon.

Soon, both had a steaming cup of coffee in hand and manned their dishes. Closeness buzzed between them, and Evelyn caught Kade staring as he flipped his second pancake.

"I'm ready to discuss it, if you are, Ev," Kade whispered.

Evelyn fought tears and swallowed. She'd waited for Kade to come to her, and now that he'd opened the door to discuss what had happened in the Nūa Library, her jumbled nerves returned. She removed crispy bacon to cool on a piece of parchment and swallowed.

Evelyn decided fear was a friend of doubt, and she'd not let either foe get in the way of honesty with Kade.

"What did Circe show you?" she whispered.

Kade's shoulders stiffened, but his focus remained on cooking. "A desolate wasteland—Sorin if we fail."

Evelyn released a shuddering breath, a false sense of relief settling over her.

"She also showed me you as a young girl." Kade swallowed, voice thick. He peered down at her. "Did she hurt you, Ev?"

He'd asked Evelyn the same question in the underbelly of Nūa, but she'd not been ready to discuss it. Maybe she never would be. Shame was as oozy and thick as Circe's wretched hallucinations. But this was Kade. He was her home and heart.

"Yes."

Kade's jaw ticked. "For how long?"

Evelyn gripped her coffee mug tighter, leaning against the counter. She focused on the dancing flames inside the wood-burning stove.

"About six months," she started. "I've told you what my tutors were like, but it was Circe who convinced me I was nothing without my flame. She's a well-respected scholar, and when she requested to oversee my training, no one objected. But my flame never came naturally to me. Sure, I could conjure it, but I had difficulty *controlling* it as a child. I was naïve, impressionable. I worried I'd never amount to being Daughter of the Goddess, and Circe only fueled that belief."

The memories had faded, and Evelyn had broken the chains of the tutor's cruel whisperings, but sometimes they lingered in the back of her mind, like dormant roots she'd never fully dig up.

"What exactly did you see?" she asked, voice brittle.

Kade's tone turned gentle, cautious. "You were locked away, scared, and your hand . . ."

Evelyn shook her head, blinking back tears. Of course Circe had shown Kade one of her worst memories. All to hurt them both.

She placed her mug on the counter, crossing her arms. "When I failed lessons, she locked me away in a cupboard. She, too, used her hallucination-like magic on me. Showing my coven slaughtered by scáths. Threatening me with what would happen if I failed them."

Kade's brows knitted together, anguish dimming the gold in his amber stare. "Ev."

Now that Evelyn had started, she couldn't stop, and Kade's presence was all encouraging. *There* for her in this.

"One day, she was furious with me and . . . I was seven, not strong enough to fight back, let alone old enough to differentiate what was real and wasn't. I believed in what she showed me so fiercely her hallucination became reality. Two of my fingers snapped. Circe panicked. She'd scared me into never telling my parents what happened day to day, but broken fingers revealed her cruelty. She locked me away in my cupboard, trying to find a way out of the mess she'd made when Uzoma found me."

Kade turned off the stove and stacked pancakes on two awaiting plates. "Wait, Uzoma knew about this? Did she let it continue?"

Evelyn shook her head, grabbing the plate of food Kade handed to her. Blueberries floated on buttery syrup, and somehow, someway, she still managed an appetite.

"No, Uzoma didn't know until that day, and from that moment on, she protected me," Evelyn said, slicing into her first bite.

Kade shook his head, pain darkening his golden eyes. "I don't understand. If Uzoma knew of Circe's abuse, how is she on the Council? Once your parents discovered what happened, how did she not face consequences?"

Evelyn shut her eyes, rallying her breath. "My family, no one in my coven knows. You're the first I've ever told."

A stillness entered the cottage, the first snap of tension, but Kade rallied his shock and softly asked, "Tovi? Blair?"

Evelyn shook her head. "They don't know."

"Stars above," Kade breathed. "You've carried this alone for twenty years."

"Uzoma was there for me."

A growl rumbled through Kade's chest. "But she did nothing—"

Evelyn placed her food down and grabbed Kade's hands, making him look at her. "She protected me in the best way she saw how. Uzoma made a deal with Circe: transition my tutelage under her from thenceforth, no fuss or questions asked, or all of Nūa would learn what she'd done."

"The latter should've been the only option," Kade said through gritted teeth.

"And what if the Council didn't care?"

"What do you mean?"

"You witnessed it during the hearing, Kade. To the witches, I am a weapon . . . not *Evelyn*. They care for my power, not me. I believe Uzoma thought Circe might twist the incident in her favor, or if my parents fought too hard to protect me, they'd lose me."

"*Moons*," Kade hissed. "Uzoma wasn't only protecting you from Circe, but an unfair future."

Evelyn nodded. "I'm sorry I never told you. I wasn't trying to keep it from you; it just never came up, and I know that's not an excuse, but honestly, I try my best to forget—"

Kade grasped Evelyn's chin, stilling her words. "Never apologize for your pain, Ev, not to me. I'm always here. In stillness, silence, or to talk."

"Thank you," she breathed, wiping tears from her eyes. A lightness spread through Evelyn, like a spring breeze.

Kade pulled Evelyn into a hug. She fell into his chest. Held him back. She closed her eyes. Inhaled his scent. Relished in being together.

"Thank you for breakfast, too. It made this conversation . . . easier."

"Perhaps that'll be our thing, then." Kade offered an assuring smile, making him all that more handsome. "Pancakes with difficult topics."

"And coffee," Evelyn said, grabbing back her mug.

Kade laughed. "*Right—*"

A knock resounded on the door. Both of them winced, knowing full well they couldn't escape the inevitable on the horizon.

"Evelyn," Blair called. "It's me. I . . . I have an idea on how to get your magic back."

Evelyn and Kade shared a look. Kade mirrored Evelyn's own surprise—her sister had avoided her, even here in the Drengr Village—but what made her pause was Blair's tone.

Hesitant and . . .

Uncertain.

Chapter Twenty-Six

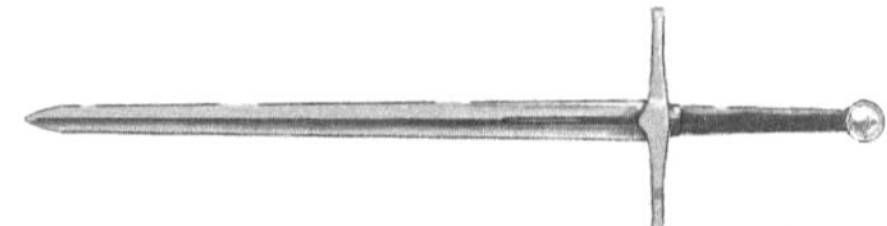

"I'm afraid, Evelyn will have to die," Blair whispered.

"Out of the question." The words shot out of Kade like he fought with his sword. Harsh, quick, and cutting. He paced inside his cottage, sending all his wolfish wrath in the scholar's direction. "How dare you suggest such an idea?"

Neither Evelyn nor Blair said a word. Embers in the hearth popped, and trees groaned outside as they stood against the howling wind's force.

The shock, the sheer horror of Blair's suggestion washed through Kade, threatening to unleash his wolf.

Or worse, the pent-up power he couldn't control.

"I don't like it either, Kade," Blair said, "but Evelyn cut a piece of her soul out. I have tried no avail to find a way to destroy the bloodstone or get Evelyn's magic out of it. I have a theory—"

Kade growled through gritted teeth. "You're willing to bet your sister's life on a mere theory?"

Blair threw out her hands, wind and static rising in the cottage. "I don't like it any more than you do."

Kade whirled towards Evelyn. "Tell her this is *out of the question.*"

Evelyn's silence rang like deafening drums in his ears. "Kade . . ."

"You can't seriously be considering this!" he roared.

Evelyn flinched, and the minimal peace they'd found earlier evaporated. Why did it feel as though fate berated them at all ends?

Moons, Kade couldn't bare it. He'd already lost Evelyn before when she was Riven's captive, and that had riddled him with agonizing worry. But *this*? Maddening.

"Did you know about this?" he asked, his words coming out far calmer than he felt.

"What?" Evelyn reared back, her anger hitting Kade in waves. "No, I wouldn't keep this from you, but I have a good idea as to why Blair has."

"Excuse me?" Kade stepped towards Evelyn, peering down at her.

She released a breath. "She probably knew exactly how you'd react—"

"Like what?" he seethed.

"An overbearing, protective mate!" she shouted.

His werewolf raged underneath his skin, threatening to shift, to protect Evelyn, just like she said, from Blair's absurd suggestion.

"You're right," Kade whispered. "I *am* an overbearing, protective mate, so why bother with what I think?"

"That is not what I'm saying!" Evelyn hissed. "We haven't even heard Blair out or have a sense of the idea."

"*Moons*, I don't care to listen to another word of this." Kade laid his hands on his hips and stared out at the snowfall in his homeland. Tried to find peace in it. Softness.

But it was no use. He couldn't rally his anger, and his control snapped, his power rising in one giant tidal wave inside him. He threw out his arms as he said, "In the cave under Nūa, we made a promise that we are in this *together*."

Evelyn's brows pinched. He didn't need their bond to know it was hurt flashing in her gray stare. Perhaps he was being harsh. Perhaps he was being hurtful. But he was so worried, so *frightened*.

"We are, Kade," she whispered.

"The concept of you *dying*, leaving me, doesn't exactly feel like it." He turned towards the door, snatching his fur-lined coat.

"Where are you going?" Evelyn asked, voice cracking.

"I need a moment, Ev," Kade whispered, not daring to look at her and face more hurt marring her gaze. He heard it enough in her tone and by her racing heart. "Right now, I don't accept this."

Night crept through the forest, and the darkness followed Kade as his legs moved on their own accord. Down the village streets and through an alley as a shortcut, he marched through the Shield-maiden's entrance.

He nodded once to Lucy and slipped through the curtains that led to his team's secluded area, and found his brother, Eldrick, lost in thought as he trailed a finger around an untouched pint.

Eldrick's head snapped up, his eyes widening. "What has you so tightly wound?"

"I could ask the same of you," Kade said.

His brother snorted. "Evelyn?"

"Tovi?"

The brothers sighed and sank further into their seats.

"Do you want to talk about the vampyr queen?" Kade whispered.

Eldrick sighed, combing his hair through his head. "It feels like my heart is the last thing I should be worried about."

"I heard what happened when Riven attacked," he said. "It isn't an easy thing to dismiss."

Eldrick didn't meet his brother's stare. "No, but it has become more apparent that we both must focus on what's best for our people. I take it you've also heard about Bjorn's decree?"

Kade nodded. "He's a fool. Riven already demonstrated he's not afraid to cross the Void and attack. To leave the Vadon Mountains without a leader . . ."

"I know." Eldrick stared deep into the depths of his ale. "What of Evelyn's magic? What of your own?"

Soot and rot was faint under Kade's nose, like he was back under Circe's influence. He brushed his fingers through his beard, exhaling the memories and scents.

"Blair has a theory," Kade said, hands itching for a drink of his own, something to burn away the fear coursing through him. "Yet, I—"

"There you are."

A voice Kade had only heard in memories jolted him out his seat.

Nadia, their mother, strode through the curtains. His heart hammered. He knew she was alive and had returned home, but seeing his mother firsthand, locking eyes with the amber stare they shared and feeling her strong, fierce presence in the air had him sprinting towards her.

He didn't care she'd stayed away. He didn't care she'd kept secrets.

He only cared that she was alive and *home*.

As they collided, his mother held him in a tight hug, but Kade lifted her in his arms and spun. A laugh escaped her, and she swatted his chest.

Kade placed her back on her feet, gazing down at her with a smile that made his cheeks ache. "Mother."

"How dare you remind me how much taller you've become." She cupped his cheek, tears glistening in his eyes. "Kade, you're . . . I'm so proud of you. *Both* of you." She spied Eldrick over his shoulder.

Kade gave her hand a squeeze and held it close. Ten years. A whole decade without her. Fuck Blair's *danu*. *This* left him off balance, but in the best way, like a piece of his heart that had never healed had been restored. Even though he'd read her name in letters from Eldrick, this was better. So much better. His eyes stung with years of emotion and joy.

"Thank you," he said, the words a breath.

Her dark brows pinched. "For what?"

"For looking after Evelyn and getting her out of Drystan," he said. "She told me everything."

His mother blinked, eyes darting to the stone ground. She set her shoulders back, exhaling through her nose. Those amber eyes of hers tracked him, uncertainty swimming in them. "Speaking of Evelyn," Nadia whispered, "I went by your cottage looking for you and found her rather . . . upset." She raised an expectant brow.

Kade opened and closed his mouth, chest tightening. "Blair knows a way to get Evelyn's magic back, but she would have to die."

Eldrick shot out of his seat. "What? That is asking far too much of Evelyn."

Nadia hummed. "What exactly does it entail?"

Kade squirmed under his mother's perusal. The truth was, he hadn't the slightest clue. Usually, he and Evelyn needed space when they disagreed on matters. It worked for them, to sort out their thoughts and feelings, but this time he'd simply left, fear herding him out of his cottage.

He swallowed. "I can't fathom the idea, let alone learn more about it, when it risks who I love most in this world."

His mother studied him, gold eyes as sharp as any blade. "You'd walk into battle with Evelyn, wouldn't you?"

The question yanked him back to the underbelly of Nūa. *No matter what we face, may it be matters of the heart or an enemy on the battlefield, we face it together.*

It'd been the same concept Kade had thrown in Evelyn's face, yet he hadn't given her space. Hadn't heard Blair out. Because he felt time slipping through his fingers. Not only the impending Blood Curse, but Evelyn's dwindling days. If they tried to get her magic back or if they failed, Kade feared no matter what direction they ventured, he'd lose her no matter what.

To rub salt in Kade's already festering wound, he, too, had to master his power, and he wasn't certain he could when his emotions ran so wild, more wolf than man.

Though, he had made a promise, one he intended to keep until his last breath.

"I'd walk by Evelyn's side through anything," he whispered.

"Then perhaps you need to remind her of that," Nadia whispered back.

His mother was right—of course. Kade couldn't take back that he'd yet again retreated from Evelyn, but he could show her something that might demonstrate how deep his commitment was to her.

"Thank you. If you'll both excuse me."

Kade left the Shield-maiden, his gait set at a determined pace. He weaved through werewolves still recovering from the aftermath of Riven's attack and past the thicket of werewolves manning the destroyed gate. Snow crunched under his boots as he listened to the surrounding forest. Night critters and wind greeted him, and as he stormed up the steps of his cottage, his wolfish hearing detected Evelyn scrubbing dishes.

He entered their cottage on cautious feet, awaiting Evelyn's wrath, but found her expectant, tunic sleeves rolled up and gray stare roaming him up and down.

Kade swallowed, rallying his courage. "Can I show you something?"

Chapter Twenty-Seven

KADE OPENED THE DOOR to a room Evelyn'd yet to explore.

Specifically, a bedroom—neat, simple, and untouched—awaited them.

A large four-poster bed, layered with white furs and quilts was pushed against the righthand wall. Beside it, there was a writing desk with a few floating shelves, dead plants wilted against stacks of books. A vanity made from a redwood tree with a matching stool sat near the large window. More books, along with dusty cushions sat on a window sill, large enough for one to sit on, like a reading nook.

It wasn't confusion flushing through Evelyn, but a keen level of interest. Kade had shown it to her for a reason, but he was silent, watching her.

She dropped Kade's hand as she rushed forward, a glinting hand mirror snagging her attention. Her heart hammered wildly in her chest. She brushed her hand over the letter '*E*' carved into it.

She stilled, assessing the room again and noticing the small, *feminine* touches as if—

"The window faces east, so you could watch the sun rise in the direction of home," Kade said with what felt like the first words in hours.

But the gravity of the space, of the room had simply hit Evelyn, suspended her and left her feeling floaty, elated, and warmly grateful. Because this was *her* room. Or, at least, it had been intended to be her room, once. The wooden walls were different from the rest of the cottage, the clay between stacked logs lighter.

A space that had been added to his already lovely home.

"You built this for me?" It came out like a question, but Kade didn't need to assure Evelyn that was the case, because she felt the rooms purpose, and she *knew* him.

Kade grabbed her hand, joining her near the window. "Back then, I didn't expect us to be married in a traditional sense, so, I wanted to give you your own space, a room that was yours, somewhere you could escape to if you needed."

Evelyn laughed, and it came out bubbly, thick with tears. "Are you kicking me out of your room, *huntsman?*"

"Absolutely not, and by the way, the room upstairs is *our* room, *princess,*" he said, tucking a stray strand of hair behind her ear.

"Then why bring me in here?" Evelyn whispered, grasping hold of his hand.

Kade sighed. "To show you and remind myself my intentions from the very beginning. Long before we met, I'd dreamed of us being partners—you and I against the darkness. Yet, the more I fall in love with you, there feels to be more at stake. I'm sorry I left. I let fear get the best of me."

Evelyn's heart skipped. "For what it's worth, I'm frightened, too, Kade."

His golden stare softened. "Then we face whatever Blair's theory is together."

Evelyn nodded, her heart swelling. "Together."

The grizzly-size fireplace beside the large table for twelve crackled, filling the air with aromas of sweet hickory. Underneath the table, Evelyn held Kade's hand as the rest of their friends filtered into Lār's meeting hall.

Tovi stood at the end of the table, hands outstretched as she leaned over the ancient wood covered in maps and missives. The remnants of battle still stained her leathers and face. Red soaked her white braid. Nadia stood off to the side, arms crossed and one foot resting on the wall. At the other end, Eldrick, with his jaw rigid as the surrounding stone, sat with his father and brother, Lorkan, the scholarly Drengr Evelyn had yet to meet.

With her sleeves rolled up to her elbows and forearms stained from ointments, Belle arrived with Todd in tow, his bun slick with sweat. They sat next to Yennifer and Bétar. They too hadn't washed after Riven's attack. The archer's bow sat on the table along with her mate's sword, as if both warriors expected another one. Last, Linx entered the hall, finding a seat next to Blair, who sat with brow set and hands clasped over a stack of books.

Kade ran his thumb across her knuckles, sending the warmth of a thousand suns through her weary being. She sighed at his touch. Evelyn appreciated the silence and the simple presence of standing by each other's side, for everything they faced was so loud, booming in her pounding head.

Riven. Circe. The Blood Curse. The Void spreading. The bloodstone—

Blair cleared her throat, and the chatter amongst them quieted. She gestured towards the prophecy on the table. "I think we can all agree that in order to defeat the Blood Goddess's hold on Sorin, we must break the curse. There are many things left to decipher in the prophecy, but one thing is certain, as it has been for centuries—Evelyn and Kade are essential to whatever that entails."

Lorkan nodded. "We've all known the last two lines of the prophecy, but the other lines within the stanza suggest weapons to aid in the fight to come, and I know where we'll find the blade of ancients."

Everyone straightened, and Nadia peeled off the wall.

Tovi's eyes narrowed. "Where?"

"Drystan. Riven has the blade." He flipped open a book and pushed it in Kade's direction. Text covered most of the page, aside from an intricate sketch of an all-black sword. "I recognized it when the prince wielded it during the attack. *That* is the sword the Moon God fought the Gods War with. It is also the weapon he gifted to the first werewolf. It disappeared eight hundred years ago."

"How in the hel did a vampyr find the blade?" Todd asked.

All eyes shifted to Nadia. She stiffened. "I've not heard him discuss the blade, let alone knew he was after one as significant as this."

"Ingrid was," Belle said. "She never mentioned it by name, but she researched weapons for the war to come. Said the gods had left them behind, why not find and use them."

Tovi hissed. "Goddess, do you think they know which blade it is?"

"Does it matter?" Evelyn asked. "It's enchanted with dark magic. I felt it when I fought Riven during the Blood Moon."

Tovi frowned. "I've sensed the wrongness within it, too. Is it of any use to Kade now with dark magic? *If* it's even the blade?"

"Is it enchanted or draining its wrongful master?" Lorkan raised a brow. "The power of the Moon God, which runs through Kade's veins, created that metal. It doesn't belong to Riven."

Kade stiffened, an edge to him Evelyn had never witnessed before. "Are you suggesting the sword is fighting back?"

"Perhaps there's merit in that theory. He could barely hold the sword steady when we fought." Tovi's gaze turned distant. "He's tired, worn. I assumed it was the curse getting worse, but maybe it's the sword."

Todd studied the sketch. "There's no denying the likeness."

"Well, how do we take it back?" Bétar said.

"I'll retrieve it," Nadia said. "Its best I leave the village for the sake of the Earl vote, and I'm more use in Drystan, anyway."

"Alright," Kade said, addressing everyone. "We have a plan for the sword. What of the ancient bones of an old friend?"

Blair sighed. "I'm not certain yet, but . . . Evelyn needs to get her magic back first and I have an idea." She looked at her sister, silently waiting for her approval.

Evelyn's insides twisted. Apprehension bled into her sister's dark stare, lips etched into a thin line.

She nodded. "Go on."

Blair circled her hands over an open book. Light shot out of the pages and onto the stone wall, projecting the content for the entire table to see.

"This is our world and its many layers," Blair said.

A grand tree, root to canopy, stretched from the bottom to the top of the page. Four shaded rings surrounded the trunk, extending to the margins—the Upperworld, the Living Lands, the Otherworld, and, blackened by smudged ink like an afterthought, the Underworld.

Hel as some called it.

"We're here," Blair said, pointing to the Living Lands, full of vibrant grass, snowcapped mountains, and a deep-blue sea separating two large continents, Sorin and Torren. She dragged her finger to the Otherworld. "This is eventually where our souls venture—the afterlife."

Blair flipped through the pages, stopping on a drawing of a heart, a speck of power glowing at the reddish center. Underneath, cloaked figures stood with an illuminated goddess, shimmering suns dotting her flowy dress.

"When I first started researching the bloodstone, my instinct was like both of yours—how do we get Evelyn's magic *out*? We're looking at it the wrong way. Right now, Evelyn's soul is severed into two pieces. What if we sent those pieces into the same realm, giving them a chance to reunite?"

Evelyn's brows pinched as she focused on the book Blair held and the ideas she'd suggested. Her thoughts tumbled through her, pulse skyrocketing, but she couldn't dismiss the theory—*something* to get her magic back, no matter the fear chilling her to the bone.

"If I venture to the Otherworld, there's a chance I can weave my soul back together." Evelyn rubbed the constant ache in her chest.

"That means you'd have to die," Tovi hissed down the table.

The rest of the team stiffened, staring with wide eyes. Next to Evelyn, Kade swallowed, jaw ticking. They shared a wordless conversation, and despite Evelyn's racing heart, he nodded, silently agreeing with her. They trusted everyone at this table with their life. This wasn't the Council, they were among friends and those they loved.

She swallowed. "We never said anything in our letters these last weeks because we feared the news might fall into the wrong hands: I'm already dying."

Her words sent a shock through the table. Belle gasped, covering her mouth. Todd cursed. Yen and Bétar's stares couldn't decide where to land, Evelyn or Kade. Tovi gripped the edge of the table as she fought to stand, and Nadia remained stoic and silent. On the other end, Eldrick and Aramis leaned forward, both alphas rigid. Lorkan observed with his chin resting on his hand, golden eyes locked on Blair past his spectacles.

"How long do you have?" Linx asked.

"Three weeks." The tense air in the hall strangled her resolve, but Evelyn pushed on. "Which is why Blair is right. We don't have time to research another option. *This* is it."

"Evelyn is my sister, and I don't like the idea any more than the rest of you, but the prophecy details this idea—*a journey to the beneath where life and death meet.*"

Stunned silence stretched in the hall, but Evelyn's heart raced with promise.

"How would we ensure Evelyn not only ventures to the Otherworld but returns to the Living Lands?" Kade asked with an unnatural level of calm.

Evelyn gave his hand a reassuring squeeze, grateful he was at least hearing this out, and nodded for Blair to go on.

Her sister sighed. "We'd use a spell that guides Evelyn there and back."

"What does the spell entail?" Belle asked.

Blair retrieved a piece of parchment, and Evelyn recognized her neat handwriting at this distance. "Spells work best with the power of three. First" —she peered up at Evelyn— "there's you, your physical mind and body. Usually, spells use timing, but because that isn't on our side in this instance, we need a location as our second element, one powerful enough to aid the spell, but also relevant to your destination. Now, hidden portals exist—like wells, lakes, the sea—across Sorin and Torren, which we can discuss as contingencies, but I think the Sun Goddess's temple in Cirrillo is our best bet."

Belle thrummed her fingers against the table. "It's ancient, and legend says built by the goddess herself."

"Exactly," Blair said. "She gifted Evelyn her flame, and perhaps her influence will aid the spell as well."

Evelyn nodded. "I've traveled to the temple before. I know how to get there without being discovered by the Guard."

After she'd run from her wedding to Kade, she'd tried to get her flame back, visiting the temple and praying to the Goddess who'd gifted her the power. Seven days, seven nights. The desert mages who tended the sacred place had found her unconscious and dehydrated from her efforts.

Kade exhaled. "What is the third part of the spell?"

"Objects, and to keep the theme of balance, it'll need to be three items strongly connected to Evelyn. The first one is simple—the bloodstone. Your magic, a piece of your soul, is already inside it. Which leaves us with two more to decide on."

"How about your staff?" Kade studied her. "It has the power to withstand your flame."

"Perhaps," Evelyn said. "But my staff was found and forged, not made by me."

Kade snapped his attention to Blair. "Does that make a difference?"

"It might," Blair said. "Made is best."

"Your grimoire?" Tovi asked. "Your parents crafted the cover and spine with your bloodline's magic, but you filled the pages and created the contents. It has to have at least two decades' worth of *you* in it."

"That's in my apartment in Nūa." Evelyn's shoulders sagged. "It's too much of a risk to go back and get it."

Blair nodded. "Fair. There has to be something else."

"What about your muince? Witches make them as a rite of passage with their own magic. It's similar to the bloodstone in that regard," Belle said. "Where is it?"

"At the bottom of the Sapphire Sea, I'm afraid." Nadia grimaced. "Thanks to Riven."

Belle's expression brightened. "Luckily, you have a witch with a water bronntanas. If we found its location, I could retrieve it."

Evelyn nibbled her lip. "It's not a terrible idea, but we would need a seer with the ability to scribe and find the necklace, which is already rare enough, *and* a witch we trust."

"Uzoma," Blair said without hesitation. "She lives in Sorin's valley now, far outside the city."

"Your old tutor?" Kade straightened in his seat. "Can we trust her?"

His question had an edge to it, as if he had layered it with another: *Is she like Circe?*

Evelyn nodded. "Yes, we can trust her."

"It's also on the way to Morrow," Tovi said. "I have a contact—a vampyr—with access to ships, so that leaves witches out of it."

For the first time in weeks, Evelyn's restless being sighed with relief. A *plan*.

"Alright, that leaves us with the third and last item," Blair said. "We could lean on your *physical* being if we must, though it wouldn't be my preference—"

"Me," Kade said. "I'll be the third item for the spell. I'm Evelyn's mate, and even if our bond is frayed, our love remains strong enough to withstand the distance of worlds and realms."

Evelyn didn't know it was possible to fall for Kade all over again, but there she was, fighting tears as they threatened to spill. She couldn't breathe. Struggled to find the words. He brought their clasped hands out from under the table and rested them atop the table for the team to see, a symbol of their unity.

"Kade," she whispered.

His kind golden eyes met hers, and the world around them fell away. The stone walls of Lār crumbled. Their friends drifted from existence. It was just *them*. Their brimming devotion brought Evelyn back to the first time they agreed to work together, sitting at the bar in the Runaway Radish as Kade cleaned glasses. The whiskey bottles glowing behind him. The scent of stew and crusty bread. And the inevitable magnitude of *something* starting. The kindle of forever in a place full of rain, clouds, and *promise*.

He addressed her, and only her. "We swore that no matter what we face, we face it together. If you must travel to the Otherworld, Ev, then so shall I." He kissed the back of her hand.

Evelyn's wounded heart swelled, and she feared she might burst from her fated's fierce love. Because she knew this was a risk. Knew, even without their mating bond fully intact, it was unnatural for him to accept this notion, to allow her *to die*. But they'd made a promise. Partners, in everything and anything.

"Thank you," she whispered.

Kade's throat bobbed. He blinked a few times, composed himself, and then his expression transformed back into the beastly warrior known as the Son of the God. He stood and addressed the group.

"Thanks to Blair, Evelyn and I have our course of action. We'll head to Morrow at dawn. While we're away, there's still Riven to worry about and the prophecy."

"I suggest Lorkan and Blair work together to decipher it," Eldrick said, glancing at the two scholars.

"What?" Blair hissed, then blinked, as if realizing she'd spoken out loud.

Evelyn froze, studying her sister. Hurt marred her dark eyes as they skittered over Lorkan, but *fucking flames*, why?

Linx slid a pamphlet across the table, and the *Morning Sun*'s block print logo taunted Evelyn. "This arrived by italog this morning. Blair's name has been added to the list of traitors to Sorin."

Blair snatched the parchment, and the temperature in the hall dropped a fraction. "They're calling for my arrest and—*blasted books*—it's a ten thousand silvers reward. Am I safe in the Drengr Village?"

Aramis sighed. "You're more than welcome here, but I think it's best you and Lorkan travel to Vísdómr. That library is a far richer resource to aid in deciphering the prophecy. Don't you agree?" He raised a brow in his son's direction.

Lorkan shifted in his seat and cleared his throat. "My father's right. It's our best chance at finding answers, and you'll be harder to arrest if you're on the move."

"I think it's a fine idea," Nadia said, mirth etched into the crevices of her small smile. "The two of you used to be thick as thieves as young scholars."

Blair's expression turned unreadable, and Evelyn rooted to her seat. She shared a glance with Tovi, whose brow was raised as if to say, *What does* that *mean?*

Evelyn didn't have the faintest idea. Of course, Blair and Mirella had traveled with their parents during formal visits to the Drengr Village when she'd stayed in Nūa, upholding the request of the Elders and alphas that she and Kade couldn't meet until their wedding day—*oh*, how circumstances had changed—but Blair had never, not once, mentioned Lorkan. Unease churned in Evelyn's gut. Perhaps she didn't know her sister as well as she thought.

Blair exhaled, inquisitive brows raised. "If I'm to travel to Vísdómr, who will perform the spell to send Evelyn and Kade to the Otherworld?"

Belle stood. "I can, seeing as I'm going with them to help retrieve her muince."

Kade nodded. "Alright, Belle will travel with Evelyn and me. Mother is headed north to retrieve the Moon God's sword. Lorkan and Blair will work on deciphering. The rest of you?"

Tovi stared into the grooves of the wooden table. "I must return home and unite Drystan under one banner. I'll write to my contact in Morrow first. They're a potential ally."

"I'll be at your side," Yennifer said.

Tovi stilled. "What? But Bétar is—"

"Yen and I have already discussed the possibility. I'll remain here, protecting the village and helping the Drengr pack win the Earl vote, while she accompanies you."

Aramis ran his fingers through his scruff. "It's important for vampyrs to understand werewolves are with you in the fight against darkness. Yen can act as an ambassador."

"With a bow and arrow, of course," the archer added. "No dresses."

Evelyn followed Kade's line of sight. Eldrick leaned back in his chair, expression otherwise observant, but his knuckles bled white as he gripped his chair's arm. He and the princess hadn't spoken a word to each other during the meeting. Even now, Evelyn's best friend assessed Yennifer, jade stare averted from Eldrick's. Evelyn pocketed it for later when she had a moment alone with Tovi.

"Are you sure?" she asked.

"Yes," Yennifer said. "Besides, what sort of friend am I if let you face this alone?"

"I think it's best I travel with Evelyn and Kade's party. Always a plus to have a healer amongst you," Linx said.

Todd whistled. "*Moons*, Bétar, you barely lasted a month as Commander. The Gray Fenris is disbanding."

The burly werewolf grumbled. "I like to think of it as dividing and conquering."

"He's right. We'll come back together." Kade smiled, but it didn't reach his eyes. "All of us. The Earl vote is in a month's time, and we should reconvene then."

A silent agreement rippled through the team, and a sense of purpose peppered the air.

Evelyn swore she'd have her flame back at her fingertips again.

Chapter Twenty-Eight

Eldrick

A BALCONY STRETCHED ALONG the perimeter of Lār's fifth story, granting a bird's-eye view above the village. Solemnity hung in the air as thick as the winter cold. Below, pyres dotted the village. Their flames roared, and embers twisted into the snow drifting on the winds. Evelyn, Yen, and Nadia held Tovi as she said goodbye to her friend Lou, the baker's pyre decorated with purple ribbon instead of Drengr navy.

Eldrick's legs tingled with restlessness, his body warring to get to Tovi, to comfort her, but his heart ached with the truth. Riven's attack had shown them that being together didn't work. It jeopardized peace too greatly.

Approaching boots echoed across the stone. "There you are."

Eldrick greeted his father with a half-smile.

Aramis rested his elbows on the balcony, spring eyes roaming over their village. "Why aren't you down there with her?"

Eldrick exhaled. His father had never addressed his relationship with Tovi, not so directly, but now there was nothing to discuss. Perhaps admitting it out loud, saying the truth to his father made it more real.

"Because that is not my place," he said, words as sharp as daggers.

The wind whipped down the balcony, but he ignored its frigid bite. Let the land rage. Let his body yearn. His heart belonged to the werewolves as it pulsed with alpha blood. *This* was his purpose, and the vampyr queen, the woman he loved, had hers.

Aramis nodded, lips set in a thin line. Snow collected in the fur of his cloak, and Eldrick paused, noting his father's many layers—dark traveling leathers, navy wool tunic, belt fastened with both his axe and sword, and riding gloves. The realization dawned on Eldrick like the slow melt of a snowflake against his skin.

"You're leaving."

His father sighed. "Yes."

"But where? The Earl vote—"

"Is yours to secure, not mine."

Eldrick reared straighter, replaying his father's words. He waited for his father to clarify or correct himself, but Aramis's sights focused below.

On Eldrick's mother.

"I don't understand," Eldrick breathed.

His father frowned. "You mother has decided to return to Drystan as a spy again, and I'm going with her. Her presence in the village will only hurt the Drengr's chances at the Earl vote, as will I—"

"Father—"

His father's adamant expression stopped him short. "I spoke to the other alphas regarding the decree, and they're no longer confident in my ability to serve as Earl. Their signatures should've been telling enough, but it is worse than I thought. Alpha Skau still questions my health. Thorn and Drabek are wary of the future. The rest simply don't trust me."

Eldrick shook his head. "That is because Bjorn has poisoned their minds against you."

His father scoffed, grasping the balcony's edge. "Oh, I'm sure of it. That prick has waited for me to fuck up as Earl for almost twenty-seven years."

"Then convince the rest of the alphas he is dividing the werewolves for the sake of his pride," Eldrick said.

Aramis's exhale plumed into the cold late-night air. "I blew that chance the moment I refused to hand your mother over to Riven."

"She is your mate," Eldrick hissed.

Aramis winced. "She is also a vampyr, son. They'll never accept her."

His father's rushed words came out pointed. Eldrick swallowed, knees locking as he understood his father's stern tone. He meant more than one *her* in this instance.

Aramis assessed the forest. "It takes a real leader to set aside their wants, Eldrick."

"I know," he said.

He'd seen it with his mother, sacrificing these last ten years for the prophecy's promise. She'd stayed away. From her pack, sons, and mate. Eldrick admired her ability to put her duty above all else, and now, his father was doing the same.

"You're ready." Aramis grasped his shoulder. "Have been for some time now."

Eldrick had craved his father's approval. All his life he'd trained to become alpha. It'd been in the palm of his hand weeks ago when his father had given him the option to ascend, but with his father healed and mother home, he'd set aside the notion.

"I feel like I'm robbing you of your right," Eldrick whispered.

His father scoffed. "When your mother became pregnant, I knew our first child would one day take my place. How and when was up to fate. But what greater honor is there than to witness the male I'm proud to call my son become the Drengr Alpha?"

Eldrick's throat grew thick. "Do you really think I have a chance of winning the vote?"

"Yes. The other alphas will trust you more than Bjorn, but it won't be easy."

Eldrick's wolf grew restless. If he didn't win, the Johannes alpha would, and werewolves didn't stand a chance in the war to come if their new leader refused to form an alliance based on prejudice.

The wind howled as the pyres shrank to cinders. Eldrick tracked the mountain range on the horizon, ignoring Opal's voice whispering in the back of his mind. *Those of these lands will unite . . .* Perhaps the line was much simpler—he as Earl, she as queen, together uniting werewolves and vampyrs under their titles.

For Eldrick's heart beat for werewolves and his alpha blood bonded to the Vadon Mountains, just like his mother and father's. He'd known this day would come all his life.

"I'd rather avoid a frilly ceremony," he finally said.

His father laughed, and the pride shining across his eyes sharpened the rightness of Eldrick's decision.

"How about a handshake between a father and son?" Aramis asked.

Eldrick rolled up his sleeve and extended his right hand out, heart pounding. He had no idea what to expect—this sort of ascension was so rare, he'd not read about it in books, only heard whispers from those who'd wondered when this day would come for the Drengr Pack.

A *given* exchange of power.

Aramis removed his glove, revealing his alpha tattoo. He clasped Eldrick's forearm, and a warm magic thrummed from his father's touch. The ink on his father's skin grew faint, and pearly white tattoos came alive on Eldrick's hand, around his fingers and wrist, and disappeared up his sleeve. They shone like the moon on a clear night as Aramis chanted an ancient tongue, words that were equally foreign as they were familiar, like Eldrick had heard them all his life.

Snow whirled around them, trapping them in a tunnel of flurries. Eldrick tightened his grip as the power bit through his skin. Like dunking into a frozen lake, the cold burned his skin.

Soon, Aramis's alpha tattoo vanished completely, and Eldrick's shined with the might of the full moon. His wolf howled in his blood, and a new sense awakened.

The whispers of his pack. The perimeters of the village. The hearts and minds of those he led.

Once the power transferred from father to son, a sonic boom emitted from them. Snow blew backward. The surrounding trees leaned. The lands shook.

It was done.

Eldrick had ascended and was now Alpha Drengr.

CHAPTER TWENTY-NINE

WHITE COATED THE SKY and the forest, encompassing the land in an unnatural stillness. The cold reminded Tovi too much of home. It bit back, sucking away the wood's beauty. She trudged through the snow, a rather tedious endeavor, but her blood supplies were running low. Tovi needed to stock up before she set out on her journey to return Drystan and assemble a force strong enough to beat Riven.

She could hear Lou's ire for leaving the fortress alone, but Lou was gone, and Tovi would never hear her friend's council again.

Despite the risk of venturing through the forest without a companion, Tovi'd encountered only a hare. It was the unlucky one, its blood now filled the vials in her satchel. The irony scent wafted from her side, and her fangs ached, refusing to retract.

She'd fed directly from the hare's neck, too, enough blood to last her a few days, but the recent taste of blood awakened the curse. Disdain battled her pride. No matter how sedated she *felt*, the curse always reared its viscous head when she drank blood. She couldn't outrun the need to feed, but Tovi had fought her baser instincts for centuries. She'd endured the thrum through her veins after fresh blood before.

Today was no different.

She exhaled, her hot breath pluming across her line of sight. She gripped her bow tighter and retrieved an arrow on light, balanced feet. She'd grabbed the weapon on purpose. A *true* hunt. Not one of agile speed or sheathed talons, but skill.

Tovi cracked her neck, shut her eyes, and breathed in the scent of pine again. Stillness. Breathe. Presence. Moments like this, weapon in hand, and out in the open air, in a land that held a similarity to the beauty of Drystan before the curse, was when Tovi felt most herself. Not cursed. Not doomed. Nor a queen. Just *her*.

With a sigh, she unbuckled her satchel and counted the vials. Four full ones. Not enough to last the month, especially if she planned to travel with haste through Drystan.

Large flurries raced from the sky. Not ideal for hunting, but another smile tugged at her lips. Her muscles vibrated with the promise of a challenge. She climbed a slop dotted with ferns and reached a stretch of colder forest, the canopy thicker. It had far less snow, and the little it did have was frozen solid. Tovi boots didn't sink, a welcome reprieve, but her heels crunched with each step.

Tovi glided on light feet to the nearest tree. Naked for the winter, the birch's branches caged her in a crooked embrace. Back flush against the unfurling bark, she inhaled, shut her eyes, and listened past the stillness of the forest.

Snow landed with a gentle crackle, and—

Huff.

An animal snorted, close enough she scented its kind.

An elk—her favorite.

It munched on frosted grass. Tovi peered around the corner, muscles tightening in readiness. The elk's antlers were rounded and wide, four points reaching to the sky. Fresh snow collected on the curves and lined its spine.

Set jaw, tight gaze, she studied the distance. Fifteen yards—a little too close.

Tovi's heart raced in her chest. She'd have to wait for it to get further. One more yard, another . . .

Inch by inch, she nocked the arrow in place. Her bow groaned as she readied it. Snow kissed the arrow's tip and caught in Tovi's lashes. She didn't move. Didn't breathe.

The elk wandered further away and turned, exposing its chest. *There.* Behind its shoulder—

Tovi released her arrow and breath.

The forest stilled aside from her shot. It whistled through silent flurries and then popped, hitting its target. Startled and injured, the elk fled, leaving a trail of blood in its wake.

Tovi trailed the beast out sight and waited. Its last, hot breaths plumed over the snow, until it slacked slowly like it fell into a peaceful slumber. Tovi sent a prayer to the Goddess, thanking her and the creature for its blood. For its life. She promised to use its blood right, to take the kill into the village and allow the werewolves to use it, too.

Vial after vial, Tovi filled them with blood to last her weeks. A shot in the morning, a droplet in her wine. Her mind played through her feeding routine, a somewhat mundane task after so many years. Lost to her own thoughts, she didn't detect someone was near until it was too late—the sensation eyes were on her itched up her neck.

Tovi whirled with arrow nocked and bow stretched.

Gem eyes glinted past the iron tip of her arrow, a splendid contrast of color compared to the white landscape.

"Eldrick?"

He held up his hands in surrender. "I didn't mean to startle you."

Tovi lowered her weapon, a response lost as her mouth dried. Sweat slicked her hands, and she shuffled to hide her vials. *Fuck.* Of all the things Eldrick could've stumbled upon, it was *this*—a blatant distinction that made her a vampyr.

But it was too late. He approached in that proud walk he always possessed, and his attention jumped between the elk's slit throat and the vials.

"Let me help."

Tovi turned as still as the forest's icicles. A soft smile, gem eyes burrowing into her's, tone reassuring, he meant it.

"You don't have to—"

"I want to."

Want.

What a dangerous word for both of them. Though it no longer mattered—she'd made her decision to leave and return home. They were allies. Nothing more. Lou was gone, but her recent warnings were fresh. Tovi wouldn't let her desire for Eldrick get in the way of uniting her people under one banner, and in turn, it allowed her to run from fate and not have to face *what* Eldrick was to her.

"I only have four more to go," she said, handing Eldrick two empty ones. "It'll go by faster if you pass them to me, and I won't say no to help with getting this beast back to the village."

Eldrick nodded, crouching on the ground next to her. He weighed the glass vials in his hand, his gaze lingering on the broken arrow lodged into the animal's shoulder. "An impressive shot, and your favorite, if I recall correctly."

Tovi's gut twisted. She wasn't sure if she appreciated the normalcy of the conversation, or if it felt entirely wrong. The fact he remembered her preference sent tingles to her toes, but it also made her fangs and core ache, desperate to weave feeding, pleasure, blood, and sex all into a blissful moment.

With *him*.

Bloody hel, Eldrick was dangerous. Tovi's hand tightened on the vial as she filled it with blood, her fingers itching to write the word out and pin it on his chest, some sort of warning label so she could keep her wits. At present, Tovi's mind raced, leaving her off-balance. Thank the Goddess they'd have miles separating them soon enough.

"This . . . doesn't bother you?" she asked. The last time he'd faced Tovi in her vampyr element, he'd been terrified. Perhaps that's why she was so unsettled—she didn't care if he judged her, but it still stung.

Eldrick sighed and studied her. "Not anymore. Drinking blood is part of being a vampyr, isn't it? Besides, I know you do this instead of feeding from . . . others."

Tovi placed the vial in her satchel and indicated for another. "It scratches the itch."

He passed it to her without even a flinch, not a shadow of disdain entering his eyes. Like two friends breaking down a hunt, nothing more. "When the curse is lifted, will you still need to drink blood?"

"Here and there," Tovi said, not meeting his gaze. "Yen once told me werewolves need to shift from time to time."

Eldrick nodded. "We do. Our inner beasts can get unruly."

"Hunger is much the same, but once the curse is lifted, we won't be bound by *needing* blood every three days. We get to determine how and when."

Eldrick grunted his agreement. "How does that look?"

So many questions . . . Yet Tovi's stomach fluttered, and she leaned into his curiosity.

"Usually, drinking blood is an intimate moment. Foreplay, sex, a sign of affection." Tovi cleared her throat. Eldrick's jaw tightened, but he handed her the last vial, nodding for her to go on. "It's very common amongst mates, too."

Eldrick's brow pinched, a borderline scowl lining his face. "I've never heard you talk about mates before."

"They're rare," she said. "Not for the reasons you may think, though. Female vampyrs are often married off before they have time to even meet their mates."

"What a cruel practice." Eldrick stared off into the forest, jaw ticking. Anger wafted off him in waves, his inner wolf bristling in the air. "But no one can outrun fate, not even the pompous lords of Drystan, marrying off their daughters." He eyed her. "Is that why you fought your parents on an arranged marriage? For the promise of meeting your mate?"

Tovi rose to her feet and released a light laugh. "I was thinking of freedom and nothing more, I'm afraid."

And now?

The question hung in the air, like the slow, tranquil snow flurries. Tovi walked through them and moved onward.

"You deserve it—freedom, all of it. Don't ever let anyone make you think otherwise," Eldrick said.

Electricity shot through Tovi's body, and *something* wedged into the crevices of her heart. It was like longing but more; beautiful but forbidden.

She unsheathed a knife, handed it to Eldrick, and found another she'd secured in her boot.

"Best we get started," she said, words thick in her throat.

Eldrick shook his head, playful smile on his usually serious face. "*Stars above*, any more sharp things I should know about?"

Tovi flashed a fang. "Ten more if you count my talons."

Their banter bled warmth into the air, and with it, they got busy skinning the beast. It wasn't long before they'd broken it down completely and divided it into two game sleds, made with tarps and twine from Tovi's satchel and sturdy oak branches Eldrick had secured.

They trudged in determined silence, side by side, as they pulled the elk behind them, the light of the morning no match against the thick clouds.

Eldrick halted, throwing up his hand for her to stop, too. He crouched, releasing his game sled and eased forward on silent, cautious feet. Tovi mirrored his movement, and hidden behind a large evergreen, they assessed the forest below.

The Johannes envoy walked the very path Eldrick and Tovi were headed for, their indistinguishable chatter crackling the air. The hairs on Tovi's arms rose, tension settling in the air.

"They'd be fools to travel home in these conditions," she said. "With their wounded, too?"

"I don't think they are." Eldrick narrowed his eyes. "I don't spy their wounded with them either."

Tovi assessed them again. Dalinda and Bjorn and two others she vaguely recognized. Weapons strapped. Light furs. Leather breastplates. Not traveling leathers nor horses. Or Sam, the alpha's son, in sight.

"They're tracking something," Tovi said.

"Or someone," Eldrick hissed, teeth grinding together. He stood on quick feet, pushing away from the tree.

Tovi grabbed his arm, ignoring the heat searing up her arm. "Eldrick, wait."

He shut his eyes, releasing an angry breath. "*Stars above*, you're right."

"Bloody hel, can you say that again?" Tovi smiled.

He gave her a pointed look. "How can you joke when they might be tracking *you*?"

She shrugged. "I'm used to others wanting me dead."

Eldrick's jaw ticked, his eyes darkening.

She squeezed his arm, making him look at her. "We can't be seen together."

He blinked and understanding flashed through his eyes. "Then we hide and wait them out. They were only looking to get lucky, not search all day. Others will venture out of the village soon enough, and Bjorn can't afford to be seen up to something."

"Alright."

They first hid their sleds under a burly evergreen, lost beyond the snow crusted branches. Eldrick led them to a small cave, large enough for two to stand. The front was covered in interlocked roots, weaved like some curtain.

Silver caught Tovi's eye, and she snatched Eldrick's wrist. Power glowed in delicate tattoos, ones that hadn't been there before, pulsing under her touch. Three parallel lines with a double-lined dash ran down his forearm, until they reached the depiction of a crescent moon, the curve following Eldrick's palm. The shapes held an ancientness to them, simple yet powerful—a magic Tovi had never witnessed but understood.

The world slipped out from under her.

"You ascended," she whispered, the words breathless with awe as well as hollowness. It spread farther and farther, with no way to stop it.

But she had no right to feel hurt.

Tovi'd made her choice, and Eldrick had made his choice.

This was for the best. For them. For their people. For Sorin. Yet, disappointment bled through her like ink blooming in water. This hurt far more than she ever imagined. The urge to say something, to put everything out in the air, danced on the tip of her tongue.

Eldrick's green eyes studied her, swimming with a thousand thoughts, and then he stepped closer. Another and another until she was backed against the enclave's wall, caged under his arms. He brushed his nose against hers. It was almost gentle, kind.

If it weren't so damn painful to feel the heat and intensity that Tovi couldn't have.

Her traitorous body arched up, planting her lips against his. He answered her kiss with a slow, methodical one. Taking his time. Tasting her. Molding his lips against hers. He wasn't hurried or hungry. Neither was she, their kiss long and slow. Tovi's body burned. Her heart ached.

Bloody hel, the kiss tasted like a goodbye.

Tovi couldn't bear it. She braced her hands against his chest, and pulled away enough to breathe, "Eldrick, wait."

His body deflated, and Eldrick leaned his forehead against hers. With clamped-shut eyes, he released a shuddering breath. Their hearts hammered together in tandem until he peeled himself off the wall, his muscles shaking with effort.

Tovi stayed, needing the stone to keep her upright.

"We can't," she whispered.

"I know." He planted his hands on his hips, staring off into the forest. He was stone, rigid and stern, the Eldrick she once knew.

She shook her head. "I'm sorry—"

"There is nothing to be sorry for," he said. "We have our own paths in this. I an alpha, and you a queen."

"Exactly."

Eldrick scoffed, forced and uneasy. "I'd hoped the prophecy meant something different. That you and I brought werewolves and vampyrs together."

Tears pricked at the edge of Tovi's eyes. "I think we can, Eldrick, just not in the way we might want. If Sorin has any chance of beating Riven—"

"We need to be united." Eldrick sighed. "I have to win the vote."

"And I must return home, secure alliances with whom I can before I return here."

Eldrick nodded, jaw rigid. It suddenly felt so final, so damning.

Tovi sucked in a breath, heart cracking. "I need you to know that I l—"

"*Don't.*" Eldrick gave her a hard stare, tone near desperate. "It is already difficult enough to walk away. Please don't make it hurt more than it already does."

"It's what's best," Tovi said, voice thick.

"I know," Eldrick said again, a sad smile marring his handsome face. "You will always have me as an ally, Tovi, and"—he broke their stare, couldn't look at her, couldn't bear this either—"a friend."

Two hearts broke in a little cave of the Vadon Mountains, and hours later, long after they'd returned to the village, passed out the elk's meat, and went their separate ways, Eldrick's promise etched into Tovi's heart, a scar to remind her of their end.

PART II

But when true love dies,
it'll be the land's demise.
Not until the land is cast in
red, a new dawn will rise.

The age of curse, a crack in the land, the
seep and sorrow of death, darkness, and rot.
Her children cast in night, whilst a
hunger for blood
will be their blight.

Chapter Thirty

S ORIN'S VALLEY REMINDED EVELYN more of the hills of Callum than the towering rocky beasts in werewolf territory. Snow hadn't breached this far past the continent's river, leaving the rolling landscape a muted green. Loblolly pines ringed the edge of the distant lake. It shimmered silver under the rising sun, Evelyn and her party's destination a few hours out.

Thanks to Blair's *danu*, they'd shaved three days off their journey. Her sister hadn't visited this territory before—it was notorious for nasty *nathracha* demons—so she'd deposited them by the river near a post she'd ventured through to reach Kade at the Void years ago.

The notorious wall of mists and darkness stood fifty miles north, and it loomed more than ever. Gray plumes broke away from the fog and dotted the sky in rumbling storms. The wind blew fiercer from that direction, too, and with no forest, there was no reprieve from the biting cold.

Evelyn slowed her horse beside Tovi's as her best friend's gaze fixated on the Void, jade eyes churning with vengeance. That was her home, ravaged by a curse Tovi had never asked for, yet she sat atop her horse with shoulders proud. Evelyn didn't know what it meant to be centuries old, fighting for her people, but she understood sacrifice.

"It'll fall one day," Evelyn said. "I promise."

Tovi exhaled, offering her a small smile. "There's not an ounce in me that doubts you, Evelyn."

They nudged their horses back into a steady walk. Ahead, Kade, Todd, and Yen led the party in their shifted forms, three wolfish beasts prowling on all fours. Belle rode alongside Linx, and Evelyn noted the orangish tips the mage had added to her pink braids, a much-needed splash of brightness in a land riddled with gray.

"Did you have time to talk to Blair before we left?" Tovi asked.

Evelyn shook her head. "No."

She convinced herself there wasn't any time. Mere hours stretched between their planning meeting and then leaving the Drengr Village, but truly, Evelyn didn't have the right words to say to her sister. Besides, Blair hadn't seemed inclined to talk either. She'd crafted the idea and spell to get Evelyn's magic back, and Evelyn hoped it was a makeshift peace offering.

For now.

Eventually, Evelyn would have to talk with her sister, but at present, it felt like there were more important matters. The thought left Evelyn squirming in her saddle.

"You?" She turned to Tovi, changing the subject.

Tovi scoffed. "Goddess no. She barely looked at me."

"I didn't expect her to be so angry," Evelyn whispered.

"Something tells me she has been for some time." Tovi sighed. "You and your sister share the same dark hair and . . ."

Evelyn raised a taunting brow. *"And?"*

"An unrelenting streak of stubbornness."

Again, Evelyn shifted in her seat as Tovi studied her with a level of intensity that lifted the veil from her friend's true age.

"The last conversation I had with Lou wasn't my proudest," Tovi said. "It makes losing her that much worse, knowing the way we left things. There's too much uncertainty not to mend things with your sister. The next time you see her, talk to her."

Evelyn's mouth turned dry, and she didn't respond as they reached Uzoma's cottage. The sun shone high above the mountaintop, and the night's frost trickled down the brass gutters of the cottage. Speckled sheep and fuzzy chickens scurried through the puddles, signaling their arrival. Flower boxes filled with rosemary scented the air with an herby sharpness.

A circular door sat at the center, painted teal and adorned with a wreath of evergreen branches, chestnut mushrooms, and dried blood oranges. As Evelyn dismounted Bleu, and the cracking bones and snapping muscles echoed from the shifting werewolves, the door clicked and swung open.

Shirtless and sweaty, Todd approached on cautious feet. "Just as I was about to admit this place was charming, the cottage had to do something creepy."

Evelyn laughed, and Kade's fingers brushed against hers. His ever-green-and-rain scent overshadowed everything else in the garden as he stayed close to her side.

"That's only Uzoma's flair, Todd." She turned to Kade. "Shall we?"

"Wait." Linx appeared at Kade's elbow—it was as if Evelyn blinked and then the mage was just . . . *there*. "You want to go in there alone?"

"We're not alone," Kade said. "Evelyn and I are together."

Linx rolled her catlike eyes. "Yes, I'm aware of that, but shouldn't we *all* go?"

Evelyn shook her head. "Scribing doesn't take long, and once we've got the location of my muince, we'll leave straight for Morrow."

Linx, standing with arms folded, didn't appear convinced.

Kade addressed them all, grasping Evelyn's hand and heading towards the cottage. "Rest, hydrate, keep watch. We'll continue onward soon enough."

They entered the cottage, and after some wandering, Evelyn found Uzoma exactly where she imagined, nestled deep into the cushions of an oversize armchair, using her layered shawls as blankets, with an old, weathered book in her hands.

At her age, Uzoma was the oldest witch in Sorin—older than Circe. Texts claimed that nurturing one's magic properly ensured a long lifespan, yet Evelyn believed a constant, reeling mind had a hand in her tutor's impressive age. Adapting it, morphing it. Uzoma had never tired.

Her hair was whiter these days, a few strands of silver throughout. The smile lines around her eyes had deepened, and her fingers had thinned, tee-tering on frail. The same wisdom rippled through her irises, and the knowing that seers possessed weaved into their state snapped from her texts and landed on Evelyn and Kade. She slammed her book shut and stood.

"You're late," Uzoma said, one brow raised.

"Always is," Kade said.

Evelyn shot him a look, but couldn't fight the smile curving on her lips. "I wasn't aware I had a scheduled appointment today."

Uzoma hummed, approaching on steady feet. She braced her hands on Evelyn's shoulders. "You've always tested fate with your punctuality, Evelyn, though I've known you'd seek me out. It's why I moved out of the city and into the valley. Something told me it was best that way." Uzoma winked like they shared a little secret.

Evelyn laughed, but unease swam in her gut. "I don't understand."

"You need a scribe, right?"

"How . . ." Evelyn shook her head. She'd known Uzoma was a seer, but she'd never revealed her visions were about *her*. Not once, not even when they'd met daily for Evelyn's lessons as a child or visits over the years while she attended university. Uzoma had regarded her Sight as "less than insightful", so often in fact, most of Nūa forgot she was a seer at all.

Uzoma's fingers brushed against the bloodstone, brows pinching, and ignored Evelyn's question. "There it is."

Kade tensed. "Have you seen it before?"

Uzoma backed away, nodding to herself. "Yes, and no."

"That seems like a very seer-like thing to say," Kade muttered.

The older witch's expression turned sympathetic. "I see flashes of things, but I don't know things for certain. Things. People. Colors. All are attached to emotions. Yes, I've seen the bloodstone, but I saw a shattered version."

Evelyn's heart skipped, mind running wild. Kade grasped her hand, giving it an assuring squeeze. Always there, always thinking of her.

Fucking flames, what if—*no, no, no.* Evelyn wouldn't accept anything less than getting her magic back. She'd travel to the ends of the world, fight any sort of demon or darkness. Not because she needed it; she was strong on her own, but because the power locked away in the bloodstone more than belonged to her, it *was* hers.

"I'm uncertain. Yet, the prophecy details the two of you defeating the darkness, does it not?"

Evelyn crossed her arms, chilled by the stretch of the unknown on the horizon. "The prophecy is more than we originally thought."

Uzoma raised a finger. "But it's being deciphered, no?"

Kade nodded. "Blair, Evelyn's sister, and Lorkan, my brother, are headed to Vísdómr to study it."

Uzoma hummed a content tune, as if Kade's news hadn't been news at all but a confirmation.

Evelyn grew hot, hands turning clammy. "What else have you seen?"

Uzoma smiled, studying her fated. "I've seen you, Kade Drengr, and that honey stare so full of *kindness*. I've felt you by Evelyn's side in a land with sprawling green hills, a forest cursed with never ending winter, and a battle that I fear approaches sooner and sooner with each passing day—"

"Wait." Evelyn reared straight. "Do you mean Callum? Did you know I'd run away?"

Uzoma laughed. "Well, of course. I knew long before the idea crossed your mind—"

"Why didn't you stop me?" she hissed. Heat surged through her body, but it was nothing like the power of her flame. It was harsher, *worse,* like she might burn from the inside out with anger.

Uzoma sighed. "That is not my place. Your fate is your fate, Evelyn. Even if I stepped in and stopped you, you'd only deviate off the path and find your way back to it."

The tear in Evelyn's soul ached, and she hated the choice she had made, ripping her magic out, but that brash, foolish decision *belonged* to her.

Or so she thought.

Everything she'd done felt like water slipping through her fingers. *Nothing* was in her grasp. Not her name that was now tarnished in the papers, not her title, chosen by her homeland, or her magic, locked away in the bloodstone.

"I thought myself broken, and you let me believe it."

"You *were* broken, Evelyn, and there is no shame in that. It is not my place to get in the way of your journey, and I can already see you're better for it. Fiercer, stronger. Far braver than you ever were. To think you're pushing back against me?" Uzoma snorted. "You'd never once questioned me before, and it's a refreshing change."

"Don't mock her," Kade growled.

"I'm not," Uzoma snapped. "At my age, you know that no words can heal wounds. That power exists only within us. But know this: When I saw the bloodstone, I didn't know what it meant or what it would cost you, my dear. Just because I've seen what may be, doesn't mean I *want* it for you."

"What about what *I* want?" Evelyn whispered. "Does that count for something?"

"Oh, my dear." Uzoma grasped her hands and held them with a tenderness she'd offered all those years ago, a gentle comfort with so much on her small shoulders. "Listen to me—"

"Did you know Circe would hurt me?" Evelyn asked, impressed with unwavering tone.

Uzoma stiffened. Her silence ballooned in the cottage, and Evelyn snatched her hands away.

"Goddess, you *did . . .*"

"Evelyn, please. You must understand—"

"What? That having my tutor tell me I was nothing made me *better for it.*"

Uzoma winced. "I *see* things, not write them. You are the Daughter of the Goddess—"

"I'm Evelyn Carson. *That* is my name." Betrayal seared through her; she'd never been her title to her tutor. On the streets of the city, amongst covens, but not with Uzoma.

Her old tutor's shoulders slackened, and pain flashed behind her spectacles. "Forgive me, I know exactly who you are and always have. I swear to you, the first visions I saw of Circe are what led me to find you in that cupboard, and once I had you away from her, I never tutored you as the Daughter of the Goddess, but as Evelyn. You must remember that."

Kade laid a hand on the small of her back, and Evelyn released a breath, finding the courage to agree with Uzoma. She did, and that was why she trusted her enough to come here today.

Circe's words. Her people's opinions. Evelyn kept telling herself it didn't matter how they labeled her, what her title was. Yet Uzoma's *knowing* made it worse, deepened the cut almost. Like she was some pawn that others moved as they saw fit.

Fuck that—she refused to accept that was the way of things, and Uzoma's next words encouraged her more in that conviction.

Uzoma laid a soft hand on her cheeks. "Things are written, yes indeed. The prophecy. The Nūa papers." The witch snorted with disgust. "But don't think for a second your fate is not in your hands, and yours only, you hear me?"

Evelyn nodded. "Yes."

"Now"—Uzoma backed up, gathering her many shawls—"I think it's time I scribed for your muince."

Chapter Thirty-One

B LAIR'S BREATH BLOOMED INTO the evening air as she folded and unfolded the note she'd received at the Shield-maiden.

Let's meet at the north gate at dusk, ready to travel. -L

She crumpled the note and shoved it into her pocket. Reading it again changed nothing—she had to work with Lorkan *fucking* Drengr, and he'd shoved a note under her door and *summoned* her.

Like . . . like . . . like some errand girl at a lead scholar's beck and call. She'd published over thirty research papers and an entire textbook entitled *The Relationship Between One's Weapon & Their Bronntanas*. As far as Blair was concerned, *he* should follow *her* lead.

But they were headed to Vísdómr, the esteemed werewolf library, and truthfully, Blair was out of her element. Her breath plumed in the evening air, blending with the fog. Frost clung to the surrounding pines, and snow blanketed the Drengr Village. She had no winter items. No heavy cloak, traveling boots, or money to buy supplies. Blair possessed the clothes on her back, her shillelagh, and Rook, though her mischievous familiar was nowhere to be found—

Blasted books, Blair was going to scream.

Ahead, the Drengr scholar emerged through the mists in the village, the plumes of gray snaking around his lean legs. He'd fashioned an all-black ensemble, a blazer-like jacket reaching to his shins and flaring behind him as he strode in her direction. Head down, eyes downcast, face hardened into a pensive expression thanks to his glasses. He held an alluring sharpness with his unbuttoned tunic revealing his taut chest.

And Rook, that thieving, pesky, disloyal bird, sat on his shoulder.

The raven clacked its beak next to Lorkan's ear, snapping him from his brooding—and *oh Goddess*, a smirk tugged on the bastard's lips.

Blair tasted chalk. How dare he be beautiful? How dare he find joy with *her* familiar? To make matters worse, Rook complimented his dark and stormy attire. They fit, as they had all those years ago when she and Lorkan had found Rook as a chick, tucked in the rafters of the Drengr Library.

"Good evening," he said, fluid.

"Ready to go?" She sent a fleeting glare at Rook.

"Of course." Lorkan tilted his head. "Lead the way."

Confusion bristled through Blair's aggravated being. Why would she lead them to Vísdómr?

She could really, truly scream, and she tried to replay the moments at the meeting table the night before. Her mind kept reeling back to that moment, replaying her silence. But what could she have said?

I'm not traveling to Vísdómr with the man who broke my heart.

That would've gone over well. Not only would she have revealed their teenage romance, but also she would have admitted that Blair's heart still carried bruises many years later.

Blair reached the edge of the forest before she realized Lorkan wasn't with her. He cleared his throat, and she whirled toward him.

"What are you waiting for?" she asked.

Rook held onto Lorkan's shoulder, beady eyes jumping between them, as Lorkan placed his hands in his pockets and strolled towards her. His eyes tracked her, and Blair had a horrible sense a predator watched her. Yet she wasn't afraid. Her heart pounded in her chest, but for entirely different reasons.

"I was waiting for you to conjure a *danu*," he said. "It would make our journey far faster."

"A *danu* to Vísdómr?" Blair scoffed. "They don't work that way."

She turned away from him, heading northwest. She'd already studied the best route. It would be on foot, slower, but it was their only option. With her face in the papers and a ten-thousand silver reward, they couldn't risk main villages, werewolf territory or not.

"I don't understand." Lorkan fell into step beside her, and Blair gritted her teeth at the sight of Rook, wedged between them both, in her peripherals. "You've traveled farther with your magic before. Nūa to Drengr Village is a bigger jump compared to—"

Blair stopped abruptly. "I'm well aware of my abilities, Lorkan, and how far I'm able to travel. You're forgetting a key component of traveling with a *danu*. I can't conjure one to places I have never been."

Lorkan's eyes flared wide. "You've never been to Vísdómr?"

"No," Blair said, turning from the emotion swimming in his golden stare. A sheen like he cared. *Bastard*. "I already mapped out our journey—"

"Completely on foot?" Lorkan's nostrils flared. "That will take days."

"Yes, seven to be exact."

"A full week," he hissed. "First, we don't have that kind of time. Second, you're barely dressed to survive an afternoon in the Vadon Mountains, let alone seven days and nights."

Winds whistled in the trees, but Blair didn't argue Lorkan's points or dare admit she had *nothing*.

"Third, why would I suggest starting our travels at night and during winter?" he asked.

Blair halted, whirling towards him. "Perhaps if you hadn't shoved a note under my door and summoned me to a meeting place, the two of us could've discussed all of this by a warm fire and cup of tea, but no, you avoided me."

Lorkan's jaw pulsed.

"Why did you agree to this?" she whispered.

He blinked, studied her and said, "Same reason you didn't object. No one knows we . . . were acquainted."

Blair snorted. Angry, loud words had become permanent residents on the tip of her tongue, it seemed, for Lorkan undermined their time together. She'd cherished his dreams, fought away his fears, recalled how he tasted like smoke and moss. That was more than acquainted. But what good did arguing about the past do for them now?

She swallowed and set her shoulders back. "It seems we're in this together, so if we're going to work well, don't summon me with notes."

"Fine," Lorkan said. "Can't you use a *danu* somewhere farther north? How about Fika?"

"No," Blair said, holding back her bite.

She *had* been to Fika. With *him*. Many, many times. It was also the village they'd agreed to meet in all those years ago. The village she'd sat in *waiting for three days*. The first fracture of her broken heart had started there. Blair couldn't even see the name printed on a map without the decade-old pain lodging in her throat. And to think Lorkan suggested it without a second thought?

Blair seethed, wishing, praying to any god who would listen to set her free of this misery. It was already bad enough that she had to work alongside Lorkan to decipher the prophecy, but to know he didn't recall the tiny details, ones that still hurt her . . .

But Lorkan was right. They didn't have days to waste—they had a prophecy to decipher and a curse to break if Blair wished to have any semblance of her life back.

"Béal is up the river," she said. "We can take the ferry the rest of the way to Vísdómr. Saves us three days. The only issue is it's witch territory on the east side."

Lorkan shoved his hands into his pockets. "Sounds like we have a plan; we'll just need to be discreet."

Chapter Thirty-Two

Lorkan

Lorkan had a plan: (1) get to Vísdómr with haste, (2) avoid Blair entirely, and (3) learn how to break the curse.

But it was already going to utter shit.

He stepped through Blair's *danu* and straight into a blizzard.

Snow plundered from the north, and white swallowed the village's buildings, and the howling winds—

Moons, they wrapped Blair's scent around him. Storm clouds and sage. His baser instincts fought to unleash while he wavered on unsteady legs against the blizzard's force. Both challenged his restraint.

"We need to head back," he yelled.

Blair's curls twirled in the erratic flurries. "I can't! My magic isn't infinite!"

He knew that. Of course, he did. As teenagers, Blair had conjured *danus* to visit him from Nūa to the Drengr Village. The distance left her spent, but after a night's rest, she'd be ready to conjure another one to return home come morning.

Which meant they had to stay the night.

Gods help him.

Blair braced against the wind, trying to stand. He reached to assist, but she flinched away from his touch. *Right.* Of course she didn't want his help—he'd abandoned her. Left her in Fika, where he'd *suggested* they travel to first, like some forgetful fool, although he recalled the reason he'd never shown every damn day of his existence.

Blair shivered, hugging herself. His inner wolf whimpered. His instinct warred within him—protect her. But he couldn't touch her, not when his bloodthirst sat at the surface.

He could use his speed and strength, traits a latent wolf didn't possess, but that gave away what he was. *Hide what you are,* his father's voice whispered. Yet, he still had heightened hearing and sight he could depend upon.

"Follow me. I know where the inn is," he lied.

Blair didn't object, and he faced north and braced against the winds. He tilted his head right, narrowed his sights away and reached for his inner monster.

It wasn't music, laughter, nor the clanging of cups he listened for, but hearts.

Thump . . . thump . . . Thump, thump, thump—no, that was Blair's behind him. Anxious, frightened, quickening her sweet blood through her veins. Lorkan tuned it out, focusing ahead. Like some beast prowling in the snow, he hunted prey. A dozen hearts beat east, the loudest concentration of them throughout the village. He squinted and shielded his eyes with his hand. Light glowed through the white, warm and pulsing.

Rook cawed, his black wings a dash through the frantic snowfall, and Lorkan almost smiled—smart, helpful bird.

After a half-mile, Lorkan pushed through the inn's double-swinging doors, and Rook flew to his shoulder, claws clamping tightly into his cloak. Blair muttered something under her breath, too quick for him to catch what, but before he asked, his attention snagged on her clothes. *Stars above,* they were so unsuitable for traveling through the Vadon Mountains, anger lanced through him.

"Aye! Good evening to you both. Horrible night to be travelin' I'd say."

The innkeeper's jolly greeting snapped Lorkan out of his reeling thoughts. The male witch with ruddy cheeks and a friendly smile scrubbed the bar top. He eyed Blair up and down. Not in an assessing way, but a knowing way, like he was used to desperate, tired patrons daily. Still, Lorkan stepped closer to her.

Big mistake, because fear heightened one's scent, and they'd just walked into a witch's inn and Blair was a traitor with a ten-thousand silver reward dangling over her head—

"Can I get you a room?" the innkeeper asked.

Hide. Lorkan's mantra roared in his mind. Get her out of sight. "Yes, two please."

"Aye, I've only have one room left for the night. The honeymooner's suite, actually. Extra big bed. Large enough for two. Even a male as tall as you will fit. Though"—he pointed at Rook—"no pets inside."

Before Lorkan could stop her, Blair stepped forward, ire lacing through her onyx stare. "He's a *familiar.*"

Lorkan winced, and the innkeeper's eyes narrowed a fraction. *Gods dammit,* had she forgotten they were in a witches village? How many witches had *ravens* for familiars? Rook practically gave her identity away. But she'd always been protective of the raven, as was Lorkan, but they couldn't afford to reveal who there were.

Not here, stuck inside a village facing a snowstorm.

They needed to get out of the scrutiny of the innkeeper before a patron sipping their stew took notice. But being trapped within four walls surrounded by Blair's scent? Lorkan's inner beast howled at the prospect, greedy, while Lorkan's insides churned with nerves. His well-laid out plan was indeed going to shit.

"How much for a single night?" he asked the innkeeper.

"A silver coin will do."

Lorkan placed three onto the bar top, and the innkeeper halted his cleaning, eyes gleaming with greed.

"I hope this pays for the room, some food, and overlooking my companion's familiar," Lorkan said.

The innkeeper swiped the money and shoved it deep into his pockets. "Ah, that'll do. Up the stairs, third room on the right. I'll have food left outside the door soon."

He pushed a key towards Lorkan, but his arms locked at his sides. Was he strong enough to endure this? One room. One bed. With *Blair.*

But she didn't seem bothered by the prospect. She grabbed the key and strutted up the steps two at a time. Lorkan sprinted to keep up. Blair didn't glance back as she entered the room. On heavy feet, Lorkan followed.

With wet hair, sodden cloak, and racing heart, her beautiful scent looped around his senses like a hypnotizing vine, and Lorkan let the sweet tendrils sink into him.

She headed straight for the laden fireplace, busying herself with the flint. Cold gripped the room, and her teeth chattered. Loud. Blaring. An unavoidable reminder of how small the space was, and because Lorkan hated his vampyrism and how he *felt* towards Blair, he lashed out.

"I had it handled down there. You didn't need to point out Rook was your familiar. He's a raven, Blair. It gives away who you are."

She rolled her eyes. "It's the middle of a blizzard. Witches . . . f-f-freak out over an inch of snow. They aren't venturing through this to get to me."

"Moons, I hope so." For the third time, he assessed her thin layers. "Did you not think to pack a more fitting cloak for the Vadon Mountains?"

Blair stiffened. She didn't bother looking when she said, "It's all I had."

"Hard to believe," Lorkan said. "You're one of the highest-regarded scholars in all of Nūa—"

"*Was*," Blair snapped.

Lorkan suddenly felt like an ass. *Because you are,* he thought.

But perhaps that's what he needed to be. It hid his feelings that had never faded for Blair, ones he had to avoid more than his wretched secret. He'd play the villain, and maybe she'd avoid *him* once they reached Vísdómr, making his plan all that much easier.

"Right, the Nūa papers have deemed you a rebel. How could I forget?"

Blair seethed, chest heaving. "That isn't true, and you know it."

"I don't know you at all, actually." His words came out smooth, *easy*. "A lot of time has passed since we last saw one another."

She clenched her fists at her sides. "Seems time made you a prick."

"Keen of you to notice." Lorkan winked.

Blair didn't respond, busying herself again with the flint. Yet, it fumbled from her shaking hands. She sank to her knees, and her teeth clattered worse than before.

Lorkan rushed to her side without thinking and cursed under his breath. Her usual rosy lips had turned a shade closer to blue. Shivers racked through Blair's body, she risked chipping a tooth.

"Stars above, Blair, you're hypothermic," he whispered.

"What?" She shot him a glare. "I'm fine."

Blair was anything but. Her clothes, or lack of, were soaked from the snow storm, and without a fire, they were stiff with frost. Her curls had lost their bounce, rigid from ice clumps. Lorkan clamped his eyes shut, listening to her heart. It beat at an alarmingly slow pace.

"Fuck." His hands itched to reach for her, but instead, Lorkan grabbed the flint, starting on the fire. A few swipes and embers caught onto the dry tuft of wool underneath wooden logs. Lorkan bent lower on his hands and knees, blowing into the flame and feeding it air. Soon, it crackled to life, but its heat was minimal compared to what Blair needed.

"Can you tap into your magic? You need to heal from the cold, Blair."

"I . . ." She winced. "I can't. The *danu* . . . we traveled far . . . and my . . . s-s-stores are depleted." Her eyelids shuttered closed.

Lorkan snatched her hands—*moons*, they were as cold as stone, her fingertips almost purple. He rubbed them between his, and perhaps she was so unwell, Blair didn't notice or care.

His next comment, though, snapped her from her haze. "You need to undress."

"Absolutely not."

Lorkan sighed, burrowing his eyes into her hers. "Your clothes are wet. If you don't, you risk getting sick or worse."

Blair's onyx eyes darkened. "This wouldn't have happened if you'd planned better."

Lorkan seethed. He could throw out the fact that if they'd traveled straight to Fika, this wouldn't have happened either, but he didn't wish to be that harsh, not when the mention of the place hurt them both.

"Says the witch with clothes fit for an outing in the city, not a journey through the Vadon Mountains. At least shed your cloak."

"It's all I had!" Blair shouted, snatching her hands from his and unclasping her cloak. Lorkan grabbed it draped it over the closest chair, hoping it'd dry by morning.

Blair reaching for her boots next. Yet, her fingers remained crooked and unmoving, unable to grasp hold of the laces.

Rook landed between them, nipping at Lorkan's own fingers and hopping between Blair, still struggling in her wet trousers and high-neck blouse, and a too still Lorkan. His stomach twisted into knots. The raven's message was clear.

"Gods, meddling bird," he sighed, scooting closer to Blair. "You need to let me help."

The love of his life stilled, but revulsion didn't glint in her eyes. Instead, apprehension mixed with disbelief. "No."

Lorkan exhaled. He wasn't the sort of male who'd touch without permission, even in a time like this. "Please, Blair. It is only to get you warm, nothing more."

Blair, albeit shivering, positioned her boot ahead of him. "Alright."

Lorkan started with the laces, pulling them loose and then eased her feet, wet and cold to the touch, free of the ruined leather. He peeled her soaked socks off next, and positioned Blair closer to the fire. Her legs tangled with his.

Another shudder racked through Blair, and she managed to unfasten the button of her trousers, but the heavy, wet suede clung to her thighs.

Lorkan swallowed. "May I?"

Crimson bloomed across Blair's cheeks. "Blasted books," she cursed and relented, nodding for him to proceed.

Lorkan, careful to touch her pants and *only* her pants, tugged them inch after inch down her legs. Over the slope of her strong thighs and past her knees. His fingers might not have brushed her beautiful skin, but the sight of under the glowing fire had Lorkan's blood heating and his inner wolf rising to the surface.

Get a grip, he roared to himself. *She's freezing, for moon's sake.*

He added her trousers to dry alongside her cloak, trying to dismiss the image of Blair's bare legs from his thoughts, but by the time he turned back around, she'd pulled free of her blouse. It landed on the rickety wooden floors with a loud *splat*, rooting Lorkan in place.

Near naked, Blair sat by the fire with breasts peaked underneath a lacy bralette—

"Stop s-s-staring," she muttered. "Not like you haven't seen it all before." She held up a hand. "My undergarments are staying. I guarantee you they're dry."

Lorkan's jaw ticked, and he hurried to the bed, blinked away every horrible, wretched thought of Blair and how very, very, very wrong she was. Yes, they'd had their fair share of teenage exploring. Clothes *had* come off. He'd had the privilege of seeing her naked before, but Blair's body was more a wonder all these years later, gifted by womanhood.

He couldn't help staring at her fuller breasts, maddening hips, or slender legs he craved to kiss from thigh to toe.

Fate was indeed a cruel, sadistic bitch, to place what he so craved, dreamt of late at night, in a small room with the snow berating the village. But he couldn't have her. No matter how badly, because physical entanglements led to hunger of an entirely different kind. He'd explored with lovers before, those like him, and he couldn't stomach revealing his vampyrism

Focus. Lorkan exhaled through his nose. *Get her warm.*

He grabbed hold of the blanket from the supposedly large bed fit for two and pulled it free.

Lorkan moved back to the fireplace, sitting behind Blair.

"Come here," he whispered.

"You c-c-can't be serious," she wheezed.

"Blair."

She stiffened at his unbending tone and scooted back into his hold. She sat wedged between his legs and arms, and Lorkan wrapped the blanket around them both. Huddled together and sitting in silence aside from the delicate snowfall and crackling fire, they found warmth entangled with one another.

Soon, Blair fell asleep in Lorkan's arms, and one of the dreams he'd had all these years, came true, and the curse didn't rear its nasty head once during the night.

CHAPTER THIRTY-THREE

BLAIR

BLAIR WOKE TO FIND the fire smoke and ash, the flames long gone. Yet, warmth encompassed her along with a considerable weight hugging her middle.

She blinked. *Blasted books*, that weight belonged to an arm.

Not just any arm. *Lorkan's*. It's owner smelled of smoke and moss, breathing evenly as he held her to his chest. To make matters worse, as if that were possible, his hand palmed her bare stomach.

Right. She'd undressed out of her soaked clothes the night before. They must've fallen asleep by the fire together.

Despite the jarring realization Lorkan held her, she found comfort in his nearness. How large he was compared to her, holding her close. But they had a prophecy to decipher, and Blair couldn't afford to lean into the desire coursing through her body.

She fidgeted, hoping to peel his arm free—

Blair froze. What in the Goddess was that pressing against her backside?

Awareness jolted through her like she was riddled with bone-deep cold all over again. She'd been wrong earlier. Things could certainly get worse. Because that was no dagger. No book. No anything but Lorkan's—rather large—manhood, hard and ready.

Blair moved ever so slightly to put room between her and Lorkan, but he woke. He stiffened behind her and an awkward stillness brimmed in the air.

Finally, Lorkan cursed, jerking backward.

Blair rolled forward with the blanket, and behind her, Lorkan fidgeted with his pants. After last night, it was his turn for a blush to creep across his cheeks.

Perhaps it was hunger, tiredness, or genuine amusement, but Blair giggled.

Lorkan seethed. "It's an entirely natural morning phenomenon."

Blair snorted. "Right. Goddess forbid you're caught being attracted to me."

He pinched the bridge of his nose. "That is not—*moons*, I just didn't want to make you feel uncomfortable."

Blair rose and found her clothes stiff but at least dry. "I've had a man's length rub against me before, Lorkan. I find it quite comfortable."

Lorkan stewed, his jaw clenching so tight, Blair feared he'd break a tooth.

"Don't suppose we should head for the ferry?" she pulled on her clothes and fastened her cloak.

Rook appeared at the window just as Lorkan opened it.

"I'm afraid the only way of travel we're using today is by way of *danu*."

No wind or flurries hung in the air, but stillness did. Blair peeked her head out, inspecting the village blanketed under six feet of snow. It towered over most establishments, blocking windows and doors. Ahead, the river didn't move, ice hardened from bank to bank.

"Blasted books," she hissed.

"We'll have to go to Fika," Lorkan said.

Blair fisted her hands at her sides. No. She refused to go there, especially after last night. The way Lorkan had cared for her. Held her. Blair's traitorous heart skipped a beat, her skin growing warm at the memory.

"There has to be another—"

Lorkan held up his hand, silencing her.

Blair saw red, marching towards him. "Lets get one thing straight: I don't take orders from you—"

In two long strides, Lorkan was upon her, hand clasped over her mouth. His golden eyes landed on the door. He listened. *Seethed.*

Blair sent out her magic and detected the magic of half a dozen others just beyond the door.

"*Lorkan—*"

But it was too late to warn him. The door burst open, and they flew across the room. Blair landed with a harsh thud, pain jarring through her head. She cursed, kneading her temple as she blinked her sights back into focus. A ringing pierced her ears, and she barely registered Lorkan's rushed words.

"Get up," he said. "We need to leave."

Blasted books, this bossy and arrogant werewolf.

"I'm *trying!*" she shouted.

Rook cawed endlessly above them. The green smoke ahead dissipated. Debris and shattered glass littered the room. Six Guards stood at the ready. Weapons in hand. Hands splayed with magic.

"You don't need to be ruinin' my inn! You hear me!" the innkeeper called from behind.

"Blair Carson, you're under arrest!" a Guard roared.

Fuck that, Blair thought instantly. She'd not spent a second in Tùir, not when she had every intention of figuring out how to break the curse.

Blair threw up her hand, sending a wave of wind through the room, knocking the Guards and innkeeper back into the adjacent wall. She and Lorkan rushed to the shattered window. Snow blanketed the street below.

"We have to jump," Blair shouted, grasping Lorkan's hand.

A shudder ran up her arm, but she ignored it.

"Take us to Fika."

Blair whirled, ire scorching through. "Stop telling me what to do!"

"*Stars above,* Fika or prison, Blair, which is it?" Lorkan shouted over the wind.

"Blasted books, let me think!"

"There isn't any time!"

But that's all Blair wanted. *Time.* A moment. The ability to grasp her newfound reality. Why was it so difficult to accept? Did the werewolf at her side have anything to do with it? Was she too frightened of stepping off that path, even if she'd been tasked with this venture?

Behind them, the Guards groaned and rose, readying to attack again.

"*Blair!*" Lorkan's growled.

Panic gripped Blair like shackles dangling at each of her limbs, and she conjured a *danu* to the first place that came to mind. A foolish, risky move, but Blair had some inkling of a plan.

Maybe.

Winds whirled above the snow-covered street. Reality shimmered, and a new street, cobblestones sleek with rain, awaited them. Rook dove through Blair's *danu* first, and together, Blair and Lorkan jumped after.

The impact broke their clasped hands apart. Blair rolled onto the familiar street, more pain pulsing around her head.

Above, her *danu* closed, shutting out the cries of the Guards left behind.

Lorkan blinked. Stars shone through the cloudless night sky. Leaves rustled on shaky branches. Autumn sat in the air, not winter.

"Blair, where are we?" Lorkan asked, wiping dirt from his shirt.

His voice came far away, and warmth coated Blair's lips. She touched them with the pads of her fingers, wiping away crimson. Goddess, she'd given herself a bloody nose.

She'd drawn up to much magic. She wavered foot to foot as she tried to stand. Her knees rebelled and gave out. Lorkan launched forward, catching her in his arms as she collapsed from exhaustion.

White dots filtered across her vision, blocking out his beautiful face.

Lorkan searched wildly. Up and down the street.

"*35, 36, 37* . . ." He rattled off the numbered homes like he knew them. His stare widened at the wooden bones that lay in a crumbled heap ahead of them, number *38* missing.

"What have you done?" he rasped.

For they'd not traveled to Fika.

Blair had created a *danu* to Nūa, the city of witches.

Chapter Thirty-Four

"Heave!" Eldrick called.

His alpha baritone buzzed through his body as he led the rebuilding efforts after Riven's attack. Sweat matted his brow as he lifted a wooden stake to repair the palisade wall. Bétar stood on the other side while ahead, other pack members pulled a rope to help hoist it into the air. They worked as a team—a *pack*—to ease the last stake left of the southern gate.

It sank with a triumphant *thunk*.

A few cheers resounded behind them, and Bétar grasped his shoulder. "That'll do, alpha."

The title conjured an array of feelings, too many for Eldrick to count, but a hollowness spread in the pit of his belly. He'd leaned into the infectious energy these last days, grasping onto the sense of purpose pulsing around him and ignoring the creeping sensation that he'd misplaced something but couldn't pinpoint what.

Without the rest of the Gray Fenris, his parents, or brothers, an emptiness swallowed the village, and of course, Tovi had left, too. She was the last thought Eldrick had before he fell asleep and the first when he woke, but then the day's tasks occupied his mind, and he busied himself in his new title. He had an Earl vote to win, but he couldn't leave to hold a council with the other alphas until Drengr Village was equipped to face another attack if vampyrs or demons returned.

"What of the new posts?" Eldrick asked.

He instructed a crew to build two hidden tree houses outside the village, doubling the watch so no one would ambush them again. He'd also order pack members to only leave the village in groups of three, and scouting parties had grown from three to five.

"They're well underway—done by the week's end," Bétar said.

"Good." Eldrick nodded. He grabbed Lucy as she passed and dropped a heavy pouch into her muddy hand. "Feed those who worked today. That should cover it."

Lucy weighed the coin. "*Moons*, it more than does, Eldrick."

"Throw in a pint or two, then."

The Shield-maiden's owner winked. "Ah, that I'll do."

Eldrick turned to thanking his pack mates for their efforts. He strategized with a few warriors on additions to the Wall and tidied the remaining mess. Soon, everyone parted ways for the night with plans in place to return at sunrise the next morning. Bétar headed home, and Eldrick headed towards Lār, intent on washing before he met with his friend. They planned to discuss his next course of action to secure the Earl vote. He'd have to meet with the alphas, one by one, and he witnessed his village come alive as he mulled over ideas.

Cottages glowed onto the streets. Between the dark indigo and warm orange, the sights and colors of home did wonders for Eldrick's tired muscles. The smithy's hearth roared, and his hammer clanged. The butcher handed out rations from the latest hunt. The baker's doors were closed and the chimney stack lifeless, but warm wheat still hung in the air. Children, some shifted into pups, giggled as their parents tried to wrangle them inside. Hoots and hollers echoed in the warrior's barracks, song and games adding to the chorus of cheer.

Hope was on the rise in Eldrick's home.

He turned a corner, and the hair on the back of his neck rose. His wolf rose to the surface—Eldrick was being followed. He sniffed and detected a werewolf, but not one from his pack. Lār's stairs ascended ten yards away, but Eldrick's curiosity got the best of him. He quickened his gait—the boots behind him quickened—and turned a corner last-minute. He fell flush against a building, holding his breath, and as the werewolf turned the corner, too, he launched.

Eldrick grasped a fistful of the werewolf's tunic and shoved him up against the adjacent wall.

"Stars above, wait!" Sam Johannes threw up his hands in surrender, panting.

Eldrick loosened his hold, but didn't let go. "Why are you following me?"

The young werewolf's eyes darted down the village streets, apprehension falling off him in waves.

"Did your father put you up to this?" he growled.

Sam's eyes widened. "No. I wasn't *following* following you but seeking you out to . . . talk."

Eldrick narrowed his gaze, releasing Sam with a slight shove. "Talk then."

"Not here."

"Why?"

Sam's voice dropped to a whisper. "Because if my sister or father discover I'm talking with you, I'm fucked."

Sam straightened out his tunic, and Eldrick stiffened. Bruises on the werewolf's chest, neck, and wrists.

"How the hel—"

"I'd rather not talk about it," Sam hissed. "Please."

Eldrick's jaw pulsed. He knew Bjorn was an ass, but the implication that he *beat* his son made his character far worse than he thought. But he wouldn't let his frustration out on Sam, and said nothing, respecting his privacy.

"Alright. Follow me. I have somewhere we can go."

Bétar and Yennifer's home sat at the center of the residential street, clay front wedged between two wooden cottages. Whitewashed with a fresh set of shingles, the door had been painted a glacier blue, *like my mate's eyes*, Bétar had said.

Eldrick knocked, and moments later, the door burst open. Bétar stood there with not a single leather or strap of armor on him, and the burly werewolf appeared relaxed in a simple set of britches and tunic, freshly showered and beard trimmed.

"Wasn't expecting you for another hour—" Bétar paused at the sight of Sam, eyes narrowing.

"He needs to talk. Somewhere private," Eldrick said.

"I see." Bétar opened the door wider. "Come in."

A hearth crackled in the kitchen, and a skillet popover steamed on the counter. Glazed short rib surrounded by roasted rutabaga rested next to it.

"Is there any chance Sam can join us for dinner?" Eldrick asked, giving Bétar a pointed look.

"Aye, of course." Bétar didn't miss a beat, setting the table for three. "Conversations are better over a meal."

Eldrick ushered Sam into a chair and sat across from him. "Excuse the two-against-one. Honestly, I'm not sure I can trust you yet."

Sam laughed. "I don't blame you. My father's a prick."

Eldrick crossed his arms and leaned back in his chair, assessing any signs of a lie in Sam, but found his words truthful and body language relaxed.

"For what it's worth"—Sam paused—"I didn't agree with the decree, but I'm glad you ascended. It gives the Drengrs a fighting chance at the Earl vote. No offense to your father, of course."

Eldrick's lips twitched into a smile. "I doubt he'd take any. He knew where he stood among the other alphas. What did you want to discuss?"

Bétar joined them and pushed the food towards Sam, gesturing for him to start. The young werewolf plated his food, but barely touched it as he spoke.

"My father hates vampyrs," he said.

Bétar snorted. "That's a revelation."

Sam's expression turned serious. "But he hates the Drengr name more."

Eldrick dished himself the meat and vegetables, releasing a heavy breath. "Hate is a strong word."

"It's the truth. Finton was his brother, you know. He was Earl during the first third born union and continued to lead vampyrs a century after my uncle's death. He's never forgotten the day when your father, a werewolf a fraction of his age, took the title from him. This isn't about vampyrs versus werewolves or defeating the darkness, though he'll easily spin it as such. It's about power. There's no way in hel he's going to let you, an alpha even younger, win. He'll fight dirty, and you need to be prepared."

Eldrick's wolf wrestled inside his blood. He sat back in his chair, appetite gone. Aramis had led with fairness and had taught Eldrick that lesson in leadership. He wasn't sure how to fight dirty and was equally certain he didn't care to.

"There are seven votes, and you must have four to win," Sam said. "You'll vote for yourself, as will my father, which leaves five alphas to convince. Skau is a lost cause."

Eldrick grunted, shifting in his seat. He'd met the alpha from the pack farthest north, a male hardened from his time so close to the Void.

"Skau should want the curse broken more than anyone," Eldrick said.

"My father doesn't have friends, but Skau is the closest thing. More than an ally. For three centuries. The Johannes have also helped the Skau pack the most in the last years, and they owe my father their vote. Thorn is tricky, but most likely a no. My father has had his eye on Thorn's land—"

"Werewolves haven't fought for land in centuries," Eldrick said. "Pack land is pack land."

Bétar nodded his agreement.

Sam sighed. "I told you: My father will fight dirty. He threatened Thorn over the land to sign the decree, and he'll hold Thorn's vote over his head at the Earl vote, too."

Eldrick reared straighter. "But then there's a chance I can sway him, if he didn't want to sign it."

"Even if there's a chance you'll win, he can't afford to piss my father off."

"But if I become Earl, Bjorn will answer to me, and I'll protect Thorn."

"Would you take that chance and jeopardize your pack's territory on a whim that a thirty-year-old recently ascended will win the vote against Alpha Johannes?"

Frustration leaked from Eldrick, and his knuckles popped as he tightened his hand.

Bétar whistled. "Way to put it lightly, Sam. Nicely done."

Eldrick cursed. "But he's right. On paper, Bjorn is the better vote, and as it stands, he has three votes—his own, Thorn, and Skau."

Sam nodded. "Exactly."

Bétar crossed his arms and leaned on the table and eyed Sam, both wary and impressed. "How do you know all of this?"

Sam shrugged. "My father drags me to his meetings, and while he thinks I tune out and don't care, I *listen*. You have one advantage—the southern packs. Alland and Lindström will vote together, and Drabek has their ear. She was the loudest voice against my father for the decree."

Thorn and Drabek are wary of the future.

Aramis had said that days ago, and Eldrick's reeling mind snagged on the information.

"Why did she sign it?" he asked.

Sam rolled roasted rutabaga across his plate. "My father got to her last, strategically. It was five against one at that point, and if she didn't, she lost her Earl vote."

Bétar hummed. "Is she a guaranteed Drengr vote, then?"

"I think so, and Alland and Lindström will follow her lead. You have one advantage, Eldrick. The Drengrs sit between the three packs to the north—Skau, Johannes, and Thorn—and the three packs to the south—Drabek, Alland, and Lindström. My father controls the north . . ."

Realization spread through Eldrick. "But that's three votes, while if I win the south, that's *four* including mine."

"Precisely," Sam said. "My suggestion? Visit Drabek first. She has the balls to stand up to Bjorn."

"Perhaps her lack of balls makes her stronger than the rest of the alphas," Bétar said.

Sam laughed. "I suppose you're right. Her wife is fierce, too. They'll be helpful allies in the coming weeks. The sooner you meet with them, the better."

"Sounds like a fine plan to me," Bétar said.

Eldrick nodded, forcing a small smile. "Indeed. Thank you, Sam, for not following me."

Sam rubbed the back of his neck. "I owe you my life, to be honest. You all saved me in Drystan, and I'll not easily forget your honor and duty."

Duty.

The word crept up Eldrick's spine like a pesky critter. He flexed his hand, where the alpha tattoo shimmered. The onset of a headache bloomed through his whirling mind. Sam had offered valuable information, and he felt indebted to the young werewolf who'd risked himself to seek him out, but his fingers itched, craving the feel of an axe in his hand, to experience the leather molding under his grip. He tasted battle on his tongue, and out of his peripherals, the mirage of a certain white-haired queen fighting at his side. His wolf howled at the thought, like his inner beast yearned for that and not *this.*

Discussions. Words. *Politics.*

He was back in his office before he set out for Drystan, discussing the missing werewolves with Claus. It felt like a different life, a different him. He'd wished for the alpha title like a starving man begged for water, and yet, now that he had it, it was like wearing a shoe two sizes too small. Equally uncomfortable as unfitting.

But his place was here, even if he didn't *like* it. Fate had presented this path since his first breath, and with his parents' absence, he understood sacrifice, inhaled it like his blood needed it to push forward. He'd trained for this. His father believed in him enough. No, it wasn't a battlefield and his heart ached with loneliness, but it was a part of the war to come.

But what sort of alpha did he want to be? Eldrick's inner wolf grunted, agreement flushing through him. Yes, he had a duty and a vote to win, but Eldrick refused to lose himself in this game. He'd not stoop to Bjorn's level—he doubted his father would respect him if he did, too.

He sighed, spying the bruises near Sam's neck again, like someone had gripped the young werewolf's throat and squeezed. His insides twisted while his wolf bared its teeth. He chose his next words carefully. "If you want to leave the Johannes Pack, there is a place for you here, Sam. I could use a werewolf as observant."

Bétar nudged Eldrick's shoulder. "Aye, don't poach the young talent. I have a team I need to rebuild, ya know."

Sam blinked. Swallowed. Shifted in his seat. "That offer means more than you know, but . . . I have someone at home who needs me."

"Who?"

Sam rose from his seat. "My younger brother. He's a scholar and rather brilliant at botany and less inclined to hold a weapon."

"Why does that matter for a second born?" Bétar asked.

The hair on the back of Eldrick's neck rose. "Because all Johannes know how to wield a blade."

Sam's jaw hardened. "I have my bruises because I protect my brother, and I'd rather it be me than him. I'm sure as one with brothers, you know what it's like?"

The hearth crackled, and Eldrick huffed, his chest tightening at the thought of Lorkan and Kade. He gave Sam a curt nod. "I do."

Sam headed to the door. "I appreciate you hearing me out, but if my sister notices I've been gone longer than an hour, my journey home will be hel."

Eldrick rose with him and shook the young werewolf's hand, grasping it with meaningful force. "I mean it—there's a place in the Drengr Pack for you *and* your brother if you need."

"Thank you," Sam whispered, and a glint shone in his eyes. "I'll remember."

He headed for the door, but as he laid his hand on the doorknob, Bétar cleared his throat.

"How far would your father go to win the Earl vote?" the warrior asked.

"He'd kill for it," Sam said without hesitation.

With that, he left, leaving Eldrick rooted to the stone, uncertain if he could play this game at all.

CHAPTER THIRTY-FIVE

I N THE LATE WINTER months, the sea's rains drenched the partying city, Morrow, in endless puddles. The gaps between cobblestones bubbled with ocean sludge, the shingles on the roof glistened under the gray, wispy clouds, and seagulls' caws mingled with the lazy lull of midday waves. Winds blustered from the Sapphire Sea, and despite their chill, a thickness hung in the air. Humid with sweat, salt and—

"This town smells like sex," Yennifer said next to her, nose wrinkling.

Tovi tried to laugh, but limbs tingled with nerves—she, Yen, and Evelyn weaved through the town revelers on their way to meet with Captain Flynn Seaver. She'd received a letter from him with a time and place, nothing more, nothing less. Though she'd written to the pirate to help with the captured werewolves months ago, she'd not *seen* Flynn in decades.

Ahead, a green sign swung on the coastal breeze, the tavern's name painted in a dark purple to contrast—The Muckie. A sea monster of some kind was etched onto the sign, slumbering like a coiled snake. Algae and mussels clung to the bottom stairs, still wet from high tide. The weathered wood groaned as Tovi and the others ascended up.

Evelyn intercepted Tovi's path before she walked through the entrance. "How exactly do you know Flynn?"

Tovi paused, debate hovering over her tongue.

"My guess is a past lover." Yen raised an all-knowing brow.

Evelyn's brows pinched, and Tovi sighed. There was no sense in lying, and she'd given up the habit of keeping up secrets. "Alright. Fine. Flynn and I were once involved *romantically*. But he betrayed my trust and it ended as swiftly as it began. Of course, Flynn hadn't meant to hurt me, he just . . . tried to protect me. In the end, I forgave him, but we haven't seen one in another in long time. Its rumored he still has feelings for me."

Evelyn shook her head. "I don't understand. If you forgave him, why not give him a second chance?"

Sadness spread through Tovi's chest. "Because once I realized I could live without him, I knew he wasn't the one."

Tovi stepped around her friend and entered the Muckie. Inside, the establishment buzzed with conversation. Fire flickered inside a hearth constructed from coral instead of stones. Witches dressed in teal dresses that resembled scales carried trays filled with drinks garnished with fruits and herbs.

Evelyn nodded towards the bar, empty aside from the female attending it. Witch, vampyr, or human, Tovi didn't have the slightest idea at this distance.

The bartender braced her hands on the bar top, revealing tattoos reaching from elbow to wrists. "What can I get you ladies?"

"We'll have the Tempest Tonic," Tovi said.

It wasn't *actually* the name of a drink, but a password that Flynn had detailed in his missive.

The bartender's eyes widened a fraction. "Salted rim or not?"

Ah, why hadn't Tovi anticipated another question that Flynn *hadn't* shared the answer for? To make her think. To make her work for it. To make sure the letter hadn't landed in the wrong hands.

Evelyn's brows furrowed. "What does that mean?"

"It's a riddle of sorts, something only I would know." Tovi rattled through her memory, battling annoyance. *Bloody hel.*

"I'd guess salt," Evelyn whispered. "Right? He's a pirate after all."

Tovi nibbled her bottom lip. "It's more than that—"

Salt always.

The pads of Tovi's fingers tingled from the distant memory of brushing her fingers over words etched into Flynn's main ship—in a place only someone close to him would've seen.

Her chest tightened, making it hard to breathed as she said, "Salt always."

The bartender smiled, flashing a fang. "Follow me."

Tension bristled as they followed the female vampyr out of the main floor and down the hallway painted black and lined with candles molded into the shape of skulls. At the end, a red door stretched from ceiling to floor, with a single brass doorknob positioned at the center. The vampyr used both hands to turn it, unseen gears clanking out of place. It eased open by itself, sighing as it revealed the inside of the parlor, gaslight lanterns lining wooden bookshelves.

"The Captain's waiting for you, my queen." She bowed and hurried off, leaving Tovi speechless.

"You're going to have to get used to hearing that," Yennifer whispered.

"She's right," Evelyn said. "We can't go into negotiations with you looking stunned."

Tovi shuddered. "I don't look stunned."

Evelyn's brows shot upward. "I might have to pick your mouth off the floor."

"You're ridiculous."

"And you're a queen."

Tovi waved a hand in the air. "I'm aware."

Evelyn grabbed her hand, giving it a gentle squeeze. "As well as my best friend, and—"

"Tovi."

Flynn appeared in the doorway, looking as if he had just stepped off his ship moments ago. His dark, wind-swept hair framed his face, while stubble lined his jaw. His dark eyes, the same smoky gray of the sea he sailed on, brightened at the sight of her.

Evelyn released her hand, and Tovi didn't glance at her friends as she entered Flynn's parlor. Like a queen. Shoulders back. Hands clasped ahead of her. With a diplomatic smile plastered across her face.

"Flynn, it's good to see you."

He nodded, flashing his signature, dashing smile. Once, that smile had the power to buckle Tovi's knees, but she stood there and felt *nothing*. Her stomach swam with butterflies, anticipation tightening her smile as she readied to convince a pirate to play politics.

"You haven't aged a day." He winked and strode over to the table with a decanter full of an amber liquid. "Ah, there's the famous Daughter of the Goddess." His slate eyes skimmed over Yennifer. "And a werewolf warrior. You brought quite the entourage, Tovi."

"I detailed in my letter that the request was on behalf of Evelyn—felt foolish not to bring her. Do you have wine?"

Flynn swirled his rum. "Already on the table for you."

Evelyn's stare pierced through Tovi's back. She ignored her, following Flynn towards the seating area. He lounged on the crescent leather chair, throwing his arm across the back. Tovi paid him no mind, snatching up her glass of burgundy wine, and headed for the one window on the north wall.

Past the velvet curtains, she peeked out and soaked in the bay's view. The Void's gray taunted her with the choices awaiting her on the horizon.

"I never thought I'd see the day when a vampyr, werewolf, and witch walked into a room as friends. Tell me, how did you manage that feat?" Flynn asked.

Tovi had to admit, Flynn was a handsome male, but against the green of his leather couch, the color reminded her of someone else—a werewolf alpha tucked in the Vadon Mountains across the continent. Tovi sipped her wine, allowing the ripe fruit to burn her throat and bring her back to the present. She'd left Eldrick behind for a reason—all to focus on what was best for her people. The wine burned worse during her second sip, as if it'd become laced with the lies and emotions she'd let fester.

There was a time when Tovi had admired her father, and back then, she'd studied his movements in meetings—how he kept his opponent on edge by moving about, standing so he remained the imposing figure in the room, and wearing a mask that appeared disinterested or bored. Her father always carried an air that he had somewhere more important to be. At first, Tovi had studied him with awe, but it grew apparent her father was pretending—a humble farmer turned monarch thanks to the snap of the Goddess's fingers. He hid his fears behind a mask, and Tovi witnessed, decade after decade, not the seed of experience sprouting into confidence, but the mask itself taking root.

If one pretended for too long, it wasn't others they fooled, but themselves as well. He donned the mask with his children and wife, and suddenly it wasn't a mask at all, but simply the king he was—above others. With Flynn at her back, remnants of the curse ahead, and the unknowns peppering the air, it felt easier to don the same mask as her father.

"Tovi helped break me out of Drystan Castle," Evelyn said, snapping Tovi back to the present.

"The rumors are true then; you *were* the prince's captive," Flynn drawled, his smile loud on his lips.

Tovi whirled, Flynn's choice of words catching her off guard. *Prince.* Had his choice of words been bait and she'd fallen for it? The urge to remain guarded prickled across her skin. She'd used secrets as armor before, so why not use the act of pretending? Temptation tasted like leather and blackberries on her tongue, yet Tovi had no interest in letting her subjects feel *little*.

Tovi could stand by the window, far from Flynn, and use the distance as a shield and pretend she didn't care, or she could be authentic, *herself*. Even if Flynn was bluffing, she could play the game too, but not like her father once did.

She waltzed over to the large arm and sat across from Flynn, relaxed and conversational—the ghost of her mother hissed in the back of her mind, demanding she sit straighter, more ladylike. Whatever the *bloody hel* that meant.

This was her. Wine in hand, heart at ease, friends by her side.

"She indeed was. What other rumors have you heard?" she asked.

Flynn's shoulders relaxed a fraction, mirroring her own posture. He sat back, pressing into the leather of the coach. "That you've gained allies in Sorin, the werewolves." His gaze flitted over Evelyn and then back to Tovi. "As well as witches. But other rumors suggest you've lost the werewolves altogether after your brother attacked. It makes me even more curious why you're here."

"I'm here on behalf of Evelyn." Tovi inclined her head towards her friend. "She needs a ship."

Flynn narrowed his eyes. "What for?"

Evelyn retrieved a map from under her cloak and spread it across the oak-stump console table between them all. The coastline of Sorin ran up the left side, while a majority of the map detailed the Sapphire Sea, its currents and tides all the way to Torren's mirroring shore on the right. Evelyn jabbed a finger at the northern fjords.

"We need you to take us here," she said.

Flynn stared at the spot for a tense moment, then eyed them. "Whatever for? That is the sea."

"Evelyn needs to retrieve something from the bottom," Tovi said.

Flynn laughed, then stopped short. "So the rumors are true. Your witchy friend here has no magic." The air in the room shifted. "Ah, yes. Whispers that she lost it travel on the wind. Little hard to fulfill that so-called prophecy without it, don't you think?"

"That's why Evelyn needs your help," Tovi said. "Her lost necklace is a key item in the spell to get her magic back."

"*A necklace?*" Flynn hissed. "What is your plan? Dive for it? Far off the coast, the sea is miles deep."

"We'll retrieve it with magic," Evelyn said, expression adamant. "All we need is to get in the general area of where it may be."

"While bracing the fog and mists of the Void, along with all the monsters lingering near the darkness," Flynn said. "Have either of you faced a sea demon before? They're not *madras*. They're far worse, three times the biggest ship here at port."

Yen smirked, crossing her arms. "Maybe the job is too risky for you, Captain Flynn."

He scoffed, shoulders shaking. "I'm glad to see you've found friends fit for your company, Tovi. I like them, but not enough to risk my crews' lives."

"How about setting them free of the Blood Curse?"

"Not my problem, not my concern." Flynn downed the last of his rum. "But I appreciate you confirming these rumors. What a delightful surprise."

Yen leaned forward. "If this information becomes, as you called it, a whisper on the wind, I'll plant an arrow in your pirate heart."

"Bloody hel, *wolves.*" Flynn rolled his eyes. "Look, I'll not utter a word about this, but I can't help, Tovi. My ships aren't available for this job."

"Alright, if not for honor, what about for money?" Evelyn asked. "We can pay you whatever sum—"

"No." Flynn fell back into the love seat, the arrogant bastard.

Heat flushed through Tovi, but she refused to let it rise too far and jeopardize their time with Flynn. Her father would yell, her mother would throw petty words, and as tempting as lashing out was, she didn't want to make the same mistake as her parents.

She set her wine down and locked eyes with Flynn. "What about for a friend?"

"We haven't seen each other for ninety years. I'd hardly call us friends."

"Fine." Tovi pulled out a folded cloth and placed it atop the map, throwing it open and revealing a ring with one small gem at the center.

A bloodstone granting Flynn the ability to walk in sunlight.

Flynn eyed the ring with such intensity, black swam in his eyes like dissipating smoke, and a mighty—perhaps centuries-old—anger brimmed under the pirate's skin. It wafted like a surge, prickling the air with static. Yen reached for her dagger, but Tovi shook her head once in a silent command. *Don't.* It was a risk, showing Flynn what he'd desperately wanted for so long. Only the royal family could give the ability to walk in sunlight, a status Tovi had denied Flynn silently for years—she'd forgiven him, yes, but she'd also not trusted him enough to grant him that freedom.

Evelyn tensed in her seat, the static in the air only worsening as Flynn grew stiller and stiller. Nothing else moved, but his gaze snapped to hers.

"Can I speak with Tovi for a moment alone?" he breathed, chest rising.

"Do you think us mad?" Yennifer asked.

"Let me make myself *very* clear: I'd never hurt her, you have my word." Flynn snatched the ring off the table, marched over to the wall lined with windows and opened a concealed door that led to a balcony outside.

The salty winds barreled into the parlor, and Tovi ignored the prickling stares of her friends. She had no other choice, did she? They needed Flynn to help Evelyn with his ship, but what rooted Tovi to the reading chair was not the anticipation of that argument, but *what* he'd ask for in return.

"Tovi." A warning wavered in Evelyn's tone, her gray stare hard.

"It's alright." Tovi sighed, not believing her own words. "Stay here."

She set her shoulders back and met Flynn at the door. Perhaps she'd not pretended earlier, but now, she refused to let him see her fear, to taste it in the air as it mixed with Morrow's brine.

The door behind them clicked shut, and it was as if the decades between them ballooned on the balcony, and the fresh winds weren't enough.

Tovi gripped the balcony's railing for balance. In the distance, waves rolled more white than blue, the sea's temperament wild, much like her thumping heart. Flynn braced the banister with his arms wide. For a moment, it was their silence, the winds, the distant roar of the waves, and the jolly tunes of the party town.

"I don't want a bloodstone, Tovi." Flynn placed it on the banister, sliding it over. The gold band reflected the mold clinging to the Muckie's bones, the red of the gem almost black under the cloudy sky.

"What vampyr doesn't want to walk in the sun, let alone a pirate?" she asked.

Flynn tucked his hair behind his left ear, revealing a bloodstone earring piercing the tip of his ear.

Hurt lanced through her. "You've already pledged yourself to Riven." She searched for exits, eyed the seam of the concealed door—*fuck*. Evelyn and Yen. She'd been a fool to step out alone, to—

He grabbed her arm, not fiercely but with a reassuring squeeze. "I'd *never*, and you know that."

She tugged free of his grip. "Then where did you get a bloodstone? It's only an honor given by the royal family—"

"Why are you really here, Tovi?" Flynn searched the sea.

Tovi blinked. "We need Evelyn's magic—"

"Fuck the ship. Why me?" He shook his head, finally looking at her and studying her. His eyes flared, and an unpleasant laugh bubbled out of him. "You're finally going to fight your brother, aren't you?"

"I need allies, Flynn. He's working with the Blood Goddess and claims to be king. If we have any chance of breaking our people of this curse, I need to stop him from ruling Drystan to its end."

"Let me guess, your plan was to hand out bloodstones for fealty?" he smirked, and Tovi's insides twisted.

"Don't patronize me."

Flynn shrugged. "If you can't offer me the sun, what can you offer me?"

"Money and land."

"I don't need money—I'm one of the richest vampyrs in Drystan. Nor as a pirate do I need land." He pushed off the banister and leaned his hip against it, driving his hands into his pockets.

Tovi tried to smile. "You could start a new business, venture out of the plundering, smuggling, and stealing."

Flynn scoffed. "Salt, always."

Impatience thrummed through Tovi's blood, but she understood how to barter, to start small and work her way up. Flynn came from humble beginnings, and despite his wealth, his status still held him back in their homeland so hell-bent on titles and lineage.

She swallowed, bracing her last hand. "I can make you a lord."

Flynn shook his head, slate eyes drilling into her. "I want you to make me your husband."

Tovi reared back. *How dare he*. After everything she'd endured with her parents. But he didn't know, didn't have the slightest clue, the hold her parents had used the prospect of marrying her off like a bargaining chip. The only other male she'd ever admitted that pain to had been Eldrick, and the moment Flynn breathed the word *husband*, it was his face that'd filtered through her mind, her heart aching with the prospect.

She shut her eyes, stilling her heart and pushing out any thought of the werewolf alpha she'd left behind. She couldn't afford to think of him, to worry about matters of her silly, foolish, poisoned heart when her fight against her brother hinged on this conversation with Flynn.

"I never imagined you'd vie for my hand in marriage to gain power," she scoffed.

Flynn didn't budge. "Every unmated male you go to for aid would ask the same."

Tovi threw up her hands. "Why not throw your name into the mix, is that it? If everyone else is, why not join them?"

Flynn leaned forward, eyes narrowing. "Did you really think this wouldn't happen?"

"Of course, I expected it! I just didn't expect it from *you*!" she shouted.

He laughed, bitter and sad. "Out of all those pompous asses who'll demand you marry them, I'm your best option."

"Is that so?" Tovi didn't hide the anger rising in her voice.

"Unlike them, I'm not after power. I have no interest in being king, only your husband—a loyal man by your side. The others won't even care that you're the queen, they'll use you as a figurehead while they rule Drystan."

Tovi seethed, blood boiling. "That will never happen, because I have no intention of marrying to secure my rightful seat on the throne."

"You might not have a choice," Flynn said, sounding like Lou.

He stepped closer—too close. His scent—fire and brine—was all wrong, clotting Tovi's senses. Her baser instincts craved spearmint and spice, the freshness of the Vadon Mountains.

"We were happy once," Flynn whispered.

"Yes, keyword, *once.*" Tovi's words were like barbed arrows, and she shot them without a second thought as to how deeply they buried into Flynn's tender flesh. Fuck him.

No. No. No.

Tovi's entire being thrummed with the word, like a lightning bolt fueled by retaliation shooting through her. She ignored her heart, fraying at the seams. Her body warred much the same, craving another male, while her mind battled reason and sense. Flynn was right. Other lords would ask. At least with Flynn, she'd secure a husband, a fleet of ships, and loyalty. Despite how her heart corroded like the idea was rust, it knew him and trusted him, even after the pain he'd caused all those years ago.

But something else warred within Tovi. It wasn't Eldrick or her heart's longing for another. It was the essence of freedom.

To have *choice.*

Deep in her bones, Tovi refused to give up the last shred of dignity she had. She'd fight for it. Flynn was only the first contact on Drystan. There were others. Fight brimmed within her, almost like a magic she could wield. She'd been so resilient for so long, perhaps she didn't know any other way than to muster on.

"If you see me as your queen like you say, then you'll take Evelyn where she needs to go."

"Tovi—"

"I can't marry you, or anyone else for that matter."

Flynn shook his head, grip tightening on the banister. "*Won't* and *can't* are two very different things."

Indeed they were, but she would not admit the truth to him.

"Am I your queen or not?" she asked.

Flynn gritted his teeth, nostrils flaring. "I'll take on the job under one condition."

Tovi sounded far braver than she felt when she said, "Name it."

"You'll take back your answer and consider my proposal." Before she had time to rebuttal, he continued, "And you owe me for that favor you asked."

"What favor?"

"When I helped smuggle the werewolves out of Drystan—join me for dinner, that is all I ask in return."

Tovi wavered. Despite feeling strong in her choice, she couldn't say no to Flynn's ask. Not when breaking the curse and setting her people free truly came before anything else. "Alright."

"It's a date then."

"It's dinner."

Flynn shrugged, roguish, and there was that smile she'd fallen in love with—dashing and fun. But it didn't brighten his features, didn't carve his usually stony, rigid scowl into a radiant beauty.

"Good night, Flynn," she said, heading towards the door.

"It was Lord Nathanaël," he called over his shoulder. "He gave me the bloodstone."

She paused her hand over the doorknob. She'd not heard the lord's name in a long while. He owned farmland to the east and had deep pockets, one's that had tempted Tovi to add to her list of diplomatic visits. But Lord Nathanaël didn't believe she had a right to the throne. *Female*, he and his wife had spat during balls at court.

"How in the bloody hel did he come by one?" she asked.

"I don't know," Flynn said. "We struck a trade deal six months ago, and the bloodstone was part of the terms. I had my crew vet it first, thinking it was a back-end way for your brother to finally gain my favor, but his greedy fingers hadn't come anywhere near it."

"Why are you telling me this?" Tovi studied him, trying to find his reasoning etched into his distant gaze.

"If Lord Nathanaël is giving out bloodstones, he has influence. Perhaps you should win him over."

Tovi bit the inside of her cheek. "I'll think on it, and Flynn, thank you for telling me."

He nodded. "Be safe, Tovi. After all, we have a dinner date on the books."

CHAPTER THIRTY-SIX

THUNDER RUMBLED FROM ABOVE and the sea's sky released its first droplets, but the icy sting of rain did nothing to distract Kade as he marveled at his mate. He'd discovered that he loved nothing more than the sight of Evelyn's resolve, glinting in her steely gaze like a sharp blade.

And tonight, she held a makeshift sword, one Kade had whittled from a broomstick. Her strikes clattered against his own practice weapon, echoing off the *Sel*'s quarterdeck.

Pride warmed Kade's chest as he blocked her next blow. She didn't meet his stare, her focus locked into their drills. Frustration leaked from each strike, and Evelyn clenched her jaw so tightly, Kade swore his werewolf hearing caught the sound of her grinding teeth.

Rough seas and winds had delayed their journey north with Captain Flynn and his crew of vampyr pirates. They stood around, watchful as Kade and Evelyn trained together, a daily routine they'd adapted—Kade taught Evelyn how to wield a blade, and she helped train him with his new magic.

Adrenaline rushed through Kade's veins. He'd fantasied moments like these, training with Evelyn. Though, their partnership, love, friendship far exceeded his wildest fantasies. His body hummed, his heart raced.

This, it sang.

Kade struck from overhead. Evelyn pivoted and swiped downward, catching Kade's attack. They both stilled. Amber collided with gray, and despite the restless and uncertainty chilling the briny air, they smiled at one another.

In two long strides, Kade reached Evelyn. He grabbed her waist and dragged their bodies flushed together, audience be damned.

"Oh, get a room!" Linx snorted off to the side.

"I believe they're called cabins on ships," Todd said.

Evelyn giggled, pushing Kade to arm's length with a small smile lighting her features. She gestured her hand towards his practice weapon.

"Your turn."

Kade sighed and relented, handing it over. More recently, they'd practiced his power in the quiet, empty hills of Sorin, far from watchful eyes.

As if she sensed his thoughts, Evelyn leaned in close and said, "There'll always be an enemy with their eye on you during battle."

Kade grunted, fighting a smirk. "Aren't you a wise teacher?"

Evelyn shrugged. "Is that so hard to believe?"

"No," Kade said quickly. "Not in the slightest."

"Practice drawing your power forth and keeping it steady." Evelyn stepped back, putting a respectable distance between them.

Kade appreciated it, averting his gaze from the burn still healing on her hand.

He opened and closed his own, reaching for this power, awakening it at his command not with emotion. He inhaled next, grounding himself to the wooden planks underneath his boots despite the ships constant up and down movement.

He focused on his hand, not the waves, vampyr pirates or Evelyn standing a few feet away. Blue glowed at his palm first, then bled to his fingers. His power surged forth, but Kade grasped hold of it, pulling it back—he, his wolf, and power aligned as one.

His hand remained the same shade of pearly blue, no more, no less.

"Kade, that's brilliant," Evelyn whispered.

He inhaled her encouragement and used it to draw a tad more.

Wind blew across the quarterdeck. The sails flapped insistently

A sphere of power formed above his palm, and blue light pulsed in circle around his hand like the light that ringed around the moon. Kade turned his wrist, flexed his fingers.

His power moved with him.

"It feels . . . a part of me." Kade glanced up at Evelyn, for once wonder for his power flushing through him.

Evelyn nodded. "Your power is you. You're one and the same. Can you call it back?"

Kade's brows pinched as he rallied more control and dimmed his power. It resisted at first, but with a stronger tug, it answered. Blue light drew it inward, and Kade's hand no longer shined with his power.

"Well done," Evelyn whispered with a smile reaching her eyes, the first in some time.

Todd hollered while Linx whistled. The vampyrs, on the other hand, narrowed their gazes, shoulders stiffening with caution.

"How do you feel?" Evelyn asked.

"Spent," Kade sighed.

The ship lurched against a mighty wave, and the Sapphire Sea splashed against the hull. Salt thickened the brisk air, and Kade's nausea roiled to life.

"Aye! Is your fur green when you shift, wolf? You're a questionable shade this evening."

A steady hand grasped Kade's shoulder, and his inner beast growled at the vampyr standing at his side. He'd spent three days near Captain Flynn on the *Sel*, and Kade wished for nothing more than to smack the vampyr's smirk clean off his face. He reminded Kade of a fox, not a wolf. An agenda lay beneath the surface of his friendly demeanor.

Beside him, the captain's quartermaster, Jasp, hid nothing from view—his disdain for Kade or vampyr fangs. His hood cast shadows across his sneering face. Kade's inner wolf bared its teeth, but he rallied his instinct to attack what he'd once considered the enemy.

Thus far, the captain had held true to his word since he agreed to take them north. The fog parted around the ship, lone fjords jutting out of the sea to the west. Ice fractured as the ship pierced through the waves.

Since the ship sailed with a vampyr crew, it buzzed with commotion at night. The sails ballooned under a cloudy sky, crewmen cried commands, and Captain Flynn winked as he left Kade and Evelyn for the stairs to the quarterdeck.

"Puke overboard, not on the deck, for *bloody hel's* sake," Jasp said.

"Here." Linx appeared at Kade's side, handing him a cup with steaming liquid.

He detected warm, comforting herbs.

"A tea to help with your sea legs. I know it's a few days late, but took me some time to dry the herbs well enough with all this mist and fog."

"Thank you," Kade said.

"I also had to make sure it didn't taste like shit," Linx said.

"Gods, I'd not trust her assessment." Todd wrinkled his nose. "Linx enjoys *cabbage*."

"With the proper care, it's a delightful vegetable." Linx frowned, crossing her arms.

"It smells rotten." Todd shivered.

"As entertaining as this is," Belle said, "we're here."

The witch held up Uzoma's coordinates and a map, pensive stare locked out onto the choppy waves.

"Anchor!" Flynn called.

The ship lurched forward, and Kade grabbed the railing for support. "*Moons*, I really hate boats."

Above, the moon's light bled through the gray sky. It glowed more yellow than pearl, and Kade racked his brain. Had the days blurred so quickly he'd lost track of the last full moon? He shook his head, blaming his worries on Evelyn's dwindling days.

"Better drink that tea." Linx winked, pushing the cup up to his lips. "You'll feel the benefits in no time."

Kade relented, and found his weapons master was right—Linx wasn't the best judge on taste. Still, he downed the musty tea all to rid the shake of the sea from his limbs. By the time the ship had stalled on the waters, and Belle had set up her space to draw the muince up from the depths, his stomach had settled.

Vampyrs lingered off to the side, their animosity mingled with the fog and under hoods, their predatory stares watched Kade and company. They seemed less than thrilled to have them on the ship, but their loyalty and orders came from Flynn, who watched Belle with curiosity.

The witch drew a circle with salt, laying the map at the center and using rocks as weight to hold the corners down. Evelyn crossed her arms, nibbling her lip, and Kade planted a kiss atop her temple.

"It'll be alright," he whispered.

"I know."

He stepped back, giving her space, but stood at her side if she needed him. Kade's own nerves, thankfully unrelated to the choppy waves, swam in his gut. The spell to get his mate's magic back hinged on locating her muince.

"I'll need a drop of your blood," Belle said.

Evelyn nodded and placed her hand in the fellow witch's. With a small prick of a needle, Belle drew blood at the tip of Evelyn's finger. She didn't wince or complain as Belle wiped blood onto a cloth, but Kade noticed for the first time a new tiredness clinging to her, one that hadn't been there in Morrow. His gut twisted—how had he not recognized it before?

His jaw ticked as Belle approached the edge of the ship. Her golden curls twisted in the wind. With Evelyn's bloodstained cloth in one hand and the other splayed above the water, she chanted.

At first, the winds whipped by at the same speed, and the waves dipped and ebbed. Then the sea hissed. Below, the waves churned, twisting like a cyclone. The winds stilled around the ship, snaking through the sails and circling above the water. Belle's magic brimmed in the air.

With eyes closed, she continued to chant in a language Kade didn't recognize. The sea groaned again, and bubbles festered at the center of the whirlpool.

Kade peered over the edge, eyeing the shift in the water. The magic in the air intensified. He caught a sweet scent, but it was gone as quickly as it came. Belle's eyes sprang open, and the surface broke, revealing a shimmering object dripping with water and seaweed.

A necklace, with an opal pendant mirroring the gray sky.

"Belle, you did it!" Evelyn said, rushing towards the banister. Wind unraveled her obsidian curls, framing her bright smile.

The young witch beamed, and across the way, Todd winked. A blush crept over her cheeks, but she blinked back into focus. Evelyn's muince wavered twenty-yards from the boat's edge. It floated towards them, and Kade's hope rose to the surface—

The necklace halted.

Belle winced, hands shaking as she focused on her magic.

"What is it?" Evelyn asked.

Sweetness entered the air again, growing more and more distinguishable. Kade's inner wolf's hackles rose. He dropped his hand to his sword's hilt, bracing as the temperature and energy shifted.

The fog parted ahead, and another black-as-soot ship emerged from the gray. Ingrid stood at the front, one hand holding a mast while her foot planted at the edge. From this distant, Kade caught the anger bleeding through her sneer.

"Oh, dear sister," Ingrid called over the waves and wind. "You're equally pathetic as predictable."

Todd growled, baring his teeth, but Kade grabbed his shoulders.

Belle flinched at Ingrid's words, but her hold on the muince necklace didn't falter. "Let go!"

Ingrid tsked. "I'm afraid I can't do that, but give me what I want, and I'll let you come back to Drystan with open arms."

"The witch is right, Belle. Surrender, and I'll drop your crimes against my court."

A familiar voice grated against Kade's resolve. The power embedded deep in his core flared to life. Riven emerged from the fog. Palish skin. White hair. Dark circles rimmed his eyes. Pride swelled through Kade at the sight of the scar Evelyn had left running up the vampyr's face. The prince appeared sickly, much like Tovi's assessment, but Kade didn't spy the sword of ancients, and he wondered about his mother and father's journey through Drystan.

"The Blood Moon is long past," Evelyn cried. "You have lost, Riven."

The prince snickered. "Always so naïve. Such singular thinking. You're a fool to think I don't have another plan. I've joined forces with another player on the board, Miss Carson. No, I don't need your magic any longer—but think of today as vengeance. If I can't have your magic, Evelyn Carson, *no one* can." He gave Ingrid a curt nod.

Ink-black winds oozed from the witch's fingertips, snaking through the air towards Evelyn's muince. Belle faltered a step, the pull of her sister's power too much. Todd lurched forward and pulled Belle to his chest, gripping his arms around her waist and whispering encouraging, stern words into her ear. Belle gritted her teeth. Clamped her eyes shut. And shook with exertion. The waves and winds around them grew angry.

Kade rushed to Flynn. "Bring the ship closer to Riven's—"

"No." There was no hesitation in the captain's answer, and heat scorched through Kade.

"If Riven gets ahold of that necklace, Sorin is doomed."

"Not my problem," Flynn hissed but something lay hidden in the creases of his eyes. Not an agenda. *Acceptance.* Like the bastard had known Riven would come.

Kade launched, grabbing a fistful of the captain's shirt and dragging him close so they were eye to eye.

"You sold us out!" he roared. "Didn't you?"

The crew shifted around them. Blades sang as they were unleashed. Kade barely registered Evelyn's distant warning. His beast and power sat so close to the edge, for the first time working alongside one another, he thrummed with furious energy

Flynn released a feline-like screech. Kade's wolf snarled. Werewolf and vampyr vied against each other.

"I'd never betray Tovi," the pirate said. "I'd rather die than hurt my queen."

Kade growled, shoving the vampyr out of his grasp. He heard the honesty in Flynn's words. The even heartbeat. The steady breath.

The pirate spoke the truth.

"Letting Riven succeed might as well be betraying her," Kade said.

Flynn stepped closer. "I promised to sail to these coordinates, that is all. I'll not risk my crews' lives for some war we've not signed up—"

A startling force rocked the ship. It tilted to the side, water spilling onto the main deck. The crew and company lost their footing, and Kade dove for Evelyn, grasping around her waist as the ship jolted again.

"Is that Ingrid?" Kade asked.

Evelyn's brows furrowed. "I don't think so—"

Riven's ship lurched too, booming with impact, the assailant unseen. Ingrid lost her balance long enough for Belle to yank the muince closer to the *Sel*. Riven cried out orders, and the dark witch threw out her hand, stopping her sister. The young witch cried out in pain, but Todd kept her steady.

A groan echoed from the depths of the sea. Fear and confusion halted them all. The waves rumbled and trembled as a dark, looming mass rose out of the sea. Above, the moon swayed past the clouds until it popped away from the gray, revealing a yellow glowing ball attached to an inky, reptilian-like appendage.

Evelyn gasped. "That's not . . ."

"Demon!" the *Sel*'s crew bellowed.

The glowing sphere shot higher and cast its light onto the face of a demon twice the size of the pirate ship. Winglike fins fluttered around its face, and rows of razor teeth dripped with sea sludge.

"Harpoons!" Flynn cried. "Positions!"

Click. Click. Click.

The demon's high frequency sounds pierced Kade's werewolf hearing, and he gripped Evelyn closer to his chest. Darkness reached across their world. The demon roared. The sea trembled. The clouds shook.

The ship's bones whined as it stopped, something holding it in place. Evelyn's frantic heart beat in tandem with Kade's, and they reared back as a pitch-black tentacle slithered up the ship like a beast in its own right, climbing higher and higher.

Kade let Evelyn go, handed her his sword, and pulled her close, forehead to forehead. Amber collided with silver, and he bore all his love into their locked stare. "Fight."

"Remember, your power *is* you," she said with a shaky breath and pivoted away, slicing the sword through the tentacle, fighting it like a breathtaking goddess with a bravery that outmatched any strength. Blood and suckers showered onto the deck with a sickening splat.

Kade heeded his mate's words and shifted into his werewolf form. Beast against beast, no matter the size.

Tentacles broke through the deck's banisters, and wood exploded. One seized a vampyr, wrapping its puckered flesh around his pale body. Lifting it into the air, the vampyr's screams only grew, until a deafening crunch silenced him and a shredded body landed on the deck.

A female vampyr screamed and cried, crawling towards the defiled body. Kade howled, but it was too late. In her grief, the female vampyr missed the tentacle reaching for her. It lifted and swung her off deck. Waves swallowed her whole.

Two vampyrs down in seconds.

The ship became a frenzy of panicked activity. Kade launched, landing on the tentacle and ripping with his claws and teeth, tearing through the demon's slippery flesh. The demon roared, shaking the entire world with its baritone. Across the waves, Riven's ship dealt with the same attack while Ingrid and Belle continued to battle over Evelyn's muince, hovering unguarded over the waves.

Stars above.

Kade tore through another tentacle, ripping it in half with his claws. He turned at the last second, almost missing one creeping from behind, but Evelyn struck his sword downward and severed it. The tentacle writhed, and black blood sprayed across their faces, the smell putrid.

In retaliation, more tentacles rose from the sea, salty water showering across the deck and drenching the *Sel*.

"Damn you!"

Kade whirled. Jasp fought relentlessly as a tentacle dragged him across the deck. Kade didn't hesitate. He shifted out of his werewolf form and called upon his power. His hand warmed. Glowed. Light shimmered at his fingertips. He focused. Inhaled. Breathed in the rightness he craved. He was calm. Collected. He recalled Evelyn's teaching.

Your power is you.

He thrust his power straight into the tentacle. Blue light swarmed across the demon's flesh, sizzling through the appendage. Jasp scrambled back, tearing off the remaining piece. Kade reached the vampyr and helped him stand. Jasp stared up at Kade with wide eyes, his mouth opening and closing.

"Thank you," he finally said.

With a small nod from Kade, a mutual understanding bled across the ship—they were all in this fight together.

"Aye, watch out!" Flynn called from the quarterdeck.

The demon reared closer to the *Sel*, teeth glinting from the ship's lanterns. "Kade!"

He and Evelyn locked eyes, and he ran. Evelyn threw his sword, and as he caught the weapon, Kade leaped up onto the ship's railing and used it to launch his footing as he jumped into the air. The demon's rancid breath brushed across his cheek, and with a warrior's bellow, Kade sliced the beast's antenna. It screeched, and the glowing ball plopped to the deck, pulsing until its dark magic faded.

The demon's tentacles retreated, falling away as the ship's harpoons pierced its flesh. Waves roiled over its body as it retreated, the sea swallowing it as it sank.

Kade panted, and a cheer resounded across the deck. Flynn threw his fist into the air, and the *Sel*'s crew joined. But Evelyn didn't share the same sentiment. Kade followed her line of sight, his heart dropping like a stone to his gut.

"Give up, Belle!" Blood dripped from Ingrid's nose. "I'm stronger, and you know it! You're nothing without me protecting you."

Belle's arm shook with exertion while tears ran down her face, but she didn't falter. "It is you who is weak, and I'm ashamed that you're my sister."

Ingrid shrieked and thrust a large ball of dark magic across the sea, straight into Todd's shoulder. Belle screamed. Her magical hold on the muince severed.

"No!" Kade roared and dove into the water, aiming for the spot the muince dropped.

Kade swam, but the current dragged him under, the weight of the sinking demon pulling water with it.

"Aim for the prince's ship!"

Jasp's commands filtered over the whooshing waves. Kade fought the waves. Evelyn cried out his name. He cursed the cold and dove. His eyes burned with the salt, but metal glinted ahead, and he pushed towards Evelyn's muince. For *her*, every ounce of effort he mustered was for Evelyn and getting her magic back.

His hand grasped the necklace's chain. The opal pendant hit against his wrist, and Kade fought as he kicked upward, the light of the surface breaking through the water.

Something twisted around his ankle and tugged. A tentacle's suckers locked onto his shins.

Click. Click. Click.

The demon's sounds mocked him. Kade gripped the muince tighter, not daring to let it go, but the demon's hold was too strong. He fell farther from the surface. Light dwindled. His lungs ached. He couldn't fail her. *No,* not like this.

A form crashed into the water. Bubbles swallowed their face, but silver glinted as they stabbed the demon. Over and over. Blood bloomed like red ink, and with one final yank, the dagger slit through the tentacle. Kade kicked free, and an arm snaked around his middle, assisting him to the surface. He gasped for air, blinking away the salt.

"Hold on!"

Flynn's voice didn't fully register until they were airborne, flying out of the water and dropping onto the deck. Kade rolled, choking up water.

"Kade!" Evelyn rushed to him, grasping his shoulders.

He pressed her muince into her hand, and her voice cracked. "Goddess, you did it."

Flynn chuckled at his side, gasping for air as he shot him a smirk. "Gods, you're heavy. What in the hel do werewolves eat?"

Kade laughed, leaning on his knees as he shook with fatigue. "Thank you."

Flynn studied and shared a look with Jasp. "*Thank you* for fighting with us and protecting my crew. I'll not forget it, Kade Drengr."

Kade nodded, peering over his shoulder. "What of Riven and Ingrid?"

Todd stood off to the side. "Belle has it handled."

The water witch did. The Sapphire Sea swirled under her command, Riven's ship caught in its unwavering grip. As the wood splintered and vampyrs cried out, they fled through the dark witch's *danu* in time before the ship succumbed to the watery depths of defeat, as he and Evelyn sat there, one step closer to getting her magic back.

Chapter Thirty-Seven

*T*AP, TAP, TAP.

Blair sprang awake. Unfamiliarity prickled across her skin, and she panicked and fell out of bed. A bed—one she had no recollection of getting in or where in the blasted books it was. Her head throbbed, and Blair kneaded her temple.

That's right—she'd hit her head when the Guards had attacked.

Goddess, *Guards*. She and Lorkan had fled, and she'd . . .

Brought them to Nūa.

Blair whirled, searching wildly in the room she found herself in. Loud colors. Vibrant art. A window facing the southern district of Nūa. Where exactly was she?

Tap, tap, tap.

Rook sat at the base of the window on the outside of the glass, demanding she let him back in. A shred of relief washed through Blair—at least her familiar trusted wherever they were.

But where was Lorkan? She replayed the night's events over in her mind as she eased open the window's latch. The last thing she remembered was her townhouse, or the lack of it.

Rook fluttered inside and landed at the door, pacing. He picked at the door's chipping paint, chucking the mint green color across the floorboards.

"*Shhh*," Blair hissed.

But she failed to remain quiet. The door swung, and Lorkan stood in the doorway. Rook flew to his shoulder and nuzzled the werewolf's jawline in greeting—*traitor*, Blair thought.

"Where are we?" she asked.

"Do you not recall the *danu you* conjured last night?" Lorkan shut the door with the heel of his boot. "Why, in the stars above, would you bring us to Nūa?"

"A book." Blair crossed her arms. It wasn't a lie exactly. She'd wished to avoid Fika, and at the last second, she'd recalled Jace's ancient text.

"*A* book?" Lorkan said. "Vísdómr has thousands, and you risked yourself for one bloody text?"

"It's written by the faerie and has information detailing the bloodstone."

Lorkan tilted his head, studying her through his wire-framed glasses. "So, you've seen it?"

"Well . . ." Blair wiggled her shoulders. "Not exactly. A peer of mine has access to it, *not* in the library, thankfully. He offered to let me see it whenever I wished—"

"Who?" Lorkan became unnaturally still.

"Jace Brookes."

"Do you think we can trust him?"

Blair nibbled her lip, shifting from foot to foot. "I don't know."

Rook cawed as if sounding his own disappointment in Blair's brashness, but in truth, Blair'd rather be stuck behind the Wall of Nūa, lurking in the shadows than stepping foot in Fika. But how would they reach Vísdómr now? Blair winced. Maybe she would have no choice, but she needed more time.

"Look, the book might have answers regarding how the gem works, and that might lead to how we can fight the Blood Goddess and her power," she said. "If we learn her weaknesses, we might discover how to break the curse."

Blair didn't mention her burn, and that she sought answers of her own.

"Fine. We visit Jace and get the book." Lorkan placed a leather satchel at the end of the bed. "I went out and grabbed clothes for you. Along with a cloak and gear better suited for the Vadon Mountains. I wasn't aware Circe burned your home, and I'm sorry."

Blair's heart raced. She'd wished to hear those words from Lorkan for a decade—for entirely different reasons, sure, but to hear something out of him that was more than discussions about books or bossing her around had flighty sensation swarming in her gut. Blair snuffed the feelings down, inspecting the clothes he'd brought her.

"Thank you," she whispered, not trusting her own voice. "Wait—how did you know it was Circe?"

Lorkan shoved his hands into his pockets. "It made front lines across the papers in Nūa, and my contact filled me in."

"Contact?"

Lorkan nodded, heading for the door. "Yes, this is her apartment."

It turned out Lorkan's contact was a witch.

A *beautiful* one.

She hummed as she cooked breakfast, red-as-holly curls bouncing behind her. Light on her feet, petite and willowy, she had an ethereal softness to her, unlike Blair's dark, sharp edges.

Bloody hel. Like a child, Blair was comparing herself to another woman. Blasted books. Why was Blair growing warm? The windows were cracked, chilly air twisting with the yeasty scent of browning toast. Oh, *right*, that was her uncalled-for, deep-rooted, scorching jealousy.

"Here's a coffee to get you started." The witch slid over a mint-and-brown-speckled mug; a heart formed in the milky foam— she was one of those who made coffee art. Pretty and talented.

Blair grew hotter in her seat.

"Oh! Here's a scone. Made them yesterday."

Blair's stomach growled, and she helped herself to a baked good bursting with chocolate morsels—*damn*. This friend of Lorkan's could also cook.

Fucking fantastic.

But Blair wasn't jealous. No, she wasn't a child either. A grown-ass woman, in fact, one who could swallow her pride.

"Thank you, ah . . ." Blair internally cursed for the tenth time that morning. She'd forgotten the witch's names. Was it Maria? No. Marya? Wait—

"Mya."

"*Mya*, I'm sorry. Thank you. For the coffee, and the food of course, and letting us stay despite . . ." Blair shrugged, "Well, you know."

She laughed, bubbly. "Think nothing of it! Helping a rebel witch? Exciting, if you ask me."

Blair disagreed, but smiled through her next sip of coffee, bouncing her foot on the metal foothold of her barstool. There was nothing exciting about discovering the man who broke her heart had a "friend" in the same city as her, a mere five blocks from her own townhome.

Blair kept eyeing the two doors on the left side of the apartment. She'd woken in the small guest room on the south wall. Lorkan had excused himself to let her get ready to visit Jace's antique store, and after emerging, she'd discovered Mya's room was the left door, but the witch had hurried out of it when she'd greeted her, and Blair hadn't caught a good enough glimpse through the door before she shut it. Not that she *wanted* to see Lorkan lounging in the bed of another—

Oh, stop it!

Why did it matter who he was entangled with? She'd fucked plenty, if she was honest with herself. Heck, today they had plans to visit Jace, someone she'd had fun with so often, she'd lost count.

Perhaps it was less that he was with someone else, but more the fact Mya was nothing like *her*, and even though comparison was a shallow trick that only ached, she couldn't help sighting the differences between them. Lorkan liking someone so unlike her—airy and vibrant—stung more than Blair wished to admit.

"What's your post in the city?" Blair bit another scone, the buttery bread turning to ash on her tongue.

"I'm an artist." Mya gestured with her hand around the flat. Murals and canvases with watercolor scenes hung on the brick walls.

"I see," Blair said.

Artists were few to none these days. With the fight at the Void, most posts were related to efforts against the darkness. No firstborn, second born, or third born was studying the arts, let alone making it. Those who were fourth or fifth born, though rare, had more freedom, if their covens permitted it. Regardless, Blair's mind nagged with the question: How had Lorkan met Mya?

As if her thoughts summoned him, the second door on the north wall—*not* Mya's door—opened, and Lorkan strode into the common area, golden eyes finding Blair's. She sucked in a breath, becoming lost in the rivets of molten amber.

"You . . . cut your hair."

Eight inches of it. Blair played with the freshly chopped tips. "Figured it counts as a disguise."

Blair usually wore her hair in a tidy bun, curls twisted neatly away from her face. Thanks to Mya's scissors, she'd shortened them inches above her shoulders and, for good measure, painted her lips a crimson lacquer.

"I think it suits you." Mya winked, giving Lorkan a pointed look.

But the Drengr scholar didn't comment any further. "We should head out."

The willowy witch's shoulders slumped, her bright and cheery features deflating. "Well, that's a shame. Breakfast isn't half started. I had bacon and eggs next. Should I expect you both a little later?"

"Maybe—"

"No," Lorkan cut Blair off. "Once we have this *ancient text*, we're heading straight for Fika."

Mya nodded. "Alright, here." She handed Lorkan a pouch, and he frowned.

"I can't..."

"Yes, you will now *go*." She smiled, nibbling a strip of bacon. "If your names end up in the papers, I know who to contact."

Curiosity had followed Blair like her shadow as they snuck through the city's back streets and alleys, but her mind lingered on Lorkan's plan. *Fika*. She mulled over the village, sourness coating her tongue.

Crinkled parchment blew in the wind, jolting Blair out of her musings. Horror shot through her, and she ripped away the wanted poster that read dangerous above a sketch drawn to her likeness. With lips in a thin line, eyes straight ahead, lost and vacant, and her curly hair twisted into a neat bun, she didn't look like herself at all.

It didn't *feel* like her either.

Lorkan scowled. "Don't pay it any mind. We have more important matters."

Right. Like figuring out how to break the curse. Blair's insides twisted. Jace's text would help, but had she been a fool to drag them all the way here? *Yes*, an infuriated voice hissed.

The street bustled with morning foot traffic, and a group of witches headed to their daily posts ambled by. Blair fell into step with them, Lorkan following. The current swallowed them, hiding them in plain sight.

Ahead, Jace's antique shop's sign, a bronze-forged medallion with his coven's name Brookes ingrained on it, hung from an iron bar.

Blair peeled herself from the crowd of witches and tiptoed up the few steps leading to the store's front door. Bronze that matched the sign above ran the perimeter of the window, illuminating Jace's coven name. Blair turned the doorknob, and—it didn't budge. *Locked.* Blair cursed. They didn't have time for this; she needed to get her hands on that book.

Lorkan glanced into the shop, honey eyes narrowing. "It appears Jace Brookes isn't in."

Blair humphed, unconvinced. Lorkan didn't know where to look for the signs. She pushed him aside, taking his spot at the window and framing her eyes to block out the light as she peered inside. *Ah,* right as she predicted. The light under Jace's workroom was lit, which meant he was here but hadn't opened the shop.

Perfect.

"Follow me," Blair said.

Lorkan made an unintelligible sound, and Blair didn't pay him any mind. If he objected, so be it. She was getting her hands on that book today, regardless of his grumblings.

She scurried around the corner and then the next, quick on her feet as she reached the back alley behind Jace's storefront. A rusted mint door was the third on the left. Blair had accessed it plenty of times, using a *danu* straight to the back ally to meet Jace for an afternoon—

"Jace!"

A woman's voice echoed beyond the door, and Blair froze, stilling her hand above the doorknob. *Goddess.*

Lorkan hovered, a smug smile tugging at his lips. "Sounds like a busy man."

His condescending, jarring tone had Blair's sights turning red, her fingertips growing cold, and the shadows of the back alley darkening. Blair fled her darkening magic and burst through the back door—

Kneeling on the ground, Jace's head was between a witch's thighs as he pleasured her with his wickedly talented tongue. Heat scorched Blair's cheeks—she'd sat at the edge of the desk in a similar position many, many times.

"Oh!" The witch threw her head back, hand tightening in Jace's curls.

Though jealousy had been a close friend of late, it never joined Blair as she stood next to Lorkan, taking in the couple. Completely lost in bliss, Jace nor his lover noticed they had an audience. Instead, heavy breathing sent a shiver down Blair's spine.

Lorkan stepped closer with the swiftness of fog over the stone floor. She peered up at him, regret snuffed the heat blooming in her belly. His eyes had turned molten, a predatory hunger gleaming in his amber stare. Blair's mouth turned dry. Not because she was afraid, but because of what it promised. Something insatiable. Something irrevocable. Something she *craved.*

"*YES!*"

The tension snapped between them, and Blair averted her attention back to the entangled couple. Flushed and panting, the witch sat scrunched like she'd lost the use of her limbs, relaxed and tight all at once. Her eyes fluttered open and instantly landed on Blair.

"Goddess!" She swatted Jace's head. "I thought you said the door was locked!"

Jace popped out from underneath her silk skirt. "It is locked, Daisy. I checked it three times!"

Daisy pointed a finger straight ahead. "Then how in the hel did they get in?"

Jace whirled and shot to his feet. "Blair? What are you doing here— *Oh my gods*, is that a werewolf?"

Daisy smirked, spreading her legs wider as she leaned back. "Oh, I've never been with a male like *you* before. Care to join us? Three is fun, but four is a party."

"No," Blair said through gritted teeth. *Ah*, there was jealousy, not so far away after all.

"We're here for research," Lorkan said. "Our visit is also *urgent*."

Daisy's stare lingered on Blair, and then she sighed. "Well, I guess that's my cue to leave." She laid an affectionate kiss on Jace's cheek. "If you'd like to finish what we started, you know where to find me."

The witch winked as she passed by Lorkan and strutted out the back door, humming a jolly tune.

"Can we trust her?" Lorkan asked once she was gone.

Blair's stomach backflipped. Surely she'd misheard the level of concern in his tone.

Jace sighed, running a hand through his curls. "I don't have the slightest idea."

Lorkan rolled his eyes toward the ceiling. "Then we'd better make this quick before you have the Guard at your doorstep. Blair claims you possess a book written by ancient fae, detailing the bloodstone. I think you're full of horseshit."

Jace smirked, boyish and unabashed. "Prepare to be proven wrong."

He gestured for them to follow him into the front of the shop.

Blair stepped to do just that when Lorkan grabbed her wrist.

"Are you alright?" he asked.

Blair opened and closed her mouth. "Excuse me?"

His nostrils flared, and he flicked his attention around the room. "Were-wolves have a keen sense of smell. It took me thirty seconds to discover . . . you and Jace were once involved."

She swallowed, and heat rose up her neck. "*And?*"

Lorkan hesitated, as if weighing his words. "We just walked in on him with another woman."

Blair snorted, and she couldn't explain the pain lodging in her throat. "Jace and I fucked on Mondays and Thursdays. Today's Friday."

She snatched her hand out of Lorkan's grip. How dare he have the audacity to care or ask? Blair shook her head as she waltzed into the front room of Jace's antique store, dismissing any thoughts of Lorkan's confusing behavior and setting her sights on getting the book.

Jace yanked a chain switch in the corner, and a dozen lights popped on, casting their heady glow onto the hundreds of items in the shop. Attached by invisible strings, the bones of a giant creature dangled from the ceiling. With wings spread wide and toothy skull roaring towards the window, the remains of a dragon were positioned in mid-flight. A tag hung from the tip of its tail, its three-thousand-year-old age written in thin cursive.

Caldrons, some too large for a table and others small enough to rest in Blair's palm, lined the tables filled with timeless items. Amethyst crystals dotted the store in specks of purple. Velvet cloaks buzzing with magic hung on a rack in the corner. On the left wall, jars of dirt, dried herbs, and potions collected dust. On the right wall, waning black candles sat on a floating shelf.

Jace paused at an all-glass cabinet. Eerier items glared up at them—a vampyr's fanged jaw, the coiled tail of a beast Blair'd never seen, the black feather of *iolair*, and a stack of ancient text. Magic filtered out from the shelves as Jace opened it, and Blair spied the grimoires, research journals, and a text that had once been detailed with gold foil but was now splitting at the spine, its brittle pages barely hanging on.

Jace grabbed the text and placed it atop an empty table. Blair's fingers tingled, the text's age prickling in the air. Her magic sensed the power within the words and those who inked them to the page. Jace flipped it to the first chapter and revealed the lost language of faerie.

"Stars above." Lorkan's voice caused Blair to jolt. She'd not heard him approach from behind as he peered down at the text. "Interesting . . ."

"That's all you have to say?" Jace asked, wide-mouthed. "This text samples at four thousand years old. I've conducted the test myself."

Lorkan made a low rumble of acknowledgment.

Jace shot Blair a pained look.

She shrugged. "How on earth did your coven come by this?"

Jace smiled, a proud glint entering his blue eyes. "My great-great gran stole it from the Nūa Library."

"Stole it?" both Blair and Lorkan hissed.

Jace threw up his hands. "Well, sort of. Apparently, after my gran had checked this book out from the library, the Nūa Library suffered a horrific fire. Checking books in and out wasn't really their concern, and she simply kept it."

Blair pocketed the information for later. "Why has no one bought the book? This is an insane collector's item."

"It's a thousand silvers," Jace said.

"*What?*" Blair asked.

"That's absurd," Lorkan said.

"It's four thousand years old," Jace grumbled.

"We can't pay that sum," Blair said.

Jace shrugged. "Then you can use it here for as long as you need—"

"Are you really going to put a price tag on breaking the Blood Curse?" Lorkan said, his voice far too calm.

Jace's eyes widened. He opened his mouth, but stopped, his attention falling outside the window. "*Shit.*"

Elder Circe waltzed across the street, heading straight for the antique shop's front door, nose high in the air.

"Both of you need to hide. *Now.*"

Blair snatched the text off the table. Jace glared, but there was no time. He ushered them into the back of the shop. A heavy knock rattled the door, and Jace sprinted to let Elder Circe in.

"We need to go—"

Blair laid a hand over Lorkan's mouth, placing a finger over her own to silence him. His eyes flared, but Blair ignored the heat searing her hand at their skin-to-skin contact.

They *should* leave, but interest nagged at Blair. Why was Circe visiting Jace's shop? What artifacts or antiques was she after? Was Jace working with her? Her thoughts tumbled alongside her churning stomach. She conjured her winds, buzzing a magic of air that concealed her and Lorkan's presence.

"Good morning, Circe—"

"It's *Elder* Circe." The witch snorted.

"What can I help you with, Elder?" Jace's tone edged with annoyance.

Circe sighed, her voice growing closer as if she moved further into the store. "I came across the most interesting information this morning. Your great-great gran checked out a text long ago. I thought it was lost to the fires as so many texts were, but imagine my surprise when I discovered it'd never been *returned* to the library. Where is it?"

Jace laughed, and Blair stiffened. He didn't know Elder Circe like she did, hadn't experienced her wrath against Evelyn and Kade.

"Why are you so certain my coven even has this text still?" Jace said.

"Because I had a colleague scribe for faerie-touched things in the city. Only one item appeared, and it is in this shop."

Lorkan snatched Blair's hand from his mouth. He glared. Jaw ticking. Golden eyes lethal. His stare screamed *Now!*

Jace's next words were louder, pointed. "Perhaps the text is with someone for safekeeping. After all, it is a priceless item."

Realization dawned on Blair—Jace was telling her to *go*. Hope. It settled over her like morning dew. Goddess, her swelling pride receded. She and Lorkan had the book. They had to leave before things escalated, like their last stint in the village. If Jace could lie to an Elder, she could face a village she'd sworn never to visit again. But could she leave him and let him face the consequences? What if Circe hurt him?

No, that wasn't it. Of course, she cared for Jace in a friend-like way, and she appreciated his help, but reflection made her face the truth—Blair was afraid of who she was outside this city. The painful memories of Fíka were one thing, but being back in the Drengr Village and being around Lorkan made her off-kilter. Here, beyond the Wall, she was safe, away from the reminder of her broken heart and from that young, foolish girl she'd been. In Nūa, she recalled her place—a second born, a scholar. She held that truth like the book she clutched to her chest.

Vísdómr was a library, one with the answers on how to break the curse, and Fika, though the village where her heart had shattered, was simply a place on the map along the way. Instead of running from the memories, perhaps Blair would be better off running into them headfirst, a cold reminder that sticking to who she was didn't get her hurt.

The back door eased open, breaking Blair from her tumbling thoughts, and Daisy popped her head inside. She motioned for them to join her, and on cautious feet, Blair and Lorkan darted out into the alley.

"I'll help Jace distract Circe. Go." Daisy slammed the door shut, leaving them in the chilly air.

Rook cawed from above, and with her decision made, Blair twisted her hands and created a *danu*.

Lorkan grabbed her elbow, eyeing the other side with narrowed eyes. "Where does this lead?"

Blair inhaled, and with Rook on her shoulder, she crossed from Nūa to a quaint town. Over her shoulder she called, "Fika."

CHAPTER THIRTY-EIGHT

KADE

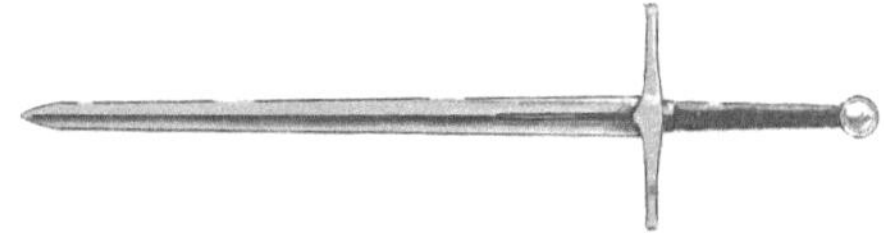

"MOONS," KADE HISSED.

Hidden under bedsheets, Evelyn's moan vibrated against his length as she took every inch of him into her mouth. With her tongue and lips, she worshiped him like some god, but truly Kade prayed to *her*. He'd forgotten they were on a boat, the sea's up and down waves no match against the pleasure she wrung from him.

He ripped the sheets off of her, and the sight of her tongue twirling over his tip as she fisted his length almost had him coming undone right then and there, but he refrained. Her heated gaze sent him a silent warning: *Don't*. And with her mouth wide around his length and her need perfuming the air, what sort of man was he to deny her?

Kade smirked—he loved his mate's sounds, skin, and body, but he also loved her unabashed *want* during their entanglements.

Outside their cabin, waves knocked against the pirate ship's underbelly, but Kade didn't care, nor did his wolf. Not when he and his mate lost themselves in the sheets of their bunk.

A growl rumbled through Kade's chest, *need* of his own coursing through him. He grasped her hair and held tight, encouraging her rhythm as she continued to suck, drawing him deeper than ever before. *Stars above*, save him.

"Ev . . ."

His warning did nothing but quicken her pace. He shut his eyes, his control at the edge of bursting at the seams, pleasure tingling to his toes.

"*Love.*"

That got her attention, and Evelyn slowed, easing him from her mouth. Hair amiss. Teary eyes. Glowing flush across her cheeks.

She still wore her tunic and trousers, and Kade couldn't bear it, craving the sight of her naked curves. She straddled him, and he leaned forward, dragging her shirt up and over her head. Evelyn screeched as he yanked and snapped the bralette hiding her breasts from him. She didn't have time as he took one nipple in her mouth, sucking, twirling his tongue, and bit down.

"*Oh.*"

Evelyn wrapped her arms around his shoulders, falling into her pleasure, toes curling as he moved to the second nipple and worshiped it the same way.

Kade moved, placing Evelyn on her back. Eyes wide and panting, she smiled up at him. He unbuttoned her trousers, taking her undergarments off with them in one swoop. Kade gripped her hips and twisted her beautiful bare body onto her hands and knees.

Evelyn gasped, peering over her shoulder. "*Kade.*"

"Hands on the wall," he said—guttural, his beast sitting on the surface.

Evelyn swallowed but obeyed, planting them firmly with fingers splayed. A tremor ran up her spine, anticipation thrumming between them. They'd been here before, lying with one another, but there was always *something* to explore.

Kade *yearned* for Evelyn, and he cherished these moments alone, and lately, they felt more precious—her three weeks had dwindled to two. Sometimes, he felt like a selfish bastard, needing her like this, but then Evelyn gave him a particular look, and he knew this was a shared desire.

Kade dismissed his agonizing, wretched thoughts and traced his fingers over Evelyn's pale, moonlight-like skin until he found her clit. Kade's touch slicked through her sex, and his length twitched—his mate was so ready, so needy, and *stars above*, he rallied his control so he could worship her, too.

Evelyn arched, her fingers digging into the wooden wall. Kade drew circles at a slow, deliberate pace. He memorized the flush on Evelyn's cheeks deepening, the way her toes curled as he quickened his circles, and how breathy she became.

"I'm close—"

"Don't. Wait."

Kade positioned himself behind her and kicked her knees wider with his, granting himself more access to her glistening sex. He drew their hips flush together. Evelyn pressed back, her wetness coating his aching length. A growl rumbled through his chest, and he pinched her clit, and Evelyn writhed against him. He released her, palming his length as he lined it up with her entrance.

"Keep your hands on the wall."

He thrust inside her fully, and Kade cursed all the gods for creating such maddening perfection. A moaned, *yes*, gasped out of Evelyn. Her arms shook, but she braced against him and took what he gave her. He drove into her. Again and again. Rough. Teetering on the edge of control.

Her small waist fit so perfectly into his large hands, and those muscular legs of hers trembled as she kept her hands on the wall, mewling as her release built through her. If Kade could bottle up the sight and sounds of his mate taking him so utterly well, he would.

"Kade . . . I *can't* . . ."

He grabbed a fistful of silky hair and yanked, making her look back at him. "You can, and you will, love."

He brought her flush to his chest, widening his knees. Evelyn whimpered as she sank farther onto his length.

"Fuck," he hissed as drove deeper than before, her sex choking his cock.

Evelyn's head fell back against his shoulder, and she peered up at him with silvery eyes, and the sight almost undid him there. He loved this woman. Unconditionally. For eternity. His heart, mind, body and soul belonged to Evelyn, and he hoped he conveyed that through his body to hers tonight.

Kade dipped his hand between her breasts, brushed against her strong stomach until he found where they meet.

"*Kade,*" she cried out as he drew two fingers over her clit. He did it again, but this time alongside a deep thrust. Her sex clamped around him, and he scented her release on the horizon, the tightening grip on his length telling enough.

"Come for me, love," he whispered.

Evelyn shattered in his arms, her body arching, stiffening, and clamping all at once. He swallowed her release with a bruising kiss. Kade's inner beast took over, and he lost control as he pounded into Evelyn.

His release ripped through him. Fierce, harsh, and unrelenting. Stars burst into his vision, but as he blinked and came to, panting with Evelyn in his arms, it was her beautiful face and sleek body tangled with his that overcame his sight. The gleam in her eyes almost pushed him over the edge again, the power within that silver his undoing.

"I love you," she whispered, breath tickling his face.

He ran his nose up hers, inhaling the vanilla-and-cedar scent.

"When we visit the Otherworld, I'll be thanking the gods for creating you," he whispered into her ear.

Evelyn sighed into his hold, and for a moment they remained still and joined as they came down from one another.

CHAPTER THIRTY-NINE

THE SUN ROSE OVER the Drengr Village, chasing the remnants of the latest blizzard with its morning rays. Songbirds washed in the puddles left by dripping icicles, and snow melted off the trees, pine needles free from tufts of white.

Eldrick's breath still plumed in the air, and he'd bundled in a fur-lined cloak and gloves for his journey south to meet with Alpha Drabek. He prepared his horse for a week's journey, though he hoped to arrive there in two days' time, *if* the sun stuck around and no storms stalled his travels.

"Fine day for a ride." Bétar entered the stables, beaming. His horse stood at the ready. Saddle packed. Blankets rolled. Swords and axes sheathed.

"Indeed," Eldrick said, spying Lucy hurrying from the Shield-maiden. He walked his horse out of the stables to meet her. "Good morning, Luc— *Moons*, what is wrong?"

Panic bled across her expression. Eldrick's hackles rose, and he listened to the morning activity, but nothing suggested an attack.

"It's the grain stores." Lucy's voice shook. "More than half was destroyed."

Eldrick's wolf howled, and his jaw pulsed. "Show me."

Lucy led him and Bétar to the storage house. A crowd had gathered, circling upturned sacks of grain. Eldrick squatted and inspected them. He sniffed and detected a musty scent.

"Mold?" Confusion rippled through him. "In the dead of winter?"

Bétar reached inside a sack and pulled out a damp cloth. Spores dotted the fabric. The Commander reached further into the grain, a frown creasing his beard.

"It's damp at the bottom," he said.

"Look."

A pack member pointed, and Eldrick rose from his haunches and followed their line of sight. In the corner, a dormant fire scorched the center of the storehouse, not large enough to cause damage, but enough to warm the inside and encourage the mold's growth.

"Moons," Eldrick hissed. "Who would tamper with our grain stores?"

Yet, as he asked the answer dawned on him like a punch to the gut—Bjorn.

He'll fight dirty, so you need to be prepared.

Sam's warning filtered into the back of Eldrick's mind. A dozen eyes settled on him, and his skin crawled. He didn't feel equipped for *this*. He'd not trained for it either. Protecting his pack against demons and scáths. Meeting with the alphas and discussing strategy. Stripping his father of his title was one thing, but a blatant assault against the Drengrs? Bjorn had robbed his pack of food midwinter—or worse, poisoned someone if they hadn't been wiser of the stench. There was no telling if this cold would linger for longer with the Void spreading, too.

Eldrick's wolf raged. Though, wasn't that what Bjorn wanted? The alpha knew Eldrick cared for his pack, so he'd hurt him where it mattered.

He turned to a set of warriors in the crowd. "Do any of you man the gates?"

"Aye, Alpha." One nodded.

"Did you see Alpha Bjorn leave?" Eldrick asked.

"Two days ago," the werewolf said. "With his entire party along with him."

Bétar approached. "Which means he left before the storm."

"And if he or anyone in his pack planted this, no one would've taken notice during the blizzard." Eldrick shook his head, a growl working its way up his throat.

"The stores won't last the winter. We'll have to trade with another pack."

"But who?" Lucy said.

"Thorn." Eldrick scoffed, tongue bitter. The pack's village sat northeast, closest to the continent's river where the central plains rolled into the Vadon Mountains. The valley-like terrain created more suitable farmland, allowing Thorn to sustain his pack's wealth by growing wheat and barley. Yet, Thorn territory was in the opposite direction of Eldrick's original plan and a much harder vote to win.

"Bjorn is leading me away from Drabek," Eldrick said, keeping his voice calm while his wolf paced inside his blood, anything but.

Eldrick itched to pinch the bridge of his nose, to lay a hand on the hilt of his axe for comfort, or to release a bottled-up howl, but expectant stares landed on him from all angles. His pack looked to him for strength and balance. How he responded to Bjorn's assault set the tone for his pack.

He swallowed his anger, suppressed his worry. *Lead*, Eldrick's inner voice said, stern and unbending, while a selfish part of him ached to prove where he stood was *right*. That his heart beat for his homeland and pack.

"Bjorn knows Drabek is the vote to win, so he's either stalling me or attempting to get to her first," he said.

Bétar's eyes widened. "*Stars above*, the bastard. What will you do?"

Think, Eldrick thought. Cold blustered through the storehouse. Gray clouds hovered on the horizon. If winter continued to rage across the mountains, they couldn't rely on hunting. Game would retreat and become scarcer and harder to hunt. Frost delayed the harvest, too. Grain fed his pack, and it didn't matter if he won the Earl vote if they were hungry and weak.

"I'll ride north and meet with Alpha Thorn," he said and marched out of the storehouse to hide his frustration, heading towards his horse.

Ice crunched under Bétar's boots as he followed close behind. "What about our journey south?"

"I have to feed the pack, Bétar. The pack comes before the vote. The Drengrs matter most in times like these." Eldrick reached his horse. He checked it twice over, making sure he was prepared for an extra few days of travel. "I'll make the most of my time with Thorn, convince him to vote for me as well as barter for the grain. While I'm gone, I leave the village under your command—"

Bétar gripped Eldrick's arm, halting him in place. "*No.* I can't let you go alone. *Moons*, what if Bjorn has set you up to do exactly that? It is too dangerous for you to travel alone. No witnesses or help? You're risking your life."

Eldrick paused. Bjorn had been scouting for someone that morning when he'd walked the forest with Tovi. Stars above, the thought of her left him off-kilter. *Rattled.* He blinked, and a gut-wrenching scene played through his mind. In the late hours of the night, they discussed all their worries, fears, and hopes in the comfort of each other's arms. His body craved her presence at his side, a teammate to navigate this with.

We have our own paths in this, he'd said as they'd parted ways as alpha and queen. What he envisioned was fantasy, and he'd chosen the silvery ink tattooed up his arm, and when he earned the Earl vote, the rightness of his decision would finally settle over him like the magic of his new title.

"I can't leave the Drengr Village undefended," Eldrick said. "Bjorn has already struck where he knew it hurt the worst—my pack. He knows I'll leave no matter the course, but what if it's an undefended village he wants? We know he's threatened Thorn and prepared his entire pack to fight. If he returns—"

"We'll face him if need be," Lucy said, with hands on her hips. She pointed down the street at her warrior shield wedged into the glinting morning light. "You forget I once held the title of Commander for forty years. I know how to protect my pack—from scáths, demons, or a bloody bastard like Bjorn if I must. You'll do what you need, and the village will stand upon your return, alpha."

Agreement rumbled through the crowd that had gathered. Arms folded. Brows set. Committal nods. Eldrick inhaled his pack's unwavering strength. Perhaps it wasn't only him who had to embody it, but a resiliency that passed through each of them.

"Aye, what do you say, Eldrick? It's a fine day for a ride after all." Bétar winked.

Several hours later, with a sodden ass stuck to his saddle, Eldrick shivered under the spilling rain. "Your words jinxed us, Bétar."

The Commander's cloak clung to his red hair, and his beard dripped with water. "Don't blame me; there's a much darker force in charge of this."

As if to fuel Bétar's assessment, berry-sized hail joined the rain, dinging off their horses, rigid exteriors, and weapons. Though Eldrick thrummed with the promise of his plan, the weather unsettled his inner wolf. This winter was proving harsher and longer than most. Branches were bare of saplings. Ferns dotted the forest floor in their dormant brown, fronds naked of leaves. Under Eldrick's horse's hooves, the land remained hardened with the cold, deep under the mud of today's rainstorm.

He'd read the paper, heard the accounts, witnessed the darkness spreading, but to *feel* it was an entirely different matter. Eldrick's blood now coursed with alpha magic. His connection to the land was like an oak's roots—deep, sprawling, and strong. The darkness's presence touched wherever it spread, much like the mold that'd ruined his pack's grain. It was a disease, infectious. In times like these, when the symptoms poured over Eldrick and chilled him deep to his bones, he questioned his efforts in breaking the curse. Was he doing enough?

The rain slowed to a drizzle, and ahead, lanterns dotted the wall surrounding Thorn Village. Patrols sounded their horns, and Eldrick held up his hand in greeting. He and Bétar slowed their horses at the gate.

"Good evening to ya both." A young werewolf Eldrick recognized—Erik, one of the werewolves they'd saved in Drystan—appeared at the wall. "What business are you here for?"

Eldrick dropped back his hood, letting the rain kiss his revealed face.

The young werewolf's face split into a grin. "Eldrick, or should I say, *Alpha Drengr*, it's good to see you. Let them in!"

The gate groaned open, and three dozen tree houses shone in the night. Crafted from enormous willow trees the width of thirty to forty men, the Thorns lived above the forest ground. Rope bridges connected the tree houses like streets. Some establishments were built on posts between trees, the Wasted Willow a tavern at the center where Eldrick had stumbled from a few too many times.

Erik slid down a ladder. "Come, you can leave the horses in the ground stables for the night, and I'll take you to Alpha Thorn. It is good to see you both."

Eldrick and Bétar dismounted their horses and shed their travels. After a fresh set of dry clothes from his pack and the stiffness of riding flushing out of his legs, he and Bétar followed Erik up a set of stairs that spiraled up the trunk of a tree.

At the top, they took a series of bridges and platforms until they reached the alpha's fortress. More longhouse than tree house, the building stretched between two willows, branches framing the front and rear. Extra posts angled in crossed patterns held the longhouse in place, and the wooden frame and roof featured carvings of dancing wolves and a waning moon.

Inside, sweet hickory burned inside a cauldron-like hearth. The smoke traveled through an open window built into the ceiling. Rain hissed against the flames but was no match for the fire's intense heat. At the end, Alpha Leif Thorn laughed with his mate while his young daughter sat on his lap. His long hair reached to his navel, covering his Thorn maroon tunic, while a thick dark beard framed his grin.

He lifted his goblet to drink, stilling it at his lips as he caught sight of Erik, Bétar, and Eldrick. His smile grew, and he rose, lifting his daughter with him and saddling her on his hip as he approached them.

"Uncle," Erik said. "I've brought Alpha—"

"Eldrick will do," he said, grasping the young werewolf's shoulder.

Leif grumbled, grasping Eldrick's arm in greeting. "Aye, let them say it. It's a reminder not just to those around but to ourselves, too."

Leif's father and mother had passed five years ago during a scáths attack. Leif had ascended as alpha at sixty years old—though he looked the same age as Eldrick—which was fairly young for an alpha. Eldrick wondered if Bjorn had bullied Thorn for that very reason and perhaps pride, the need to appear collected—a feeling Eldrick knew all too well—was why Thorn hadn't leaned on the other alphas.

"I hope we aren't intruding, but we're here on urgent matters," Eldrick said.

"Come. Sit," Leif said. "Are you both hungry?"

"Starving." Bétar rubbed his hands together.

"As am I," Erik said.

Leif rolled his eyes, nudging his nephew with elbow. "I know your mother feeds you, Erik. You emptied half of Thorn's stores with that endless appetite. Alpha, Commander. Join us. Eat. Please make yourselves comfortable. Ah, and this beautiful werewolf" —Leif planted a kiss on the female's temple— "is my mate, Rue."

Leif busied himself pouring goblets of mead and pushed them across the table.

"It's nice to meet you," Eldrick said to Rue. "We appreciate you letting us interrupt family dinner."

"I don't mind at all." Rue smiled up at him, and it reached all the way to her warm brown eyes. "Your visit gives me a chance to say thank you for saving Erik, my sister's son. I hear you both were part of the team that got him." Her eyes danced as they skated across Eldrick and Bétar. "Along with the vampyr queen."

Eldrick assessed both Rue's tone and Leif's reaction to the mention of Tovi, but unlike Rue's gratitude, Leif bristled. Perhaps discussing Eldrick's alliance with Tovi wasn't wise.

"I appreciate that," Eldrick said, "but I think the bravery of those young werewolves is overlooked."

Bétar nodded, lifting a mug towards Erik, who was far too consumed with the potatoes he dipped in gravy.

"Well, you can all blame Erik. He never gives us a chance to commend what he endured. He goes on about you all nonstop. *Eldrick this* and *Eldrick that*, and *You should've seen the vampyr queen in action!*"

"What about me?" Bétar scoffed. "I was there, ya know?"

Rue wiggled her brows. "Well, we did hear all about your mate, the archer. She's never missed a shot, according to Erik. He's mentioned her skills at least a hundred times."

The young werewolf paused mid-bite. "That isn't true."

The female alpha scoffed. "It is so, and hush, or I'll tell your ma you're arguing at the alpha's table."

Erik narrowed his gaze and sank deeper into his seat, sights falling back to his plate of potatoes.

Leif's grin faltered a fraction. "Are you here to discuss the Earl vote?"

"Yes, but my pack also needs to bargain for some grain," Eldrick said.

"Grain?" Leif and Rue shared a look. "Did you lose it during Prince Riven's attack?"

Eldrick shook his head and sighed. He'd mulled this over during his journey. Played out different scenarios and conversations. What did he gain if revealed Bjorn had done this? What did he lose? Did he appear weak, tattling to the other alphas, or did they deserve to know who they were voting for?

"Mold has infested half, and there's evidence it was planted." He ran his fingers over the rim of his cup, again gauging their reaction.

Rue straightened. "That bastard."

Bétar leaned forward in his chair. "You'll have to be more specific. There's been more than one as of late."

"Bjorn," Leif said, hand tightening on the arm of his chair. "He didn't tamper with our grain, but he stole our resources before the decree vote."

Rue growled, baring his teeth. "His daughter carried out the siege under Bjorn's command. I welcomed her into our village, not knowing she had an agenda. She's a fucking snake."

Eldrick weighed his next words carefully. "If you're well aware of Bjorn's true character, why vote for him?"

Leif and Rue shared another silent conversation, and with a small nod from his mate, Leif handed his daughter to Erik. "You're on uncle duty. Eldrick, there's something my mate and I'd like to show you."

Bétar shrugged, pulling his plate closer. "I'll remain here, where it's warm and not raining."

Eldrick rolled his eyes. Leif and Rue led the way up stairs that climbed through the longhouse until a hallway deposited them onto the upper level outside. A single bridge across led to the northern section of the wall. Those on watch bowed their heads to the mated alphas and whispered good evening to Eldrick.

The three of them stopped at an overlook tower. Light flickered ahead, and Eldrick narrowed his eyes.

"Do you have scouts outside the village?"

"No, Bjorn does." Leif braced his hand on the balcony. "They watch our village, intimidate my pack if they leave the walls. The harvest this autumn was brutal."

Anger flushed through Eldrick, but he inhaled and exhaled. *One, two.*

"Why didn't you seek my father's help?" he finally asked.

Rue crossed her arms. "Claus was in Bjorn's back pocket and whispered too much into your father's ear. We worried that spreading news of his argument, merging the Thorn and Johannes packs, would make it all that much louder."

Eldrick winced. He agreed with Leif's assessment and hated the truth—he'd have put aside pack and pride and only looked at the angle of strength and numbers. Facts, not his heart. Now, his wolf howled at Bjorn's disrespect towards Thorn land and Leif's right as alpha.

He rallied his breath. "If I earn your vote—"

"Bjorn took twenty of my best werewolves, Eldrick," Leif said. "I can't cast my vote and say your name. There's no telling what he'll do to them."

"Why, in the stars above, did he take your pack members?"

Rue blinked back tears, and Leif grasped her hand. Both their wrists gleamed with the alpha tattoo, the intricate design a continuation from one to the other. The sight of them together as a united front jarred the whisperings of the prophecy in the back of Eldrick's mind, and sadness settled over him like the wet clothes had stuck to his skin. The night cold didn't sting as much when he felt alone, at least.

"Bjorn asked for a trade, twenty of my best in exchange for my resources back," Leif said. "We were going to refuse, but our warriors volunteered. The pack came first, and we needed the resource to last the winter."

Eldrick shook his head. "It'll only get worse if he wins the vote, Leif. You've had to consider that. He might not permit your werewolves to return home, not with the war looming."

"But what is worse? Having them taken from us or hurt because of my decision?" Leif's nostrils flared, and Rue tightened her hand over his. "You've not been alpha for very long, Eldrick, but it is a series of weighing pros and cons about how to protect your pack."

"But it's more than our packs now." The words shot out of Eldrick before he thought them through. He'd come here intending to get grain for his pack above all else, Leif's vote secondary, but the more he stepped foot into the weeds of politics, the more he discovered how unnecessarily tangled it all was. This was more than surviving the winter, more than protecting their territory.

It was defeating the darkness.

Perhaps it *was* the whispering of the prophecy that fueled his next words. Eldrick was certain he believed them down to his soul.

"There is a curse to break and a homeland to save. Bjorn will not lead the werewolves to that future. His pride may as well be a demon wreaking havoc across the Vadon Mountains."

"How do we protect our pack against either future, Eldrick?" Rue asked. "We are damned either way."

"If Bjorn hurts the Thorns after the vote, you have the Drengrs as allies," Eldrick said, hating the last word—this was werewolf against werewolf when it shouldn't have been.

Leif shook his head. "If Bjorn wins the vote, can we fight the magic of his command? The Earl title possesses a magical baritone alphas must answer to."

"Then vote for me." Eldrick jabbed his finger into the air. "Tomorrow I will travel to the Drabek territory, then Alland and Lindström. If I win them over, that is four votes, including my own, against Bjorn. Be my fifth and guarantee the title falls to the Drengrs."

Leif hissed, pulling out of his mate's hold and leaning his elbows against the tower's balcony. Wind whistled through the night. Sleet *tinged* against the tree house village. Rue slid her hand up her mate's back, giving his shoulder a squeeze.

"He's right, my love."

Leif shut his eyes and hung his head. "I know."

Rue moved her hand to his chin, making Leif look at her. Silence rang as they stared at one another, and as their expressions shifted, Eldrick recognized that they were mind-linking, something he'd seen his parents do during meetings, too.

He shifted on uneasy feet, waiting. *Moons*, if Leif agreed, it'd make the scar running across his heart worth it.

He cleared his throat. "I'll give your village ten warriors from the Drengr Pack."

Both Leif and Rue whirled.

"What?" she said. "If we take them, we're no worse than Bjorn—"

Eldrick shook his head. "This is different. Thorn is a fraction of the size of the Johannes and Drengrs. To have lost twenty of your best during these times is too great a risk. I'll send word and have them arrive within the week. Hopefully, it should show the type of Earl you'd vote for."

Leif nodded, a sound of agreement rumbling through his chest. "It does, Eldrick. You have the Thorns' vote, but on one more condition."

"Name it," Eldrick said.

"I'm coming with you to visit the southern packs."

CHAPTER FORTY

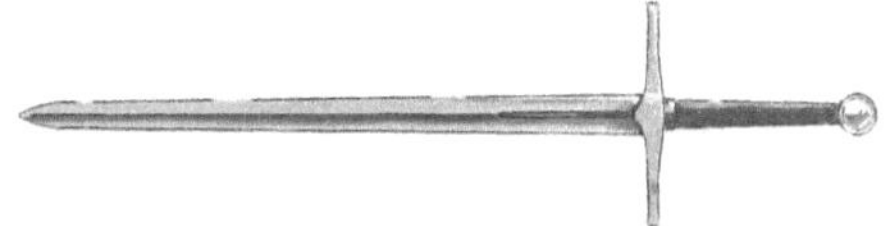

KADE BLINKED, A PURPLE haze blurring his vision, and stretched out his stiff muscles. A sensation gripped his knees, as if the world had been sucked hollow. An eerie emptiness skated across his wolf, and he peered up at the sky, searching for the moon.

Snow fell from above—no, not snow, ash. It piled into his outstretched hand. The gray flurries didn't sting as they hit his skin, nor did they melt as they landed on his bloodstained leathers. It blanketed the endless hills around him and danced on the wind.

Kade inhaled, scenting destruction, burned flesh, and infection. His stomach churned with nausea from his flooded senses and from worry—where, in the *stars above*, was he and where was his mate?

"Evelyn!" Kade's desperation cracked in his voice. Fear coursed through his blood, racing his heart. *This isn't real*, he tried to tell himself.

But it *felt* real.

He was back in the dark, desolate wasteland Circe had made him see. How had she reached him this far away? Was she near? But he found no answers, no ability to wake up. Only ash and smoke covered the ground.

Boom. Boom. Boom.

War drums echoed in the distance, and so Kade walked. To find someone, to *get out* of this horrific dream. Step after step. Miles passed. Wind whipped. His legs and resolve ached. Occasionally, he felt the sensation of rising, *up* and *up*, only to come crashing down, the unseen impact making him falter a step.

His body thinned. His throat dried. Kade stared at his bloody, broken hands.

Tiredness took over, and Kade crashed to his knees. His power flickered like a lantern. Cold, paralyzing anxiety rooted him in place, and yet all wished to do was run, to be free of this horrid cage inside his own mind.

You did this.

A voice he knew in all its forms. Disheartened. Joyful. *Resilient.* Evelyn's words snaked through the air. Kade clamped his eyes shut, pushing away the voice, the pain that came with it. Behind his eyelids, a powerful light glowed from his hands. He tried to rein in his new magic, tried to gain control.

Kade!

A thousand voices grated across his skull. His fear amounted to a tidal wave.

Wake up, he chastised himself. He pictured steely blue eyes, obsidian hair, and a laugh that brightened the darkest days. He imagined her rare, beautiful smile, and the way her left brow furrowed so deeply. He thought of the little time they'd spent together, and yet how magnificent it had been no matter how short. He inhaled her courage and exhaled the promise of *them*, and the future they were fighting for—

"I wondered when we'd meet again."

Kade whirled, finding Tenebris, the dark witch he'd encountered in Tùir, standing a few feet away, a mirth-etched smile spreading across his face.

"You're not real," Kade growled.

Tenebris laughed and stepped forward with hands clasped behind his back. His scythe was nowhere in sight, but he wore the same cloak, but this time, less tattered. Pressed, freshly washed, *crisper*. With his hood back, he revealed dark hair cut to his shoulders. The color drew out the half circles rimming his two-colored eyes. The milky-white one latched onto Kade, while the other observed the wasteland.

"I'm a messenger, Kade," Tenebris said. "Your line of connection to the darkness."

He stumbled back, tripping over a body. He didn't dare look at their faces or wounds. Flies buzzed around him as he continued to retreat from the dark witch.

Thunder rumbled in the distance, mixing with the moans of the dead. To the east, a village that shared a likeness to his home burned, but it was the flames of pearly blue that danced in the wind and devoured the cottages. The center fortress crumbled, its descent sending a ground-shaking boom across the land. To the west, birds circled a long-since destroyed city. The Carson coven's banner, ripped and bloody, swayed on the breeze.

You did this, the thousands of voices rasped again.

Get up, Kade screamed. *Snap out of it!*

The sky trembled, but there was no pain lancing through his head like when Circe had controlled his mind. He was simply *here*. Like his mind had visited the horrors that had never truly let him go.

"Aren't you the least bit curious why the darkness has called upon you?"

Kade said nothing. He thought of the things that mattered most: Evelyn, their love, his parents and brothers, the Gray Fenris, the prophecy and his *destiny*.

Tenebris laughed again, wet and sticky. "How can one fulfill their destiny when they don't even know who they are?"

Kade growled, charging towards the dark witch. "I am Kade Drengr, third born and Son of the God."

Tenebris didn't flinch.

LIES! Evelyn and Circe's voices both shrieked like thunder across the sky.

Kade's heart dropped like a stone to his gut. Tenebris circled him, and his scythe appeared from the shadows.

"Have you ever wondered why your power doesn't feel right?" Tenebris asked.

"Stop," Kade hissed.

"It is because you haven't accepted where it came from."

"You're wrong," he bit out.

Tenebris tilted his head and sneered, revealing his decaying teeth. "It is chaos and destroys. *You are darkness.*"

Kade's chest heaved. It wasn't this place that was hollow; it was *him*. Uncertain, frightened. He was losing the one he loved most in all this world, and he didn't know how to help her or fix it because he *didn't know who he was*.

The realization paralyzed him.

"No." Kade shook his head. "I'm prophesied to defeat it."

Tenebris tsked, snaking out his tongue to lick his bottom lip. He leaned on his scythe like a walking stick. "Only you can accept this, Kade. Until you do, I will visit. Messenger and helper! Ah, yes. The darkness's task for me is so sweet and honorable."

"Honorable?" Kade charged, grasping hold of Tenebris. Surprise shot through—the man *was* real. The fibers of his cloak itched Kade's palm, felt the male's weight as he held him off the ground. "That doesn't exist within those who follow darkness."

"Until tomorrow night." Tenebris snapped his fingers and disappeared.

Kade woke with a start, the rush of panic lingering in his limbs. He throat tightened, and he gasped for air, like fear was a hand grasping his throat. He ran a hand down his face, the feel of ash still at his fingertips.

He turned, reaching for Evelyn, to feel her against him and find some comfort as the hours ticked by before began their journey to the Sun Temple, only to find her side of the bed empty.

CHAPTER FORTY-ONE

Evelyn

E VELYN WRETCHED FOR THE second time, last night's dinner splattering against the sandy street below. She wiped the back of her hand against her mouth and slumped against the roof's wall.

The sun rose over Cirrillo's major port city while to the right, gulls cried the morning hour, and the *Sel* was nowhere to be found on the horizon, long gone after dropping them off in the lands desert mages called home. After Kade's valor during the demon attack, Flynn had more than begged to help in any way he could, and when they revealed their next destination, the vampyr witch had taken them around witch territory. Flynn had saved them from being discovered, but Evelyn's days still dwindled.

Dying *really* hurt.

She wretched again, barely making it over the balcony. A sharp pain lanced through her stomach. There was nothing left in it but bile and—

Blood.

Evelyn patted her lips. Crimson smeared across her fingers, and the taste of iron coated her teeth.

Fucking flames.

She clamped her eyes shut, grasping the wall for support. The hole in her chest was widening. The frays had unraveled while she'd fought on the ship with Kade's sword in hand, but she hadn't the courage to tell him her body was failing.

She'd not considered it or discussed it with Mirella. Evelyn thought she had a severed soul and a ticking time clock, not a deteriorating body. They still had three days before they reached the Sun Goddess's temple. Could she even make it?

She *had* to.

On shaky legs, Evelyn rose. She couldn't let anyone see her like this, not when they needed her to keep the group together. It was *she* they risked everything for. Her sisters, Kade, his pack and friends. She'd not let some sore soul stop her progress in getting her magic back.

Her body screamed in retaliation as she wobbled down the steps. Sore was an understatement. Pain radiated deep in her bones. Evelyn bit her lip to muster through it, tasting more blood.

"*Fuck—*"

"Evelyn." Belle appeared at the bottom of the stairs, concern pinching her brow.

"I'm alright," Evelyn whispered, stumbling down the last step.

"You're a terrible liar." Belle held her steady. "Has anyone told you that?"

"Don't tell Kade," Evelyn breathed. "That's all I ask."

"Why?" Belle studied her with too-beautiful eyes.

Because . . . Kade had conjured his power with control on the *Sel*, wielded it. Evelyn's skin crawled, and she tried to blame it on the desert air, but she was too familiar with shame to ignore it. It whispered in the same tune as doubt. If Kade learned she faced this pain, that her body ailed her, would it jeopardize the progress he'd made with his power?

Evelyn didn't have the stomach to admit that to Belle, so she lied.

"He's already worried enough, and more won't aid in our journey to the temple."

Belle frowned. "I suppose you're right. Here."

She passed Evelyn a waterskin, and she rinsed out her mouth, cleaning her face and hands.

"Thank you," she said. "Should we head back to the inn before anyone notices I'm gone?"

Belle nodded, and they fell into step with one another.

"How are you doing?" she asked.

The witch shrugged. "Dandy. Happy to be off the ship. Well, Todd is, I mean. He won't admit it, but I think he hates boats as much as Kade."

Evelyn smiled and grabbed her friend's hand. "I meant about your sister. You both said some harsh words."

Evelyn left out the part where Belle had caused a whirlpool to suck Ingrid and Riven to their demise, an angry side of her she'd never seen before.

Belle stared off at the market square and scoffed. "Ingrid will always be my sister, but we are on different paths now."

Evelyn thought of her own sisters. She and Blair had *disagreed* of late, but they'd not reached that fork in the road where they went in different directions. The possibility ate at Evelyn's nerves.

"There's a chance Ingrid's not herself, you know?" Evelyn said. "Using dark magic is a risky power, and perhaps it's *changing* her."

Belle stopped on the main street. Cirrillo buzzed around them. "We're both witches with magic. It's what we do with it that divides us. Ingrid's choices led her down that path, and she may believe she did it to protect me, but I think she did it for herself, and now she no longer has an excuse for who she is."

They walked into the main dining area of the inn, and Evelyn let Belle's words settle over her. In the corner, their team sat at a long table, hunched over breakfast. The smell of sizzling oil and coffee floated in the heady air.

"How do you feel about the spell?" Evelyn asked.

Belle had been studying it since they left the Drengr Village, collecting items and tweaking Blair's theory here and there.

"Good, but actually, there's something I want to talk to you about—"

"There you are," Kade called from the bottom of the stairs. He reached her in two long strides, grasping her face. "You gave me a fright. *I'm* usually the morning person."

Evelyn rested her hands over his. "You looked like you needed the extra rest." But tiredness clung to him, and she noted it for later. "Can you give me a second with Belle?"

"Sure." Kade kissed her forehead and walked off to join the others at the table.

Belle paused, deliberation warring in her gaze. Once Kade was out of earshot, she sighed. "Look, I won't tell Kade or any of the others how I found you, but"—Belle emphasized the word with a bashful roll of her eyes—"take it from someone who ... *maybe* ... I don't know ... there might be a chance, I guess—"

Evelyn laughed. "Goddess, Belle, tell me."

Belle bit her lip and fought a smile. "As someone who might have a werewolf fated sensing everything and anything, you can't hide what you're going through, broken mating bond or not."

She stilled. Open and closed her mouth. "Are you saying what I think you're saying?"

Belle nodded furiously, and as if it were possible, her bright smile made her even more beautiful. She practically beamed like the sun inside the inn.

She held up her hands. "Nothing is official-official. Todd thinks I'm rather young for something so binding, but we agreed to take it slow . . . Though, fate has a mind of its own, I suppose. The whole feeling of one's emotions comes in handy for exploratory activities." Belle winked, and a faint blush spread across her cheeks.

"*Belle.*" Evelyn gasped, grasping her friend's arm, unable to fight the giggles working their way up her throat.

By the time they joined the others at the table, Evelyn's aches and pains had vanished from her thoughts, and her stomach had settled to a manageable churn, and she sipped her coffee, finding solace in the small moments with friends.

"It has more legs than I do in my shifted form!" Todd held up a piece of squid, battered and fried to a golden crisp. A heaping plate of them sat at the center table, tossed with sweet peppers and over-easy eggs on top, the runny yolks adding a rich sauce.

Linx shoveled them into her mouth two at a time. "I think they're delightful."

"*Delightful?*" Todd grimaced. "It's unnatural. May I remind you that many legs is reminiscent of the demon we fought a two nights ago?"

The mage shrugged, popping another fried squid into her mouth. "Much like that beast, we're making quick work of these.

The table laughed, and Todd turned to Kade. "So, what's the plan?"

"A day in the city would do us good." Linx sipped her coffee. "A day to rest."

"There isn't time," Evelyn blurted out, not thinking before she spoke.

Kade rested a hand on her knee under the table. "Evelyn's right. We don't know what we'll encounter on our way to the temple. It's better to start our journey sooner rather than later and get ahead of any delays."

"We just stepped back on land." Linx, wide-eyed, looked to other members of their team for support. "One day can't hurt us, not when a full day's rest and meals better than vampyr pirate stew will give us the strength we need to journey in a place new to all of us."

"Not all." Evelyn planted her hands firmly on the table. "I traveled through Cirrillo to visit the very temple we're headed to when I lost my magic. I know the journey. It isn't easy. Sandstorms, bandits, and sand-dwelling demons."

She stressed each one, but withheld the real reason—a day in the city might allow the others to rest, but she might wake up unfit for travel. Evelyn couldn't afford to delay. The sooner they reached the Sun Temple the better.

"Besides, we may have avoided Nūa, but that doesn't mean we won't cross paths with witches this far south. The port city is teeming with witches and mages. It's best to get on the road and keep moving so Circe doesn't learn our plan. I know the route to a village near the temple," Evelyn added.

The table nodded as she spoke, even Linx relaxed, her frown turning into an expression of understanding.

Kade nodded. "Then it's decided—today, we start our travels through the Cirrillo Desert."

Chapter Forty-Two

Tovi's body exhaled at the sight ahead, the limestone brick and slate shingled roofs a welcome sight in her cursed homeland.

Despite the time since she'd lived here, over two decades now, the ivy hadn't overgrown as much as she'd expected. The trees were trimmed, and the ferns known to pop up along the walls thanks to the lack of sun from the curse were nowhere in sight. It was neat, not an estate in shambles.

"You said you had a manor, not a castle!" Yen said, shaking her head with a wide grin.

"It's small compared to Drystan Castle. It could fit in one of its wings comfortably," Tovi said.

"It's far nicer though," Yen said, eyes bright. "Less drab. Suits you actually."

Áilleacht Castle had many names. The summer house, the princess's estate, and the king's grand gift. But Tovi preferred its given name—*áilleacht* meant beauty in the old language of Torren, and her father had selected it as a nod to the nickname he'd used for her. She'd been his beauty, and Riven had been his cleverness.

It wasn't until decades later that he saw her beauty as something to sell.

Tovi sighed, dismissing those distant memories. She loved Áilleacht Castle for the older memories, the ones where her mother and father hadn't fallen too deep into their greed tied to their titles as king and queen.

The primary structure of the castle was a square-cornered tower. Four stories tall, it reached to the Drystan mists with a hip-style roof and four turrets at each corner. Delicate purple flags, a shade that reminded Tovi of creeping phlox, stood tall in the winds. An enclosed bridge constructed from the same limestone brick crossed over a tranquil creek. Many, many times, Tovi had ventured to the bridge with a book, sat in one of the glassless windows, and allowed her nerves to balance with its gentle sound of the calm water.

Yen guided her horse forward, riding ahead of Tovi. "I know what Flynn asked of you. Werewolves have keen hearing, too."

Tovi shifted in her saddle. "Did you tell Evelyn?"

"No," Yen said. "But she's smart. I'm sure she put it together herself."

Tovi sighed. "Is this where you tell me to take the offer?"

Yennifer brought her horse to a stop, halting their progress across the bridge halfway. "How could you possibly think that?"

"The offer is the wise choice. It proves to my people I'm putting them first."

"You are already a queen without fighting for the title, Tovi. You don't have to prove anything."

"This isn't the Vadon Mountains, Yen. You, Nadia, Lucy . . . You're all honored and respected for your fierceness and abilities to fight. Here, vampyrs measure females on their smiles, poise, and mundane talents to pass the time."

"You are none of those things. Why fulfil societal expectations you loathe? It is *marriage*."

Tovi shook her head. "Flynn would be more than a husband. He has a fleet of ships."

"Other lords have armies and resources. What makes the pirate different? Because it once worked? You deserve better."

Like a gentle kiss to her temple, Eldrick's words zinged through her—*You deserve happiness.*

Yen's horses stepped side to side as the archer tightened her grip on the reins and her expression hardened. "Do you simply want to become queen or do you want to change Drystan, Tovi?"

Tovi swallowed a hiss, staring out at the gray-infested land around them. She could practically smell the curse in the air, feel the smaller particles creeping across her skin. Dancing in the shadows, seeping from the tree sap, embedded in the stone below the horses' hooves.

She sighed, setting her shoulders back, tone unbending. "Breaking the curse is my priority, and the chance to make change will come after my homeland is restored."

"If you marry Flynn, you show your subjects that the status quo *is* the way. Not even their queen can break free of society norms, so how can the rest of them? Why not prove that you can do this on your own? Set the tone for

Drystan's new era. Or better yet, stop sacrificing bits of yourself, because as your friend, I fear by the time the curse is broken, there won't be anything of you left." Yen urged her horse back into motion.

Tovi's chest grew tight. A yearning for the future her friend spoke about rooted in her heart, but her stomach twisted into knots. Nerves like pesky minnows nibbling at her resolve. Could she afford to think about herself and what she wanted? In truth, it was why she had said no to Flynn, but hadn't forgotten his proposal. It was an option she had to consider, right?

Yet, the touches of green in her homeland, the color leeching past the curse, taunted her with another promise. What if *he* was the choice she wanted to make?

"Yen," Tovi called.

The werewolf stopped at the end of the bridge.

"When did you know Bétar was your mate?" she asked.

Yen smiled, eyes brightening at her warrior's name. "The moment I met him."

The urge to ask Yennifer more questions rose in a mighty wave. She clucked her tongue and caught up to Yen with her horse. What if she simply learned? What if Tovi finally admitted what she was afraid to say out loud?

"Auntie!" the gleeful shrieks of children broke through the mists.

Juni and Bryn, her niece and nephew, sprinted towards them with mud-splattered welly boots, and grins so unfitting for Drystan's gray, Tovi forgot about it all entirely.

Tovi dismounted her horse and caught them as they launched into her awaiting arms. She spun with them, their giggles infectious.

"Why, I missed you both!" she said, holding them on opposite hips. "What are you doing here?"

"Playing werewolf!" Bryn said.

"*I'm* the werewolf," Juni said, but the many syllables blurred together and sounded more like "wee-ulf".

Yennifer snorted and dismounted from her horse, gathering the reins of both steeds. "Now, that is a first that I've heard of such a game."

"Did you bring an elk?" Juni asked.

"Bryn! Juni!" Opal and Sven emerged from the castle gardens, their gloves coated with dirt. Sven held shears while Opal carried a shovel. They lowered their makeshift weapons at the sight of Tovi, and her brother released a whooshing breath.

The main door to the castle groaned open, and Tovi's uncle, Bran, stormed out. "I swear those children are too fearless for their own good, running off—" He blinked past his gold-wired glasses. "Well, I'll be damned. You came."

Tovi set the children down, who rushed off to their parents. "I'm glad to see you made it here, Sven."

"We wouldn't be without your help and Cass's guidance," her brother said, dragging her into a tight hug.

Uncle Bran, his mate, Cass, nowhere in sight, descended the stairs—he wasn't her real uncle, but he'd been her father's best friend all those centuries ago in Callum, and who'd fled Torren and survived the voyage to Drystan's shores with her family. He'd been one of the first vampyrs turned. Not a Verena by blood but circumstance. Like Sven, Bran shied away from court, but he'd grown to be one of Tovi's most trusted connections, helping her run her merchant business from afar.

He pulled her into a tight hug, palming her cheek. She'd not seen him since she'd left for Callum all those months ago to spy on Riven, leaving him Áilleacht Castle if he chose to stay here.

Silver had peppered Bran's well-shaped beard before he'd turned, remaining long after immortality had touched his blood. It suited him and matched the gentleness that had never vanished from his hazel eyes.

"It is good to see," he whispered. "My *queen*."

She pushed his shoulder. "Please, for the love of the Goddess, don't call me that."

"You'll have to get used to it someday," Yennifer said.

"Here," Opal said. "Let me help with the horses."

Uncle Bran clasped Tovi's hands. "I'll get us some wine poured. Dinner's just around the corner."

With a shower, a change of clothes, and enough laughter to cause a stitch in her side, dinner with Tovi's family had eased the tension and travel. Her earlier conversation with Yen was long gone from her mind, but politics weren't. As good as it was to sit at the table, sip wine, eat a delicious meal, and tease her niece and nephew, she'd trekked to Áilleacht Castle with a purpose.

"What have you heard about Lord Nathanaël? I discovered he's dealing out bloodstones."

Sven paused mid-drink, and Opal's eyes widened.

Bran poured more wine, sighing as he leaned back into his seat. "There have been rumors of such these last few months, that he discovered a deposit nestled in his farmland."

Tovi ran a finger over the rim of her glass. She and Riven had discovered the bloodstone's properties by accident after the curse. Yet, in pursuit to find more, she and Riven had also learned how rare the gem was, and to prevent chaos around a gem that vampyrs might die for, they created a narrative that bloodstones were the official gem of the royal family. If discovered by anyone, they were to be handed over to the Verenas.

"Lord Nathanaël's audacity to withhold them isn't just cheeky, it's treason," she said.

"He knows you and Riven are too busy to do anything about it," Sven said.

"Do we think he's vying for the crown himself?" Yennifer asked. "He could earn fealty with the bloodstones, no?"

Opal shook her head. "Drystan's lore is so deeply woven with the Verenas, most would fear putting an another on the throne that doesn't please the Blood Goddess."

Tovi nodded. "Nathanaël has always been vocal about not wanting a female on the throne, but he's never had eyes for it."

"Indeed," Uncle Bran said. "His power is in money, and he's one of the wealthiest lords and landowners in Drystan. He has also written to your merchant company, proposing to do business with them."

"For?"

Uncle Bran rose from his seat and sifted through a pile of letters on his desk. He handed her one with the Nathanaël house's seal. "He's building an army, Tovi, and has considered you as the buyer. These came last week."

"What?" She flipped through the letters, which were written more like proposals. Lord Nathanaël claimed to have an army "large enough" to win a war. "*Bloody hel*, he wants to profit off the divide between my brother and me."

"If this lord doesn't want a female on the throne, why consider Tovi?" Yennifer asked. "It could it be a trap, a way to lure her to his lands and then capture her for Riven."

Tovi shook her head. "Yen's right. Why write to me and not Riven? He's the preferred heir."

Uncle Bran held up a finger. "There's only one problem with that: Your brother is broke, and Lord Nathanaël knows it."

Tovi snapped straighter, her brow pinching so fiercely pain lanced through her forehead. "How is that possible? His merchant company is not much smaller than mine. He possesses Drystan Castle's troves, too, seeing as he controls vampyr court."

"Your brother hasn't conducted business with his merchant company since he left for Callum. He also assumed the ruling role in court with your absence, taking up much of his time, too. As for the castle's wealth, you and your friends buried it all under rubble during your mission to break out the Daughter of the Goddess."

Yennifer whistled. "That's a splendid surprise. I'll be sure to let Linx know how very effective her explosives were."

The others laughed, asking questions about the Gray Fenris, while Tovi slumped in her seat, tapping the wooden table. Was her next move visiting Lord Nathanaël? Could she stomach conducting business with a mercenary who detested females like her?

Boots clattered down the hall, heavy and quick. "I swear, my senses must be failing me. It smells distinctly like a werewolf—"

Uncle Bran's mate, Cass, halted in the dining room's doorway. He frowned, but a playful sheen coated his dark eyes. "Well, Goddess. I thought *I'd* be the first to invite a werewolf to the castle's table." He held his arm out, ushering others into the room.

Nadia and Aramis appeared—traveling leathers worn, cheeks reddened from the cold, and jaws tight.

Tovi and Yen sprang out of their seats. The archer greeted her once alpha, and the werewolves exchanged hushed, excited words.

"Far too much wine in this country," Tovi heard Aramis grumble.

"It's not the Shield-maiden, that's for sure," Yen laughed.

Nadia rolled her eyes at their conversation but gripped Tovi's shoulders. "What brought you here?" she asked.

Tovi's brows shot up. "I can ask you the same thing."

"Running," Aramis threw over his shoulder as he introduced himself to Sven, Opal, and Uncle Bran. The measured grump of the alpha reminded Tovi of another Drengr werewolf, and she snapped her attention back to Nadia.

Her friend shot a glare in Aramis's direction. "We are *regrouping*."

"From what exactly?" Tovi asked.

"Your sister, Visha," Aramis said. "She caught us snooping inside the castle, and we barely got out alive."

Nadia threw up her hands. "But we got out!"

"*Barely*—"

"How about some wine?" Uncle Bran's friendly announcement cut through the tension.

Opal dragged Nadia closer to the table and invited her to sit—at the opposite end of the table from Aramis, Tovi noted.

"They're in vampyr territory, and yet, their biggest enemy is themselves," Cass whispered into Tovi's ear, his voice just as deep as his brown skin. "About did my head in getting them here."

"Why were you so far north?" Tovi asked.

Cass smirked. "Spying, per my queen's orders. How do you think your uncle comes by all this useful information?"

Tovi crossed her arms, finding the energy to smile. "Well, what did you find?"

"Two fools who failed to steal back the Moon God's sword," Aramis said from the far end of the table. Servants entered, bringing additional plates of food. In the corner, Juni and Bryn slept on the oversize reading chair, wool blankets tucked to their chins.

Nadia's grip on her wineglass threatened to snap the stem.

"Is Riven the crowned king like he claims?" Tovi asked.

Nadia cut her attention away from Aramis. "No more than I was a war advisor on his council. He's playing pretend with the title. Visha entertains the court, and the Drystan Village remains loyal to you. Though Riven is preparing a small legion, and . . ."

"And?" Tovi pressed.

Nadia frowned. "We discovered Riven's next move."

"That's worthy news, is it not?" Yennifer asked, peering up and down the table.

Aramis said nothing, and Tovi suddenly realized where the eldest Drengr brother had learned the art of stewing from.

"What is it?" Tovi asked.

"Ingrid is working on a spell to widen the Void and spread the curse all over Sorin."

"Goddess," Tovi breathed. "I guess if they can't give vampyrs the sun, they'll send darkness everywhere instead."

"Precisely," Aramis said through gritted teeth.

Uncle Bran leaned forward in his chair, adjusting his glasses. "When does Ingrid plan to conduct the spell?"

"We didn't find that information in time before Visha found us reading through Ingrid's things," Nadia said. "But neither the prince nor his dark witch were in the castle, both away on business."

Tovi crossed her arms, bitterness coating her tongue. "Still, we must assume its tomorrow or the next. We must stop them."

"You will need an army of your own to face him, Tovi," Nadia said. "Sadly, the werewolves aren't a guarantee."

"I know." She picked up Lord Nathanaël's letter. She'd come to Drystan to secure allies, but with news of Ingrid's spell, she didn't have time on her side. Flynn had already proved what she'd feared—marriage. Yet, what if there was a way to protect her heart, to keep her choice, but also do right by her people?

Dance their dance, Lou had said.

The lords of Drystan thrived off prestige, land, and wealth, and unlike Riven, she had money, perhaps enough to buy *exactly* what she needed to face him.

"Is Lord Nathanaël married?" she asked her uncle.

He nodded. "Yes."

"Any sons?"

"No, only one daughter," Uncle Bran said.

Perfect.

Tovi addressed the table full of expectant stares, her plan settling over her like the summer sun rays. "It's time I replied to him about buying an army."

Chapter Forty-Three

Blair

Fika wasn't frozen in time, but a season.

Strings of buzzing lights connected the village's quaint buildings, lighting the cobblestone streets in a magical glow. Cinnamon perfumed the air no matter the time of day, and pine wreaths decorated cottages and business's doors. Witches called the season Yule, and though they were weeks past that holiday, Fika remained this warm and festive all year round.

Though, this distance from their respective homes had drawn Blair and Lorkan here all those years ago. It wasn't a village that belonged to a certain pack, but a base town for the buzzing mountain of Vísdómr.

If Blair raised her hand out ahead of her, she could place her index finger on the mountain's peak; *that* was how close it sat on the horizon. It was a half day's ride with a well-rested horse and favorable weather, and she and Lorkan had plans to leave within the hour. She'd enter the most prestigious library in all of Sorin by sunset, perhaps with an ancient text in hand by dinner.

Blair sank further into her reading chair, wishing the cushions would swallow her whole so she could dismiss the shame she held for her own stubbornness. She was a fool not to have brought her and Lorkan here in the first place, but at least the detour to Nūa had been worth it.

Jace's ancient faerie text indeed discussed the bloodstone. Three entire chapters. Though her reading was slow going given she had to translate every word, she'd already learned something fascinating—this text was written before the great war amongst gods.

"Anything interesting?" Lorkan waltzed into the reading area she'd sought for some solitude.

She'd agreed to travel here, but not to endure the painful memories with the male who'd given them to her. But they were working together on figuring out how to break the curse, forcing her to have to speak to him.

Blasted books.

"Yes." Blair turned the text around for him to see. "This details what we already know—the gems are made from the blood of fallen gods—but faeries discovered that the phenomenon *only* happened if the god was slain by a fellow god. Faerie believed they left the memories behind in the stone, a warning of sorts to other gods. Though I haven't made it far enough to translate *how* they came to that conclusion."

Lorkan positioned his glasses so he could inspect Blair's translations. "It would align with its properties, hiding vampyrs from the Blood Goddess, like the fallen gods were protecting them. Any mention of her?"

"Actually, no." Blair frowned, flipping the page to a previous chapter. "There's no direction mention of her, but the faerie referred to the One, capitalized just like in the prophecy."

"That can't be a coincidence," Lorkan said, brows pinched. He leaned closer, skimming the page.

"I agree—" Blair stilled, red catching her attention. "Blasted books, are you wearing a bloodstone?"

She snatched the leather cord threaded through the ring—careful not to touch the gem—and inspected it. Yet, she realized, until it was much too late, that she'd dragged Lorkan down to her level. His breath tickled her lips, and his eyes darkened to amber.

Time stopped. Sense vanished from her mind. If she brushed her lips against his, a hair's distance away, would he taste of smoke like all those years ago?

Lorkan, achingly gently, pried her fingers from the necklace and, inch by inch, rose away from her. "My father found it after Riven's attack and gave it to me to research."

"You're just *now* telling me?" Blair swiped her hand in the air. "Scratch that, *were* you going to tell me?"

"We've been a little busy." Lorkan shoved his hands into pockets, attention falling outside the window. "You know, being chased across the continent."

Blair ground her teeth together, but before she could comment, the shop owner, Aina, entered the reading area with books stacked to her chin. Lorkan rushed to assist, grasping half of them out of the elderly werewolf's hands.

"Thank you, my dear." She swiped sweat from her brow as she busied herself stacking books in their respective places.

An awkward silence bled into the shop, Saga & Spines. The bookstore held a special coziness, fitting for Fika, and it was the one part of the town Blair still held dear. She'd visited often with Lorkan during their relationship, but even after it ended, Aina had mailed her special copies of books she thought Blair might love—adventurous romances that were a breath of fresh air compared to her scholarly work. To this day, Blair's heart expanded with the sentiment, but not enough to visit.

"Should I get a pot of tea going?" Aina asked, rubbing her hands together. "Cold always wanders inside these days. No escaping it."

Lorkan smiled, but Blair noted the slight sadness etched into his mouth, and how his focus kept falling outside the window.

"I'm afraid Blair and I are headed out soon." He turned to Blair. "I'll meet you at the stables in twenty minutes."

His quick gait suggested he had somewhere to be and was late. Blair furrowed her brows, unease swimming in her gut.

"It is so lovely to have both of you back in my shop again." Aina sighed. "I can remember your first visit like it was yesterday."

Blair recalled it too, walking in hand in hand and so consumed with staring into the other's eyes, they'd bumped into one of Aina's intricate displays and knocked down over fifty books. They spent the better half of the day helping Aina with the mess, which turned into tea, then dinner, and then . . . They popped into Saga & Spines every time they visited Fika—a tradition.

Lorkan had shattered that tradition when he'd never shown at the inn. She'd wandered into the shop, crying her eyes out, and Aina had made her tea and patted her hand, promising everything would be alright.

Blair didn't think the kind werewolf had lied; she just believed her to be wrong.

She rose from her seat and gathered her things, eager to get out of the village and make it to Vísdómr and continue her research. "It was good to see you, Aina, and I'd like to thank you for the books you've sent over the years. You know my reading taste so well."

Aina laughed, pulling her in for a hug. "Oh, I can't take the credit. Lorkan's the one who picked them out."

Blair stilled, blood turning to ice. "I'm sorry. What did you say?"

The shop owner nodded with a wry smile. "Aye, I figured you didn't know. Those packages might be from Saga & Spines, but they weren't from me, my dear. They were from him."

She pointed out the window at Lorkan, who stood with a man Blair had never seen before. Lorkan pinched his brow, frustration leaking from him, even at this distance. Rook landed on his shoulder for the hundredth time, and Blair saw red.

Why?

The question rattled through Blair related to many, many things, and she wasn't sure she could contain her anger towards Lorkan any longer.

Why had he never shown? her shadows whispered inside her blood.

Blair marched out of the bookshop, ignoring the question coursing through her like some angry storm. She needed to reach Vísdómr before she did something she regretted.

CHAPTER FORTY-FOUR

LORKAN

Lorkan cracked his neck from side to side, trying to shake away the sight of Blair peering up at him. Lips parted. Fathomless eyes wide. Heart skipping. It took all his strength not to crash his lips to hers and do every delectable thing he'd imagined since he was a seventeen-year-old lovesick fool. Her storm-and-sage scent had stained the leather cord holding his bloodstone, sitting right under his nose. *Stars above*, the curse heightened his hunger.

He imagined sinking his teeth into her neck and dipping his fingers into her sex, drawing out her pleasure as he lapped up his.

Lorkan growled, snuffing his desire with the fact that he had to hide what he was. With one misstep with Blair, there was no telling where the line between desire and hunger lay, and may it be her lips or blood—that line blurred too deeply.

To make matters worse, Alvin stood in the shadows of the stables, a scowl carved into his face like stone.

Rook landed on his shoulder as he stepped out of the sun's light. "I'm sorry—"

Alvin held up a finger. "You haven't written, not *once*, not even to confirm you'd made it to the Drengr Village." With hood up and against a wall shaded in shadow, his friend stayed clear of the sunlight peeking out from the clouds. "I thought you were dead, and a letter from Mya filled me in on your little adventure. I risked leaving the mountain, figured I'd sit and wait here and maybe cross paths with you. Then, by some luck"—he pointed to Rook perched on his shoulder—"I spotted that menace in the village. What the *fuck*, Lorkan?"

He pinched the bridge of his nose. "There hasn't been time."

"*Time?*" Alvin spat. "What about the pack? They're running out of time with the tea. Rations are lower than ever before—"

"I'm working on it," Lorkan hissed. "Did Mya mention I'm working on deciphering the prophecy? I'm trying to break the curse." The one flowing in our veins, he thought, but didn't say in earshot of those in the village streets.

"I don't want messages from Mya." He jabbed his finger into Lorkan's chest. "I deserve to hear from *you*."

Lorkan seethed, "Well, here's my update: My father forbade me from telling anyone what I am, or the pack for that matter. He also forced me to work alongside a particular witch, so forgive me, Alvin, if I haven't time to spare and send a message while a traitor as my partner has chased me halfway across Sorin. And let me not forget that my bloodlust is worse than it's ever been because it's *her*."

Alvin paused. "I guess that explains it."

Lorkan grunted.

"Is that gem doing anything?" He nodded towards the bloodstone.

"It hides what I am," Lorkan said. He knocked back his hood, and Alvin jumped. "Helps me with the sunlight, too, but does nothing for my thirst."

Alvin nodded, shoving a few vials of blood into his hand. "Since you haven't written, I'm taking the fun out of guessing. Bear."

"That's rude."

His friend shrugged. "You know, I might know a solution to your current problem."

"What's that?"

"Tell her."

Lorkan's blood ran ice cold. "What? No, Sorin isn't ready for what we are, not until the curse is broken."

"I didn't say Sorin, I said *her*."

Wind blustered through the village, and snow drifted off the rooftops. Lorkan froze as solid as the icicles dangling off of the clay shingles.

"My father—"

"Isn't here," Alvin leaned in close. "I wager, if he were though, he'd understand if it prevented you from the task at hand: figuring out a way to break the curse. What's your plan exactly?"

"Avoid her," Lorkan bit out the words. He couldn't believe they were having this conversation.

Alvin scoffed. "How's that going so far?"

"It'll be easier once we're at Vísdómr," Lorkan said, sweat tingling at the back of his neck.

He lied to himself because he knew they'd have to work together to get answers about how to break the curse. Yet, he'd told Alvin about the girl he loved and left behind after he'd turned, breaking her heart to protect her from what he was, but he'd not told him the entire truth.

Not how this village flooded his memories of their love, and yet he'd been turned on his way here. He'd marched out of the Drengr Village to finally *lay* with the woman he loved. To start anew, to tie their souls together. No, it wasn't what he was that he feared, but how he hurt Blair.

Farther down the street, a cottage overgrown with vegetation sat as empty as Lorkan's heart. It pained him to spy it, to know its promise died the day he'd turned into a monster.

Alvin cleared his throat, glacier eyes focused on something behind Lorkan. He whirled and found Blair scowling, arms crossed, ire directed at Rook and then at Alvin. Her eyes widened, and she blinked, jumping her attention between all three of them.

"Who are you?" she asked.

"Alvin." He outstretched his hand to hers.

As his friend introduced himself, Lorkan's wolf bared its teeth. Unwarranted territorial thoughts wheeled in his mind, but Rook tapped his feet on Lorkan's shoulder, snapping him to the present.

"Blair. How do you know Lorkan?"

Suspicion lay in Blair's tone, and wariness gripped Lorkan.

"I'm a fellow scholar," Alvin lied.

"Really?" Blair's dark eyes roamed over his warrior braids, running tightly across his scalp.

"He's also a friend," Lorkan said.

Blair snorted. "Didn't know you had those."

Alvin laughed, slapping him on the back. "I'll let you two get on with your travels, aye? It was good to see you, and *stars above*, write. Nice to meet you, Blair. I hope the next time we have more time to chat."

His friend fell into the village streets and stuck to the shadows, leaving Lorkan yet again alone with Blair.

"Shall we?" he asked.

She didn't grace him with a response, turning on her heel and stormed towards the stables.

After four hours of silent travel, the valley Vísdómr sat beyond the hills they trekked, and the sun inched below the overlapping mountain peaks in the distance, the horizon sharp, blazing, and pink.

Lorkan's horse snorted, continuously disagreeable about allowing him to ride, which was an improvement compared to Lorkan's usual relationship with animals. He thanked the bloodstone's properties, perhaps not hiding *everything* he was, but just enough so their travels weren't delayed.

Beside him, Blair's curls whipped in the wind, and her eyes brightened at the sight of the infamous library. Carved into the caverns of an actual mountain, windows shimmered as if pieces of broken glass were sewn into the rocky crevices. The mountain sat alone in the valley, miles away on each side from others in the Vadon Mountain range. Its brothers and sisters stretched far beyond, but its peak towered over them, the tip lost past the clouds.

"It's a wonder, isn't it?" he asked.

Blair's nostrils flared, and she dismounted her horse, using the beast to separate her and Lorkan. He followed suit, leading his horse towards the narrow, winding path that reached to Vísdómr's front entrance.

"You haven't said a word since we left Fika," he said.

Blair winced at the town name, and the winds whirled through the valley, bowing the long, frostbitten grass in its mighty current.

"That is our normal, Lorkan. You and I don't talk."

Which wasn't far from the truth, and Lorkan should've preferred it that way, set the tone before they entered Vísdómr. He wanted distance between them, *needed* it, but Alvin's "solution" had replayed in the back of his mind for miles, and with each passing hour, Blair had turned more rigid, and it was the first time since being at her side that he realized that . . . that . . .

He'd fucking *missed* her. *Moons*, she'd been his anchor in this world. After he'd turned, he'd lost the one person he loved most, and like some selfish bastard, he enjoyed having her back at his side, and now, she was rigid, cold, and so—

"You're angry," he whispered.

He hadn't meant to say it out loud, and he realized his mistake too late. Blair halted her horse on the path and charged towards him. "That is the understatement of the century."

"Blair—"

"Don't say my name," she hissed. Dirt swirled around her boots as her wind bronntanas awakened.

Rook descended from above, landing on Lorkan's shoulder and cawing in Blair's face. Red rose up her neck, spreading towards her cheeks. Her midnight stare flared, murderous.

"He is my familiar!" she yelled. "Not yours, *mine*!"

"We both found him together. Don't blame—"

"No, that doesn't make him yours. It is my magic he tied to, and *you*"—she balled her fists and gritted her teeth—"abandoned us." Tears welled in her eyes, and the instinct to comfort her and keep his distance warred within him. "At least, that's what I thought."

"What do you mean?" he whispered, unease creeping us his spine. Had she overheard his conversation with Alvin? Did she know?

Blair dug into her trousers and retrieved something. She snatched his hand, pressing items into it. She stepped back, and a mixture of disgust and anger marred her face.

Lorkan opened his hand, and Rook peered down at the treasures he'd collected, a pleased caw squeaking out of him.

"I recognized the beads in Alvin's braids," she whispered. "For years, Rook has brought me shiny trinkets. Sure, I noticed a few had markings from the west, but I never once thought he visited you, or imagined, not for a single second, that you had the audacity to be around my familiar after what you did to me."

"Please—"

She stepped closer, tears streaming down her face. "Aina told me about the books, Lorkan. That it's been *you* sending them all these years. Why? Was it your way of a sick apology?"

Lorkan winced. His fondest memories were visiting Saga & Spines with Blair, reading books in the comfort of one another's presence, talking adventure and story with Aina, sipping tea like the snowfall didn't matter.

"You sent me romances, Lorkan," Blair's voice cracked. "Books about *love*. Why would you be so cruel?"

Lorkan swallowed, nausea whirling in his gut. "I didn't want you to give up on it, not after what I . . ."

"After you what, Lorkan?" Blair yelled. "You can't even say it, can you? You're hiding what you did to me, ignoring it."

Hiding.

Lorkan lost strength in his knees and almost crumbled to the grass, but words stuck to his tongue. He couldn't move, speak, or breathe under her fury. But he deserved this. *She* deserved to say her piece finally.

Blair's chest heaved, and tears laced her words. "My heart didn't just break; my entire being fractured, and I have never, ever been the same since you. I've suffered in silence because no one knew what we were, but you got to spend time in the places we fell for one another, picking out books for me from afar, being with my familiar as if you had a right, all while a piece of me died."

Tell her, a voice whispered. *Hide*, his father had instructed. Lorkan might burst with indecisiveness.

"I was afraid," he whispered a half-truth, a false lightness washing over him.

"Do you think I wasn't?" Blair wiped tears from her eyes.

"It wouldn't have worked," he whispered. "We were both young and fools, Blair. I am a werewolf; you're a witch."

She shook her head. "But did I not deserve at a letter? A goodbye?"

Lorkan swallowed, words like knives in his throat. "I thought silence was answer enough."

Blair scoffed, wiping away her tears. She clicked her tongue, and Rook flew to her shoulder, staring off at the mountain and ignoring Lorkan. "Stay away from me inside Vísdómr."

Relief should've washed over Lorkan, but dread crept up on him instead, like the shadows of the descending night. But he was the villain, right?

"Gladly," he said. Cold, hard, *meaning it* so he could convince himself.

Her hand connected with his cheek, a deafening crack echoing across the valley. He kneaded his sore jaw, blinking past the radiating sting.

They stared at one another. Blair's chest heaving. Lorkan stunned into silence.

Something within him broke. How had they come to this? He couldn't bear the pain lacing Blair's midnight stare, not for one single minute longer. He'd hidden for so long and tried to find the honor within the shadows, but there was none in the way he'd hurt Blair or denied himself. The power beating through his soul for her outmatched the wretchedness of the curse.

Love.

Lorkan couldn't admit what he was, but what if he revealed his heart instead?

"Fuck it," he breathed, and in two long strides, Lorkan crashed his lips against Blair's.

Chapter Forty-Five

L ORKAN KISSED BLAIR LIKE she was salvation. He tasted of smoke and things she shouldn't want. His lips molded to hers with a demanding desperation, like his kiss was a plea, and Blair's body betrayed her, falling into him.

This is wrong, a voice whispered in the back of her mind.

The valley vanished. Like her body lifted from the grassy ground, a sense of suspension locked into her knees. But Lorkan held her close. Stars above, he'd grown a full foot since they were teenagers, towering over her, but his one hand cupped her cheek and while the other gripped her waist, keeping her steady as she stood on her tiptoes.

It began to drizzle, but neither of them cared. The stinging cold and roaring winds only drew Blair and Lorkan closer. Droplets pelted Blair's face, and rain and tears mixed with their kiss. Lorkan tilted her head farther back, driving his hand into her curls, and Blair swore she heard him curse.

You need this, her thoughts continued.

Thunder clapped above, and temptation zapped through Blair like lightning. She'd believed she was a strong woman, one who could face her vices, and yet, as she opened her mouth wider and encouraged Lorkan's kiss, she'd found the one thing that made her weak.

Him.

He'll hurt you again.

Blair's doubts blared in the back of her mind, and her bones rattled with the truth, not the booming storm brewing in the valley, but she didn't care—it was as if she'd been locked in a cage, days without water, and Lorkan was her first sip. *Blasted books*, she would enjoy this.

Even if she never kissed him again. Because she couldn't—right? Her palm stung from slapping Lorkan across the face, and yet there wasn't much juxtaposition from that moment to this one. Both hurt.

Blair threaded her fingers through his hair, tugging Lorkan closer, drowning out the storm and her doubts. She embraced his touch, craved his harsh hold on her hips and the tentative hand against her cheek.

A muted growl rumbled through his chest—she'd not known he was capable of making the sound. Beastly. Reaching to her toes. But Blair's surprise was short lived. Lorkan bit her bottom lip—not hard enough to draw blood—but enough to tug her lip and tease her with a delicious pain.

Yet, the more Lorkan kissed her, her heart expanded, threatening to burst. The tendrils of her soul tightened, and the scars running across her soul itched. Ached. Lorkan's lips against hers didn't soothe the hurt he'd caused, but reawakened them.

This is wrong. But this time, it wasn't a phantom voice blaring in her mind but her own. This *wasn't* right.

Winds whirled around them. Cold bit her fingertips and nipped her cheeks, and—

Blair opened her eyes during their kiss and spotted shadows leaking from her hands, intertwining into Lorkan's dark hair. But he was none the wiser—her shadows mingled with the whirling winds and chilly rain, a part of the storm. Yet, the sight reminded Blair of stepping off the path, of what she herself had to hide from.

This will only cause you pain.

Panic jolted through Blair, and she pushed Lorkan away.

She hid her hands behind her back. Her shadows answered, rushing inward with a cold hiss, and Lorkan stumbled forward at the loss of contact. He blinked, water racing down the lens of his glasses.

They stood in silence in the wake of what they couldn't take back. Hair matted by the rain, lips swollen and red from their kiss, Lorkan was untethered.

It reflected the unraveled heap of Blair's heart.

He'd hurt *her*—and how dare he try to silence everything between them with a kiss? Blair had already stepped down this path with Lorkan, and shadows aside, she refused to do it again

He stepped toward her, reaching for her. "Blair—"

"I can't, Lorkan," she said over the storm.

He halted, and hurt flashed through his eyes. Blair's stomach roiled at the sight, but she ignored the pang of guilt—this pain brewing between them was fleeting compared to the hurt they'd endure if they were fools again.

"We've been down this path, and it only leads to more hurt," she whispered. "I won't endure it a second time. I *can't*."

Rain ran down Lorkan's sharp nose. "I'm sorry for everything. For what I did. For abandoning you. For not explaining why."

Blair's heart raced. She'd waited years to hear those words from him, and yet they did nothing. For his apology felt like a lie, and it wasn't good enough.

"Then tell me the truth. Right here, right now. If you cared for me these last years, enough to look after me, why didn't you come?"

Lorkan blinked. Flexed his hands at his sides. "My fear is the truth."

It couldn't be that simple. Blair's instinct screamed with apprehension. She'd been afraid at seventeen, frightened to tie herself to a male she'd have to keep secret for the rest of her days. She'd lied to her parents and sisters, even to this day. Yet, she'd traveled to Fika, not chained by doubt but rebelling against it.

Like a fool, she'd stepped out of line. Entertaining a romance with Lorkan was her first offense. Seeking out Kade had been her second. Saving Evelyn from Circe had been her last. What did her efforts outside being a scholar bring her? Nothing but pain.

"I can't," she said again, not to Lorkan but to herself.

Everything ached—her chest, head, and lips. Goddess, her bones and limbs weighed her down like stones. Lightning flashed above the sky, shining across Lorkan's beautiful, sharp features, and in that moment, Blair realized she wasn't as weak as she thought; she could walk away from this. *Would*.

Vísdómr loomed in the distance. She had a purpose, a scholarly task to attend to. That kept her safe. Books, research, and the confines of a library.

"What makes now any different?" she asked.

"We are older," Lorkan breathed.

"You're right." Blair smiled, sadness sour on her tongue. "We are also wiser, Lorkan. You and I know better. What sense is there in hurting ourselves all over again? I plan to figure out how to break the curse, Lorkan. *That* is my place here. If we must work together, so be it, but that is all we are to one another: peers."

Blair marched towards Vísdómr. The storm raged above the mountain and valley, but its might was nothing compared to the one brewing in her soul.

CHAPTER FORTY-SIX

UNLIKE Áilleacht Castle, the curse had dug its sharp claws into House Nathanaël's manor and allowed no light to shine through. The black velvet curtains covered the windows in the grand dining hall, and the fireplace sat dormant, allowing a draft from outside to sneak in through the chimney.

Two candelabras lit the table. At one end, the black flame flickered across Lord Nathanaël's auburn beard and neatly cropped hair. After deliberating with her family and friends, Tovi had written to his estate, and to her surprise, he'd extended an invitation for dinner within the same day.

The haste unnerved Tovi—was it desperation or eagerness? So, she'd brought Nadia and Yennifer with her. Yen sat on her left, while Nadia sat on her right. Down the table, Lady Nathanaël shifted in her seat, casting wary glances in the vampyr and werewolf's direction, while her daughter, Anastasia—her scarlet hair and olive-green eyes the only bright color in the estate—snuck curious glimpses towards Yen over the rim of her goblet.

"Tell me, Queen Tovi," Nathanaël drawled, shooting all three of them a rueful smile, none the wiser to the werewolf alpha and vampyr spy—Aramis and Cass—nestled in the forest surrounding his manor, lying in wait if anything were to go awry. "What other lords have you met?" he asked.

Tovi placed her silverware down. "You are the first."

Not a lie. Flynn wasn't a lord, and Tovi had no intention of revealing she'd met with the pirate captain. Nathanaël might have done business with Flynn, but that didn't mean he respected him—the lords of Drystan looked down upon her ex-lover, all because he didn't have a title in front of his name.

The edge of Nathanaël's lips twitched as he fought a smile. "I'm delighted. Am I too bold to say there is interest in my army?"

Tovi sipped her wine, swallowing her disdain. *This is for your people,* she told herself, *and you can protect your heart.*

"No," she said. "It's not—I find myself *very* interested."

It was dangerous to lay out her cards so candidly, but lords loved to have their egos stroked. She could practically hear his purr down the table. Nadia sighed, falling deeper into her chair while Yen picked at her food, the werewolf's nose wrinkling.

He chuckled. "I thought you might. You were always one to test the other lords with your . . . *rebellious* ways."

Lady Nathanaël snorted, and Tovi raised an inviting brow.

"You've come such a *long* way since the early days at court. I can't imagine how proud your mother would be." Lady Nathanaël sipped her wine, sharp eyes narrowing as she smiled like a cat before it pounced on its prey.

Tovi pushed back from the table, her chair scraping across the stone floor. She leaned back, crossing her legs in an exaggerated motion.

Lord Nathanaël choked on his wine, while his wife blushed, averting her attention back to her plate of food. The servants straightened at the side walls, and their eyes skittered about, unsure where to look.

For Tovi wore leather pants, and she'd been sure to make sure they noticed. Skintight and forming to her muscular legs, she'd not dressed in the finery of a queen nor the layers of a lady.

This was her, ready at a moment's notice to retrieve the dagger at her boot and slay a demon. Not some poised female sitting at attention. She was the heir by right, not by the lords of Drystan's approval.

"I think my mother is rolling in her grave." She raised her glass in the air as if the truth were something to cheer for.

Yen and Nadia smiled, and young Lady Anastasia bit her lip.

Lord Nathanaël laughed and pulled at the cravat tied around his neck. "Yes, yes. Very different females, indeed. It is a shame I can't vie for your hand like the other lords or a son to match you, though"—he patted his daughter's hand—"my daughter has made a match that has made me beyond proud, one that has allowed this business deal to even exist, my queen. For my daughter is to wed Lord Oziel, drawing together our two houses and interests."

Tovi blinked. Shifted in her seat. Yen spat out her wine.

"I'm sorry," Tovi reined in the surprise in her tone. "It was my understanding Lord Oziel was dead."

"Ah, yes. The *former* Lord Oziel had a tragic passing. I believe bits of him washed up in Drystan Village. Lord *General* Oziel is the late Oziel's brother. Shame the lord passed away, but because he had no wife or heirs, his lands and wealth were inherited by his brother."

"General Oziel is a fine match indeed. Just the man for my fiery daughter," Lady Nathanaël said.

Anastasia had turned as rigid as stone, not with surprise but disdain. The announcement wasn't new, but she hated it. Yen pressed her boot into Tovi's, and subtly, she followed her friend's line of sight.

A soldier, high ranking by his armor, stood in the corner of the dining hall. Eyes ahead, jaw pulsing. He didn't move a muscle, but Tovi caught the uptick of his heart rate and the slight pop of his knuckles as he fisted his hands behind his back.

Something passed between Anastasia and the soldier, and Tovi noted it for later.

"Will I meet General Oziel?" she asked. "I'd like to know more about the man leading my potential army."

Lord Nathanaël smiled. "Oziel is on business rounding up more recruits in the smaller villages in the west at the moment, but if you're ready, I'd like to show you the army I've put together and what makes it *very* special. Of course, I'd prefer this to be between queen and lord."

Tovi rose out of her seat, giving permission for the others to stand as well. "Lead the way."

"Just know, Lord Nathanaël, the last vampyr of your standing to insult Queen Tovi lost his head at the hands of a werewolf." Yennifer winked.

The lord swallowed, and his wife paled. Tovi sent her friends a reassuring smile and followed the lord of the house and the stiff soldier up a flight of stairs. It spiraled until it deposited them at a wrought iron gate leading to the roof of the manor. The metal groaned as Lord Nathanaël opened it for Tovi and ushered her to emerge into the night first.

She hated placing the two males behind her, but she tuned into her keen senses. Listened to their hearts. Smelled their sweat. Even, cool. Aside from an excited *thump, thump* from the lord, neither gave any sign they'd hurt her.

Tovi sighed and set her shoulders back, and as she breathed in the night air, the sound of laughter, song, and metal clanging buzzed in the distance.

"Come, come," the lord said, gesturing to the balcony overlooking the back half of his lands. "Here is the legion you need, my queen."

Anticipation thrummed through Tovi. Her left hand itched for the dagger at her boot, the other tight and ready to defend if need be, but she grasped the balcony's banister for purpose and held back a gasp as surprise zapped through her.

Three thousand soldiers sprawled across a destroyed forest. Campfires, tents, longhouses, and training grounds dotted the land like a city ripe for war.

"That . . ." Tovi blinked, trying to make sense of how Lord Nathanaël had successfully built such a feat.

"Twice the size of your brother's forces, and his aren't nearly as well-trained." Lord Nathanaël snapped his fingers. "Come."

Tovi bit her tongue, drawing blood. His tone grated against her resolve, so like her demanding father in his last decades. The soldier strode over to them, bowing in Tovi's direction.

Lord Nathanaël gestured to the soldier's armor, and that's when Tovi noticed the small flecks of red embedded in the black metal.

"Bloodstones," she whispered.

"Indeed," Nathanaël said. "You can take this legion wherever you wish."

"All of them have armor like this?" The deposit of bloodstones Nathanaël must've found had to be miles long.

"Yes, crafted into their breastplates and weapons."

"Why would I have a need of an army that can fight in sunlight if my enemy is here?" Tovi asked.

Nathanaël sighed. "This army was never intended for you, but your brother. Now seeing as he no longer has the funds to afford it . . ."

Tovi's skin crawled. "You're seriously only after money. Has it ever occurred to you that your wealth could help end the Blood Curse not bring more darkness upon Drystan? You're fueled by greed."

"Does it matter?" he asked. "You have a choice: pay a man who only wants your money or agree to marry a lord. You and I both know which one you loathe more. Greed may fuel me, but you can't afford to be fueled by pride."

"How dare you speak to me that way?" Tovi hissed, baring her fangs.

"I have the cards, a legion that can squash your brother's claim to the throne within an afternoon siege."

Tovi seethed, not daring to draw back her fangs. "I could have you arrested for treason. You used bloodstones without the consent of the royal family."

"And then what? This legion answers to General Oziel, and he only answers to gold. You may not like it, but you need us."

Tovi set her shoulders back. *Need.* What a dangerous overreach. She sighed, playing the act of a bored lady. "I wonder how much it costs to fund an army of this size . . . I bet your coffers dwindle by the day, but of course you never expected my brother's empty pockets, did you? I'd tread carefully, Lord Nathanaël . . ." Tovi stepped closer to him, peering up at his palish face and not buckling under his red-tinged eyes. "It is you who needs me."

Nathanaël narrowed his gaze. "Then I expect your answer come morning of agreement to fifty thousand gold coins, as I have no time to waste."

The lord turned on his heel without so much as a good night or a bow. The commanding soldier, though, inclined his head and followed the lord off the roof's balcony. Tovi faced the sprawling army ahead and released a pent-up breath.

The legion promised the same victory as Flynn's fleet, but she'd have to give up gold, not her hand in marriage. The word conjured memories of a certain spearmint scent. Fresh, enticing. Her skin tickled with the memories of him traveling down her neck or how his tongue had worshiped her there.

Tovi clenched her thighs, hating how her mind wandered to such distracting places. *Goddess*, perhaps she should marry Flynn and save her people from the thrall the werewolf held over her. But that would be a union in title only, not body or heart.

The night's cold nipped at Tovi's skin—she could barely *think* his name, let alone admit all those things belonged to him.

Steps grew louder behind her as someone climbed the stairs, and Yennifer crested the last step, wheat-colored hair blowing in the breeze. Her nostrils flared and eyes widened at the sight of the city of soldiers.

Her friend handed her a glass of wine. "Thank you."

"I should thank you," Yen said. "Lord Nathanaël's disgruntled return gave me the perfect opportunity to slip out. That manor smells like death."

"Is the Drystan air any better?" Tovi scoffed.

"There are hints of promise." Yennifer winked.

"Nadia?" Tovi asked.

Yennifer waved her hand. "Frightening Lady Nathanaël with tales of being a spy. She's covering for us while we talk." Yen turned her archer-like focus onto the legion ahead. "There it is then, what you need to win against your brother."

Tovi sighed, resting her forearms on the roof's wall. "It is."

"What are you thinking about?" her friend asked, leaning against the wall with her.

"My father and brother, and the things they'd do for power." Tovi's words felt like an admission of a fear she'd harbored to herself for weeks. "*Buying* my way to the throne feels a lot like them."

Yen shook her head. "Your father and brother didn't make their choices for anyone else but themselves. You make it not for power but for your people and a better future for Drystan, one without the curse."

"Do I?" Tovi shook her head. "Lord Nathanaël is the type of male I loathe in vampyr society—pompous, arrogant, selling his daughter to the highest bidder. I doubt General Oziel is any better. Here I am, about to conduct business with him. Flynn is a good male, one who could help create change alongside me."

"The perfect choice isn't always the right choice, though, and the fact you're thinking of your options is better than Riven, a man so easily fooled by the Blood Goddess. Why haven't you sought *her* help?"

Tovi scoffed. "That's wrong."

"It's weak," Yen said. "You and Riven may be twins, but your opposites."

Tovi considered her words—she didn't feel as wild and off-kilter as her brother and father, but the fear remained. She wished to grasp certainty with an iron grip, yet it wasn't a tangible thing, like the tendrils reaching out from the mists of the Void, playing tricks on her wary mind.

"I wasn't completely honest with you the other day." Yen didn't meet her gaze, studying the burgundy liquid in her cup.

"About?" Tovi asked.

"Bétar." Silence stretched until Yennifer continued. "You asked when I knew Bétar was my mate, and yes, the moment I met him, but it took me two years to finally admit it to myself, and then another until he and I admitted it to one another."

Tovi's chest tightened. "You fought your feelings for three years?"

"Yes, along with the mating bond."

"Why?" Tovi asked.

"I'm from a family of five children, and I'm the youngest. In werewolf society, those after the third born have the freedom to choose what post they take up. After losing two siblings to the Void, I had my sights on being a protector, you know, continue to make Sorin a better place—much to my parents' dismay. Their disapproval ate at me, but if I became the best archer, how could I have made the wrong choice?"

Yennifer paused, composing herself, keen stare tracking more than the army ahead, but memories it seemed, too.

Tovi waited, giving her the space she needed.

The werewolf went on. "When Kade asked me to join his team, I didn't hesitate. Years of hard work got me to that point, but then I met Bétar." Yen scoffed, shaking her head. "Like a dark cloud, it suddenly felt like I might lose everything, all because my heart *yearned*. I'm not a queen like you, but I'm a warrior, bound by duty, too, and I was afraid if I chose Bétar, I'd lose sight of it. The worst part? The more time I spent with Bétar, the more I actually *liked* him. Not all mated pairs are love matches, ya know? There I was, falling in love with a male I denied myself."

"What changed your mind?" Tovi breathed, afraid to learn the truth.

Yennifer laughed. "Well, after too much blueberry ale at the Shield-maiden, Bétar declared his love for me. The whole tavern fell silent, and he turned beet red, and I knew right then and there I'd lose him forever if I said nothing, and then I realized it was okay to choose me once in a while. So, I walked straight up to him, kissed him, and said, 'I'm glad to hear it, because I love you, too.' Not all sacrifice is valiant, and it doesn't make us neglectful of our duty when we choose ourselves."

Tovi clamped her eyes shut, something within her warring against the blissful promise Yen's story gave her. "What if I'm not like you and Bétar? What if I'm like my brother and father? What if it consumes me? Where is the line between choosing myself and being a queen?"

Yen shook her head and grasped Tovi's hand as she said, "You, Tovi Verena, are one of the strongest people I know, and that makes you different from your father and brother."

Tovi sipped her wine, trying to swallow some sense of believing that she was indeed like Yennifer said. She wasn't used to this doubt. Yet, she wasn't used to foreign feelings related to a male either, all battling her pursuit of doing right by her people. The answer sprawled out, all for the fine price of fifty thousand god coins—

The color red caught her attention, and below the manor near the gardens, Anastasia, Lord Nathanaël's daughter, snuck through the shadows, glancing back at the manor every few feet.

"Yen," Tovi breathed, jutting her chin in the vampyr's direction.

Yennifer hummed. "My guess is she's off to meet that commanding soldier her eyes kept finding during dinner."

"It's a good thing I'm wearing pants," Tovi said, setting her goblet down and searching for a way to get down the side wall of the manor. Anastasia disappeared beyond a gate overtaken by ivy.

"Are you planning on following her?" Yen asked.

"Yes," Tovi said. "If Lord Nathanaël's daughter is sneaking out of her house and heading towards the legion I'm supposed to pay for, I want to know why."

"You're hoping she'll reveal more about her father and General Oziel."

"Precisely." Tovi found a metal gutter running down the gray brick. *Perfect.* "Cover for me?"

Yennifer nodded. "Yes. If you need to hurry back, you'll know it."

Tovi planted her hand at the top of the metal, and swung over, allowing her grip to guide her momentum downward. As her boots hit the stone, she somersaulted across the stone patio and rolled off onto the path, hoping to go unnoticed from the manor's windows. She remained crouched and followed the same path as Anastasia.

The ancient gate groaned as she slipped through it, entering a garden tunnel with more ivy. Voices murmured ahead, and on light feet, Tovi crept further down.

"You're late, Ana," a male voice drawled.

"I'm glad to see you waited for me, Bash," a female responded—perhaps Anastasia.

Bash remained silent, and as Tovi peeked around the ivy-covered archway, she found Anastasia changing into fighting leathers and the commanding soldier without his armor, stripped to a black tunic and trousers, practice swords in hand. He threw one right as Anastasia finished lacing her boot. She caught it, albeit almost a moment too late. The soldier smirked, and *Goddess*, Anastasia, blushed in return and attacked.

Bloody hel, the soldier was training the lord's daughter to fight.

And *well.*

Their wooden weapons clashed, but the sounds were swallowed, as if muted somehow. Tovi searched the fighting area, spying enchanted rocks in each corner. *Interesting.*

Mentor and mentee danced more than they fought—fluid, breathless, and in tune with one another, until they both attacked at once, clashing in a tight embrace.

The soldier stared down at Anastasia. Their lips almost touched, and the intense sheen in their eyes had Tovi turning back around the corner, averting her gaze from such an intimate moment between them.

Not just training—the two were clearly *entangled.* But Anastasia was betrothed; how in the Goddess was the young female getting away with this right under mother and father's nose?

Clanging wooden swords turned to something else entirely, and Tovi headed down the ivy-covered tunnel, retreating from the very specific *noises* that she had no business hearing. Instead, she waited for Anastasia at the end of the garden tunnel.

Once night had begun its descent and Tovi's ass had gone numb, Anastasia crept through the iron gate—training leathers gone and the multilayered skirts of a lady returned. Tovi emerged from the ivy she hid behind and found the tip of a dagger at her throat the next second. She raised a brow, peering down at Anastasia. Tovi's own dagger pressed into the young vampyr's belly.

The young female gasped, covering her mouth, and backed away. "Bloody hel—I mean—fuck—no, I'm sorry—you're the queen. Oh my word, I just tried to stab *the queen*."

Tovi rushed over and grasped Anastasia's arms. "Shhh, you're fine. Unless you want us to get caught."

Anastasia blinked. "Why are you out here? Did you . . ." Her eyes flicked to the gate, and she swallowed.

"I will not tell your father and mother what I saw," she said.

"How can I trust your word?" Anastasia asked.

"Because I was once a female used as a bargaining chip. Then, I found inner strength and the power of a well-handled blade. I want every female in Drystan to experience what you did this evening."

Anastasia's chest heaved. "Fine, but we can't talk here. The manor's guards will catch us from the roof."

Anastasia led them deeper into the garden, and the wedges grew taller, towering over them and obscuring them from sight.

Tovi studied her. "How are you hiding your scent from your parents? It's a dangerous line you're walking with your soldier."

She blushed. "I'm taking a tonic. There's a witch on Bash's unit. Well, a vampyr-witch."

Tovi stilled, trying to detect a lie in her words. "I've never known a vampyr to wield magic before."

"She was turned and kept her powers. Though from what I've learned, they're different now." Her green eyes widened, and Tovi gathered she talked when she was nervous. "She's nothing like that Ingrid, if that's what you're thinking."

Tovi's head spun. "You know Ingrid?"

"She and your brother have visited General Oziel many times in the last few weeks."

"But not your father?"

Anastasia sighed, crossing her arms. "No. Look, my father might try to play part owner of this legion he's promised you, but the general is pulling the strings."

"What else can you tell me?"

Anastasia wavered from foot to foot, and a shadowy figure emerged from the hedges—Bash.

"Stay right where you are." Yennifer's bow groaned, and as she stepped out of the hiding, the nocked arrow glinted in the night's dim light.

Anastasia stepped in the line of Yennifer's shot, and Bash hissed, "*Ana.*"

Tension rose in the gardens, dropping Drystan's already cool air.

"I can say with confidence that all of us are on the same side—ensuring we break the curse," Anastasia said.

Yen peered down her arrow. "What are you two lovebirds doing about it?"

Bash stepped forward. Arrogant and proud, Tovi almost wondered what he'd been before he turned—that's when she spied his most peculiar pointed ears.

"Planning to take General Oziel's army from him," he said.

Bash's words jarred Tovi to the present, her curiosity regarding what he was, short-lived. "How?"

"Killing him," Anastasia said.

No hesitation, no lie. But truth *and* want.

The archer lowered her arrow. "*Moons.*"

"What about your father?" Cold prickled up her skin. "I just made a deal with him to use the army against my brother."

"Make the deal with me instead," Bash said.

Tovi ground her teeth. "You don't have an army to make deals with, only a plan, one that hinges on mere hope."

"As do you," Anastasia said. "One that makes Drystan better by breaking the curse."

Yennifer snorted. "She has you there."

Tovi snarled, agitation leaking from her body. "You're all downplaying the risk I take here. I *need* that army."

"General Oziel doesn't care for your future, Queen Tovi. He craves the curse and enjoys it. He's simply waiting for your brother's next move."

Tovi's heart skipped a beat. "You're aware he plans to draw the Void all over Sorin."

"Riven's plans are far worse than that," Bash said. "He will unleash darkness, but by opening the gates of Hel. The Void will be a reprieve in comparison."

The snowfall slowed as if time itself did, too. Tovi's blood ran as cold as ice. Yennifer's being deflated, shock rippling across her expressions.

"Where? When?" Tovi asked, her voice shaking.

Bash shook his head. "I don't know. Ingrid hasn't shared that with Riven, let alone Lord Oziel."

Yen muttered a curse. "We need to return to the werewolves with this information, Tovi."

"You're right. I need to warn Eldrick." Tovi halted, while the others stilled, too. She'd not meant to say his name out loud. *Bloody hel*, she'd not *thought* his name these last weeks, and yet, with the grave news of Riven's plan, Eldrick was the first she considered in this world.

Tovi could argue he was an ally, a leader amongst the werewolves, and to maintain that alliance, she needed to warn him, but it was her heart that had found those words, not politics.

Of course, there were plenty of others who needed to know. Lorkan and Blair, those researching prophecy. Perhaps they knew where the gates of Hel were. Not to mention Evelyn and Kade, if they were back.

But Tovi refused to return south empty-handed. She couldn't dare waltz into the Drengr Village without the forces to defeat Riven. That was what she'd set out to do, her part in defeating the darkness.

"When can I expect this army to be under your command?" she eyed Bash.

The vampyr with pointed ears tilted his head, and Tovi guessed he'd been predatorial being before he was turned.

"Two weeks."

"Goddess," Tovi breathed. "I can't believe I'm considering this. What are our next steps here? Ana's father expects me to have a decision on the legion in the morning."

"Give it," Bash said. "Delay your funds until our plan is finished. Trust us. I'm not from this world, Queen Tovi, but I'm willing to sacrifice my life to save it from the Blood Curse."

What a fickle, stomach-churning concept in this world. *Trust.* Yet, Tovi assessed Anastasia, a young lady much like she once was, stepping out of the norm and rebelling against vampyr society expectations for females. Distain coated Tovi's tongue that her subject had to sneak out of her home and hide that she'd mastered a blade, but perhaps that boldness and risk-taking attitude was what she needed to harness now.

"You both have yourselves a deal," Tovi said.

Chapter Forty-Seven

S NOW HAD MELTED IN the southern werewolf territory. It left the pines and evergreens bare, a deep green stretching across Eldrick's homeland, a welcome contrast to the gray blanketing the sky. Songbirds shot from tree to tree, their chirping a spirit-lifting sound. Winter still lay in the breeze, but so did saplings and wet dirt after a rain shower. If Eldrick and his traveling companions, Bétar and Alpha Thorn, kept pace, they'd reach the Drabek Village by sundown.

"Tell me, Alpha," Leif stared. "Where is the vampyr queen?"

"North," Eldrick said. "Gathering support of her own."

Leif grunted. "Any news?'

Eldrick shook his head, keeping his expression neutral. "Not of late."

He bent the truth; Eldrick hadn't heard from Tovi since they'd parted ways at the cave. He tried to convince himself that no news was good news, but their last conversation replayed in his mind, and he wagered the lack of correspondence was also avoidance. But did she owe him an update?

"The other alphas will care if there's progress in the north," Leif said. "Does she plan to meet with the alphas before the Earl vote?"

Eldrick's brows pinched, and he studied Thorn. He found the alpha trustworthy, kind-hearted in a world so hel-bent on finding darkness, but also direct.

He sighed, weighing his next words. "No, she and I feared her . . . *presence* might hurt my chances of securing the vote. She is a vampyr after all."

Leif hummed, eyebrows shooting up. "Ah, that's probably wise."

Eldrick tightened his grip on his reins, heart dropping like a stone to his gut.

Bétar snorted. "How can the alphas believe she's any different than Riven if they don't allow her to demonstrate it?"

Leif shook his head. "It's centuries' worth of prejudice. She can't undo it in weeks."

Eldrick reared straighter, failing to rally his frustration with the alpha's flippant attitude towards Tovi. "If it wasn't for her, your nephew wouldn't have made it out of Drystan."

"Which I'm grateful for, but"—he peered over at Eldrick, tone turning serious—"I was there that night when they killed my parents, ya know? It's not something I'll easily forget, especially when I come face-to-face with the vampyr queen, knowing her family started the curse that created scáths. Perhaps an alliance with her is necessary, but it doesn't mean she deserves a warm welcome in the Vadon Mountains."

Leif trotted his horse ahead, leaving Eldrick with his reeling thoughts.

"I don't agree with him," Bétar said in a hushed tone. "The Gray Fenris changed their opinions because we got to know Tovi. The other alphas simply need to give her a chance."

Eldrick sighed. "It's a shame none of you can cast a vote for Earl."

"I suppose you're right," Bétar said. "Though, I think if the other alphas witnessed your relationship with Tovi, they'd understand."

"But we aren't just allies, Bétar. It's messy. *That* might hurt us."

His friend raised a red bushy brow, expression suggestive. "I believe the word I used was *relationship*."

Eldrick's backside melted into his saddle, and Bétar laughed at his expense, pointing an accusatory finger at his face. "Take it from a male who avoided such things, that's far messier."

He trotted his horse to ride alongside Leif's, and the two older mated males murmured amongst themselves. Eldrick stewed in his own thoughts, tracing the silver ink of his alpha tattoo.

He'd chosen this, not Tovi. For good reason, it seemed. Leif was less inclined to accept Tovi, considering his past with vampyrs, and he wasn't the only werewolf that had been hurt by the curse.

Eldrick, for a long time, had hated vampyrs, too. But his opinion changed after he'd gotten to know Tovi. *Relationship* aside, he admired her for being a fierce leader to her people *and* Sorin. Could he convince the alphas of that? Could Tovi?

He didn't doubt it, but instead feared the mess he and Tovi were in. Would it distract them both? Draw them farther and farther from their duties? If Eldrick lost the vote because of his heart's yearning, he'd never forgive himself. He'd lose what he'd trained for all his life, what his heart beat for.

Home.

Yet, as Eldrick repeated the words to himself, his heart didn't expand at the sight of the trees but at the reminder of a softer green and the power that gaze had over him.

Eldrick sighed as they entered rockier terrain. Pebbles covered the path, and around them, boulders jutted from the ground. Trees clung to the stony surface with gnarled roots. The temperature dropped, and the songbirds ceased singing.

Eldrick's wolf surfaced, alert. Ahead, Leif and Bétar had straightened in their saddles. The commander tilted his head, listening while Thorn scanned the forest.

Movement had them halting on the path. Eldrick sniffed the air, while one hand dropped to the hilt of his axe.

"It's friendly folk." Siv Drabek emerged from the trees with another werewolf Eldrick recognized, Gyda, two werewolves they'd saved in Drystan, and—

"Sam," Eldrick said, a smile fighting through his rigid exterior from earlier. He dismounted his horse and tipped his head in greeting.

"Alphas," the young Magu said, nodding to both Eldrick and Leif. His attention fell to Bétar next. "Commander."

"Aye, does this mean your father's visiting the Drabek Pack?" Bétar asked.

"I'm afraid so." Sam frowned.

Eldrick shared a knowing look with Bétar and sighed. "Still, Drabek Village is farther south. What brought you three up this far?"

Gyda frowned, sharing a grave look with Siv. "We were scouting and smelled anise on the wind."

"It led us here," Siv whispered. "The air felt too similar to Drystan."

"Like dark magic?" Bétar asked, raising a rusty-colored brow.

Sam shook his head. "No, like the land was touched by the curse."

A chilly sensation crept up Eldrick's spine, his wolf growing restless. As if the land mirrored his instinct, the ground beneath his boots quaked. Pebbles tremored. Dust burst from the cracks in the cliffs, the land cracking. Their horses reared back and retreated, despite Eldrick's attempt to keep them calm. The air thinned like all its moisture had been sucked away.

They stood. Waited. Held their breath. And then—

Screams ripped across the forest followed by a demon's roar, and Siv unsheathed her sword and charged north.

"Wait!" Eldrick hissed, chasing after her.

Sam cursed while Gyda shouted after her friend. Leif and Bétar raced after them.

Eldrick grasped his axe, mindful of his steps against the still shaking ground. He grabbed Siv by the elbow before she burst from the trees.

"Let me go!" she snarled.

"Yield!" Eldrick growled, using his alpha baritone.

Siv shuddered, lowering her weapon, and backed up a step. "I won't allow the things I endured in Drystan into my homeland," she breathed.

Eldrick's chest heaved, and he rallied patience and used a gentler tone as the others caught up. "You have no idea what's out there and revealing yourself unprepared won't help your cause."

Siv gritted her teeth and remained silent, anger blooming in her young eyes.

Eldrick ignored the ire as he tread on light feet to conceal himself behind a tree, then dropped to his haunches.

Across the glade, three ialtóg demons attacked a farmstead. The demons resembled bats but were ten time bigger. And far hungrier.

One feasted on an unlucky goat, its flat snout covered in blood while another flapped its black leathery wings and lifted a cow into the air. The third chased after half a dozen werewolves retreating into the storehouse. They shut the door just as the demon collided into it.

Its deafening screech grated up Eldrick's spine.

The other two ialtógs grew tired of their half-eaten meals and joined the larger of the three. They climbed up the storehouse and began tearing into the straw of the thatched roof.

"*Moons*," Bétar breathed.

"Ialtógs this far east and out in the open," Leif whispered, hunkered behind another tree a few yards away. "That's bizarre."

Eldrick agreed—ialtógs preferred the mountains, dwelling in caves. He rallied his wolf, sniffed, and sensed the land. Darkness sucked the liveliness from the forest air and replaced it with a sticky otherness. "We need to help them—"

"What we should do is attack." Siv fisted her hands at her sides, knuckles whitening.

"May I remind you of your place amongst alphas," Eldrick said cooly.

"These are Drabek lands," she said. "I'll not stand around and do nothing."

Eldrick ground his teeth and marched towards the unit, seething. They didn't have time for the hearts of young valiant warriors that were borderline foolish.

"Acting out of anger will only get us killed and the farmstead will be no better off than when we found them. If you wish to make a difference, you'll listen to my command."

"He's right, Siv," Sam said.

Siv blinked, relaxing a fraction, recognition and trust passed between them.

"Fine," she huffed. "What's your plan?"

"There are three demons, six of us. We divide into teams of two and each face one of the ialtógs."

Bétar unsheathed his sword. "This should be fun."

"Sam, you're with me," Eldrick said. "Leif and Gyda pair off, and Siv and Bétar, work together. Let's go."

With axe in hand, Eldrick led the charge out of the trees and released a warrior's bellow. Two ialtógs took notice, launching off the storehouse and gliding on leathery wings towards them.

An arrow pierced one of their wings, and the smaller of three lost it's balance in the air.

"Nice shot!" Leif called to Gyda.

The female werewolf nodded, nocking a second arrow. She released, and it hits its mark, lodging into the demon's belly.

The other ialtóg screeched, baring its long, black fangs. It dove towards Bétar and Siv, who braced with swords at the ready.

Eldrick turned his attention back north. The ialtóg dug its scrunched snout into the roof, and the werewolves in the storehouse emerged, dashing in various directions. Chaos ensued as Sam and Eldrick reached the fray.

Irritated to find no prey inside the storehouse, the demon fidgeted on its perch, searching, searching, searching—

Its pointed ears flicked back, and all six fathomless black eyes focused on Eldrick. He growled and tightened his grip on his axe. Beside him, Sam mirrored his defensive stance.

The demon crawled using its wings and back legs. It launched, landing with a harsh thud ahead of them. Anise wafted from its greasy fur, roiling Eldrick's stomach.

Sam attacked, cutting his sword across the ialtóg's wing. It turned, giving Eldrick the oppurtinuty to step forward to slice through its other wing. This time, the demon whirled and pushed off into the air. Dust billowed upward in a mighty gust.

The demon dove, grasping Eldrick's shoulders with its taloned feet. They rose higher and higher into the air. Eldrick fought, hacking his axe against any inch of the demon he could reach. Its talons dug deeper into his shoulder, breaking flesh. He roared, and with one last swing, Eldrick struck his axe deep enough to sever bone.

The demon screeched, releasing him.

Moons, Eldrick fell and fell—

Another force barreled into him from the side right before he hit the ground. Eldrick plopped into a pile of hay. A familiar plum-and-lilac scent, stronger than the sweet grass under him, invaded his senses. He blinked, chest heaving, and found Tovi staring down at him.

"How, in the stars above, did you . . ." *Find me.* Eldrick didn't finish his question, too frightened he misunderstood why she'd returned to the Vadon Mountains.

Tovi smirked. "You and Bétar were creating quite a ruckus. Yen and I practically heard it from the Void."

Eldrick smiled, and it was as if the sun had peeked out of the clouds for the first time after three days of straight rain.

A scream cut through their lighthearted moment. Both of them jumped to their feet. Ahead, a farmer shielded his daughter from the prowling ialtóg.

Arrows—Yennifer's—fell from the sky and pierced the demon's flesh. But it didn't care or notice, six black eyes solely focused on its next meal.

White blurred in Eldrick's peripheral.

"Tovi!" he snarled.

She sprinted towards the beast, drawing her sword free from the scabbard strapped to her back. The silver glinted in the dim light, and Eldrick chased after her, hands itching for the axe he'd dropped in the scuffle with the ialtóg.

But it was no matter.

Tovi leaped as the beast was distracted and landed on its back. It had no time to react.

With all her might, Tovi whipped her sword ahead and plunged it straight into the demon's skull. It shuddered, stilled, and crumbled to the ground, Tovi with it.

Darkness peeled away from the demon's body in small flecks and blew away in the breeze. It rose into the air, whipping around Tovi like the petals of battle circling a warrior queen.

"Well, that was quick work," Bétar laughed, reuniting with Yennifer in a silent and still embrace.

The farmstead's werewolves and Eldrick's makeshift unit gathered together. Gyda carried three stained arrows, and Leif's sword was soaked in black blood, their kill long gone from the world.

Leif's attention fixated on Tovi. Eyes narrowed, assessing. Eldrick stepped ahead of her, and Leif blinked as if coming back to himself.

Siv and Sam joined them last, and the Johannes Magu bowed as he greeted Tovi.

"Queen," he said.

"Sam," she nodded in return.

Siv smiled, the first crack in her usually serious demeanor. "Talk of today will make its way to the Drabek Village by night's end. You should journey with us. Stay and recoup, if you'd like."

"I don't think that's a good idea," Leif approached, shoulders tight. "Alpha Johannes is in the village, and I have no doubt Alland and Lindström will make an appearance, too."

Eldrick swallowed a growl, heat scorching through him. The demon's blood stained Tovi's leathers as much as it did Leif's sword. How could he so easily dismiss her help?

Tovi stilled, glancing at Eldrick then back at Siv. "My errand is with Alpha Drengr, nothing more I'm afraid."

Alpha Drengr, not Eldrick. It sounded wrong on her lips, in her voice. Eldrick's wolf agreed, growling at the wrongness. Which also implied Tovi's return south was for political reasons.

Before he had a chance to inquire further, Siv beat him to it. "Nonesense. My mothers, the *alphas*," the young werewolf sent a glare in Leif's direction, "of the Drabek Pack, would be delighted to finally meet you."

Eldrick racked his brain for an excuse, but words died on his tongue.

Tovi, on the other hand, swallowed. "Alright. I'd hate to turn down Drabek hospitality."

Siv beamed. "Excellent. Let's hurry, then. You can tell Alpha Drengr your matter on the way there. Oh, lets not forget there's a festival in two days."

Wariness and tension brimmed between Eldrick and Tovi, but neither had any room to argue with Siv. Eldrick fisted his hands at his sides, searching for his axe. As he mindlessly scoped out the farmstead, he rallied control and purpose.

He'd traveled this far south to win the Earl vote, and Tovi's return didn't change anything.

Chapter Forty-Eight

Tovi

Grime and tension clung to Tovi as night settled over the forest, and she and the others rode in silence as they left the farmstead behind. She exhaled, her breath pluming like the prowling fog, and despite the distance they put between them and the ialtógs, tension refused to leave her limbs.

She'd recognized the look in Alpha Thorn's eyes, the *blame* glistening in his hard stare, ripe enough she could smell it.

The horses trudged through the gray, and Tovi fidgeted in her saddle, trying to focus ahead. It didn't help that a taut, muscular werewolf male sat behind her.

Because their traveling party had outnumbered the horses, and with exhaustion and injuries, shifting hadn't been discussed amongst the seven werewolves, and before Tovi had any grasp over the situation, Eldrick had saddled the same horse as her and together, they rode at the back of the group, Siv, Gyda, and Sam riding the front and leading them towards the Drabek Village.

"Are you alright?" Eldrick whispered into her ear.

Tovi fought the shiver running down her spine. Instead, she gripped the reins of their horse, spying the black blood staining her hands.

"Demons are nothing new," she said over her shoulder.

"That isn't what I asked, Tovi." His tone was unbending, then dropped to a mere breath. "You never need to pretend with me."

Tovi clamped her eyes shut. "It isn't just you here, Eldrick. Alpha Thorn clearly doesn't trust me. Despite Siv's excitement, I have no doubt she'll report to her mothers everything that happens. We can't jeopardize your Earl vote."

He sighed and remained silent for ten dreadful seconds until—

"I'm confident in Leif's vote, and I'll worry about the Drabeks' when I get there. Right now, I care about you."

"You don't need to," Tovi muttered. *Caring* was dangerous territory, one they'd abandoned weeks ago. Yet, during that time, it was as if Tovi had lived underwater and being near him was like coming up for air and breathing again.

He tensed in the saddle, his legs growing tighter in line with hers. "I haven't heard or seen you in weeks. Not a letter. Nothing."

"Eldrick—"

He grasped the reins out of her hands and reared the horse to a halt. The rest continued on, none the wiser to their pause on the path, and once they were a fairer distance behind, he clicked the gentle beast back into an easy walk. Trees, ferns, and yards separated them from the rest.

"There. We're out of earshot," he said. "It's just you and me."

Tovi peered over her shoulder, ready to tell him being alone was a horrific mistake, but stopped short. Eldrick's gem eyes were alight. They ensnared her, drinking her in like she was the only thing in the forest.

Tovi sighed. She trusted Eldrick with the truth. In fact, the weight of it begged to be unleashed.

"It never gets easier," she whispered. "Seeing ripples of the curse inflict horror across Sorin. Yen and I fought our fair share of demons through the Void, and scáths, too, in the Vadon Mountains. I should feel relief when I slay them, and yet instead, its anticipation for the next—the horrifically cold question: Will this ever end?"

Eldrick studied her, and Tovi turned back ahead, unable to bare the intensity of his understanding, like it wasn't her words he heard, but instead her heart.

"Thank you," Eldrick whispered, chest vibrating behind hers. "For being honest with me."

"I find it easy with you, wolf," she whispered.

They fell into silence for a moment, and Eldrick's heart raced inside his chest. Its tempo vibrated through Tovi's bones.

The path grew denser. Ferns replaced the rockier terrain, and the horse trudged through the sprawling green. Tovi swore she spotted purple flowers dotting mossy roots, the first signs of spring pushing through the harsh winter. Tovi pocketed the promise, holding onto it as her hand stiffened with the dried blood of her latest kill.

"What *matters* did you want to discuss?" Eldrick asked.

"I've secured an army," she said.

"How?" Eldrick asked. His hands tightened on the reins, and Tovi's insides backflipped at his reaction.

"With gold." Tovi explained Lord Nathaniel and the army with bloodstone armor.

Eldrick sighed, and their bodies molded to the other as if he relaxed at the news.

"Do you trust this Bash or Anastasia?" he asked.

Tovi shrugged. She recalled Bash's peculiarly pointed ears, but also the love he had for Lord Nathaniel's daughter. "I trust their intentions but not entirely their allegiance to me, but I don't have much of a choice. What of your efforts?"

Eldrick chuckled behind her, and Tovi realized he didn't do it often enough. "Nothing as impressive as an army, I'm afraid."

"But you have another alpha with you," she said. "That has to count as something, no?"

"Leif is a good male," Eldrick said. "I'm grateful to have him during discussion with the Drabek alphas."

"And do you trust him?" Tovi asked, studying the alpha from behind. If he heard them discussing him twenty-five yards aways, he made no indication. Thankfully, Leif and Sam appeared to be in deep conversation.

"I trust that Leif will do what's best to protect his pack, and I must ensure that means I'm the right choice." Eldrick detailed Bjorn's offenses since she left, and his strategy with the southern packs.

Tovi cursed. "I should leave before you reach the Drabek Village then, regardless of what Siv said. You can't afford for me to jeopardize—"

"No," Eldrick said too quickly. He huffed, and she could feel his body brush against hers as he shook his head. "I think its best if you stay."

"Why?" Tovi's mouth turned dry.

"I think the alphas of the south should meet you, face-to-face. They won't trust my assessment of you alone; they need to make one from themselves. If you win over the Drabeks, you're halfway to winning Lindström's and Alland's favor, too. And . . ." Eldrick audibly swallowed. "Because I missed you."

Tovi clamped her eyes shut.

Tell him that isn't reason enough to stay. Tell him that's exactly why you should leave.

But Tovi's traitorous heart took over, robbing her rational mind of any sense. How could she when his basil and spearmint wrapped her in a fresh and spicy cloud?

"I missed you, too," she whispered.

What she'd give to be alone, to feel his bare skin on hers, to taste his release on her tongue and to scream hers in his arms. She leaned back in the saddle, pressing closer to Eldrick's chest. A deliberate invitation she'd regret, but Goddess knew, after weeks of being away from Eldrick, the worries mounting like bricks on her shoulders, she needed him.

Eldrick remained as rigid as stone, and then . . . he leaned his head against hers, and the simple touch almost unraveled her.

"Touch me," she breathed.

Eldrick swallowed a growl that vibrated through his chest, shaking Tovi's rib cage. One hand let go of the reins, and he dragged his fingers up her filthy leathers, pausing at her trousers. Eldrick bit her ear, and Tovi hid her pleasure by falling farther back against him, giving him more access to dip two fingers under her waistband and undergarments.

His touch seared her skin, the power reaching to her toes. The others at the front kept riding on, in the midst of the conversations of their own as Eldrick teased her with his touch. Goddess, if she could have this one moment to sedate her need. To breathe him in and feel him against her—

Eldrick pressed a finger against her clit, and he ran achingly slow circles over it—just the way she loved it—and the crescendo inside Tovi's core began to climb, the precipice between pleasure and ache amounted to an incredible, shattering force.

Blood hel, he thrummed her pleasure like he'd written her body's song. *Yes*, she wished to cry out. *Don't stop*, she let her body beg—

Eldrick snatched his fingers away and withdrew his hand, leaving Tovi cold, breathless, and at the edge of combusting.

His lips tickled the edge of her ear. "No."

Tovi lurched forward, putting as much distance as she could in the saddle between them. Her need slicked between her legs, and *UGH*— "You bastard," she said through gritted teeth.

Eldrick laughed, and the sound reached Tovi's desperate sex. He dismounted the horse, peering up at her.

She seethed, unsure if she wanted to flee into the forest and escape this embarrassment or slap the smirk dripping with male pride right off his face.

The latter sounded far more satisfying, but both revealed to the others that *something* transpired between them. Tovi gripped the reins to still her eager hand.

Eldrick's expression turned serious, if not a bit saddened. His gem eyes dimmed. His shoulders snapped straighter. "If I can't have all of you, Tovi—heart, body, mind, and soul—I don't want any of it."

The earlier heat coursing through Tovi's body vanished. She froze to the saddle, stunned into silence as she tried to read Eldrick's thoughts, to find a chink in his usual, stony, alpha armor and find the lie, but there was only adamancy wafting off him in waves. Tovi opened and closed her mouth, unable to respond. Eldrick smiled without showing any teeth, breaking off their stare and walked off.

Werewolf horns bellowed in the distance, fracturing the tension gripping Tovi's limbs and yanking her back to the present.

They'd arrived at the Drabek Village, and she rode through the gates with Eldrick's rejection searing through her like some dark spell.

Chapter Forty-Nine

Evelyn and the team had traded a midnight-blue sea for a terra-cotta one. Waves of sand rippled across the horizon, and the dusty sky reflected a muted orange. Sand danced across the dunes, shimmering under the angry sun.

As she rode atop Bleu with Maxie curled in her lap, the scorching rays beat across Evelyn's resolve, and she questioned if the Sun Goddess raged against what she'd done, as if this close to her temple, the deity spied her selfishness. The bloodstone heated against her chest, the locked-away flame awakening in a land so reminiscent of the power Evelyn had once wielded at her fingertips.

They were on day two of their trek across the desert, and the blurry outline of a village sharpened on the horizon as they grew closer.

"*Stars above*, civilization," Todd breathed.

Belle, riding a horse to Evelyn's left, rolled her eyes. "I'm the one with a water bronntanas, and yet I haven't complained *once*."

"*Please*, can we rest for the afternoon?" Linx said from behind them. "As the team's healer, I must advise that traveling in this heat for such long periods of time isn't wise. We'd be better off resting, hydrating, and continuing our journey at night where the sun isn't as angry as a scáth."

Evelyn sighed and caught Kade searching her face. He'd wrapped his hood close around his head, drawn his shirt up and over his nose and mouth, revealing only his golden eyes that stared at her in question. It was her choice if they stopped, but the rest wasn't for her, was it? Truthfully, Evelyn couldn't rest until she had magic back, but it wasn't fair to make the others suffer. They'd yet to encounter a demon or any other obstacle to delay their journey.

"Alright," she breathed. "We rest and resume our journey after sundown."

The mage village bustled with a central market. Todd and Belle disappeared into the throngs of spice vendors and merchants while Linx excused herself to find an herbalist to restock her healer's supply. After a meal in the tavern, some much-needed time out of the sun, the team reconvened on the outskirts of the village near the stables. They'd found shade under the rows of a farmer's fig trees. Kade and Evelyn had both agreed that not lingering in the market prevented unwanted sightings in the village. At least Evelyn hadn't spied wanted posters this far south. *Yet.*

"Now these"—Todd juggled the purple fruit—"are the type of snack I'm on board for."

Evelyn laughed and turned to Kade. "Should we train a little, since we missed our usual morning session?"

"Let's." Kade tied his hair back from his face, twisting his golden waves into a bun.

Kade's lack of apprehension about his power put a pep in Evelyn's step. She shot him a pleased smile and began creating a makeshift target with stones, fallen tree branches, and a wine bottle she found sticking out of the sand. She planted her hands on her hips, gesturing towards the stack.

"You're getting better at drawing it forth, so let's work on your aim. Try to knock the bottle to the ground."

Kade wiggled his fingers and stepped up to the challenge, but Evelyn guided him ten steps backward.

"There," she said. "Now try."

She'd placed him twice the distance away from the target compared to the proximity between him and the tentacle on the *Sel*. It had been an impressive shot, but it was at close range, and it was best to train Kade on all the possibilities. His enemy might stand a hundred yards across the battlefield. Some fights called for different weapons—some a sword and others for a bow and arrow. Magic was much the same.

"I love your challenges, Ev." Kade inhaled, chest rising as he set his sights on the bottle. Time traveling across the plains and at sea had deepened his sun-kissed tan to a golden-glow. Rugged and handsome, like all those months ago when they'd met in Callum.

The team stood off to the side, silent as they waited for him.

"Draw up the power like energy, but harness it, dictate where and how you use it. Don't let it lead you, you lead it," Evelyn said.

Kade nodded, not breaking his focus, but hearing her instruction all the same. His fingers glowed first. The light pulsed pearly to blue, swirling around his fingers and hand, blue twinkling in the air. Evelyn had seen nothing like it before. The uniqueness of Kade's power made it all the more beautiful, and it *suited* him.

The dry air prickled with anticipation as Kade mounted more and more power in the palm of his hand until his digits disappeared from the sphere swirling ahead of him. Silver rimmed the gold of his eyes, and Kade *changed*. The energy of his power rippled from head to boots. Shoulders straighter. Feet planted firmly into the sands.

Belle sprang to her feet, and Todd dropped his figs, cursing. Evelyn held her hand up for them to stop—if Kade sensed their unease, he'd lose the progress he'd made on his power.

Linx appeared at Evelyn's side, making her jump. "He's drawing too much."

"He's fine," Evelyn said.

Linx frowned. "You can't feel the magic in the air, Evelyn, but we can—"

"Trust in his power goes beyond him," Evelyn hissed, hating how Linx mentioned her *lack* of magic and doubted Kade all in one sentence. "If all of you fear it, so will Kade."

The mage seethed, crossing her arms and stepping back.

Todd positioned Belle behind him. The horses shifted on uneasy legs, yanking at their reins tied to the tree. Evelyn's instinct pricked at the back of her neck, but she believed in Kade—he *could* do this.

Goddess, please.

Kade released the sphere. It landed on its mark, but as Linx had predicted, the energy was too much. The rock, branches, and bottle exploded, and the force ricocheted back. It blew Kade across the dunes, and the fig trees bowed against the sonic boom.

Evelyn internally cursed as she ran towards Kade and dropped at his side. He groaned, kneading his temples as he struggled to his knees.

"Kade, are you alright?" she asked.

He shook his head, eyes springing open. No silver remained. "I hit the target."

Evelyn paused. "I suppose you did."

"That sounds like there's a but in there." Kade peered up at her.

"Well . . ." She nibbled her lip, spying no injuries but bruised pride. "Your aim is good, *but* the amount of power you call upon we can continue to work on—"

Someone barreled into her, and pink blurred across her vision. Linx shoved her out of the way.

"You're a fool for not listening to me." Linx inspected Kade's limbs, putting her hands on him. Evelyn's ears rang. She couldn't think straight, couldn't pinpoint the array of unwarranted emotions scorching through her. Who, in the *fucking flames*, did Linx think she was?

"Moons, I'm alright," Kade said, pushing the healer at arm's length. "I drew too much power—"

"No, you're not alright." Linx jabbed a finger into his chest. "She's pushing you too far!"

She, as if Evelyn wasn't standing right there—she saw red.

"He must learn it," Evelyn yelled.

Linx whirled. "At *his* pace, not yours!"

"Stop," Kade growled.

But Linx didn't, she fisted her hands at her sides and crowded Evelyn's space. Pebbles in the sand trembled. "Just because you don't have your magic doesn't mean you get to abuse Kade's!"

Evelyn reared back as if Linx had slapped her.

"*LINX!*" Kade's roar ripped across the sands, shaking Evelyn's bones. He stepped between them, shielding Evelyn at his back. "Don't talk to Evelyn that way. *Ever.*"

Linx's catlike eyes flashed. She opened and closed her mouth, but her gaze landed on Evelyn as she said, "We're not a team anymore because of her."

Hurt shot through Evelyn at Linx's words, and the sting didn't stop. It bloomed. Reaching to her chest, belly, and bones. Her ailing body swallowed the insult, and Evelyn couldn't hold back.

Evelyn stormed off. Head down. Gait quick. She ignored Kade calling her name, finding the farthest fig tree and clutching the trunk for balance. A sharp pain pierced her stomach, and Evelyn toppled forward, clutching her middle, but before she crumpled to her knees, strong, tentative arms caught her, and Evelyn and Kade fell to the ground together.

"Hey, look at me."

"I'm fine," Evelyn breathed, wiping away the tears she'd let escape.

No. No. No.

Strength, resilience, resolve. She grasped for them like weapons in her arsenal, but they slipped through her fingers like the sand beneath her boots. Evelyn couldn't allow Kade to see her like this. She had to remain strong, rebellious against what fate handed her and forge ahead—

"It's okay to not be okay, love."

Kade's words broke her, and Evelyn dug her face into his chest and cried.

"It hurts," she whispered. "I hate that it hurts."

Kade held her as she cried, letting the fears of the last weeks finally descend upon her. The bright sun mocked her, as if the Sun Goddess shot her immense power yet did *nothing*.

Evelyn pulled out of Kade's hold, shaking her head and not meeting his stare.

"Linx is right—"

"She was out of line," Kade growled.

"No, I'm asking too much of everyone. Especially *you*. I keep telling myself it's alright, but the more I feel this—*death*—I can't accept you taking the risk. If I truly die—"

"Then I die too. We are mated, Evelyn."

Tears streamed down her face. "But our bond is broken. There might be a chance . . ."

Kade blinked, and every inch of him went rigid. "No," he breathed. "I don't accept that. I'll not walk this world without you. I can't—"

"Perhaps fate doesn't care what we want," Evelyn whispered, rising.

Kade grabbed her wrist, and his golden amber stare begged. "Ev . . ."

Evelyn swallowed her tears. "I just need some space. Alone. To think. *Please*."

Her fated nodded, letting her go. More pain lodged in her throat. She hated walking away, but Goddess, her mind whirled like a speeding wheel. Evelyn didn't stop until she'd ventured to the heart of the desert village and found the solitude of an alley. She leaned her head against the wall, the shaded stone pleasant to the touch and cooling her heated exterior.

Evelyn screamed into the rock. Beat her fist against it. Cursed the Sun Goddess for ignoring her prayers. She'd been here before, in this unforgiving land vacant of green, water, or clouds, begging for her magic, *fighting* for it, only to be left sunburnt, ignored, and near such fatigue, she'd lost conscious on the temple's altar, found by the desert mages who'd offered her refuge.

Why *her*? Rage twisted its nasty vines around her ankles and wrists, and for the first time in a long while, Evelyn's defenses against doubt fell. A sob broke out from her. How did she make her fate a *path* and not an endless loop?

Evelyn slid down the rock and put her head between her knees. *Breathe*, she tried to tell herself. *You can do this*.

Something—*two* somethings—pressed into her shins. Soft, plush, small.

"Meow."

Evelyn blinked and wiped tears from her eyes, finding Maxie rubbing her forehead into Evelyn's legs.

"Oh, Maxie," Evelyn said.

Maxie wiggled her nose. Flicked her tail. And completely invaded Evelyn's personal space as she climbed into her lap, assuming it as her position to sit and rest. A shadow fell over Evelyn, and a much larger beast nibbled her hair. It tickled and Evelyn laughed, spying Bleu's distinct coat in her peripherals.

"Hello to you, too," Evelyn whispered.

Bleu snorted, shaking his head as if to say, *You're alright.*

Her familiar's purr vibrated through Evelyn's taut being, and the sound and feeling calmed her racing heart. She pulled Maxie further into her chest, crying into her reddish fur.

This simple, tender moment had to give Evelyn hope, right?

Chapter Fifty

BLAIR SAT AT A desk nestled into a cozy enclave twelve stories high in the library. It possessed both a view of down below and a window revealing the Vadon Mountain range. This high into the library's structure, snow inched up the window's glass on the outside.

On the page Blair studied, the high sun illuminated a gold circle created by interlocked roots and branches of a tree, the trunk at the center. *The power of light* and *darkness*, the faeries had described. Roots remained underground, *in the dark*, while the leafed branches *looked to the light*.

The last line reminded Blair of the opening one of the witch's creed: *Eyes to the sun*. But the only god mentioned in the faerie text was the One. Blair gathered the god was wicked, cruel, and unpredictable, one the faerie did not respect but feared. The tree circle was a theory, a way to banish the One, to lock them in a cage of a new realm.

But the text was prewar, and without a text detailing the actual war that banished the Blood Goddess, Blair had no context if the faerie we're successful or not. Had they helped the others gods banish the One?

Blair slumped in her seat. Despite the little she'd learned from the faerie text, why had Elder Circe wanted it so badly?

Questions and anxious pent-up energy propelled Blair into motion. She drew her oversize turtleneck higher up her neck and abandoned her study

"

area to find additional texts, Rook in tow, flying above her. She descended six flights of stairs and wonder bled through her wary muscles.

Accounts hadn't done Vísdómr justice. Inside the mountain, the library functioned like a fine-tuned city run by books, research, university classes, and eager werewolf scholars. Some prowled the many stories in their werewolf forms, and Blair didn't know ruggedness, magic, and books could fit all in one place, but at Vísdómr it worked.

The stained-glass windows created a twinkling light in the rocky structure. Stairs spiraled around stalactites, and tunnels carved with shelves were stacked with endless books.

Blair reached the ancient historical section. A golden gate closed off the entrance, and a female vampyr with wheat-colored hair braided with daises sat at an oversize desk, stamping paperwork as she categorized a stack of weathered, dusty books.

Blair cleared her throat, standing on her tiptoes. The clerk peered down at her over crescent moon spectacles.

"I need to find additional texts such as this." Blair slid over the faerie text. "Given its age, I believe similar titles are within your ancient historical section."

The clerk inspected the title and sighed. "Unfortunately, Miss Carson, I can't permit you into this section of Vísdómr without a written reason from a superior."

Blair exhaled through her nose. Despite being a traitor to her own people, Vísdómr had at least welcomed Blair, but her "visiting" status came with limitations.

Rook landed on the clerk's desk, picking through things, no doubt searching for something shiny and silver. "Surely, given my circumstances, you can overlook that certain protocol."

The clerk frowned. "No, unless you had a Vísdómr leading scholar as a chaperone—"

"Blair Carson can enter the section with me."

Blasted books—Lorkan leaned up against one of the cavern like columns. Yet, Blair was relieved to see him. Per usual, his collared shirt was unbuttoned, revealing his pale, muscular chest. He'd forgone a vest, suspenders in its place, clipped to his high trousers folded above his ankles and revealing his laced boots. His dark hair stuck out in various directions, like he'd combed his hand through it too many times.

They'd not crossed paths in three days, yet the remissness of their kiss prickled on Blair's lips.

"Professor Drengr." The clerk jumped out of her seat, running her hands down her wool skirt stitched with flowers to match the ones in her hair. "Why, of course"—she tipped her head towards Blair—"I'll open the gate."

The clerk dashed from behind her desk, and moments later, the unseen gears of the gate clanked, and Lorkan held out his hand, motioning Blair to go through first. Her insides swam with nerves, but she hid them with a passive expression. Rook flew ahead, disappearing into the lofted ceiling dotted with rocky stalactites. In three long strides, Lorkan met up with Blair, and they walked down the ancient section's main hall, the silence between them thick as honey.

This section was more cave than library. Bookshelves were built into the rock, study areas were carved under stony nooks, and stalagmite-like columns kept the structure from crumbling with the weight of ancient texts and artifacts.

Lorkan drove his hands into his pockets. "I was actually on my way to find you."

"Oh," Blair said. "Did you find anything regarding the curse?"

"No, I wanted to apologize."

Blair halted, and Lorkan paused an arm's length away. High ranking scholars in their dark chestnut werewolf cloaks bustled about. Blair felt like all eyes were on them, but also she and Lorkan stood in their own world, a place they'd discussed visiting together. How different the circumstance, and yet the energy between them had grown.

"Lorkan, this isn't necessary," she breathed.

He shook his head. Without his cloak or glasses, he was bare and open as he stood ahead of her. "If you and I have any hope of being successful, we need to work together, but that isn't possible with everything that has happened between us, and I don't mean three days ago in the valley, but long before." He swallowed, like the next words pained him. "You say you hate me, but there is no one who hates me more than I hate myself. Excuses seem meaningless ten years later, all fueled by the foolish fears of a teenage *boy*, who believed he was protecting us. I can't undo the unforgivable pain I caused, but know I'm sorry. For it all."

Every inch of Blair turned taut, her wild emotions vibrating. Shadows crept up the jagged halls, but Blair didn't have the strength to rein them in. In fact, the sight of them and the cool breeze under her fingernails brought her comfort. She *could* storm out. Refuse to accept Lorkan's apology, but a cold, hardened corner of her heart softened, and her shadows kept her steady.

"I'm sorry, too," Blair whispered, and the weight of a thousand tons lifted from Blair's chest.

Lorkan reared back, eyes widening. "What for—"

"I should never have slapped you, and I'm sorry," Blair said, swallowing.

"Forgiven." Lorkan opened and closed his mouth as if he wanted to said more but then the gold in his eyes dimmed. "Shall we figure out how to break the curse?"

Blair nodded, offering Lorkan for the first time, a smile. Though, a sliver of disappointment melted on her tongue. Lorkan had apologized, but that was that. Nothing more. Maybe a part of Blair had hoped a small part of Lorkan still felt the same all those years ago, but he moved onto breaking the curse, their *very* important task at hand. Still, this newness between them was like an uneven path Blair had to navigate in heeled boots.

Lorkan led them to a mahogany door wedged between bookshelves. Inside, Lorkan revealed a dark yet cozy office. Floor-to-ceiling bookshelves lined the north and south halls. A grand fireplace crackled to life on the east wall with a leather sofa and two reading chairs to match. At the opposite end, a desk sat with a large wingback chair, but by the long table at the center of the room, it appeared whoever occupied the space used the studying table and large reading chair most often. Blair didn't spy a window but instead oil lamps lighting the place.

It smelled of moss and smoke, and as Lorkan shut the door, Blair spotted the brass plaque just in time.

"Goddess, this is *your* office?" she whispered, gazing around with more wonder.

It was so . . . *him*.

"I like to be away from the all the noise."

"Lorkan, this is a library," Blair laughed.

He shook his head, placing his glasses back on as he fiddled with a tea kettle on a corner nook. Lorkan prepared two tea mugs.

"You've not explored the university yet," he said. "Werewolves aren't like witches. We're beastly no matter our posts."

Except, Lorkan wasn't beastly as a latent wolf. Well, aside from his looming height and lean build. Blair walked the perimeter of the office, and much like his hideaway in the Drengr Library, she wondered if Lorkan found the most secluded place in Vísdómr to escape the reminder of what he didn't have.

A wolf. Though, it didn't stop the wolfish details throughout the office. Dancing, howling, and snarling wolves were carved into the wooden fireplace.

"Why did you come seeking texts in the ancient section?" he asked.

Blair spun on her heels, finding he'd joined her near the fireplace, two mugs in hand. She tapped the cover of the book clutched to her chest. "This is prewar, or before they banished the One, and I wanted to see if there were any other texts dating after the war of the gods."

"You know, I had a similar thought this morning and found them myself." Lorkan smirked and handed her a cup of tea. "Citrus and cinnamon."

"That's my . . ." Blair trailed off, unable to stomach the truth.

"Your favorite, I know."

Blair sipped, hiding her smile and disdain all once. "And? Did you find anything?"

Lorkan set a stack of books onto the table. Burnt and destroyed.

"Blasted books, what happened to those?" she whispered, joining him at the study table and placing her books and satchel down.

"A fire."

Blair paused, a memory resurfacing. *The Nūa Library suffered a horrific fire*, Jace had said.

"You don't mean . . ." Blair shook her head. "Wait, a fire here? At Vís-dómr?"

Lorkan nodded, lips downturned in a grave frown. "In this very section."

"Two fires in the largest libraries can't be a coincidence." Blair's head spun, and she grasped the edge of the table for balance. "These books belong in the same section, perhaps even the same shelves. You heard what Jace said, this text wouldn't have survived if his great-great grandmother hadn't checked it out. It's almost like these books were—"

"Targeted," Lorkan finished.

"Precisely." Blair's brows pinched. "When was the fire at Vísdómr?"

"1895."

"That's the year the vampyr curse fell. Again, that can't be a coincidence," Blair said. "Is there a way to confirm when the fire happened in Nūa? I don't recall it from my history of the library."

"I've written to Mya to learn more for us," Lorkan said. "Until then, I think it's safe to assume these are related events."

Blair nodded and rummaged in her various items and papers. "These are parts of the prophecy Evelyn discovered in Drystan Castle. She had to etch the words with a pencil, because they'd been scratched out and painted over."

"Which not only means someone wanted to destroy something, but they were close enough to vampyrs to be in the castle."

Blair sighed and hugged her tea mug, allowing the heat to permeate through her hands. "That leaves us the question, who and why?"

"The prophecy is a given. It helps us learn how to defeat the Blood Goddess by breaking the curse," Lorkan said.

"But ancient faerie text? What do they have to do with either? They left this world thousands of years ago."

Lorkan lay a finger over his lips, pensive as he asked, "*Why* did they leave?"

Blair shrugged. "Humans in Torren drove them underground."

The edge of Lorkan's lips twitched. "I'm not so sure I believe that anymore. Have you ever read that account or been told that lore passed down from generation to generation? It's easy to dictate an account when the subject is no longer around to defend the truth." He patted his hand on the faerie text.

Blair's mouth grew dry, and the threat of misinformation rattled her nerves, but she didn't disagree with Lorkan, in fact, she had reason to believe it, too.

She slid the ancient text over to him. "There's a theory described here, about using the magic of tree roots and branches to entrap the One, like a mighty ring of life and light."

"Were the faerie successful?" Lorkan asked.

"They never go into detail if they used it. I found a more robust text to help translate the text and found an interesting passage detailing that *One became Three, so they set her free.*"

"*Her?*" Lorkan scratched his jawline. "The Blood Goddess?"

"That's the thing, I haven't found a single account of her name yet," Blair said. "Not in the faerie text at least."

He sighed and slid over the burnt texts. "I don't suppose we can restore these texts with magic." Blair inspected them, careful with the brittle pages as she flipped through them. Her fingertips buzzed with energy not magic, as if they had been burnt the old-fashioned way. *Fire.* "Yes, luckily I have experience with restoring ancient items."

Lorkan smirked, in the way that reached his honey eyes. "I thought you might."

Blair grabbed a piece of parchment and scribbled a list of items for a potion she knew by heart. "Do you think we can find these items in Fika? I'd much rather not travel back to Nūa."

Not yet anyway. With the fire behind her, the caverns of Vísdómr surrounding her, and exciting books to decipher, ease caressed Blair like a summer breeze.

"I'd prefer to avoid Guards myself." Lorkan inspected the list, pushing his glasses up the bridge of his nose. "Well, there's only one way to find out. It looks like we need to visit Fika."

Chapter Fifty-One

Kade

K ADE FOUGHT SLEEP AS he tossed and turned on his bed role, but Circe's mind control wrapped its thorny vines around his conscious and dragged him back to the wasteland.

A raven sat atop Tenebris's scythe. The dark witch was nowhere to be found as the bird pecked at the blade, *ting, ting, ting,* echoing across Kade's mind. It pinned Kade in place with one large menacing eye at the center of its head.

It cawed.

Wake up.

Evelyn's gentle whisper caressed his mind. His insides twisted into knots. They'd not spoken since their training session. Both of them needed distance and a moment to breathe, but the more unsaid words that peppered the air, the more anxious Kade became.

They didn't have time to not work it out, and Kade wondered if his crippling anxiety led him to the wasteland.

She showed you your greatest fear . . . that's what she does, Kade.

He let Circe in. As the days grew nearer to Evelyn's last, and he grappled with a power he feared, his guard had dropped. His weary mind had no defenses, not when his heart ached for his love and body raged to do something. All his energy was being dumped into putting one foot in front of the other, but the more he walked through the wasteland, the more real it became.

Doubt strangled Kade's lungs. Was this a fear or the future?

"That is a fair question, my friend." Tenebris appeared at his side. He walked in step with him, bare feet and too-long toe nails digging into the ash-covered ground.

"You're not my friend," Kade growled.

Moons, he was talking to a hallucination now. Engaging with him. Taking part in Circe's sick mind games.

Kade should shift, outrun this nightmare in his werewolf form—

His wolf didn't answer. No howl. No beastly energy. No pacing inside his blood. Icy panic shot through his veins, and Kade reached and reached and reached for his shifting magic, to no avail. He found himself hollow like the expansive wasteland around him.

"How is she reaching my mind from afar?" he growled.

Tenebris hummed. "Once darkness has been let in, it is so easy to invite us back."

"I didn't let any of you in," he hissed.

"What about the time you attacked Todd?" Tenebris asked, hands clasped ahead of him.

Kade stumbled. "I didn't attack—"

"You were trying to protect Evelyn, but he was in your way, so your instinct took over, and you tried to get rid of him."

"That isn't true!" Kade roared.

Tenebris didn't even flinch from his anger. "You know what I find interesting, your power arose in a land seeping in dark magic. *Ah*, you thought it surfaced because you met *her*." Tenebris tsked his tongue, disappointment flashing across his face. "Torren is where the One began, and that day at the docks, darkness filtered on the wind. You *smelled* their sweetness, and I believe it awakened what has lived in you since you took your first breath."

How, in the stars above, did a dark witch locked in the Tùir know these details? *It's in your mind*, Kade realized. His memories lived here, of course Circe's hallucination pointed to the facts embedded into him.

"This isn't real. You aren't real. Get the fuck out of my mind!" Kade roared to the sky, praying to the Moon God to help him against Circe.

The raven flew towards them, and Tenebris winced. Thunder rumbled, and the hold on Kade's mind tightened. He buckled to his knees, driving his hands through his hair as pain threatened to split his head open.

Tenebris stood close, looming over him like a demon, not a witch. "Is it so hard to admit the possibility of which side you belong? You left your precious mountains behind, abandoned your friends, blew up a historic witches' building, *hurt* the woman you love. You're even working with those touched by the curse—vampyrs."

"Not all vampyrs are evil," Kade breathed, but each wrongdoing Tenebris mentioned had slashed across his skin like a knife's cut.

"Once darkness has touched another, it blooms, Kade. There is no out-running evil." Tenebris threw out his hand and the wasteland rippled from gray to sprawling green. The clouds above faded, the fiery sun sucking them from existence. Spring sweetened the air. Honeysuckle, grass, vanilla, and cedar—

Kade whirled, and atop a hill, two figures stood hand in hand. Their faces and details were blurred and faded like fuzzy lines, like they'd been drawn with oil pastels—one had golden hair long and reaching his shoulders, and the other, obsidian hair braided to the side. Crowns sat atop their heads.

A king and queen will emerge . . .

"See," Tenebris exclaimed. "Even a bit of truth has been weaved into the lies witches have foretold. There is no escaping the future. You're meant to rule this land, Kade. Not save it."

The Drengr Village built itself back up, Nūa too, brick by brick. A new crest tangled from banners, a silver wolf against a black velvet, fangs dripping with blood.

Wake up, Evelyn whispered, and at the beautiful, soul-rousing sound, Kade's wolf finally surfaced. It howled at the scene around them, baring its canines.

Denying. Fighting. Rebelling against the notion.

"No," Kade bit out.

He rose on steady legs and grabbed Tenebris by the throat. "I am *not* darkness."

Tenebris tipped his head back and laughed. The clouds flew back across the sky. Grass died under Kade's boots. Ash blew the image of him and Evelyn away, the pastel colors swirling into black whisps.

"Let us show you a much more frightening future if you don't accept your place amongst us, Kade Drengr, *Son of Darkness*."

Tenebris vanished, and inky shadows slipped through Kade's fingers. The sudden loss of weight in his grasp had Kade stumbling forward and landing face-first into the dirt—*no*, not dirt.

Rotting flesh.

Kade had fallen into a pile of dead bodies. He tried to regain his balance, to crawl his way out of the heavy, stiff limbs and putrid stench—

"No!" Kade scrambled back, jolting to his feet.

He wretched into the ash, his heart shattering. Yen's lifeless eyes stared up at him, resting atop Bétar's chest. His friend was palish blue. Unmoving, bloodied. *Dead.* Todd's strong, tattooed arm reached out beneath Yen and Bétar, fingers still reaching for his bloodied weapon.

Moons, what sort of hel was this?

The ash shifted direction, winds whirling across the wasteland.

"Kade."

Ahead, the ghosts of his friends stood side by side. His blue power dotted their injuries. Yen's bloodied head, Bétar's gaping chest where his heart should've been, and Todd, the wound he'd given him previously reopened and gushing. His brothers, Eldrick and Lorkan, stood at the end with their stares vacant and empty.

All five of them talked at once. *You are the One's son.*

Kade covered his ears, an all-consuming horror taking hold. What if this wasn't a hallucination? What if it was *real*? The voices dug their way into his mind, and they bounced off his skull. There was no way to escape them, and he didn't have the power to wake up.

"Kade," someone shouted.

"*My son,*" another hissed.

"Com . . . mander," a painful choke came from behind.

His eyes sprang open, and he found his team no longer dead, but on the brink of it.

"Yen!" Kade rushed to her, dropping to his knees. Blood trailed down her temple, a gash festering with his blue magic. Kade, without a second thought, pushed the body laying limp over hers.

Bétar groaned, eyelids flickering. "Aye, it'll be alright soon."

"No!" A cry cracked out of Kade.

"K-a-de." Yennifer's plea came out broken, but it didn't compare the crack cementing in Kade's chest. "You did this." The blood coating her words made the hiss all that much worse, all that much deeper of a cut across Kade's soul. "It was you who brought the darkness."

"No—"

His name. In that voice. Full of such anguish. Kade spun wildly. Searching for her.

Searching for *Evelyn.*

She cried out again and again, each one more desperate than the last. Kade tried to grasp his wits, tried to slow his racing heart, tried and tried to grasp some sense of calm. He turned back to Yen and stilled, his heart skipping a beat and dropping like a stone to his gut. She was gone. The mounds of bodies had vanished with her.

"*Kade!*"

"Evelyn!" Kade roared, rising to his feet and searching, running, sprinting in the direction her voice came from the loudest. But it echoed, bouncing off the walls of this wretched place.

"Kade." The last plea came out a whisper, and Kade snapped his gaze downward.

Something in Kade fractured. His heart, his chest, his entire being. Kade couldn't be sure. The pain was blinding, the tear running through him so violent, he lost his knees and collapsed.

The moan he released wasn't of mortal or of this world.

Evelyn was dying, her entire body scorched and still. She lay at the center of a concaved indent in the ground, like the aftereffect of a powerful boom. Smoke rose from the still-hot ground, and her silvery blue eyes never left his. Orange embers didn't dot her burns, but blue, tantalizing sparks. *Stars above*, he'd done this. She shined with *his* power. He'd hurt her.

Killed her.

His mate, his love, the one person who mattered most in the world.

"No, no, no." Kade's words were frantic, desperate—the mumblings of a broken man.

"I couldn't stop you." Tears fell down her beautiful face.

"I'm so sorry, Evelyn. I love you, please—"

She snapped up, like her body was a puppet and her limbs were pulled by strings. She grabbed a fistful of his shirt and dragged him eye level.

"You're wrong," she rasped. "We're all wrong. *You're her son, Kade.*"

A thousand hands gripped him from behind. They belonged all to the same people—Eldrick, Lorkan, Bétar, Yennifer, and Todd. Dozens of those he loved. Lifeless, but moving. Tinged blue with death. Dragging him farther and farther away as blood spilled from Evelyn's lips, creating a river of red and heartbreak.

Kade lurched awake with the sight of his dead mate tattooed on the back of his eyelids. Coated in sweat, his pants and blanket clung to him as he shook with the horrors of his mind.

"Hey." Evelyn sat up, tiredness rimming her eyes, and rested a hand on his cheek. He didn't know he'd shed tears of his own until Evelyn brushed them from his cheek.

"You're alright, you're safe. *We're* safe."

Kade shook his head, heart racing, he thought it might burst from his chest. He couldn't find the right words, not without admitting the atrocities he'd committed and seen.

She studied him, blue eyes flashing with pain of her own as she took him in. "Talk to me, Kade. Don't shut me out, not now."

Kade wavered. How much of the truth did he divulge?

It was only them. Earlier that night, tired and shaken from Circe's attack, they'd found a tavern with available rooms in the mage village near the Sun Temple. The others had retired to their own rooms, leaving Kade and Evelyn alone.

She waited, sitting in the silence with him, and her unbending silver gaze encouraged him to be honest, creating this sense he could tell her *anything*, no matter how horrific it was.

"Circe still has control over my mind. She's shown me a vision, a wasteland that I create with my power and killing everyone I love, including you."

"Kade . . ." Tears laced her words, and she rested her forehead against his. "What do you need? In this moment, right now. How can I help you?"

"Your heartbeat," he whispered. "I need to hear it. I need to hear that you're alive."

She nodded, urgent understanding bleeding into her sad smile. "Okay."

Evelyn dragged Kade into her arms, and they fell back onto the bedroll as he lay his ear flush against her sternum. *Thump, thump, thump.* The sound calmed his own heart. Evelyn simply held him, but the rawness of this moment, the vulnerability she gave him had him wrapping his arms around her, not daring to let her go. He breathed in her vanilla cedar scent, counted her heart rate, evened his breathing to match her pulse.

He was with Evelyn. She was alive.

"I'm alright. You're alright," she whispered. "We're together."

"This is real?" His words muffled into her tunic. He wasn't ready to let go, to be away from her, which made the days leading up to their agonizing ordeal all the more frightening.

"Yes, love." Evelyn combed her fingers through his hair, brushing it back and drawing faint circles over his temple. "Whatever Circe showed you, it isn't real. *This* is real. We're real. "

"But it felt real, Ev," he whispered. "I—"

He broke off, biting the words back. The scent of death remained in his nose, the sights of his dead friends. Evelyn's hold kept him from retching.

"It's okay to not be okay," Evelyn whispered.

Kade swallowed, remembering the words he had told her. The truth was, he wasn't okay, maddened with worry about who and what he was.

"My power is chaos, and it makes me question everything. What if . . . What I'm not the Son of the God? What if this magic is from the Blood Goddess?"

"What if it is?" Evelyn asked, expression unfazed.

Kade blinked, trying to read whatever swam in her eyes. There was nothing. No judgment. No fear. No worry. "But then this power—"

"Belongs to you, not her." Evelyn shook her head. "Belle said something the other day. Both her and Ingrid have magic. It isn't light or dark that makes them different, but what they choose to do with their power."

"That makes it all sound so simple," he whispered.

Evelyn steadied her gaze and glided her hand over his heart and palmed his chest. "I know your heart, Kade. It is kind. *That's* what matters."

Kade ran his thumb over her pinched brow, smoothing the worry from her features. "How did you get rid of Circe's mind control?"

Evelyn sighed, staring off into the distance. "I didn't have nightmares like you, but when I believed in myself, not my flame or title, but me alone, her words vanished from my thoughts."

Kade considered Evelyn's words. "But I hate this power, Evelyn. It's like a poison running through my veins."

"Then perhaps you're not ready to master it or fight Circe's visions until you've accepted it."

Yet, how could Kade accept everything else but this? He accepted his love for Evelyn to be real, that their bond was good and right. That his place in this world was as a protector and third born. If only he could accept the immense power in his veins, but he feared he'd never accept what it was, until he knew the truth.

Evelyn and Kade held each other and spoke of their fears and dreams late into the night. They didn't fall back asleep. Their time was slipping away like the sands whipped up and carried away in the desert breeze, and Kade cherished Evelyn's voice, listened to her words and heartbeat and *held her*.

For tomorrow, they ventured to the Otherworld.

CHAPTER FIFTY-TWO

A FEW DAYS LATER, Lorkan's study was filled with the scent of Blair's potion, bubbling away in a copper soup pot—the closest she'd found to a cauldron in the werewolf village. Luckily, Blair's go-to potion for repairing or restoring damaged books included echinacea, goatweed, and star anise, which didn't smell half bad when brewed over maple wood.

But the process was time consuming. Blair brushed the potion on the damaged pages with tied lavender, dandelion and wool all while muttering a certain spell she'd written herself. As a leading scholar, she practically recited the spell in her sleep.

With her wind bronntanas, the texts and pages dried quickly. Their ink, parchment, and contents salvaged. Lorkan had read as Blair worked, and it wasn't long before both of them pored over the ancient texts, reading in content silence like they had as teenagers.

Hours went by, and without windows, Blair had no measure of time, aside from Lorkan's dwindling stack of firewood. They remained silent and focused as they scoured the text for any remnants of words, images, or clues.

"Is this the tree you read about in the faerie text?" Lorkan asked, flipping a book around for Blair to read it.

The trees roots and branches connected into one large, interlocked circle. "Yes, that's similar."

Blair thumbed the stacked books, a sense of awe coming over her at the several-thousand-year-old texts so easily available to her. She found the one they'd retrieved in Nūa and flipped to the page detailing the tree. They were similar, but the branches and leaves slightly different.

"This is the tree of life to werewolves, also known as the elm," Lorkan said. "In ancient myth, the trees create balance and possess protective properties."

"Do werewolves use them for anything?" Blair asked.

Lorkan didn't meet her stare as he said, "Carving bows and arrows, that's about it. But this is also similar to our realm's map with the various realms."

Blair's brows pinched. "Here, the faeries called it an ever tree."

Lorkan reared straighter. "Did you say *ever*? This text detailed a seed with such a name, how the faerie used it to create pocket realms."

"Like going underground?" Blair asked.

He shrugged, pushing his glasses up the bridge of his nose. "Perhaps. But I found an interesting passage about a forest called the Gray Wood. It's not a faerie-written text, but written by humans in Torren. They claim the faerie left this world under those hills and can be spotted in the roots of the trees."

Blair jumped out of her seat and peered over Lorkan's shoulder. "That's in Callum."

"You know it?" Lorkan turned, their noses almost touched.

Blair nodded. "My sister Evelyn saved a young woman inside it when she was solving the murders. It was enchanted with dark magic at the time, but she—"

"Set it free," Lorkan whispered.

Blair shook her head. "What?"

"*With the old bones of friend now set free,*" Lorkan laughed. "It's a line from the prophecy. So, your sister undid the dark magic?"

"Yes," Blair roamed her gaze over all the texts and notes, finding the parchment with the written prophecy. "But what would the Gray Wood give her?"

"A *seed sown from elsewhere.*" Lorkan pointed to the second to last stanza and then to his translations of a faerie text.

Blair froze. "Are you suggesting the Gray Wood is a forest of *ever* trees?"

"Why not?" Lorkan shrugged. "It's no coincidence your sister is detailed in the prophecy, and there's a supposed connection between the faerie and this forest. Further, the Gray Wood didn't dot a single map until after the Gods War."

"As if they'd created it to avoid the conflict, leaving our world entirely," Blair said.

She scribbled their collective notes into a journal, drawing conclusions to the various stanzas, too. The fire popped and the increase sense eyes were on her caressed her cheek. She snapped her head up, finding Lorkan staring at her.

"What?" Blair asked.

Lorkan offered a small smile. "It almost feels like the evenings we spent in the Drengr Library together."

Blair bit her lip, hating to think of those old times but also appreciating the similarities. "I'd say your office is far more spacious."

"True," Lorkan sighed. "But nothing can beat that view in the reading nook."

No, it can't, Blair wished to agree, yet she refrained. She liked spending more time with Lorkan. Researching things. Experiencing his quick wit. Working *together*. Blair's insides swam, and she tasted apprehension with her next swig of tea. She didn't want to fracture this normalcy they'd found working together.

Especially if they were figuring out more and more about the prophecy.

Blair cleared her throat. "So, Evelyn and Kade get this seed, and then what?"

Lorkan shrugged. "Based off the properties I know of, we plant it at the epicenter of the curse."

"The Void then," Blair said. "*The age of curse, a crack in the land, the seep and sorrow of death, darkness, and rot.*"

He nodded. "I'd say this is a start."

Blair rose, gathering her things. "Should we continue tomorrow?"

Lorkan stood up, too, helping her stack the books and tidy the space. "Yes. Let me walk you back to your room."

"That isn't necessary—"

"I'd like to," Lorkan said. "Please. Vísdómr is a different beast at night. It's easy to get lost."

The last bit of fire dwindled, but his study grew hotter. Thicker. Blair swallowed, throat going dry, and all she could manage was a small nod.

In silence, they ventured to the visiting dormitories.

With the few windows glowing from the sun, the central library was dimmed with glowing lanterns. Shadows rippled across the stony exterior, and Blair hugged her arms tighter around the books she carried.

Few werewolves browsed the shelves at this hour. Some were so lost to their books, they didn't notice Blair and Lorkan passing by. Others recognized Lorkan from afar and greeted them with enthusiastic smiles.

They finally reached Blair's hall. Tiredness clung to her bones, sleep beckoning after a night of dedicated research. They stopped outside her door and turned to the other.

"Thank you, Lorkan," she whispered.

He stared down at her, golden stare as bright as sconces lighting the hall. For the first time since being together again, a stillness bled in the air between. The *comfortable* kind. The one Blair had looked forward to when she visited him. Darkness ran in her veins, and yet, Lorkan quieted that storm. Even now, after so much time.

And when he stared at her, the sharpness of his reserved demeanor softened. There was a hint of the boy she'd fallen for. The quiet, thoughtful werewolf who'd worn glasses and faced being a latent wolf without an ounce of resentment.

They stepped closer, as if an invisible thread tugged them together. A breath passed. Yearning replaced the storm in Blair's veins and then—

Lorkan stepped back, shaking his head. "I'll see you tomorrow at half past nine. Have a goodnight, Blair."

He retreated from her door, and Blair exhaled.

She wasn't certain if her sigh was full of relief or regret.

CHAPTER FIFTY-THREE

E VELYN EXHALED THEIR JOURNEY and inhaled the sight of the Sun Temple, her soul no longer in its last days, but hours. As if her body knew the end neared, an instinct urged her forward.

Sand blew down the other side of the canyon like rusty waterfalls. Through the shimmering dust, Evelyn made out the simple archway carved into the cliff, the etched sun above it barely visible at this distance.

Kade stepped up to the canyon's edge, and a thousand words swirled in his golden stare, but he said none and gave Evelyn a committal nod instead. They were here, and there was no going back.

Haste filled everyone's steps as they descended the hundreds of stairs down the cliff into the canyon's valley. Evelyn and Kade led the front, Linx at the center, and Todd and Belle at the rear.

Sweat collected rose-colored sand across everyone's skin, and as they reached the walkway across the valley, Evelyn swore the winds bellowed. Maxie dashed ahead, meowing insistently. Evelyn peered at her familiar and stilled. A pebble by Maxie's paw trembled.

"Run!" Kade roared.

Bleu ran past, and in a single move, Kade swung upon his horse and headed for Evelyn. She braced, waiting for his outstretched hand, but another force barreled into her, knocking her across the sand.

She landed with a bone-rattling thud, but she didn't have time to regain her wits. A nathracha—a snakelike demon—launched at her. Evelyn threw her hands out and grasped its bared fangs. Fathomless black eyes stared down at her, the acidic scent of its deadly venom puffing into her face. Its long, legless, scaled body writhed, muscles trembling as it fought Evelyn's hold, intent on driving its fangs into her flesh.

Evelyn growled, arms shaking as she fought the demon's attack, and slacked as metal sang through the air and the head landed on her chest.

"Evelyn!" Kade thrust the beast's head off her, sword soaked in black blood.

She shook as she rose on unsteady legs, panting.

"Are you alright?" he asked.

Evelyn patted herself for injuries but found none aside from scraps left by the sandy rocks. "I'm fine."

"Kade!" Todd called

The ground trembled, echoing through the canyon.

Todd shifted into his werewolf form, and two more nathracha demons sprang out of the sands. The tips of their tails glinted red, their stingers dripping with venom. The droplets sizzled in the sand where they fell, burning through the rocky terrain.

"Stars above," Kade hissed, squatting into a fighting stance.

One demon circled Todd, Belle, and Linx, and the other slithered towards Evelyn and Kade.

"Goddess," Evelyn breathed, hoping the Sun Goddess heard this close to the temple. They didn't have time for an attack.

"Stay close," Kade called over his shoulder. "If I tell you to run, you listen."

Evelyn nodded. Any other time, she'd argue and refuse to let Kade face a demon alone, but she wasn't in any shape to assist, putting *him* at risk. Tiredness clung to her bones, and her soul disintegrated yards away from the temple.

The demon struck, but Kade pivoted right, slicing near its neck. The blade clanged off its tough scales, barely leaving a scratch. It whirled, lunging at Kade again as its tail rattled, the tension rising in the air. It struck again, and Kade deflected its blows by scraping his blade across its bared fangs.

Evelyn trailed Kade as he circled the demon and fought. Maxie weaved between her legs, frantic and hurried, while Bleu paced—the other horses had long abandoned them, specks on the valley's horizon.

Belle and Todd fought a demon together. The witch attacked, stepped back, and before the demon recovered, Todd sliced the demon's softer underbelly. Linx somersaulted across the sands, joining Kade, and the teammates began the same tactic.

Uselessness vibrated through Evelyn's tired muscles. Her head ached, and while her heart raced, an icy chill, unfitting for Cirrillo's desert air, ran in her blood.

"*Oof!*"

Evelyn swiveled her attention back to Todd and Belle. The demon had used its scaly tail to knock them off their feet.

A screech cut through the air. Linx had thrown an explosive at the other nathracha, giving Kade the chance to lunge close enough and strike his sword through the demon's underbelly. Flesh tore. It screeched louder. Kade pulled out his blade. Black blood splattered on the sand, but he'd exposed himself. Unguarded. Unaware.

Evelyn shouted his name, but it was too late, and her instinct screamed, *move*, and she did, jumping in front of Kade—not thinking, not caring if she died, but only that Kade *lived*.

Shielding Kade, she took the other nathracha's strike.

A sickening crunch rang in Evelyn's ears, and all she became and knew and breathed was pain. Agonizing, hot, eroding pain.

Evelyn screamed.

Yet, fate and the gods were nowhere to be found so near their temple.

For the nathracha pulled out its stinger, the barbed end shredding Evelyn more on its exit.

Kade bellowed her name, his horror rattling her to the bone. His blue power fizzled in the air. It grabbed hold of the demon's tail, still wet with her blood, and climbed. The demon grew powerless, unable to fight or slither away from Kade's hungry power. It devoured its scales, flesh, and bone until only blue remained, peppering the air with Kade's immense energy.

Evelyn crumpled into his arms. Her hands turned black and spidery from the venom taking root in her veins.

She didn't have hours. She had minutes.

"Kade . . ." she fought for breath and words and consciousness. "I . . . I love you."

"*NO!*" Kade scooped her into his arms and ran. "Get to the temple!"

The ground trembled—or was that Evelyn's teetering consciousness? The world flipped. Screeches of more demons echoed across the cliffs. Kade's heartbeat echoed like war drums to her impending doom against her ear as she slumped in his arms.

Stay awake, someone shouted far, far away.

Remember the spell. We're almost there, another said. Gentle, closer.

Belle—that was sweet, beautiful Belle. A friend Evelyn had found in the darkest of places. A witch who added light to the world. *Brightness.*

Evelyn lost feeling in her toes and fingers, and fire roared in her veins. Not her power, pure unapologetic flame burning her from the inside out. It inched closer and closer to her already failing soul. The darkness fed on her weakness. Grew stronger from it.

Evelyn fought the venom, grasping onto Kade's shirt. "It hurts. It always hurts."

"I know, love, I know. But listen to Belle, we're going to start the spell. Stay with me."

Evelyn obeyed. Tried to. The sun became lost, a sky of rocks, carvings, suns and nymphs dancing across the terra-cotta colored ceiling. Familiarity caressed its gentle presence over Evelyn as Kade laid her down on cold stone. She'd been here before—a different version of herself, but also wanting the same thing.

To get her magic back.

"Evelyn, listen to me," Kade whispered, his voice so urgent and gentle all at once as he stroked her hair. "I love you—with all my heart and soul, in this life and the thousand more to come. Meet me there, Ev. Meet me in the Otherworld."

Her handsome, kind fated. *Fucking flames.* How was she dying and happy all at once? Because of him, she had *lived*. It was with him she'd discovered herself. She'd found happiness, laughter, and love. Even without the mating bond, their love withstood the darkness they fought against. They, together, prevailed.

As would their love, long after Evelyn was gone.

Darkness, the sweet kind that fell before a blissful sleep, wrapped itself around Evelyn, and she closed her eyes, succumbing to the fall.

CHAPTER FIFTY-FOUR

KADE

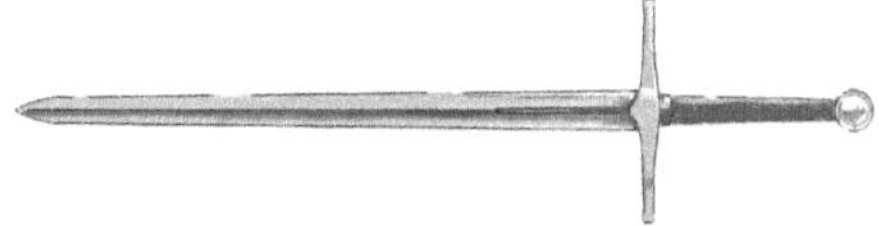

THE WALLS OF THE temple shook as Kade held his dying mate in his arms.

Thump, thump . . . Thump . . . Thump . . .

Evelyn's heartbeat grew fainter and fainter, and Kade couldn't breathe. This was true horror—not Circe's visions, but feeling the life drain from the love of his life's body.

"Belle," Kade gritted his teeth. "I'm losing her."

The witch fumbled with her supplies, tears streaming down her face. The temple walls trembled again, knocking over her candles and whooshing out their flames.

"Gods damnit," she hissed.

"Here." Linx tipped a murky liquid past Evelyn's motionless lips. "It'll thicken her blood and slow the venom from reaching her heart."

"Moons." Todd sprinted towards the temple's archway, blades drawn.

Past his weapon master's silhouette, dozens of nathrachas burst from the sands, slithering over one another as they raced to get inside the temple first.

Rooted to the stone and clutching Evelyn in his arms, Kade had no rational thought, no reason on what to do, only to hold Evelyn close.

Save her.

Protect her.

Stop this.

An ear-splitting scream rocked through Kade. Belle rushed ahead of Todd and threw her hands north. The air stilled. The demons still approached. The trembling shifted.

And a river roared.

"Goddess," Linx breathed.

In the desert, in a land devoid of water, Belle conjured it from nothing. She made it. Drew from nothing and created a river with her magic. It surged past, drowning each demon with it. When the water settled, not a single one remained alive.

Belle stumbled, chest heaving.

The young witch had saved them all. Including Evelyn.

"There's still time," Linx said, helping Belle gather the items for the spell.

Belle created a ring of salt. Laid out candles. Lit them. Dug for Evelyn's muince, motioned for the bloodstone, and Kade handed it to her.

"Shall I do it?" Linx asked.

"What?" Belle hissed. "No, I've studied the spell for weeks."

"You just used a lot of magic, Belle," Linx said.

"I can do this," Belle pleaded, looking at Kade. "Please."

War raged in Linx's eyes, but Kade shook his head.

"There isn't time to debate. If Belle says she's ready, I trust her."

Linx said nothing more on the matter, and Belle ignored her stare. She sat, crossed her legs, and positioned herself ahead of Kade, but outside the circle. The notebook she held was Blair's, and there were notes scribbled.

"I can't guarantee this won't hurt," she whispered. "For either of you."

"I understand."

Belle exhaled. "Alright. Don't let go of Evelyn, not here nor there. You're a part of the threads Kade, keeping her tethered to this world. You can't lose her."

Kade nodded, his soul yearning to hear Evelyn's voice again, to have her open her eyes once more. Even if it was just their souls in the Otherworld.

Belle began to chant in a language Kade didn't understand but recognized as Olde Script. She shut her eyes, holding her hands out. Water droplets formed in the air and began to twist like small diamonds. Sand whipped from the stone, and soon a tunnel of water and sand whirled around Kade and Evelyn, thin enough for him to still make out Linx and Todd manning the archway and Belle sitting ahead of him.

The muince glowed, then the bloodstone next. They rose on either side, floating in the air. Magic brimmed between them and shot towards Kade. Above, the etched lines of the carvings glowed with the spell, even the markings on the ground. Kade and Evelyn sat atop a full sun, and the rays shot outward, illuminating the temple in a glow that reminded Kade of stars. His wolf howled at the powerful magic in the air.

"Close your eyes."

Kade obeyed. Something cracked, and he flinched, wondering if it was the bloodstone. A similar sound echoed to his other side—the muince.

Something ripped through him, like a scythe had cut him neck to hip. He was open, bare, splitting from the inside. Evelyn slacked in his arms, and her final breath eased from her like a sigh while she slept. Kade fought with everything he had, a battle raging within him as the spell took hold. It battled everything that he knew was right and natural. His wolf threatened to unleash until she collapsed.

"Steady, Kade," Linx called, unseen.

He'd known he'd lose her. He'd been told. But nothing prepared him for the ricocheting agony as his mate's soul left this world first. He cried out. Breaking from the inside.

Together.

Evelyn's voice whispered in the back of his mind, and he grasped onto her like she was his anchor in all of this while a numbness overtook him, a hollowness in his chest.

Kade rocked Evelyn to the cadence of Belle's chant, calling to his mate.

"I'm coming, love. Wait for me."

Chapter Fifty-Five

THE DRABEK VILLAGE BUSTLED with preparations. Werewolves worked to hoist an amethyst banner near the north gate. Others climbed trees and hung glass orbs on invisible string, muted in the cloudy morning. A woman with delicate braids handed out evergreen wreaths for families to decorate their cottages, and garlands filled with baby's breath lined the palisade wall. Ahead, two young girls fought with wooden shields and swords, embodying what the festival celebrated—shield-maidens.

Yet, the sky remained gray, and an ominous chill crawled up Eldrick's skin. How did the Drabeks find the ability to celebrate anything with darkness so vividly on the horizon?

Hair white as snow caught his attention, and around the bend, Tovi walked beside the Drabek Alphas, Ragna and Asa. Their daughter Siv trailed them, hands clasped behind her back.

Eldrick's inner wolf reared to life, quickening his alpha blood. His legs grew restless, the instinct to be near hear all-too-consuming. In a village filled with werewolves who might hate her kind, his rationale abandoned his place as Drengr Alpha and instead stood at her side.

As her protector, lover, and friend.

Though Drabek werewolves nodded in greeting, some offering her wide-toothed smiles and others grasping her hand, welcoming her to the village, Tovi's shoulders were set back, proud, and there was an underlying smile tugging at the edge of her lips. His inner wolf sighed with relief at the sight.

The moment her jade gaze found him, her expression faltered.

The world vanished, and for the first time in weeks, the invisible thread connecting them pulled taut. Eldrick's inner wolf howled. The energy thrumming between them had the power to buckle Eldrick's knees but also fill his limbs with enough adrenaline to fight across a battlefield.

"Aye, there he is!" Ragna called from yards away, throwing her hands into the air. "The three of us were just discussing you, Alpha."

Eldrick bristled at the use of his formal title. "I've known you for too long, Ragna. Please, my name is fine," he shouted back.

Ragna and Asa were like aunts. Eldrick's mother, Nadia, had originally been a Drabek, a pack full of the fiercest shield-maidens in all the Vadon Mountains, before she met Aramis.

Their mating had brought the Drengr and Drabek packs closer despite the distance separating the territories. Ragna and Asa had also been the most supportive to his father after Nadia's death, though, the more Eldrick reflected, he wondered if their presence was because of their apprehension towards Claus.

Leif, washed and presentable after days of travel and battle, approached. "You're never going to get comfortable hearing the title if you don't let people use it."

Eldrick exhaled, crossing his arms. "It's bizarre coming from Ragna and Asa; they've been alphas longer than my father's been alive."

"Time does not matter amongst your political peers. We're all alphas; that is what connects us."

Eldrick swallowed. "I'm still adjusting to the sound of it. Doesn't feel . . . real."

Leif hummed. "You and I are both firstborns, Eldrick. We didn't know our paths, but we always knew the destination: to lead our packs. Are you certain it's realness you're struggling with or *rightness*?"

Eldrick whirled to face Leif, but the alpha's unbending gaze had Eldrick's rebuttal turning to ash on his tongue. How could he argue with a male who saw right through him?

Leif grasped his shoulder. "The two are as similar as they are different. Think long and hard, Eldrick. Sacrifice is valiant until we're shells of ourselves, falling into a persona rather than a purpose. But listen to this"—Leif pointed at Eldrick's chest, right above his heart—"not this." The alpha tapped his own temple.

Tovi and the Drabek Alphas neared. Ragna's wheat-colored hair was braided to the side with baby's breath blossoms dotted through the fishtail pattern. She wore a simple metal band around her head, keeping her hair in place and signaling her alpha title with the ruins carved into the steel. She wore layers of shawls and furs, appearing delicate and bundled all at once.

Her mate, Asa, wore fighting leathers and a lavender fur-lined cloak. Asa's features were as sharp as her the axe on her belt—thin nose, narrow eyes, defined jaw, hair pulled into a tight bun—but her gray eyes were soft with an apparent kindness.

They moved as one, and Eldrick imagined after four hundred years of being mated, one expected as much.

Leif strode towards them, bowing in the presence of Tovi. "I hope it's alright if I steal the queen. We haven't had a chance to meet, officially."

Asa huffed, rolling her eyes. "If you insist, Leif, but then you must allow us time with Eldrick."

Leif peered over his shoulder and winked. "The alpha is all yours."

Tovi dipped her head in greeting and said her thanks to the Drabeks. She ignored Eldrick —rightfully so, after he'd teased her with his fingers and robbed her of release—and laced her arm with Leif's. They re-entered the activity of the village, and the busy streets swallowed Tovi from sight, and Eldrick sighed.

He'd not only robbed Tovi atop the saddle yesterday, but himself. Every inch of him ached with what he denied them, but he'd done it to protect both of them. Much like Leif had mentioned, if he and Tovi started down that path, Eldrick knew the destination.

Hurt and heartache.

The sides of his face itched, and to Eldrick's dismay, he found two sets of ancient eyes borrowing into him as if they read his soul not his expression.

Asa whistled.

"That bad, huh?" Ragna snorted.

Asa snapped her fingers and pointed ahead. "I think our discussion is best had at the tavern, don't you think?"

"It's morning," Eldrick said.

Asa waved her hand in the air. "Feelings rarely care about the time of day."

Eldrick huffed but followed the mated females to the Drabek's central tavern, the *first* Sheild-maiden. Guilt panged through Eldrick—he'd not dare mention this visit to Lucy, though the rivalry between distant cousins was in jest. Mostly.

Carved into the trunk of a redwood tree stump, the tavern was ten warriors wide and four stories tall. Asa and Ragna led the way to the top, slapping a pitcher of gourd ale down on the center of the table and three metal pint mugs.

"How long have the two of you been sleeping together?" Ragna asked.

Eldrick choked on his first sip of ale—it was far too early for beer or this conversation. "We're not."

"But you were?" Asa asked.

Eldrick seethed, gripping the edge of the table. "Why does it matter?"

The females laughed at his expense, and Ragna flashed a teasing smile. "You're so like your mother, I feel like I've fallen back in time."

"Aye," Asa whispered. "Was at this very table where your mother denied her mating bond with your father, ya know?"

Eldrick shook his head. "Tovi is a vampyr, and I'm a werewolf. That possibility—"

"Is something we have no grounds to even dismiss. How could we, seeing as vampyrs and werewolves have lived separately on this continent?" Ragna snorted. "Who knows if it even exists amongst witches and werewolves, another resident of Sorin we've lived away from."

"There aren't the right signs," Eldrick said, but the omission was barbed on his tongue, as if it were a lie.

"Like?" Ragna pushed.

"Feeling ones' emotions. Mind-linking . . ." Eldrick shook his head, withholding the thread he felt pulling at his heart every time his eyes fell on Tovi.

Asa sipped her ale. "Those parts of the bond don't usually arise until both parties accept it."

Eldrick's wolf bared his teeth. Hadn't he accepted what Tovi was to him after admitting his love? He wrestled with denial, because the truth was, he hadn't. But his stubborn streak roared to life, ruffled by the fact *she'd* not said those words back to him. That was entirely unfair, considering what he knew of her past. Eldrick stewed and sipped his ale. There was no one to blame—they'd each made their choice.

For once, though, it wasn't the whispering of the prophecy that played in the back of Eldrick's mind but Leif's earlier words. *Rightness.* Eldrick couldn't deny that feeling yesterday of having Tovi back in his arms, *feeling* her radiating strength and greeting his beastly energy. What did rightness have to do with anything when his body thrummed with want while darkness crept over the horizon?

"War *is* coming, and the darkness has entered Sorin worse than ever before. *That* is my focus," he finally said.

Ragna narrowed her gaze. "Your statement feels pointed, Eldrick."

"Why bother hosting the festival?" he asked. "There are far more important matters. Defenses, perhaps even making the other alphas reconsider the Earl vote."

Asa sighed, leaning back in her chair. "Strategy is a mere fraction of what it means to lead. The festival is a centuries-old tradition. Canceling it because of clouds in the sky and demon sightings rips the village out of normalcy. The festival also creates something far better and rarer than defenses—hope."

Ragna nodded. "We feel the shift in the land, and our alpha magic is practically tremoring as we speak. You're right, war is coming, but it is hope I want strapped to my warriors and their shields when we face Riven, not fear and tiredness."

Eldrick exhaled, attempting to release the tension wound in his pent-up being. He didn't disagree with them, but his mind fixated on his task at hand. "What of the Earl vote? Are you considering myself or Bjorn?"

Ragna's gaze narrowed to slits. "I'm insulted you'd think we'd entertain Bjorn's name."

Eldrick shrugged. "I'm aware of Bjorn's methods to gain power, and my guess is he was here before my arrival."

Asa nodded. "You're correct, but we're neither afraid of Bjorn's bark nor his bite."

"Indeed," Ragna said. "We offered him the stables to sleep in or the forest outside the village. He isn't welcome in our home."

Eldrick shook his head. "I'm sure that angered him."

"Bjorn was born angry," Asa whistled between her teeth.

Eldrick laughed, uneasy. "Do I have your vote, then?"

Asa and Ragna shared a sad, silent conversation. Ragna addressed him first, and Asa grasped her mate's hand and gave it a comforting squeeze.

"Yes, but there is something you must know first," Ragna said.

"Tell me," Eldrick said.

"My Time has come," she whispered.

The statement jarred Eldrick in his seat. With his father's once ailing health, he'd heard it before, but it was a rare phenomenon. Time was when a werewolf's magic and wolf began to fade. Their soul wavered between the land of the living and the Otherworld, leaning closer and closer to the latter. It was the gradual descent of old age, though the signs were less external, and felt from within.

"But I don't understand . . . you're . . ." Eldrick failed to find the right words.

"I'm one of the oldest werewolves in the Vadon Mountains," Ragna said.

"Though she doesn't look it." Asa's gaze shined with pride and sorrow.

"How much longer do you have?" he asked, his tone gentle.

"Somedays it feels as though it's my last and others feel like I have another six months," Ragna said. "If the war to come doesn't take me first."

Eldrick weighed his next words carefully. "Does Siv know?"

Ragan nodded. "Our entire pack knows. That is why we need your support once I'm gone. Since Asa and I are mated, her Time is weaved with mine. We've always known, seeing as I'm older, but we didn't prepare for our succession. After our Time has passed, the Drabeks will be left without an alpha to lead the pack."

"What of Siv?" Eldrick asked. "I know she is your adopted daughter, but the land will choose her, no? She is a firstborn after all, right?"

Ragna and Asa sighed, their clasped hands tightening. "Siv doesn't want to become alpha."

Eldrick's inner wolf rose to the surface, and he fidgeted at the word *want*, like the foreign weight of it pressed down on him. "Then your planned successor?"

"It'll be left to a vote within the Drabek Pack only," Ragna said. "But that'll result in our village being vulnerable in the meantime."

"Do you think Bjorn will interfere?" Eldrick asked.

"I have no doubt," Ragna said. "He'll argue our pack needs protecting and secure the territory under the Johannes name. If he succeeds, he cages both the Drengrs and the Thorns. Skau is already in his back pocket, and Lindström and Alland are far too small to face *five* packs under Bjorn's command."

"He'll start a civil war," Asa said.

A growl rumbled through Eldrick's chest, and he ran his hand through his hair. "*Moons.* You must convince Siv to accept the title."

"No," both Asa and Ragna said at once.

"There is no want when it comes to duty," Eldrick said through gritted teeth.

Ragna tilted her head. "Aramis and Nadia may have raised their children to think that way, but we have not. Siv has made her chose, and we have made ours: to accept her wishes. Our pack has as well. Siv wishes to be a warrior, and as her mother, I see that she is her truest self with a sword in one hand and axe the other."

Choice. The word groaned in Eldrick's ears like a village's warning horn. It was foreign and chilling and jealousy-inducing all at once.

"Why not host the vote now, let a pack member ascend?" Eldrick said, trying to think of another option to avoid Bjorn's pursuit of power interfering.

"A transition of the title would leave us just as vulnerable," Ragna said. "Bjorn threatened to take our vote for Earl away if we didn't sign the decree. This close to the vote, there's no telling if Bjorn will suggest the same."

"Bastard twists anything to get what he wants," Eldrick muttered.

"Which is why we can't give him anything to twist," Asa said. "All we must do is make it to the Earl vote, and all we ask in exchange to vouch for your name is to assist the Drabeks transition once we are gone."

Transition came with more than just assisting the votes. It came with protecting the Drabeks from Bjorn's pack leering down their necks. Eldrick tightened with frustration. They shouldn't have to worry about facing their own kind, not with Riven's hold on darkness casting farther across Sorin. Tovi had an army. He had the Drabek's vote. But who knew when the prince would strike again.

Eldrick had to lead the Vadon Mountains as Earl and unite with Tovi, Drystan's queen. That was how they followed their duty.

Eldrick rose from his seat, tipping his head in both Asa and Ragna's direction. "You have my promise and future support."

"Good," Ragna said. "Thank you, Eldrick. Now, will we see you in attendance at the Dísablót Festival?"

Eldrick smiled. "I wouldn't dare miss an evening to celebrate the Vadon Mountain's shield-maidens, and if my mother ever learned I skipped the holiday, she'd have my hide."

Asa laughed, almond-shaped eyes glinting with a tease. "Perhaps you can celebrate another warrior, too, *hmmm*, a certain queen from the north?"

Eldrick's nostrils flared. "Perhaps."

"Let him go, Asa," Ragna whispered. "He's practically running from the subject."

Eldrick nodded, not feeding into either of their bait to discuss Tovi.

He descended the tavern's steps and strode back into the village. With each step, he didn't envision celebrating Tovi, he dreamed of worshiping her. With his tongue, fingers, lips, and cock. A festival wasn't enough to honor the strength, poise, and bravery Tovi embodied. She deserved a scattering of stars across the heavens, to join the constellations of gods—

A hand grasped hold of Eldrick's wrist, and he was dragged into an alley and thrown behind a stack of barrels, sweet and sticky from aging gourd ale.

The ethereal beauty Eldrick had lost his thoughts to stood before him. Panting. Rosy cheeked. Tovi's eyes darkened with *want*.

Eldrick answered, stepping towards her, and their lips clashed in a frenzy. Tongue, lips, and teeth clanged as a desperate hunger claimed them both.

Tucked behind barrels and in the shadows of the alley, their kiss was hidden from those on the street, but not their sounds. Eldrick stilled his rising wolf, fighting the urge to growl through their frenzied kiss.

Stars above, Tovi tasted of salvation and ruin all once, and he didn't care. He loved it. *Loved her.* He was kissing her, tasting her exquisite lips, feeling her silky strands between his fingers, and relishing in her taut body pressing flush against his.

Tovi moaned as his hand grasped around her throat.

Eldrick planted a thumb over her lips. "*Shh*, dove. We can't have the village hearing the beautiful sounds you make."

Something flashed in her jade eyes—a challenge? She raised a brow, and Eldrick's hackles rose. She found his belt buckle and unclasped it without breaking their intense stare. She peered up at him, and Eldrick stifled a curse as her hand dropped into his trousers and fisted his length. He moved to kiss her again, but Tovi reared back, taunting him with her blissful expression.

Tovi dropped to her knees, attention falling to his length that she pulled free into the morning air. The sight was Eldrick's undoing. He loved and hated it all at once. Stars above, he was a male after all, and Tovi was beyond beautiful as she stared up him, but *moons*, she was a goddess in her own right, he should be on his knees for *her*—

"That isn't where you belong—"

"Do you want me to suck your cock or not?" she whispered.

"Godsdamnit, dove," Eldrick hissed, tilting his head back and shutting his eyes.

Tovi didn't wait for his response. She licked his length base to tip, teasing him with the attentive promise of her wicked tongue. It swirled across his tip next, and as she ran circles over it, driving Eldrick closer and closer to the edge, the village fell away, and Tovi brought him near oblivion.

Eldrick almost roared with need when she took him inside her mouth. Fully. Deeply. Tightly. One hand gripped his waist, nails driving into his skin while her other fisted the base of his length, pumping him as her lips sucked. Up and down.

He was going to die today, Eldrick realized. Right here, right now. He opened his eyes, daring to peek at the glorious sight he found himself in, and *moons*, he was nearing his end.

Once, he'd believed Tovi an enchantress. Now he knew it, had *seen* it. Her reddened cheeks, determination and heat glinting in her eyes. She enjoyed this, making it all that much better and worse, and Eldrick didn't just know from the eagerness thrumming from her being, but the scent of her heady plum-and-violet need pooling between her legs.

Eldrick sat at the edge of release. Morning turned to night because he saw stars. He had to warn her, beg to find his release deep inside her—

His length popped free of her mouth, meeting the cold air, and Tovi vanished.

A breeze *whooshed* past Eldrick, and he stumbled back. He searched for Tovi, and found her, standing at the end of the alley. She wiped her wet lips with the back of her hand, a triumphant smile splitting across her face.

"Tovi," he hissed, guttural with his beast a hair below the surface. "What the fuck?"

She shrugged. "Consider us even."

Even.

Moons, because he'd edged her all the same. Of course she had no intention of letting him get away with that. Smug, Tovi winked and fell into the current of werewolves walking the street. She disappeared into the village, leaving Eldrick stunned, his cock hard and aching with need.

"Eldrick?" Bétar's voice boomed down the alley. "What in the stars above are you doing down there?"

He cursed, shoving his length into his trousers and adjusting himself to appear somewhat put together.

Bétar rounded the corner, and his pinched brows shot up. "For the love of gods, you reek of—"

"Don't," Eldrick grumbled, storming out of the alley and leaving his friend and bruised pride behind.

He needed a goddamn shower.

Chapter Fifty-Six

T**RUE DEATH WAS LIKE** a blink.

Light shined for the briefest moment, and then darkness flashed. Evelyn was in the living world and a breath later, zapped to nowhere.

Weightless, she fell through a realm of a thousand stars.

Her perception kept shifting. Here, there, and everywhere. At one angle, she stared at a fathomless black, falling from the light shining above, and the next she blinked, Evelyn witnessed herself from afar, a speck in the vast oblivion of nothingness, free-falling.

"Evelyn!"

She twisted, heart bursting at the sight of Kade falling alongside her. Evelyn grasped his outstretched hand and fought the tears that threatened to spill.

"I've got you," he whispered.

With hands clasped, Evelyn and Kade fell, fell, and fell. Oblivion waited below, waiting to swallow them whole. Kade held true, jaw tight, but amber eyes shining with determination.

For the first time in weeks, pain didn't bloom through Evelyn. Her chest was hollow, but something tugged at the edge, like the taut yank of a thread.

Her hand ripped from his grasp, and her fated growled, trying to get to her. It was as if an invisible rope had gripped Evelyn's ankles and tugged her in the opposite direction. *Away* from Kade.

Their fingertips brushed over the other, one last feathery touch before they drifted too far apart. Kade's bellowing protest was muted. Lost.

Kade vanished.

"No!" Evelyn cried.

Was it the spell? Was it the Otherworld? Why were they ripped apart?

Below Evelyn, the nothingness ripped like a sliver of paper, and another world's light burned her eyes—

Evelyn awoke to the warm kiss of the sun's rays, birds singing in the distance, and bees buzzing. She blinked and immediately searched for Kade.

Fucking flames, where was he?

She found herself in a pasture of wildflowers. Buttercups, purple and blue cornflowers, daisies, and foxgloves reflected the colors of the sky. Glowing bees bobbed from flower to flower and zoomed past to follow a creek bending into a forest of magnificent trees.

White bark peeled to a darker flesh, and the leaves shined like luminescent gold, reminding her of Kade's eyes.

He, who was nowhere in sight.

His name lodged in her throat. She was desperate to call out to him, but she gripped the ground, plush and dewy grass tearing in her grasp. As beautiful as the place was, her gut swam with distrust, like it wasn't real.

What was to say she'd even landed in the Otherworld?

She tried to grasp the mating bond, testing to see if it was back, but found nothing. Though the frayed threads of her soul had woven together, it wasn't whole again, and her magic was still missing.

With an ounce of relief washing through her, Evelyn stood and teetered foot to foot. Still weightless but grounded. Her insides stretched like summer-spun sugar. Her clothes were the same—traveling britches and tunic, but her boots were gone, toes digging into the grass.

Tones of blue and pink swirled in a cloudless sky, rivets of purple weaving on the horizon. The sun, or *a* sun, glowed like a golden, contained orb. It sat so large and low in the sky, Evelyn reached out to touch it, her movements feathery like the whoosh of mists.

Something tugged at her heart, and Evelyn stilled, holding her breath. It wasn't Kade. It was fainter and farther and . . .

Evelyn turned north, and an ache bloomed in her chest. She palmed the spot and rubbed it, soothing the absence.

Tug.

"Fucking flames," Evelyn hissed, stumbling forward.

Tug, tug, tug.

The pesky sensation pulled from the north, up the creek and into the forest of impressive, ethereal trees. Evelyn's instinct screamed for her to keep going in that direction. Was it her magic calling to her?

A branch snapped, and Evelyn whirled.

"Kade?" she whispered.

No one answered, but movement caught Evelyn's eye. In the trees, it was too difficult to see who or what hid between the shimmering leaves, but they rustled enough to indicate something was about. Evelyn backed up a step and halted.

A giggle reached towards Evelyn's heart, the infectious bubbliness washing over her like a sunny day in Callum. Hope and caution warred within her as she took a steady step forward, throat going dry.

"Who's there?" she asked.

Green wool peeked between the leaves—it was an oversized sweater layered under overalls. That outfit. That green. Evelyn clenched her fists, the thumping of her heart echoing in her ears. Goddess—

"Evelyn!"

"Aster?" she breathed, stunned to her bones.

Her sweet and round-eyed friend jumped out from behind the tree. Sticks and forest debris stuck out of her red ringlets, and her bare feet were covered in mud. But despite the wear of the forest, she looked well, happy, and *alive*.

With hands. Small, delicate, freckled hands.

A sob cracked out of Evelyn, and she barreled into Aster, pulling her into the tightest hug. She inhaled her fern-and-daisy scent, memories of Pages and Leaves transcending through her.

"I'm gone, and now you like hugs." Aster's words came out muffled against Evelyn's chest as she refused to let her go.

"I'm so, so, sorry, Aster. For what happened. For—"

Her friend wiggled free, grasping Evelyn's hands and giving them a squeeze. Those bright, russet eyes roamed over her, and instantly, warmth spread through Evelyn's chest.

"What happened is not your fault," Aster said.

Evelyn shook her head, vision blurring. "But I—"

"No." There was that fierceness she missed from her friend. "I refuse to let you blame yourself. The White Lady killed me, Evelyn. She also lied to you—it wasn't at my shop, and I never cried out your name. I was picking buttercups when suddenly I was here. There was no fear, Evelyn. No pain. My death was swift."

Evelyn swallowed, throat thick with tears. "We killed her, Kade and I."

Aster's smile was small. "I know. I actually know a lot of things now."

Evelyn tilted her head and studied the knowing etched into her friend's glowing face. "Let me take a wild guess, you know why I'm here?"

"Yes, in fact I do!" Aster released Evelyn and planted her hands onto her petite hips. "You sacrificed your magic, Miss Evelyn Carson. And"—she raised a finger to stop Evelyn's protest—"I don't want to hear how *it was the only option*. I thought we'd been over this—your magic is a part of your soul. Rather foolish, don't you think?"

Evelyn laughed, brushing away her tears. "*Goddess*, I've missed you."

Aster's ire softened. "Well, I'd be lying if I didn't say I missed you, too, or at least mention that what you did wasn't a little bit brave."

"Only a bit?" Evelyn smiled so wide her cheeks bruised.

Aster pinched her forefinger and thumb together. "A bit, about the size of a poppy seed."

Evelyn threw up her hands and rolled her eyes. "If it makes you feel any better, it hurt like shit."

"How do we think it felt for us?"

"Us?"

Aster gestured around them. "The Otherworld. Your power barreled in like a fallen star not too long ago, thanks to your little trip here."

Evelyn snapped straighter. "You know where my magic is?"

Her friend bounced from muddy foot to muddy foot. "That's why I'm here. The Sun Goddess asked me to retrieve you. I'm your guide." She puffed out chest, every inch of her proud.

Evelyn wrestled with so many tumbling emotions. On one hand, she was relieved to see Aster, but saddened by the circumstances. This was Aster, yes, but it was her soul because—

She shook her head, snagging on something Aster had said. "Wait, *the* Sun Goddess? The one who gave me my power? Is Kade with her?"

Aster studied her. "Kade has his own journey in the Otherworld, and I wouldn't worry. The Moon God is a fairly nice god. He isn't like . . ." The freckles on Aster's nose connected as she scrunched her nose in thought. She sighed, lowering her voice to a whisper as she said, "Look, I believe the Sun Goddess gifted witches the power of magic long ago, but . . . Your flame is yours alone, Evelyn."

Evelyn shook her head, peering up at the sun. "It's her power, no? It's a Goddess-given gift."

A smirk cracked Aster's freckled features, and she leaned in closer, one brow raised. "I thought you didn't care for titles anymore. How did you put it?" Aster schooled her features to a deadpan, lowering the pitch of her voice as she said, *"Titles don't define us, actions do."*

"I don't sound that deep," Evelyn giggled. "Fucking flames, are you eaves-dropping on all my private conversations?"

Aster shrugged. "Perhaps a few. This plain of existence is beautiful, but at times boring."

A breeze blew past, raising goosebumps on Evelyn's skin. Her blood turned to ice, and she tried and tried to find some sense of relief that Aster was here.

Aster's death wasn't her fault, but old thoughts about mistakes and deci-sions, and what-ifs spiraled through her mind. She tried to shake them and convince herself they didn't serve her while trying to get her magic back.

Evelyn swallowed and grounded herself in what she'd visited the Other-world for.

"Where exactly is my magic?" she asked.

"The palace, of course," Aster said, pointing down a winding path through the forest.

A crawling sensation crept up Evelyn's spine. She'd only ever encountered one goddess before, and she still felt the Blood Goddess's cold mists on her skin when she closed her eyes and thought of her time in the Drystan dungeons.

But why would her instinct feel unease with the Sun Goddess? The two were entirely different deities—the two couldn't be more different, right? Perhaps it wasn't unease, it was nerves. To meet a deity or enter her palace, no less. What did she think of Evelyn's latest actions? Did she think Evelyn was foolish like Aster?

Stop worrying, she told herself.

"Let's go," Evelyn finally said, far calmer than she felt.

Aster led the way, and the two fell into step together.

"How is the beastly huntsman?" Aster bumped her shoulder into Evelyn's, wiggling her brows.

Evelyn laughed. "You tell me, eavesdropper."

Aster clutched her chest. "Goddess, a hug and a tease? Who are you, Evelyn Carson?"

"A lighter version of me, I suppose."

"Well, you've come a long way, and I can't help but think Kade played a bit of part."

"He certainly did," Evelyn sighed.

Aster smirked. "Oh, I know it. Unfortunately, any time I've checked in with your mate in the room, things go in a direction I'd rather not see. Kade's rather . . . voracious."

A blush crept over Evelyn's neck, but there was no point in arguing with Aster—she'd always been so direct, so honest. "He is indeed."

Her friend hummed to herself. "To think, we were once on a walk, much like this, and you denied your attraction to him because you 'worked together'"—Aster mocked Evelyn's once-haughty tone—"and now you're mated."

"Was," Evelyn said. "I mean, in our hearts we feel as though we are because of our love, but as my soul frayed, the thread that tied us unraveled."

"That'll mend when you reunite with your magic," Aster said.

"I believe it," Evelyn sighed. "I'm glad I was wrong in the beginning, though. I don't think I was ready for us. Falling for Kade as Cyrus . . ." She shrugged. "Even though we were both pretending to be someone else, I think we were unabashedly our truest selves. We had our secrets, sure, but we didn't have the weight of our titles and duties, and therefore there weren't any expectations. We were able to fall for one another as we were."

Evelyn wasn't entirely sure they weren't the huntsman and barmaid anymore, either. They'd met as Cyrus and Saige, and a small part of her believed that beginning had laid the foundation of what they were now. Partners. Had that ever changed? No. Even now, as they both journeyed through the Otherworld, separated, Evelyn knew they'd find one another.

"You in love is a wonderful sight, friend," Aster said.

The two smiled softly and fell into a gentle silence. Birds continued to sing unseen in the trees, and a breeze had the gold leaves rustling together.

"So, how does it work?" Evelyn asked. "Visiting our world but having your soul here?"

"It is similar I think to how you're here, actually," Aster said. "My soul is tethered to the Otherworld in death, while your physical being in the land of the living. Think of our world as layers, our essences rooted in the one of which we belong."

A faint breeze snaked around Evelyn's ankles, and she turned back in the direction from which the chill came from. Across the creek, mist swallowed lone trees on the other bank. Beasts screeched and moaned, their sounds of protest contrastingly dark to the songbirds and bees. Farther inland, crooked branches reached downward like outstretched claws, with leaves so dark it appeared they'd been dipped in ink. It reminded Evelyn how the curse touched vampyrs.

"Is that Hel?" Evelyn whispered.

Aster paused. "Remnants of it. Like the living realm, the Blood Goddess's darkness seeps through the cracks."

"Wouldn't that harm souls that are here?" Evelyn asked. "What does the Sun Goddess do about it?"

Aster molded her lips together, nostrils flaring as she exhaled. "The Moon God and Sun Goddess planted this forest. His lights and her life outshine the dark."

"Why not destroy it though?" Heat flushed through Evelyn—why did she get the sense the gods weren't doing enough?

"Why cut back a weed that grows fiercer when trimmed?" Aster shrugged. "There's a harmony between the two, darkness and light. Think of the moon. When does it shine the brightest?"

At night.

Evelyn didn't voice her answer out loud as Aster led them onward. She stewed instead as confusion rippled through her. She hadn't failed to miss how Aster was apprehensive whenever Evelyn mentioned the Sun Goddess—why did her friend hold back? She turned back again, catching a glimpse of the darkness below. Was the Blood Goddess's power that fierce that even the gods couldn't fight it? The more she thought about it, the more her head ached. It left her increasingly unsettled that Aster said her flame wasn't a Goddess-given gift. Even worse, if her power wasn't a gift from the Sun Goddess, how exactly was the Goddess aiding those who followed her?

Voices filtered from ahead, and Evelyn slowed, trying to discern who or what they'd come across. A god? Another soul like Aster? Or perhaps a creature of this world? Except, the voices became distinct, so familiar, Evelyn halted.

"For what it's worth, Evelyn," Blair said, "Mother would've loved it."

Evelyn's lungs ballooned and contracted, an emptiness forming in the pit of her belly. Since arriving in the Otherworld, her body turned cold and sweaty. She ran. Sprinted towards the sound of her sister's voice. Why was Blair in the Otherworld? Had something happened?

Goddess, no.

Breathless, Evelyn ignored Aster's pleas to slow down. She had to see, had to prove she was wrong and hadn't heard Blair's voice—

She pushed between two trees and burst into a clearing, yet again stopping in her tracks. As a child, Evelyn and her sisters attended musicals in the arts district of Nūa, and the scene before her was like that of a play, a staged setting with props and a backdrop.

A shop—*the* shop she'd purchased her wedding dress from—had sprouted from the roots of the surrounding birch trees. Wooden floorboards weaved through the grass, branches held up the walls; gold leaves snug between the dresses hanging on racks and displays.

Yet, this wasn't a scene; it was a *memory*.

At the center, standing atop a velvet-coated dais, Evelyn stood as seamstresses poked and prodded the white gown, molding it to her lithe frame. Moonstones had been sewn into the crepe material, their reflective light scattering across the fitting room. Even past the tulle of the dramatic veil, the misery etched deep into Evelyn's expression seeped past the grandiose. Dark circles rimmed her distant, vacant eyes.

She hardly recognized herself, and yet the grief and heaviness of that day rose through Evelyn as if it were yesterday.

That had been the day she'd run.

Her sisters had been none the wiser. How could she blame them? Mirella's face was hard as stone, not cold nor ambivalent like she remembered, but lost. Vacant even. Blair had darker circles than Evelyn, curls wild and untamed.

In their own ways, all the sisters had been battered by their parents' death.

Tears welled in Evelyn's eyes. Why had she navigated fate this way? How had she missed the grief etched into her sisters? Had she missed the same signs in Blair more recently?

Yet, that version of her was so young and lost, and though blind, she'd tried to protect them all. She'd known the anger and hurt she'd leave in her wake.

Aster appeared at her side, lips downturned.

"Why is a memory of mine here?" Evelyn asked in a hushed whisper.

Her friend tilted her head, russet eyes studying the other Evelyn hugging her sisters—she'd held them a little too long, the goodbye so evident on the outside looking in.

"Memories are part of your soul, Evelyn. Its who we are. You may come across them as we walk this forest. Everyone does when they first enter the Otherworld."

Evelyn and her sisters faded. The roots and branches groaned, the scene before them shaking. The grass grew longer and grasped hold of the floorboards, pulling them deeper into the soft, plush ground. The bark of the trees opened, engulfing the walls and dresses until the memory was gone, any evidence lost to the wonders of the bright forest.

She was the one who said titles didn't matter but actions did; what did this memory say about her?

More voices resounded ahead. Shouting. Glass breaking against wood. A certain word, a certain name, carried on the wind along with the silence that followed, and Evelyn winced. Unlike the previous memory, she recognized the latest one immediately.

Aster, this time, didn't protest as Evelyn headed towards the voices. She found her old apartment above Pages and Leaves, wedged between two trees. Sheppard's pie and red wine seeped into the pine floorboards dotted with creeping phlox.

She and Kade stared at each other, chests heaving, moments after he'd revealed his true identity.

Kade Drengr, Son of the God.

The omission seemed to boom through the forest. Pain contorted both their faces. Weakness clung to Evelyn, and *fucking flames,* the fear set into Kade's golden eyes had Evelyn clutching her stomach. Each and every word from him cracked with heartache as he tried to reassure her, tried to reason with her.

Goddess, she was so bloody stubborn, refusing to see that he loved her long before he said those words, weeks before they'd been reunited and completed their fated mate bond. His actions had been loud and clear, declaring his intent and feelings for her, and yet what had she done? She'd sent him away, pushed back the notion that anyone could ever care for someone broken like her when that someone was standing right in front of her the entire time.

Shame washed over Evelyn like the mists of darkness had slithered into the forest. Was she too consumed by what she thought was right? Was she too steadfast in her decisions? The possibility had her insides twisting and turning on themselves like a dried, curled leaf.

As they continued onward, they passed more and more memories. They bled into each other like a street lined with circus acts. To the left, city bells chimed on the morning of her parents' funeral, and high atop the Wall, the three Carson sisters argued. Mirella threw out Evelyn's wedding arrangements as a weapon, the news causing her to flinch. The night of her parents' death echoed in the next clearing, her father's pleas to believe raising the hairs on the back of Evelyn's neck.

The next—and last, Evelyn hoped—memory was the night of the Blood Moon. Red tinted Evelyn's pale skin, the darkened blood smearing her face and clothes. Patches of snow buried the forest's bright-green grass, and unlike the others, Evelyn paused at the determination set into her brow all those weeks ago. She stared and stared and stared at the bloodstone in her hand while the clanging of swords and axes chimed unseen around them. The decision had been quick, but she'd debated.

"What are you doing?" Ingrid's voice boomed through the forest.

Evelyn didn't hesitate as she fisted the bloodstone. Magic whirled and—

Her magic ripped from her soul, planting into the bloodstone.

Aster held her hand, and Evelyn appreciated the stability. But it wasn't pain Evelyn felt, but certainty rocking through her.

She'd made the right decision that day, no matter what the cost.

A faint tug pulled from the north, as if her magic agreed, too. This had been the right decision. Rash, foolish, or otherwise, it was still *her*. Her path of decisions, no matter the twists and turns, Uzoma had said she'd grown, and Evelyn believed that truth, but also understood that sort of change wasn't pretty, comfortable, or glamorous.

It *hurt*.

But the chaos of grasping fate with one's own hands was also a beautiful power.

All these memories, all these choices Evelyn had made were hers—not based on the prophecy or the expectations of others. Not even the sting of her mistakes, the scars of past heartache, or the mind tricks of the Otherworld could take choice away from her.

A breeze gusted through the forest, the birch tree branches swaying in one mighty, golden wave. The memories ahead of them shifted—her laughing into Kade's chest, enjoying a glass of wine with Tovi, snuggled into Blair as they read together by a roaring fire, even older memories with Aster at the Runaway Radish. Evelyn's heart swelled with why she made the choices she'd made and *who* she fought for.

"Let's keep moving," Evelyn said.

Aster didn't say a word, a slight smile playing on her lips, and Evelyn's memories evaporated and became mists of the Otherworld.

CHAPTER FIFTY-SEVEN

THE TENDRILS OF AN unseen power took hold of Kade and pulled. The nothingness ripped below, blinding light shining upward. The opening sucked Kade through and swallowed, thrusting him into the cold night of another realm.

Kade fell through the night sky, a forest of pines awaiting him. He crashed through the canopy with a growl, the branches scratching across his skin. His vision blurred to green and brown. Like a heavy stone, he landed with a thud. His bones groaned with the impact, but the pain didn't compare to the ice running through veins.

"Evelyn!" he shouted, righting himself. He turned in frantic circles as he searched for any signs of her. "*Evelyn!*"

Only crickets and the peaceful night responded. He sprinted from the forest and into a glade. Fireflies bounced and sparkled from blades of grass, mirroring the stars dotting a cloudless, midnight-blue sky. The moon, so large Kade's fingers itched to reach out and touch it, shined a pearly light across the forest.

Was this the Otherworld? Where had Evelyn gone?

Wood clattered, like the scraping of a chair against a table, and Kade whirled.

At the edge of the glade, a squat, circular cottage sat beside a centuries-old redwood tree. It held a likeness to the ones in the Vadon Mountains—a hodgepodge assortment of stone, but inviting, nonetheless. In fact, the forest, the sky, and even the white-tipped mountains in the distance reminded Kade of home. Yet the air was still. *Too* still. The temperature too perfect, like it didn't shift. Kade's wolf paced inside his blood, uneasy as he approached the cottage on light feet to investigate who or what resided inside.

Moons, what was to say whoever was inside was friend or foe? Instinct warred for him to find Evelyn, while another part of him—his power and wolf—urged him forward.

A fire glowed orange beyond the hazy windows, and smoke rose in lazy puffs from the cobblestone chimney. A figure cast their shadow across the hearth, and Kade squatted, falling lower than the windowsill and out of sight. Kade held his breath, heart racing—

The door swung open, and the light from inside outlined a tall, muscular frame.

A male built to massive proportions stepped into the moonlight. He appeared Eldrick's age, at least physically, but there was something different about his features. Sharp, angular. Stonelike.

"Kade Drengr," the male voice boomed like thunder. "You're here early. Come, the stew's about ready."

He abandoned Kade, bewildered, outside, leaving the door open. Kade tried to gain a sense of the risk, and yet his inner wolf didn't pace with its usual restlessness. In fact, a jarring sense of calm went through him. The moon, the forest, the night. All of it eased his anxiety, stilling the cold tingling from his toes to the tips of his fingers.

But what of Evelyn? Where'd she gone? Would they see on another again?

The last horrifying thought had Kade's heart thumping wildly in his chest, but it also got his legs moving. He entered the cottage, mind wary, and assessed his surroundings. The fire crackled, and the gamey scent of venison and onions braising over an open fire enticed his appetite.

"Sit," the male said, motioning towards a stool at a small table. "I'm sure the journey jostled your bones a bit, per the sound of that landing." A wry smile played on the male's face, sharpening his jawline even more.

"My mate," Kade said. "Did you hear her land, too? Can you tell me where she is?"

The male nodded, indigo eyes glinting with silver. "Evelyn has her journey, while you have yours. Sit."

A growl rumbled through Kade's chest. "You don't understand. I'm part of a spell to get her to the Otherworld as well as back. We can't be separated—"

"The spell worked. Welcome to Otherworld." He spread his arms wide, like the cottage spoke for itself.

"But Evelyn—"

The male grunted. "Not like you to doubt her. Do you believe her incapable of making this journey?"

Kade pinched the bridge of his nose, inhaling so deeply his chest rose and fell. His next words came out shaky despite his efforts. "No, of course not."

"Then *sit.*"

A baritone rang in the man's tone, something that reached Kade's wolf and made him pause. It was like the tug and power of an alpha's command, something Kade, as Son of the God, had never felt before. His wolf relented, and Kade followed suit, sitting on the stool.

"So, this is in the Otherworld," Kade asked.

"Indeed, it is." The male waved his hand in the air, and the pot of stew appeared on the kitchen table.

"Who are you exactly?" Kade asked.

"I'm Odin."

Kade paused, his haggard expression staring back at him in the bowl of stew. The name snagged a memory, and Kade paused.

"Wait . . . It can't be." He shook his head and rubbed his hands down his thighs. He had to be wrong. There was no way. "You're not Matilda Moore's lover, are you?"

Odin frowned, pausing his spoon at his lips. "That was a long time ago. A different life, a different path."

"How are you here? Are you a soul?" Kade rushed. "You died."

"*Died?*" Odin burst with laughter, so loud the walls of the cottage shook. "My kind don't die."

"What do you mean by *your* kind?" he asked.

Odin stirred his stew and sighed. "I should've known a relaxing meal wasn't in the cards tonight. You're always wound so tightly, so restless. But a god can always dream."

A god.

Kade swiveled his attention out the cottage window. The moon sat so close to the glade's edge, it was like a pearly boulder resting in the grass. He reached to his inner wolf, and it sat to attention, recognizing the likeness to something he'd looked to his whole life.

"You're the Moon God."

Odin tipped his head. "It is so good to finally meet you, Kade."

Disbelief coursed through him. Stars above, the Moon God sat across from him. The god of his people, and supposedly who Kade was gifted by.

You're her son, a hiss shot through his mind, disputing.

Kade gripped the edge of the table, knuckles whitening.

But he dismissed that doubt, a hundred questions tumbling through his mind.

"I don't understand," he said. "Odin was a witch, plagued by visions. If you did not die, what happened?"

Odin leaned back in his chair. "I chose a mortal life."

"Why?"

"Why else?" Odin said. "There was a woman, and my heart couldn't let her go. Gods experience the same bond you and Evelyn share. Our hearts, too, seek a mirror to the soul, and there is only one, even for us, in this life."

Kade wrestled with what he had learned. "How did you meet Matilda?"

"By accident," Odin said. "Unlike the other gods in this realm, I get bored and leave from time to time, visiting your realm. Nūa was a new, lively city, built on such hope after years of violence and heartache in the human world. It possessed an infectious energy. I enjoyed it, second best though, compared to Vadon Mountains. Yet, there she was, reading over a text like her life depended on it. When our eyes connected, I knew what she was to me before my next breath."

Odin's eyes became lost, the silver dimming. A howl in the distance broke him out of his trance. Wolves. Kade's chest grew warm, his heart swelling at the sound much like his inner beast and his new power. It buzzed at his fingertips—

You are darkness.

Kade winced as a thousand voices shouted in his mind. Instinctually, he fisted his hands and pulled them onto his lap.

Odin's gaze narrowed, but he continued. "I changed, became the kernel of an idea before life touched me and was reborn into a witch. It was decades before my path crossed with Matilda again, but for an immortal, time passes like a flurry on the wind. Decades felt like days, and with her, I found the purest happiness in my existence—I even questioned the lover I'd had in the past, told myself I was wrong, that *she*, Matilda, was the one. So lively and colorful. She always made me laugh, even on my darkest days."

Kade leaned closer. "Were you aware that you were a god? Did you have the same power as one, but as a witch?"

Odin sighed, frown deepening. "In my mortal life, fate blessed me with two sisters. We were three, you see, all arriving in the living world together. I believe my immense power was too great, my Sight as a god plagued us all. But unlike my time as a god, I had no way to control my sisters, no way to harness the power. All three of us, Opal, Orla, and I, were cursed with visions of a wretched future."

"Why didn't you leave or become a god again?" Kade asked.

Odin grunted, leaning back in his chair. "Would you ever leave Evelyn, the woman you love, in a different realm?"

Kade's wolf howled at the notion. "No."

Odin raised a blond brow. "Aye, so you know the workings of a heart. I couldn't leave Matilda, but I sought a way to heal myself, for her sake at least."

It hit a similar note with Kade—he hadn't tried to heal himself, but mastering his power had been for Evelyn. Not only to protect her, but to stand by her side as the partner she deserved.

"That's why you traveled to Drystan, to the vampyrs with Opal."

"Yes, but they held a frightening familiarity." Odin tugged his upper lip into a snarl and, for the first time, revealed his teeth.

No—his *fangs*.

They were thicker than Tovi's, but two sharp fangs, nonetheless.

Kade sat frozen in his chair, gaze jumping between the god's eyes and the fangs of a predator. Kade already knew power sat across from him—and merciless power at that—but he'd never imagined the god his people followed, or the one woven into his prophecy, shared similarities to those cursed in Drystan.

"I don't understand. Are you a vampyr?" Kade asked.

Odin shook his head. "No, though they are made in our likeness."

"Our?" The center of Kade's forehead ached.

"The gods," Odin said, grim. "I knew their creator was a god or goddess, and I feared which one."

"The Blood Goddess."

"That is a new name she has bestowed upon herself." Odin leaned across the table. "We called her the Mother of Darkness." He settled back into his seat, eyes settling on the fire like the flames brought him to enough time. "In the time before witches and werewolves, my equal amongst the gods was Morrígna. She shined bright in the day, and I at night. It was not just our powers but our hearts that were a match. The other gods looked to us to lead. Yet, Morrígna had wickedness to her, a dark part of herself that many of us feared. War, famine, death. Yet, there was also the light, too, and when Morrígna's time was threatened in this realm, she devised a plan to rid herself of darkness completely. She split herself into three, creating a tri-fold of what mortals call souls. One became the Sun Goddess, the other the Mother of Darkness, and the third vanished, a shred of divine existence, a ghost on the wind."

Kade pinched the bridge of his nose. "If I understand this tale correctly, the Sun Goddess and the Blood Goddess are one and the same?"

Odin tilted his head. "Yes and no. They're more like soul sisters. Imagine a piece of silk spun from the same line, yet it is cut in two. One piece is sewn while another is woven elsewhere. The Sun Goddess and Blood Goddess, as you call her, are as similar as they are different. A mirror of opposites, and the Mother of Darkness earned her name by the reflection she represented."

"The Sun Goddess created her greatest enemy within herself," Kade said.

"Yes," Odin said. "Morrígna failed to understand that there is no darkness without light, nor light without the dark. The moon shines brightest at night, no? Darkness exists, but with light there is balance. Morrígna fractured the balance. Without her fertility, light, and life, the Blood Goddess had nothing but darkness as her power. War ensued, but the Sun Goddess feared if we killed her, we destroyed her as well. Morrígna had been my mate, the mirror to my soul. Her rebirth had altered that, broken our bond, but I still could not destroy the Sun Goddess, knowing what she'd been to me once. Instead, we banished the Mother of Darkness to Hel for a thousand years. She was dormant, silent, waiting out her sentence until an accidental blood sacrifice and the cries of a heartbroken man reached her."

"Tovi's father," Kade whispered.

"Yes. With the curse, she's been planting her darkness in your world for centuries. Though I can't understand why, as her banishment ends in the next fifty years. There has been discussions to extend it, considering her transgressions against Sorin, but I fear we can't contain her darkness."

"If that is the case," Kade said, "what have you been waiting for?"

"You," Odin said. "Fate cursed me with Sight during my life as a witch, but with it, I've seen you defeat darkness, Kade. Aramis and Nadia Drengr are your parents. You are their son, but it is my power in your veins."

Kade's head swam with a thousand retorts, but he could only manage to blurt out, "Take it back. I don't want it."

Odin tsked. "You will need it in the fight to come."

"I've done well enough without it."

"Indeed, you are a fierce warrior, which is why I gifted it to you when the time was right—*after* you met Evelyn. You are the light that shines in the darkness, Kade, she is life. Together—"

Kade shot forward, crowding the god's space. "Did you not hear me? *Take it back.*"

The Moon God barely blinked. "No."

More anger, maybe fear, shot through Kade. "Call me ungrateful. Call me a coward. But I have seen what this power can do it. It is evil—"

"*No!*" The boom that echoed in the cottage shook not only the walls but also the forest outside. The ground trembled, like a quake in the foundation of the Otherworld. The power, the tone, it jogged Kade's memory.

"You," he breathed. "It's been you in my dreams."

"Driving away the darkness, yes." Odin grunted. "Forgive me, this will hurt."

Kade didn't have time to prepare as the Moon God covered his face with his hand. Power radiated off his palm and stung Kade's flesh. He fell to his knees, losing his eyesight as the pain sliced through him like a knife into the soft sponge of his mind.

"*STOP!*" he roared.

Mists, shadows, the darkness of the wasteland that had plagued his sleep for weeks flashed across his thoughts. Terror beat against his skull like a caged beast, frantic to be let loose. The wet slick of Evelyn's blood coated his hands, the lifeless eyes of his friends stared back at him.

"Don't fight me, Kade."

The throbbing in his head traveled to his stomach. It churned and flipped, nausea rolling through him. Odin let go, taking a step back to give Kade a wide berth as he wretched, a blackish worm plopping onto the floor soaked in stomach bile. It reared back, hissing and baring its tunnel of teeth, rows and rows of razor-sharp needles.

"Destroy it," Odin said, expression hard.

Kade hurried, reaching for the empty mug beside his bowl of stew. He tried to use it as a weapon, tried to smash the slithering beast with sheer force. How, *in the stars above*, had that been in him? Distrust for the god standing off to the side only worsened the cold sweat matting Kade's forehead. He wasn't helping. He wasn't doing anything as the worm scurried out of Kade's reach.

"Fuck," Kade hissed as he got too close and the tiny beast bit his hand.

"Use your power," Odin said.

"*No.*" The worm hurried closer to Kade, who scrambled back and kicked it away with his boot. "Help, damn it!"

"You don't need my help. You are enough."

Kade felt absolutely, positively ridiculous. He chased the demon-like beast around the cottage amidst an unbothered god. He turned over the sofa, knocked over vases and jars. Fuck this. Fuck the Otherworld. He should've been with Evelyn, by her side—

"This magic isn't mine, it's yours," he said through gritted teeth, "and I don't want it."

Odin stepped in the path of the retreating worm, locking it between him and Kade. He bent down, grabbing it as it writhed in his grasp. "It's not that you don't want it, you're afraid of what it'll do."

"Stop."

Kade didn't like hearing the truth, his heartbeat echoing in his ears.

"Our powers aren't darkness, Kade. It's what we do with them that makes them dark. Light and dark together create balance, we ourselves tip the scales with intent and malice," he said. "There is nothing dark about your soul or your intentions. There never has been."

"But . . ." Kade's chest rose and fell, the fear coursing through him so horrific he didn't have the ability to say the words out loud. Didn't have the courage to ask.

Odin inspected the squirming worm. "You are not her son. One of her servants infiltrated your mind, made you believe it. Even if you were, there is far too much light in you. You'd outshine the darkest nights she created, no matter the thicket of shadows in your making." He threw the worm at Kade's feet and leveled his indigo stare on him. "Destroy it."

"I really don't want to blow up your cottage," Kade whispered.

Odin smirked, fangs glinting. "Then don't."

Kade rallied his breath, inhaling the truth of Odin's words. He hated to admit it, but he'd needed to hear who he truly was. He brought his magic forth, and an odd sensation buzzed through him as a tantalizing blue glowed from his hand. He'd always considered *what* he might do with his new power, but not once had he considered who *he* was.

You and your magic are one in the same.

Evelyn's words whispered through his mind. His heart thumped, once, twice, a third time. With her teachings and the Moon God's truth at the forefront of his mind, Kade became centered.

He and his power were one.

And Kade was light.

He twisted his fingers, the blue light sparking an inch higher. He didn't cast or thrust his power at the darkness slithering and hissing below. Instead, he pulled his essence from the surrounding ether, feeling its presence in the air particles. Like the gravity of the moon, it rose and lapped, pulling and tugging. Twinkles of blue formed around the worm. Its screeched louder, bending and twisting as Kade's light overtook the darkness.

There was no violence. There was no fear.

Kade drew from within, understood the goodness, the *light*. How he'd wield this power was his choice—not who gave it to him, not the foes they faced. *Him.* His power destroyed the demon until there was nothing left, not even a shadow in its wake, and he left no scorch marks on the cottage's floorboards, no evidence of his power. He released a breath as he brought it back into himself, slowly, in control, his outstretched hand no longer glowing. Kade's wolf howled; his beastly strength, tracking ability, and magic danced together in his blood.

As one formidable power.

"Good," Odin said, slumping into his chair. "That was good."

Kade blinked, noticing the god's face had gone paler, blond hair streaked with gray. A stone dropped in his belly.

"You didn't gift me with a kernel of your power, you gave it *all*," Kade whispered.

"Yes, indeed. My power now belongs to you," Odin said with a sad smile. "There's no one in this world I'd rather give it to."

Kade shook his head. "Why not join the fight yourself?"

Odin's gaze, all indigo with no silver, roamed Kade up and down. "Because I've fought the remnants of Morrígna before and lost. I've seen glimpses of the war, and it's you with my sword in hand, leading the charge. That sword doesn't answer to anything but my power."

Kade inhaled and exhaled, trying to grapple with the unknowns on the horizon. "But why me?"

"Love is what beats in your heart, and it's all around you. What better reflection of light is there than love?" Odin raised a brow, his tone sarcastic.

Kade swallowed, staring at the floorboards where the worm had been. His insides felt bruised, like too many days of a stomach illness.

"And speaking of love, I think it's about time we find your mate." Odin tipped his head.

Evelyn's silvery gray eyes flashed in Kade's mind—

"Is she in danger?"

"Oh, the Sun Goddess is dangerous, perhaps the most flippant of Morrígna, but I have a feeling your mate can take care of herself. Care to witness it with me?"

"Absolutely," Kade breathed, hands itching to hold Evelyn once again.

Odin headed for the door, grasping a few weapons resting near it and sheathing them at his belt.

Curiosity nipped at Kade's mind, and a missing piece of Odin's story made him pause. "Wait, you never mentioned what happened to Matilda Moore. Did you find her again?"

"Ah." Odin held up a finger. "Sadly, no. Though I searched for her. I believe, since Matilda had a mortal soul, she died when our fated mated bond was severed."

CHAPTER FIFTY-EIGHT

ELDRICK SHOOK ALPHA LINDSTRÖM'S and Alpha Alland's hands as they committed their support to his Earl vote. In the corner, Johannes and Skau sneered. Guests of the Dísablót Festival, Eldrick had sought them out first, and as the two males walked away, Eldrick found himself relishing in triumph. Though it was a mere verbal promise and not voting day, Eldrick was one step closer to earning the Earl vote and protecting the Vadon Mountains from Bjorn's personal agenda.

Spheres of blown glass—greens, blues, and whites—hung all throughout the Drabek Village. Enchanted light glowed from within them, creating the effect of fallen stars. A garland of snowdrop flowers weaved into pine branches lined a long table. A smoked venison sat at the center surrounded by a few roasted ducks, flaky meat pies, glazed vegetables, and bowls of spiced wine Eldrick knew better than to drink unless he wished for a mind-numbing headache for the next two days. Small fires dotted the outskirts, winterberry incense sweetening the air, and laughter and song traveled on the wind, warming Eldrick's insides.

The infectious joy of the festival seeped into his skin, and he inhaled the hope Ragna and Asa had mentioned. Tonight was a peaceful reminder of what they all fought for—the land, the people, and the light that continued to outshine the curse.

"Stars above," Leif whistled. "Are you actually enjoying yourself?"

Eldrick rolled his eyes, but offered his new friend a small smile. "I know how to have fun, Leif."

The alpha snorted. "Fooled me with how high-strung you are."

Eldrick opened his mouth to argue, but found no retort. He sighed. "Tonight brings back fond memories."

Females wore whimsical, airy dresses and crowns made of holly leaves. Hand in hand, they giggled as male werewolves lingered to the side, knuckles white as they held their ale, mustering the courage to ask someone to dance.

Eldrick had been there, beside Kade and Lorkan once—nerves burning through his alcohol before he finished a pint. Festivals like these had been a night to let loose. To forget titles and duties. And perhaps have a little *fun*. The kind that had him sneaking off into the woods with a lover, naked and breathless under the moonlight.

"I was wrong about the vampyr queen." Leif kept his attention averted ahead, mapping out the festivities. "I was thrown off after witnessing her wield a blade, but after talking with her today, I'm certain the other alphas are fools not to trust her, and . . ."

Eldrick shifted on uneasy feet. Images of Tovi on her knees flashed across his mind, and their unfinished business left him taut. It was his turn to focus on the dancing crowd, ignoring the itch of Leif's penetrating stare.

"I think you're the biggest fool of us all not to love her."

Eldrick snorted, downing his ale and wishing it was stronger. "Those your wise words, Leif? Love?"

Leif shrugged. "When I met my mate—"

"It isn't the same," Eldrick snapped. "Rue is a werewolf. You were both born of the same land and people, while Tovi and I aren't just from different worlds but different kingdoms. You also said it yourself: we're up against centuries' worth of prejudice. It would never work."

Leif studied him. "How you do know for certain?"

Eldrick didn't, and the cold, harsh realization had his inner wolf's hackles rising. Had he and Tovi even given themselves a chance? But deep down, Eldrick feared it wasn't him holding back, but *her*. Did she even care to try? Did she love him like he loved her?

Eldrick shook his head, the questions leaving him off-balance.

"I'm a leader, Leif," he said. "Sometimes what I want doesn't matter."

Leif nodded. "Perhaps you're sacrificing the wrong thing. Don't forget that rightness I mentioned earlier. My soul sings for both these lands and my mate. Can you say the same?"

The alpha walked off, leaving Eldrick to stew on his parting words. *No*, the answer flushed through him. He glanced up at the glowing spheres, latching onto one and wishing upon its power like it were a true star.

It was foolish and useless, but he dared to imagine a different time, an alternate universe where the curse didn't exist. What if relations between werewolves and vampyrs were peaceful? What if he and Tovi met at a festival like this? Not as a queen or alpha, but simply two beings drawn to the other where they could dance with friends and wander off and get lost to the tastes and sounds of the other.

But what of his parents? What of the sacrifices they made for werewolves? Was he lesser of a leader because temptation crept through him? Would his inability to squash want lead him to fail his people?

An indescribable sensation yanked at Eldrick's heart. He snapped his attention east.

There. With shoulders back and proud, laughing over something Yennifer whispered in her ear, Tovi entered the festival with an arm linked through the archer's.

An emerald velvet dress enveloped the dips and curves of Tovi's tantalizing frame, bare feet already muddied from the village's roads. The neckline ran straight across her chest, revealing her collarbone and slender neck. The moon and its phases were sewn onto the bodice with silver twine, drawing out the snowy white of her hair, which was braided and pulled to the side, as button-like silver beads dotted each knot.

Stars above, Eldrick took back his wish.

He would never regret how they had begun—at the Shield-Maiden, discussing blueberry ale. It had been messy. Axe drawn, fangs bared. Eldrick winced at the memory, but he wouldn't give up the mess to have the easy. Not when Tovi robbed him of breath and drowned out the sights, sounds, and smells of the festival. *She* was a marvel, a woman to be worshiped and celebrated.

She and Yen headed towards Bétar, and the others, and Eldrick lost sight of her. He stood taller, trying to glimpse her snowy hair. Ragna and Asa walked into his line of sight, and Eldrick greeted them with a smile, hiding his earlier intentions.

"You've outdone yourselves this year. I believe it's the grandest in the Vadon Mountains," he said.

Ragna snorted. "Quit with the flattery, Eldrick. You already secured our vote."

Asa kissed her mate's cheek. "Oh, I think he has a point. Your efforts this year are exceptional, love."

Ragna softened under Asa's praise. "Fine, I'll take a compliment from you, but I'm not convinced Eldrick isn't confusing the beauty of tonight with a particular queen." She raised a far-too-knowing brow.

Asa hummed. "Actually, speaking of Queen Tovi, now might be a time to tell you our *wonderful* idea."

Eldrick's legs grew restless, his instinct screaming to retreat from their scheming stares.

"There are more"—Ragna leaned closer, voice dropping to a whisper—"*official* ways to unite the vampyrs and werewolves. A quicker, more formal, political alliance."

The warmth of the festival vanished, and Eldrick froze in place. "What are you suggesting?"

"Marry her."

Ragna might as well have punched him in the gut.

"What?" Eldrick hissed. "That's . . . absurd."

It wasn't the thought of marrying Tovi—*that* wasn't ridiculous—but using marriage as a political alliance? An *arrangement*? He shook his head, fighting the bile working in his throat.

"Why not?" Ragna whispered. "You're clearly both interested in each other. Love would blossom over time—"

"That isn't the point." Not that he'd admit his reasoning to Ragna—that was Tovi's past and wounds. She owned them, not him, and he'd damn well protect her integrity and secrets. Eldrick wouldn't reveal the pain Tovi's parents caused, and he certainly wouldn't use her like a pawn like they'd been so inclined to.

Ragna shrugged. "Are you sure? If I recall a line in the prophecy, there's something about uniting, and what brings two people together more than marriage? Besides, it's difficult for the other alphas to question your alliance with her when she's your wife."

Wife. How could he want something so adamantly and loathe the idea so violently all at the same time?

"I've already secured Lindström's and Alland's votes tonight," he said through gritted. "I would *never* marry her."

"Eldrick, there you are!" Bétar grasped him on the shoulder.

The commander, Yen, and Tovi joined Eldrick and the alphas. Tovi's hard jade stare pinned Eldrick in place.

Ragna cleared her throat and held her hand out to her mate. "I think it's time we dance."

Bétar grabbed Yen by the hips and tugged her close. "Shall we?"

Yennifer laughed into his hold, and the mated couples disappeared into the throngs of dancers, and silence stretched between Eldrick and Tovi as they were left alone.

Werewolves lingered in the corner, eyes drinking in Tovi like they weren't sure if they wanted to kill her or ask her to dance. A territorial instinct rose up in Eldrick, and damn him, he had no right, but he stepped closer to her. Perhaps for tonight, he'd honor what he wanted, and in the morn, refocus on his duty.

"Would you care to dance with me?" Eldrick held out his hand, heart hammering like he was moments away from stepping into battle.

"Yes," she finally said, placing her hand in his.

Their skin-to-skin contact zapped through Eldrick like a magic.

He swallowed and led them away from the thicket of dancers and to the outskirts, closer to the musicians beating goatskin drums and plucking lyres. Eldrick pulled Tovi to his chest, and flush against the other, they swayed and stepped side to side. Tovi peered up at him, and Eldrick down at her, and the festival vanished. It was just them, dancing in an empty forest, with only the trees to witness their rare gentleness and the sound of their racing hearts as song.

Green overtook Eldrick's senses—Tovi's emerald dress, forest spruce—but nothing compared to the jade in her eyes, ensnaring deep into his soul. The two didn't whisper a word, silent as their gazes never left the other. They twisted to the thrums of the harp, turned to the tune of the splendid flute.

By the third song, Eldrick showed Tovi simple footwork, and they joined the circle of dancers, overcome with laughter as they spun hand in hand with the Drabek pack. When the fourth song turned sad and slow, Eldrick pulled her close again, and Tovi melted into him, hand molding perfectly to his.

"Welcome to your first Dísablót," he whispered into her ear.

"What exactly does it honor?" Tovi asked, eyes alight with such curiosity Eldrick swore the first glimpses of spring sprouted in her irises.

"Warriors, female ancestors, and the winter season we've made it through and the spring harvest still to come."

"You celebrate halfway through?" she whispered.

Eldrick marveled at the joy lighting Tovi's features. "Yes. We also honor fate herself, the one that carries us forward with each passing season. It is good to give thanks even in the harshest of winters, for spring always arrives. Thanks to fate. Ancient songs and ballads say our female ancestors ride along with her, too."

"Fate," Tovi molded the word on her lips, "I've never heard of it as an actual entity. Is she a goddess?"

Eldrick shook his head as they continued to dance. "No. She's as elusive as time and passes like the seasons. She moves on the wind as a bluster or a breeze. Tales claim she's older than the Moon God, that perhaps she is even the mother of the gods."

"You speak of it with such pride," Tovi said. "Like you truly believe it all."

The edges of Eldrick's lips tugged into a smile. "How can I not? Look at it all." He gazed at the gathering, peered up at the trees, and turned in the direction of the mountain peaks, cloaked in the night. "The Vadon Mountains are a wonder—werewolves, too. My people have stayed true to their roots. Fate, the Moon God, the land. We honor and prosper, and I can't help but find *that* magical, shifting and abilities aside."

Tovi reared slightly back, the glisten in her eyes dimming such a fraction as she roamed over his face. Her expression slacked. Had Eldrick said something wrong? Eldrick's heart dropped like a stone in his belly.

Tovi shut her eyes, a small smile spreading across her beautiful face. "The way you love your people and home is one of the many things I admire you for, Eldrick." Her tone and words were true, but that smile—it was forced. "I hope one day, in Drystan, vampyrs can have the same culture, the same pride and celebrations werewolves have."

Eldrick laughed, trying to breathe out the unease prickling across his skin. "Perhaps you celebrate Dísablót? Fate is for all of Sorin, I dare to say even Torren, not just the Vadon Mountains and the werewolves. She is everywhere, in all the lands. Besides, everyone should honor their female warriors, no?"

Tovi sighed. "I fear vampyrs still have a ways to catch up in how they treat their females."

"A queen will shift things, Tovi," Eldrick whispered. "*You* already have."

"I know," she whispered, mouth remaining open as if she debated on saying something else.

"Eldrick!" a large hand grasped his shoulder and gave it a generous squeeze.

Bétar grinned at them both, Yen standing at his side with sweat soaking her wheat-colored hair.

"Care to grab a glass of wine?" she asked Tovi. "I could use a break from the dancing."

"Avoid the wine." Eldrick released her. "Trust me, dove. Stick to the ale tonight. You'll thank me in the morning."

Bétar laughed. "Aye, a true gentlemen! He is right. The wine is rather potent this far south."

Yen rolled her eyes. "Overprotective males. Ale it is, I guess. Maybe even a slice of meat pie—I'm starved."

Tovi laughed, but that light, that joy Eldrick had seen earlier was gone. Something plagued her mind. Eldrick felt it in his bones. But what? Were her worries regarding Drystan's future? What he'd told her of fate?

"Thank you for dancing," Tovi said before Yen dragged her away.

Her words rang like a goodbye. Eldrick paused, never losing sight of her as she weaved out of the dancing crowd, whispered something into Yen's ear—who's lips down turned and shoulders slumped—and headed back into the village, leaving the festival in a rush. Eldrick's insides backflipped. How could such a magical night also feel like shadows closed in around him?

"Do you want my advice?" Bétar asked, hand still gripping his shoulder.

Eldrick grunted, eying his friend. "You're going to give it to me anyway, why ask?"

Bétar shrugged. "I like to hear that you want it."

Moons. Eldrick palmed his heart. "Tell me, Commander, what is on your mind?"

Bétar released him, beaming as he crossed his arms. "Go after her."

Rightness.

It thrummed through him like power—there was no question on what he needed to do. No, he didn't have the exact answer, but he had choice and the strength. He knew Tovi like breathing, recognized a fear she didn't share. She was guarded, reserved, and if was something close to her heart, she'd not utter a word of it. He had to show her it was alright—that he'd be there for her. No matter what.

"Thank you." He eyed Bétar as he backed out of the crowd. "*Oh wise Commander.*"

His friend's boisterous laughter followed him through the crowd, filling each of Eldrick's steps with jittery confidence.

CHAPTER FIFTY-NINE

TOVI SLAMMED THE DOOR to her guest suite, slumping up against the ancient wood and tried and tried to calm her racing heart. Her eyes stung while her stomach twisted—she wasn't sure if she needed to cry, wretch, or both.

No.

This wasn't who she was. She didn't crumble. She didn't break. Yet, why did her heart ache?

I would never.

The room shrank, the walls closing in her around her as Eldrick's earlier words, laced with such disgust echoed. Tovi hadn't meant to hear. She'd simply made it through the crowd quicker than Bétar and Yennifer and found Eldrick first. He, nor the alphas, noticed when the word *queen* caught her attention, and then her vampyr hearing took over. She'd listened to every word, every protest Eldrick had uttered. And it had hurt.

Then he danced with her like Tovi was the only thing that existed in this world, and she hurt all the more.

Tovi rushed to the side table to pour herself a glass of wine. Sip after sip, she reminded herself it didn't matter. She shouldn't care. They'd agreed to remain allies.

The Vadon Mountains are a wonder—werewolves, too.

His people, his home. *Bloody hel*, how could she forget he was an alpha, destined to lead his own people one day? Of course he didn't want to marry her. Perhaps that's why it hurt. They both had their duties, their people to consider. Yet, out there, they'd been celebrating fate, thanking her for the marvelous gift of being carried through life, and yet Tovi cursed fate for weaving her heart for a male she could not have. What a silly, foolish, girlish fantasy—

The door slammed open, and Eldrick charged in, only stopping when his gaze spied the tears on her cheeks. Heat flushed through Tovi, and she wiped them away.

"Vampyrs are accustomed to knocking," she said, hating the tremor in her voice. She swigged more wine.

"What's wrong?" Sincerity laced his tone, and his chest rose and fell like he'd rushed here.

Like he'd *ran* to find her.

Tovi swallowed, bracing her hands on the side table. She could lie, demand he leave her room. A large, aching part of her wished to. But she wasn't a silly girl. Withholding what she knew was childish. It was better to let it out, to be honest. To finally clear the air and be done with this mess between them. To brace for the pain to come.

Tovi talked to the groves in the table, unable to meet Eldrick's beautiful stare. "I overhead your conversation with the Drabeks. When Ragna suggested a marriage between us, you . . ." Tovi cursed, swallowing her pride and turning to him. "You shot it down so quickly like . . . Like it was a wretched idea. *Bloody hel*, I have no right to care because we agreed, but your rejection—"

"*Moons,*" Eldrick breathed, raking a hand through his hair. "Tovi, I'd marry you this very hour if you'd have me."

Tovi stilled, anger and disbelief warring inside her. "I don't understand—I *heard* the disgust in your voice, Eldrick. "

The alpha planted his hands on his hips, for once untethered and lost as he struggled to finds words. Tovi braced, waiting for the gauntlet, the "but" of his reasoning, to hear the speech about Eldrick's duty to his pack and homeland. She understood it more than anyone else, and she had to accept it.

Finally Eldrick sighed, leveling his gem stare on her and not breaking it. "Marrying you would be the greatest honor of my life, but basing it off a political alliance would also be my greatest crime."

Tovi sucked in a breath, rocking back at the intensity of his words.

He stepped closer. "Your parents threatened your happiness with an arranged marriage, suitor after suitor, decade after decade. I know the pain they caused you. A match made for political reasons feels far too close to what they wanted for you, and you deserve to be cherished. To be *loved* by the male you one day marry. I refuse to rob you of that chance . . . to find a partner you also love."

Eldrick's voice cracked on the last sentence. *Goddess*, he'd been thinking of her. *Respecting* her. Even when it's what he wanted. This male. This werewolf. Tovi refused to hold it in any longer—physically *couldn't*. Not when he was so honest, so true and patient with her and wrong about how she felt.

"You *are* the male I love."

Every fiber and muscle of his being stilled. "What did you say?"

She shook her head, unable to contain her emotions. Weeks. *Weeks* she'd let this fester inside her. "I'm in love you, Eldrick Drengr, and have been for some time now."

Eldrick blinked. "Then what are you so afraid of?"

Her blood ran cold. She battled reason and sense. What was best versus what she wanted. "I am a queen—"

"No." Eldrick took two long strides so they were toe to toe. He cupped the sides of her face, tilted it so she was forced to peer up at him. "No, you don't care what people think. You don't care for status or titles. You may love your people, but this has *nothing* to do with ruling Drystan. You're afraid of something. I can *feel* it. Have for weeks. Tell me what is. Let me support you. Together we can figure it out."

He knew her, read her so well. "Eldrick . . ."

If only it were that easy—if only she truly understood why she wanted to run from this. There it was, that pull, that instinctual tug to lean into him, to accept it. Her body and mind didn't feel like her own, yet her heart ached for him.

"Tell me, Tovi." He caressed her cheek, and she shuddered at his touch. "Trust me."

Oh, how this ground felt familiar. They'd been here before, only it had been her asking him for trust. It'd taken time, but Eldrick had. He'd allied with her, killed for her, and admitted his love for her. She could do the same for him, *wanted* to do the same for him. When she blinked, the memory of that night when the Blood Goddess had created her family into vampyrs tattooed the back of her eyelids.

"I witnessed what love did to my father," she whispered. "What it made him do. It's what drives Riven to destroy Sorin, all so he can bring back his wife and child. What if I'm like them?"

Eldrick's expression softened, and he brushed away her tears with his thumb. "You're not, Tovi."

"No?" she scoffed. "I'd go to war for you. I'd burn this entire world to save you. If we stood on a battlefield against Riven and it was you or my people, I'd chose you. *That* is what frightens me, Eldrick."

He tucked a stray strand behind her ear and gripped her chin, making her look at him. "Why not agree to love each other fiercely but also accept our responsibilities to our people?"

Tovi shook her head. "It's not that simple."

"If we feel this way about one another, we can make it work." Eldrick's tone wasn't a plea but a declaration. His beastly energy wafted off him waves.

Tovi swallowed, blinking back tears. "When we have children, where will we raise them?"

"I . . ." Eldrick blinked. "I always envisioned my children in the Drengr Village."

Tovi nodded. "And I always saw my children running through the halls of Drystan Castle."

Eldrick rested his forehead against hers. "I'm not saying it'll be easy. *Stars above*, I know that. We'll split our time between our homelands. We'll figure it out."

"What about us?" The past, present, and future blurred through Tovi's mind. She tried to think straight, rationally while Eldrick's spearmint scent engulfed her. "Will we live separately? Will our beds be empty of the other while we lead our people?"

Eldrick was silent for a moment, and Tovi felt his heart beating in his chest. It was surprisingly calm, and Tovi found solace in the tempo, like he grounded them both. He pulled away and placed his hands on her hips.

The look he gave her, thank the Goddess he held her upright, undid Tovi's resolve at the seams, and only one thread remained. The one connecting their souls.

"You're right. There are challenges we might face, but all I ask is that you give us a chance. To just be together. This love between us is real. I know it. I've never trusted anything more in my life."

They'd stood like this once before, being pulled together. They'd agreed for so very little from one another. No feelings. No distractions. Now, they were about to walk a path that asked everything of them.

Tovi was frightened.

She didn't trust her heart, but Goddess, she trusted Eldrick. Not because she second-guessed her answer. Fears regarding her fierce love for him aside, Tovi understood, or at least suspected, the gravity of this love, this bond between them. Yet, this decision was of her choosing.

"Okay," she whispered. "Let us try, Eldrick Drengr."

Eldrick's gem eyes drank her in. He leaned down, inch by inch, and placed his lips against hers. His kiss was slow, hesitant, as if at any moment she might run from the room and take back her answer. Yet, Tovi felt the smile through their kiss.

He paused for a single breath. "Turn around. Let's get you out of that beautiful dress."

Tovi, tingling with tension, obeyed, exposing the crisscrossed laced back. Eldrick took his time, pulling each and every loop loose, the dress's release from her body was like a tease, the process agonizingly slow. Eldrick paused every so often, lining kisses up and down her neck, occasionally nipping her shoulder, which shot pleasure to her toes. He turned his attention to peeling her sleeves off, the dress falling inch by inch and finally collecting at her feet. A silk underdress remained, Tovi's nipples peeking through the thin fabric.

She turned, sucking in a breath at the sight of want in Eldrick's eyes. Raw, unabashed desire. Green, dark, and beastly. Tovi drew her finger down the sharp edge of his square jaw and—Eldrick snatched her hand away and crashed his lips to hers. His desire shifted to hunger. Tovi matched it, opening her mouth wider, running her tongue along his. A growl rumbled through his chest, and Tovi pushed him backward.

They grew clumsy, a mess of steps and limbs as they fumbled with Eldrick's tunic, releasing it from his waistband and tossing it across the room. His pants came next, his britches last. Tovi hissed as Eldrick's fingertips grazed up her thighs, grabbing fistfuls of her underdress to pull up and up and over her head. Tovi blinked and became airborne, squealing as Eldrick picked her up and deposited her onto the bed. He crawled atop, and their naked bodies molded to the other.

The tempo of their kisses built, and Tovi savored the taste of him, the feel of his lips on hers. Heat hummed through Tovi, only growing as Eldrick kissed down her neck, peppering her skin with promise. He gripped the back of her thighs and gave them a gentle, glorious squeeze as he opened them wider and dipped two fingers into her ready sex.

"Stars above, dove," he hissed.

He circled her clit, and Tovi's chest rose and fell, her breath turning ragged as release built, built, and built within her.

"I need you," Eldrick whispered.

Tovi understood and nodded. This was different than the other times they'd laid together. It suddenly felt all the more real. *Meaningful.* It wasn't urgent or hurried. They'd declared their love for one another, and their bodies begged to celebrate it, to mirror their words' pleasure.

Emerald and jade clashed as Eldrick aligned himself at Tovi's center. Their stare didn't break as he pushed into her entrance, inch after inch, until he was seated to the hilt. They both moaned and shuddered, and Eldrick rocked into her. Once, twice, a third time, and Tovi melted around him, adjusting to his size.

His pace was slow, thoughtful, to the point Tovi felt every ridge of his manhood, the pleasure and tingle reaching to her toes. Eldrick leaned his forehead onto hers, and their breathing turned ragged and spent. Wine, sweat, *love*. It all mingled and burst in the tiny room.

A crescendo built at Tovi's core. She ran her hands down his back, memorizing the dips and bends of his muscles. She trailed her fingers up until they weaved into his tousled strands.

"I love you," she whispered.

The gem light in his eyes flashed an otherworldly shade. "And I love you."

Their declaration to one another sent them over the edge. A wave of beautiful, blissful release cascaded through Tovi, and Eldrick growled into the nape of her neck, trembling as his own release filled her to the brim. Their hearts, their breath, their pleasure beat in tandem—a tune that felt like one they had weaved, not fate herself.

CHAPTER SIXTY

GOLD RAN THROUGH THE marble of the Sun Goddess's palace, shimmering under her namesake. The grand stairs led to a floor of open rooms, billowing curtains, and monstrous columns that held up the three-story structure. It sat on the edge of a rocky cliff. Beyond, a body of water with no current or tide lay still like a mirror, reflecting the jeweled-colored sky.

For a Goddess known for fertility, Evelyn failed to find life and vibrancy on the palace grounds. In fact, the grass and golden-leaf trees stopped in a definitive line, leaving yards of kicked-up dirt between them. Fountains flowed in rectangular pools, naked sculptures poured water from spotted pottery, but no birds visited, not even the sludge of mold was at the waterline.

Laughter, a kind that reminded Evelyn of the fighting rings in Drystan Castle, trickled from inside, grating against her resolve. Beside her, Aster's smile had fallen into a straight line. Evelyn'd never once seen her friend so quiet.

"What's the matter?" she asked.

Her friend swallowed, brown eyes going wide. "Well . . ."

Evelyn stepped closer, dropping her voice to a whisper. "Aster, you know you can trust me."

Aster eyed the palace, not meeting her stare. "The Sun Goddess isn't what witches believe. You need to be prepared for anything, Evelyn."

Trust with Aster went both ways, which left Evelyn wary as she considered her friend's words. Her stomach churned, but she schooled her expression as they climbed the stairs and entered the palace's grand foyer.

The columns stood on catlike paws, their claws digging into the marble floor for a ferocious effect. Above, a mural depicted the sun at the center with its fiery rays swirling into starry spirals to the west and a cloudless blue sky to the east.

Marble statues lined the walls—warriors in mid-battle, queens addressing their subjects, werewolves in their shifted form, witches casting their magic. Metal plaques detailed a name, but they moved too quickly for Evelyn to read them.

The Sun Goddess's namesake, aside from the mural, continued to lack—the palace was sterile and cold. Evelyn's bare feet slapped against the marble, loud enough to hopefully drown out the racing of her anxious witch's heart. Her instinct screamed, *Get in and get out*, but the notion had her peering over at Aster, an ache forming in the pit of her belly. She'd only just reunited with her.

The distinct sounds of a party sharpened as they traversed farther into the palace. Glasses clanked. A harp thrummed. Someone recited poetry.

"Isn't it marvelous," a commanding voice called.

Evelyn quickened her gait.

For an insatiable *tug* compelled her forward.

Golden gates groaned as Evelyn and Aster turned the corner. With no moment to compose herself, they walked straight into a grand hall.

The crowd—gods or souls, Evelyn wasn't sure—fell into an eerie silence. A hundred eyes scraped across her skin, and a glint of hunger shined in each one. They stared at Evelyn and Aster like they'd waltzed into the party on silver platters. Evelyn feigned indifference with shoulders back, steps sure, and gaze alert. Once deep in the throngs of those draped in silks or wearing nothing at all but gold body paint, the crowd parted to reveal a stunning female.

The Sun Goddess.

She needed no formal introduction—every inch of her shined with the likeness of golden light, and an aurora of power pulsed around her. At the center of the gathering, she assessed Evelyn with hands clasped at her waist, waiting almost expectantly. She was an ethereal, breathtaking beauty. A petite nose, a bluish-green stare, and hair not red or blonde but perfectly in-between, like rose gold spun silk, piled high atop her head. Her sheer white dress draped against her glowing yet palish skin, her nipples pebbled and piercing the thin fabric of her dress. A lace undergarment covered her sex, but golden chains holding the piece in place followed the divots of her protruding hip bones, lines leaving little to the imagination.

The Sun Goddess smiled with no teeth, and Evelyn's instinct flared. Not her magical kind, but a baser sense. *That* smile wasn't real—it was posed. The twinkle in the goddess's eye wasn't delight either. It was the hint of knowing more than the other and feeling smug about it.

"Evelyn Carson, do not be frightened," the Sun Goddess said, her voice tickling the back of Evelyn's mind. "You are more than welcome in my hall. After all, this party was thrown in your name."

The crowd chuckled. Evelyn's guard hardened, and she searched the room for Kade, but found no sign of him.

Interest in Evelyn waned, and the crowd turned back to their festivities. They drank, ate and conversed—and some continued activities tangled on chaises, moans and gasps echoing off the walls. Evelyn hadn't envisioned attending some lavish party while in Sorin witches and werewolves fought demons, scáths, and the Void—a darkness destined to destroy them if they didn't break the Blood Goddess's curse, one of *their* own. It wasn't for a lack of power—it vibrated in the palace, the marble turning porous and absorbing the immense energy like a sponge.

The Sun Goddess approached closer, her bare toes dipped in golden paint shimmering against the marble floor. She circled Evelyn and Aster and paused at her friend's side, who dipped her head in respect. The Goddess laughed, patting—*patting*—Aster on the head. Like some pet. Evelyn fisted her hands at her sides, knuckles popping, but the Goddess didn't seem to notice as she smiled, flashing—

Fucking flames, the goddess possessed fangs.

The paler complexion, the beauty beholding her.

The Blood Goddess made us in her likeness.

Tovi's words from weeks ago filtered through Evelyn's mind. She eyed the goblets and other sets of fangs flashing in their direction. Blood dribbling down their chins. Red staining their teeth. Crimson stains on their garments. The many, many bite marks on Aster's neck. Evelyn's own blood ran cold.

"Where's my mate?" she said, tone bold and demanding.

Aster winced, and gods that lingered close ceased conversation.

The Sun Goddess stepped closer, peering down her nose at Evelyn. *Nothing* witches had prayed to the Goddess for shined in her eyes.

"You're one stubborn witch, aren't you? Placing your magic in the bloodstone was unexpected, even for me." She bent lower, but Evelyn didn't move. She didn't cower under the Goddess's perusal or power.

"I was left with no other choice."

But what choice did these gods have? While those of Sorin suffered at the hands of the Blood Goddess, they were *partying*—drinking and fucking as if their demise was something the celebrate.

The Sun Goddess leaned back, humming to herself. "True. If the prince had succeeded, I fear the alternative dawn that would've arisen. What an interesting thing, fate, is it not? *You*, a young witch, single-handedly shifted the tides of the fight to come. I must say, your resilience is a treat for us all."

Evelyn blinked. *A treat*. Like she was entertainment.

"Indeed," a god said, sauntering over from a lingering group. His dark curls intertwined with a crown made of stars. Tattoos, the phases of the moon in fact, lined his inner forearm. His midnight gaze roamed her up and down, brimming with interest and a dangerous hunger. "You're a marvel to watch. Forgive me, but I've fantasied about meeting you too many times."

Evelyn snapped her shoulders straighter. "And you are?"

He wasn't the Moon God, despite the tattooed moons, Evelyn was sure of it. There was no likeness to her fated, and she felt that truth deep in her bones.

"I'm the God of Night." He flashed a fang. "Slumber, pleasure, and dreams are my affinities. It's a pity you're mated to such a delightful male, for I'd take such care in showing you my talents—"

"Step away from my mate, or I'll fucking gut you."

Sheer immense power radiated with those words, and Evelyn shivered.

The party ceased. The music died, and the gods stilled. Attention swiveled to the main entrance where two newcomers stood—Kade and a sharp-edged god.

But Kade was anew. Himself, but *more*. His golden stare flared with power. His walk radiated unmatched strength. It rippled off him in waves. Alluring, deadly.

Kade stood before Evelyn in room of gods a god himself.

The magic within his soul weaved into something anew.

Yet, there was still that goodness in him—the kindness that had shined from his eyes since the day Evelyn met him.

"Odin," the God of Night said, but his hungry gaze lingered far too long on Kade. "Not only have you graced us with your presence after centuries, but you've also brought us such a delectable specimen."

Evelyn stepped closer to the God of Night. He swiveled towards her, a predatorial smile cracking his far too beautiful face.

"My, my—"

"Call my mate anything but his name, and it's *me* who will gut *you*," Evelyn hissed.

Both the Sun Goddess and the God of Night blinked, and then tipped their heads back, roaring with laughter. Murmurs of more laughter rose on a wave through the hall, but Evelyn ignored it all, locking eyes with Kade. She didn't miss how they were separated by mere feet, but the god and goddess before her had blocked his path. Beside him, the Moon God stood tall, proud, and eyed those in the hall like one regarded pests. *Fucking flames*, he looked like a werewolf, like those he'd gifted his power to.

"Now, my treat"—*oh*, how Evelyn hated that term the Sun Goddess used—"with what powers do you plan to fight a god with?"

Shadows marred the gold of the Sun Goddess's eyes and dissipated like mists, far too like the ones that had entered Evelyn's cell in the Drystan dungeons. Her brows scrunched together, her mind reeling.

"But that's what you're here for, isn't it? Aster, won't you do the honors, my little pet?"

Aster winced, and Evelyn saw red. Her instinct screamed to do something, to defend her friend, but Aster scurried ahead without a backward glance, small dainty hands wringing together. *No.* That wasn't right. Aster was fearless, bubbly. Evelyn cut a glare towards the Sun Goddess—how fucking dare she dim the light of the brightest soul.

Yet, everyone focused on the dais at the north end of the room. Something draped with a crimson silk sheet stood at the center. The feet of a lone column stuck out, and whatever lay atop it, wiggled and writhed, as if starved for air and fighting for release.

Aster, hands shaking, pulled back the sheet, revealing an orb of flame. *Evelyn's* flame. Like sang to like. It was her power. A piece of her *soul* on display as if it were some coveted artifact for all to see, no different than the marble statues she'd passed in the foyer.

Pain seared through Evelyn's chest, the gaping hole near her heart pulsing and festering. She fought the urge to crumple to her knees. Kade lurched forward, but the God of Night countered his approach.

"Step aside, Nótt!" the Moon God boomed through the hall. Candles whooshed out, even the sun dimmed, casting shadows on the depravity of the party. Gods, goddesses, and souls cowered, huddling closer to one another and backing away from the center of the hall.

The Sun Goddess clucked her tongue. She molded her hand slowly onto the God of Night's shoulder, pronouncing her slender, clawed hands. She held him back with glistening eyes set on the Moon God.

"You're no fun, Odin," she tutted, fanning a pout. "We've been dreaming of this day for centuries."

"A day that never would've arrived if it weren't for your brashness, Macha," Odin said, ushering Kade forward.

In two deliberate strides, Evelyn flung herself into his arms, not caring what god or goddess witnessed their love and touch. Power thrummed through him. She smelled it in his scent. In every muscle and fiber of his being, he was raw with it.

Kade *was* power.

The God of Night whistled while the Sun Goddess clasped her hands to her chest, knotted knuckles paler than before as she shook with excitement.

"Mortal love," she whispered.

"In its purest form. Rare, so rare . . . I find myself utterly . . ." The Moon God searched for the right word, running his tongue across his needlelike fangs. "*Captivated.*"

He sneered, spreading his arms wide to encourage those in the hall. They whispered and laughed, causing bile to churn in Evelyn's stomach. She and Kade molded closer to the other, hands interlocking. He kept her steady, kept her grounded as she threatened to empty the contents of her stomach onto the palace floor. She and Kade were a spectacle. They were nothing to the gods but something to fill the boredom of immortality.

It was no different than the papers of Nūa—a fabricated tale in the *Morning Sun* for covens to gossip about. Yet, these gods had power, sight, and the ability to help. Not that witches and werewolves didn't, but these were their creators, ones with the ability to shift the trajectory of fate, and here they were, gawking at Evelyn and Kade as if one of their own wasn't destroying Sorin.

Ahead, Evelyn's magic flared higher, illuminating the hall's walls. Embers sparked towards the ceiling, mirroring the angry heat flushing through her. Evelyn swore she spied silver in the dance of orange and red, but the painting, the depiction of a battle on the walls had Evelyn stepping forward for a better look. Aster hurried down from the dais, joining her side as she studied the oiled swirls.

A dark-haired goddess, skin ashen, was bound in chains. The Blood Goddess's namesake dripped down her chin and stained her taloned hands. She was so different than the others, so monstrous. The other gods glowed with faint auras—Macha yellow, Odin pearl, and Nótt indigo—and the splatter of blood, dirt, and war didn't mar their beauty.

With mighty weapons in hand, they dragged her to a fissure in the land's surface. Mists swirled around it, and the painting depicted the darkness beneath the land—crooked roots, barren trees, glowing mushrooms, and prowling madra.

"You've defeated her before." Evelyn whirled towards the Sun Goddess. "Why have you done *nothing*?"

The Sun Goddess snickered. "Is that what you think? I gifted you *my* power."

"My magic is *mine* and mine alone," Evelyn said through gritted teeth.

The Sun Goddess blinked. The murmurs in the hall had fallen to apprehensive whispers. The air shifted to unease. The God of Night eyed Evelyn and Kade, slinking back a step. The Moon God, on the other hand, burst into a wide, toothy smile. Was that pride flashing through his tired eyes?

Evelyn's words had left her lips before they'd even fully registered. The belief flushed through her so aggressively she rocked back on her heels, shocked by her own revelation. Of course, she'd not considered her magic belonged to witches, but it went deeper than that.

Yes, the Sun Goddess had gifted witches a kernel of power all those years ago, and Evelyn was the third born in the prophecy, but she was *nothing* like this goddess.

Neither was her power. Distrust snaked through Evelyn for the Sun Goddess's intentions, her nature. Cruel, arrogant, pompous. She'd witnessed her struggles, *marveled* at them. Had she laughed the times Evelyn had called out to her? Even those days, years ago, when she'd first traveled to the Cirrillo and prayed at the temple, had the Sun Goddess sipped her wine, leaned back, and enjoyed the show?

There'd been a time in Evelyn's life when she would've cowered from the thought, her skin crawling and prickling from embarrassment. But now all she felt was rage. Being played like a puppet wasn't fate, but cruelty.

The Sun Goddess's behavior, her decisions, what she'd done—or lack thereof—was a reflection of *her*, not Evelyn. She'd trained, fought, run, bled, and loved these last years—*that* reflected who she was. She wasn't some story the Nūa papers crafted, nor a show the Otherworld could watch.

Every part of her, even her magic thrummed with truth. Ahead, it flickered as if agreeing, and for the second time, Evelyn spied rivets of luminescent silver.

"My magic is mine, no one else," Evelyn repeated, stepping towards the goddess. "I'm here to take it back."

"Silence!" The Sun Goddess's command grated against Evelyn's mind, and the distinct smell of mildew and cold, wet stone filtered through her memory—

"Ungrateful, pathetic, and selfish mortal!" the Sun Goddess shook. "You come into my palace, my world—"

Kade growled, eyes brightening to a pearly blue. The same shimmer glowed at his hands. Controlled, yes, but immense, too.

The Sun Goddess stiffened. "What have you done, Odin?"

"Ensured the world survives," he whispered.

The goddess remained still, too still, like hundreds of thousands of years wheeled through her distant gaze. Calculating.

Then she giggled.

Slow, throaty until it grew into shrill laughter that threatened to crack the hall's windows. The crowd joined, and instinctually, Evelyn drew closer to Kade.

"Oh, sweet, gentle Odin . . ." The Sun Goddess gathered her skirts. "The Son of the God was never the problem. So duty bound and loyal to the prophecy. So very, very much like *you*. No, no, no . . . The fate of Sorin has always rested in the hands of a witch, desperate to control the path *I* wrote for her. Now, because of her selfish decisions, she is left with no choice but to make an ultimate sacrifice, or else her power, magic, and soul will remain here, dooming everyone she loves to the curse."

The God of Night smirked, licking his lips at the prospect.

Evelyn fisted her hands at her sides, stilling the icy cold rushing through her veins. "What sacrifice may that be?" she asked.

The Sun Goddess flicked her hands for Aster to come, beckoning her forward.

Evelyn stilled, and Kade grasped her forearm, holding her back. *Wait.*

Odin whispered into Evelyn's ear, his words a mere breath. "Remember, your power is life *to ride the shade*."

The god annunciated the word *your*—he agreed, knew her power was hers and hers only.

The Sun Goddess sighed. "You severed your soul so greatly, Evelyn, it needs more than patching but something extra. Sweet Aster has volunteered, waited all these months for you to arrive."

"What does Aster have to do with this?" Evelyn asked, words getting stuck in her dry throat.

The God of Night prowled to the Sun Goddess, grabbing her waist. "Let her come to the conclusion on her own," he whispered into her ear, "You know I delight in how clever she is."

"I'm going to fucking gut him," Kade breathed.

The Sun Goddess smiled, and when Evelyn blinked, she saw Visha—beautiful, sneering, and cruel. "Think of it like this, Aster will now always be with you."

"What?" Evelyn demanded.

"Aster Arkwood has always been such a wonderful witch," the goddess drawled. "She knew how to guide you in the living world. Why not let her help you from this day forth? Aster's power grows life, Evelyn. It'll only strengthen your ability to defeat the Blood Goddess once and for all."

Aster grabbed her hand. "My magic, it's yours Evelyn. Take it."

The suggestion, the implication had Evelyn's insides twisting so violently, she thought perhaps a knife had lodged into her gut and shredded her from the inside. Kade kept her standing, but she felt his riled wolf, the beastly energy brimming in the air.

"Your magic is your soul. What will become of you?" Evelyn whispered.

"It's alright," Aster said, but her eyes screamed with a lie. She was afraid—*terrified*.

"No." Evelyn shook her head. "*No.*"

"How dare you ask that of her?" Kade roared. "Of either of them!"

The Sun Goddess's eyes flared. "I do dare! As powerful as you both are, time is not on your side. The Blood Curse grows with each passing—"

"And who is to blame for that?" Evelyn shouted. "Aster is kind, she is gentle. She has always believed in goodness and the idea of *you,* and now you ask her to become nothing."

"Your friend's fate has been written—her death a part of the plan."

"You . . ." Evelyn swallowed back bile. "You knew she'd die, and you did *nothing.* The other young woman, murdered. Riven's plans. And yet still, *you did nothing.*"

The goddess tsked. "Fate is sometimes a misfortune. What is written, is written. Aster's fate was decided long ago, and more importantly, she accepted her path and walked it happily. You now must do the same. Use her soul to mend yours and draw back your magic, or remain here, Evelyn Carson. What will you decide?"

Evelyn remained passive, drawing a false frown to her lips. She pinched her brow, and to others, appeared perhaps distraught but she was *thinking.* For the Sun Goddess doubted one strength Evelyn had not lost these weeks—*belief.*

One emotion rushed through Evelyn as strong as any power—rebellion. From this day forth, Evelyn answered to no one's plans but her own. She resisted the goddess's notion of fate with every fiber of her being, but she played the obedient mortal as she set her shoulders back. Evelyn rose on her tiptoes and planted a kiss on Kade's cheek.

"Trust me," she breathed into his ear.

The crowd parted as she walked to join Aster on the dais. The Sun Goddess smiled like a cat who'd caught its prey, and Evelyn bowed, playing the mortal who conceded to her whims. She didn't use words, the capacity to lie impossible as she thrummed with her plan.

The Sun Goddess stepped off the dais, joining the God of Night's side as the crowd grew, fixated on the scene about to unfold.

Evelyn dragged Aster into a tight hug.

"Everything's going to be alright," she whispered.

She released her friend and stepped closer to the sphere of power, the hole in her chest warmed. The walls of the palace shook as she called upon her power to return. Her magic answered the call, soaring through the air and crashing into her chest. Evelyn's soul and magic collided, and she sucked in a breath and—

Evelyn shot off the ground, suspended, as her back bowed. Silver engulfed her. Down her arms and legs, lifting her obsidian hair. Light flared around in luminescent flames, dancing in tandem with her. Never had Evelyn felt so centered, so *right*.

Mine, her heart beat as silver threads weaved across her soul.

Evelyn was not remade, she was reborn.

As Evelyn descended back to the ground on steady feet, she crackled and burned with pure power. Fiery orange flames no longer ignited at her fingertips, but silver ones, a power that was a truer reflection. Not some goddess-given gift, not power mentioned in a prophecy or magic adored by her people. It was *her*.

Evelyn was silver and strength.

And life.

For safe measure, and because she could thanks to the infectious rebellion flushing through her veins, Evelyn outstretched her hand and reached for the sun in the sky outside the main window. After all, the Sun Goddess had said she needed something a little extra.

So, Evelyn *plucked* the light of the sun and stole it.

It fueled the power of life already flowing in her veins, a power she intended to use as she saw fit.

Starting with Aster.

Evelyn addressed the Sun Goddess, piercing her with an unabashed stare. "Fuck fate."

She snapped her fingers.

Aster stumbled back, layers vibrating, as Evelyn drew upon her power. She was so familiar with the threads of souls and life and light now, weaving something anew was as easy as breathing.

Aster patted her chest, her face, tears welling in russet eyes. Her friend was whole again. "I'm . . . You brought me back to life."

"No!" the Sun Goddess raged, charging towards Evelyn and grasping her by the shirt. "What have you done?"

"What is written, is written." Evelyn thrust her silver flame ahead of her, throwing the Sun Goddess back onto her ass.

The hall erupted into gasps and shouts of protest. The Otherworld skies darkened.

"Seize them!" the Sun Goddess roared.

The God of Night took one step forward, eyes focused on Evelyn, and then cried out in agony. He crumpled to the floor, clutching his stomach as his entrails splattered to the marble floor—Kade's promise to gut him fulfilled.

Her mate stalked through the frightened crowd, hand alight with his power. Their bond vibrated between them, not fully intact yet, but tied by a thread once again. He joined her side, and they were more powerful than ever.

"Can you feel Belle's spell?" he shouted over the chaos.

"No," Evelyn shook her head. "It's like something's blocking me from the living realm."

Kade nodded. "Me too ."

"Are we stuck?" Aster asked.

The Sun Goddess rose, and fire leaked from her powers. "You will not leave the Otherworld, Evelyn Carson. How dare you steal from *me?* How dare you have the power of a goddess?"

Ahead, the God of Night's body twitched, entrails drawing back into his stomach as he writhed back alive.

"Fucking flames," Evelyn breathed. "They can't be killed."

"We need to get out of here," Kade shouted.

Panic flushed through Evelyn. "I can't feel Belle's spell."

"You don't need a spell to guide you home. Your power is infinite now. *Use it,*" the Moon God shouted over his shoulder, positioning himself ahead of them. "Work together, and I'll hold them off as long as I can."

Kade grasped Evelyn's hand, and with an unbending look of devotion and strength, they weaved their powers together.

Evelyn reached her hand out to Aster. "Hold on!"

Silver and blue shot upward. The ceiling cracked open. The palace shook. Columns fell and shattered. The Sun Goddess's cries chorused with the Moon God's last efforts as he fought her.

Evelyn and Kade sent their powers through the Otherworld and ripped open the tethers between realms, carrying all their souls into the Living Lands once again.

Chapter Sixty-One

B LAIR WOKE REFRESHED, REMEMBERING not to step out of line of her scholarly path. She'd brought that mindset with her into the next research session with Lorkan.

The fire never ceased, Lorkan's firewood restocked. Librarian aids delivered food throughout the day, and Blair never ran out of tea either.

Lorkan read with his spectacles resting at the tip of his nose, and though they'd said little to the other, that peacefulness of just being together hugged them all around.

Blair had found a few interesting terms in her readings—the One, the Three, and an interesting term she had spent the last fifteen minutes trying to translate. The first was only a few letters, *m, o,* and ending in *r*. The center word was the most difficult, practically impossible, while the third was simple enough, reading *darkness*.

"Mother," Blair breathed after her fourth attempt at figuring out the word.

"What did you say?" Lorkan whipped his head up.

"The Mother of Darkness," Blair said, reading all the words together. "It's the closest title to the Blood Goddess I've come across so far. It's reminiscent of the prophecy, too, a mention of darkness we're supposed to defeat."

"This text includes the term, too." Lorkan grew closer to her, pushing the book between them and caging Blair with his arms as he stood behind her. "This illustration survived."

Depicted in a drawing, a beautiful woman stood in the chaos of the battlefield. An army of demons stood behind her while a row of glowing figures—gods was Blair's guess—marched from the other side. At the top of the page, the illustration was labeled *The Mother of Darkness*. She thrust a sword in the air like she led the demons into battle.

"Blasted books," Blair hissed.

"What?" Lorkan said, peering down at her.

She hadn't meant to say anything out loud, and she nibbled her lip, trying to come up with an excuse, a lie of some sort, but Lorkan's gaze dropped to her mouth. The tension between them rose, crackling with the fire. Blair had daydreamed of nights like these. Almost entangled in one another's arms, reading books and theorizing. Just like their teenage years. The separation between work and pleasure, a fragile line, thrummed in the air like a plucked bow string, and the fact she'd tasted him days ago made it all that much worse.

Blair fought the instinct to lean in, to press her lips to his, but the burn on her palm itched, reminding her that this wasn't their small hiding spot in the Drengr Village, and the fate of their homeland rested on how soon they figured out how to break the curse. Besides, she belonged in this spot, with a book in hand and researching, not falling for the whims of her treacherous heart, so hel-bent on dragging her from the path fate had laid out for her.

She cleared her throat, severing their intense connection, and pointed to the goddess's sword. The hilt was the line of three moons.

Just like her burn.

"I've seen the shape before," she said.

Not a lie, but not the full truth, and she kept her wrapped hand underneath the table, out of sight.

Lorkan blinked and studied the illustration. "Wait, so have I."

"Really?" Blair blinked, mouth drying.

Lorkan rushed to his bookcase. Blair's legs moved of their own accord, and she followed, trailing behind him as he ran a finger over the spines.

"Here," he said, pulling out a small, dainty book no more than twenty pages. "It's a werewolf fable related to the cycle of the moon, and the three stages are called the Mother, Crone, and Maiden."

"Three . . ." Blair said, leaning into Lorkan's space to trace her fingers over the symbol etched into the leather cover. Lorkan flipped through the pages, and the symbol continued on throughout it.

"Bizarre," Lorkan mused. "That 'One became Three' is written along with the Mother of Darkness . . ."

Blair's mind ran wild. "Who would be the maiden and the crone?"

"If I had to guess, the maiden is the Sun Goddess, right? Life, light, joy, and abundance, but the mother in this fable doesn't align with the Blood Goddess."

"This would also suggest they are one and the same, no?" Blair shook her head. "Like the Blood Goddess and Sun Goddess were once 'One' and the second?"

"But who is the third, the crone?" Lorkan said, eyes distant.

Blair considered, and the mark on her palm ached. What was the connection between her burn, the symbol in the werewolf fable, and the Mother of Darkness's sword's hilt? Blasted books, was there a connection between *her* and all these elements, or was it simply the properties of the bloodstone? Yet, the ring rested on Lorkan's bare chest, not bothering him at all.

Blair crossed her arms, teetering between admitting the burn, but would her connection to the Mother of Darkness damn her again? They were finally working together, and she didn't trust that the truth wouldn't set back their progress, not when she was getting so close to having something worth reinstating her tarnished name.

Chrome lettering snagged her attention, and Blair pushed past Lorkan to a set of books—no, not a set, an entire shelf, dedicated to *her* published works.

"I don't understand . . ."

Lorkan didn't respond behind her, and Blair turned, inch after inch, finding him so close that if she reached out, her hand would land on his chest. His honey stare zeroed in on her, and heat flared to life in the pit of her belly. Blair wasn't sure how Lorkan could appear so cutting and dark yet have the light of a thousand suns shining in his eyes—a pure contradiction.

She'd be lying if she said that wasn't one of the reasons she'd been drawn to him all those years ago. The dark allure. Manhood clung to him in sharpness and angles now, dark strands flicking over his forehead, and his perfectly thin nose. Blair had always hoped her attraction to this male would fade with time, and yet, her yearning for him was worse than ever.

He studied her, his eyes so ensnared, she wasn't sure what he was looking at—her or her soul. Lorkan stepped forward first, and instinctively Blair matched his step backwards, her shoulder blades coming flush against the bookcase. She was trapped. Not only under Lorkan's hungry, appraising stare but also against the shelves holding her upright.

Neither of them said a word—what was there to say?

The thread that pulled them together could no longer go ignored. The air between them had grown increasingly hot. So much so, Blair was sure she couldn't breathe. Tonight felt different. This moment, this time. Perhaps it was the late hour, the dimmed light in Lorkan's office. It was just them. Two beings pulled together by something they didn't understand or know how to sever. They stood inches apart, their breath mingling together.

The scar across Blair's heart pulsed, yet another sensation rested on her shoulders like the weight of a thousand boulders. But she was tired of fate's rigid perimeters. Her heart burst to be set free, and Blair obliged, screwing consequence. She grabbed Lorkan's tunic and dragged his lips to hers.

CHAPTER SIXTY-TWO

LORKAN LOST ALL SENSE. The crackling fire in his office was swallowed by howling winds, and he braced against storm and sage, answering Blair's need.

Moons, her body melted against Lorkan's as he pushed her into the bookshelf. He drank her moan by opening her lips and gaining access to sweep his tongue across hers. Lorkan dug his hands into her curls, reveling in their softness as they tangled around his fingers.

This is what he'd wanted. Not the desperation or sorrow-laden kiss in the valley, but to have Blair's sweetness amongst books with the warmth of a fire, untethered during the late hours of the night.

His hands dropped to her waist, and he lifted her into the air and—

A low growl rumbled through his chest. Blair wrapped her legs around his waist. *So fucking responsive.* She gasped, breaking away from their kiss. She rested the back of her head against the books, midnight stare studying him as he repositioned himself between her legs.

"Blasted books," she breathed as he pressed into her core.

Their stares locked, ensnared by the promise separated by the thin layers of their clothes.

Blair's eyes darkened, and her heady scent of want entered the air. Lorkan's manhood twitched, swearing he felt her wetness despite both their trousers. *Moons*, he wasn't certain they'd leave his office with them on.

But he stilled, caution washing over him. Above all else, he respected Blair's need in this, and he'd gladly let her push him away again, if she wished. Yet, Blair's legs tightened around his waist, drawing him closer, and Lorkan's body answered, rolling his hips in a circle, letting her feel him.

"Do you see the power you have over me?" he whispered, lips brushing against hers. "Even after all this time."

"Show me," she breathed. "*Please*, Lorkan."

Blair's plea unleashed years of restraint. He crashed his lips back to hers and Blair leaned into what he gave and demanded more. They were fervent for one another, desperate for just a single taste, and once they started to drink, they couldn't stop.

As their lips molded against the other, Lorkan's free hand skirted under Blair's sweater, and he found her breast swollen inside the silk of her bralette. He ripped the fabric away and ran his thumb over her hard nipple. Blair cursed and Lorkan smiled through their kiss.

He dropped his hand to her wool trousers and fumbled with the buttons. "Tell me to stop."

"No." Blair's hand grasped his wrist, urging her his hand down.

Lorkan's fingers dipped past her undergarments, and he found Blair slick and ready, his wolf growling with hunger.

He kissed her jawline as his fingers explored for her pleasure, and unlike the fumbling touch of a seventeen-year-old boy, his fingers were deliberate, methodical, drawing slow, tentative circles.

He increased his speed as he studied Blair beneath him, listening, feeling, watching her unravel as he worked her. This was for her as much as it was for him, and if he could paint a portrait of her like this—parted lips, flushed cheeks, and molten stare—he'd hang the art above his fireplace.

"Don't stop," she whispered. "I'm . . ."

Lorkan did. He removed his fingers from her clit, and Blair whimpered with protest, but it was cut short as he plunged two fingers into her ready sex.

She cried out, and the sound outmatched all his fantasies. Lorkan pumped his fingers inside her as his thumb found her clit again, and he pressed.

Blair dipped her head back, granting him access to her neck. Lorkan accepted her invitation. He trailed kisses across her collarbone, up her neck, and right over the vein that pulsed. Hunger of a different sort reared to life, but

Lorkan was so drunk off Blair's mounting pleasure, he ignored it. Her sex squeezed his fingers, and the sight of her shattering was almost his undoing.

She screamed out, and as she slumped into his arm, Lorkan rested his forehead against her shoulder. He smiled, triumphant, but he lost all sense and reason. Her racing heart echoed beneath him and reached his baser instinct. A red haze of hunger flashed across his eyelids. The curse reared to life, his wolf snuffed by insatiable hunger for one thing, and one thing only.

Blood.

His fangs ached, and Lorkan palmed his hand against the bookshelf to keep steady. No, this couldn't be happening. Not with *her*, the woman he loved. Lorkan fought for control, but it was like reaching for a rope coated in oil. It slipped from his grasp, and his mind only registered blood rushing through Blair's veins and his need to feed—

"*Lorkan,*" Alvin's voice hissed from behind.

Blair and Lorkan sprang apart. Hair amiss and panting, there was no hiding what they'd done, and embarrassment bloomed across Blair's cheeks.

"I should leave," she whispered.

Lorkan tremored, gritting his teeth, and fought with all his might not to reach out to her and unravel the scant bit of control he'd found. Blair discovering he was a vampyr was one thing, but *hurting* her was an entirely different horror Lorkan couldn't live with.

He didn't object to her retreat, letting her walk away. Blair gathered a few books, and rushed out of his office. Lorkan released a sigh of relief as the door clicked shut. In the absence of her racing heart, silence rang in his office, and he blinked away the haze of hunger.

"You nearly bit her," his friend whispered.

Lorkan seethed, but there was no denying it. His fangs pierced his bottom lip. He hadn't been prepared for how the scent of her need had heightened his hunger, and the whole study thickened with the promise of a rainstorm. And now he felt wretched. The curse had almost driven him to feed from the woman he loved.

"You're the one who told me to tell her what I am." Heat flushed across Lorkan's skin, and he abandoned his spot and reached for the decanter of whiskey near the fire place. His fangs and manhood ached as he poured himself a glass, and the first sip of liquor added more pain as it burned down his throat.

"Did you or was your plan to explain *after* your fangs sank into her neck?" Alvin snatched the bottle of whiskey from his hand.

Lorkan growled. "Watch yourself."

Alvin poured himself a glass and chuckled. "Look who's talking. If Blair is what I suspect, you know feeding goes hand in hand with that sort of territory. We've seen it in our own pack. It is inevitable."

Cold washed over Lorkan, and he stared into the dying fire, its dwindling embers a reflection of his hope to have anything with Blair. Alvin was right. Vampyr mates fed from one another, and Lorkan's insatiable need to feed from Blair wasn't the first sign that she was his mate. He'd known because of the thread that had formed long before he turned into a vampyr. Blair was the first thought he had every morning and the last before he fell asleep. Lorkan suspected Blair knew what they were to each other, too, but that didn't ease his worry.

Lorkan was still a vampyr, and starting down this path shackled her to the curse alongside him.

"She'll never accept it." Lorkan downed the rest of his drink, reaching for another.

Alvin relented, filling his glass. "For someone who has dedicated their life around research, you state an adamant claim with no facts to back it."

Lorkan shook his head, an animalistic hiss wheezing through his gritted teeth. "You don't know Blair. Vampyrs killed her parents. I abandoned her because of what I turned into it. Her sister is destined to defeat the curse running through my veins. She has plenty of reason to reject me."

"I think the witch might surprise you."

"What proof do you have to support that statement?" Lorkan asked.

Alvin snorted. "Pure observation. Not of Blair, but of *you*. How can you trust anyone will accept you're a vampyr, Lorkan, if you haven't accepted it yourself?"

Lorkan's hold on his glass threatened to shatter the material. He set it down on the mantel, flexing his hands at his sides. His inner wolf paced, ruffled by the truth of Alvin's words. Damn his friend for being right. *Again*. Perhaps he was so used to hiding what he was from others, he'd hidden from himself, too. Lorkan stared down at the whiskey decanter, but there wasn't enough drink to drown out that sad realization. He sighed, his reeling thoughts too much to sort out. He had to either come clean to Blair or walk away, and both prospects rooted him to the stone floor, chilling him to the bone.

"Why did you come to my office in the first place?" he asked, changing to subject.

The painting to the right of the fireplace was slightly ajar, and a cold draft escaped from the shadows. The hidden door led to the tunnels that reached deep under Vísdómr where their pack lived, out of sight from others and protected from the sun.

"I actually came with good news," Alvin said.

Lorkan pushed Blair to the back of his mind and centered his focus elsewhere.

"What is it?" he asked.

CHAPTER SIXTY-THREE

THE NEXT MORNING, THE sun shine high in a cloudless sky. Songbirds darted across the blue backdrop, and the pines, their green color no longer muted by frost, swayed in the breeze. A whisper lay in the air, as if the lands sang their approval for Eldrick and Tovi's evening together.

The wolf and dove.

Though, the Drabek Village didn't mirror the crisp, bright morning.

A few sleeping werewolves hadn't made it to their beds. Bent over with their faces planted against wooden tables, they'd fallen asleep with their festival wine in hand.

He weaved through fallen petals, abandoned streamers and lost flower crowns. Not a single establishment had their doors open, and not a chimney billowed with smoke. He found the sleepy village almost peaceful.

Eldrick had left Tovi, begrudgingly, to clean and wash for the day, with plans to meet at the training grounds before the mid-morning feast.

His own room sat waiting at the *first* Sheild-maiden, but as he entered through the main door, his inner wolf's hackles rose. *Something* lay in the air, and it wasn't the stench of ale or the sweaty patrons snoring at the tables.

Eldrick sprinted up the stairs to the hallway of guest rooms and halted at the top.

At the end, Bétar, Yennifer, and Siv were huddled by his door—no, around someone. Siv sniffled, mumbling someone's name. Eldrick quickened his gate, boots thudding against the walls, and the Gray Fenris commander caught sight of him.

"Eldrick," he whispered.

Bétar turned, and Eldrick recognized the unmoving figure slumped at his door.

"Sam—"

Bétar grasped Eldrick's shoulder and held him back from the horrific sight before him. If it weren't for Sam's hair, he'd have not guessed by his face. Both eyes were swollen shut, purple and bulbous. Blood streamed down his crooked nose, running into the rivets leaking from his split lip.

Eldrick blinked, anger and worry warring within him. He tried to detect a heartbeat, tried to listen for signs—

"Is he alive?"

Siv nodded, adamantly. "Yes, but we need to move him."

"He was left here," Yennifer said, words thick.

Eldrick shook his head. "Outside my door . . ." He trailed off, noticing for the first time the makeshift sign hanging from Sam's neck like some necklace.

BANISHED one side read. Eldrick dropped to his haunches and flipped it over. HE'S ALL YOURS, DRENGR the other side read.

"Moons," Bétar hissed.

"He was punished because of me," Eldrick whispered. "Bjorn did this—"

"It doesn't matter," Siv hissed. "Sam requires a healer, *now*."

Eldrick sighed. "You're right. Bétar?"

"Aye," his friend nodded.

"We'll carry him," Eldrick said. "And you lead the way Siv."

The female werewolf fought tears. "Alright."

Together, Bétar and Eldrick lifted Sam. Eldrick held his shoulders, keeping his head steady, while Bétar grasped his legs. Sam moaned in their arms, and the two werewolves were careful with his bruised and beaten body.

Back in the village, the too-bright sun blinded Eldrick. The several werewolves now awake stopped and stared as he and Bétar rushed after Siv, Yen at their back. The Drabek werewolf pushed through double doors of the village's infirmary, calling out commands to the healers on duty.

Eldrick and Bétar lay Sam on an empty cot, and Eldrick's inner wolf growled at the sight of his beaten face again. He inhaled, detecting more than one scent on the young wolf.

"Bjorn *and* Dalinda did this," he snarled. "His own father and sister."

Healers huddled around Sam, pushing Eldrick and his friends back. Siv tunned them all out, bringing up a stool and grasping Sam's hand.

"But why?" Yennifer whispered. "Why would they banish Sam?"

Each werewolf in the vicinity stiffened. Banishment, though a rare practice in the last century, was the ultimate punishment, a horrendous sentence to any werewolf. It meant they were officially removed from their pack by their alpha.

It was exile for Sam, meaning he couldn't return to Johannes lands.

Eldrick's stomach backflipped. He'd offered to let Sam join the Drengr Pack, but he'd never intended it to be under these circumstances. He'd hoped it'd be the young werewolf's choice, not forced upon him.

"There you are," Tovi said, breathless. Her gaze fleeted over Sam and Siv, then back to Eldrick. "I heard whispers in the village and came as quick as I could."

Eldrick swallowed, suddenly needing her presence like an anchor in this harrowing turn of events. He assessed Sam again as the healers who applied a cooling ointment to his swollen eyes. Another readied twine a needle for the gash running through his brow, another injury Eldrick hadn't accounted for.

He fisted his hands at his sides, knuckles popping.

"Look at me." Tovi grabbed Eldrick's hand. "This isn't your fault."

"But it is. Sam warned me about his father. He told me to travel south," Eldrick said.

"Bjorn must've figured out his son tipped you off," Bétar sighed. "But Tovi is right. Sam's father did this, not you."

"The other alphas deserve to know," Yennifer said.

"What if they already do?" Eldrick asked. "I spotted Sam's bruises the moment I met him. They can't be that oblivious."

Tovi shook her head. "Yet, they'll still vote for him?"

Eldrick's jaw ticked. "They're afraid of him."

"They should be more afraid if he becomes Earl," Siv said, peering up at them all. "If this is what he will do to his own son, the Johannes Magu, I'd hate to think of his wrath against anyone who defies him."

"What will you do?" Tovi asked.

Eldrick debated, the same question of late tumbling through him: what sort of leader did *he* want to be?

"I refuse to be afraid. I'll confront Bjorn." He searched Tovi's face. "I need to do this—"

"Alone." She nodded. "I know."

Because though they'd decided to try and make this work between them, they weren't Evelyn and Kade. They couldn't waltz into a room together, hand in hand. At least, not until Eldrick secured the Earl vote, and that was still a strong, unknown *maybe*.

He inhaled and stormed out of the infirmary, swallowing the bile of leaving the woman he loved behind and wishing they could face this together. But he'd not let Bjorn's cruelty remain in the dark any longer.

Eldrick pushed both twelve-foot doors open into the Drabek's longhouse. The remaining festival cheer continued as hungover werewolves piled food atop their plates, drank herb-infused drinks, and reminisced on the previous evening's affairs.

At the center, Bjorn roared with laughter with Alpha Skau at his side. Dalinda was nowhere in sight. Eldrick didn't care, he marched straight for Alpha Johannes. Werewolves took notice, conversation lulling to a murmur.

Bjorn's attention snapped to Eldrick, and he smirked, eyes glinting with amusement.

"I see you got my gift." Bjorn snickered, *laughed* about beating Sam and dumping him outside Eldrick's door.

Blood still stained the bastard's knuckles, and Eldrick's control snapped.

He slammed his fist onto the table and whirled to face the hall. "Is this the Earl you all wish to lead the Vadon Mountains?" Eldrick shouted.

Conversation quieted, and ahead, the Drabek Alphas paused their hushed conversation in their alpha chairs. Alland and Lindström pushed off the wall where they stood, falling deeper into the crowd.

"Werewolves need a true leader to help face the battle to come," Eldrick said. "Yet, the male you all consider is nothing but a bully."

Skau sneered while Bjorn chuckled. He pushed out of his chair, the legs scraping against the stone and cutting through the rest of the conversations.

"I suppose you're a better fit, pup?" Bjorn said. "Will your mother join you on the battlefield so you can suck from her tit in between foes? You're far too young, too naïve to lead packs that have run these mountains for centuries."

"You are right about one thing, Alpha Bjorn," Eldrick said. "I am young, but I'm not hardened by ego and prejudice like you. I ask, alphas, what sort of leader is it that you want? A bully who beats his own son into submission? Banishes him when his efforts didn't work?"

The hall bristled with tension, shocked murmurs snaking down the tables. Eldrick's heart hammered inside his chest. Never had he felt so centered, so certain in his conviction.

"That is Johannes business. How I discipline my pack members is of no concern to you."

Eldrick snorted. "Only a coward hides his actions. It matters more what one does when no one is watching. *That* is a true testament of your character."

He turned back to the werewolves in the hall, making sure to find the other alphas, too.

"If Bjorn leaves bruises on his own flesh and blood, how do you think he'll treat the rest of us?" Eldrick asked. "I'll admit one thing, the Johannes Pack produces formidable warriors, some of the best in the Vadon Mountains, but Bjorn leads with hate. He thrives off malice and power. Elect Bjorn as Earl of our homeland, and you will not only doom us all to lose the war ahead, but ruin werewolf history."

"What are you suggesting?" Alpha Drabek descended the dais from her chair.

The hall parted, letting her pass. Lindström and Alland followed suit, and Leif moved into position behind Eldrick, giving him a swift, approving node. All six alphas stood near, and Eldrick's wolfish blood sang, and the Vadon Mountains answered in a steady chorus.

Yes. Yes. Yes.

"I say we cast the Earl vote now," Eldrick said. "Why waste time when our people need a leader?"

Bjorn's laugh grew uneasy as a hundred eyes fell to him. "The decree—"

"Never explicitly set a date for the vote," Leif said. "It was simply part of the discussion."

Bjorn growled and pointed his meaty finger at Eldrick. "Is this truly who you all wish to vote for?"

"By all means, Bjorn," Ragna said, "state your case if it is your name we should consider instead. We're all here."

Bjorn chucked off his cloak and unclasped his breastplate. "I'll not waste words when I can simply show you."

The centuries-old alpha leaped across the table and shifted. Eldrick braced just in time as a pure muscle of wolf form barreled into him. He and Bjorn tumbled, he still in his male form, and Bjorn's beastly claws digging into his wool tunic.

An alpha-on-alpha brawl hadn't taken place in centuries, but an embedded custom rippled through the hall. A respect for their one-on-one fight was ingrained in the magic of the werewolves' inner beasts. As Eldrick and Bjorn wrestled, bumped against table and chairs and circled the other, those gathered gave them a wide berth and created a makeshift ring at the center of the Drabek Hall.

Bjorn snarled, dark, angry eyes focused solely on Eldrick. The hundreds of werewolves disappeared from Eldrick's peripherals. He bared his teeth, facing off against his opponent full of ire.

Weeks' worth of turmoil thanks to Bjorn brought them to a brawl. Eldrick unsheathed his axe. Adrenaline buzzed through him, his axe's shaft molding to his hand as he gripped it tighter, squatting lower into a defensive stance.

Waiting. Anticipating. Tasting the air for Bjorn's next move.

The alpha launched. Eldrick braced, holding his axe at both ends out horizontally. As Bjorn pushed him to the ground and snapped his teeth, Eldrick shoved his axe into the alpha's mouth, driving it between his teeth.

Bjorn growled, but it came out more like a huff, fanning Eldrick in his reeking breath. He shook his head, struggling to break free of Eldrick's axe. But Eldrick's grip wouldn't loosen on the right side, and if his opponent swiveled left, he risked the bladed end slicing through his lips.

Pain pierced Eldrick's side, and he yanked himself free. He kicked Bjorn and scrambled back, clutching his side. Eldrick peeked down, he caught blood soaking his hands. Claw marks ran across his ribs. As Bjorn circled him, a single paw left a bloody print.

Eldrick set his shoulders back and tremored head to feet. He called upon his inner wolf and grasped the magic to shift into his beastly form. Bone stretched, muscle tore. His skin sprouted hair and then a thick coat of brown fur. His shins elongated and his thighs widened. Eldrick grew taller. Stronger. More at one with magic and wolf than ever before.

He held onto his axe, standing on his hind legs, and attacked.

Bjorn roared, rising on his hind legs too. He used his claws as a blade, blocking Eldrick's blows, forearm against forearm. Frustration leaked from the alpha. He was larger, stronger by many years, but Eldrick was swift. Despite his looming weight, a foot-taller than Bjorn, he moved with ease.

Eldrick fought with every fiber of his being and heart. His hits and jabs at Bjorn did not reflect hate, but instead were full of hope, purpose, and promise.

The fight no longer belonged to Eldrick. His brawl against Bjorn was for the Vadon Mountains. The packs. And a future he so desperately wished for. Envisioning his goal with each blow of his axe and swipe of his claw, Eldrick stepped forward, herding Bjorn back into the crowd. He inhaled the promise of his homeland free of the Blood Curse, Sorin finally at peace. Witches, werewolves, and vampyrs all thriving.

He thought of the four seasons in the Vadon Mountains. Experiencing his first Drystan summer with his love. Witnessing his future littles running through the halls of Lār, readying to play in the snow.

With that, he ducked and averted one of Bjorn's blows, thrusting a punch straight into the alpha's gut. Power—from the lands, gods, his wolf, Eldrick wasn't certain—embedded into the jab. It rocked Bjorn back so harshly the alpha shifted from his beast form to his male form, falling to the stone.

A deafening silence leached through the hall, and wolfish energy stood to attention as Eldrick shifted to his male form, striding towards Bjorn.

Eldrick held his blade at Bjorn's throat, halting him from rising. He'd beat him, for all the alphas to see.

"Be done with it." Bjorn didn't meet his stare, lethally still with rage.

Opportunity presented itself to Eldrick. He'd drawn his weapon's blade across another male's throat before. Shoved poison done another's. But his heart begged him to ask another question.

What sort of leader was he?

Eldrick sheathed his axe. "I'm not like you, Bjorn. I won't cut another while they're down."

Eldrick swallowed his triumph, and amid the crowd, Tovi stood with Bétar and Yennifer, a slight smile playing on her perfect rosy lips. Eldrick tore his gaze away from the most beautiful woman in the room, and assessed the other alphas. He cleared his throat, heart thudding in his chest.

"Alpha Thorn, what is your vote?" Eldrick asked

"Drengr," his newfound friend Leif said without hesitation.

"Alpha Drabek?" he asked next.

His aunt nodded, a prideful smile reaching her eyes. "Drengr."

"Yours?"

Skau spat at Eldrick's feet. "Johannes."

Eldrick cracked his neck, at least admiring Skau's loyalty. He dropped his attention to Lindström and Alland next. Both alphas voted the Drengr name.

"I vouch for my own name," he declared to the hall.

Eldrick turned to the last alpha and outstretched his hand, offering to help the alpha stand.

Bjorn swatted it out the way with snarl and rose. "Fuck off."

"Do you care to vote?" Eldrick asked.

The alpha rose. "I cast my own name, Johannes."

Eldrick nodded and swallowed. "Let it be known, the vote tallies at five for the Drengrs and two for Johannes. The Drengrs reinstate their claim to the Earl vote."

Cheers erupted. Bétar hollered Eldrick's name.

Alpha Bjorn bumped his shoulder and whispered into his ear, "You will regret sparing my life. Mark my words, pup, I'll never answer to you as Earl."

"So be it, Bjorn," Eldrick whispered. "Damn the Johannes for all I care, the other alphas will answer to me."

Bjorn sneered as he retreated out of the hall. "We'll shall see. There is still a ceremony to be had, pup."

Eldrick let the male walk away, refusing to let him rile him or his wolf any longer. He had won the Earl vote. Across the way, the woman he loved stared with arms crossed, sword strapped to her back, and a wine cup in hand. She lifted it, saluting him.

Leif gripped his shoulder, giving it a fierce shake. Bétar approached, smile wide, and—

"Stars above, are you crying, Commander?" he asked.

"Aye." Bétar rested his hands on Eldrick's shoulders. "It is a wonderful thing to be proud of one's friend, *Earl*."

Eldrick grimaced. "For the love of moons, please don't call me that."

Leif chuckled. "You'll have to get used to it. *After* the ascension of course."

"Right," Eldrick said. "Soon enough."

Thunder rumbled in the distance as a snowstorm prepared on the horizon. Cold crept up Eldrick's back. Like a tug he couldn't avoid, his attention found Tovi in the crowd again, the cheers and congratulations drowning out. Despite everything falling seemingly into place, Eldrick wasn't sure he'd ever get use to the title he'd earned.

PART III

After a storm between mistaken enemies,
the wolf and dove,
the clash of the light and night,
those of these lands will unite.

A sowing of seeds, a journey to the beneath where
life and death meet. A king and queen will emerge,
with the seeds sown from elsewhere, life to rid the shade
and make way for the Prince to
walk with Light.

CHAPTER SIXTY-FOUR

EVELYN

E VELYN GASPED UPRIGHT, LUNGS burning. Death still ached through
her body as new life and magic thrummed through it, jolting her stiff
limbs. She coughed, her throat brittle as she blinked her eyes back into focus.

A sense of wrongness gripped Evelyn's bones, like the ancient power she'd
placed into her soul was stitched too tightly, bursting at the seams.

"Kade! Evelyn!" Linx's said, tone echoing in the cave. "Can you hear me?"

Small, gentle hands lay on Evelyn's shoulders, and Belle's beautiful face
sharpened in the dim light of the Sun Goddess's temple. Sweat, dust, and the
remnants of spell work hung in the air.

"You did it," Belle said. "I can sense your magic!"

Tiredness ringed Belle's eyes, her hair a bit dimmer than the last time
Evelyn remembered her—why did she care?

She didn't. Ambivalence shot through Evelyn so violently, it was like a
harsh lashing. She fell into the sting, not bothered by it but almost . . . *liking*
it.

Besides, Evelyn had done it. She'd made it back to the Living Lands.

Ev.

She whirled, heart thudding inside her chest. Righting himself, Kade rose
to his looming height. Her heart burst at the sight of him—she stilled, rooting
to the sandy floor.

It was more evident back in their realm that Kade Drengr was no longer
the son of a god but remade into one himself. Power brimmed off him in the
light of the moon, etched into his sharper-honed muscles and keener, brighter
eyes.

A transcendental energy clung to him. Blue embers flew around Kade's frame, barely visible at all. Yet, his soul remained the same, bursting with kindness, loyalty, and love for Evelyn that spanned between worlds and realms.

Evelyn stood on steady legs, pushing Belle off to the side. She, too, rose taller, sharper than before. It wasn't only her ailing soul that was now restored. A newfound strength rippled through her as she grew used to her new body and magic. It was fiercer, not singing through her blood but chanting with the power of a thousand. It practically roared for her to draw it forth to her fingertips and wield it.

Evelyn fisted her hand, drawing back its eagerness. She sucked in a breath, equally shocked at how well it answered her and unnerved by its mightiness.

She snapped her gaze up—there'd be plenty of time to explore the magic she'd created in the Otherworld. Right now, all Evelyn cared for was to breathe the air of Sorin and reunite with her fated.

Kade, she whispered his name through their mating link.

In two long strides, they met each other halfway and grasped hands. Kade leaned his forehead against hers, and Evelyn clamped her eyes shut, relishing in the fact they made it home.

Together. Partners. *Always.*

"I'm so proud of you, love," Kade whispered.

Evelyn squeezed his hand, running her thumb over it. His power didn't greet her magic, nor his inner wolf, but the thread of their mating bond connected their souls again, begging for them to complete the bond and draw it tauter with their weaved powers.

A ravenous hunger lit in the pit of Evelyn's belly. She inhaled Kade's scent, and *fucking flames*, he smelled divine—

"Who are *you*?" Linx asked.

"Oh my word, Evelyn," Belle whispered. "Did you bring a soul back to life?"

A small, tentative sniffle quipped from behind, and naked as a newborn babe, Aster sat on bent knees, brushing tears away from her russet eyes. "Where am I? *Who* am I?"

"Moons," Kade hissed.

He pulled his hands out of Evelyn's grasp and grabbed his abandoned cloak. He wrapped Aster's small trembling frame in it, and Evelyn pressed her nails into her fleshy palms, using the pain to stall the scorching heat of jealousy flushing through her.

That . . . was uncalled. *Irrational.* This was Aster and Kade, and above all else, *they'd made it back home.*

Evelyn exhaled, sauntering over to Aster and falling to her haunches. Her wide eyes wildly roamed the cave, seemingly unsure which of them to rest her sights on. As Evelyn reached out a hand to comfort her, Aster recoiled.

"It's me, Evelyn," she whispered. "I brought you back."

Tears ran down her friend's face, and Evelyn reached her magic out, trying to greet Aster's gently, but she met nothing. A hollowness spread through her, the hair on the back of her neck standing up. Aster had no magic, no earth bronntanas.

"I don't know who you are," Aster whispered. "I don't know any of you. Why am I here? Where did I come from?"

Evelyn clutched her stomach, trying to fight the bile working its way up her throat.

"Does someone want to explain who this is?" Todd asked, standing back from them all while keeping an eye on the temple's entrance.

"Aster Arkwood." Kade busied himself with retrieving a decanter of water from their supplies, handing it to the frightened witch. Wait—could Evelyn call her that if Aster no longer had magic?

"As . . . ter . . . Ark . . . *wood*?" she annunciated her name.

Evelyn nodded. "Yes. You're from Callum, remember? You own Pages and Leaves, a plant and bookstore, because they're good company for one another."

Aster's ginger brows pinched, and she frowned. "Did I ask for this? I don't remember wanting this. Why am I here?"

"I brought you back to life," Evelyn whispered, heart cracking. "I gave you a second chance."

Linx cursed under her breath, reaching for clothes inside her travel sack. "Did you not think this through, Evelyn? Did you not consider reviving a soul would have ramifications?"

Evelyn gritted her teeth. "She didn't deserve to die in the first place. I was righting a wrong."

Linx tsked, pink buns bleeding into red as anger etched her expressions. "That isn't your call to make. There is a balance to things, Evelyn."

What a fool, Evelyn thought. *Silly, naïve mage.* "Fate is in our hands," she said, leaving her stare on the Gray Fenris healer. "The gods are liars."

A laugh boomed inside the temple. The stone bones trembled, and dust puffed from the cracks. Kade gathered Evelyn in his arms, and their team braced against the quaking earth.

"Did you truly think, Evelyn, that you could steal from a god and not pay a consequence?" The Sun Goddess's voice traveled here, everywhere and nowhere.

Evelyn couldn't differentiate if it filtered through her mind or directly in the temple. The shrillness. The way the goddess's voice *boomed*. Familiar.

"You have forgotten your place in this world, Miss Carson," the Goddess said. "Allow me to remind you. You stole a soul from me, and it is only fair I take from you."

"What—*no!*" Evelyn screamed.

But it was too late.

Like the Sun Goddess had snapped her fingers, a clap echoed in the temple.

A growl vibrated behind her, and Evelyn expected to find Kade buckling to his knees, but it was Todd, rushing towards Belle.

The water witch's eyes rolled backward, and she collapsed. Limp, almost lifeless. Todd caught her in his arms, calling out her name.

"Belle, wake up. Come on now, listen to my voice. *Wake up,*" he said.

Evelyn tuned into her enhanced hearing. Her friend's heart still thumped, slower, but . . . *there*. She was still alive. *Barely.*

"What have you done?" Linx whispered, stare jumping between Evelyn and Belle.

A friend for a friend.

It wasn't the Sun Goddess's voice hissing in the back of Evelyn's mind but her own. She'd traded kindness for kindness. Two witches who'd aided her during times of darkness. Two beautiful souls, and she'd brought one back only to lose another. The blatant show of balance rocked through Evelyn. She reached for remorse but found . . . *nothing*.

The Sun Goddess's echoing chuckle reached Evelyn's mind this time. The others didn't notice, didn't flinch as she whispered, "You'll soon experience the rest of your mistake. You're more my daughter than you've ever been."

An audible crack shot across the temple's ceiling. Rock came lose and crashed to the temple's floor.

"We need to get out of here. *Now,*" Kade said, his tone rattling with authority.

Evelyn took hold of Aster's hand, tugging her along as rocks showered from above. She jumped back as one landed a few feet ahead. Another rattled above. Evelyn braced, drawing Aster under her, but nothing came. She blinked, finding blue embers showering above her, the rock gone.

Kade gathered Aster in his arms, carrying her like she weighed nothing. "Run, Ev."

She didn't protest and used Linx's brightly colored hair to find her way through the fray of falling rock and shifting ground. She kept hold of the mating bond, certain Kade continued to follow close behind her.

Outside, the ground still shook, the entire canyon echoing with the temple's destruction. Yet, none of them slowed. They ran across the dried-out river, not daring to stop for a breathe as the Sun Goddess's anger rippled beyond Cirrillo.

As they grew farther and farther away, a deafening screech pierced their ears, and Evelyn stumbled, staring back at the temple. A dozen *nathracha* demons burst from its entrance.

Kade roared. A power that outmatched the Sun Goddess prickled in the dry air. He slammed a fist into the sands, still clutching Aster's form in his other arm.

A thousand fractures in the rocks echoed in the canyon. A *whoosh* of wind traveled down it, whipping Evelyn's hair back and knocking Linx and Todd off balance. Evelyn stood her ground, relishing in the power Kade wielded.

He pulsed with acceptance, but perhaps not yet control.

A tidal wave of his power, like the magnetic yank of the moon above the sea, pushed forward. Blue collided into the adjacent canyon, and the rock burst on impact.

The ancient structure lost integrity and crumbled under Kade's sheer strength. Blue swelled far beyond the cliffs, eroding the terra-cotta for miles and miles.

After a beat, blue surged back into him. Kade's efforts left behind a wasteland, the temple buried under sand.

Evelyn released a pent-up breath, and Kade's wide, surprised gaze snapped to hers. His mouth lay in a thin line, his amber stare ripe with something close to apprehension. Was it towards her or the power he'd finally accepted?

Evelyn pondered his expression for the rest of the climb up the cliff's stairs. There was no flighty sense flushing in her pit. No anxiety. No *doubt*. In fact, nothing but hollowness spread inside her.

You're more my daughter than you've ever been.

The Sun Goddess's parting words nipped at Evelyn's heels. She climbed two stairs at a time as they reached the canyon's edge, leading up the rolling sands and dunes. Evelyn crested the last step and the horizon bled with dusk, magenta lining the dunes in a pinky glow.

Kade made it over the edge last, and he placed Aster beside her.

He turned his attention solely to Evelyn, laying a hand on her cheek. "We made it. That is all that matters right now."

Evelyn tried to find comfort in Kade's words, hope, resolve, *something* that felt remotely like herself. Flame ignited in her soul, the piece she'd plucked from the Sun Goddess.

Stole, she corrected.

The reminder tugged her gaze to Belle, but she couldn't stomach her kind, sweet friend's unconscious form and Todd's ravaged stare as he combed her hair back tenderly.

Despite the emptiness inside, Evelyn's being buzzed with one question: What had she been reborn into?

Chapter Sixty-Five

Blair

B LAIR SPRANG AWAKE, HER breath pluming in the cold air.

Her shadows hovered over her bed, and the howling wind beat against the glass of her visiting-scholar dormitory. Something lay in the air, not just at Vísdómr, but all across Sorin.

Rook landed at her feet and nibbled her toes.

Blair hissed, shooing him away with her hand. "Did you forget your beak is sharp?"

Rook ruffled his feathers and avoided her gaze as if the reminder was an insult.

Blair checked the time on the enchanted clock above the door. Embers glowed in the small hearth, the warmth lingering. She yawned, rubbing tiredness from her eyes. Blair had only slept a few hours, restless and agitated. The book she'd read before falling asleep still remained on her lap.

Rook cawed, bouncing foot to foot by the door. He flapped his wings and pecked at the lock in mid-flight, demanding for Blair to open it.

"Blasted books."

Cold and tired, Blair obliged her familiar and eased the door open. Rook shot free of the room, but remained a few feet down the hall, tilting his head at her. The wind continued to howl, no sing, and Blair paused. A name hovered on the wind.

B...l...air.

Not any name, *her* name.

Blair, follow my voice.

It was the whisper of a female. Gentle but stern.

Blair blinked, shaking her head. *No.* She was still asleep. This was a bizarre dream. Why would someone call her name on the wind? Who? *What?*

Hurry, the voice sang.

Its power reached out and caressed against Blair's soul. Like understood like. Storm, shadow and winds. All of it cooled in the air. Ice crawled across her window. The fire in the hearth froze over. Blair's skin tightened as cold prowled through the dormitory.

Rook flew down the hall and landed, waiting. Expectant.

Do you want to learn what you are?

Like a bucket of ice had been dumped over Blair's head, she stilled, the question chilling her to the bone. *Yes, yes, yes*—the darkness slithering in her veins sang with the wind.

Rook gave Blair one last look and took flight. His black feather wings grew distant, and Blair didn't think any longer, she darted out of her room and raced after her familiar.

Left, right, down and down. Blair paused to catch her breath only for Rook to shoot down a hall she'd yet to explore.

She cursed through clenched teeth and turned. The bookshelves loomed over her, titles peering down with disappointment as her bare feet slapped against the stone and disturbed the quiet hour.

Ahead, Rook sat atop a werewolf's paw carved from marble. The heel pressed against a row of books, its twin at the other end. As Blair reached Rook, he flew from the statue with enough force to knock the appendage back. A click sounded, and the bookshelf—no, hidden door—swung open and revealed a dark corridor leading beyond.

Rook purred, pressing his head against Blair's jaw.

Follow my voice.

It came from all angles, and yet Blair's familiar flew through the dark corridor. Despite every instinct screaming for her to not, Blair followed. She snapped her fingers, and in the confines of darkness, she drew out her gray shadows which provided a bit of light to the darkness. Like a spiraling tower, the corridor tunneled downward, and the temperature grew colder and colder.

At the edge, Blair encountered the most peculiar area: a well set up reading nook. Leather chair, red rug, oiled lamp, and a wool blanket, threads snagged from use. A stack of books lay on the floor, the first bursting open as a breeze caught hold of the cover.

Blair.

Rook darted through a crack in the wall, and as Blair wedged herself through, night and forest greeted. The winds welcomed her, pushing her in the direction of Rook flying into the forest.

"What . . ." Curiosity warred with caution, but Blair grasped the first and ran through meadow and dashed into the trees.

"Rook," she hissed.

He descended from the canopy and dove east, staying only a few feet ahead. Moonlight kissed the tips of his onyx feathers, a shimmering beacon as Blair grew further into the forest and then landed on a lone tree. White trunk, red leaves, crooked branches. It didn't belong in the Vadon Mountain, not with the oaks, pines, and redwoods. It was of a different time and place.

Light from the canopy cast a spotlight on it, shimmering the well of water pooling at its circling roots.

A strikingly beautiful female with a sharp hawklike nose, hair twisted into a studious bun, coal smudged around her eyes, and red-stained lips stood with arms folded, deep-blue eyes expectant. She wore black trousers, and a collared shirt—she could easily pass as a scholar in the Nūa Library if it weren't for the unfitting accessory strapped to her back.

A sword with three moons lining the hilt.

"You're the Blood Goddess," Blair whispered, stepping back.

That is not my name.

The female didn't move her lips. Instead, the winds carried her voice. Calm, at ease, so unlike the accounts of the Blood Goddess, but she possessed the sword from the illustration Lorkan and Blair had found. The three-moon symbol sneered at her, and a question lay on her lips—

The woman shifted, moving like mist hovering over the forest ground. She wasn't physically there, but a transparent figure spun between realms.

Wait. Blair gasped and rocked backward. *No,* she might've said out loud.

Shadows wavered in the air—the same gray tendrils Blair conjured with her magic. They awakened beneath her skin, snaking with familiarity. In the midnight air, likeness caressed likeness. It was different from witches' magics greeting one another, but power of the same power saying hello to a long-lost friend.

Blair rooted to the forest floor as rigid as the pines around her.

"I don't understand," she breathed, driving her fingernails into her palms, wishing the sting woke her from this bizarre dream. "How is that possible? What am I? If—"

There is no time for me to explain—your sister's rebellion against the gods has allowed me a mere moment to speak with you.

"But if you're not the Blood Goddess, who are you? How can I trust you?" Blair rushed.

The woman stepped closer, her stare hard and unbending. *You won't, which is why you must witness the truth for yourself. Crack open the blood of my fallen brothers and sisters, and witness a memory.*

"I don't want a damn memory!" Blair charged but tripped straight into the woman's shadowy figure. Desperation clung to her skin like the cold particles that drenched her oversize tunic. "I want to know what I am!"

A bloodstone will lead you to the truth. Then find me, Blair Carson. I will give you the answers you seek.

Branches creaked. Thunder rumbled north, and the winds shifted. Magic bristled under Blair's feet, and layers of earth shook with it. The rest of the trees leaned with the winds, and as they straightened, the air stilled once again.

The mysterious female vanished, leaving her alone in the forest.

"No," Blair whispered, chest tightening. She spun in a circle, the forest closing in around her.

She ran.

Blair chased after nothing. She'd tugged at her curiosity, a lifelong unfed need for Blair to understand these shadows swimming in her veins. Like a moth to flame, she'd rushed out of Vísdómr, only to be fed riddles and false hope. Her shadows leaked from her fingertips and snaked around her ankles.

They might as well have been shackles.

"Tell me what I am!" Blair screamed.

Yet, Blair's demands were swallowed by the angry winds. Something icy-hot shot through her veins. Was it adrenaline or desperation? Trees twisted with the whipping winds. Voices traveled closer to Vísdómr, and false hope urged her legs to move.

Midnight hair she recognized in an instant snagged her attention, and Blair darted behind a tree. She called upon her bronntanas, using her winds to conceal the sounds she made and her scent.

Lorkan, chest bare and gleaming in the moonlight, continued to pluck blossoms from a tree, unaware she watched. Why in the Goddess was he out at this hour? What sort of tree was that? Blair hadn't studied botany during her time as a scholar, so her mind came up blank. *Not* because of the sight of Lorkan, shirtless, chest, arms, and abdominal muscles straining under his pale skin as he worked.

She'd not crossed paths with him since he'd riddled her senseless in his office. Blair had wondered if he was avoiding her, but in truth, she'd been avoiding him, riddled with uncertainty on what they were and terrified of the path she'd started down.

The trees beside Lorkan rustled, and his friend, Alvin, emerged. He held a basket filled with blossoms, and Alvin's smile reached his glacier eyes. Blair studied his attire. Cloak, traveling leathers, hair braided like a werewolf warrior. Alvin wasn't a scholar, or at least, didn't appear to be one.

"You must admit this was an excellent find," he said.

Lorkan grunted his agreement. His glasses were absent, giving Blair an uninterrupted view of his pinched brow and concentrated gaze. He handled the blossoms with deliberate care as he lay them between the fabric of a handkerchief.

Blair pressed flush against the tree she hid behind, mind reeling with questions. What was so special about this tea?

Alvin placed the basket on the ground and retrieved a leather flask from his satchel. He swigged and passed it to Lorkan.

Lorkan added his blossoms to the basket and sniffed the leather skin. He was silent, and the forest sat suspended in time as he considered. *What exactly?* Blair was confused more than ever—

"Rabbit," he finally said.

Blair's insides twisted into knots. What in the Goddess did that mean?

"Impressive, as always," Alvin chuckled.

"Are you two guessing animals again?"

Blair whirled. Mya waltzed into the clearing, oblivious that Blair stood yards away. Despite the frigid air, Mya didn't wear a cloak or wool, only a flowy linen dress stained with paint. Her luscious curls trailed behind her back, and she carried a basket of blossoms, though not nearly as full as Alvin's. In her other hand, she grasped a gnarled branch, but at this distance, Blair couldn't make out the details.

"You're jealous because you're horrible at our game," Alvin said.

"Blood is blood." Mya shrugged.

Every inch of Blair's body froze. *Blasted books*, did the leather flask have rabbit blood inside it? *No*, she silently screamed. That didn't make any sense—

A ringing pierced through Blair's mind, and she couldn't think, could only stare on in horror.

For Alvin's smile widened, revealing a set of fangs. Sharp, needlelike, glinting in the moonlight.

Vampyr.

Blair's instinct screamed to flee while her magic rose to defend, wary and wild. But reason warred within her, or was it denial? For Alvin had handed the flask to Lorkan. Who'd taken a sip, too. Who'd guessed rabbit. Who displayed a rare smirk, revealing his own red-stained fang. It jutted over the very lips Blair had kissed days ago.

Lorkan was a vampyr, and Blair's world ripped out from under her.

Lies, deceit, betrayal. It all latched onto her heart, mind, body, and soul. Blair couldn't think or see straight. It was like sitting in her kitchenette again, learning the truth of why Evelyn had left. She'd lost her magic, a horrific reality Blair couldn't possibly understand, she knew that, but it wasn't the truth she detested but the wretched *knowing* that her sister hadn't trusted her with that secret. She'd squirmed under reality's heavy thumb, the message clear: *You're not good enough.*

Not enough to be seen. To be told. To be loved.

Lorkan hurt worst off all.

All Blair's emotions—desperation, fear, curiosity—were snuffed out. A sharp, unbound newness gusted through her veins. It wasn't her wind bronntanas or shadows.

It was a storm fueled by rage.

Chapter Sixty-Six

Glowing lanterns hung from the cavern's ceiling, draping Lorkan's secret village in a heady glow. While those of Vísdómr Library slumbered, half a mile under the mountain's base, a pack of witches and werewolves now turned vampyrs lived.

It wasn't as grand as the city built into Vísdómr or full of the same charm as the Drengr Village, but for those who had to live their life away from the daylight and fear the sun, it was a place of refuge, and *that* gave Fjall it's beauty. Those like Lorkan, with little choice from what fate handed them, had a chance.

With rock surrounding them on all sides, the quaint but bustling village echoed. Built into larger caves, establishments conducted business. Bakeries handed out savory bread stuffed with cured meats and well-aged cheese. Another storefront handed out fruit and vegetable preserves, jars that lasted years on the shelves if properly stored. At the edge, another distributed smoke trout—something Lorkan had never taken a liking to. Instead, he sipped a mug of barleywine and nibbled on peppered almonds while assessing the fallen branch Mya had found during her foraging.

The crooked branch looked as though one had pulled a string from inside and scrunched the once mighty oak. The one leaf that remained hung limply, flesh burnt from frost. The bark curled to reveal an onyx fleshy exterior, and inky sap oozed from the cracks.

"Smells like licorice," Alvin whispered.

"And death," Mya added, frowning.

"How close to Vísdómr did you find it?"

Mya gestured towards the baskets. "Near the elm trees."

"That is the farthest south we've come across signs of the Void," Alvin said.

Lorkan trailed a finger over the rim of his mug. "I'll have to write to Eldrick."

But he had nothing else to report. Aside from some vague connections, he had no answers on how to break the curse, nothing to soften the negative news that their land was infected.

"What else was it near?" he asked.

Mya's brows furrowed. "Trees and more trees . . . *Actually*, I spotted the most peculiar tree, and there was a small pool of water wedged in its root, tremoring from the storm."

"Odd storm for the winter months, don't you think?" Alvin said, lips downturned in a frown. "Felt like something was watching us, still does."

Mya hummed. "I don't think we can count on anything normal with the Void spreading. Weather has been unpredictable in Nūa, too, these days."

Lorkan sighed. "But Alvin has a point. It felt more than the land tonight."

Mya didn't reply, her eyes fixated elsewhere. Lorkan followed her line of sight, but he didn't catch anything of interest across the street, aside from a weaver handing out thick, wooly sweaters. He caught sage on the slight breeze funneling through the tunnel, his inner wolf rising to the surface at the familiarity. But to think it was Blair was a foolish notion—his pack cooked inside their homes, restaurants, and taverns. No doubt there was to be hints of the woody herb in the air.

"Did you find anything regarding the fire I wrote to you about?" he asked Mya.

She nodded. "It happened in 1895, the same year as Vísdómr's. Days apart."

Alvin's brows pinched. "No one found that incredibly coincidental?"

"It was within the same weeks as the Void splitting across the continent," Lorkan said. "I imagine their attentions were elsewhere."

Mya nodded. "I found something else interesting. That wasn't the only fire that night within the city walls of Nūa."

Lorkan gripped his mug, hair rising on the back of his neck. He couldn't shake the sense Alvin was right, and they *were* being watched. He shook it away, focusing on Mya again. "Go on."

"A printing house suffered an incredible loss. Their warehouse and pressroom were scorched to the ground. Records, too, destroyed," Mya said. "But I was able to study their printing logs. Guess who had their next installment and anthologies fresh off the press?"

Both Alvin and Lorkan leaned inward and asked at the same time, "Who?"

"Matilda Moore," Mya said. "It would've been her last work before she disappeared. Every last copy was burnt, even the manuscripts' master copies."

Lorkan stilled—he'd learned from Evelyn and Blair that the famous witch scholar had close ties to vampyr history with her fated, a seer seeking solitude from his visions, along with her journal full of personal accounts.

"That work might've covered the original history of vampyr *before* the curse," Lorkan said.

"Which means, whoever destroyed this information never wanted us to learn that vampyrs were different before the curse," Alvin said.

Lorkan shifted in his seat, still unsettled that vampyrism wasn't darkness but instead touched by a curse.

"But why?" Mya shook her head, the usually optimistic witch saddened. "What exactly did they gain by destroying that information?"

"Curses can be broken." Lorkan crossed his arms, pensive. "Without the truth, it kept 'darkness' ambiguous. Without the rest of the prophecy, Sorin has little solution other than the Son of the God and Daughter of Goddess. Someone was intent on making sure no one discovered exactly *how* to defeat the darkness."

"We've all been led astray so the Blood Goddess was able to grow in her power," Alvin muttered.

"It seems so." Lorkan sipped his barleywine, but the pleasant maltiness melted on his tongue and left behind a sour taste.

"Was or *is*?" Mya said. "How are we certain this someone isn't still controlling the narrative now, or worse, seeking more desperate measures?"

"Perhaps it's that ghastly prince you've mentioned." Alvin jutted his chin towards Lorkan.

He shook his head. "From what I know, Riven wasn't working for the Blood Goddess that soon after the Void formed."

Mya sighed, voice tentative as she spoke. "I don't suppose you and that witch can put your heads together and figure it out?"

Alvin snorted. "He'd have to speak to her in order to accomplish that, and Lorkan's barely been in the same room as Blair for days."

Lorkan tensed at the sound of her name, hating to hear it in the place he'd visited to escape her. No matter the distance or stone he put between them, he couldn't outrun what he was, and instead of hiding his truth, the surrounding rock closed in on him.

Moons, he still tasted her on his lips, could feel the aftershocks of her release on his fingers, but more importantly, he missed the sight of her studious stare or the twitch of her lips before she smiled. He yearned to simply be in the same room as Blair, to cherish her presence. What would it be like to have her as part of his world, sitting amongst his friends and theorizing to break the curse?

Sorin still isn't ready for your darkness, his father had said. Yet, Blair wasn't Sorin. Lorkan's insides twisted. He could pretend he feared harming Blair, his blood thirst too great, but he'd never hurt her, he knew that. He feared what she'd think, how she'd react to him being a vampyr. He feared the unknown, and yet one thing was certain—he had to find her and discuss what Mya had discovered. Perhaps their time at Vísdómr was coming to end, and they had to take their research elsewhere.

"I think Lorkan knows what's right, he's just afraid." Mya rose from her seat, downing the rest of her barleywine. "Now, as splendid as your company is, I need to get these blossoms ready to dry before the sunrise."

Alvin got up from the table, too. "I'll join you. Goes faster with two."

"How long will it take to create the tea?" he asked.

"Ten days," Mya said. "Albeit that's only if the storms hold off and we get a sunny day tomorrow."

Lorkan nodded. "I'll visit you both then. If there's anything urgent in the meantime, you know where to find me."

Alone and swallowed by darkness, Lorkan ventured up the north and most narrow tunnel, leading to his study. His thoughts ran wild as he climbed—Blair, the curse, taking care of his pack, worries for his brothers and parents. The latter had an ache blooming in the pit of his belly. The longer he walked, the tauter the knots grew. These last years, keeping what he was a secret had been relatively easy. Hiding had been like breathing, but Blair had waltzed back into his life and shattered the grip he had on his secret. Regardless of how his bloodthirst rose in a mighty wave in her presence, his heart yearned for her, a thread he'd ignored for ten long years.

As darkness surrounded him and doubt wrapped its thorny vines around his mind, Lorkan wished the shadows would swallow him whole and save him from this torment.

But Lorkan's legs keeping moving, one foot in front of the other—a Drengr family trait thick and through—like his cursed body was tired of his weary mind.

At the end of the tunnel, he placed his palm flush against the hidden door and pushed. Warmth and coziness reached him on the other side as he stepped into his study and positioned the large painting back in place.

The hairs on the back of his neck stood up. Another presence bristled in the air, and Lorkan froze and inhaled. Sage and storm mingled with the crackling fire, and he whirled.

Blair sat on the leather couch, not even looking in his direction. Her wild curls stuck in various directions and mud reached above her shins. Healing ointment and a bowl of water sat on the cushion beside Blair, and she cleaned a cut on the bottom of her foot with a washcloth.

Lorkan didn't think, he moved, snuffing a growl that vibrated up his throat. The sight of her hurt riled his inner wolf.

"Moons, Blair, what happened?" Lorkan dropped to his haunches, snatching the cloth from her and inspecting her wound.

She didn't answer, nor did she object as he took over cleaning the cut. Not deep enough to require stitches, but large enough to stain his rug.

Foolish, a voice shouted in his mind, but in that moment, Lorkan's bloodthirst didn't rise within him. He only thought of Blair, her pain, and the insatiable need to protect her.

Blair didn't object as he dipped the cloth into the bowl of water mixed with her oils and ran it across the cut, cleaning out dirt and debris. Smaller cuts lined the tops of her foot and shins, and—

Beautiful thighs.

For she wore no pants. A sleeping tunic, tattered and dirty, too, reached just past her hips. He followed the slope of her muscular legs, watched the slow rise and fall of her chest, her peaked nipples pressing against the thin fabric. *Stars above*, had she run through the forest in the dead of night? But how could Lorkan focus on the right questions to ask when the exquisite slope of her neck beckoned him to lay kisses up it?

His gaze snapped to hers, and Lorkan's grip on her ankle tightened. The heat in his study rose. Midnight clashed with honey. A storm raged in her eyes and ensnared his inner wolf, conjuring a beastly hunger inside him.

"Blair—"

"I'm surprised"—she tilted her head, studying him with a level of intensity that tugged his world out from under him—"it isn't more difficult to be around blood, seeing as you're a vampyr."

Lorkan's secret out loud turned him to stone like Blair had uttered a spell. He blinked. Swallowed. Tried to convince himself he'd misheard. How did she know? He opened his mouth—

"Don't waste your breath denying it."

Lorkan's heart cracked at the emptiness in Blair's voice.

"I saw you tonight in the forest, and I believe the blood you shared with Alvin was rabbit, right?"

His heart raced inside his chest, the rapid thump echoing in his ears. Blair tugged her foot back, and Lorkan let her go, the simple act feeling far more damning, like he stood on the precipice of losing her forever.

"I can explain," he managed.

"There's no need," she said, expression void of anything.

Blair stood on steady legs, forcing Lorkan to his full height. She stepped forward, and Lorkan matched the distance by retreating back. The fire hissed and embers popped, but the heat at Lorkan's back was nothing compared to the cold radiating deep in his bones. His heart ached, and Blair's next words chilled him in place.

"I followed you, down the tunnels and deep under Vísdómr. I walked the village—"

Lorkan growled, angling closer. "What? That is a cave full of vampyrs—"

"Ah." Blair's brow shot up, like they were having a conversation over ancient texts, not a decade-old truth now out in the open. "That confirms my suspicion. Every one of them has been turned, then? Even Mya?"

Lorkan gritted his teeth, sensing everything he tried to control was slipping through his fingers. "Yes, it's a safe haven for those who were once werewolves and witches."

Blair nodded, and the darkness of her stare wasn't the fathomless beauty of night, but a vacant oblivion. Lorkan couldn't breathe. His hands itched to reach for her, but his mind warred at the notion.

"When were you turned?" Blair whispered.

The curse snaked through his veins, hissing and mocking at his predicament. He thought he had time to tell Blair these secrets himself. To be honest. To come clean. Now he was robbed of choice, the when and how.

His next words rose up his throat like shards of glass. "Ten years ago."

Blair scoffed and blinked back the glistening in her eyes. "Answer this one question, and I'll never ask anything of you ever again."

"Blair—"

"Is that why you never met me in Fika?" she whispered.

There it is was—the ugliest truth of all. It wasn't Lorkan's vampyrism, his bloodthirst, or the curse. It was the choice he'd made to not go to Blair, to not seek her out when he needed help.

"*Answer me.*"

"Yes!" Lorkan roared. "But I stayed away to protect you—"

"There's nothing righteous about breaking my heart, Lorkan," she hissed. "Lie to yourself all you want."

Lorkan shook his head, and it was his turn to invade Blair's space and make her step back as he peered down at her. "I was attacked on my way to meet you, and as the scáths fed from me, my instinct to live reached something I never thought existed—my wolf. I shifted for the first time, and overcome with that transformation and the venom in my veins, the rest is an absolute blur. I awoke two days later, unsure where the fuck I was, let alone that I was a vampyr. My skin burnt when the sun touched it. I had a new ability, wild and *hungry*. Not to mention that insatiable thirst and haze of red, and the chanting of the curse in my mind. Then, there were the bodies. Their blood covered my clothes, stained my fangs and filled my belly. I'd slaughtered a home, Blair. A farmer. His wife. Their child. There was no way to deny it. Their blood coated my new fangs."

"Are you telling me this to scare me?" Blair said through gritted teeth.

"You should be," Lorkan breathed.

"No. I won't let the way you feel about yourself be thrown at me." Blair jabbed his finger into his chest. "You should've come to me. I could've helped. *Goddess*, I love you, Lorkan, and you shut me out."

Love. Not *loved*.

Lorkan's heart cracked, and he almost fell to his knees. "We were seventeen, Blair. You would've been frightened. Being near me was a danger."

"And? I'm frightened now, and yet I'm here. Regardless of what you are, I'm here."

Lorkan exhaled. "Your perspective is jaded by everything you know now. Sorin was a different place then, *we* were different people. What about Evelyn? Your sister is the Daughter of the Goddess—destined to kill those like me."

"I know that. Perhaps you're right. But you didn't give me a choice." Blair clamped her eyes shut, and when they sprang open, tears brimmed at the edges. "You were my anchor in this world. Everyone has cast me aside, but you made me feel *seen* for the first time in my life."

"I've never stopped, Blair." Lorkan grabbed her hands and lay them on his chest.

Blair sucked in a breath, eyes landing where right over his pounding heart.

"You are all I see. During my days, thoughts, and dreams. It is you, and only you. I hear your name on the wind. Think of your midnight stare on a constant measure. Trace the shape of your smile with ink throughout my notes—"

Blair snatched her hand away, chest heaving. "Those are all just pretty words."

"Then what do you want? Need? Tell me, and I'll give it."

Lorkan waited. Silence threatened to swallow him whole, and his heart hardened as he studied the pain he'd caused in Blair's midnight eyes.

"Space . . . Time," she finally whispered. "I . . . I accept what you are, Lorkan, and I don't want you to think for a second this is because you're a vampyr. It's your lie I must come to terms with, and I need to process your reason. *Please.*"

Lorkan swallowed, fisting his hands at his sides and fighting his inner wolf raging at Blair's request. His body warred with the idea of time. He'd spent enough of it away from her, but that had been his own damn fault, hadn't it? She was right. He'd not given her a choice then, but he'd not dare make that mistake again.

"If that is what you wish," he said.

Tears brimmed at the edge of Blair's eyes as she stepped back. "There is still the prophecy and what we learned. We need to meet everyone back at the Drengr Village—"

Fear jolted through Lorkan like a zap of lightning.

"You must not speak of this to anyone," Lorkan said. "They can't know."

Blair scoffed. "Have you learned nothing tonight?"

"It's different. Eldrick must keep the Earl vote. If the other alphas discovered what my father has hidden—" Lorkan stopped short, raking his hand through his hair. Stars above, he hadn't meant to reveal that.

"But your brothers have loved you unconditionally all these years. Will you make their decision, their judgment for them?" Blair asked, her ire rising in her voice again.

"For now, it is what best."

Blair shook her head, blinking back tears. She stepped closer—one, two, three strides—until she placed a gentle hand on his cheek, making Lorkan look at her. "You can't hide forever, not even from yourself."

She rose on her tiptoes and gave him one last parting kiss before she left him alone.

The instinct to crawl deeper into the mountain and hide roared to life now more than ever.

CHAPTER SIXTY-SEVEN

THE SUN GODDESS'S WORDS haunted Evelyn for hours.

She stood with arms crossed, admiring the change in scenery as well as her heightened senses. Ahead, steam rose from heated pools, their shores thick with moss. To the right, a small waterfall roared over jagged rock. An elk huffed as it trudged through the night. Smaller critters rustled in the forest floor, and the *drip... drip... drip...* of dew beat with the whistling breeze.

Evelyn breathed in the cool air of the Vadon Mountains. The hint of pine and the promise of rain relaxed her tired mind, reminding her of a certain werewolf. Here, back west, the sense of home anchored Evelyn after her time in the Otherworld.

Still, Evelyn and the team had two days of travel north before they reached the Drengr Village. Her body craved Kade's cottage. Her feet ached for the creaky floorboards, her skin eager for the many layers of fur warming their bed.

As if her more promising thoughts conjured him to existence, Kade's presence tickled her instinct, and after a beat, he wrapped his strong arms around her middle.

He kissed her temple in greeting. "You seem relaxed. Lighter."

"It feels like home," she whispered.

"You have no idea how happy I am to hear that." Kade buried his face in her neck.

Evelyn shivered from the contact. Her body had always responded to Kade's touch, but there was a heightened awareness now, like his mere nearness might set her aflame.

A pang of guilt shot through Evelyn, though. Despite the kernel of fire festering in her soul that tried to eclipse her emotions, her truth remained.

She cared for her friends. Or should care. *Ugh.* Protectiveness was a fierce streak that ran through her, but it lay dormant.

Evelyn rooted for who she was like one dug through sand. The deeper the hole grew, the more sand that fell, burying Evelyn's sense of self and making it impossible to reach.

"Do you feel different?" she asked.

He remained silent, thoughtful until— "Yes."

Something close to relief settled across Evelyn's skin like the gentle kiss of dew. Perhaps she wasn't lost, but new, and it'd take time getting used to it.

"How are the others?" she asked, finding the courage.

Evelyn'd left the campsite earlier, needing space from the sight of Linx tending to Belle who still hadn't awoken since they left Cirrillo. Todd remained on edge, and Aster hadn't muttered a single word, stuck in a state of shock.

"Everyone is resting," Kade said. "As should you."

"There's too much on my mind."

"Like?" Kade's voice tickled the shell of her ear.

"I'm grateful we're back together and home." Evelyn swallowed, hating the taste of vulnerability on her tongue. "But I feel like I've brought back more mess."

Mess put it so fucking flames lightly, Evelyn dug her nails into her arms. She'd stolen from a goddess. Brought her friend back to life. Doomed Belle to who knows what—

Kade turned her around, prying her fingers away from her arms and not only unraveling her tense mind but her body. He placed a finger under her chin, making her look up at him.

"We were successful in our task. We repaired your soul, and you're *alive*, Ev. Yet, we always knew we'd return to mess. There is still the Blood Curse, after all."

"Have I not made everything worse?" Evelyn breathed.

"No." Kade tucked a stary hair behind her, and his eyes glistened like honey. "You did what you thought was right by saving Aster. The Sun Goddess is who hurt Belle."

"Because of me." Evelyn shook her head, unable to bear the kindness in his eyes.

"It doesn't take away the fact it was *her* choice." Kade tugged her chin, refocusing her attention back on him. "There is nothing more we can do, not until we return to the Drengr Village, but . . ." He stepped closer and dropped his hand to cup Evelyn's cheek, running a thumb over her bottom lip. "I'm not going to so easily dismiss that *we did it*, Evelyn."

She swallowed. They'd not traveled miles to find one another, but realms. They'd left this world, traversed an emptiness full of stars, and then endured what the gods had thrown at them. *Together.*

Kade was right. More hardship awaited them, and she'd not waste this moment of peace they'd found. Not with the trees so still, the breeze gentle and the night beckoning them.

"That is what I care most about," Kade whispered, eyes fixated on her lips. "Perhaps I'm a selfish bastard for it—"

Evelyn grabbed a fistful of his shirt and dragged him into a kiss. Tenderly and eagerly all at once. Instantly, her wound-up being relaxed and buzzed and turned aflame.

Kade opened up her mouth wider, pulling at her bottom lip with his teeth. The delectable pain shot to Evelyn's core, and a moan escaped her.

Kade pulled away and smiled. "Will you come with me?"

Evelyn's insides warmed. How could she say no when he looked at her like that? As if nothing else mattered. As if war didn't wait on the horizon.

"Always," she said.

Evelyn took his hand, and Kade led her towards the waterfall. It fed into a waist-deep pool, steam lapsing over the mossy shores like waves. Without a word, Kade started unlacing his boots and stripping his leathers.

This male. Carved from stone and etched by the gods, his muscles rippled as he tore off his shirt and exposed that delicious V-shape outlining his abs. Scruff lined the center, disappearing past his waistline, and Evelyn's mouth turned dry.

"Done staring?" Kade asked, dropping his trousers and undergarments in one swift move, revealing his taut ass and half-ready length.

Evelyn smiled, a *real* one, and it had been so long, her cheeks ached.

In the best way.

Evelyn took her time as she removed her leathers, pulling the laces one at a time. She chucked her boots off next.

Kade's stare didn't leave her as he stepped back into the thermal pool. He submerged waist deep, and his eyes roamed every inch of skin Evelyn revealed by tossing off her trousers and throwing off her tunic. Her chest wrapping came next, and Kade's eyes darkened as her breasts met the cold, nipples peaked.

She abandoned their pile of clothes at the edge of the pool and entered the steaming water, following Kade's lead. Warmth tickled her toes and climbed her legs. The water reflected the scattering of stars in the midnight sky, like moonstones floated through the steam.

But the most breathtaking sight wasn't the sky, waterfall, or the forest but Kade. He ran a wet hand through his hair, drawing his sun-kissed waves off his face. Jaw tight, eyes set, muscles on display. They way he looked at Evelyn had eagerness rushing through her veins.

Kade's patience snapped when she stood an arm's length away. He gripped her bare ass in his strong hands and lifted her. Evelyn hooked her legs around his waist. His rigid length glided through her folds, and a small breathless whimper escaped her lips.

Evelyn drew her legs tighter around him to gain more access, relishing at his size and needing it *now*—

Kade nipped at her jawline, his next words tickling her ear. "You'll have to wait for that, love."

His guttural words reached Evelyn's baser instinct, and that thread between them pulsed.

She dug her hands into his hair and pulled Kade into a kiss. He answered, devouring her mouth with sweeping strokes of his talented tongue. The thought of it in another place, like her pulsing sex, almost sent her over the edge.

Their kiss tasted of the past, present, and future. How they'd once kissed with rain-coated lips in Callum, with snow falling around them in Drystan, and now in a land they called home, the red sands of Cirrillo washing off them, like they shed death and were reborn in each other's arms this time.

Kade broke away from their kiss, and for a moment, they stared at the other. The power Evelyn had stolen was no match for the love teeming in their hearts. It could not outshine the truest emotion she possessed. *Nothing* came between her and Kade. Not even a power she still had to grow accustomed to.

Evelyn yelped and giggled as Kade held her tighter and moved deeper through the thermal pool. Steam parted as they reached the waterfall. It roared around them, and as Kade carried Evelyn under the cascading water, she understood why he'd picked the spot.

It'd drown out the sounds of their pleasure.

Past the waterfall was a cave. The pool continued a few more feet, bumping up against a smooth, rocky ground. Kade lifted Evelyn and planted her on the ledge. Around them, indigo-colored moss coated every inch of the cave, soft and plush under Evelyn's bare skin. Tiny holes carved into the ceiling revealed the starlight, illuminating their wet skin.

Kade gripped Evelyn's ankles and tugged, and she squealed as he brought her ass to the edge. He leaned over her, peppering kisses down the slope of her neck.

"Kade . . ." she said, drawing her fingers down his cheek.

His face hovered inches over hers. His hand skated across her stomach, traveling closer and closer.

"Fuck," Kade growled as his fingers dipped between her folds.

His golden eyes bore into Evelyn, and her chest rose and fell. She couldn't utter word, could barely think as her body tingled from head to toe with such promise.

"I plan to make you come three times," he said, lips brushing over hers. "First"—Evelyn's back bowed as he delved into her core—"with my fingers, then"—Kade swept his tongue over one of her nipples—"my tongue, and lastly . . ."

He didn't finish but smirked as Evelyn's sex tightened around his pumping fingers.

Fucking flames, she was already so close. She writhed for more, but Kade removed his fingers. Slick with her readiness, he glided them upward. Kade drew torturously slow circles over her swollen clit. He kissed her, and all Evelyn could do was surrender to his lips and touch.

Pressure and pleasure built at her core. She sat at the edge of oblivion, a place Kade so artfully brought her to time after time.

The thread between them pulsed again, and a growl rumbled through Kade's chest. He quickened his pace and—

Evelyn shattered, her first release like a mighty wave that crashed against all her nerve endings. Kade swallowed her cry like a man starved of water.

He pulled away, planting kisses across her chest and belly, her tingling skin burning after her release. Evelyn gulped for air, trying to gain some sense of balance and reality, but Kade gave her no time. He lowered his face between her legs, her sex inches from his parted lips.

Then my tongue, he'd promised.

With the first lick through her already ready sex, Evelyn's worries and thoughts vanished. In fact, she could only think and breathe the pleasure Kade gave her as he darted his tongue into her opening and made circular motions.

She arched back. Dug her hands into the moss. She was blinded by pleasure. On the brink of losing consciousness. Evelyn couldn't be sure of the pleas she gasped, but they only encouraged Kade.

This was what being remade felt like. Not the games orchestrated by the gods. Here, tucked inside a small cave, with Kade lapping his tongue over her clit like he wrote the power of his love across her flesh.

Kade showed no mercy, sucking on her buzzing bundle of nerves. She'd not even settled from her first release, the growing pleasure far fiercer and wilder this time.

"Fucking flames." Evelyn threaded her fingers through Kade's hair and grasped his wet strands like they might anchor her in this world. "*Kade.*"

Evelyn fell into oblivion, and a thousand stars burst at her core. Their remnants rushed through her veins, leaving her suspended in her second release. Male pride gleamed across Kade's face as he stared up at her with a triumphant smile.

"You alright, love?" His words tickled her sex.

Evelyn sat up, limbs feeling floaty, and planted a hand on Kade's shoulder, tracing his facial features with the other. His proud nose, sharp jaw hidden underneath his beard, the scar running through his right brow.

More than alright, she said down the bond. *I never knew love could feel like this.*

She didn't dare speak words aloud or fracture this moment, not when they might reweave their bond.

Kade's eyes widened. *Like what?*

Infinite. Beautiful. Unyielding.

Evelyn dunked her hand into the water and fisted Kade's length. He sucked in a breath, eyes darkening. Evelyn continued a slow and steady motion, sliding her hand up and down his rigid manhood.

Kade watched her with a beastly intensity, and then he snatched her hand away and grabbed her waist, encouraging Evelyn to wrap her legs around him. She obeyed, draping her arms around his neck. He ventured left, finding shallower water that reached knee deep. Steam remained, encompassing them in a comforting warmth.

Evelyn never stopped soaking in his handsome face, not until her back hit moss-covered stone. Kade's length twitched against her molten sex, and she dropped her head back, eager for what she craved.

"Are you ready, love?" He lined himself at her entrance.

"Yes," she breathed.

He eased in, inch by glorious inch, until he sank to the hilt. Their moans echoed in the cave as they came together. Kade moved. Once, twice, a third time, allowing Evelyn's sex to grow accustomed to his size at this angle. Evelyn's toes curled at the friction.

Then he drove into her, over and over. Evelyn's moans turned to screams. She *loved* it when Kade unleashed. When he didn't hold back. When his inner beast sat at the surface as he pumped into her.

Fuck, of course there was a mess. A curse. A war. But there was also *them*, and nothing seemed impossible with Kade.

Their bond glowed. Infinite and beautiful like she'd said. The thread that unraveled began to weave itself together again. Kade moved inside her, drawing her legs a little wider and—

"*Oh,*" Evelyn cried out.

He found a new angle, and *that* spot inside her lit a fire to her toes. Evelyn was heat and life and light, and she didn't know where either of them began or ended. The threads of their bond tangled with their building pleasure.

Evelyn's third release began, blooming at her core, and she came and came and came, until she bled into sweet, sensual nothingness. Every inch of her tightened around Kade, even clenching around his length, and his brows pinched.

"Evelyn," Kade breathed her name like a prayer and curse all.

He shuddered, slowing his pace as he found his own release, filling Evelyn to the brim.

Their souls touched. Sang. Life and light met. Their powers caressed the other. The last thread that needed to be woven inched—

Something hot, fiery, and wrong flared in its way. Evelyn whimpered, and Kade stiffened, brows pinching fiercer.

The glowing thread between them dimmed. Their bond stood on a precipice. Closer, but not rewoven. As if they'd failed—

"Look at me." Kade pressed Evelyn further into the stone, keeping her steady, as he cupped her face. "*Everything* will be alright."

"I know," she lied. "I love you, Kade." *That* was the unbending truth.

The rest of Evelyn's words died on the tip of her tongue. Fear lodged in her throat. So instead, she kissed Kade to reassure him. Molded her lips to his, tasted his kindness.

They moved to another place, another position. Celebrated their bodies with pleasure and release and flesh. Again and again, until Evelyn drowned out her suspicion.

For she believed the power she'd stolen from the Sun Goddess had *blocked* their mating bond.

CHAPTER SIXTY-EIGHT

ELDRICK

ONE NIGHT LYING BESIDE Tovi turned into three, and upon their return to the Drengr Village, Eldrick escorted her to his alpha quarters inside Lār.

That night, they simply held the other close under layers of furs and talked about everything from dreams to the simplest things. Their favorite colors. The things they loved during childhood. Palm to palm, they studied their hands flush together, listened to the other's heartbeat, and whispered ridiculous teases until the fire went out and they surrendered to sleep.

Eldrick woke first with Tovi nuzzled into his side. He surveyed her curved figure like it was a magnificent mountain range, stretching from the head to the foot of his bed. The peaks of her breast, the valley of her muscular legs.

Stars above.

He wished to trek every inch of her, to study the terrain of skin, the edges of her mind, and the depths of her soul. Each and every piece, he wanted to learn and know it as if it were his second homeland.

And yet, his heart raced like some petrified rabbit. It was like every minute with her would be his last, as if their time was limited. There was still so much left ahead. Eldrick *wanted* to make it work.

More than anything.

More than . . . Eldrick shook his head. *No.* Was it possible he wanted to be with Tovi more than being Earl? Why couldn't he have both? He'd never ask Tovi to renounce her title as queen to be with him. He'd rather die under her blade than utter that selfish ask. Not when he knew how important it was to her.

Tovi stretched, sighing as she found her new position, resting her head on his chest. Right then and there, as their bodies rose and fell together, Eldrick swore *this* was what he, his soul, and inner wolf yearned for.

The rightness should've brought comfort to him, but instead, a jolt of anxiety shot through him. What if *he* abandoned his duty?

A knock resounded on the door, and Tovi shifted awake.

"What time is it?" she murmured as she rubbed the sleep from her eyes.

The door swung open, and Yennifer barged into the room.

"It's half past nine," she said, leaving the door wide open.

"Moons!" Eldrick snarled, grasping the quilts to cover him and Tovi.

The queen's head snapped up, and she released a brittle, ear-splitting screech. "Yen, what in the *bloody hel*?"

Yen, positively unbothered, called over shoulder. "You lot owe me ten silvers!"

"Ten silvers?" Eldrick stuttered. "What in the—"

"Aye!" Bétar stuck his head into the room. "My mate's telling the truth—they're both in here."

The commander waltzed into Eldrick's room next, chest puffed out and eyes focused ahead like some warhorse on the battlefield.

"Leave," Eldrick said, a growl vibrating from his chest. He was far too aware that Tovi wore a silk slip and nothing else, barely covering her breasts and sex.

Bétar only chuckled.

Yen approached the end of the bed, arms crossed and a huff exhaling out of her as the archer's sky-blue eyes widened with hurt. "Here I thought we were friends."

Tovi shook her head. "We are! Did you really need to barge into our room to confirm that fact? Could it not have waited until breakfast?"

"Well, friends sleep and tell, Tovi," Yen whispered. "I'd thought you'd have the decency to tell me yourself that you and Eldrick are . . ." She shrugged.

Tovi threw her hands in the air. "Bloody werewolves and their nosy ways. If you all must know, yes, Eldrick and I are—" She stopped, eying his expression. "I swear to the Goddess, Eldrick, if you utter one contradiction, I'll stand atop this bed and strip my nightgown off."

"You'll do no such thing," Eldrick growled. He wrapped his arm around her waist and pulled her close. "Please tell me there is another reason you disturbed our morning?"

Bétar wiggled his brows and nudged Yen's shoulder. "Did you hear that? *Our*."

Tovi bared her vampyr fangs and hissed a slew of curses in their direction. Red bloomed across her cheeks, and Eldrick liked seeing the usually poised and proud queen caught off guard. A smile tugged at his lips, his territorial wave receding.

Tovi swiveled her attention towards him and swatted his arm. "Don't you dare enjoy this, *wolf*."

"But I love the sight of you in my bed." Eldrick winked.

"Goddess, I should've trusted my instinct!" Linx's fiery-orange buns peeked past the door frame. "I knew the two of you couldn't resist one another."

Tovi's mouth hung open. "Wait . . . if you're here, Linx . . ."

"Ah!" Bétar clapped his hands together. "That's also why we visited. Kade and Evelyn have returned. A bit *different*, I'll warn you both."

The mage planted her hands on her hips. "Indeed they are, but they retired to Kade's cottage, wanting a bit of privacy."

"What a novel idea," Eldrick muttered.

Tovi leapt from the bed, and Eldrick reached for her, but she was quicker, darting out of his reach

"Tovi, get back in bed. *Now*."

She stopped, planting a hand on her hip. It made everything worse. The strap on her nightgown slipped, deepening the dip of fabric between her breasts. The tension in the room thickened. Dangerously so. Suddenly, it wasn't just friends teasing friends—Eldrick's wolf was screaming *mine, mine, mine*, moments from unleashing and annihilating everyone in the room.

Stars above, it reminded Eldrick of Kade when they'd rescued Evelyn out of Drystan Castle. His mate. The thought—the similarity—worsened his wolf's protective instinct.

It also made his mouth go dry.

Of course, what Tovi was to him had crossed his mind before. Before, Eldrick had let the thought come and go. It had been fleeting. Silly almost. She was a vampyr. A queen. He a werewolf.

Now, here in his room, there was no denying it, and the earlier fear he had about losing her grew. Because losing Tovi would be like losing a part of his heart. The thought turned him clammy, made the sheets stick to his bare torso while his blood rushed through him, cold and frigid and rooting him in place.

Which part of his heart could he survive losing?

"Your alpha voice thing doesn't work on me," Tovi said, breaking Eldrick from his racing thoughts.

She grabbed the nearest robe—Eldrick was certain it was actually his not hers. As she wrapped it around herself, she swam in the fabric. An evergreen velvet, one that drew out the undertones in her eyes.

"Better?" Tovi asked, her taunting brow making him really wish no one else was in the room. What he'd give to get on his knees before Tovi, disappear under the robe, and riddle her senseless with his tongue.

All to ease his worries with the sounds of her pleasure. A *distraction*.

Bétar coughed. "*Moons*. Let's get out of here before something unfolds before us."

Eldrick smirked, masking his bundled nerves, and Tovi's jade eyes brightened, none the wiser.

CHAPTER SIXTY-NINE

KADE STOOD BY THE fireplace in his cottage, studying the flames as they danced.

"How did Bjorn take it after you beat him?" he asked his brother.

Eldrick swirled a glass of whiskey in his hand. "Not well."

"Do you think he'll be a problem at the ascension ceremony?" he asked.

Eldrick had won the vote amongst the alphas, but unlike the power transfer from Aramis to his firstborn, the *land* had to accept Eldrick next.

Eldrick shrugged. "Why bother? The werewolves are united under one leader. Tovi has her army. I've also written to the other alphas, letting them know you and Evelyn have returned. Why jeopardize everything as we grow closer to defeating the darkness?"

"There is still the matter of the prophecy. Bjorn would be a bigger fool than ever to interfere with breaking the curse," Tovi said, sliding an affectionate hand down Eldrick's back as she passed by them.

Kade raised a brow at Eldrick's wistfulness, dazed as Tovi sauntered over to join Evelyn in the reading chairs.

His brother grimaced when he caught Kade staring. "Don't give me that look. You're just as bad when it comes to Evelyn."

Kade grunted and said nothing more on the matter. There were still hard days ahead. A battle to win. Riven to defeat. And . . .

The front door clicked open, and Blair and Lorkan arrived.

"I hope you all are ready. We learned how to possibly break the curse," his scholarly brother announced.

The Drengr brothers greeted each other, and as Kade embraced Lorkan in a hug, he spied another reunion over his shoulder.

Evelyn shot from her seat, and Blair halted. The Carson sisters faced off, and after several long, dragged-out beats, they collided into each other's arms. Kade swallowed, overcome with a foreign emotion at the sight of his mate happy after such hard, tiring weeks.

Still, a new sharpness honed Evelyn. They'd not rewoven their bond, a fact that left Kade unsettled, and ever since their time in the thermal pools, he had an inkling Evelyn withheld something from him.

But so much had happened, and each time he went to ask, he didn't know where to start. Then, he recalled the prophecy and the curse. Kade resigned to say nothing, especially with seemingly more important matters to address. *Moons*, he loved Evelyn, but sometimes, their duties came first.

Like what Lorkan and Blair had discovered in regard to breaking the curse.

"The new hair suits you," Tovi said.

"Thank you," Blair said, hugging the vampyr queen. "I . . . missed you."

"I missed you, too," Tovi whispered.

The three females moved to the love seat, squishing themselves onto it and pulling a large fur blanket over their laps.

Kade's mate wiped tears from her eyes, and he spotted a glimpse of the woman he loved past the mask she'd worn the last two days. "Alright, how do we break the curse?"

Lorkan's pushed his spectacles up the bridge of his nose. "There is something called an ever tree. It was used to create another realm by the faeries who fled the Blood Goddess's wrath."

Kade crossed his arms. "Is that the seed mentioned in the prophecy?"

Blair nodded. "That is our theory, yes."

"Where do we find one?" he asked.

Lorkan sighed. "Our hope is that the Gray Wood would possesses one, or better yet, gifts it to Evelyn."

Tovi's brows shot up. "In Callum? The forest Evelyn released from dark magic?"

Lorkan nodded, an amused smile on his lips. "Precisely. *An old friend now set free.*"

Evelyn's stare jumped between Blair and Lorkan. "So, what's the plan, then? I just waltz into the Gray Wood and . . . ask for an ever seed?"

Blair crossed her arms. "Perhaps. Do you recall what the forest was like?"

Evelyn's left brow furrowed as she thought. "Alive, buzzing. It was hurting from the Far Darrig's darkness but not controlled by it. At one point, it did answer me when I need it to."

"It also joined our fight and helped us defeat the faerie tribe." Kade crossed his arms.

He recalled how he and Evelyn had lured and trapped the Far Darrig with Evelyn's flame and the Gray Wood had helped finish them off while they escaped the forest.

"Well, let's hope it's much the same since you left," Blair said. "It appears our next venture takes us to Callum."

"Us?" Evelyn sat up straighter.

Lorkan's jaw ticked, and Kade noticed how his brother tensed underneath his usual relaxed demeanor.

"Blair has done the most research regarding the ever trees. It might be wise to bring a guide," he said.

"What about you?" Kade asked.

Before Lorkan could answer, a knock sounded on the cottage's front door, and everyone shared an apprehensive look. The meeting only included the six of them.

"It's your mother and father," Nadia called on the other side. "May I remind you, it is quite cold out here."

Kade hurried towards the door and let his parents into the cottage. Nadia carried a long object wrapped in a fur blanket, and silence ballooned in the space at the possibility of what she held.

Eldrick set his whiskey down, shaking his father's hand as he eyed the item. "Is that what I think it is?"

"Aye." Aramis nodded. "The sword of ancients."

Tovi blinked. "*Bloody hel*, you both did it."

Nadia snorted. "Don't sound so surprised."

Tovi smiled. "Not in the slightest, but also how did you manage it?"

"That is a tale for another day," Aramis sighed.

Kade's parents smiled, though small and timid considering the circumstance. For the first time since they'd been reunited, he noticed true affection, wonder even, shining in their eyes. Whatever journey they'd been on, it'd brought them closer together.

He averted his attention from the bite mark peeking out from his father's tunic. He'd rather think of a thousand different things than his parents—

"Unfortunately, we have more pressing matters," Nadia said. "We discovered where Riven plans to open the gates to Hel: Lake Glenn. Though, can't say I've heard of it."

Blair sat straighter. "That's because it's in Torren. It's east of Callum, actually."

Evelyn nodded. "Kade and I have been to it."

He tipped his head. "Fought a nasty kelpie."

"*That* sounds more like a guard of Hel," Lorkan said, his stare connecting with Blair.

Eldrick crossed his arms. "Does it help keep the Blood Goddess in or—"

"Serve her, I'm afraid," Blair mumbled. "Demons and creatures are from her domain. If I had to take a guess, it recognized Evelyn and Kade and"—she shrugged—"thought to protect its master."

Tovi stood. "Regardless of what we'll face, it sounds as though we're all headed to Callum, hopefully before Riven gets there."

"You're coming, too?" Evelyn asked, glancing at Kade.

Tovi sighed. "If I recall, the Gray Wood and Lake Glenn are on opposite sides of each other. We need to divide and conquer. You and Kade focus on finding the ever seed, while the rest of us stop Ingrid's spell."

Kade nodded. "It's a solid plan, though it'll take three weeks to reach Callum."

"Ingrid isn't ready for the spell, and Riven hasn't the slightest idea we learned the plans," Aramis said. "That's a bit of good news."

Nadia laughed. "Yes, the prince was far too concerned that we stole this." She handed Kade the sword of ancients and tugged the leather twine loose.

Kade set it down on the wooden table in the seating area and unfurled the wool. An onyx-colored sword revealed itself, glinting in the hearth's light.

He ran his fingers down the blade, and his power and wolf rose to the surface. Promise buzzed at his fingertips. He gripped the hilt, and the moonstone embedded into the pommel glowed the same blue as his power.

"It suits you," Evelyn whispered.

Kade found the energy to smile, and as he met his reflection's gaze, he prayed to the Moon God that his mate was right, and he was worthy of such a magnificent sword.

Chapter Seventy

THE NEXT DAY, EVELYN leaned against the doorway in Mirella's infirmary. At the farthest bedside, Belle lay motionless in a cot, wool blankets brought to her chin. Her eyes remained closed, the one indication she slept the slow rise and fall of her chest. Todd sat at her bedside, holding her hand like a lifeline.

"She'll be fine, Todd." Kade gave his teammate's shoulder a squeeze.

"You don't know that," Todd whispered. "We have no idea the cost Evelyn had to pay."

Evelyn stilled. She hated seeing Belle unconscious, stuck in some magical sleep state, but she had no *feelings* on the matter.

Her insides were vacant of anything. Evelyn tried and tried to reach for *something*, anything to say to Todd to make matters better before they left for Callum.

"Evelyn," a small voice said from behind.

She whirled. Aster, wrapped in shawls and shivering from the city's cold, approached at arm's length. Her bare feet slapped against the teal tile of the infirmary's hall.

"Aster," she whispered. "You're not dressed to travel."

"I'm not going," she said, tired and sad. There wasn't an ounce of her friend left. No bubbliness or brightness. No small quip to lighten the mood.

"You're from Callum. It's your home." Evelyn reached for Aster's hand, but her friend recoiled. "Your parents—"

"I don't remember them—I mean—" Aster shut her eyes, gripping her shawls tighter around her small frame. "I'm not ready to face them or . . . this . . . yet."

This, as in coming back to life. Words turned to ash on Evelyn's tongue, but at least she managed, "I'm so sorry, Aster."

The kernel of power she'd stolen from the Sun Goddess reared to life. It eclipsed the empathy brimming in Evelyn's soul. She clamped her mouth shut, trying to fight the callousness reaching forth.

Aster blinked. Swallowed. Stared at her with those wide russet eyes that had brought her so much joy and hope in the past, twinkling with nothing but lostness.

"I believe this is where we say goodbye, Evelyn Carson."

Something pierced Evelyn's heart, but the pain was gone as quickly as it came. The flame in her soul scorched it away, and by the time she recovered, Aster had already retreated down the hall, disappearing into the infirmary's next wing.

She blinked back tears that never came. *Fucking flames*, this was Aster. Someone she loved. Why did she feel *nothing*? What was happening to her?

A faint cackle tunneled down the hallway, as if they Sun Goddess sneered at her from above. Goose bumps pricked up Evelyn's arms, and she shivered, trying to rally her resolve.

Could she at least make it right with Todd? Say her goodbyes to Belle? She turned, ready to march into her friend's room when movement caught her attention, and Maxie followed the wall as she scurried with ears flicked back.

Evelyn crouched to her familiar's level, but Maxie stopped. Her hackles rose like orange spikes down her spine and hissed.

Evelyn reared back. Why was her familiar acting so strange? Their familiar-to-witch bond still existed like a thread connected their souls, but much like with Kade, it was distant, as if something infected the connection.

"Maxie, its alright," Evelyn whispered. She reached out—

Her familiar swiped, clawing the back of her hand. Beads of blood bloomed across her skin.

"Gods damn it." Heat scorched through her. Fiery. *Angry.*

Maxie's stare narrowed, and with her tail low and quivering, she darted into Belle's room, finding her spot in between Kade's legs.

He sighed, a deep kind that Evelyn hadn't witnessed before. He caught her in the doorway and stiffened. He turned his attention back to his friend.

"We'll visit upon our return," Kade said.

"Don't bother," Todd muttered. "I don't want to see her, not until Belle wakes up. I can't, Kade. My wolf . . ."

Kade's frown reached his eyes. "Okay."

Evelyn fell back into the hall and retreated, not daring to let Todd catch sight of her. Kade caught up to her before she made it out of the infirmary, the city blustering with a harsh winter cold. Flurries twisted on the wind, a rare sight in Nūa, leaving the street emptier than usual. The once crimson-and-copper trees were bare, and the potted marigolds wilted with frost.

Kade took Evelyn's hand, making her pause on the street. "He's scared, that's all. You can't take it personally."

"But I should," Evelyn whispered. "The Sun Goddess is punishing me for bringing back Aster. Not only does she barely remember who I am, I've lost Belle to who knows what."

"Our time in the Otherworld was tense," Kade said, running his thumb across her knuckles absently. "You were trying to protect someone you love."

Love. Why did the word feel and sound so foreign? Yet, Evelyn searched the gold rivets in Kade's amber eyes. She loved this man, and no matter the foreign feeling festering in her heart, she believed that to her core.

"Is there something you're not telling me?" he whispered.

Evelyn's insides backflipped. "I . . . don't need to talk right now, but instead a distraction. Let me show you this city. A proper tour this time."

Kade studied her, a thousand words warring in his stare. As if to support his objection, wanted posters flapped in the wind.

It technically still wasn't safe to wander the city without their names officially cleared, but Evelyn was tired of hiding in a place she'd once called home. These were *her* streets as much as they were any other witch's.

"I don't think that's a good idea, love," Kade said.

Evelyn's chest tightened. "Please. I'll take us a way that leads straight to the harbor, and we'll keep our hoods up."

Kade sighed. "Evelyn, what are you frightened of? What are you hiding from me?"

"Nothing." She marched past him, but Kade grabbed her wrist.

"Ev, don't be angry with me—"

"I'm not." She tugged her hand free of his grasp, throwing her hands into the air. "I'm angry that I fight for this city, and yet, I can't even enjoy it. I have a price over my head, despite everything I've endured. How, in the *fucking flames,* is that fair?"

"It's not," Kade said in a hushed tone. "But you're quite accustomed to the injustices of this world. *Moons,* you don't sound like yourself—"

"I damn well don't feel like it either!" Evelyn roared.

Kade's eyes widened. "Talk to me."

He'll never understand. The thought came and went like a hit to the back of Evelyn's knees.

No.

Kade understood her more than anyone else. They'd promised one another, no matter what they faced, they'd face it *together*.

She swallowed. "Aster said goodbye, Maxie won't come near me, Belle might be gone, and you're . . . *distant*. The mating bond didn't weave back together—"

"Our love is more than the bond, Ev," he said. "What is it that you're so frightened of? You're holding back from me. I can feel it."

Lie, a voice whispered, one embedded deep like it wasn't in the crevices of her mind but embedded in her soul.

Like the Goddess's power.

Evelyn ignored it, refusing to let it control her. "I thought I'd come back whole again; but I feel less like myself than when I didn't have my magic. My soul's repaired, and yet, I'm not . . . *me*."

Wind barreled down the street, howling in the wake of Evelyn's words. The trees groaned as their trunks bent, and the branches clattered against one another.

Kade reached her in two longs strides, grabbing hold of her wrists. "Before we met in the Sun Goddess's palace, what did you encounter in the Otherworld?"

Evelyn blinked, trying to remember. *Oh.* "Memories. Not of things I necessarily regret, but difficult decisions I made."

"Like?"

She swallowed, words thick. "One of them was when I sent you away after learning you weren't actually Cyrus."

Kade's eyes softened. "You faced those memories as a test."

Evelyn shook her head, shutting her eyes. "I know, and in the moment, I accepted my choices and efforts, but now I've hurt two people I love, Kade. What do I do now?"

He nodded, understanding rippling across his face. He placed a hand over her heart. "We trust in what's here. We travel to Callum, stay the course of the prophecy, and when we return, you'll make right by your friends."

Your actions define you.

Evelyn tried to remind herself of that as she and Kade hurried to Nūa's harbor.

But how could that bring her any comfort when her late actions hurt not only herself, but those around her?

439

CHAPTER SEVENTY-ONE

Rook nibbled at Blair's curls, unbothered as the Sapphire Sea groaned for miles. At the end of the docks, a ship named the *Oilliphéist*, the very vessel that had brought Evelyn to Callum before, awaited their team, all thanks to a large sum of money from Tovi. The sun shined like a silver dollar behind the clouds, its descent towards the horizon a sign they had less than an hour before they left the shores of Sorin.

Nerves prickled across Blair's skin. She'd never left the continent, but she had every intention of putting as much distance between herself and the Drengr scholar who'd volunteered to remain at Vísdómr to continue research regarding the prophecy.

Workers at the harbor eyed her familiar, wariness bleeding into the calm sea breeze, but their murmurs stopped short as they spotted the towering presence standing to Blair's right.

Lorkan.

Though he planned to return to Vísdómr, they'd stuck close to one another since they'd left the north, moving as one like a river bent and curved through the land. Yet, unlike when they'd researched in Lorkan's study, Blair found no comfort in the silence ringing between them.

"You didn't need to travel all the way to Nūa," she whispered.

The Sapphire Sea's winds barreled into them, unforgiving and cold, as if they detected Blair's lie.

Lorkan peered down at her. "I'd not dare let you leave for another continent without a proper farewell." He stepped closer, and Rook shot into the air.

Some witches sent prayers to the Goddess to protect them against the bad omen. Blair almost laughed, considering what Evelyn had detailed about her time in the Otherworld, but Lorkan invaded her space further. His smoky moss scent unraveled her senses, and she fisted her hands, digging her nails into her fleshy palms to keep her wits.

The winds picked up, and the waves lapped up and over the docks. Salt and brine clung to Blair's bones as she braced for the hundreds of words swimming in his golden eyes.

"I know there's a rift between us as large as the sea separating Sorin and Torren," Lorkan said. "There was a time once when I'd accepted it, left it as is, but I'll not make that mistake again. The truth is, Blair—"

"There you are!"

Lorkan stiffened as Eldrick grasped his shoulder. The alpha wore traveling furs, a large sack thrown over his shoulder. Beside him, Tovi held her plum cloak close to her face, her Verena hair tucked away and out of sight.

She glanced at Blair, her ancient jade eyes assessing her too closely.

Blair exhaled, breath pluming like smoke. If only she could step foot on the ship, lock herself in her cabin, and get a moment's peace from curious glances and Lorkan's presence.

"Are you sure you're not joining us?" Eldrick asked his brother.

"No," Lorkan said, rather quickly. "There are matters I need to attend at my post."

Blair ground her teeth together, tasting chalk. Lorkan didn't lie exactly. He had his pack to look after and a secret far too difficult to conceal on a ship. But it was his relaxed nature she couldn't stomach. How easily he deflected his brother's question.

It left her off-balance, as if she had fallen into the waves and was at the mercy of the current. What if his earlier words weren't genuine but rehearsed, too? Would she trust him again?

Blair swallowed, running her hands down her black velvet cloak. "Tovi, would you like to head towards the ship with me?"

Beside her, Lorkan's jaw ticked. Tension bristled in the air. Eldrick cleared his throat, and Tovi forced a small smile.

"Alright."

She looped her arm with Blair's, and they weaved through harbor workers. Fish flew across the docks, sailors hollered commands, and boats bobbed against the slick docks.

"What's going on with you and Lorkan?" Tovi whispered.

Blair winced. "Nothing."

Tovi snorted.

"What?" Blair couldn't help herself.

The vampyr peered down at her, one brow raised. "You and Evelyn are so alike. She acted much the same with Kade."

"Why do you think that is?" Blair asked.

Her friend shrugged. "Fear? Who isn't afraid when it comes to love."

Tovi glanced back, her stare landing on Eldrick. The Drengr brothers laughed together, and Blair all but wished Lorkan recognized the care shining in Eldrick's eyes as he gazed at his brother. Being a vampyr wouldn't change his brother's love. She felt that truth to her bones.

She sighed, insides twisting. Yet, it wasn't love Blair feared, but herself. When she stared into Lorkan's honey eyes, her own secret reflected back at her.

Secrets, Blair chastised herself.

Because it wasn't just the shadows any longer. She had a scar from touching Evelyn's bloodstone, a symbol associated with the Mother of Darkness. Not to mention, that goddess had visited Blair when the veils between worlds had thinned.

Hypocrisy weighed heavy against her limbs like shackles. Blair questioned the anger she harbored, too. Perhaps it festered worse because she and Lorkan were more similar than she wanted admit.

Both had secrets weaved with darkness, and neither understood how to forge ahead with those they loved, all hel-bent on saving Sorin from the curse.

"*Psst,*" someone hissed a few yards away.

The Carson coven stood at the end of the docks, mingling near the *Oil-liphéist*'s ramp. Roderick, Josepha, Artie, and Emmett stood with their hoods back and cloaks fastened, though they'd chosen various colors and not Carson crimson. Mirella and Ruth, on the other hand, had their hoods up.

Mirella pursed her lips, fighting tears. "Were you really going to leave Sorin without a proper goodbye?"

Blair reached her sister in two long strides and answered her with a tight hug. Mirella wrapped her arms fiercely around Blair, as if she'd never let go.

"Must you leave?" her sister whispered, words thick.

No, a phantom voice said in the back of Blair's mind. Evelyn and Kade had all they needed to enter the Gray Wood, but where else could Blair venture? She couldn't stay in Nūa with a bounty still over her head, and Vísdómr included Lorkan, and avoiding one another hadn't worked before.

Perhaps halfway across the world, she'd find some solace.

Mirella released her and lay a hand on her cheek. "I'm proud of you."

Emotions lodged in Blair's throat, and Mirella's words were a fraction of being truly seen, but Blair inhaled them like a starved woman.

"Thank you," she whispered.

Goodbyes peppered the air for the next few moments as Blair hugged the rest of the Carsons. Artie handed her a pack full of supplies, cinnamon and citrus tea wafting from inside, and Josepha gave her a few books, ones from Blair's townhome she'd managed to restore.

"I wish there'd been more to save but . . ."

Blair clutched them to her chest. "This is enough, auntie."

"Aye, take care of yourself, books," Artie said.

The Carson coven begrudgingly stepped away from the ship's ramp, giving Blair and Tovi the space to board. Her friend grasped her hand, giving it a gentle squeeze as her family sent tender, backwards glances her way, but commotion up the docks severed the harbor's peace.

Blair and the Carsons whipped their attention to the culprits gaining all the attention.

Kade weaved through the workers with Bleu trailing behind. Yet, the Son of the God's face was concealed under his hood. Fisherman inspected his looming height, but it was Evelyn who captured their attention fully.

She'd dropped her hood back, and her obsidian hair twisted in the wind, declaring for all to see she'd returned to Nūa. A sharpness lay in her stare as she dared the witches around her to say *something*.

Kade followed the Carsons' line of sight and cursed, but before he had time to say anything to Evelyn, Blair beat him to it.

"You're a fool," she hissed.

Evelyn blinked. "We're about to leave. If Circe hasn't spotted me yet—"

"That isn't the point," Blair said. "You jeopardize the coven, even our plans!"

Evelyn stood toe to toe with her. "I'll not cower in a city that is as much mine as it is any other witch's in Sorin."

Blair reared back. She didn't recognize the edge in Evelyn's stare nor the way she said *mine*, like an angry, spiteful hiss. Blair shook her head,

"Evelyn, this isn't who are you—"

"By orders of a council member, step aside!" a Guard roared.

"Bloody hel," Tovi said.

Merchants, traders, and sailors parted on the docks, making way for a unit of Guards to pass. Circe marched at the front, rail-thin hands gripping her skirts as she avoided muck. She sneered and pointed a crooked finger in Blair and Evelyn's direction.

"Arrest them!" Circe shouted.

Guards rushed forward, but the Carsons fell into a line, blocking their path. Kade knocked back his hood and unsheathed his sword, standing ahead of Blair, Evelyn, and Tovi.

"Move!" a Guard yelled. "We don't want to fight you!"

"Pathetic!" Circe pushed the Guard out of the way and cast her magic out. Artie and Josepha didn't block in time. They collapsed to their knees, screaming from the horrors Circe's visions showed them.

Anise filtered on the wind, and the docks erupted into chaos.

Circe sneered, "Surrender, Evelyn Carson—"

"No." Blair stormed towards Circe, calling forth her winds and using them as an invisible shield against the witch's possible attacks. *Blasted books*, she'd give Evelyn a piece of her mind once they were safely aboard the *Oilliphéist*, but she'd not let the Elder near her.

"My sister is the key to breaking the Blood Curse," she said. "Let us leave."

"Is that so, *scholar*?" Circe laughed. "It is such a pity you decided to run from your proper place."

"Blair, don't listen to her," Tovi whispered from behind. "We need to get on the ship. *Now.*"

Circe's eyes widened. "The lot of you aren't going anywhere."

She thrust a wave of her magic, and Blair braced against it with a wall of her own, digging her heels into the planks of wood. Fighting clattered down the dock. The Carsons, Evelyn, and Kade fought the Guards.

"Turn your sister in, Blair, and I'll reinstate your position at the Nūa Library," Circe said.

Never, the promise vibrated through Blair like a storm rumbling across Sorin's plains. She didn't announce it out loud, not when she harnessed enough power to show Circe.

Yet, Blair called upon too much. Perhaps it was the disarray around her or the sheer audacity that Circe would suggest such a thing, but she lost her grip on her shadows. They unleashed in her next blow. Inky tendrils snaked out from her fingertips, heading towards Circe.

Blasted books, Blair had revealed her secret, and the Carson coven took notice. Bewilderment thickened the briny air.

Circe eyes widened—

Then she laughed. Cackled. The sound grated up Blair's spine. Circe pivoted, and with a flick of her wrist, deflected Blair's shadows to the left.

"*NO!*" Blair and Evelyn screamed at once.

Blair's shadows hit Mirella square in the chest. She jolted. Gasped. Spidery veins bloomed across her skin. Blair's eldest sister collapsed to her knees, and it wasn't sweet anise in the air anymore, but death.

"No, no, no," Blair sobbed.

She didn't care for Circe's continued laughter, Evelyn's own shouts of rage, or the ripples of shock through the crowd. Blair ran to Mirella's side. Her sister shivered, and blood seeped from her mouth. Her blue eyes grew darker and darker—no, that was life fading from her.

"Mirella." Blair's voice broke. She couldn't contain the tears streaming down her face or the tremors racking her own body. Blair didn't know where to put her hands. Didn't know what to do—

"Somebody help!" she shouted.

But *Mirella* was the healer. The firstborn. The *leader*.

"Blair," her sister rasped. She palmed Blair's cheek. "My smart, brilliant sister."

Pain pierced Blair's heart. It cracked. Ripped in two. The power running through her veins had done *this*.

"No!" Emmett crashed to his knees. "Mirella—" He winced, drawing his fated into his arms.

The pain lancing through Blair's heart spread like thorny veins scraping against her insides. Her sister didn't only face death; Emmett did, too. Strong arms grasped Blair and pulled her back.

"What are you doing—"

"Blair, there's nothing you can do," Lorkan breathed into her ear. "Let them be together."

The sound of his voice broke Blair even more. She'd pushed him away, all because of the darkness within herself. The kind that killed. Yet, he was still there for her. Near. She fell into his embrace, gripping his arms like a lifeline.

Emmett rocked Mirella in his arms, and the two stared at one another until the life in Mirella extinguished entirely. An unnatural sound broke from Emmett as he held her tighter, drawing her lifeless body to his chest.

Soon, he became lifeless, too, and Blair's mind echoed with nothing but the jarring truth.

She'd killed them.
She'd killed them.
She'd killed them.

CHAPTER SEVENTY-TWO

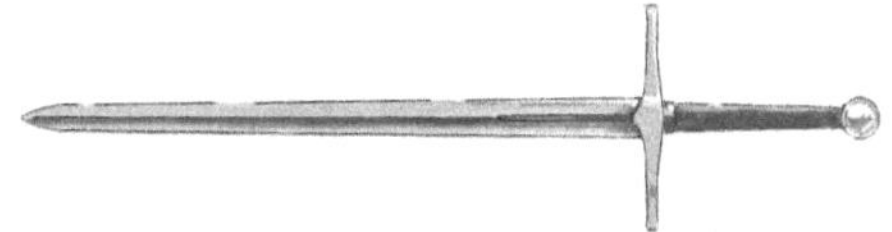

DISCONNECT BRISTLED AT KADE'S fingertips.

The sword of ancients hummed under his touch, but its power didn't caress his own.

Perhaps it was the fact he didn't wish to kill with it but disarm. His stomach backflipped as he bashed the hilt straight into a witch's temple. The Guard crumpled to the dock. Not dead, but unconscious.

He drove his fist into the gut of another, knocking them back. To his left, a witch twisted her hands and drew up her power. Before she thrust it in his direction, Kade threw out his arm, sending a wall of his own power and casting her off the docks. She landed with a splash in the tempestuous waves.

Disarm, not harm.

Kade refused to kill witches today. Not when they were technically on the same side. Damn the Nūa papers and city gossip. He refused to let his actions feed into their narrative.

"What's the plan?" Eldrick fell flush to Kade's back, axe at the ready.

"We get on the ship and avoid bloodshed," he growled.

"Got it," Eldrick breathed.

The brothers sprang apart, fighting their own opponents. Kade grasped the shoulder of the Guard he fought and threw him across the docks. A second Guard landed in the waves.

Anguish barreled down the mating bond, and Kade whirled.

His mouth turned dry. His own heart ached.

Mirella lay dying in Blair's arms.

And there was despair and loss and *pain* brimming in Emmet's eyes as he crawled to his fated.

The sight rocked through Kade, reaching his inner wolf. He searched and searched and searched for his mate—

"*Ev,*" Kade hissed.

She fought Circe, and he didn't recognize her nor the type of rage gleaming in her eyes. Sure, he'd fought side by side with her angry, but this version of her was different.

Fiercer. Wilder. *Darker.*

Silver flames twisted with wisps of red, and for the first time since he'd met Evelyn Carson, he didn't know who she was.

Or *what.*

Get to her, his instinct roared.

Kade hedged through the fray, but two Guards, one wielding a metal staff and another wearing Burns coven green, intercepted his path.

Kade cursed.

The Burns witch tightened his fist, and magic rumbled underneath Kade's boots. The dock trembled, and everyone shouted as the planks loosened. It threw Kade off balance, but his werewolf hearing detected Evelyn's cries of frustration off in the distance.

He conjured a sphere of blue power and threw it ahead. The Guard on the left used her staff to deflect it. Boldness bled into their expression, and they charged forward, driving him back.

Farther from Evelyn.

She drove her own staff into the docks and lit the dragon bone aflame. Silver and red climbed and hissed and—

Between blocks and jabs, Kade caught the flames eating away at the material.

Burning it.

Kade reared back as the Guard's staff came inches from his face. Ahead, Evelyn's longtime weapon crumbled in her hand. In her moment of disbelief, Circe backhanded her across the face. His mate fell to the docks, clutching her mouth.

Kade's inner wolf rose to the surface, and his resolve snapped. He couldn't think straight at the sight of Evelyn's blood, and his new ancient power wouldn't let him stand by and do *nothing.* He swiped his blade across the

Burns Guard's belly. Blue glowed down the blade, alighting the bloodstain. The witch stared, wide-eyed, and fell with a deafening thud to the docks.

Dead.

No, no, no.

He hadn't meant to, Kade told himself. It *wasn't* his intent. He blinked, tightening his grip on the hilt of his sword, yet the metal burned, as if refusing to mold to his hand. *Moons*, he wasn't darkness, right? No, he was gods damn poor circumstance.

He searched for Evelyn again. An orange mass of fur shot through the chaos and landed on Circe's face. The Elder screamed, and the feral cries of a tiny beast echoed against the ships. Flesh tore, and the Elder's pathetic pleas only egged her assailant on.

Maxie attacked Circe as Evelyn stood on unsteady legs.

Kade called her name, but it was no use. The winds swallowed it, and even down their bond, *something* blocked his plea.

The Guard wielding the staff screamed as she advanced, tears welling in her eyes as her dead comrade lay a few feet away.

Kade blocked her weapon with his blade just in time. Metal and wood shook with exertion as they pushed against the other.

A growl rumbled through Kade's chest. "We don't want anyone else to get hurt. Let us continue our journey, and no more blood will be spilled."

He pushed one last time and released a hint of his power, hitting the Guard straight in the belly. She tumbled into two more Guards, disarming Eldrick and Tovi's opponents.

They all rose, huddling into formation. Their dark uniforms sucked the little color from the docks.

"Despite what you've been told," he said, "we're all on the same side. I promise you, Circe is leading you astray."

Wide-eyed, stunned, breathless, the Guards shared a silent conversation. One nodded, and the others followed. Their shoulders slacked, and the tension across the docks dropped. Eldrick, with Tovi at his side, lowered his axe. The Carsons too, spent, lowered their hands, magic dissipating from the air.

For a moment, relief crept through Kade.

"All such pathetic fools," Circe roared.

Metal pierced through flesh, and a broken cry unleashed from Evelyn. Pain like nothing before shot down their bond. Kade almost crumpled to his knees.

"*MAXIE!*" Evelyn screamed.

Behind him, Circe had stabbed Evelyn's familiar through the belly, the hilt of a letter opener pressing into her fur. Maxie whimpered, and before Kade reached them, Circe withdrew her blade and thrust Maxie into a cluster of netting and fish traps.

"No!" Evelyn cried, dashing after Maxie.

Kade moved to join her, but Circe intercepted his path. Dozens of cuts across her face seeped with blood with one eye swelled shut from a bruise.

"Kill them!" Circe roared to the Guards. "The Goddess's flame is *mine*, and I'll not be leaving these docks without what was promised to me!"

Ah. It didn't confirm the witch was Riven's contact, but Kade had wondered why Circe wanted Evelyn's bloodstone. Circe's obsession with her flame when Evelyn was a child made all the more sense, too. But how did she plan on getting it now that Evelyn had her magic back?

A female Guard stepped forward, shaking her head. "Elder Circe, Kade and Evelyn are a part of the prophecy—"

Power rippled down the dock, and the Guard flew yards away. The rest stumbled back, eyes wide with horror.

"If you won't listen to my orders, allow me to *make* you listen." She snapped her fingers.

Licorice drenched the docks in its sweet anise scent. The Guards stiffened. Even witches who'd hid amongst the merchant stalls and harbor supplies emerged. Their shoulders snapped back, and lips fell in a thin line like they stood to attention. Their eyes shifted to an eerie all-black color.

Dozens under some sort of trance charged.

"Stop!" Eldrick tried to reason with them, but they attacked with killing blows.

"She's controlling their minds," Tovi said, mindful of her blade as she deflected advance after advance.

Kade braced as a Guard thrust barrels towards him. He flicked his wrist, sending out his power, and they disintegrated into blue shimmering dust around him.

"We can't kill them," he shouted over the fray.

"Kade is right," Ruth yelled. "It's what Circe wants."

Yet, the Guards continued, black eyes void of emotion.

Circe.

Kade grabbed a Guard by the breastplate and chucked him across the docks. He set his focus on the cruel Elder.

Circe smirked. "I wonder what she'll become if I take you from her."

Kade charged, and power collided with magic. Anger mixed with salt. Winds weaved with Kade's blue power, and he dug his heels into the wooden planks. He positioned his sword ahead of him, like an extension to his taut being.

He swiped down and spun, attempting to deliver a death blow to this wretched witch once and for all. His sword came down and hit an invisible wall.

Circe had thrown up her arm, a shield of her magic blocking him.

Kade reached for more of his power and pressed down. Circe stumbled slightly. She gritted her teeth, rage flashing in her eyes. She threw out her other hand, bony fingers flexing at unnatural angles, and her words speared through his mind.

One of you will fall to darkness. Don't you see?

But Evelyn was *good*. A protector who cared.

Kade faltered. His sword suddenly grew too heavy, the weight of it all too much. Darkness no longer lived in the crevices of his mind, but a weed of doubt festered in his soul instead. Circe's words were like fresh water, reviving it. He worried, now more than ever, if he was worthy of the power he'd accepted in the Otherworld and if he'd fail Evelyn.

Like he was now.

A phantom hand gripped Kade's throat, closing off his airway. He dropped the sword of ancients, and it clattered across the docks. White dotted his vision, and he clawed at his invisible assailant.

This isn't real, he tried to convince himself, but Circe's hold tightened.

Unleash your power. Show them who you really are.

No, Kade bellowed inside his head. Losing and hurting, perhaps . . . but he was *not* darkness—

Circe's hold vanished.

Kade buckled to his knees, snapping his attention ahead. Circe stared, her wide eyes void of anything. Her body, completely slack, swayed. Steam rose from a hole in her chest—where her heart should've been.

The dead witch fell forward, revealing her killer standing behind her. Circe's still pumping organ was clenched in Evelyn's hand—no . . . her *talons*. Evelyn's nails had elongated to sharpened tips, black as ink. Like . . . like a *vampyr*.

Yet, no spidery veins ringed her eyes or fangs jutted over her bottom lip. Instead, her eyes brimmed crimson, matching the wisps dancing in her silver flame as it disintegrated the heart she'd ripped from the Elder's body.

"What . . ." Tovi's brows pinched, her mouth falling open in utter shock.

Kade balked, too. He thought he hadn't recognized Evelyn before. *This* wasn't simply a rage-filled version anymore but an entirely different witch.

Evelyn smirked, eying Circe's body with triumph. Blood dripped from her hand, down her forearm, soaking her leathers.

Moons, she *had* saved him, but viciousness gleamed in her eyes, not protectiveness. His knees rooted to the dock as his mind reeled with possibilities and questions, leaving him off-balance, as if he floated endlessly in the Sapphire Sea's waves.

What had his mate become?

Someone grabbed his arm in a fierce and unbending grip, snapping him from his harrowing thoughts.

"Uzoma?" he whispered.

The ancient witch didn't pay him any mind, her sights set on Evelyn past her spectacles. "It's far worse than I thought."

"What's happening to her—"

"She made a choice and is suffering the consequences." She snapped her attention back to him. "We must get you all to Callum."

Except Guards, bewildered with Circe's mind control gone, blocked their path to the *Oilliphéist*. Uzoma dragged Kade to his feet and released him. She conjured a crooked and worn staff similar to Blair's and jabbed it into the wooden planks. Winds from the east and west traveled from the plains and sea, twirling at her command. Wisps of air circled, spiraling until the docks shimmered from existence, and a new place—ale-soaked floors, fresh baked bread, and cheery song—manifested on the other side.

Kade almost—*almost*—allowed himself to feel relief.

"Go!" Uzoma shouted to the others.

Eldrick grasped Tovi's hand, and they darted through her *danu*. Lorkan, holding Blair tightly in his arms, hurried after them. The Gray Fenris, Bétar, Yen, and Linx, rushed forward next, weapons still in hand.

Evelyn stormed towards the *danu* last. She clutched Maxie to her chest, and Kade spied the familiar's chest rising and falling ever so slowly. Evelyn didn't acknowledge Uzoma, nor peer in Kade's direction, a vacant look bleeding through her eyes, their natural gray once again.

His heart dropped like a stone to his gut, and despite it all, his hands itched to reach for her—she'd been there for him all these weeks, reassuring him, and Kade knew Evelyn's soul like breathing. No, that hadn't been her earlier, but *Evelyn* was still in the there. He believed it to his bones.

"Listen to me, Kade Drengr." Uzoma's stare pinned him in place. He had one foot in Callum, another in Nūa. "The next days ahead are a test. Now more than ever, both of your destinies hang in the balance. Remember, fate is in your hands, and your hands only. *Go.*"

Kade grabbed his sword, strapped it to his back, and marched into the Runaway Radish Inn, hoping to leave the dead and doubt behind.

CHAPTER SEVENTY-THREE

FAMILIARITY WRAPPED EVELYN IN a warm embrace, but deep inside, she remained cold. A wretchedness clawed its way up her throat and wrapped its fiery tendrils around her heart.

She, along with others, stood in the middle of the Runaway Radish Inn. The band atop the dais stopped playing their harp and flute. Dancers stilled. Conversation lulled to a whisper as the inn's guests stared, open mouthed. Whiskey bottles lined the shelves, and the scent of hearty rabbit stew perfumed the air.

"Well, I swear them faeries be playin' tricks on my agin' eyesight. Evelyn Carson and Kade Drengr are standing in my inn!"

Miss Patricia, the sweet and kind owner of the inn, rounded the bar. Exactly as Evelyn remembered her, with flour coating her from to head to foot.

Evelyn had no words, her mind reeling as recent events caught up to her. Kade's presence itched up her neck. She stiffened as he joined her side, brushing his arm against hers. She couldn't look at him. Couldn't stomach the blood crusting her cuticles and staining her leathers.

Circe's blood.

Evelyn *had* killed before. But not for vengeance. Not with any other intent but to protect or fight darkness. She'd never . . . liked it.

She deserved it, a hissing voice whispered in the back of her mind.

Evelyn winced. Yes, Circe had been a cruel witch, but she didn't wish to feel that way about anyone. It felt so far away from who she was at her core. She pulled Maxie closer to her chest, her familiar's heartbeat growing faint.

"Let me take a look." Linx brushed her small hands over Maxie's belly covered in blood.

The mage's magic shimmered an array of colors, and when she finished, Maxie fidgeted in Evelyn's arms. The thread between their souls thumbed with life again.

Evelyn couldn't think, couldn't move but she managed to whisper, "Thank you."

The mage healer smiled, though it didn't reach her eyes. "Of course, Evelyn."

Whispers peppered the inn. *Magic. Werewolves. Blood.* Evelyn had almost forgotten they had an audience, but with Maxie safe in her arms and healed, she didn't care.

Kade cleared his throat. "If it isn't any trouble, we need a place to stay."

Miss Patricia inspected Evelyn up and down. "No trouble at all."

"Aye, aye. Nothing to see here! Carry on, carry on!" Commissioner Charles Doyle, uncharacteristically standing *behind* the bar, waved a cleaning rag at the band.

The harp player wiggled their fingers, and a bright melody filtered through the inn. The barmaids busied themselves with handing out overflowing pints to the tables. Soon, the crowd grew disinterested of the newcomers soaked in blood and brine, lost to the band's majestic song and malty beers.

"Follow me." Miss Patricia wrung her hands in her apron.

Solemness leaked into the air as Evelyn and their traveling party followed the innkeeper through the kitchens and out the back door. Her mind wavered between the present and a red haze. Keys rattled. She caught the tail end of Miss Patricia mentioning the inn's expansion and Charles, her new husband. Bétar and Yen disappeared. Linx too. Lorkan muttered something about taking care of Blair.

She killed Mirella, those nasty voices whispered in the back of Evelyn's mind.

Before Evelyn had time to register their meaning or fight the nastiness of them, she was shoved into a chair. She blinked, the red haze disappearing from her vision. Inside a small room with a queen size bed to the left, Tovi, Eldrick, and Kade stood ahead of her. Her fated placed Maxie onto the bed, making sure her familiar was comfortable near the pillows.

"What—"

Tovi grasped hold of her chin, trying to pry Evelyn's mouth open.

"Fucking flames," she muttered, swatting her best friend's hand out of the way. "What are you doing?"

"Checking for fangs," she whispered with a frown.

Evelyn had never witnessed her friend so . . . *rattled* before. It caught her off guard, and the tension in the room rose.

"I didn't see any," Kade said.

With arms crossed, his body remained taut while indecision warred in his golden eyes as if he couldn't decide to touch her or remain an arm's length away. His stare prickled up Evelyn's skin, and she squirmed under his assessment. It was as if they were back in Callum, but *she* was the beast he investigated.

"But she had talons." Tovi glared at him.

"I'm *right* here," Evelyn hissed.

From the small hearth in the corner, the fire crackled in the wake of her cutting words. Wind howled outside the window. Kade's jaw tightened, and Tovi clamped her eyes shut.

"We should all take a breath," Eldrick said. "A lot happened."

An understatement, Evelyn almost said.

Mirella, her loyal and steadfast older sister, was dead. Evelyn had transformed and killed Circe. By some luck, Uzoma had saved them, yet she barely recalled her tutor's parting words or if they'd spoken before she left Nūa.

"Do you remember what happened?" Tovi whispered, tone gentler.

"Some things," Evelyn said.

The moments after her sister's death were a blur, and the more Evelyn thought and thought, glimpses of the red haze returned.

Tovi placed her hands on her hips and paced. "Did you see or hear anything when you killed Circe?"

"Tovi," Kade said, an edge to his tone.

"It's what happened," Tovi hissed. "You were different, Evelyn. As your friend, I'm just afraid."

"I know," she breathed, not feeling she deserved Tovi's concern. "I don't remember what or how, but only why. I was angry. There were voices. And then there was a red haze."

"Fuck." Tovi stared up at the ceiling.

"What is it?" Kade asked.

Tovi frowned, shared an apprehensive look with Eldrick, and sighed. "It's what happens to vampyrs during bloodthirst or intense hunger because of the curse."

Panic washed over Evelyn like icy rain. "I'm not a vampyr. I don't crave blood. I swear it."

A tense beat passed in the small inn's room.

"Alright," Eldrick said. "How do we explain the talons, red haze, and your eyes, then?"

"My eyes?" Evelyn reared back, looking to Kade.

"They turned crimson," he whispered.

Evelyn's insides twisted. She didn't know what she wanted more—to melt into the chair and disappear or bolt from the room.

Kade met her in two long strides, got down on one knee and knelt to Evelyn's level. He caged her in his arms, and she exhaled at his nearness. The day's events barreled into her, and she stared into his golden eyes, the kindness shining in them grounding her.

"Whatever this is, whatever you face, we face it together, remember?" he asked.

Tears welled in Evelyn's eyes, and all she could manage was a nod.

"Talk to me."

He'd asked her the same thing back in Nūa, and Evelyn hadn't been truly ready to share what she fear. Yet, she'd stopped running from fear and doubt a long time ago, and despite the grief festering in her heart and the hovering unknowns, she'd face them.

"It's the power I stole from the Sun Goddess," she said. "It make me feel as though something's *wrong* with me."

Kade's eyes softened, and he rubbed reassuring circles on her hips.

There's nothing wrong with you, Ev, he said down the bond.

Evelyn fought tears, grasping hold of the reassurance Kade gave her while uncertainty wormed in her gut.

Tovi shook her head. "Why would the Sun Goddess's power invoke similarities reminiscent of the Blood Curse?"

"I . . . I don't know," Evelyn said, suddenly feeling weightless and spent, as if they had taken the journey across the Sapphire Sea.

Kade stood, turning to Eldrick and Tovi with crossed arms. "We aren't going to figure this out tonight. Instead, we should focus on rest."

Evelyn rose, too, and headed towards the north-facing window. Night shrouded the green hills in darkness, but future rain sat in the air, soaking into the inn's wooden bones.

"Kade's right," she said, turning to the others.

Tovi sighed, crossing her arms. "You should go and find Blair."

"No," Evelyn said too quickly, snapping her attention back to the night.

Perhaps a choice she'd made was a mistake. She never should've stolen from the Goddess or brought Aster back to life. Those were her faults, and she'd own them, but she didn't have the capacity to face her sister; not so soon after

Mirella's death. Evelyn didn't hold anger towards Blair, but she couldn't sort out the feelings coursing through her. Frustration, grief, betrayal. They ran hot and cold and all at once, and that wretched kernel that didn't belong in her heart heightened them, too.

Evelyn feared she couldn't control her emotions or what she'd say to Blair. That's why she couldn't speak with her. Not yet.

"Tomorrow, we head to the Gray Wood," she said.

Tovi tsked her tongue. "Bloody hel, Evelyn. Mirella is gone—"

"I'm well aware, but our task in Callum remains the same. Uzoma gave us a three-week head start. Let's not waste it. If we're lucky, you'll beat Riven and Ingrid to Lake Glenn."

Tovi's lips fell into a thin line, and apprehension bled into her jade stare.

Finally, she said, "Alright. We'll see you in the morning before you head off. I'm so sorry about your sister."

Evelyn's eyes stung, but she didn't reach for her friend. Instead, she gave her a curt nodded and didn't relax until the door clicked shut.

Once alone with Kade, she let the tears fall. He tugged her into his strong embrace, and her sobs didn't stop, they worsened. She cried for so many things.

Mirella. Blair. Belle. Aster. Sorin. *Herself.*

For the first time in months, doubt crept over Evelyn like a shadowy cloak, draping her in fears.

Later, the rain started and pelted against the inn. It seemed Callum was just as saddened as Evelyn.

CHAPTER SEVENTY-FOUR

BLAIR SAT MOTIONLESS IN a copper tub. Steam rolled across the water, kissing her exposed shoulders with warmth. Outside, rain pattered against the room's window. Droplets raced down the glass, and she found reprieve in following their paths instead of lingering on the ache spreading through her chest.

If she fidgeted amongst the honeysuckle-scented suds, a piercing pain lodged near her heart. When she winced and closed her eyes, Blair witnessed the life extinguish from her sister's eyes over and over. Despite the hot water scalding her skin, Blair remained still. For minutes, hours, days. She had no concept of time as grief gripped her.

Occasionally, the winds howled through the coastal town, hauntingly like Emmet's bellow when Mirella had died.

All because Blair's shadows had manifested, and they'd killed Mirella.

She'd killed her sister.

The door to the room clicked open.

In the window's reflection, she spied Lorkan. Rain had matted his hair and soaked his clothes, but he held a tray of food. Soup. Bread. Tea. Tucked under one arm, he'd arrived with fresh clothes, and in the other, a large, weathered book.

Neither spoke as he set the items down.

Blair focused back on the suds, counting the various colors wavering in the bubbles. If she could dunk under the water and not resurface, she would, but by Lorkan's fierce hold on her as he carried her through the *danu*, she had a sense the Drengr scholar wouldn't let her go any time soon.

Lorkan's boots thudded against the wooden floorboards. He pulled up a stool and sat, rolling up his sleeves. Still, they said nothing, and Blair appreciated that he leaned into the quiet and allowed Blair to sit in it.

He grabbed the small sponge and soap next and dipped his hand into the tub to pull Blair's arm free. She swallowed as he busied himself with washing her skin clean. Shoulder to elbow to wrist and back up. Not in a sensual manner, but in a tender sort of way.

The gesture threatened to unleash Blair's tears building up.

"Aren't you angry with me?" Her first words in hours burned in her dry throat.

Lorkan didn't stop washing her, moving the stool so he was positioned behind her. She leaned forward, and he rubbed the sponge tentatively down her spine and followed the lines of her muscles.

"Why should I be?" he asked, voice far too gentle.

Blair sucked in a shuddering breath. For not only had she killed her sister, but she'd also revealed her darkest secret.

"Because I kept something from you all these years. I'd not be surprised if you thought me a hypocrite—"

"That is the farthest from what I think of you, Blair," he whispered, resting his hands on the edge of the tub.

Blair peered over her shoulder at him. "How can you be so certain?"

"Because I love you," he said, honey stare pinning her in place.

She didn't doubt him for a second. He'd held her since Mirella had died. Been by her side. He'd carried her through the *danu* to Callum, abandoning his duty at Vísdómr and risking his own secret traveling so far from home. He'd chosen her above it all, and his presence and actions spoke louder than his four words.

"It's what I planned to tell you at the docks, but then—"

"I killed Mirella," Blair said, voice breaking on her sister's name.

"No." Lorkan shut his eyes and shook his head. His shoulders tensed. His jaw ticked. When his eyes sprang open again, a sharpness burned in them, as if his predatorial side lay just below the surface. "Circe killed your sister. I smelled the dark magic that witch used. *She* manipulated your shadows."

"You don't know that—"

"Lean back, Blair," he whispered.

She swallowed. Obeyed. Her head rested against Lorkan's chest, and he grasped her hand holding the edge of the tub.

"Draw your shadows forth," he said into the shell of her ear.

"*What?*" Blair lurched forward, but Lorkan's arm clasped across her chest, holding her in place. "I don't want to hurt you."

"You won't. I trust you. There's not an ounce of darkness inside of you, Blair."

She shook her head, unable to fight the tears any longer. "You don't know that. The Blood Goddess visited me when Evelyn visited the Otherworld. Bloodstones *burn* my flesh. I don't know what I am or why—"

"We'll figure it out," Lorkan whispered, voice slightly different. "Blair, look at me."

She turned, slowly, in the tub.

The scholar seated behind her, the man she loved, had released his fangs. Slightly thicker than a normal vampyr, they jutted over his bottom lip. Black spidery veins ringed his eyes, making their honey color gleam more like gold. Something sharper than fingers brushed across Blair's knuckles. She turned to their touching hands and didn't balk at Lorkan's talons hovering over her pebbled flesh.

Lorkan abandoned his stool and kneeled at the side of the rub, peering up at her.

"You're not afraid of me?" he asked, his words barely a question at all but full of *knowing*.

"Of course not," she breathed. How could she be when he'd chosen her in these last difficult and harrowing hours?

He raised a brow. "Why?"

Blair swallowed. Shook her head. Tears stung the edges of her eyes, and gods knew her heart ached, but something else—mighty and pure—beat inside it.

"Because I love you."

Lorkan's lips twitched into an almost smile. Slowly, hesitantly, he placed a taloned hand on her cheek, cupping her face with the gentleness of falling snow. Blair placed her hand atop Lorkan's, encouraging and welcoming his touch. She gripped his hand like her life depended on it; as if she didn't sit on solid ground and his touch anchored her in the present.

"Show me your power," he whispered.

Blair shut her eyes. An old, stubborn streak in her roared in retaliation. *Don't step out of line,* it screamed. Yet, Blair already had. She'd conjured her shadows in her home city. Shown her coven, sister, and Lorkan. Perhaps it was inevitable she'd one day reveal them, for they were a part of her. Could she truly outrun what she was?

She called upon them. The power sang in her blood like a whistling wind. Cold caressed her fingertips.

Lorkan sucked in a breath. Not of fear but of wonder.

Blair opened her eyes, and below, in the water's reflection, she witnessed her shadows tangling themselves between Lorkan's talons. Curious. Gentle. Like smoky wisps at the end of a storm.

"See?" Lorkan whispered. "Beautiful."

He shifted back to his scholarly form, all evidence of vampyrism gone. Blair drew back her shadows and stood out of the tub. Lorkan helped wrap her in towels and blankets, carrying her to the bed. Once dressed in an oversize sweater, she nibbled on sourdough dunked in soup.

"Thank you, Lorkan," she said in their comforting silence. "For coming with me and being by my side."

He ran a hand through his damp hair. "When I was seventeen, I let fear control me. Believed Sorin wasn't ready for what I was—perhaps they still aren't—but I was a fool to think you were amongst them. Your anger when you discovered I was a vampyr makes even more sense. Our otherness brought us together long ago. Your shadows, my latent wolf. I see now that keeping that I was a vampyr from you must've hurt because it confirmed your fears about your own power. I'll not abandon you like I did all those years ago; I'm with you in this. Forever and always."

Forever and always, Blair repeated to herself.

Lorkan's declaration was mighty and soothing all at once.

Blair and Lorkan entangled themselves in the bed's quilts. She fell flush against his back, sitting between his legs as his arms draped over her. A steaming cup of tea wafted between them, and Lorkan opened the book he'd borrowed from the innkeeper, *Faeries & Their Tales,* and the old spine creaked over the constant rain.

Lorkan read to her late into the night. His storytelling tone calmed Blair's aching heart. She still thought of her sister, but she managed the pain better in Lorkan's arms. He spoke of monsters and creatures tucked into the green hills, recited limericks, and began the longest tale: a faerie king who sacrificed it all.

The moment brought her back to their hiding place inside the Drengr Library. So similar, yet also different. They were still two tender hearts drawn together by otherness, but they'd revealed their secrets. It made the comfort all the more real.

Eventually, sleep found Blair. She didn't dream amongst smoke and moss encompassing her, but soon hours passed, and a knock resounded on their door.

Day had arrived, and it was time they traveled to the Gray Wood.

CHAPTER SEVENTY-FIVE

T HE NEXT MORNING, EVELYN, Kade, and Blair braced the rainy Callum morning as they traveled south past Dinberry and over the green hills leading to the Gray Wood. They rode in silence, the unsaid words between them pounding as loudly as Bleu's muddy hooves.

She and her sister hadn't spoken yet. Not once since loosing Mirella. But Evelyn still didn't trust this unnatural callousness gripping her and faced the forest's entrance.

She'd face what happened with Blair after they completed this task.

The Gray Wood had changed. The once curved trunks had straightened, creating a prouder army of trees and taller canopy. Healthy pine needles covered the smoother branches top to bottom, and delicate berries with a silver sheen sat at the tips, dripping with rain. The bark still peeled and unfurled from the trunks, but without the Far Darrig's dark hold over it, no foxy-colored flesh remained, but instead verdant green.

"It feels like a lifetime ago we were here," Kade whispered, droplets collecting in his beard.

"But at the same, like it was just yesterday," she said.

She'd been Saige. He'd been Cyrus. A barmaid and a huntsman, solving murders that led to far more than they anticipated. To think, this is where it all started, and they found themselves back at the same place.

Evelyn brushed her fingers against Kade's.

His gaze snapped towards her fingers intertwining with his, and Kade released a shuddering breath and grasped Evelyn's hand. "I love you," he said.

"Yesterday, today, tomorrow, and the far distant future, when my soul is but essence floating in the wind. Remember that."

Evelyn swallowed, the words reaching a part of her soul that was smothered with *other*. Not the mating bond, not the thread connecting the souls, but the simplistic fact her heart belonged to Kade, no matter what else she'd weaved into it.

"Kade, I—"

"Are you two ready?" Blair snapped.

Evelyn blinked, finding her sister at the precipice of the Gray Wood's entrance, map in hand. She sighed, her sister's ire not in nasty words but a piercing gaze that might as well have been a blade slicing across the back of her knees.

"Let's go," Evelyn said.

Rain showered through openings in the canopy, drenching clusters of wildflowers. Songbirds chirped unseen, and small mammals scurried across the path, their noses twitching as they sniffed the wet air and inspected the forest's visitors.

Evelyn paused halfway down the path and dropped her hood back. Memories flushed through her. Here, she'd heard the drums of the Far Darrig and communicated with the Gray Wood the first time. Her fingers itched to speak with the forest again, to confirm they were in the right place.

Tentatively, she placed her palm atop the closest tree, molding her hand over the peeling bark. It was softer than it appeared, plush like moss.

At first, nothing happened.

Birds hopped from branch to branch, animals scurried through foliage, and rain ran down Evelyn's neck, hot and steaming, like the Sun Goddess watched her efforts from the Otherworld. Heat built underneath Evelyn's palm, the branch growing hotter and hotter until—

Evelyn hissed, snatching her hand away. A red, angry burn bloomed across her palm, but it healed as quickly as it came.

Confusion rippled through Evelyn, and she inspected the tree she'd touched. The green flesh bloomed a foxy red, and no ancientness caressed her magic, no indication it recognized her.

Evelyn released a breath and continued to follow Kade and Blair. As they trekked ten yards down the path in stewing silence, the canopy above shook. Evelyn braced, and Kade unsheathed his new sword.

Branches snapped. Thunder rumbled. The commotion echoed from behind, and the three of them whirled towards the entrance.

"Fuck," Kade muttered.

Roots slithered through the mud and puddles, connecting with the others across from it. The trees bent, curving towards one another so the branches intertwined, too. Leaves sprouted in bulbous puffs, blocking out the misty hills of Callum.

The entrance to the Gray Wood closed, locking them inside.

Blair eyed the entrance and then Evelyn. "Any idea why that happened?"

"How should I know?" Evelyn asked.

Blair shrugged. "Perhaps because the prophecy claims this place is an old friend."

Yet, the Gray Wood didn't answer Evelyn, and Blair's tone hurt like she'd pinched Evelyn's skin. In retaliation, the flame in her rose in one mighty wave.

Scorching. Fervent. Angry.

Demonstrate your power. Show her your wrath.

She fisted her hands at her sides, snuffing down the unwarranted reaction. The sense of unbalance rocked through her. What if she leaned too far the wrong way? What if this wrongness took her? What if she *liked* it?

"Come back to me," Kade's voice whispered.

Evelyn hadn't realized she'd closed her eyes. Hadn't felt the silver and crimson flames dancing at her fingertips. Hadn't known she'd fallen into numbness, unaware of the forest sprawling around her.

She blinked and met Kade's kind amber stare. "I . . ." Evelyn's voice cracked. "I don't understand who I am anymore."

"I know, love." Pain pinched Kade's brow.

"Look out!" Blair cried.

Evelyn peered down as panic crept down her spine. Branches snaked towards Kade's boots and wrapped around his ankles. He flinched and sprang away from Evelyn, but that only caused the branches to tighten their hold.

They yanked him back, and Kade slammed into the forest floor.

"Kade!" Evelyn shouted.

She twirled her fingers, conjured her flame, and thrust a sphere of magic at the branch. It reared back, releasing one of Kade's legs, but the other dragged him away.

Evelyn dashed after him as Blair rushed to her side. Winds howled, her sister's brotannas mixing with rain and whirling through the forest. Kade twisted, swiping his sword through the brush. Yet, it was no use. Their efforts only awakened more trees.

They converged ahead of Evelyn and Blair, drawing together like the Gray Wood's closed entrance. Trees crawled on creeping roots, moving from one place to another. Branches overlapped and tightened, like a weaved tapestry of wood and leaves. With a loud *thunk*, the Gray Wood stilled, separating Evelyn from Kade.

"No!" she roared, slamming her fists against the trees.

A branch reached out and hit Evelyn square in the gut, knocking her back. A scream unleashed from her, and she thrust out her hands. Silver and red flames awakened, raging up her forearms.

"Wait!" Blair shouted, stepping in front of Evelyn. Her midnight eyes bore into her sister's, desperation shimmering across them. "Can't you see that isn't working? Fighting the forest only makes it worse!"

"How dare you?" Evelyn hissed. "Are you seriously going to give me a lecture on how to use my magic when yours killed Mirella?"

Blair reared back like she'd slapped her. "It was an accident."

"Is that what you're telling yourself?" Evelyn scoffed, a wet, hollow laugh falling from her. "Take some fucking accountability."

Her sister cried out in anger and cast her winds in mighty wave, thrusting Evelyn across the clearing. She landed, pride and bones rattled.

Fucking flames, she hadn't meant to say those words. To allow her grief and anger to take over.

Blair strode towards her, magic leaking from her fingertips. "Fine. I'll admit it. It was my magic that hit our sister's heart. Now, where's your accountability?"

"*Mine?*" A red haze fell over Evelyn's sights. She hurried to her feet, drawing her own magic back up. Flames ignited at her fingertips. They hissed as rain pelted from above. Gods, she was *so angry*.

The forest's energy fluttered through the air, greeting Evelyn for the first time but with an angry, definitive *Stop*. Evelyn didn't understand the meaning of the word.

She hurled a ball of flame towards her sister. "What, in the hel, did I do?"

Blair blocked her attack by drawing it into her winds. The tendrils of their magic weaved together until Evelyn's was snuffed out.

"We had a plan! To get in and out of the city, to meet at the harbor and hurry to Callum, but you waltzed down the docks like there'd be no consequence. If you weren't so arrogant, so *blasted books* blinded by what you always think is best, Circe never would've attacked, and Mirella would still be alive!"

Evelyn's chest heaved, and the red haze dimmed for a moment. "I'm sad she's gone, too, Blair."

"I'm not sad. I'm fucking angry!" Her sister pressed her palms forward, hurtling winds towards Evelyn.

She threw up her arm, drawing a wall of flame ahead of her, using it to block Blair's blow. Evelyn dug her heels into the ground, sliding through the dirt. Blair called back her winds, and both their magic burst outward from the lack of tension, scattering across the sodden forest.

Blair's curls twisted wildly, her winds like a cyclone around her. Evelyn couldn't differentiate between the rain and tears dripping down her sister's beautiful face.

"None of this would've happened if you'd just stayed the Daughter of the Goddess. If you had told me about your lost magic—"

"You can't patronize my secrets when you've had plenty of your own," Evelyn said through gritted. "You possess shadows!"

Blair flinched. "That sort of power gets a witch thrown into Tùir. At least I stuck to my path. I remained a scholar and worked hard at it. I understood my place. I'm not so hel-bent on rebelling against fate!"

"What about Lorkan?" Evelyn said. "I see the way you look at each other. Noticed it during our first meeting in Lār. You've met the Drengr scholar before, haven't you?"

Venom, not magic, coursed through Evelyn's veins, and she wished to dig deeper into Blair's pain. Craved it. The hunger festering in her belly had a mind of its own—she dared to call it darkness. A curse of her own making.

"Lorkan isn't any of your damn business," Blair seethed.

She whirled her hands and attacked, and her winds turned into shadows. Evelyn spun, and the two Carson sisters fought one another. Anger, hurt, all of it leaked from their magics.

"Nūa was my home once," Evelyn's shouted above their chaos. "Witches are my people. Do you know what it's like to walk the streets of your kind's city and not be seen for what you truly are? As if everyone that passes by just sees *through* you?"

Blair stumbled, drawing back her magic. "Of course I do, Evelyn. That has been my life every day for as long as I can remember."

No, a voice shouted inside Evelyn's mind. *How could she possibly understand?*

Evelyn attacked harder. Fiercer. Her magic and body moved without her. She was so off-kilter with her mind and heart. Fathomless. Empty. Hope fell through her fingers like sand.

Mirella was dead. The Blood Curse still loomed over Sorin. She and Kade couldn't reweave the mating bond. She'd gotten her magic back, restitched her soul and *more,* and it still wasn't enough. She kept running from her title and replacing it with purpose, but were her efforts worth anything?

It wasn't doubt that wrapped around Evelyn's resolve. It was horror. She stood in this very forest and fought against the demons of her mind before, but she was so tired. So done. So *angry*. What if Evelyn didn't have a grasp on her fate as strongly as she thought? What if she'd forever be a pawn?

Never.

The hiss echoing in the back of Evelyn's mind wasn't resilience. Bred from malice and vengeance, it reared its fangs like a serpent, hypnotizing her with the promise of the power pulsing in her heart. Evelyn fell into the haze, its willing victim.

The flames at her hands roared to life, red overtaking the silver. The Gray Wood's temperature rose like the Cirrillo desert, baking under the heat she emitted. Steam rolled around her like a fire-breathing beast.

"Evelyn, stop!" Blair shouted. "This isn't who you are!"

Her sister's voice traveled from far away. Instead, ahead, a dark witch with shadows at her fingertips that Evelyn didn't recognize threatened to *put her in her place*.

Never.

For her place was above them all. She'd make them bow and cower from her power. What a wonderful, delightful prospect.

The witch's face fell. "Evelyn . . ."

Your darkness is not welcome here.

The Gray Wood's deep, soft voice yanked Evelyn back to reality. A breath whooshed out of her, and she stumbled forward. Spent, wary. Evelyn blinked, finding Blair yards away, hands still twirling with her winds. Pure horror etched across her face.

A branch shot out of the thicket of trees, grabbing one of Blair's wrists. Then the other. Evelyn's sister screamed as the branches tightened, snuffing her magic. With arms splayed wide, the Gray Wood held her sister in place.

"Let her go," Evelyn whispered. "Please!"

Why have you come?

Evelyn shook her head. "Release my sister—"

What do you seek?

"A seed!" Blair said, wincing. "We are here for an ever seed."

"To defeat the darkness," Evelyn shouted to the canopy. "To rid the shade and make way for the light. Like you helped the faerie long ago."

Chose, the Gray Wood said.

"What?" Evelyn asked.

Blair stiffened, the branches at her wrists going taut.

One of you wields wretchedness, darkness that is not welcome. Choose wisely, and we will give you what you seek.

Evelyn's mouth went dry. Her heart pounded inside her chest.

"It means my shadows," Blair rasped. "It has to. Let it have them."

Is that your choice, Evelyn?

She met her sister's gaze head-on. Her midnight stare pleaded. Begged.

"Yes," Blair said through gritted teeth. "It is my choice. Take them!"

Light glowed from the branches holding her sister's wrists, and Blair unleashed an earsplitting scream.

"No!" Evelyn shouted, dropping to her knees. "Stop!"

She dug her hands into the Gray Wood's soil, connecting with the enchanted forest through touch. Something eclipsed Evelyn's earlier ire. It was of the same making as the pulse in her heart for Kade. It sprang upward, like a buttercup popping past the dirt in spring.

Your actions define you.

Evelyn's newly weaved heart pounded in her chest while a sense of knowing bloomed in her belly. Evelyn still believed her title was just words. But there was a core part she'd never shed. *Protector.* How could she willingly hurt her sister? Shadows or not, Blair was not darkness.

But you could rule—

No, Evelyn said. Adamant, final. Silencing the power she'd stolen from the Otherworld. The flame that she'd let corrupt her soul. The darkness that wasn't hers at all.

There you are, the Gray Wood whispered.

"I give you my magic," Evelyn replied. "Not my sister's. *Mine.*"

"Evelyn," Blair rasped. "What are you doing?"

How much are you willing to give?

"All of it."

"No!" Blair said. "Don't do this. I'm not worth it. Our sister is gone because of me—"

"I'll not let you be swallowed by blame like I once was. For I thought I killed our parents. Yes, I played a part. Could've made different choices. But in the end, it was vampyrs who killed them. Circe killed Mirella. Not you." Evelyn swallowed a shaky breath. "I love you, and I refuse to take away what makes you *you*, Blair. I see you, and I'm so sorry it took me this long."

Blair blinked and tears streamed down her face. "Evelyn, no."

She dug her hands deeper into the soil and surrendered.

The Gray Wood's roots sprawled up and over her, and Evelyn sank into the forest of ever trees orbit. She embraced the bark tightening around her. Gave into it. She'd give it all, she decided. To defeat the darkness. To save those she loved. Her soul, magic, *life*.

Everything.

Ancient, powerful magic rushed around her. Roots and branches intertwined. It was one magnificent circle of light and dark, death and life.

The purest form of balance.

You have passed our test, Evelyn, the Gray Wood whispered. *We would not dare take away your life and light.*

Because her efforts mattered, but so did choice. The Sun Goddess's power possessed a callous nature, so, Evelyn gave it back. Not to the Goddess, but to the earth and energies of this world.

Evelyn reached inside herself, found the kernel of the power she'd stolen, and plucked it out of her soul. Her body writhed in pain, the sensation entirely unnatural. She choked, coughed, couldn't find her breath as fire rolled up her throat and she spat it out. The swirling sphere of crimson landed in the palm of her hand, floating in its red-and-orange glory. She let it roll off her fingers, and gave it to the Gray Wood.

Its ancient magic swallowed the flame whole, and the Sun Goddess's power bled into oblivion, nothing more.

Evelyn inhaled. Exhaled. Fully herself again. *Enough.*

And for what you have given, here are the bones of an old friend, the Gray Wood said.

A newly formed staff bubbled from the ashes of what Evelyn had sacrificed. Made from gray roots of the forest, it stretched to her full height. At the tip, branches twisted around a silver gem, reminiscent of Evelyn's true magic.

Chapter Seventy-Six

K ADE ROARED, BEATING AGAINST the interlocked trees separating him from Evelyn.

Her turmoil rushed down their bond. When he closed his eyes, his tracking ability flared to life of its own accord, her emotions vivid. They bled copper, rust, and black. He'd never experienced his mate so wild, so . . . *fragile.*

Kade's chest heaved, and he backed away from the wall.

Rain pelted against his fighting leathers. Soaked his hair and beard. Trailed the bridge of his nose. Thunder boomed above, mocking him.

Moons, he had to get to her. He had to assure Evelyn it'd be alright. They'd get through this. They were partners. They loved one another.

Evelyn, can you hear me? he asked down the bond.

But the wall ahead separated them physically and mentally. His words ricocheted off the enchantment. Kade snarled with frustration, his inner beast rising to the surface. The words he'd said weren't enough. *Moons,* he was a fool. Fate was so hel-bent on pulling them apart, why hadn't he prepared to lose her again so soon?

A branch snapped behind him, and the scent of anise tickled underneath his nose. Kade reached for his sword only to find it missing from behind his back, discarded fifteen yards away. *Stars above,* he must've dropped it during the chaos.

Across the clearing, steam rose from a tree. The birch-like bark furled back and bubbled, as if the trunk boiled from the inside out. Knots smoothed into fingers. Knees pressed outward. A figure peeled themselves free of the bark, sap pulling webs behind them. With shoulders hunched forward, the humanoid figure cracked its neck side to side. Steam rose from its rounded head and pale shoulders. Hair sprouted, growing thicker as bark shifted to skin. Like the delicate billow of a sheer curtain, a cloak fell across thin, pale shoulders. The figure smiled in greeting, and Kade's knuckles popped as he fisted his hands at his sides, the familiar face riling him and his wolf.

Tenebris, the witch from his nightmares, stood in the Gray Wood.

"It's lovely to see you in the flesh," the dark witch said.

Kade shook his head, not bothered by the rail-thin witch. He turned his back, refocusing on the wall and getting back to Evelyn. If he was visited by such foes, who and what did Evelyn face?

Tenebris chuckled behind him. "You can't save your mate from her fate. Both of you must pass these tests apart."

The next days ahead are a test, Uzoma had said.

The word blew through the forest like a stormy wind. An ancientness clung to it, and for a moment, Kade considered that perhaps Kade and Evelyn's journey started and ended here, in a place where they'd fought side by side as Cyrus and Saige.

Tenebris sucked his lips between his teeth, ruddy and milky eye pinning Kade in place. "No longer trapped in the confines of your own mind, I see. Such a strong, promising king."

Kade bared his teeth. "If this is a test, then what the fuck are you doing here?"

Tenebris raised a bony finger, nails gnarled and yellowish with neglect. "I am here to ask: Are you worthy, Kade Drengr?"

Hearing the question that haunted his thoughts was like a punch to his gut. Kade rocked back from the rawness and truth, the air peppering with his rancid fear. Yet, he'd accepted his power, and as a reminder to himself and the Blood Goddess, he drew it up. His fists glowed, lighting the overcast forest in a shimmering blue.

"Yes," Kade bit out, despite how doubt ringed his wrists and ankles.

"Let us see, shall we?"

Tenebris morphed into something anew for the second time. He grew taller, wider. His limbs ballooned with muscle. Dark stubble turned blondish and filled out. The same-colored hair overtook his dark strands, pulling back into a bun tied away from his face—

Not Tenebris's, Kade's.

His own face stared back it him. He stood yards away from *himself*. Frighteningly similar, and yet jarringly different. Sharper jaw, a smirk etched with mirth, and golden eyes darkened with a stomach-churning edge.

"Hello, Kade," he crooned, a throatiness to his voice like he'd swallowed smoke.

"You're not real," Kade said through gritted teeth.

His other self laughed, throwing out his arms wide. Fangs, not like a vampyr's, but similar to a god's, glinted.

"I am your shadow self. Your potential. The part that you fear the most but perhaps also *want*."

A growl rumbled through Kade's chest. "We are nothing alike."

"Are you so sure?" His stare skidded over the sword of ancients laying between them. "Have you wondered why it won't answer to you?"

A chill crawled up Kade's spine. The hair on his forearms rose, and his inner wolf paced, snarling at his shadow self.

Across the way, his twin amber stare narrowed, and they both dashed for the blade. They reached it at the same time. Kade's fingers brushed against for the hilt, but his shadow self backhanded him across the face.

Stars above, he didn't realize how strong he was. How hard he hit. Fuck. He wiped blood from his spit lip, tasting iron on his tongue. Vines reached across the ground and drew back the sword, curling it into the roots and away from either of them.

His shadow self laughed, and the sound cut across Kade's back like a lashing. He couldn't outrun the horrific realization that *this* lived inside his soul. That *this* was a part of him.

"Are you frightened of darkness in me or the promise? Becoming me would be so easy. The world would bow at your feet. A god king amongst mortals."

"I have no desire to rule," Kade whispered. "I wish to break the curse."

"The Blood Curse or your own?" he tilted his head.

Kade darted towards the sword, something in his soul and power chanting for him to possess it. To wield it. His hand wrapped around the hilt, and it burned. Kade reared back, holding out his injured hand.

"Pity." His shadow self prowled closer. "Maybe you need me after all."

He reached down and grasped the hilt. The vines loosened, and his shadow self pulled the blade free. It sang through the air, the black metal reflecting Kade's wide-eyed stare.

His opponent attacked, swift and deliberate. Kade deflected left, but his shadow self didn't fight his finesse. It was all brawl. He tackled Kade to the muddy ground and pressed the blade closer to his throat.

"You aren't good enough for her anymore. She craves something different. Evelyn doesn't want a protector, she wants a destroyer. A king to rule this world with!"

Kade's growl turned louder as he shifted. He planted his elongated feet onto his shadow self's chest and kicked him off. In his werewolf form, the breeze snaking through the forest seemed to say, *Yes, yes, yes.*

He charged on all fours, tackling his opponent to the ground. They wrestled, and Kade knocked the sword from his hand. The blade clattered over sprawling roots, and his shadow self bared his teeth and shifted, too.

Kade's shadow self possessed the same burly build and gold-streaked fur, but scars lined his limbs and dotted his muscles. He flicked his ears back, the left missing the tip. He bared his canines at Kade, the two larger ones, thinner and sharper, jutted far past his bottom jaw. He circled Kade, dragging his crimson-stained paws through the dirt.

Lightening streaked above the canopy. Thunder shook the forest floor. Rain worsened, soaking Kade's fur.

He matched his shadow self step for step and no longer stared into a reflection. Shifted and in his beast form, he witnessed the least resemblance. It fueled his resolve to dart left.

There you are, an ancient voice said.

His shadow self roared, but Kade shifted mid-jump. Lighter, Kade flew through the air and grasped the blade.

It answered, the power within the ancient metal singing on contact. He skidded to a halt, planting his legs in a sturdy, defensive stance. Kade lit his blade blue. Embers popped around the black metal, and as his shadow self snarled with rage, he braced.

He was Kade Drengr. He was a third born and a protector to his core. He was good and kind. His heart was full of love and his life abundant with friends and family, and until his dying breath, he'd fight for a future full of peace.

Even if he had to kill a part of himself.

His shadow self launched, and at close range, Kade grabbed his shoulder and drove the sword of ancients into his exposed belly. The sickening, wet sound of tearing flesh echoed in his ears. His own stomach lanced with pain. It was his own demons he destroyed, slaughtered like a foe on the battlefield.

Tears fell down Kade's face, and he cried at the weight of what the test had caused him.

Doubt evaporated like a summer's mist off his shoulders. An internal click rushed through his strong body. The power of the moon, his inner wolf, his unique tracking ability, the sword of ancients. It all wove in his soul.

Kade drove his sword further into his shadow self, watching the life leech from his shock-riddled gaze. Blue shimmered across the dead body in his arms, and behind him, the trees crawled to their original places.

The Gray Wood returned anew.

The rain stopped, and across the way, Evelyn stood, a newly made staff in hand, and her magnificent steely eyes, *her* stare and nothing more, met his.

Kade breathed her name, and then he was running.

She met him halfway, launching into his arms.

"I'm back," she whispered through thick tears. "It's me. I'm whole again."

"*Stars above,*" Kade said, dragging her closer and resting his forehead against hers.

And for the first time in weeks, Evelyn's magic and Kade's power caressed the other.

"Let me see! Let me take a look!" a tiny voice said, breaking Evelyn and Kade apart.

"*Blasted books,*" Blair said from the other side of the clearing. "Faeries."

Sprites and brownies, the first Kade had encountered outside of story-books, wedged themselves out of the trees.

"She's prettier than I imagined," one with a branch for a nose said, peering at Evelyn with a bashful stare.

Kade drew her closer under his arm, and she fit so perfectly at his side, it made him hold her tighter.

A seam split down the trunk of a stout tree, and a male, one unlike Kade had ever encountered before, wedged himself free. Too sharp and delicate to be a mortal, but there was no magic to speak of, at least not of the kind witches or werewolves possessed.

An ancient kind, like the one buzzing through the Gray Wood.

A simple crown ringed his head, holding back his hair and revealing thin, pointed ears. He was equally alluring as he was alarming

"Who are you?" Evelyn whispered, peeling free of Kade's hold and striding towards the newcomer.

"The King of Elsewhere," he said, brushing debris from his shoulders. He leveled his gaze between Evelyn and Kade.

Kade didn't find the male threatening, but he was at least on guard and healthily cautious. "Your tests created quite a ruckus in my world."

"We have no desire to disturb your realm," Kade said. "We only wish to save our own from the Blood Goddess's curse."

The king's eyes narrowed. "I don't know a deity of that name."

Blair stepped forward. "But you and the faerie were successful in sealing away the One, right?"

He frowned, a distant look clouding across his eyes. "No. She proved too powerful, so we escaped the wrath of the One by creating a new realm for ourselves. Though it came at a cost."

"What exactly?"

"Abandoning those of this world. It wasn't a decision taken lightly, but we knew of an era that would set this realm free, so we've waited." He reached inside his pocket and withdrew a glowing seed. "Which is why I have come to bring you a gift from Elsewhere."

"An ever seed," Blair breathed.

The king nodded. "I believe the Gray Wood also granted you a gift, and I feel the power of life coursing through you and" —he turned his attention to Kade— "the balance of light and dark within you. You have all you need to break the curse."

With a tentative, slow hand, Evelyn grasped the ever seed from the king. She let it rest within her palm, and the winds, land, and sky sang. Flowers—yellow, purple, and white—sprang around her muddied boots. A beautiful beaming smile brightened her features. She faced Kade, tears welling in her eyes. "We can do this," she whispered. "We can defeat the darkness."

Kade nodded, his own words thick with emotion. "I know, love, and I believe in us more than anything in this world."

CHAPTER SEVENTY-SEVEN

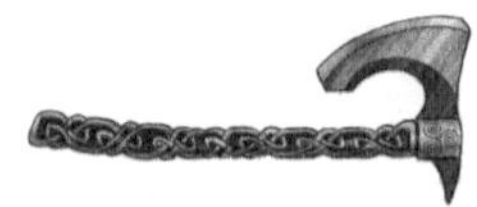

THE SMELL OF RAIN barreled in from the western coast. An unnatural cold hung in the air. Not the chill of winter like in the Vadon Mountains, but an emptiness. Eldrick's wolf wrestled inside his blood. He inhaled, exhaled. Something lay in the land of Torren, and it left him wary.

"To think Kade and Evelyn fell in love in such a wet and miserable place," Bétar muttered as he drew his hood closer to his face.

"It has its charm some days, too," Tovi said from ahead.

The vampyr queen hadn't bothered to use her hood. Rain soaked her white-as-snow braid, and her determined brow gleamed. The sword strapped to her back matched the purple undertones of the bulbous clouds blooming overhead.

Beside her, Yennifer scanned the hills dotted with jagged rock. Linx rode in an unusual silence, pink brows pinched as her golden eyes swam with deep thought.

They'd parted ways with Kade, Evelyn, and Blair, who'd headed to the Gray Wood while Lorkan had remained behind, keeping an eye on the coastal town in case Riven arrived by ship. There was still no telling if Ingrid would use a *danu* to travel from continent to continent. Kade was certain she'd been on the ship when Evelyn was captured in Callum, but if the dark witch had *touched* the ground was still a mystery.

Eldrick sent a small prayer to the Moon God—that they'd beat Riven and Ingrid to Lake Glenn and if they faced him, that their small party of five was enough.

Ahead, a wagon pulled by a mule shook as it trudged through the muddy path. The farmer manning the reins didn't stop as he said, "Aye, I'd turn back if I were you all. Something strange is brewing at the lake. Rain doesn't help either."

Tovi and Eldrick's gazes snapped to the other. The thread didn't pull taunt, but a knowing passed between them.

They had to hurry.

Eldrick clicked his tongue, urging his horse to move quicker, and the others followed. The muddy path turned rockier as they headed east. Thunder rolled across the gray sky, and the occasional streak of lightning flashed across the sheets of rain, making the water droplets glisten like a million sparkling gems.

Soon, the path became too difficult for the horses to carry them. They all dismounted and released their beasts back west. Eldrick and the others continued on foot, following one after the other in a uniform line. The hills converged closer and closer, until they trekked through a canyon filled with pebbles and patches of moss.

At some sections, Eldrick's shoulders brushed against the stony walls. He hovered his hand over the hilt of his axe, his inner wolf unsettled from the unfamiliar and tight terrain.

Ahead, the peaks of ancient mountains reached to the wispy edges of the storm clouds. The scent of stale murky water tickled his nose, and Eldrick's wolf rose to the surface.

Linx halted beside him. "Did you hear that?"

Everyone paused on the path. Eldrick closed his eyes, focusing on his werewolf's sense of hearing, but he detected nothing over the howling wind, pattering rain, and distant thunder. He opened his eyes, finding Tovi's stare almost pleading.

"What if he's already come?" she asked.

"If Ingrid opened the gates to Hel, we'd know," Eldrick said.

Yet, wariness clung to him like the mist soaking into his cloak.

A boom echoed north, and they all whirled.

"Look out!" Linx shouted, pushing Eldrick away.

He knocked into Bétar while Linx ushered Yennifer and Tovi up the path. Rocks trembled underneath Eldrick's boots.

Tovi shouted his name.

But it was too late. Boulders three times the size of their horses tumbled down the north hill. Eldrick scrambled back, dragging Bétar with him, as the avalanche headed toward the path. The descending rocks boomed across the mountains, joining the drumming thunder.

The last thing Eldrick saw on the path was Tovi's wide-eyed stare. The boulders came to a standstill on the path, separating him and Bétar from the others.

"Tovi!" Eldrick rushed to the wall of piled rocks, pulling smaller ones free. "Can you hear me?"

Eldrick's ears rang with panic. His inner wolf roared in his blood. He had to get to her. *Now.*

"I'm here!" Tovi's voice grew louder as Eldrick tugged a rock lose, revealing a gap between the rocks just small enough he spied her jade eyes and the freckles across her nose.

Bétar cursed as he tried to move one of the boulders. "They're far too big to move, and it's too tall to climb."

"We have to figure something out," Eldrick said through gritted teeth.

"No, you and Bétar need to reach Lake Glenn," Tovi said.

Eldrick balked. "I can't *leave* you."

She sighed on the other side. "If Riven and Ingrid are there, they need to be stopped. Sorin—this world—depends on it."

What Tovi didn't say out loud blared through Eldrick's mind. She was guiding him to choose their mission and not her. It left Eldrick sick to his stomach, but she *was* right. Eldrick fisted his hands at his side.

"We will find another way to meet you there, but Eldrick, you must go," Tovi said.

"Okay," he said and nothing more.

It wasn't the place or time for pretty words.

With haste, Eldrick and Bétar continued east on the path despite every fiber in Eldrick's being raging to return to the woman he loved.

They reached a cluster of trees, and Bétar cursed, dragging Eldrick behind one for cover. Below, lit black candles surrounded Ingrid as she stood with arms outstretched over Lake Glenn. Fog glided over the water, concealing its watery surface as rain spilled from dark clouds. It lapsed over the shores, wetting Ingrid's boots.

The witch didn't falter.

Even at this distance, Eldrick spotted the red running from Ingrid's nose. An eerie sound beat from the skies, but Eldrick wasn't certain if it was thunder or drums. The methodical tempo locked into his knees and matched his heart's pounding cadence.

"We need to stop her," he breathed.

Bétar grunted, and Eldrick followed his line of sight. Riven, no longer dressed in silver or sword of ancients strapped to his back but adorned in an embroidered vest and trousers, stood with arms crossed. Waiting. Seething. Dark circles rimmed his eyes, and perhaps it was a trick of the light, but his eyes appeared red not jade.

A dozen Drystan Castle guards flanked his side, watchful of the tree line on the north shore. Eldrick headed west, Bétar at his heels. They hid from rock to rock, and fell into the thin tree line on silent feet. By some god-given miracle, the winds blew in their direction, drawing their scent away from their foe.

Eldrick found a squat pine to hide behind and grasped hold of his axe. *For Sorin. For his people. For Tovi.* He chanted his reasons to himself.

Bétar tilted his head towards him, and Eldrick nodded once.

Now.

The Commander drove his heel into a fallen branch, the snap just loud enough over the lake swirling with dark magic. Guards averted their attention in their direction, and Eldrick fell deeper out of sight as three entered the trees to check on the disturbance.

Eldrick's breath bloomed in the frigid air, and he held out his hand and pressed a sharp tip of his axe into his forefinger, nicking his flesh. Blood beaded to the surface, and he ran it up the side of the tree trunk.

The soldiers stiffened. One hissed, and another quickened their gait. Eldrick inhaled, easing his heart to slow. Bétar winked across the way, and Eldrick's grip tightened on his axe. He sniffed, the sharp lemony scent of the vampyr burning his nose.

The soldier turned, and Eldrick launched.

He grabbed him from the shoulder, sure to pull him out of view, and from the back, sliced the vampyr's throat. The soldier dropped to his knees and crashed face-first into the ground.

To Eldrick's right, a vampyr sprang ahead of him, baring his fangs, but Eldrick planted his axe's blade in the soldier's shoulder before his screech alerted the others. Beside him, Bétar lowered the third dead solider to the ground, laying him with the others without a sound.

"Let's keep moving," Eldrick whispered.

Bétar grunted a sound of agreement, and they eased closer to the lake's shore, trailing from tree to tree. Tension thickened in the air, and Eldrick recognized the heady scent mingling with dark magic.

Death.

Riven shouted at the remaining soldiers. Confusion washed across the shore, and Ingrid's chanting turned to a bellow of deep-rooted pain in her wavering voice. The fog crept from the lake and up and over the rocky shores, dissipating into the crooks and crannies of the surrounding mountains. The water shifted from a gray to a gleaming black, like ink filled the lake instead of water.

More soldiers fell into the trees, but there was no time to be swift. Eldrick and Bétar charged, cutting down four more. Metal sang as it cut flesh, and Eldrick's hands molded to the leather of his axe's shaft, and he thrummed with beastly energy.

Eldrick and Bétar emerged from the shadows of the trees, and as rocks crunched under his boots, Riven whirled.

"Protect the witch!" he roared.

With eyes rolled back into her head and only the whites showing, Ingrid stared up at the sky as lit candles around her flickered in her winds.

Vampyrs charged, one with a sword and another with their inky talons released. Eldrick deflected the sword with his axe and ducked as talons reached an inch from his face.

Eldrick gritted his teeth and swung his axe upward. It hit true, lodging into his enemy's stomach with a deafening crunch. He pulled his weapon free, and blood and entrails released onto the shore.

"You damn dog!" the other soldier screeched, driving his sword down.

In his rage, he left himself entirely open, and Eldrick lunged forward and pivoted, drawing his axe across the vampyr's back, slicing through bone and flesh. Blood bloomed through his uniform, and as Eldrick stood to his full height, the dead solider dropped to the ground.

Ten soldiers remained, and Ingrid's grasp on her magic held strong, shaking the earth. Above, clouds churned, and the air dropped to an alarming chill.

Ahead, Bétar fought a vampyr, sword against sword while another crept up behind the commander. Eldrick roared his friend's name, but he was too far away, too slow to do anything. Vampyrs stood in his way, and Eldrick fought to reach his friend, blood running cold—

Something whistled in the air, followed by a distinct pop. An arrow quivered out of the vampyr's eye, and he landed with a harsh thud on the ground, dead.

"Yennifer," Bétar breathed, whirling to search the forest.

Yet the archer didn't appear, but instead announced her presence with another arrow, killing Bétar's second attacker.

Riven spun. "I smell you, dear sister! Show yourself."

Tovi emerged from the trees, and Eldrick's breath whooshed out of him at the sight of her. Her narrowed gaze was as sharp as the sword she held, glinting in the low light, and the emblem of a silver dove glistened on her breast plate.

Eldrick's soul sang.

Her jade eyes landed on him, widening a fraction as her chest heaved, and then her attention snapped back to Riven.

The Verena twins launched at one another. Their swords clashed, and sparks flew with the intensity of Tovi and Riven's blows.

Eldrick sprinted to Tovi's side, and he relished in her nearness. It was not the power of his alpha blood or wolf rising within him, but something deep within his heart. Poised back-to-back, with gritted teeth, Eldrick didn't protect Tovi, he fought *with* her. They moved as one. Riven attacked left, Tovi blocked his blow and Eldrick struck, his axe clanging against the prince's desperate attacks.

More vampyrs joined the fight, aiding Riven. They attacked in groves, more rushing from the trees. High-ranking soldiers rode atop horses, shouting commands and pointing their swords ahead.

"To the king!"

Arrows descended from the gray sky, killing some, but it was no use—they were outnumbered.

Yet, with two swords in hand, the Commander had transformed into a warrior splattered with blood, and Yen and Linx worked as a team to take down vampyr after vampyr. Eldrick fed off their valor and killed two more vampyrs, his axe dripping with blood.

A soldier atop a horse charged between them, bringing an empty horse with them.

"My king," they shouted over the fray.

Riven seethed, snarling at Tovi. Haggard, thinner, and with bloodshot eyes, the male before him was a fraction of the vampyr Eldrick had encountered on the night of the Blood Moon.

"You're a coward," Tovi cried.

"Yet, I am winning. There will be no running from the darkness you so detest after today." Riven mounted his horse and kicked the beast into action.

His soldiers followed, retreating.

"No," Eldrick growled, rushing after them.

Tovi grasped his arm, yanking him back. "Let him go. Ingrid is our concern. We can't let her succeed in opening the gates to Hel."

An eerie chant carried on the wind in a language he'd never heard before. It was not thunder he heard earlier but drums, and the haunting tempo resounding through Torren drove his inner wolf into overdrive. His alpha power ached as he *felt* his distant homeland hurting, as if the dark magic Ingrid bore into their world scratched at his skin.

He charged towards the witch, axe at the ready, but something barreled into him from the side. Bodies rolled, and a heavy weight landed on his chest as his attacker climbed atop him.

Jade eyes. Snowy hair. The likeness to Tovi rocked through him, but the freckles across the bridge of Visha's nose and the evil glinting in her stare gave her away.

She laughed and raised her taloned hand high, readying to strike. "Nothing will be sweeter than taking you away from her."

Metal flashed above, and blood sprayed across Eldrick's face. Time slowed, and Visha's hand dropped to the ground next to his head.

Visha screeched, clutching her bloody stump to her chest and—

Tovi drove her sword straight into her sister's heart.

CHAPTER SEVENTY-EIGHT

R ED, RAIN, AND RETRIBUTION sang in Tovi's blood.

This was for Lou. For the werewolves Visha had killed in the fighting rings. For the vampyrs she'd hung in Drystan. And most importantly, for Eldrick.

Because there was no world, no breathing without him in it. Tovi's mind nor heart could fathom that bleak future.

"You will cause no more pain, Visha," Tovi said through gritted teeth, plunging her blade farther into her sister's chest.

Visha stared, wide-eyed. Blood dripped from her mouth. She swayed—once, twice—before she slumped forward.

Dead.

"*NO!*" Ingrid shouted, falling to her knees and trying to crawl towards Visha's body. She writhed in the mud. "No."

Her spell stopped. The dark magic ceased. The lake settled. The clouds stilled, and fresh rain began to overtake the scent of anise.

"You killed her," Ingrid sobbed. "You killed *your own sister!*"

Tovi panted, heart pounding in her chest. She waited for the guilt to shower over her or the for the curse to rise and feed off her sweet vengeance, but it was rightness of the blade in her hand that grounded her. The blood dripping from it. The sight of Eldrick—the man she loved—*alive*.

Callum's winds, not Ingrid's, blustered over the lake and kissed Tovi's cheeks, engulfing her in truth—their world was better off without her sister.

485

Ingrid collapsed, writhing in pain and clawing at her chest. Alone and broken, the witch sobbed.

"What's happening?" Yennifer asked amongst the gathered group.

"They were mates." Tovi pulled out her sword, coated in Verena blood, and strode towards Ingrid. "She'll die, too, along with her darkness and that wretched spell."

Ingrid's bloodshot gaze snapped up to meet Tovi's, and pure hatred pierced through her. Eldrick joined her side, his beastly energy wafting off him in waves.

The witch laughed and cried and wheezed. Blood coated her teeth and lips, yet she kept cackling. "You and your prophesied friend have doomed this world. She's coming, *princess.*"

"Your spell failed," Tovi hissed. "We won."

"You're wrong. I have nothing else to live for." Ingrid slammed her hand onto the lake.

Magic prickled in the air, and the inky water slithered up Ingrid's arm, and the witch began to chant. She resumed the spell with twice as much force as before.

"Stop!" Tovi yelled.

She took one step, and shadows as sharp as glass burst from Ingrid. They bled across the lake's shore and sliced Tovi's exposed skin. Eldrick growled and tackled her to the ground, and they huddled together, bracing against the onslaught of Ingrid's dark magic. Eldrick's arms circled around her, and Tovi buried her face against his chest.

The entire world rattled with Ingrid's last efforts as she drained her soul. Her skin shriveled and turned silver. Ingrid became nothing but a husk and then mere dust swallowed by the rain.

Ancient tongue hissed on in the wind, and then the land stilled. Tovi peered up at Eldrick, and for a breath, they studied one another.

The water of the lake burst into the skies, and both Tovi and Eldrick scrambled to standing. With weapons drawn, they gathered alongside the others as the land trembled.

Ingrid's ether dissipated into the lake. The ceremonial candles burst into flames, and the same gray in Tovi's homeland blanketed the sky above Torren.

The water in the lake vanished, revealing a set of ancient weathered stairs. At the bottom, a wrought iron gate hung lose off its hinges. Three moons were etched into the stone above the entrance, and deep beyond the darkness, demons screeched and bellowed.

Their cries grew louder and louder—

"Brace!" Bétar shouted.

Madras burst from the gates and sprinted up the stairs. A whole pack of them. They hopped from stairs to rocks, launching out of the drained lake and dashing up the mountains. Arrows flew one after the other past Tovi, hitting their marks. Two madras crumbled. The rest didn't care.

Nathracha followed, slithering up the stairs. Linx threw an explosive. Pink burst across the stage, and the rock crumbled. One nathracha survived, snaking out of sight. Three italogs emerged and took flight, disinterested in Tovi and the others. The rain clouds swallowed their inky bodies whole.

One last italog, the largest of them all, pushed through the gates and crawled up the stairs.

"Tovi," Eldrick said, grasping her wrist and pulling her back.

For a woman—no, a Goddess—rode atop the demon's back. Beautiful and sharp. Hawklike nose. Hair pulled into a tiny bun. Deep-blue eyes pinning Tovi in place. She clicked her tongue, and the italog shot into the skies. A sword strapped to her back glinted.

"Who was that?" Eldrick asked, voice a mere breath.

"The Blood Goddess."

She and the others turned to find Blair, Lorkan, Kade, and Evelyn standing at the tree line. Soaked, panting.

"How are you certain?" Tovi asked, dread creeping up her spine.

"Because Lorkan and I have seen that sword before in our research," Blair said. "It appears Ingrid's spell worked. We were too late."

Tovi stumbled back as if Blair's news had hit her in the gut.

A newness clung to the Daughter of the Goddess and Son of the God, and Tovi's mind whirled with questions, but she couldn't form any of them with the jarring truth flushing through her.

Tovi had *failed*.

Her greatest fear had come true. She'd chosen her heart, not her people. Of course Visha had been wretched, but Tovi had killed her to defend Eldrick. She hadn't thought of consequence. Hadn't considered Ingrid retaliating.

For she had forgotten entirely what and why she was fighting in the first place. Suddenly, her breastplate grew heavy. It pressed and pressed against her chest.

Love *was* a poison, and she'd let it infect her.

Tovi had helped release the Blood Goddess, the very deity who'd cursed her people.

CHAPTER SEVENTY-NINE

THREE DAYS HAD PASSED since the gates of Hel had opened, and the Blood Goddess hadn't made herself known.

Lorkan counted it as a bleak blessing.

For the Drystan's gray had bled all across Sorin. The curse spread. Demons emerged from portals, and vampyrs, brave enough to trek through the still desolate Void, invaded. Scáth attacks doubled.

Werewolves and witches worked in a frenzy to protect their own. After Blair had created a *danù* to take them back to Sorin, she'd revisited Nūa to relay the recent events and hopefully encourage the Guard to prepare. Eldrick awaited his ascension ceremony, and Kade and Evelyn had joined forces at the Void, protecting Sorin. So, Lorkan had returned to Vísdómr to check on his pack.

Lorkan's secret nipped at his heels worse than ever. Blair knew, and his heart swelled at the fact she'd accepted him. He didn't doubt Eldrick and Kade would, too, but with darkness crawling across his homeland now more than ever, he feared his vampyrism would risk his brother's ascension as Earl. They couldn't afford any more problems.

Orange lined the snowcapped mountain range as sunrise teased its arrival on the horizon. Vísdómr, in all its might, stood to the north, the background light casting the library in a fiery spotlight.

Lorkan played with the bloodstone ring tied at his neck. Even with its advantages, Lorkan didn't know how to *not* worry about the sun and its gradual ascent in the sky.

"Best hurry," Alvin said. "Not all of us have a nifty bloodstone to protect us."

Lorkan's friend winked as he walked on by, and Lorkan almost smiled at his friend's natural ability to add lightness to any moment.

Lorkan, along with Mya and Alvin, marched deeper into the forest to check on the elm blossoms. Mya had set them up in a clearing, far away from Vísdómr's trails and the traveling paths of werewolf territory. Rain nor cloud coverage had interfered with the blossoms and Mya's sun-drying technique, and Lorkan hoped the blossoms were ready.

He craved Blair's presence, though he understood her duty to the witches. *I'll see you in a few days,* she'd promised.

Lorkan wished to show Blair his efforts these last years; perhaps the tea first, and if she agreed, he'd lead her to Fjall's Village through the tunnels.

Mya pushed a branch out of their way, and Lorkan entered the clearing and halted.

"Moons," Alvin hissed.

They walked straight into destruction. Mya's makeshift tables were overturned, and dried elm blossoms danced on the wind. Lorkan fell to his knees, trying to collect as many as he could, but it was no use. Brittle, they crumbled in his hands.

"Stars above," Mya said, squatting and brushing her hands over the blossoms floating in a puddle and ruined by dirt. "Was there a storm we missed? I secured the tables and wire racks like I always do . . ."

Alvin growled. "It appears this was intentional."

Lorkan's friend held up a broken table, split down the middle like someone had hacked it with a blade.

"But who?" Mya hissed. "Why?"

Lorkan reared straighter, fear pulling him taut like a bowstring. His boot edged close to a patch of prints, but not just any sort, *paw* prints.

"Werewolves—" He clamped his mouth shut, the scent of three others prickling in the air. "Both of you need to get back to village *now.*"

"And leave you?" Alvin hissed. "*Stars above,* who do you take me for?"

"My loyal and brave friend," Lorkan whispered. "But day will be here before we know it, and I have a bloodstone. It'll protect me from the sun and conceal my vampyrism. If werewolves destroyed these blossoms because they had an idea of what we were creating, there's a chance they're searching for Fjall as we speak. We need it defended and monitored."

"I don't like this," Mya whispered. "You want us to hide while you risk yourself."

"I'm tired of retreating, Lorkan," Alvin said. "Of not fighting for what we are and what we've built."

Lorkan shook his head, grasping his friends shoulder. "This isn't the time. Not yet. Let me take this risk and discover what pack these werewolves are a part of, and then I'll meet you in the village, okay?"

Objection rippled across both Alvin's and Mya's face, but after sharing a look, they relented and nodded.

"Be careful." Alvin squeezed his shoulder back. "My life would suffer without your gruffness."

Lorkan's friends left him, and he let his nose lead him through the thicket of trees. He stalked the werewolves like prey, crouching onto his knees. The clouds peeking through the canopy lightened to a slate, and birds chirped their morning greetings. Frost and pine tickled Lorkan's nose, but over the fresh scent of winter, he caught the wear and tear of travel—sweat, stench, and wolf.

Snickering bounced off the trees, and Lorkan squatted lower to the ground. Green cloaks blended into the landscape. Lorkan recognized the shade, leading him to believe it was Johannes warriors sitting by a fire, throwing pine cones into the flames and watching them burst. But why would they be this close to Vísdómr? Had they vandalized the elm blossoms?

Voices hissed in the back of Lorkan's mind. The curse reared its nasty head. Lorkan blinked. Cracked his neck side to side. Red flashed across his vision, and hunger bloomed in his belly, wretched and ferocious. Lorkan swallowed, fighting the urge to release his fangs. Why in the *stars above* was the curse so close to the surface—

Lorkan spotted the red smear running up the tree he leaned against. As he found the first, the other markings popped to life. Iron, sweet and beckoning him closer. Horror jolted through Lorkan. *Blood* marked trees all around him.

"*BOO!*" a werewolf jumped from a cluster of trees, landing in front of him.

Lorkan reared back, baring his teeth—no, his *fangs*. For they'd released of their own accord, all thanks to the blood berating his senses. He stepped to defend, but metal kissed his neck, and he found a female with her blade drawn, herding him into the clearing.

Her nose remained scrunched in a permanent snicker. The others sprang to their feet, hands falling to their weapons.

"Seems we found what we came here for boys," she said, her sights never leaving him.

A male with a shaved head and rune tattoos running up his neck sized Lorkan up and down. "Your father is going to be *so* pleased, Dalinda."

The others laughed, and Lorkan fisted his hands at his sides. Her name tickled in the back of his mind, and it took him a moment to recall who she was. Dalinda Johannes. Alpha Bjorn's daughter. *Fuck.* Lorkan's father had feared this exact discovery, and here he was, walking straight into their trap, revealing what he was with his fangs and jeopardizing Eldrick's ascension.

Lorkan studied Dalinda and her unit. Six against one. The odds weren't in his favor, even if he shifted.

"What exactly does your father want with a Vísdómr scholar?" he asked.

Delinda pressed her blade harder, threatening to break skin. "We don't give a shit about your birth order, second born. You're an abomination to our kind, just like your mother."

Lorkan growled, leaning closer. "Careful."

Dalinda laughed, and the others joined in, and the sound grated against Lorkan's control over his inner wolf. "It's you who must tread carefully." She flicked her wrist, and more werewolves emerged from the trees, dragging two figures tied and gagged.

Alvin and Mya.

Lorkan charged. "*No—*"

Dalinda swiveled her blade from his neck to theirs, running it parallel across both their throats. She fisted Alvin's braids and yanked his head back, while another werewolf pulled Mya's red hair. Both his friends flinched, and Lorkan growled.

"Don't touch them, or I'll fucking—"

"Kill me? They'll be dead before you step any closer."

"Then I'll still rip your throat out," Lorkan seethed. "You might *think* you know what I am, but you can't fathom what the vampyr curse does to a werewolf."

The werewolves stiffened. Even the breeze stilled. Dalinda narrowed her eyes, debating her chances and snarled, kicking the back of Alvin's knees. The other warrior threw Mya to the ground. Lorkan's friends' eyes pleaded with him, their voices muffled by the tightly tied gags. They looked to the canopy, the sky—

Moons, the sun was minutes away from shining its light into the forest.

"Please," Lorkan rushed. "Let them go. Whatever you want from me, I'll give it."

Dalinda scoffed. "Moons, I should've known a Drengr would be so fucking easy to manipulate. You're all so . . . *pathetic*, sacrificing yourself for others. I wanted to kill that whore of a queen to drive your brother to his end, but my father said it would be too messy. Yet, you'll do just fine proving how unfit the Drengrs are to rule the Vadon Mountains. Lorkan Drengr, his pack's ugliest secret, finally unveiled." She jutted her chin at the others. "Bind his wolf."

Lorkan's inner beast raged at the kiss of metal as it clamped around his throat. Twin shackles clanked around his wrists, and for safe fucking measure, the bastards added a three-part chain that connected the horrid pieces. Enchanted and soaked in wolfsbane, it tamped his wolf fangs and talons—anything related to his shifting abilities.

But it didn't quiet the rage of the curse.

"Tie them up," Dalinda ordered the others.

Lorkan reared out of the werewolf's hold only for three more to grasp him back from reaching his friends. "We agreed—"

Dalinda hit the blunt end of her axe against his jaw. White dotted Lorkan's vision, but he fought to get free as the others dragged Alvin and Mya away and tied them against tree trunks.

No. No. No.

Lorkan's beast began to unleash and then stopped, fur retreating back into his skin as the enchanted shackles bound his magic. Hopeless and empty yet bursting at the seams all at once. His chest heaved as he tasted blood on his tongue, for his fangs had pierced his bottom lip.

"I never agreed to let them go." Dalinda used the tip of her blade to pull Lorkan's necklace lose, balancing the bloodstone on the tip of the blade. She hummed. "I didn't spy one of these gems on your fellow freaks. So, I decided not to touch them, just like you requested. After all, why waste my time when the sun can do the work for me?"

Something glinted deep in Dalinda's eyes, and Lorkan discovered that darkness lived outside the curse. It wasn't a tangible trait only bestowed upon vampyrs or those touched by the curse. Darkness embedded itself wherever one let it take root and nurtured it to bloom. Darkness wasn't innately evil either, unless one grasped it and wielded it as such. Like Dalinda, feeding her hate until it manifested into darkness.

As five werewolves dragged Lorkan away from his friends, it wasn't the curse that reared to life. It was love, in all its hurt and enormity. He roared as his heart fractured.

He'd done this—told Alvin and Mya to run and *hide* and not fight.
Now, they'd die, and the light they brought to this world would extinguish.

CHAPTER EIGHTY

NO AMOUNT OF WINE or sparring buried Tovi's failure.

But at least in the stolen moments while the world slumbered and the sun attempted to rise past the blanketing gray, in Eldrick's arms, Tovi found some reprieve.

She kept an unhurried pace above him, rocking sensually so she felt every inch of him. With each sway of her hips, she chased distraction.

Tovi fell dangerously close to that spoiled vampyr princess she'd once been. Running from responsibility. But this was different, right? *This* was Eldrick. She just needed a moment before she faced the curse now infesting all of Sorin, a few more minutes relishing in his touch, scent, muscles, and lips.

And he let her. Welcomed it. Eldrick worshipped her as she took her time, kissing and nipping her flesh while his thumb brushed the sensitive spot between her legs.

They didn't speak, cry out, or say the other's name. Racing hearts. Breathy pants. That was enough in the early hours of morning—if Tovi were to guess given the scent of porridge in the war camp, drafting through their tent.

Eldrick stiffened beneath her and tightened his arms around her torso, his release moments away. Her own crested the wave of oblivion, threatening to crash through her. She rested her head on his shoulder, and the beautiful tempo of his heart—*thump, thump, thump*—reached her baser instinct.

Feed, the curse hissed. It sat so close on the precipice between pleasure and vice.

Goddess, she hated it. Loathed the darkness swimming through her veins. Despised herself for letting it near the one thing in this world she cared most about.

Her stomach twisted into a bundle of knots. The bond she shared with Eldrick, including the threads she refused to accept or weave, made her feelings for him that much worse.

Red and memories flashed before her sights. The color of the curse. The Blood Goddess riding off into the clouds.

Tovi picked up her pace, chasing something that would rid her of the ironlike guilt resting on her shoulders. It was no use.

FEED, the curse roared in her veins.

Tovi fought her fangs that ached to be released and sink into Eldrick's neck. She imagined it for a moment. Without the curse, darkness, and the wretched duty queenhood held over her. Something between them, and nothing more. A *beautiful* something that would tie their souls together for eternity.

Tovi's orgasm burst through her, and she bit her bottom lip, stifling a cry. Eldrick found his own release and gripped her waist, stilling her rocking hips as he trembled beneath her.

They remained intertwined for a few heavy breaths until Tovi peeled herself from Eldrick's hold, not meeting the stare she felt skating across her bare skin. She sauntered over to the water basin to clean herself off and readied her clothes for the day.

"You're distant," Eldrick said, pulling a bedroll up and over his naked bottom half.

"I'd hardly describe what we just did as distant," Tovi said over her shoulder.

He grunted. "I know your mind, dove. You're as taut as a bowstring."

"It doesn't matter, and there's no time." It wasn't the place, either, to talk feelings and worries. Not with the Void on the northern horizon, a visual reminder her homeland sat a hundred yards away. "I also have a strategy meeting this morning that I can't be late for, and—"

"Tovi—"

"—*you* should be on your way back to the Drengr Village, preparing for you ascension, not here . . ."

With me.

Tovi didn't dare speak the last two words out loud, but her heart held onto them. Things between her and Eldrick were more confusing than ever. No, that was an understatement. Bewilderment didn't grip Tovi. In fact, the sensation that whatever they had, for a very brief moment, slipped through her fingers. Perhaps Eldrick felt it too, and that's why he'd traveled here before his ascension.

She didn't have the stomach to ask.

Tovi could practically hear Eldrick's pinched brow as he said, "What happened at Lake Glenn isn't your fault—"

Tovi spun to face him, throwing on a knee-length tunic. "I'm seven centuries old, Eldrick. Lying to make me feel better is a lost cause."

His jaw ticked and a thousand words burned in his eyes. He rose, stalking through the tent in all his naked glory and found his clothes. After a long exhale, he met her stare head-on, calm and steady. "You didn't fight that fight alone. We had a unit—myself, Linx, Bétar, and Yennifer. We *all* let Ingrid succeed. *Moons,* we let Riven get away, too."

Tovi shook her head, a bitterness coating her tongue. "But my family is to blame for this curse, and now my actions set the Blood Goddess free—the very deity who is hel-bent on destroying Sorin. Of all people, I should've known better, considered the consequences of killing one's mate."

Love is a poison.

"I didn't think, I just did. I failed because—"

"You saved my life." Eldrick's tone turned hard, and he didn't meet her gaze, gem eyes dimming as he slid his axe into his waist strap.

"I don't regret protecting you," she whispered. "I swear it."

He sighed, attention snapping back to her. "I know."

"I love you," she breathed.

Pain flashed across Eldrick's face, and he remained an arm's length away. "Maybe love isn't enough for those like us. The truth is, you're right. I can't stay. I should be back in the Vadon Mountains, ascending and then readying werewolf forces, which is why I'm leaving first thing."

Tovi blinked. Was it a morning breeze or fear chilling her in place? His tenderness earlier. The kisses he'd dotted across her skin, like he committed her to memory.

Eldrick had been saying goodbye.

"We both have our duties in this, and now more than ever, it's important we lead our people to defeat Riven." Eldrick strapped his leather breastplate into place and draped his fur-lined cloak across his shoulders. "But please, I swear to the moon and all the stars, I love you."

"I know."

Tears didn't prick at the edge of Tovi's eyes. She was too tired, too hollow to feel anything at all. Even surprise. For she'd anticipated this, knew who and what they were always triumphed over their love.

In two long strides, Eldrick kissed her. His lips molded to hers, urgent and hurried.

Like it might be there last.

Then he was gone, leaving Tovi alone inside her tent. Sweat, sex, and sadness seeped into the air, and Tovi exhaled it all away, continuing to ready for the morning.

With fighting leathers, hair braided to the side, and a fur cloak snuggly fastened, Tovi braced for the misty morning and marched towards the largest tent at the center of camp.

Werewolves and witches rose for the morning while those on night watch retired to their tents. To the north, no wall of fog hid the desolate wasteland separating Sorin and Drystan. Rot and decay jutted from the earth, blurring for miles.

Archers and scouts manned the front lines. A demon's screech cut through the air, but as it emerged from the plumes of gray, an arrow lodged in its eye before it reached the Void's edge.

Ahead, Evelyn emerged from the large tent. She'd twisted her hair into a neat bun, and her pressed navy uniform molded to her frame. Tovi's friend looked . . . well, formidable, and more herself than ever.

Evelyn's eyes widened at the sight of Tovi, and she hurried to meet her halfway. "A vampyr arrived early this morning, requesting an audience with you."

"Who?" Tovi asked, peering at the tent as if she might spy the newcomer past the fabric.

"He claims his name is Cass."

"*What?*" Tovi rushed towards the tent.

Outside the flaps, Evelyn grabbed her wrist. "I don't think he arrived with good news."

Tovi sighed. "If Cass traveled through the Void, I figured as much."

Evelyn frowned. "If you need me, I'm here."

"Thank you," Tovi said with a nod.

Inside, a fire crackled at the center, and smoke and embers escaped through a hole cut into the tent's canopy. Cass—lips set in a thin line—stared at Kade who stood with arms crossed, beastly powers wafting off him in waves.

"It's alright, Kade," Tovi said, unclasping her cloak in the warmer space. "Cass is a friend of the family and a spy of mine."

Cass tipped his head in her direction. "My queen."

Tovi scowled, shooting him a glare.

A growl rumbled through Kade's chest. "Fine." He grasped Tovi's shoulder, his expression endearing but serious. "Evelyn and I won't be far."

"Understood," she said, fighting the nerves tightening in her belly. "Why are you here? Is it Sven and the littles? Are they alright?"

But even as she asked it, graveness clung to corners of the tent, like the clothed walls closed in around her.

Her spy stood and handed her a missive. Tovi brushed her fingers over the already broken seal, her resolve threatening to snap. It belonged to Lady Anastasia Nathanaël.

Tovi didn't have the stomach to read it, so she peered up at Cass. "What's happened?"

"Turns out Bash was less than trustworthy. He had no intention of giving you the army. Lady Anastasia declared in the letter she planned to take matters into her own hands, but . . ."

"*But?*" Tovi asked, heart sinking like a stone in her gut.

"I visited Nathanaël's estate. Discreetly of course. I believe she failed. She's set to marry General Oziel in two days, and Bash remains his most loyal solider. As for his army, it serves Riven."

Tovi lost her knees, crumpling into the nearest chair.

"No, Riven has no money, no funds to pay for it. Lord Nathaniël needed gold—"

"Somehow he got his hands on enough. Whispers of the deal are on the Drystan wind, Tovi."

"Bloody hel," she hissed "Do we have any word on when Riven will march?"

"No," Cass said.

"What about the Blood Goddess? Any signs of her in Drystan?"

Cass shook his head. "Still, time isn't on our side. If the werewolves hear of this—"

"They won't," Tovi said. "I'll find another way before word gets out about this."

Tovi clutched the table for support. Sorin didn't stand a chance against Riven's army, even with the combined forces of werewolves and witches. Innocents would die, all while her brother fought to stop Evelyn and Kade. Tovi couldn't let that happen. She *had* to figure out another way.

Cass sighed, heavy and long. "This was also passed along to me in Drystan Village, from one of the pirates."

Unlike Lady Anastasia's letter, the turquoise seal pressed with Flynn's crest remained intact.

"You didn't bother reading it?" Tovi whispered, throat turning dry.

Cass shook his head, dark eyes studying her. "No. Your Uncle Bran usually opens the letters, but I decided to hide this one from him. I have a feeling if he opened it . . ."

Tovi'd never gotten eyes on Flynn's words. Most didn't like the pirate after he'd broken her heart. She bent the envelope, splitting the seal down the middle. She unfurled the letter and gritted her teeth at the single, arrogant one-line:

Don't forget. You owe me a dinner.

But as his voice played in the back of her mind, it was another statement Flynn had made that Tovi hung on to.

With my fleet, you'd crush your brother in a fortnight.

With securing Lord Nathaniël's army, she'd forgotten about Flynn's proposal.

I want you to make me your husband.

Tovi turned to stone. Cold. Hardened. She racked her brain. Did she have any other choice? Did she have time to find another way to beat Riven? The idea may as well have been Tovi falling atop her own sword—the pain lanced through her so violently. She thought of Eldrick, still felt him between her legs. Heard his declaration of love singing in her soul.

Despite the pain, Flynn *was* an option. A card to play. She had to give Sorin a fighting chance, even if she broke Eldrick's heart—and her own—in the process. Perhaps, too, she'd venture down a path where she put her people first, not love.

"What are you going to do?" Cass asked.

Tovi sighed, swallowing the bile working up her throat. "I owe Flynn a dinner, and there are important matters to discuss."

Cass tilted his head. "Tovi . . . What of the alpha? It's no secret that you love him—"

"I am a queen," Tovi said, tone so unbending she didn't recognize her own voice. "Eldrick and I both know our duties to our people come above all else."

Her uncle's lips fell into a thin line, a thousand words playing in his serious stare. "You're Uncle Bran is going to kill me if Nadia doesn't beat me to it."

"She knows better than anyone that duty requires sacrifice," Tovi said.

"If you asked her what her biggest regret is, I believe she'd contradict that statement."

Tovi didn't have time to ask or to care. She left Cass in the tent, marching out into the war camp with the intention of writing an urgent letter and sending it by iolair.

She collided into a mass of werewolves, along with one witch, huddled out outside, eavesdropping. Yennifer, Bétar, Evelyn, and Kade stared at her with a mixture of despair and pity.

Yen opened her mouth, but Tovi beat her to it.

"What did we all set out to do?" she asked, setting her shoulders back.

They all shared a grave look, and Evelyn's earlier frown deepened. "To defeat the darkness."

"Precisely," Tovi whispered. "There's nothing any of you can say to stop me, so please, for Goddess's sake, don't bother."

With that, she turned on her heal and stormed through the war camp, leaving her friends behind.

The Queen of Drystan had a proposal to accept, a fleet to secure, and a damn war to win.

CHAPTER EIGHTY-ONE

ELDRICK

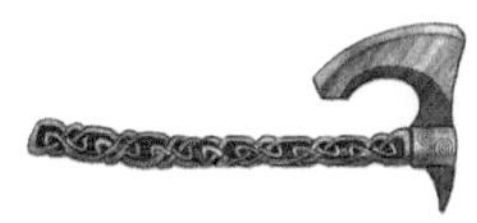

ELDRICK'S ASCENSION ARRIVED ON a cold and snowy day.

As was customary, the ceremony took place in the ascending alpha's village. With war sitting on the Vadon Mountain's doorstep, minimal decorations dotted Lār's largest hall. Evergreen garlands draped across the tables while Drengr navy banners hung from the ceiling's rafters. On either side, the enormous fires crackled, warming the space and making more sweat prickle at the back of Eldrick's neck.

He paced away from the gathered crowd, hidden in the front corridor. His pack buzzed with excitement, while all visiting alphas wore expectant stares. They would hold council and discuss preparations against Riven once the ceremony was over.

Eldrick exhaled, his pluming breath fading into the zigzagging flurries. He searched the village, wishing his werewolf sight was good enough to spy Tovi all the way to the Void. He'd received no updates aside from missives from Kade. They'd left things so final the last he'd seen her, and yet, he turned back to the hall, his alpha chair calling to him.

Hooves pounded in the distance, and Eldrick snapped his attention outside Lār's open entrance. A traveling party arrived, but through the thick snowfall and under heavy cloaks. Yennifer and Bétar dismounted first, leaving their horses with the nearest stableman. As they climbed the fortress stairs, their hardened stares filled Eldrick with unease.

"What is it?" he asked.

His mind whirled with possibilities. Was someone he loved injured, or worse, dead? Had Riven stormed into Sorin?

Past his friends, the two other figures sharpened amongst the snowfall. Tovi dismounted from an all-white horse, regal in a fur cloak and purple ensemble. He couldn't decide whether she was fit for battle or a throne.

Yet, someone else reached her side—a male Eldrick didn't recognize at all. Pale, dark-haired, staring down at Tovi like he knew her.

"Who the fuck is that?" he growled.

Yennifer sidestepped, blocking Tovi from view. "That is Captain Flynn Seaver."

Eldrick blinked. *Captain.* He didn't recall Tovi using his full name, only specifying that he was a contact. Yet, her late friend Lou had made her disdain for him clear. Like some possessive mated male, Eldrick's hackles rose.

"The pirate? Why is he here?"

"Aye." Bétar grasped his shoulder, and it was remorse bleeding from the friend's stare. "She believed she had no other choice."

Choice. What in the stars above did that mean?

Bétar released Eldrick, entering the hall.

Yennifer opened her mouth, but no words came out. She thought better of it and followed Bétar without a word.

Before Eldrick grasped his bearings, Tovi marched up the stairs and left the supposed pirate by the horses. Her boot crested the last step, and Eldrick couldn't hold back the bite in his words.

"Tovi—"

"I lost the army, Eldrick."

He stiffened. Not only did Tovi's news rock through him, but so did her eyes. They'd lost the life in them, as if something—or someone—had sucked the spring from their once magnificent green. She'd always been sharp, *beautiful*, and yet, she'd turned as cutting as stone. He hardly recognized.

"I . . ." He swallowed, trying to find solid ground in this unknown terrain. But his duty roared in the back of his mind. Riven. The war. Saving Sorin. *That* was his priority.

"I don't understand," he said. "How? Lady Anastasia and Bash swore—"

"Lord Oziel remains alive, and his army serves Riven." Tovi sighed, eyes pleading. "Eldrick, there is something else we must discuss. It can't wait. I found another way. I *had* to."

Movement shifted behind Tovi. Flynn talked with the stablemen as the snow quickened. Eldrick's heart hammered in his chest like a flighty bird.

"Why is he here?"

Tovi flinched, and *moons*, he was such as ass.

Eldrick reached for her, but she matched his step backwards, retreating. She clasped her hands together, and a ring glinted on her finger. A sapphire stone sat at the center of the gold band. It was all wrong. The color, the metal, the shape. It didn't suit her, didn't feel *right*.

His entire body turned taut. He fought his wolf, every instinct raging to kill the male twenty yards away.

Tovi followed his line of sight. "Flynn has a fleet large enough to face Riven's army—"

"So, you agreed to marry him?" Eldrick hissed.

Tovi said nothing, and his world yanked out from under him. He leaned closer, and Tovi stood her ground.

"Have you already married him?" he breathed, crowding her space. A territorial flush fell over him. Hot. Angry. All-consuming.

"*No,*" Tovi said.

"When?" he whispered, shaking.

"Before . . ." Tears welled in her eyes. "Before the fighting starts."

It was as if Tovi had pierced Eldrick's heart with a dagger. Pain lanced through him. "Will you think of me when you consummate the royal marriage?" he asked, tone flat.

Tovi seethed, rearing towards him. "Don't be so cruel."

"How dare you?" he growled. "You're the woman I love, and you come to my home, to my territory, to tell me you're engaged, as if I should be happy. *That* is far crueler than hurtful words."

"It secured me an army, Eldrick! It'll give Sorin a chance," she said. "I now have something to offer you and your people. I couldn't risk the other alphas learning I'd lost forces following my banner. I did this to guarantee our alliance and your ascension—"

"Don't you dare say this is for me, because that is a lie." Eldrick raked a hand through his hair, pacing back and forth.

Thunder rumbled in the distance, and the scent of frozen pine and ice prickled in the air. The land raged alongside Eldrick.

He halted, his anger too much to contain. "You could've waited until I became Earl, but you didn't. This is about you and your fear of *us*." Eldrick shook. Bone. Muscles. Limbs. Down to his breaking heart. "Does he know what I am to you?"

Tovi stumbled back. Her loose strands of hair twisted in the snowy wind, and her lips fell in a delicate *o*.

Eldrick stood straighter, fisting his hands at his side. The flurries stung as they landed on his heated cheeks. "Does he know I'm your *mate*?"

"Eldrick." A breath shuddered out of Tovi, and she blinked back tears. "*Please.* You have to understand I didn't *want* this. I had no other choice—"

A light in Eldrick's soul extinguished forever. "But you did. You're so terrified of fate and the prophecy bringing us together, you chose someone else."

"I'm far more terrified of failing my people, Eldrick." Tovi gritted her teeth, nostrils flaring. "Would you walk away from yours? Would you turn your back on the werewolves?"

"You know I can't." Eldrick's words shot out of him too quickly. They were like shards of glass shredding his throat.

Tovi snorted, and she peered up at the sky. She wiped away her tears before they fell. She was so pale, so different. Eldrick fought the urge to reach out and take her away from all of this. But that wasn't who they were, was it?

Good leaders sacrifice.

His inner wolf snarled in his blood, retaliating against her earlier words. Love and duty warred within Eldrick's chest. He couldn't see past his hurt, nor shake the itch crawling up the back of his neck. The woman he loved—his mate—stood ahead of him, while his responsibility awaited him in the hall.

"The thing that brought us together will always drive us apart. Like you, I serve my people," she said, turning to leave.

"Tovi."

She paused, peering over her shoulder.

"On the battlefield, we will meet as allies. That is all. Now leave, and never set foot on my lands again."

Eldrick turned away. He physically ached, like he'd ripped his heart out and left it on the step beside Tovi. He no longer knew how to breathe, but he knew how to move his legs, and he walked away from her. Walked, walked, and walked until he could no longer detect her scent and found his place at the front of the hall.

He let the cold bite his skin, let the horrid winter tighten his exterior.

Why not, when now he had a hardened heart?

CHAPTER EIGHTY-TWO

FOR SAFE MEASURE, OR because Dalinda kept equally wretched company as herself, a werewolf kicked Lorkan for the third time in the same spot. An audible *crack* bounced off the nearby trees. *Moons*—they'd broken a rib.

Lorkan was losing count of the days, beatings, and the whispers of his captors. Had it been a week? Three days? With the sky permanently gray, day and night bled together. Lorkan had no sense of where exactly they traveled to, either. He'd grown too busy fighting pain and his bloodthirst. In some cruel joke, he was grateful for the shackles binding his wolf. With the curse so close to the edge, hissing to feed, he feared he'd lose control.

Another werewolf kicked him straight in the gut, and Lorkan clamped his eyes shut, driving his fingers into the dirt. The moment darkness fell across his vision, his mind flashed with images of Alvin and Mya's scorched bodies steaming in the daylight. They'd left before he'd witnessed their deaths, but his mind replayed the horrific possibilities.

Perhaps he'd take this beating as atonement for the friends he'd failed, for the pain lancing through his side was more than an inconvenience compared to the loss of Alvin and Mya.

A werewolf glared down at him, and another came into view, its silhouette blurred into multiples and transformed into his father's. Lorkan sat on the brink of losing consciousness.

Sorin still isn't ready for your darkness, the mirage said.

A fist connected with Lorkan's nose, and as his head snapped back, a boot rocked into his jaw, jolting him to the side. Blood rushed over his lips, and his body ached like one giant bruise.

The warrior dropped to his haunches, tilting his head as he sneered down at Lorkan. "It's a pity we can't fucking kill you."

Kill me, Lorkan had once begged his father. *Don't let me live like this.*

Now that death stood near, Lorkan recoiled from the notion. There was too much to live for—his brothers and pack, Fjall, still needed him. As did Blair. His beautiful, smart mate. Was this how she'd felt when he'd never shown up in Fika? Alone, frightened, hurting.

Hate beat down on him as fists and boots, the hurt he'd feared from his people all his life. *This* was why his father had told him to hide what he was. Aramis had been right all along.

"You're pathetic," one hissed.

Lorkan spat blood out. "Says the pup using a chained werewolf as a punching bag—"

"You're *not* one of us," the male said.

"Is that so?" Lorkan laughed, part delirium and part snark. "Release me, and I'll show you my wolf."

He bared his fangs and launched—

Someone yanked the chain connected to his collar, violently pulling him back. The force knocked the wind out of him.

"Don't have too much fun. I need him alive," she called. "We're almost there."

They chuckled, stepping back from him. Dalinda wrapped the chain around her wrist and dragged him towards her horse. Lorkan struggled, but pain lanced through him with each movement. She tied his chains to the rope attached to her horse, planning to drag him through the forest, like livestock, an animal—

An abomination.

For the next few hours, rattling chains, horses' beating hooves, and laughter echoed in Lorkan's ears.

Dalinda pulled him without an ounce of grace. He couldn't find balance or a position of reprieve. If he braced the tug, his arms remained upright, and after a time, his shoulders screamed. As he stood tall, the wolfbane's effects trembled through his tired legs, and he stumbled through ice and mud. When exhaustion won and he dozed off, his father's figure appeared in the trees, his disappointed gaze trailing him up and down.

Our secrets will tarnish the Drengr name.

That's when Lorkan smelled it—the familiar warming wheat scent of his village. He snapped back to the present. He peered up at the trees. Assessed the terrain. He knew these hills and the paths snaking through the pines.

The very ones where he'd spotted Riven all those weeks ago.

An agonizing chill raked down his spine, and it wasn't from flurries collecting on his damp clothes. He'd assumed Dalinda was taking him to the Johannes Village, but his home's palisade walls became clearer and clearer through the wintry thicket.

Decorative banners hung on the wall, and Lorkan's mind reeled. *Stars above*, today was his brother's ascension. It had to be. Dalinda planned to ruin his brother's chances, all because he was a—

"No!" Lorkan roared.

He tugged the rope attached to Dalinda's horse and dug his heels into the ground. Lorkan gritted his teeth; he refused to fail his father or Eldrick—

Dalinda reared her horse to a halt, and Lorkan's rope slacked. He fell face-first into the snow. She laughed, and her unit joined in.

"I guess you figured it out, haven't you?" she asked. "My father deserves to become Earl, not your pathetic excuse of a brother. You're going to ruin it for him. After the other alphas witness the Drengr's worst secret, they'll have no choice but to rescind their votes and choose my father."

"I won't let you," Lorkan said through gritted teeth.

He stood on shaky legs, rallied the last shred of strength he had and *pulled*.

Dalinda's horse stumbled, crashing to the snow. It whined and flayed on its back, and Dalinda scrambled away.

Lorkan released his vampyr talons—it was so easy with the curse rearing so close in his blood. He gripped the rope attached to his chains and hacked away at the tender material. It frayed and *snapped* as Lorkan released himself. No, he didn't have access to his wolf with the shackles soaked in wolfsbane, but that didn't bind his vampyrism.

He ran.

"Stop him!" Dalinda's shrill command cut through the forest.

Lorkan kept moving north, putting distance between him and the Drengr Village. Something whizzed by his ear and planted in a nearby tree. An arrow trembled as he sprinted past it. More arrows shot through the forest. One, two—

Lorkan growled, falling to the ground. An arrow stuck out of his calf muscle, and crimson bled into white. He righted himself onto his back, crawling further and further back—

Another arrow lodged in his chest on the right side. Lorkan writhed as two arrows stuck out of his broken body.

Move, damn it. Move.

But it was no use. Lorkan was too weak for his healing ability to kick in. The wolfsbane worked against him, too, and Lorkan's resolve dissipated like fog. His chest heaved as he fell deeper into the snow, wishing the winter terrain would open wide and swallow him whole.

The Johanneses caught up, and Dalinda pushed through them, rage warring in her gaze.

She growled and whirled towards her unit. "I told you I needed him alive!"

"They weren't kill shots; I merely slowed him down."

Dalinda seethed. She unsheathed her axe and in one swift movement, knocked the blunt end of it into Lorkan's temple.

Black eclipsed his consciousness, and for a moment, Lorkan found peace, not pain.

Lorkan reared awake and instantly regretted it. The arrows, with their fletchings broken off, remained lodged in his chest and leg. Blood stained his clothes and seeped into the stone floor beneath him.

He blinked. The surrounding gray sharpened, and Lorkan recognized the inside of Lār. Ceremonial hymns echoed nearby, and his heart raced. Ahead, beyond a small door, the great hall awaited him.

How did Dalinda know the fortress so well? How had she gotten him inside?

"Ah, there you are. Awake at last." The wretched werewolf in question squatted on her haunches, inspecting him up and down. "Just in time, too. Your brother's ascension is about to start."

Lorkan gritted his teeth, tasting chalk. He didn't have time to wonder how Dalinda had pulled this off. He had to focus on tamping down his scorching anger. It only heightened his bloodthirst, and Dalinda's sneering face did nothing to help.

Kill her, the voices of the curse hissed. Horrific images of shredding her throat flashed through his mind.

Lorkan flinched. No, that *wasn't* who or what he was. He inhaled, exhaled. But his wolf was so near, sitting at attention—

He stiffened, inspecting himself. *Ah,* the arrows remained, but they'd removed the wolfsbane-soaked shackles. Nothing restrained his wolf, and with the curse worse than it had ever been since Lorkan had been turned, he had little control over his inner beast.

Dalinda's smile grew. She held up a waterskin and unscrewed the top. A beautiful, sweet and distinct scent reached Lorkan's senses. His bloodthirst reared to life, and his fangs released. He snarled and charged.

Eager. Wanting. *Hungry—*

"How long has it been since you fed? Does your kind need to feed as often as scáths?" Dalinda asked.

"*Stop,*" Lorkan hissed, feeling his fangs scrape against his bottom lip. "You're risking everyone's lives, even your own."

"Then cooperate." Dalinda tilted her head. "Reveal your identity with some shred of dignity left, or I drag you into that hall as the monster you are. Which is it?"

Dalinda had him. If she spilled a drop of the blood, he was fucked.

Think, Lorkan, think.

A beating echoed beyond the wall, and Eldrick—maybe even his father—waited on the other side. His entire pack. His *people*. Sure, Dalinda knew. His secret *was* out. But gods save him, not like this. Lorkan wasn't ready.

His wolf danced in his cursed blood, but another instinct, one far fiercer and familiar, rose to the surface.

Hide, hide, hide, it screamed.

All Lorkan needed was time. For Eldrick to become Earl. For the Drengr Pack to lead the Vadon Mountains. Then he'd swallow his pride and face what he was.

"Alright," he lied. "I choose dignity."

Not an ounce of him felt anything close to the word. His skin crawled, like his shame oozed from his pores.

"Good. Now get up."

He tracked Dalinda's movement as she screwed the waterskin's top back on. He stood on shaky legs.

"Move." Dalinda nodded her head towards the door.

Lorkan waited three beats and then tackled her to the ground. She released the waterskin, and Lorkan kicked it out of reach. Breathless, he righted himself and ran—straight into the Johannes werewolves from earlier. He'd miscalculated. Panicked. He hadn't heard them over his hounding fear.

They charged, herding him back into the small room. Dalinda kicked the arrow lodged in his calf, and Lorkan stumbled.

"Hold him steady."

They grabbed his arms and dragged him towards the door. Lorkan had no time to prepare as Dalinda burst into the hall. Light from the candles and the fireplaces blinded him, and the ceremony halted.

Lorkan's heart thudded in his chest, the only sound in the entire hall as all eyes fell on him.

Including Eldrick's.

Shock rippled through his brother's deep-green gaze, but something else lay in his expression. Something...*deeper*. Eldrick appeared lost and worn, as if he stood in the center of a battle, not a ceremony honoring his new title.

"Lorkan..." Eldrick shook his head and snapped his attention to Dalinda. "What is the meaning of this?"

Dalinda, with her nose high in the air and waterskin clutched in one hand, addressed her father, who stood at the front of the crowd with a wide grin. Alpha Johannes crossed his arms in triumph as pure pride glistened in his hard stare.

"What have you done to my son?"

Amid the stunned crowd, Aramis fought his way to the front, Lorkan's mother not far behind. Her horror-stricken face roiled his stomach.

"Unhand my brother," Eldrick said, lethally calm.

He stepped forward, but Bjorn and the other Johanneses intercepted his path.

"Lorkan Drengr, second born and scholar, is a vampyr!" Dalinda unscrewed the waterskin and threw it near Lorkan. "The Drengrs have kept secrets from us all!"

Blood splattered across the stone floor, and the sweat and delicious scent awakened his wolf.

Stars above. Sweat prickled on Lorkan's brow, and his heart raced inside his chest. He fought the werewolves holding him in place, but they didn't relent, pushing him to his knees. He searched for a way out. *Something.* But it was no use. The hundreds of eyes ahead pinned him in place, his secrets laid out bare for all to see.

His brother's chest heaved, a thousand emotions swimming in his eyes.

"Eldrick, I'm so sorry." Lorkan's voice broke.

As did his heart.

He growled, and his wolf—so hungry, wild and *cursed*—unleashed.

Sound and reason vanished. Lorkan became broken bones, pain, and hunger as he shifted into his wolf form. Midnight-black fur sprouted from his pale skin. As his face changed and a snout formed, his glasses fell and shattered against the stone. His clothes, not enchanted, split at the seams and shredded as he grew two feet taller, fragments piling around his elongated feet.

The werewolves holding him sprang out of reach, but all Lorkan *felt* was red. *Blood, blood, blood,* the curse chanted in his mind. He swiped left. Flesh shredded. More blood seeped into the air. He bit into the shoulder of another next, chucking them across the hall.

Swords unsheathed. Some werewolves shifted in the crowd, on the defense. Others shouted his name.

But Lorkan forgot he was anything but a monster.

With fangs released and talons dripping with blood, Lorkan howled to the ceiling, his days of hiding long gone.

CHAPTER EIGHTY-THREE

A BEAST STOOD BEFORE Eldrick, the kind that prowled in one's nightmares.

And yet, it was his brother.

The reserved, stern Drengr scholar was a vampyr—and *not* latent—and Eldrick's shock rooted him in place. When had Lorkan found his wolf? How long had he kept this secret?

The great hall spun. Eldrick didn't know where it began or ended, or what in *the stars above* to do. A hundred werewolves stood on the defense, eyeing his brother—

No. They looked to *Eldrick*, waiting on *his* command.

Because he was their future Earl. Eldrick's hands and face were still wet from ceremonial paint. Incense wafted the air, herbs that represented leaders, rite of passage, and new beginnings. But Eldrick smelled a standoff between expectations and his racing heart.

They'd never finished his ascension. By vote, he remained Earl, but the magic of the Vadon Mountains hadn't solidified it. As if fate presented another test, he had to walk the thin line between pleasing his people and protecting someone he loved.

What a cruel twist, hours after Tovi had broken his heart, too.

He took a cautious step forward, holding up a hand like he soothed a wild animal. His stomach churned. Two dead bodies lay at Lorkan's clawed feet, and his talons dripped with their fresh blood. His eyes, usually the same color gold as their mother's, now glistened crimson.

He took another step. "Lorkan—"

His mother grasped his arm. "The signs are clear. He hasn't fed in days, Eldrick. The curse—"

"If it truly had hold of him, he'd be far worse," Eldrick said. "I don't see a scáth—I see my brother."

Nadia swallowed, tears glistening in her all-knowing gaze. She shared a silent conversation with Aramis, who kept his distance. His jaw ticked as his attention jumped between sons. When he caught Eldrick looking, Aramis grimaced ever so slightly. *Moons*, had his father known what Lorkan was—

Eldrick ignored the questions tumbling through him and refocused on Lorkan. He stood taller than any werewolf Eldrick had faced before, but he had a lithe frame compared the muscle rippling in other werewolves prowling in the crowd. Vertebrae by vertebrae, his brother hunched onto all fours and bared his fang-like canines.

A deep growl—Bjorn's from the sound of it—echoed in the silent hall. "Fucking do something—"

Eldrick threw up his hand, silencing the alpha but not bothering to look in his direction. He kept his sights on Lorkan. Arrows still stuck from his chest and leg, the blood seeping into the wooden shafts old and dry.

"Lorkan," Eldrick whispered, "it's me, your brother, Eldrick. Can you hear me?"

His brother's ears flicked back, and he took a tentative step as Eldrick grew closer. Werewolves in the crowd heaved forward, hands dropping to their weapons.

"Stop," Nadia hissed.

The hall returned to a silent stillness. Eldrick picked up Lorkan's cracked glasses, grasping something that was familiar, anything to conjure his brother back to himself.

Lorkan's head tilted to the side, and Eldrick stood close enough to touch him. He reached for his inner wolf, bringing it close to the surface in case he needed to shift, and inhaled a deep, rallying breath.

Eldrick laid a hand atop Lorkan's chest, right over his heart. His fingers threaded through his thick midnight fur, and the distant *thump . . . thump . . . thump* of Lorkan's heart beat beneath his palm.

"Come back to us, brother," Eldrick whispered.

The land vibrated under his boots. He'd not used his alpha baritone, but a certain power lay in his words.

Lorkan trembled, and his fur slowly vanished. His limbs shrank. Bones snapped, and his face returned to the sharp scholarly Drengr Eldrick recognized.

Tears glistened in his once-again golden eyes. "I'm—" Lorkan winced, falling forward as pain rippled across his face. Eldrick caught him by the shoulders, keeping him steady. "S-s-sorry."

Words dried on Eldrick's tongue. He didn't know what to say or feel, and there were too many questions to count. *Later*, he told himself.

"Mother, get the healers—"

"Healers?!" Bjorn seethed, storming towards Eldrick.

His father intercepted his path, hand falling to his axe strapped to his belt.

Bjorn's face reddened. "This matter no longer concerns you, Aramis. You are no longer an alpha, and despite your efforts to keep this a secret from us all, it is now known."

Eldrick reared straighter. Bjorn confirmed his suspicion—his father had known Lorkan was a vampyr.

The crowd murmured among themselves. Leif Thorn emerged from the crowd, chest heaving.

"What is Bjorn talking about?" the alpha demanded. "How long has your son been a vampyr?"

Eldrick's being burst with the same question, but the tension inside the hall rose. The ceremonial incense faded, and the paint on his hands and cheeks cracked as it dried. They were moving further and further away from him becoming Earl—and *moons*, he was a right bastard for thinking of himself and not Lorkan in this moment, but the fate of the Vadon Mountains depended on him ascending.

"Lorkan Drengr was turned a decade ago." Dalinda thrust a handful of letters up into the air. "There are more like him—an entire pack of cursed werewolves. The Drengrs have lied to us all. Aramis has corresponded with their pack leader, Lorkan, for years."

The crowd grew unruly, and the cold from the outside crept through the hall. Eldrick's skin tightened like frost crawled across his skin, and his wolf bared its teeth. Dalinda was more fox than wolf, her timing impeccable—she and Bjorn had orchestrated this reveal, all to jeopardize his ascension.

He was a fool to think they'd not try *something*.

"*This*"—Bjorn's voice boomed in the hall as he addressed the werewolves—"is who you have placed your faith in, a pack who knew some of our brothers and sisters might still be alive, that the curse was more than it seemed, and allowed vampyrs to walk amongst us!"

"That isn't true," Aramis said. "I am to blame for these secrets. Eldrick knew nothing."

"You expect us to believe you kept your eldest son in the dark?" Alpha Skau shook with rage, his pack members stalking closer towards Eldrick and Lorkan. "How can we trust a word you say?"

"Eldrick's shock is just as genuine as all of ours." Ragna frowned, trailing Eldrick up and down with ancient eyes. "He didn't know what his brother was."

Bjorn growled. "That is hope blinding you, Ragna."

"I'd rather be blinded by hope than full of hate like you," she hissed.

Alpha Alland pointed his blade towards Eldrick's mother. "Perhaps Bjorn's instinct is just. We can't forget Nadia Drengr, who we all thought was dead, is also a vampyr. The Drengr Pack seems to be woven with secrets."

Ragna blinked, and Eldrick sent her a pleading stare, but a shadow fell over her gaze. His grasp on control was slipping.

He took a mighty breath. "It is fair to be frightened of the unknown, but we must judge cautiously. They curse is unkind, but it doesn't define all vampyrs—"

"*They* are an abomination!" Spittle flew from Bjorn's lips as he pointed a meaty finger towards Lorkan. "And this monster slaughtered two of my pack members. We all witnessed it. He is no different from a scáth."

Next to Eldrick, Lorkan flinched. He turned paler and paler as the minutes went on, and at the sight of the arrows sticking out of him, Eldrick's anger rose in a hot, fiery wave.

His boots slicked through the blood seeping into the stone floor, and Dalinda's waterskin lay a few feet away.

"Your daughter spilled blood first," Eldrick whispered. "She is just as guilty for their deaths."

"How fucking dare you?" Bjorn marched towards Eldrick and grasped him by the collar of his tunic. "I demand retribution!"

Eldrick swatted Bjorn's hand away, reining in his inner wolf. He held his ground, standing between Lorkan and Bjorn. *Moons,* he couldn't let the Johanneses win.

He searched the alphas for his allies—Drabek, Thorn, and Alland, Lindström—but they stayed back, away from him and his brother.

"Can you see what Bjorn is doing?" Eldrick shouted to them. "He is dividing us to become Earl."

"We deserved to know this, Eldrick!" Thorn's jaw ticked. "All vampyrs are cursed, even those who once were werewolves, and they have cast darkness on our lands for far too long. How can we trust you when you chose them over our own kind?" He gestured towards the dead bodies.

The crowd burst with agreement, nodding and muttering *aye* all around. Leif spoke Eldrick's fears out loud, and sweat prickled at his brow.

How could he undo this?

Bjorn held up his hands, silencing the crowd. He turned to Eldrick. "Perhaps you didn't know your brother was a vampyr, but this is a chance to show us you're not like your father. What kind of Earl will you be, Eldrick Drengr?"

Just. Kind. *Nothing* like Bjorn. His heart beat with rightness.

Before he had time to answer, winds circled above the dais. A scene grew sharper and sharper as the winds spun, revealing another place—a forest dense with snow and frost. At the center, Blair Carson, dressed head to toe in black and a raven on her shoulder, stepped through her *danu*. Her mouth fell open at the sight of Lorkan, horror flashing across her face.

She rushed to his side and draped her cloak over Lorkan's body.

Dalinda growled, stepping forward. "Stop her!"

Blair screamed, releasing a wave of her shadows. They knocked a dozen werewolves back, and she gathered Lorkan in her arms, cursing as she spied his various wounds.

Shadows converged up the walls, darkness draping over the crowd. The lit fireplaces and candles *whooshed* out, the cold worsening.

"A dark witch," Bjorn muttered.

Eldrick tasted winter, storm and chaos in the air.

But it was love brimming in Blair's eyes as she held Lorkan. Fierce and strong and real. More real than any title, duty, or fate's path. The truth knocked the breath from Eldrick, for it was not what sort of Earl he would be, but the type of werewolf.

"Stars above," Dalinda hissed.

She aimed her axe and threw it in Lorkan's direction. Time slowed, but Eldrick's heart didn't miss a single beat of the power he'd possessed earlier when he'd laid his hand over his brother's heart.

Out of love, not duty, he stepped in the line of Dalinda's attack. The axe hit true—square in his chest—lodging into his breast plate. He stumbled back, blinking past the searing pain. The blade pierced skin, though thank the stars above, not deadly deep, but enough Eldrick forgot how to breathe and crumpled to his knees.

His mother might've screamed. Perhaps his father roared. Lorkan definitely rasped his name. But when he blinked, it was a phantom voice of a vampyr queen he heard, her one word like a whisper in the wind.

Choice.

For Eldrick had made his, and he'd loose *everything* because of it.

Tears glistened in Blair's eyes. She opened and closed her mouth, but no words came out.

"Go," Eldrick whispered.

Wisping shadows swallowed his brother and the witch whole, and as Eldrick stared deep into Blair's vanishing *danu*, he fell farther and farther into darkness until oblivion held him like a dear friend.

Chapter Eighty-Four

Blair

Lorkan crumpled in Blair's arms as they landed in his office at Vísdómr.

It was the only place she could think of. She'd been so jarred, so consumed with protecting Lorkan, she'd only thought of somewhere that felt like home. Somewhere safe. *Warm*—

Except, Lorkan's office was anything but. An enchanted lamp on his desk lit itself upon their arrival, and in the dim light, Blair's ragged breath plumed in the air. The stone walls converged around them, worsening the cold. Ahead, the fireplace hadn't been used in days.

"Fuck," she hissed, crawling across the carpet.

Behind her, Lorkan shivered and grew paler than usual. Blair'd forgotten he wore *nothing* but her cloak. It was too small for his tall, lean frame, reaching his shins and revealing the blood coating his bare feet. The velvet material clung to his sharp muscles, leaving little to the imagination.

But it wasn't only his beautiful physique she couldn't tear her eyes from, but the injuries marking his body. Burns ringed his wrist and neck. One eye was black and bruised, his brow split open. He winced when he sat back against the sofa, and Blair guessed he had broken bones, too.

Why, *blasted books*, wasn't he healing?

Blair's insides heated, her shadows leaking from her fingertips. She hated the sight of him in pain. *Hated* how she'd reached Lorkan too late, and his own people had hurt him for what he was.

Rook tapped his beak against something metal, guiding Blair. *Ah—there.* She reached the stack of wood and flint, and her hands shook as she attempted to start the fire. By some luck or fate overlooking them, sparks fell onto the firewood and smoke rose. Using her wind bronntanas, Blair fed the fire until it crackled and danced to life.

She reached for Lorkan and grasped his face, stroking his cheeks and making him look at her. His golden eyes were so vacant, her chest cracked.

"Where can I find supplies?" she asked.

"Desk drawers on the left," he said.

Blair nodded and sprinted off. She discovered a few bottles of healing ointment—their scents conjuring memories of her late sister, Mirella—a washing rag, dressings, and a small bowl. Near the table with tea and a decanter of whiskey, she found a pitcher of water.

Blair busied herself with creating a cleaning station, like she'd seen her sister set up many times. She assessed Lorkan next, her hands shaking as she pushed her cloak from his shoulders to inspect all his wounds—

She froze. "Lorkan . . ." Blair didn't fight the tears. What was the point when her heart broke at the sight of him like this?

An arrow remained lodged in his chest, crooked at a wrong angle because *someone* had snapped the shaft. She assessed him up and down and cursed, finding another arrow in his leg, far deeper than the first.

Thought and reason vanished from Blair's mind as she stared at his wounds. *Think, damn it, think.* But Blair wasn't a healer. She wasn't Mirella. She was a scholar. She researched books and papers and—

No, she was Blair Carson. The man she loved *needed* her, and above all else, she was resourceful.

Rook landed by her side, staring up at her with his beady eyes. He clicked his beak and stomped his feet into the carpet, as if agreeing with her.

But how did she help Lorkan? She could clean a wound, but the arrows . . . She didn't have the bronntanas or skills to get them out.

Rook flew to the painting hanging by the fireplace, tilting his head.

Fjall Pack. Of course. Werewolf-vampyrs she could trust.

Blair assessed Lorkan again. She'd already used too much magic traveling from the Drengr Village to Vísdómr to create another *danu*, and he was far too heavy to carry. She could leave him and wander the tunnels herself, but the thought paralyzed her to the carpet. Her entire being couldn't bear leaving him.

Rook cawed, ruffling his wings. He tapped the painting again as if—

"Smart, clever bird," she whispered.

Blair rushed to him and opened the secret door that led to the underground village.

"Go," she said to Rook.

Her familiar shot into the darkness, his onyx feathers glinting until he disappeared completely.

Blair returned to Lorkan's side. No, she couldn't remove the arrows herself, but she could clean his other injuries while she waited for help to arrive.

She started with a few minor cuts, wiping blood away, and found too many bruises to count, as if someone had beaten him for days.

Blair's shadows hissed—*why* wasn't he healing?

With his head tilted back on the sofa, Lorkan fought consciousness as Blair worked. Beside them, the firewood dwindled as an hour passed.

Blair had cleaned the worst of it, aside from a nasty bruise and cut festering on his side. She dabbed the cloth with ointment and water, and as she pressed, Lorkan shot forward and growled, baring his fangs at her.

Blair didn't flinch as Lorkan's golden eyes drank her in, more predator than scholar. But he wouldn't hurt her. She believed it in her bones.

He blinked, face falling as recognition flashed across his face. "I . . . Blair, I'm so sorry."

"It's alright," she said.

"It's not." He tried to sit up but sank back as his strength gave out. "I failed Eldrick. My father. Alvin and Mya are dead—"

"Do I resemble death to you?" a woman's voice called from the hidden doorway.

"Aye, Lorkan, you look like shit *and* like you've seen a ghost." Alvin laughed.

Blair tried to find some relief in their playful banter, but something wild and fierce, like a storm raging within her, rose to the surface.

"Someone shot him with two arrows," she said, rising to meet them. "He's not healing."

"Aye, we figured someone was in awful shape. That bird of yours caused quite a ruckus in the village, stealing the healing supplies we'd need."

Mya shrugged her shoulder, showing Blair a sack packed to the brim.

"Rook is a familiar," Blair said as he landed on her shoulder, raising a brow at Alvin.

The werewolf-vampyr grunted. "Rook is a menace and owes me thirty river pearl beads."

Rook purred, proud and triumphant.

"How about we chitchat later and take care of Lorkan?" Mya said, skipping towards him.

He couldn't stop staring at his friends, mouth opening and closing. "I thought . . ."

Alvin grunted. "We were close to it, but Blair found us just before the sun rose. She must have a knack for saving lives."

Blair winced. The memory of her sister's death was still fresh. It plagued her dreams and even waking thoughts if she wasn't careful.

"How about you get some food from the Vísdómr kitchens?" Mya asked. "Lorkan will be fine with us for a little while. I promise."

Suddenly, the last few hours hit Blair like a gust of wind. It didn't help that she'd been tracking Lorkan in the mountains for days, trying to find him after learning what Dalinda had done. She wasn't a third born, yet the urge to protect Lorkan had become as intrinsic as breathing. Too, the closer she got to him, the fiercer his emotions had become.

She'd felt them as if they were her own—his despair, panic, and helplessness.

Blair had finally found Lorkan because of a bond she'd always suspected, and now, he was watching her with his beautiful golden eyes as if *he* could not only read her emotions but her thoughts.

She swallowed. "Alright. I'll be back soon."

Blair lied. She didn't exactly take her time, but she didn't rush either. She simply needed a moment to breathe. To *think*. Or for once, not.

She visited her temporary dormitory to wash and put on fresh clothes—an oversize sweater to finally remove the days-old chill in her bones and high-waisted trousers her sister Evelyn would love. She tied back her curls once they were dry, sighing at her reflection in the small mirror near the door.

Every so often, the bond between her and Lorkan pulsed. Each time, she paused, equally filled with wonder and nerves.

After a few flights of stairs, a wrong turn and two right turns, she found the library's messaging post and sent a letter detailing the latest events and her worries regarding Eldrick Drengr by iolair. The beast of a bird shot out the room's weathered window, its mighty wings causing ripples in the lingering snow clouds.

Eventually, Blair found food at the Vísdómr food stalls on the ground level—a steaming bowl of winter squash soup and a crusty bread baked with cheese and an herb butter to pair. The secretary manning the ancient text section allowed her inside the department without question, and after a long, mighty breath, she entered Lorkan's office with the tray of food.

Lorkan pressed his lips into a thin line and furrowed his brow while Alvin and Mya giggled amongst themselves. As she shut the door behind her, his attention swiveled in her direction.

"Blair," he said, sitting up.

He still wore no shirt, but at least the blanket draped across his shoulders fell over a pair of black trousers. The bruises had slightly faded, and the arrows were nowhere in sight. A dark purple paste caked the wounds they'd left behind.

Alvin clapped his hands and rose out of his seat. "I think that's our cue to leave."

"Oh, you're quite right," Mya said. She pulled up a seat for Blair and gestured to it.

Blair set Lorkan's meal down and grasped the fellow witch's hands. "Thank you for helping."

Mya's beautiful face beamed as she smiled. "Thank *you* for saving us, all of us. I don't think Fjall Pack will forget what you've done."

Blair walked Alvin and Mya to the painting and let them into the tunnels. Once they were off, she sealed it shut, and ventured to the fireplace. She fed the fire a few more logs and hovered near the warmth.

"Blair," Lorkan whispered, gentle but stern, "look at me."

She shut her eyes, her name on his lips was like a caress down her back. She turned, inch by inch. Lorkan's eyes were a plea and declaration all one, as if he gazed upon the stars and heavens, not *her*.

"Come here. *Please*."

He needn't added the latter. Blair met him in two long strides but reached for his food. "You need to eat—"

Lorkan grasped her wrist. "What I need is to hear that you're okay."

"*Me*—" Blair shook her head. Blinked. "I'm not exactly the one we need to worry about, Lorkan."

He titled his head, studying her in that way of his. "Blair."

She huffed. "I'm fine, but I'd feel better if you'd eat something."

Blair raised a brow, and Lorkan rolled his eyes, releasing her and grabbing the bowl of soup. She stepped back from his orbit, feeling suddenly cold despite the fire and her thick sweater. She curled up in the chair ahead of him, tracking his movements to make sure he ate.

"I sent word to Kade and Evelyn." Blair crossed her arms. "I didn't think it was safe to write to the Drengr Village and risk anyone discovering I brought you here but . . . Someone needed to know what happened, and we can trust them."

Lorkan nodded, a graveness etched into his features. "Eldrick won't become Earl."

"You can't blame yourself," Blair whispered. "What they did to you . . ."

She tore her gaze away from him, staring into the fire instead. Movement rustled against the sofa, and suddenly, Blair was moving as Lorkan grasped hold of her chair and dragged it closer.

"Mya is right you know," he said. "No one will easily forget what you did, especially me. I thought my friends were dead, and you saved them."

"But I was too late when I found you—"

"You can't blame yourself," Lorkan repeated Blair's own words, and a fraction of the weight she held on her shoulders fell away.

She sighed, trailing her fingers across his chest. She paused near the arrow wound. Red seeped past the purple paste.

"You're still not healing." Blair rose out of her seat, turning towards the painting. "I'll fetch Mya and Alvin again—"

Lorkan grasped her hips, pulling her back towards him. "It's alright. My healing will simply take a little longer."

"Why?"

Lorkan's gaze dropped to the carpet. "I haven't fed in a few days."

Blair swallowed, sinking into her seat again. "What about the curse? Don't you need blood?"

He traced the groves in her palm, still not looking at her. "Yes, but Mya gave me a cup of elm tea before she left, which should help my hunger until I'm rested enough to go hunt."

"But you're in pain," Blair whispered. "If blood will help you heal quicker, then why not—"

"Blair."

"—feed from me?"

Lorkan's honey gaze snapped to her in an instant. His nostrils flared, and he released her. "You have no idea what you're asking."

"Then explain it to me. I've read Matilda Moore's journal, Lorkan. Vampyrs feed from one another . . . those that are in intimate relationships, and I'm *not* afraid of you. I trust that you won't hurt me—"

"It's far more complicated than that, Blair," Lorkan hissed.

"Why?" Blair's question came out a mere breath.

Lorkan didn't miss a beat. "It'll solidify our mating bond."

His honey eyes bore into her, pinning her in place. Blair's heart raced inside her, but there was no point in denying it now, was there?

"That's how I found you," she whispered. "The—*our* bond. Weeks ago, we stood here in a similar position. Do you remember what you asked me?"

Lorkan's released a shuddering breath. "What do you want? Need? Tell me, and I'll give it."

"You," Blair whispered. "It's always been you, I've needed Lorkan Drengr, and tonight, I want—"

Lorkan gripped her hips tighter and dragged her flush against his chest. She fit so perfectly between his legs, and with his leering height, they came face to face, so close they breathed the same air.

His eyes darkened as he studied her from brow to nose to lips. He laid his own gently against hers, but as Blair opened wider for him, he pulled away, teasing his tortuous touch to her jaw, nipping and kissing as he trailed downward, towards the slope of her neck.

Lorkan's hand caressed up her back until—

He grabbed a fistful of her curls and yanked her head back, exposing her throat and giving him full access to her soft flesh. He dragged his teeth—

No, those were the tips of his fangs touching her skin. It was gentle and wicked and delightful all at once.

Blair's toes curled. She instinctively moaned and held onto Lorkan's shoulders for support.

"Is this what you want?" His words tickled her already aroused flesh. "Is this what you need?"

"Yes," Blair breathed.

"Then you'll need to be patient."

Blair became airborne. Lorkan carried her towards the table, depositing her at the edge. He bent down and kissed her. His lips molded to hers, widening them so their breaths escaped and tongues brushed together. His hands found the buckle to her trousers, and with an audible snap, he popped them open, not missing a beat as he devoured her mouth.

Lorkan pulled away. "Lean back."

The authority ringing in his tone had Blair's insides heating, but she narrowed her gaze at him. Lorkan smirked, leaning closer. His fingers dipped into her pants and passed her undergarments, finding that spot between her legs. Blair hissed, and he chuckled.

"Lean back."

Blair, begrudgingly, obeyed, anticipation alighting across her skin.

Lorkan tugged her pants and undergarments in one mighty pull. Bare before him, Lorkan's honey eyes didn't break contact with hers.

"If you need me to stop, you tell me to stop. Understand?"

Blair swallowed, her mind hollowing out at the possibilities of what Lorkan had in store. "You won't hurt me."

Lorkan knelt. "No, you're right. I'd never harm you. But this might be intense."

"I trust you, Lorkan," Blair whispered.

He sighed, breath tickling her warm sex. "Good. Now, relax for me."

Blair exhaled, allowing her body to mold to the table as Lorkan spread her legs wider. The sight of him kneeling before her, eyes glistening with worship, was almost her undoing. Lorkan ran his nose down her thigh, marking his descent before his tongue swiped through her sex.

Blair whimpered. Of course, they'd done things. Touching, innocent exploration. But they'd never ventured to something so raw, so primal.

Lorkan feasted between her legs with no restraint. He sucked her bundle of nerves and lapsed at her entrance. Blair's insides felt as though a storm brewed in them, hot and electrical. She dug her hands into his hair, and Lorkan pulled away, peering up at her.

"Tell me to stop."

"Don't you dare," she hissed.

Even with eyes closed, Blair felt his smile pressed against her thigh, and he replaced his lips and tongue with his fingers. He pressed into her core, and Blair's back bowed against the table. She writhed, pushing books and papers, and pencils onto the floor.

"Are you ready?" Lorkan whispered.

At first, his question didn't register. Then he glided the tips of his fangs down the inside of Blair's leg. Oh. He meant to drink from there.

"Yes," she breathed.

"I love you, Blair Carson. Everything I am, belongs to you." Lorkan sank his fangs into her flesh. Slowly. With care. A slight sting shocked through Blair's system, like the jarring prick when one grasped hold of a rose. Blasted books, his fangs were sharp, but then he started to suck.

To drink.

Euphoria rushed through Blair's veins, and she cried out his name. Not from agony or pain, but utter bliss. Beastly, guttural sounds rumbled from Lorkan's chest. Lorkan never stopped pumping his fingers into Blair's core as he drank, and her release climbed a steep, beautiful mountain.

Perhaps it was their bond. Perhaps it was Lorkan's natural tenderness despite the sharpness of his fangs. Within it all—the sensation, the atmosphere, them—Blair finally understood why vampyrs referred to it as a sacred act in her research.

Lorkan pierced her with his honey gaze as he drank. Blair placed a hand on his face and brushed back his hair. He curled his fingers inside her, and Blair ascended the steep mountain of release.

She fell and fell and fell, her screams of pleasure echoing off the stone walls.

A tingling sensation washed over her, and Blair's heart thumped. Once, twice, a third time. With the gentle caress of snow floating on the wind, the thread tied to her soul reached out to Lorkan, and their beings wove together as one.

Lorkan shuddered and eased out of her with as much care as he'd bitten her with. His eyes shone like mined gold, and color flushed his cheeks.

Their bond beat like a whirling storm, magnetic and beastly.

"Are you alright?" he breathed, staring at her like nothing else existed or mattered in the world.

Blair nodded, unable for words.

"Can you handle more?" He smoothed his thumb over her bite mark.

Still breathless, Blair used her body to show him. She sat up, finding the laces on his trousers and pulled them. His pants fell to the stone floor, and Lorkan stood before naked and taut.

They kissed. Nipped and sucked and tasted the other. A copper sweetness lay on Lorkan's tongue, and Blair's insides heated again.

Lorkan grasped her sweater and pulled it over her head. Her bralette came next, and their clothes lay in a heap on the floor. He tugged her closer to the edge until her feet planted on the stone—

Blair sucked in a breath as Lorkan twisted her around. His one hand palmed her belly while the other gripped her throat, making her lean back as he devoured her mouth again. Flush against him, Blair surrendered to him.

His fingers brushed against her swollen bundle of nerves, and she panted in his hold. His manhood grazed her backside, and ever so gently, Lorkan bent her over the table.

She peered over her shoulder as he traced his fingers down the slope of her spine. A question brimmed in his eyes, and Blair answered him by pressing her backside into his hips.

Yes, she sent down their newly woven bond.

Lorkan shuddered and grasped hold of her waist with one hand while the other fisted his length. Much, much longer than she remembered, it pressed and stretched at her opening. She braced, and Lorkan took his time, bending down to mold his lips against hers as he pushed the last few inches.

Both of them cursed as they came together at last.

Ten fucking years of wanting had led them to this point, and pleasure coursed through Blair as she embraced the feel of Lorkan.

He rocked his hips forward, and Blair cried out, pressing her face into the table to drown out the sounds she made. Lorkan grasped a fistful of her curls, yanking her head back.

"I've waited so long for this," he whispered between thrusts, "I plan to hear every one of your sounds, Blair."

"Fuck," she cried.

Blair gripped the side of the table, clawing at something as if to gain a grip on reality as Lorkan drove into her again and again, his pace deliberate and equally sweet. Blair craved the roughness. Yearned for the loss of abandon. Cried his name as another climax crested over the mountain of release. She'd thought the way he worshipped between her legs earlier had been primal, but this was wilder.

Lorkan's usual reserved demeanor was nowhere in sight. He became un-tethered, monstrous as he moved into her, drawing out her pleasure as he chased his own. His grip on her hip or hair didn't relent, and Blair loved the kiss of pain amongst so much pleasure. Their first time was so them. So perfect.

Their bond rumbled in Blair's chest, and like the zap of lightning, her body turned alight. Lorkan bent over, caging her in his arms as he found a deeper angle. They kissed. Messy, fervent, wild.

"Lorkan," Blair whispered.

He pressed his forehead against hers, breathless. "I've got you. Come for me."

She did.

Lorkan found his own release, stilling inside her as their bond wove tighter and tighter.

CHAPTER EIGHTY-FIVE

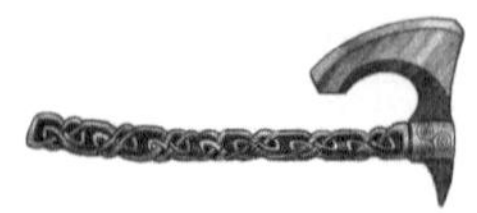

E LDRICK'S CHEST ACHED AS he blinked awake.

Outside the infirmary's window, snow fell in delicate sheets. The Drengr Village bustled with winter activity. Farmers dragged fire logs through the icy streets. Children threw snowballs, their smiles wide. The distant *ting, ting, ting* of the smithery could be made out over the whistling wind. It almost—*almost*—appeared to be a serene winter afternoon.

No curse. No scáth attacks. No war on the horizon.

Yet, fate was far crueler. Eldrick spied only Drengr navy amongst the werewolves. No shields with Drabek amethyst or breastplates painted Johannes green. How long had he been out?

"Three days," his father said, as if reading his thoughts.

Aramis stood in the doorway with arms crossed and a tiredness etched into his frown. He entered the infirmary, and the snow collecting in his furs dried instantly from the heat emitting from the center fire. Embers zigzagged up and up into the tiny opening carved into the ceiling, hissing as heat and cold collided.

Eldrick sat up, fighting the stiffness in his sore muscles. "Lorkan?"

"I received word that your brother is safe." Aramis pulled a stool up next to his bedside. "All thanks to you."

"Bjorn?" he asked next.

His father sighed. "Ascended as Earl not an hour after your mother dragged you to the infirmary."

Eldrick waited for bitterness to coat his tongue. It never came, and instead, a heaviness clung to his limbs. What now?

Restlessness bristled through Eldrick, and he swung his legs out of bed, planting his feet on the floorboards. He gripped the mattress for balance and studied the grooves in the wood, as if they might have answers.

"I don't regret my decision," he said without meeting his father's stare.

"I figured as much," Aramis said, "considering you asked about your brother first instead of the Earl seat. You care deeply, Eldrick. Always have."

Eldrick scoffed. "Can you at least *sound* disappointed?"

"That would be an impossible feat when it is the farthest thing I feel."

Eldrick shook his head, glaring at his father. "But I lost the vote and failed our pack. *Failed* the Vadon Mountains."

"The first is true—and I, too, am to blame, Eldrick—but the latter is yet to be seen." His father glanced out the window. "Why aren't you angry with *me*?"

Eldrick debated, his shoulders loosening as he said, "Because I respect your decision to keep Lorkan safe."

His father hummed. "Yet, I led you both astray, and for that, I'm deeply sorry."

Eldrick's heart skipped a beat. "Your more than forgiven, father."

Aramis sighed as if he'd released a thousand tons off his shoulders. "Thank you, son."

For a moment they sat in the welcomed silence.

Eventually, Eldrick sighed. "How am I to take orders from a male like Bjorn? How can I keep my head held high and lead the Drengr Pack after such a defeat?"

"Perhaps there's a way you can avoid all of that."

Both Eldrick and Aramis snapped their attention to Sam Johannes, who stood with his arms crossed leaning in the doorway. The young werewolf had healed, aside from a greenish bruise lingering around his once closed-shut eye. He wore leathers more suited for a battle and adorned with an interesting color choice: lilac. Behind him, a few other young werewolves lingered—Siv, Gyda, and Erik—their gear dotted with a similar shade.

"How do you propose I do that?"

Sam entered the infirmary. "You're not the only one who doesn't agree with my father, Eldrick. There are werewolves who wish to fight to free Sorin of the curse, alongside the vampyrs."

Never set foot on my lands again, he'd told the vampyr queen. Yet, he no longer had such authority nor a guarantee they'd be allies. Perhaps accepting a marriage proposal from Flynn had been for the better—

Eldrick pushed images of Tovi to the back of his mind. His body ached too much for him to linger on his bruised heart, and now his head spun with Sam's suggestion.

"I can't disobey your father as Earl. It is woven within the magic of the werewolves," Eldrick said.

"Perhaps if you remained an alpha," Sam said, lips twitching. "But speaking as a banished wolf, I'm not bound by the magic of these mountains any longer, and it's quite liberating."

Eldrick shot to his feet, unable to hide the bite in his tone. "Are you suggesting I leave my pack and let them face your father's wrath?"

"No," Sam said, his tone far too hard for someone his age. "But perhaps you can forge a new path for yourself, one more befitting for where you truly belong."

"That still doesn't ensure the well-being of the Drengrs." Despite Sam's enticing idea, every fiber of Eldrick's being fought against abandoning them.

"What if they had a new alpha?" Sam smirked. "Someone who could fight his command."

Eldrick scoffed, placing his hands on his hips. "What werewolf has that power? They'd have to be more god than werewolf—" He stopped short, rearing straighter as the realization shot through him. "Kade . . ."

Aramis scratched his beard. "If your brother is alpha and doesn't answer to Bjorn, neither do the Drengrs."

Sam crossed his arms, a newfound glint shining in his eyes. "That's an entire pack who'll go to war, regardless of Bjorn's choice. That doesn't include those that'll follow you, Eldrick. Trust me, there are more than you think."

The promise of a certain future rippled through him while a word echoed through his mind.

Choice.

Could he rise to the occasion? Would he rebel against the path fate had laid out for him?

> *After a storm between mistaken enemies,*
> *the wolf and dove, the clash of the light and night,*
> *those of these lands will unite.*

The whispers of the prophecy tickled the back of his neck, like the stanza carried on the breeze drafting through the infirmary.

For the first time in his life, Eldrick saw the world with crystal-clear sight. Perhaps fate had presented a path all along, but he'd let titles and duty get in the way. Eldrick's heart *sang* as he realized his rightful place. With an axe in hand, fighting for his lands . . . all by the side of the woman he loved. Yet—

"Kade must want this, too," he said. "I'll not thrust a title onto someone unless they truly wish for it."

A deep rumble vibrated through Aramis's chest. "You can ask him yourself. Blair wrote to him about what happened, and he and Evelyn arrived yesterday evening. You'll find both of them at the cottage." His father grasped his shoulder and gave it a reassuring squeeze. "I've learned recently there are certain things not worth sacrificing, Eldrick. Our hearts are certainly not one of them. Go after her, or you'll regret it for the rest of your days."

Eldrick nodded, the emotions rising within him too fierce for words.

Sam stepped out of the infirmary. "We're staying at the Shield-maiden. Find us when you're ready."

Later, flurries danced around Eldrick as he marched through the forest to Kade and Evelyn's cottage. He'd dressed for a long journey ahead—traveling leathers, a thick wool tunic, boots that molded shin high, and a fur-lined cloak. Not a hint of Drengr navy adorned his ensemble aside from a thin piece of fabric newly tied to his axe's shaft.

"A reminder," his father had said, "where you came from and are always welcome."

Farewell tasted crisp like the start of spring, and as Eldrick's boots trudged through the snow, he spied creeping phlox underneath the cold. The purple flowers contrasting against white quickened his gait. It was as if the land said *go*.

Kade stood with arms crossed in the doorway, one brow raised. "Shouldn't you be resting in the infirmary?"

"I'm afraid I have something to ask of you and Evelyn," Eldrick said.

Kade assessed him hood to boots. "I see. Come in."

The door shut behind Eldrick, and the warmth from the hearth encompassed him. In the kitchenette, Evelyn prepared coffee. Her and Kade's power brimmed in the quaint space, and Eldrick wondered if either of them was aware of how much they'd truly changed in the last weeks.

> *A King and Queen will emerge,*
> *With the seeds sown from elsewhere . . .*

Eldrick fought a smile. Perhaps they were, and *he* was the one late in accepting the prophecy.

"This ask seems serious," Evelyn said, handing him a steaming mug.

She took her place next to Kade, and their shoulders touched ever so slightly.

Kade tilted his head, studying him. "You're leaving."

Eldrick nodded. "I wish to, yes, but I refuse to leave our pack without a leader. The alpha baritone has never worked on you, Kade, but now more than ever, you're strong enough to fight the Earl's command." A nervous laugh escaped him. "If you ask me the truth, I think you've been the rightful leader of the Drengrs all along, but" —Eldrick turned to his brother's mate— "this also affects you, Evelyn, and if it is not something you *both* wish for, then I respect your decision."

Because if Kade accepted and Eldrick *gave* his brother the title, Evelyn would become the female alpha of the Drengr Pack.

Evelyn gave Kade a small smile, and by the unsaid words shining in their eyes, Eldrick guessed they discussed his ask over mind-linking.

Kade nodded and approached Eldrick with his outstretched. "I'll happily agree to it, brother, but where will you go?"

Eldrick's heart swelled. "I intend to find the woman I love."

PART IV

*With bones of an old friend now set free,
and the blade of the ancients
the truest of unions between the third-borns of
the Sun and Moon will defeat the darkness.*

Chapter Eighty-Six

STEAM ROLLED THROUGH THE cottage's upstairs bathroom as Evelyn and Kade emerged from the shower. In the mirror ahead, Evelyn spied the alpha tattoo shimmering from her mate's fingers to his elbow. Without the right light, Kade's new mark was practically invisible.

As was hers.

Evelyn brushed her hair as Kade combed his beard, attention fixed on the mirror.

"Bjorn will be furious," she said absently.

He humphed. "That's nothing new. He's always angry about something."

"I suppose the difference is he won't be able to do anything about it."

Kade paused, eyeing her through his reflection. The edges of his lips tilted into a proud smile. "Indeed. I—*we'll* lead the Drengr warriors to the Void, whether he likes it or not. He'd be a fool to make a move against us. He risks losing favor."

Evelyn sighed. "He'll lose werewolves regardless, Kade. Now that Eldrick has left, demonstrating it can be done, others will follow, and there's many that believe in the prophecy, and therefore you."

"As well as you." Kade stepped closer, tucking a strand of hair behind her ear. He brushed his fingers underneath her chin and tilted it up, making her peer up at him. "Do you feel the alpha magic?"

"Yes."

Among the *many* senses Evelyn had gained since returning from the Otherworld and giving the Sun Goddess's flame to the Gray Wood, like heightened sight and smell, she had a unique awareness of the Vadon Mountains—how the roots twisted through the dirt and distant creeks curved through the rocky terrain, glacier water rushing over weathered rock. Whenever she closed her eyes, the gentle tune of songbirds greeted her silver flame, and everything smelled distinctly of rain and pine.

Kade studied her, golden eyes drinking her in. "You didn't hesitate when Eldrick asked."

Evelyn raised a brow. "Should I have?"

His brows pinched as he ran a finger across her collarbone. "It binds you to these lands, not as though you can't ever leave, but—"

"I'm aware of what I agreed to."

"I know." Kade shut his eyes and exhaled.

Evelyn grasped his hand, tracing the delicate lines running through his palm—the ones untouched by the alpha mark. "I feel at home here, especially in this cottage and most certainly when I'm by your side. *You're* my home, Kade, and the promise of what we'll build together—a future for werewolves and witches, a family—is what I fight for because I can see it and *taste* it as if it's nearer than ever."

Truth and vulnerability bled from Evelyn's words. So much had happened so quickly, but they were ready for this. Evelyn had gotten her magic back, and it was more hers than ever. Kade had mastered his powers and possessed the sword of ancients, and she had the ever seed.

They were more than ready.

Yet in the morning, they'd journey back to the Void to prepare for war, and the unknown lay on the horizon.

Evelyn took a shaky breath. "There is still so much we must face, but I believe in us. Of course, I'd be lying if I weren't a little afraid. We're going to war and . . ." Evelyn shook her head, ridding herself of intrusive thoughts. She'd not think of the worst.

"I don't want to take *this* for granted. The here and now. Us together, bound in more ways than one. I want to cherish tonight, not because I believe or fear it is our last, but because it is special. We—our decisions, challenges, and triumphs—are special because they led us to this moment. I believe it in my bones."

Kade had moved closer as Evelyn spoke, entering her orbit. Fresh soap wafted from his skin, mixing with his own scent. He swallowed, hesitant. She gazed up at the man she'd fallen in love with. Every day, she swore she fell a little more. It was easy, surrendering to someone so patient and supportive. It didn't hurt that Kade was dashingly handsome in all his rugged glory either.

With muscles rippling across every inch of him, he appeared to have walked straight out of the Otherworld, a god all along.

Evelyn's lips parted as hunger bloomed in her belly. Kade grasped her wrist and planted kisses across her palm and down her forearm. He tugged her to his chest, and Evelyn released a small gasp as she leaned against him.

"I like the word *cherish*." His words came out gravely.

Evelyn raised a brow. "What exactly does it mean to you?"

Kade smiled, his eyes blinding. "I'm much better at showing than telling."

She laughed. "Oh, I don't know. I'd say you're pretty good with words, *huntsman*."

"Well, then. How about this?" Kade laid his lips against her throat. Slowly. Gently. "I'm eternally grateful that you chose me, no matter what we face." He placed a kiss right under her left ear and the sensation sent a jolt of electricity to Evelyn's toes. "Your unwavering resilience has the power to buckle my knees, Evelyn Carson, and it inspires me every day."

Evelyn closed her eyes, and Kade planted his lips on her shoulder. She lost her senses as he unraveled her with a feather-like touch. She blinked through the haze, finding him staring down at her. His amber stare ensnared her, rooting Evelyn in the infinite expanse of their bond and love. She didn't need to hear his next words—their power glistened in his eyes and already beat in her heart.

"My love for you spans wider than the realms, and it'll burn longer than existence. No matter what world or lifetime, my soul will always belong to you."

Wetness traveled down Evelyn's cheeks, and *gods*, she'd not realized tears had sprung in her eyes. Silent, *real*. She grasped Kade's cheek, sending her love down the tethered threads of their bond.

"I love you, Kade Drengr," she whispered. "There's nothing in this world that brings me more honor than being your mate."

Kade's next kiss pressed against Evelyn's lips, and amid the bliss of his touch, she heard the *plop* as her towel dropped to the bathroom floor. Another followed as Kade lost his own. Their nakedness fueled Evelyn's eagerness, and as she arched under his touch, he grabbed her ass and lifted her into the air.

Evelyn wrapped her legs around his waist and drove her fingers through Kade's hair. Past their molding lips and brushing tongues, she realized they were moving. Warmer air greeted her goose bump-laden skin, and the fire in their bedroom crackled in the background of their ensuing pleasure.

Two souls beat as one, both their powers awakening. Flame collided with the moon, and Evelyn's toes tingled with promise.

Kade laid Evelyn on the bed, the furred blankets sticking to her damp back. He broke their kiss and remained standing at the edge, his admiring gaze as molten as the fireplace.

"Gods, every inch of you is beautiful," he said, leaning down to nip under her breasts while tightening his hands around her waist. "And *mine*."

Evelyn reached down and grasped his length. He hissed between kisses as she ran her hand up and down it, relishing in how rigid it grew from her touch.

"Yours," she declared, "it's all yours."

Kade's fingers found where Evelyn loved it most, drawing tortuously slow circles over the bundle of nerves, sending her closer to the edge of existence he had mentioned earlier. His tongue lapped over her nipples, one after the other, and Evelyn arched off the bed, whimpering his name.

"I need you," Evelyn breathed.

She hooked her feet behind Kade's backside and pulled him closer between her legs. He gripped her hips and yanked her to him, giving her what she begged for. His length brushed against her ready sexy, and a deep growl rumbled through Kade's chest.

Fucking flames, the sound had heat blooming in her belly.

She'd never tire of *this*, of him, of how their bodies came together. Fervent, hungry, and brimming with love. Evelyn swore she'd crave their pleasure until her dying breath. How could she not when Kade stared at her like nothing else existed or when his hands traced the curves of her thighs like he penned poetry?

Evelyn's heart beat to the tune of their bond, and at the other end of the frayed thread, Kade's own matched the same tempo.

Thump. Thump. Thump.

What a beautiful, methodical song.

Tonight differed from the thermal pools, even disparate from when they first completed the mating bond in the small cottage in Drystan. They were whole again, anew. Souls reborn, powers reignited.

Kade lined himself at Evelyn's entrance and pressed in. Inch after glorious inch, her walls opened and clenched around him, and when he finally reached the hilt, they both released an agonized shutter.

"*Moons*, Ev," he breathed and then started rocking into her.

Evelyn relished the feeling—the ache, his size, the glorious friction—and traced her hands over his shoulders and arms. She mapped his rippling strength to memory as he moved inside her. Thoughtfully, *lovingly*.

But *fucking flames*, need coursed through Evelyn like raging fire, and her body begged for Kade's beastly and untethered side.

"*Please*," she rasped, widening her legs.

Kade smirked and lifted one of Evelyn's legs, hooking it over his shoulder.

He sped up his pace, and Evelyn swore she fell through oblivion again, the rafters above transforming into a scattering of stars. He drove into her again at a mind-altering angle—

"*Oh.*"

Kade bent closer and swallowed her cry in a bruising kiss. Evelyn couldn't think straight, let alone see or touch, through the thin line between pleasure and pain. She held onto her mate, entangling her fingers in his hair, and surrendered to the pleasure he gave.

He released her leg, and Evelyn repositioned her limbs around his waist again. He caged her face with his hands, and they began breathing the same air, chest to chest.

Kade reached with one hand to where they came together, finding the bundle of nerves aching to be touched. Evelyn writhed as he drew rapid circles, showing no mercy.

Take it, love, he said down their bond.

She moaned, allowing her body to open further and draw him in deeper as she wrapped her legs tighter.

Kade lay his forehead against hers and, with his other hand, dragged Evelyn's arms over head. He grasped her hands and pressed them into the furred blankets. They were so entangled and tightly joined, Evelyn didn't know where she ended or he began. Yet, there was the thread that connected them, an unyielding anchor that grounded them in the world's chaos.

"I love you," she whispered.

Blue flashed through Kade's golden gaze—rippling and magnetic. "I love you."

In his stare, Evelyn witnessed her own eyes reflecting silver back at her.

"Beautiful," he whispered. "So godsdamn beautiful."

With a will of its own, Evelyn's flame ignited at her fingertips. Kade's power surfaced too, and silver and blue danced together amongst their intertwined digits.

Warmth of the gentlest kind caressed Evelyn's skin, and she sighed with contentment at feeling *all* of Kade, especially the power he once feared.

Magnificent, she said.

Evelyn held Kade tighter as he drove into her again and again, her release building and building. They became lost in their pleasure, moans, and haughty breaths.

War awaited them in the days to come, and yet the curse creeping across Sorin receded from the magnitude of power radiating off Evelyn and Kade. It didn't fear the flame or the moon, though. It recoiled from abundance compared to its emptiness—from the love Evelyn and Kade had found and forged, the challenges they'd triumphed over, and the hardships they'd grown from. Together, they'd created light and love, and deep in the Vadon Mountains, it rose brighter and stronger than the curse.

Their powers exploded in a cosmic wave of silver and blue. They both found release. Evelyn's walls constricted around Kade's length as she screamed his name, and he roared hers, his beastly cry loud enough to be heard for miles.

Sparks and flames floated around them, clinging to them like sunshine and snow. Breathless, Kade stilled inside her, whispering endless words of love. He held Evelyn while blissful aftershocks wrecked her limbs and oblivion burst through every cell of her being.

A thousand argent and sapphire threads wove a tapestry of their love. Evelyn's flames hardened it, and Kade's power tempered it, until their mating bond transformed into something as unbending as a blade and impenetrable as stone.

Nothing could break them, not even death.

Chapter Eighty-Seven

"Now that the Void has fallen, my brother will bring the war to Sorin's border. We can't let him lead General Oziel's army that far south."

At Áilleacht Castle, Tovi and her closest allies had gathered inside her office. The fire crackled behind her back, but it was the map ahead of her that had sweat prickling her brow. *If* she defeated Riven before he marched to meet Evelyn and Kade, perhaps they could avoid a war altogether.

But time was running out, and they had to act fast. Cass had scouted Lord Nathaniel's lands, and signs suggested the army readied to travel.

Uncle Bran adjusted his spectacles. "What do you propose?"

She exhaled, studying the inked lines drawn into the map depicting her homeland. "We need to take Drystan Castle. It'll not only weaken Riven's stronghold and defenses, but it'll bruise his ego."

Cass scratched his chin. "It's a sound move. Our fleet would have the advantage on the river."

Our. Tovi winced. Flynn's ships still belonged to him by technicality. They still hadn't married, an event she'd been avoiding the last few days after leaving the Vadon Mountains. Though Tovi's pirate fiancé didn't stand amongst her council, absent from the meeting.

Her left hand splayed near Drystan's snaking river on the map, her finger ringless. She'd abandoned it on her desk a few paces away. The metal had itched her pale skin, and each time she glanced at the blue gem, bile rose in

"

her throat. She couldn't afford to wear it during the meeting when she needed complete focus.

"What about the Blood Goddess?" Yennifer leaned against a bookshelf with arms crossed.

Ever since Tovi had accepted Flynn's proposal, the warrior had said little to her aside from anything related to defeating the darkness. Cowardice clung to Tovi like grime. She hadn't bothered to have a conversation with her friend, but she'd rather not hear Yen's opinion regarding her engagement.

It seemed Tovi had chosen *avoidance* as her actual strategy. Eldrick. Flynn. Yen. She might have been deceiving herself about confronting her brother.

But Sorin didn't just face Riven, but the Blood Goddess, too.

"There have been no sightings of her since Callum." Tovi's mouth grew dry—another reason they had to make a move sooner rather than later. The Blood Goddess's absence taunted her.

"Perhaps she's waiting it out with Riven," Bétar grunted.

"Why stall?" Tovi said. "Besides, if she was with my brother, he'd be parading around Drystan with the news."

Uncle Bran sighed long and heavily. "Indeed. I've heard no whispers of it. Not even a celebration in her name."

Tovi nodded. "We don't have time to wait—"

The door burst open, and the fresh scent of the sea wafted in. Tovi ground her teeth as Flynn waltzed into the room with an arrogance unfitting for his tardiness.

His gray eyes landed on her, and her only. "I'd like a private moment alone with the queen."

No one moved. No one breathed, not even Tovi. She'd expected this—Flynn had finally come to demand they marry. She flinched, but of course, she'd agreed to marry him before they used his fleet.

"Leave us," she said.

Everyone funneled out of the office, Yennifer last. She lingered in the doorway with a deep frown etched on her face. A hundred words churned in her glacier-blue eyes, yet she left without saying a single one.

The door shut in her wake, and despite the fire at Tovi's back, cold nipped at her skin. She tried to focus back on the map, but the Vadon Mountains region caught her eye. She ripped herself away from the table and marched towards her desk.

"You're late to the meeting," Tovi threw over her shoulder.

"I needed some time to think." Flynn's boots clattered against the stone floor, and Tovi braced as he neared the desk.

She turned to face him, but his dark gaze peered down at her engagement ring. He picked it up and inspected it further, brows furrowed and lips set in a thin line.

"Drystan doesn't have time for you to *think*. We must start preparing—"

"Tovi, I can't marry you." Flynn set the ring down, finally looking at her.

Tovi reared straighter, hugging her arms tightly around her middle. "I . . . I don't understand. *You* asked for my hand in marriage, and I *need* your ships—"

"I fucked it up once between us, and like some selfish bastard, I saw my chance at undoing my mistake of losing you. I wished only to make you happy, Tovi. Now"—Flynn laughed, staring up at the ceiling—"I'm afraid that'll be an impossible task when your heart belongs to him. *That* is why I can't marry you."

Him. The magnificent deep green of the Vadon Mountains flashed before Tovi's eyes, and the scent of basil and spearmint wafted under her nose.

"He's your mate, isn't he?" Flynn asked, tone distant, like he grieved something.

Tovi blinked. He didn't need to specify a name. Flynn had been there when Tovi broke the news of their engagement to Eldrick, and she was a fool to think snow and wind would've interfered with a vampyr's sense of hearing.

There was no sense in denying it, and the thought of lying about what Eldrick was to her had Tovi's insides twisting—*violently.* Still, she couldn't admit it out loud, afraid the truth would swallow her whole and she'd fail her people.

Tovi instead remained silent while her one triumph—securing his fleet—these last weeks slipped from her grasp. She could practically read it etched in Flynn's eyes.

"It . . ." Tovi swallowed, words like shards of glass. "I'm a queen with a people who need her."

The vampyr pirate scoffed. "That doesn't mean you don't deserve to be happy, especially after everything you've done for Drystan."

"I released the Blood Goddess," Tovi said.

Flynn shrugged, a hint of his boyish smirk tugging at the edge of his lips. "And you'll still help break the curse."

"With what army?" she asked, boots melding to the floor.

Flynn exhaled, pocketing the ring. "My ships will answer their queen's call. I won't be late to the next meeting, promise. And Tovi"—he took a shuddering breath—"just because you took on the responsibility of breaking the curse doesn't mean you should blame yourself for it. The only similarity you share with your father is his name. Don't let his failures chain you."

He left, and Tovi found she couldn't move. Breathe. Her fingers itched for a glass of wine, and without thinking, she found a bottle stored in the cabinet near her desk, though not a glass in sight.

"Fuck it."

Tovi cracked the wax seal and pulled the cork free. She swigged it straight from the top, and stewed berries and oak rushed across her tongue, followed by a harsh burn.

Tovi didn't care, taking another sip. Then another.

The bottle weighed considerably lighter in her hand as she moved to her desk, leaning against it. Her heart yearned for the possibilities that lay outside the window—to run and not stop until she reached the land she'd been told never to return to.

Yet ahead, the inked lines of her homeland seemed to come alive and slither towards her like wicked, thorny vines.

Was she weak for wanting the first more than the latter?

The door burst open, and Yennifer stormed in. Cold painted her pale cheeks red, and her wheat curls unfurled from her braid. She glanced at Tovi head to foot, eyes landing on her bottle of wine clutched in her hand.

"I take it the wedding is off." Yen walked towards her, outstretching a hand and gesturing for the bottle.

Tovi obliged. "Yes."

Yen grunted and knocked back the bottle. She grimaced. "That—"

"Is a ruby port, aged for forty years."

"You know, one doesn't have to wait so long for ale," Yennifer said, handing back the bottle. "It's simply good in a month's time."

"Hard to find in Drystan, I'm afraid," Tovi said, trying to fight a smile.

"Oh, I've noticed," Yennifer laughed. Her attention fell to Tovi's sword leaning near the window, where the amethyst stone reflected the fire's blazing orange. "Do you know what the name of your sword means?"

Tovi eyed the six letters etched down the blade. "I'm afraid I don't even know how to pronounce it, let alone its meaning."

"*Saoirse*," Yennifer said. "It means freedom."

Tovi straightened, and the word vibrated down her spine. "What?"

Yen shrugged. "The sword was Nadia's idea, Todd designed it with my and Bétar's input, and then Lou thought of the name."

Never forget what you're fighting for, her late friend had said.

Tovi'd held that truth in her hands all these weeks. She'd defended innocents from demons and slayed Visha with it. Soon, she planned to march across the battlefield with that sword, its given name exactly what she was fighting for.

"Lou tried to remind me of that before she died," Tovi said. "She always believed I could break the curse."

Yen sighed, reaching for the sword and trailing her finger across the amethyst stone. "I don't think Lou chose the name because of the curse or even Drystan, and I remember Nadia saying, 'It suits her.' I've known you a short while compared to them, but it doesn't take one long to understand what you're after."

"It's all I've ever wanted," Tovi whispered. Centuries of desperation coursed through her veins like acid. "For Drystan and my people."

Yen gave her small smile. "I think Lou meant *your* freedom more than anything. It was freedom for yourself and for everything you've fought for. From your parents, brother, and Drystan's expectations. To fight, lead, and perhaps love however you want."

Love.

Tovi suddenly realized she'd never been frightened of anything before Eldrick. She'd marched into ballrooms with her shoulders back and held high, bracing for the judgment to come. She fought demons without a second thought, and yet, the pulsing thread between her and Eldrick's souls left her paralyzed.

Perhaps choosing Eldrick, *loving* him and acknowledging the thread between them, awakened a different sort of freedom, one with no abandon. *That* frightened her—the vast promise of them.

Maybe Tovi held guilt for choosing happiness too. How dare she, when the Verena name had started the curse?

With her sword gleaming from the fire, alcohol buzzing in her knees, and in the company of a good friend, Tovi decided she *would* dare. But—

"Eldrick never wants to see me again." The wine sloshing in her stomach threatened to rise back up.

Yen scoffed. "That was his bruised heart speaking. Eldrick is a stubborn male, but he loves you, Tovi."

Hours later, the howls of Drystan's wind and distant demons haunted Tovi as much as her thoughts. She found sleep impossible. The wine's effects only lasted so long, and the chill from outside the castle crept under her quilts. A restlessness buzzed in her legs and traveled up to her hammering heart. Mentally spent, she sprang from bed and didn't bother to dress aside from wrapping her cloak over her shoulders. She snatched up her sword leaning by her bedside and ventured outside.

Cursed, sure, but the cold air granted Tovi some reprieve. She breathed in the promise of snow, allowed frost to crunch under her bare feet, and exhaled the earthy scent of ferns.

The morning shined a luminescent silver. Fog rolled across the southern part of the estate's lands, kissing Tovi's knees. She trudged through the long grass with no sense of direction, but to simply *move*. She wished for body and mind to catch up with one another—

Ahead, a branch snapped. Tovi gripped the hilt of her sword tighter. Perhaps she wasn't alone, and something or *someone* navigated through the fog, too. *Bloody hel*, she was a fool to have ventured out onto the castle grounds alone. She sniffed the air but didn't detect another a vampyr nor demon. Maybe it was an animal—

Tovi stilled. Her breath hitched. And her heart skipped a beat.

Twenty yards south, a figure sharpened against the fog. The male, smelling of basil and spearmint, stalked through the mists of gray until the plumes parted and revealed his lean, muscular build.

Eldrick marched towards Tovi like he stormed a battlefield. Determined, focused, and unbending. His gait held more than purpose, but restraint as if he wished to run to her. His green gaze became brighter as he grew closer, a striking color against so much gray.

Tovi blinked, unsure if she had imagined him. Yet, she tracked the edges of Eldrick's sharp jaw, fighting leathers molding to his strong thighs, and his hands flexed at his sides. He was real. He was there. *Goddess,* the thread between them *pulled*.

Glowing. Vibrant. Alive. *Fuck*, the curse didn't exist in Drystan with them so near to one another. How and why had Tovi been such a fool?

Apologies tickled across her lips, and she opened her mouth to express them all. She had to make everything *right* between them. She needed to confess the truth—

Eldrick reached her, and in one swift motion, got down on one knee.

Tovi forgot how to breathe. She lost all sense as the grass, fog, and castle grounds faded around them. With Eldrick staring up at her, his love and heart etched into his emerald-green eyes, they were the only ones that existed.

Armor clung to Eldrick's chest and arms. Underneath, black leather covered his physique. He'd strapped two axes to his belt on either side, while a dagger gleamed, tucked into his left boot.

He didn't dress like a Vadon Mountain's alpha. Nothing screamed were-wolf, not even furs, aside from his beastly energy prickling the air. That's when Tovi noticed the lack of Drengr navy. Instead, Tovi spied a light purple on the inside of his velvet black cloak—a similar shade to the gem in her sword's hilt.

Carved into the metal above his heart, a new crest depicted a wolf and dove interlocked in a circle.

Tovi stepped back, the sight jarring her, but Eldrick grabbed her wrist, keeping her in place. She stilled.

For his alpha tattoo didn't gleam across his hand, his skin simply touched by the sun and battle scars.

"I don't understand," she breathed.

"I've been a fucking idiot, letting my duty bind me to a land where I don't belong," he started. "The truth is, I think I've known my rightful place since the moment I saw you outside my office window for the first time."

Tovi's breath hitched. "Eldrick—"

"I love you," he said, voice steady and certain, "more than anything in this world. My place is at your side, and I'm sorry it has taken me this long to accept it and leave—"

"*Leave?* But your title . . . your pack," Tovi whispered. "It's what you wanted and worked for—"

"What I want is *you*. Now, forever, and until Time takes us, if you'll have me."

The vulnerability in Eldrick's words had Tovi falling to her knees. Her sword fell from her grasp, and she clutched his hands instead, staring up at him as he unraveled before her.

"My heart, body, and axe are yours, always and forever. Nothing will bring me more honor than loving you every day. Let me lead your armies. Make me whatever you wish. You are my queen, my love, my—"

"Mate," Tovi finished, her own words thick with tears. "I'm your mate, and you're mine."

Eldrick swallowed, leaning closer. "*Moons*, say it again. *Please.*"

Tovi cupped his cheek, and her heart sang as she admitted, "You're my mate, Eldrick Drengr, and I love you."

His lips crashed against hers. Tovi gasped at the intensity and met Eldrick with the same hunger and devotion. In a cursed land, two souls kissed as they finally accepted what they were. Despite the fog, only light and love encompassed them.

Tovi pulled Eldrick closer, and she tasted the smile and excitement on his tongue as it brushed against hers. He held her waist like an anchor in uncharted waters, and Tovi's heart swelled so large, it threatened to burst out of her chest.

Goddess knew they'd both been stubborn fools, and henceforth, Tovi refused to let fear or anything of the sort get in her way.

She pulled away from Eldrick, peering up at him. "Will you ever forgive me?"

He brushed his thumb across her bottom lip. "I already have, dove."

Tovi kissed Eldrick again, relishing in the fact this male was *hers*.

"Wait." She pushed back a fraction, narrowing her gaze. "Did you seriously journey through the Void by yourself?"

Eldrick smirked. He stood, pulling Tovi with him. "I've not come alone. If I'm not mistaken, you need an army."

She followed Eldrick's line of sight through the fog. He released a deep growl and moments later figures—*hundreds*—emerged from the trees. Dressed in black with hints of amethyst, an army of werewolves had arrived at Áilleacht Castle.

Stunned into silence, Tovi stared at her mate. She'd never imagined choosing happiness—choosing *them*—would make her feel weightless. Suddenly, everything she faced seemed possible. Breaking the curse. Winning the war. Defeating her brother.

Love didn't make her weak—it gave her strength.

CHAPTER EIGHTY-EIGHT

LORKAN TRAILED HIS FINGERS down Blair's arm, marveling at her beauty. Her curls, wild and lose, spilled against the cushions they'd pulled from the sofa to create a makeshift bed on his study's floor.

She sighed in her sleep, perfectly curled into his side. Ahead, the fireplace danced with warmth and cast flickers of light across the bite mark at her neck. Lorkan waited for shame or disgust to creep up his spine.

But nothing of the sort trickled through his lithe being.

Instead, he buzzed head to foot with their mating bond. Lorkan tried to wrap his mind around the immense wonder of it all. He still tasted her blood and emotions on his tongue. Sweetness tangled with love, and he swallowed, tamping down a new wave of desire awakening his wolf.

Like she'd felt it, too, Blair stirred, arching against him—

He cursed as she pressed her backside into his groin, and Blair bit her lip as she fought a smile, still feigning slumber.

"Is there something you want?" He brushed his lips against her earlobe, and she shivered under his touch.

Stars above, she was so responsive.

"This a matter of *need*, Lorkan," she breathed. "Not want."

He opened his mouth to argue, to perhaps suggest she needed rest, knowing he'd left three bite marks across her body, but stopped. He understood.

Felt it, too. The insatiable hunger to have her, not in the *drinking* sense, but in body and soul.

Besides, Lorkan and Blair had denied themselves for so long, he refused to for a minute longer. Even if they lost themselves to one another in his study for days and never emerged.

He slipped his arm underneath the blanket, following the slope of her body with his fingers. Blair's midnight eyes glazed over, and she hissed as he dipped his fingers between her legs. Her wetness and remnants of him still coated her, and a deep growl rumbled through his chest.

Territorial, beastly. His mind kept chanting *mine, mine, mine.*

"Lorkan . . ."

He answered her wish, running his thumb up and down her clit. Blair arched further into him, giving him more access to thrum her pleasure. Lorkan's beast howled. He adored the sounds that came out of her and loved discovering how to draw them out of her, one precious pant at a time.

Soon, she grew breathless and wide-eyed as her heart raced. Lorkan's manhood ached, and he pulled away his touch.

"Lift your leg for me," he whispered.

Blair obeyed, widening herself so Lorkan could align himself at her entrance. He pushed in, and she relaxed as they came together, like she too was filled with pure bliss.

Lorkan grasped under her knee, keeping her leg up and high so he could find that angle to rock into Blair. She tipped her head back, whispering his name like she prayed to a god.

It only increased his own pleasure and pace.

"Touch yourself."

Again, Blair obeyed, and Lorkan moved in her, spying where they joined. Her muscles constricted around him, and his chest brimmed with so much emotion and feeling, he could burst.

Feed—

Lorkan silenced his hunger by meeting Blair in a fierce kiss. He tasted her lips, not her blood this time. He craved them and only them. No feeding. No blood.

Release brimmed at the end of their bond. Blair writhed under him, twisting and pressing her face into the pillow. With his free hand, Lorkan grasped the back of her neck, keeping her in place and making her look at him.

"Eyes on me," he said. "I want to watch as you come."

"Fuck," she hissed, the first sign of resistance to his command.

Lorkan found he enjoyed her sass, too. He rolled his hips against hers and increased his pace. Fiercer, deliberate. Blair's entire body tensed, her moans growing louder and louder. She mewled nonsense, her sentences a cross between prayers and curses until—

She stilled the fingers touching her sex.

"*Oh.*"

Every beautiful, glorious inch of her stiffened, even the muscles around Lorkan's length. She unraveled beneath him. It was almost too much. Witnessing her release, feeling it down their bond. Ecstasy burst through Lorkan next. He spilled into her, whispering Blair's name like it might save him from the suspended fall as his body and mind unraveled, too.

They untangled from one another with tenderness, kissing, nipping and sighing. Drunk off each other and their climaxes, they stared at the other until the fire dwindled to embers.

"We can't say here forever," she whispered.

Lorkan sighed. Again, he searched for the fear he'd harbored for years, and though apprehension lingered, he *could* envision a conversation with his brothers about what he was. Yet, he couldn't figure out how to be useful in the days to come. Would their research on the curse be enough to break it?

"No, I don't suppose we can," he finally said.

Eventually, Blair's breathing evened out as sleep took her again. As much as Lorkan wished to hold her, restlessness festered in his chest. He peeled away from Blair with care. He pulled on a spare pair of trousers and fed the fire to keep his study warm. Behind him, the stack of books they'd collected during their research called to him, and Lorkan sank into a chair, becoming lost to the pages detailing the Gods War.

Hours passed. Blair slept. Lorkan read. He slipped out to find food for breakfast, thoughts reeling, and once he returned, he found Blair wearing his tunic, flipping through the text he'd left splayed open. She smiled at his return, and like some lovesick fool, he greeted her with a kiss.

"Eat." He pushed a plate of cheese, fruit and honeyed biscuits towards her.

"*Blasted books.*" She plopped a berry into her mouth. "You're rather bossy."

Lorkan smiled so wide, his cheeks ached. "I don't recall you minding earlier."

She narrowed her gaze and humphed. "Why are translating these again? We've read them front to back, Lorkan."

He swallowed, pinning his gaze to the one text they'd retrieved from Blair's peer in Nūa. The depiction of the bloodstone stared back at him. Above it, he had his own notes parallel to the ever tree.

"What if breaking the curse is not enough?" he whispered. "I have this dreaded feeling there's something else we're missing."

Blair nibbled her lip. "There is perhaps something we can do."

Lorkan assessed her. Apprehension and excitement traveled down their bond. "What did you have in mind?"

Her shoulders slacked. "When the Goddess visited me—"

"The Blood Goddess?"

Blair shook her head. "I mean, it *was* the same goddess we witnessed leaving Hel, but she claimed that is not her name."

Lorkan's brows pinched. "Is that so? Did she give you another title to use?"

"No." Blair shrugged. "She was more concerned with encouraging me to witness the truth."

"How?"

Blair brushed a finger over the red gem dangling from Lorkan's neck. "By cracking open a bloodstone to witness a memory."

He shook his head, stomach twisting into knots. "Is that possible? You researched how to get Evelyn's magic out of a bloodstone but came across nothing that helped destroy it."

"True, but I wondered . . ." Blair trailed off, shaking her head. She plopped another berry into her mouth, as if to put an end to the conversation.

Lorkan grabbed her chin, stilling Blair mid-bite. He rose a brow. "Don't you dare hold back on me now."

Her midnight eyes churned as she swallowed. "Again, *bossy*."

"Blair."

She cursed. "Look, I share the same magic as her, and I think there's a reason she visited me. What if it's because my shadows have the power to crack a bloodstone open?"

Lorkan's feet melded to the carpet. It wasn't Blair's revelation that rooted him in place, but the thought of *losing* his bloodstone.

"What exactly would that accomplish? Opening the bloodstone?" he asked, throat turning dry.

"My research revealed that only the blood of a god slain by a fellow god creates bloodstones, and it can hold memories, or warning of sorts."

Stars above. That meant insight into the gods, and perhaps vital information considering the one they'd banished to Hel had been released.

Lorkan would be a lying bastard if he didn't admit he enjoyed walking in sunlight or hiding his vampyrism. Yet, the word *hiding* chilled him to the bone. Years of outrunning what he was nipped at his heels, but Lorkan's legs didn't buzz with the familiar sensation to bolt. In fact, he fiddled with the bloodstone like what it represented itched his skin. Now, he regarded it as an opportunity—not only would he let go of an old habit, but perhaps they'd learn more about the gods.

"Then we should test your theory." Lorkan pulled at his necklace, and the twine snapped. He placed the bloodstone onto the table and slide it towards Blair.

She shook her head, frowning. "We don't need to use yours. I'm certain Tovi has another—"

"There's no sense in wasting time," Lorkan said.

"But you'll lose the ability to walk in sunlight," Blair whispered. "Others will sense you're a vampyr."

Lorkan smiled, tucking a curl behind her ear. "Many already know what I am, and I also no longer wish to hide this side of me. Besides, I'll freely walk in the sunlight once the curse is broken."

Blair's being softened as her midnight stare turned molten. She trailed a finger down his jaw, and pride rippled across her beautiful face.

"Alright." She eyed the bloodstone. "Are you sure we shouldn't consider the risks?"

Hmmm, fair, Lorkan thought. It could be a trap after all. But time wasn't on their side.

"Perhaps its best we don't."

Blair cursed under her breath. She flexed her fingers at her sides, drawing up her shadows. Anxiety prickled down their bond.

You can do this, Lorkan whispered into her mind.

Blair snapped her attention to him, shadows pulsing as if exited at the sound of his voice. *This . . . this is new.*

He smiled and nodded towards the bloodstone. *Crack it open.*

Lorkan's wolf sensed Blair's magic in the air, crackling like the static rising before a thunderstorm. Lorkan swore he heard the howling winds past the thick, rocky walls of Vísdómr, too.

Inky mists kissed Blair's fingertips, and her shadows climbed up and over the table, slithering to the bloodstone. Blair winced, and through their bond, Lorkan experienced the same burning sensation as her bronntanas touched the bloodstone. He placed a hand at the small of her back, grounding her. Her breaths came out ragged as she pushed past the slick sensation of wrongness and wrapped her shadows around the bloodstone.

The light in Lorkan's study dimmed. The fire whooshed out, and a dangerous chill crept through the space. Their breaths plumed as they waited, and with one last mighty inhale, Blair snapped her fingers.

Her shadow sliced through the bloodstone like a blade cutting through flesh. Red boomed in a wide circle, and crimson tendrils of magic—dark nor light in nature—snaked upward until the gem lost all its color, glistening clear on the table.

Lorkan dragged Blair behind him, his wolf baring its teeth at the sheer ancientness weaving in front of them.

A scene—*no*, a memory—painted red sharpened to depict two figures. The first had beautiful hair the color of spun gold. She stalked towards the other, dagger dripping with blood, in one hand. The latter stumbled back, color draining from his face from the dozens of wounds dotting his body. Death seeped from the magic of the bloodstone.

Dread prickled across Lorkan's skin, and he held Blair tighter.

"Tell me where my sister hides, and I'll spare your life," the goddess hissed.

The other god laughed, blood spluttering out of his mouth. "You'll never outrun your true nature, Macha. The others will soon learn the truth. Badb will make sure of it."

The goddess named Macha released an ear-splitting scream and launched.

"No!" another goddess appeared from a plume of wispy shadows, dark-blue eyes wide with horror. The sword strapped to her back gave away her identity before her face emerged from the shadows.

The Mother of Darkness.

But she was too late.

Macha swiped her blade across the god's throat, and blood sprayed across her rage-filled face. The Mother of Darkness sprang forward, catching the god as he collapsed. He landed in her arms and stared up at her with reverence.

"I-I-I'm s-s-sorry I failed you," he whispered.

Tears filled the Mother of Darkness's eyes as she rocked him back and forth. "You were brave. You were just. Rest, my *cara*, and find peace."

The god slackened in her arms, and his blood seeped into the forest ground. As the life dwindled from the god's eyes, the red tendrils of ancient magic faded, swallowing the conversation between goddesses whole.

"*Blasted books*, what did we just witness?" Blair whispered, gripping Lorkan until her knuckles bled white.

Sweat prickled at Lorkan's brow as realization rocked his center of gravity. This memory challenged everything he knew of light and darkness. Lorkan swallowed.

Moons, think.

"Perhaps we were wrong about who the Mother of Darkness truly is." He released his hold on Blair, allowing his sense of urgency to rush down their bond. "We have to tell the others. *Immediately.*"

CHAPTER EIGHTY-NINE

F OG SLINKED ACROSS THE Void. It moved between Drystan and Sorin as if the fracture had an army of its own. Gray and angry, its slow crawl sent a shiver up Tovi's arms.

Yet, the actual army she needed to defeat hadn't arrived. Though Cass and Bran had received word that Lord Oziel's legion marched south and were due any day now, Tovi's insides tightened and buzzed. The energy in the war camp had shifted, too.

Witches had arrived from the east, led by Evelyn's Aunt Ruth. The witches wore wariness as tightly as their fighting leathers. They'd not warmed up to fighting alongside vampyrs.

Still, Tovi exhaled in relief. Thanks to Evelyn and Blair's efforts, Nūa had joined the fight instead of waiting it out behind the Wall. Tovi had heard grumblings about the proximity of the Void, too.

"For eighty years I loathed this place, and finally to be here amongst friendly folk . . . It's nothing I'd ever expected."

The very Carson who'd whispered those words assessed her with one eye. Ruth stood among those gathered at the training grounds. Some practiced drills. Others sharpened their blades. Most had gathered near where Tovi and Eldrick sparred. Werewolves stood by and watched, too. Word had spread through the mountains of Eldrick's decision, and those brave enough to leave their packs and rebel against Bjorn's orders had arrived in droves. It helped, too, that the Drengr Pack, led by Kade and Evelyn, no longer answered to the Earl's magic either.

No—Sorin didn't have the numbers compared to Riven's legion, but these witches, werewolves and few vampyrs didn't fight based on greed or gold, but fueled instead by bravery and honor. Tovi'd take the latter pumping through a comrade's heart any day.

Flurries fell from above, almost delicate and peaceful compared to the clanging of weapons and the ominous horizon. Eldrick bared his teeth and advanced. Tovi parried the down-strike of his axe with her blade. Metal grated against metal as they sprang apart.

Tovi's leathers clung to her sweaty skin. She brushed away the hair sticking to her forehead, but Eldrick gave her little time to recover. He lunged to the right. She pivoted, jabbing the hilt of her sword into his back. He growled and spun, kicking the backs of her knees.

Bloody hel.

Tovi stumbled forward and whirled into a lunge. She bared her fangs and hissed. Eldrick tossed his axe from hand to hand, a slight tilt to his lips. He didn't hold back, and Tovi appreciated it—there'd be no such mercy when she faced Riven on the battlefield.

She rallied her vampyr speed and launched. Eldrick shifted, his newfound Verena purple detailed leathers enchanted to fit his larger form.

A beast and a monster met in an ensemble of swift movements. Tovi's heart hammered in her chest to the tune of their beating weapons. Her opponent didn't relent. Pure muscle and strength, he sparred with true force.

Minutes ticked by. The air grew tense. The gathered crowd reared closer. Eventually, sweat drenched Tovi like she'd plunged into the Sapphire Sea.

She grunted as Eldrick landed a blow to her stomach. *Damn him.* Yet, she had no one else to blame but herself. Tovi grew sloppy. Fatigue gripped her.

Eldrick backed away, tilting his head as if to say, *Don't let it.*

Tovi inhaled and with the next exhale, charged. She sprinted at full speed, sword angled ahead of her. Eldrick braced, but Tovi didn't attack.

She jumped over him. And spun.

Eldrick turned, but it was too late.

Tovi's blade ran parallel to his russet-colored fur.

He snorted, snot twitching as he eyed the blade and then her.

He shifted back to his male form and smiled wide and bright, brimming with pride. "Well done, dove."

Applause and cheers sounded across the crowd. Tovi didn't have the energy to smile, but she lowered her sword and outstretched her hand. Eldrick took it, and the two shook after their match.

"Nice effort, *wolf.*" She winked.

Eldrick scoffed. "Next time, I'll go easy on you."

They both stifled a laugh. Eldrick hadn't held back during their match, nor had Tovi. Love certainly tied them together, but so did a mutual respect. For who they were, what they might face, and their duties to this land. Those who had traveled to fight had witnessed it, too.

The next sparring match began, and Bétar and Ruth circled the other. A somewhat friendly competition started between werewolves and witches. The snow continued, and the Void remained vacant of anything but endless fog.

As Tovi and Eldrick refreshed near a watering station, Bran and Cass approached. Both wore fighting gear with a lilac emblem sewn above their hearts. Few vampyrs remained in the war camp. Most had boarded Flynn's ships, long gone now.

Take Drystan Castle, Tovi had commanded.

The captain hadn't objected. In fact, he'd left with a pep in his step, as if he looked forward to the challenge. Thanks to recent missives, Flynn had mentioned her brother's absence from Drystan Village, confirming Riven marched south.

Her uncles were a welcome sight, but their deeply etched brows and down-turned lips screamed grim news.

"Lorkan and Blair just arrived from Vísdómr with more fighters," Cass said.

Bran nodded. "Indeed, with a dozen vampyr-werewolves like Nadia."

"Place them in a unit with the werewolves under my command," Eldrick said. "Sam Johannes will welcome them."

"I'll see to it," Cass said. "Lorkan and Blair also requested to speak with you both. They're with Kade and Evelyn already in the council tent."

Bran pushed his spectacles up the bridge of his nose. "Seemed urgent if you ask me."

Tovi sighed. The two scholars were the last to arrive among their allies, and she wondered what sort of news they'd brought.

"Alright, we'll head that way now. Thank you."

Cass and Bran tipped their heads, bowing towards her as they left. Weeks ago, she'd swatted them away for such formal behavior, and they would've enjoyed her torment. Yet, her title didn't leave her squirming in her boots anymore, nor the polite customs that went with it. *Queen* clung to Tovi like her well-tailored leathers.

It *suited* her, she realized.

She turned to Eldrick and caught him staring after Cas and Bran. Her uncles shared glances with one another. Their expressions shifted often, indicating they communicated over mind-linking.

Tovi and Eldrick weaved through the war camp, as silent as the snow that landed near their muddy boots. Tension leaked from him and then—

"Do vampyr mates have the ability to speak mind to mind?" His jaw ticked, brow level.

Tovi nodded. "Yes."

His nostrils flared, and he exhaled. "Yet, we can't—is it because I'm a werewolf and you're a vampyr?"

She halted, stopping on the path towards the council tent. Three flags—the Drengr's, Nūa's, and Tovi's—stood tall, pierced into the dirt outside the entrance. Between their flapping, the camp's bustling preparations, and the chilly wind, Tovi and Eldrick's conversation belong to them, and them only.

She opened and closed her mouth as Eldrick studied her. "We haven't *technically* completed the bond, Eldrick."

His brow pinched as he studied her, then something flashed like lightning in his gem eyes. "You once told me feeding is very common among mates."

"It is," Tovi said, breathy.

Eldrick stepped closer, so close their noses almost touched. "You also told me drinking blood is an intimate moment."

Heat shot straight to Tovi's core at the sound of *those* words in *his* voice.

"It can be, yes."

"Say it out loud, Tovi," Eldrick whispered.

Tovi's stomach twisted into knots. "Doesn't it disgust you?"

Eldrick's eyes softened. "Nothing about you disgusts me." He leaned down, his lips brushing against the shell of her ear. "In fact, I've fantasized about you feeding from me many, many times."

An array of images filtered through her mind. The positions they'd explore. The taste of him on her tongue. *Fuck*—

She stepped back, the distance between them like a bucket of ice.

Eldrick frowned. "Tovi—"

"I want to—gods, you have no idea how badly I do."

"But?" He tilted his head, hands fisted at his sides like he braced for something.

"Feeding from one's mate is a sacred act, Eldrick, and I . . ." She inhaled, setting her shoulders back. "When I feed from you for the first time, I don't want the curse coursing through my veins. I won't it to be just *us*. It doesn't make me want you any less, I swear it—"

In two long strides, Eldrick reached her. He took her face in his hands and kissed her. He said a thousand words with his lips.

I love you.

I hear you.

I respect you.

They broke apart, Tovi's lips bruised and sore like her worked muscles from training. Eldrick laid his forehead against hers, so they shared the same breath.

"Then we wait," he said.

"Are you sure?" Tovi asked.

Eldrick grasped Tovi's hand, placing it over his heart. "I don't need mind-linking to affirm our bond. Our love is real, and that is all that matters."

Tovi released a shaky breath. "I know, but . . . "

Tomorrow or even in the next hour, they might be in the thick of battle, death lingering over them. Without solidifying the thread that connected their souls, they risked one of them having a miserable existence if the other perished.

"Mind-linking could be useful in the days to come, and if we aren't fully bonded . . . " Tovi trailed off again, words regarding either of their deaths lodging like stones in her throat. Her chest grew heavy, the prospect more frightening than whatever Riven threw at her.

Eldrick sighed, and his gem gaze roamed over her face as if committing it to memory. "I'd rather respect your wish than complete our bond because of poor circumstance. It is our choice when and where, Tovi. And . . . " He swallowed, tone turning adamant. "If one of meets fate on the battlefield, we must promise that the other will *live*."

"Eldrick—"

"You have fought too hard to break the curse. Promise me, you will live and find happiness."

Tovi didn't need a fully woven thread to feel the truth of Eldrick's words. She had an ask, and this was his. Like he had for her, respect vibrated through her.

"I promise."

Moments later, Tovi and Eldrick entered the council tent hand in hand. Eldrick gave her a parting smile and released her to join his brothers by the fire. He and Lorkan stared at each other, and after a breath, the scholarly brother dragged Eldrick into a hug. When they parted, they spoke in hushed voices, but from the bright glint in their eyes, Tovi recognized the signs of pleasant words.

Two hearths at opposite corners kept the enclosed space warm, their metal flues traveling up and out openings in the tent's ceiling. Near the center table, Blair and Evelyn smiled together, a rare sight in recent months.

"Will you ever tell me how long you two have…?" Evelyn trailed off, raising a sly brow and jumping her attention between Lorkan and Blair.

She smiled. "Perhaps when all of this is over, we'll have time for that story. Over a bottle of wine—"

"And breakfast for dinner."

"Yes, exactly that," Blair finished.

Evelyn nodded. "I look forward to it and to having someone to talk to about having a *werewolf* as a mate. They can be rather—"

"Territorial." Tovi approached them with arms crossed.

"That puts it lightly," Evelyn grumbled.

The three old friends laughed.

"You know," Blair said, eyeing Tovi, "you're technically a sister to us now, seeing as our mates are brothers."

Tovi blinked, and Evelyn straightened. The three friends stared at one another, and something new and promising blossomed between them.

"I suppose you're right," Tovi whispered.

Rook shot between them, escaping through the tent's flaps. An orange ball of fur dashed after him, and Maxie growled as she darted outside.

Tovi grinned. "It's too bad neither Eldrick nor I had a familiar as a sign that we were mates."

Evelyn snorted, shoving Tovi's shoulder. "Oh, there were signs."

Tovi shook her head, not letting their light banter seep too deeply into her skin. She turned to Blair. "Cass and Bran let me know you wanted to see Eldrick and me."

The three Drengr brothers marched towards the table.

Lorkan crossed his arms. "I'm not sure there's a right way to say this, but we think there's a chance we've misunderstood the Mother of Darkness."

Tovi straightened. "Who?"

Blair rummaged through a stack of books. She flipped to a page depicting a goddess with onyx hair and a sword strapped to her back, the hilt embellished with a three-moon design.

Tovi shook her head, muscles tightening. "Wait, that's the Blood Goddess. We all saw her fly out of the gates of Hel."

Lorkan sighed, sharing a glance with Blair. "Indeed, we did, but this deity claims that is not her name."

"Why does her name matter?" Tovi's ire prickled in the air, but she didn't give a damn. "She could've changed it since the Gods War."

"She herself told me it's not her name," Blair said.

Tovi reared back, crossing her arms. "Have you spoken with her? Have you seen her since she entered our realm?"

"No." Blair shut her eyes and humphed. "When Evelyn and Kade traveled to the Otherworld, the veil between realms thinned." She jabbed her finger into the illustration of the Blood Goddess. "*This* is who visited me."

"Did she promise you something?" Tovi whispered, studying her friend like she might spy the same madness that had taken hold of Riven.

Blair wavered from foot to foot. "Yes, but—"

Tovi scoffed. "That is what she does, Blair. She manipulated my father with something he wanted, which is how the curse started, and now has done the same to Riven. You can't trust anything she says."

"She didn't promise me anything other than the truth about my shadows—"

"The Blood Goddess found your weakness, but there is *nothing* wrong with your power," Tovi said, tone soft but full of understanding. "My mother was my father's weakness, and Riven's dead wife and child are his. Again, this is what she does."

Evelyn grasped hold of her hand. "Tovi, I think it's worth hearing Blair out."

Her friend's gentle words stilled her anger for a moment, and Tovi met Blair's stare and braced.

"The Mother of Darkness instructed me to crack open a bloodstone and learn the truth." Blair shared a quick glance with Lorkan, and he nodded. "My research revealed that only the blood of a god slain by a fellow god creates bloodstones, which hold memories. At Vísdómr, I did as she said, using my shadows, and witnessed the moments of a god before they died."

Blair explained the memory from the bloodstone, and Tovi's limbs grew heavy as she tried to make sense of it all.

"From what Blair and Lorkan described, it sounds as though the killer was the Sun Goddess," Kade said. "Golden hair. Beautiful. Slightly deranged."

"And?" Tovi asked, heating from the inside. "We already learned she's not kind. It doesn't mean the Mother of Darkness isn't."

Evelyn shook her head. "Yes, but the Sun Goddess's power ran through my veins when I showed signs of vampyrism."

Snow escaped under the tent's walls, skittering across the ground. Silence rang in Tovi's head. She'd not so easily forgotten that her friend's hands had shifted into talons or the red haze she'd claimed to have experienced. It had made no sense in Callum, and now Tovi had one foot in denial, while the other pivoted towards the harrowing possibility that everything they'd believed was a lie.

Her soul raged against the notion. "So, what? Both goddesses could be equally wretched."

"She mourned her friend," Lorkan said. "Held him as he passed."

"Ingrid wept when I killed Visha. It means *nothing*." She yanked her hand out of Evelyn's grasp. "Have you all forgotten the Blood Goddess cursed my people? For all we know, she's laid out a new trap."

"That's an interesting theory."

All of them whirled. At the tent's entrance, a striking female stood amid wisping shadows. She wore tattered clothes stained the color of ink. Holes here and there revealed her pale skin. Draped across her shoulders, a patched cloak billowed around her, frayed so violently its edges appeared like jagged teeth. She pushed back her hood. Her windswept hair fell free, though her deep-blue eyes remained dark, thanks to the coal smudged across her eyelids.

Beautiful yet *ancient*. And that sword. The back of Tovi's mind tickled at the sight of the hilt.

Bloody hel. Her instinct flared to life. The *Blood Goddess* stood before her—the cruel deity who'd *made* her and used her father like a pawn.

Tovi unsheathed her sword. Eldrick growled her name. Evelyn cursed, and Kade shouted for her to stop. She didn't listen and charged. Without thinking. Without reason. Only fueled by vengeance.

Yet, the air ahead of her whirled and shifted, and Blair stepped through a *danu*, blocking her path to the goddess.

"Wait!" She held out her hands for Tovi to stop.

She halted but didn't lower her sword. "Get out of my way!"

Her heart hammered so wildly in her chest, it threatened to beat free. The rage coursing through her blood slithered alongside the curse, rousing it from the depths of Tovi's baser instinct. Its wicked, monstrous chant echoed in her ears. She winced, but it was too late. Her sight faded to a red hue.

All because of this goddess and her damn curse.

"Blair, I swear to *bloody hel*—"

"She's a goddess, Tovi. If she wanted us dead, she'd already have done it." Her friend's midnight stare bore into her, *pleading*.

"How can you be so sure?" Tovi tightened her hold on her sword.

"Because I'm your friend, you know *me*, and—" Blair unraveled the fabric around her hand.

Revealing a mark that matched the goddess's sword.

CHAPTER NINETY

"I BELIEVE THE MOTHER of Darkness and I are connected."

Surety rushed through Blair's veins like the stormy winds of her bronntanas. For years, she'd hidden parts of herself—her love for Lorkan, her shadows. Now, she'd embraced both. She'd mated with her love, and her shadows danced at her fingertips freely.

She'd also set out to break the curse; revealing what she knew of the Blood Goddess—if that was actually her name—might help. Could she be so bold? Would she step out of line?

Why in the *blasted books* not?

Tovi lowered her sword in inch, and over her friend's shoulder, she spied pride gleaming in Lorkan's golden eyes.

"Blair, how did you get that mark?" Evelyn whispered.

The goddess stepped forward, and three *very* territorial werewolves growled.

Kade came forward, immense power radiating off of him. "That's far enough."

The Mother of Darkness halted, deep-blue eyes scanning him. The sword of ancients remained strapped to his back, but at his sides, his fingers twitched. The goddess's expression remained blank, not an ounce of emotion rippling across her face. She addressed Evelyn next, and Blair readied herself for the truth.

"My power runs in your sister's veins, third born. She is weaved with my very essence, which includes the sadness I carry for my fallen brother and sisters. When she touched the bloodstone, the burn was but a fraction of the pain I carry."

As if to prove her point, dark wisps leaked from the goddess's boots and hands. They reared towards Blair, and she swallowed. For most of her life, she'd believed such magic would get her thrown in Tùir. As if the land understood her fear, thunder boomed above, much like the storms that had hit off the coast of Nūa and barreled into the prison. Her gut clenched.

"I don't understand," she whispered. "Plenty of witches, *dark* witches, wielded shadows—"

"Or did they choose darkness? Because those are two *very* different things." She tilted her head, inspecting Blair. "One is natural, no different from your winds, while the other is a *choice*. Though Macha twisted the perception of shadows over the centuries, steeping fear into witch's lore, much like other beings of this world." She averted her attention to Tovi.

"How?" the vampyr queen asked through gritted teeth.

"*She* is your maker, not I."

"You're lying!" Tovi hissed, stepping closer.

The goddess laughed, raspy and dry. Her venomous smile revealed two fangs, far thicker than a vampyr's. More like—Blair reared straighter. The wildness wafting from her, and those *canines*. The Mother of Darkness reminded her of Lorkan—a werewolf-vampyr.

"The entire tale of vampyrs is based on a lie. The Blood Goddess is not real, but a fictional character."

Tension rippled from Eldrick. "If you are not her, then what is your true name?"

"Badb," she said. "I'm one of the Three."

Rook flew through the tent's entrance and landed on the goddess's shoulder. He picked at her tattered cloak and rubbed his head affectionately against her cheek. Blair swallowed, blood turning to ice. Her familiar and the goddess *knew* one another.

"He was a gift, too." Badb scratched under his beak, and Rook shuddered from the touch. "A loyal companion to share in your *otherness*."

Evelyn approached, flanking Tovi's side. "Wait, what would the Sun Goddess gain by creating the vampyrs?"

"Control," Badb sighed. "As you all know, I was banished to Hel after the Gods War, but my banishment wasn't for eternity. It was a time for atonement, away from my brothers and sisters. Isolation was supposed to *teach* me something. Yet, the Gods War began because of Macha's own fears of herself. She split her soul and hence divided her power amongst the Three, but wickedness lived in her still, because light and dark lives in us all. Macha couldn't control her nature any better than she had before, and instead of accepting what she was, she pointed a finger at me, a seemingly easier figure to pin darkness and death upon."

"Why didn't you fight for that truth? Why let her win?" Blair asked.

"Because so many of my brothers and sisters had died during the war, and Macha's influence grew too vicious. Beings of this realm, like the fae, were fleeing. I had to stop the senseless bloodshed, and time for us gods is but a blink compared to mortals."

"You surrendered to Hel willingly." Kade's brow pinched, apprehension gleaming in his assessing stare.

"Yes, but over the centuries, Macha grew restless as the end of my sentence neared." Badb continued to stroke Rook absently. "I'd remained patient and silent in my kingdom of demons and darkness, unlike her in the Otherworld, toying with souls like playthings. Along with Macha's wickedness, greed rushes through her veins like a raging river. She thrives on the worship she receives in this realm, and she feared she'd lose it if the truth was unveiled. So, she orchestrated a plan to ruin my reputation."

"The Blood Curse," Tovi whispered.

"Precisely."

Maxie emerged from the outside and sat to attention near the goddess. Yellow eyes wide. Ears up. Tail flicking back and forth. Not as friendly as Rook, but not hesitant either. Tovi's eyes widened, and Badb lips twitched.

"Vampyrs *are* created in their maker's likeness, and you are far more similar to my soul sister than me. Your court in Drystan brims with the same nature of her castle in the Otherworld. All gods drink blood, but the bloodlust is a direct reflection of *her*. The Daughter of the Goddess experienced Macha's wretchedness, too, after stealing some of her power."

Blair shook her head. "Are you saying the goddess who made a bargain with Tovi's father was the Sun Goddess?"

Badb nodded. "Yes. She recreated another story to paint me as the goddess corrupted by darkness, and the other gods so easily believed the new tale, as they had during the Gods War."

Evelyn shared a look with Tovi. "It makes sense. The King of Elsewhere had never heard the name before."

"The fae fled the One," Lorkan said. "While later texts recounted the Mother of Darkness."

"But that was after Morrígna split herself into three souls," Kade said.

"I don't understand." Tovi turned a shade paler than usual. "Why not intervene sooner and stop Macha?"

"Hel suffocated my influence," Badb said. "But I tried my best to send *something* near to those in the prophecy, a demonstration that darkness is not necessarily evil. Much like the Moon God and Sun Goddess gifted their power, I did the same. "

Tovi blinked, eyes going wide. "That's why you gave Blair your shadows."

Rook cawed, stomping his feet. Badb stroked his wings, absently. "Yes. Sight told me she'd one day cross paths with you, Tovi Verena, a valiant queen who fought against a curse, and Evelyn Carson, the one to rid darkness once and for all."

Finally, Badb managed a small smile, the deep blue of her eyes no longer held wisdom, but sadness. "To think what connected you all was far more than circumstance, but love. After thousands of years, I almost lost hope until you, Blair Carson."

Hope.

Blair inhaled the word as if she was parched and desperate for water. To think this goddess had endured far worse than she'd feared—persecution, misjudgment, isolation—and yet, Badb still held onto something far mightier than power or magic.

Blair had once thought fate a cruel bitch. *Blasted books*, she'd revered the concept a majority of her adult life, resenting her shadows along the way. How easy it would've been to lean into that anger. To let it fester and spark into rage. Yet, she hadn't. Instead, she'd tamped down her shadows and stuck her nose in books.

Suddenly, relief trickled through Blair like she'd cleansed herself in a rain shower. A choice always existed, and Blair'd leaned into her true nature. She'd never let outside influence, temptations or labels dictate otherwise.

"Does Riven know who the Blood Goddess really is?" Tovi asked.

Badb sighed, and Rook flew from her shoulder, finding another place to perch as he preened his feathers. "I'm not certain. She lost a great ally when Circe was killed. Ingrid, too. I know she never revealed her true self to your father, but as for your brother, she may have grown desperate enough to tell him. He, too, is mentioned in the prophecy. *Light* can be interpreted in many ways."

The news settled over the group, and wariness spread through the tent. It all clicked. The Sun Goddess's nature. The discrepancy between lore and

Blair's research. Which meant Macha's hold over Sorin was the darkness detailed in the prophecy. Blair's inside swam with more uncertainty.

"Is breaking the curse enough?" She crossed her arms, sharing a look with Lorkan.

"No," Badb said, tone adamant. "But it'll piss her off enough that she'll leave the Otherworld. To fulfill the prophecy and truly defeat the darkness, you must end her, too. Break the curse's hold on Sorin first and then defeat Riven. Snuff out those forms of darkness, and you'll have a fighting chance of beating her. When she emerges, I'll fight alongside you to take down a goddess."

Evelyn shook her head, left brow furrowing. "In exchange for what?"

Badb's lips tilted into a smirk, her namesake glinting in her gaze. "All I ask is that I'm the one to deliver the death blow."

Kade's gaze narrowed. "Odin said Macha couldn't destroy you because it would do the same to her. If we succeed, you'll die as well."

"So be it," Badb said. "I'm ready to leave this world a better place."

"What of the third soul sister?" Lorkan asked. "If she still exists, will darkness truly be defeated if fragments of the One remain?"

"Nemain was a mortal soul, unlike Macha and me. I haven't felt her tethered to this world since the curse fell. I believe Odin's theory—she died when their fated bond was broken," Badb said. "You all have everything you need—"

Thunder clapped from above, and everyone braced. The temperature dropped ten degrees, and the fires *whooshed* out, draping the tent in darkness. More thunder rumbled in the distance, shaking the ground beneath Blair's boots.

The storm's energy pierced her chest and yanked her to *move*. Something wasn't right. She answered the land's call and sprinted from the tent. Lorkan growled her name, but she ignored him, and faced the sky. The others exited the tent, gathering around her.

"*Bloody hel,*" Tovi whispered.

Above, the amethyst clouds churned above the Void. Snow turned to sleet, scrapping across Blair's exposed skin. Tents in the war camp swayed in the wind's force. Horns blared across the plains, signaling formation. Mists shifted to dark shadows, and the methodical beat of wings joined the storm's crescendo.

A hundred italogs circled above, and the ground shook with the approach of marching foes. Prince Riven, atop a ghastly beast that resembled a kelpie, led at the front.

Yet, it wasn't vampyrs flaking him a half-mile wide, but a legion of demons.

569

Chapter Ninety-One

K ADE'S INNER WOLF HOWLED, and his immense power tingled at his fingertips.

Madness descended on the war camp. Rain poured. Thunder boomed like Linx's explosives. Lightning streaked across the sky, illuminating the demons weaving through the tents and pouncing from victim to victim. With the sword of ancients, Kade slew a monster that charged, slicing its wolflike head clean off. Ahead, four more feasted on a warrior he'd not reached in time.

He released a frustrated growl. He'd expected *soldiers*—to fight blade to blade—not demons.

"Where did Riven get them? How is he controlling them?" Evelyn asked, chest rising and falling.

Black blood splattered across her face. She held her staff firmly in her grip, black leathers forming to her figure. They'd had barely enough time to dress, let alone assemble units before the demons swarmed the camp.

"*Moons.*"

Ahead, Bétar wrestled with a *béar* demon. Much like its namesake, it possessed a burly build. Four stocky legs, thick ink-colored fur, and claws sharp enough to shred bone. Yet, its face was nothing but a skull. Teeth bulbous, eyes fathomless. Positioned behind its ears, antlers, better suited for an elk, reached towards the storm clouds.

Kade conjured his power. Gravity yanked from all around as he drew up his might. Blue swirled at his finger tips, and he thrust a sphere of power towards the demon. He hit his mark.

The *béar* bellowed. Its moment of hurt allowed Bétar enough time to step back and drive his sword into the demon's belly. It grunted and thrashed, swiping its clawed paws.

"Bétar, look out!" Kade said.

Evelyn readied her silver flame. It danced at the tip of her staff. Steam rose from the luminescent tendrils as the rain spilled. She spun and cast her magic at the beast. Silver burst across its back.

Kade stepped closer, narrowing his gaze. *No*—it had to the trick of the light. Where Evelyn's magic traveled, the dark-colored fur lightened to a brown. As if—

Something whistled from the east, and a resounding *pop* followed, yanking Kade from his reeling thoughts.

A werewolf's arrow stuck out of the demon's all-black eye. It stiffened. Swayed.

And then burst into a cloud of gray dust.

Yennifer marched between two tents. "The west side is completely overtaken."

"Riven?" Evelyn asked.

"He remains at the Void," the archer said, bitter.

"Are there any signs of General Oziel's arm?" Kade asked.

Yen shook her head. "No, Riven's forces are entirely made up of demons." Confusion rippled through Kade.

Evelyn furrowed her brows, mirroring his bewilderment. "I don't understand. He'd need dark magic to control them."

"What if it's this 'Mother of Darkness'?" Bétar asked.

Kade looked at Evelyn. Her steely eyes didn't waver, not a hint of doubt in them. "I don't think it's her—"

Bétar roared. A madras had bitten into his shoulder and dragged him through the muck. The commander thrashed, but the demon didn't relent, digging its canines deeper into his flesh. Kade flushed with panic.

"Bétar!" Yen called, readying another arrow.

Kade raced after his friend, Evelyn following behind him. The hairs on the back of his neck rose—rot and sweet licorice thickened in the air. A scream ripped from behind him, and he spun.

"Kade!" Evelyn pointed to the sky.

An *italog* carried Yennifer up and up, soaring north. She thrashed against the beast—*alive*—but it flew far away from the camp and towards the Void.

"No!" he shouted.

Kade's insides stretched as if he were being tugged in too many directions. His friend's shouting for help. His love's distress shot down their bond. The sound of the dying weaving with the storm. The gray, death and loss brought him back to the nightmares he'd experienced, as if the horrific future Tenebris had showed him sat on the horizon.

No.

Kade roared internally, and his wolf howled alongside his resolve.

He'd fucking fight for a different one.

From the north, a horn blared. Unlike the deep bellow werewolves used to warn others, this tremored for miles, reaching Kade's bones. Like dark magic had been woven into the sound. Nearby madras paused, becoming disinterested in their recent kill. With ears slicked back, they waited, oily, black fur bristling up their backs. The horn blared again, and they sprinted off, funneling out of the war camp.

Evelyn and Kade followed, racing ahead. At the edge, Tovi, with Eldrick at her side, faced off her brother. Hundreds of witches, werewolves and vampyrs stood behind them.

No one moved. No one breathed.

Except the storm raged on. Thunder, sleet, gusting winds. The land didn't relent as those of Sorin waited.

Riven dismounted his kelpie, pacing with a sinister smile. Clad in ghastly armor, the metal swam on him. The prince had lost more weight, rake thin with sunken cheeks. Black rimmed his eyes while his irises shined red instead of jade. Whatever dark power he possessed, it drained him. Kade's wolf bared its teeth, and Riven's gaze snapped in his direction.

His smile grew wider, and more malice festered in the air.

"Ah, the prophesied union! It is so nice of you to join us," Riven drawled. "I was just telling my dear sister this could all be over soon."

As Kade and Evelyn reached Tovi's side, Riven stepped back, giving them a clear view deep into his legion of demons.

Evelyn gasped, and Kade froze. Their loved ones had been taken as prisoners. Nadia and Aramis. Bran and Cas. Bétar and Yennifer. They were all tied together, their pleading words muffled by the gags tight around their mouths.

The Gray Fenris members struggled towards something—no, *someone*.

"Linx," Kade breathed.

The mage healer lay motionless on the ground. Blood rushed into the muck, the wound on her side angry and deep.

Next to them, the Carson coven members sat chained to one another—Artie, Rodrick, Josepha and Ruth. Remnants of battle stained the witch protector, and her one-eyed stare was like a dagger aimed at Riven's back.

"*No.*"

Kade grasped Evelyn's arm and dragged her behind him. She swallowed, trembling as she fought tears.

The Carsons weren't the only ones captured from Nūa. Todd, with arms bound behind his back, kneeled by Belle, the magical induced sleep still clinging to her.

"It's easy to win against those so easily manipulated by the heart," Riven said, running his tongue across the tips of his fangs.

Tovi stepped forward, shoulders straight. "There is no winning in this, brother! Countless will die for *nothing*!"

"Iona and Oli are not nothing!" Spittle fell from Riven's lips. "My wife and son will walk at my side by dusk, mark my words."

Kade stepped forward, stilling his rage and rallying a collectedness. "You've been deceived."

Riven's stare narrowed, his focus falling past Kade's shoulder.

Boots squished through the mud, and the army parted to make way for the Mother of Darkness. She scanned the horizon as if searching for someone. Her blade dripped with blood, her tattered cloak soaked from the rain. Behind her, Blair and Lorkan followed. The witch's shadows whirled at her boots, and Kade's brother prowled in his beast form. Blood coated his fur, but he didn't spy any alarming injuries on Lorkan.

Thank the stars above.

"There is no Blood Goddess to bring back your loved ones," Badb declared, her voice booming with ancient authority.

For a moment, Riven's face fell. Horror streaked across his face.

Then he tipped his head back and—

Laughed. He shook, his metal armor clanking together as he cackled.

Riven wiped away tears and tsked his tongue. "Oh, I see. You think me a fool." He jabbed a finger into his chest. "Much like you, I recently learned the truth, but the difference is, *I'm* on the right side of this battlefield. Darkness will prevail!"

Kade's wolf grew restless. The winds shifted, and a tremor vibrated through the ground. Demons dispersed, fleeing as the dirt bubbled and steamed.

Those of Sorin stepped back from the jarring sight. A *crack* followed, more deafening than the thunder. Before them, the Void fractured again. It opened wide, the ground trembling with the aftershocks. Steam rose and lapsed over the edge. Rain hissed as it collided with the hot air. Minutes of stillness followed, and everyone braced.

A delicate hand curled up and over the edge, and the Sun Goddess hoisted herself into their realm.

Kade straightened—of course, Riven wasn't working with a dark witch. He'd allied with the Sun Goddess—

Light.

For the Prince to walk with Light.

Not redemption. Not goodness. Not true light.

But to align with the goddess who claimed to embody it.

Gold-plated armor framed Macha's lanky, tall frame, shimmering with each step as she stalked towards them.

More gods emerged from beneath. Kade bared his teeth at the sight of the God of Night. He rolled his shoulders and flashed a dashing smile, appearing far too pretty for a battlefield. The bastard had the nerve to roam his predatory gaze over Evelyn.

"Patience, Nótt," the Sun Goddess purred. "Your loyalty will be rewarded soon enough."

Kade stepped forward, but it was Evelyn's turn to grasp his arm and hold him back. A growl rumbled through his chest, and the gods snickered.

All one hundred of them. Larger than mortals by a foot, sometimes two, rippling with pure lethal muscle. They held swords with serrated edges, staffs with sharp points, and cross bows that fit three arrows at once.

The Sun Goddess, tallest of them all, wrapped her thin hands around Riven's shoulders. She whispered into his ear, stare never breaking from Evelyn and Kade. "You've done so well, King Verena."

Tovi hissed, and Eldrick growled. Metal sang in the air as their forces released their weapons. The Sun Goddess merely smiled.

"My, my, isn't this a sight? It seems despite my meddling, you've proved triumphant. After my soul-sister was released from Hel, I decided I had to take matters into my own hands. So, *here I am.*"

Kade ground his teeth together. His inner wolf roared to be released.

She turned her attention to the prisoners and snapped her fingers. Fire flared to life, creating a ring around them. "Now, isn't that better?"

The sleet didn't stand a chance against the goddess's power circling his those he loved. Red and orange cast across their faces, and heat bristled in the air.

The Sun Goddess released Riven, stalking closer to Kade and Evelyn. "The choices are simple—hand over the ever seed or there will be war, one that you can't win."

Kade seethed, his power rising and rising in his blood. Outmatched, outnumbered. The Sun Goddess had a point, but she was wrong about one thing: Sorin could win.

"Your hold on this realm ends today, Macha," he said, tone unbending.

Murmurs peppered through the army of gods. The Sun Goddess sneered at the sound of her informal name.

"Very well." She raised her hand, and the gods assumed position all at once. Demons stopped their pacing, facing Sorin's army with razor teeth bared.

Kade turned to Tovi and Eldrick. "Lead the charge against Riven." He glanced at Lorkan and Blair next. "Free our friends and family." He addressed Badb last. "End her. Evelyn and I will break the curse."

A knowing flushed through Kade. Winds from the east and west collided, salt and pine mixing. He'd tasted today before, like he'd known it since his first breath.

He shared a swift glance with Evelyn.

I feel it too, she said.

Seers had whispered of today's battle. The possibilities coursed through their prophesied blood.

I love you, he whispered.

Then he charged.

A thousand battle cries followed, and the tempo of war beat against Kade's heart.

Chapter Ninety-Two

Eldrick had envisioned war many times. Had woken from night-mares fueled by it. But nothing compared to the grime—the limbs yards away from their owner, entrails unraveled like fleeing snakes, and the maddened mutterings of the damned. Even the gods wished for something in their last moments.

Eldrick tried to channel the *rightness* drummed through his taut being. His axe's shaft strained under his grip. In his other hand, his sword's hilt imprinted into his palm. His beastly energy drove him forward, kept him strong and at the ready.

He spun and slayed an approaching *nathracha* demon. Its split body writhed, and more blood rushed into the current of black and red.

Yet, more demons kept entering Sorin. For every one he killed, two emerged. Scáths emerged from the fogs of Drystan, answering the call of their dark maker. Worse, too many of Eldrick's own kin lay dead, vacant eyes staring up at the ashen sky.

His heart raced in his chest, the instinct to search and find his mate like an insatiable pull. Eldrick spun east, then west. A ringing vibrated through his head. He didn't spy Tovi anywhere. No sign of her gray leathers or white braided hair—

There.

Ten yards to Eldrick's right, Tovi fought a god. His sword was as long as Tovi was tall, and her arms shook with each blow.

Get to her, his wolf roared.

Eldrick ran, but something grasped hold of his ankle and tugged. He shot into the air and rose higher and higher above the ground. Blood rushed to his head, and Eldrick blinked through the nausea roiling in his stomach.

Stars above, focus!

A demon—one Eldrick didn't have a name for—used a furred tale like an appendage, wrapping itself around his ankle. Eight beady eyes stared at him, fangs quivering. *Fuck.* Two pincers reached up and snapped.

Eldrick thrashed, the demon's attack missing his neck by inches. Its tail tightened around his leg and yanked him to the left. He braced, keeping a tight grip on his weapons.

Yet, more blood rushed to his head. The ground grew farther away.

Mate.

Tovi's pained cries jolted him into action. He reached upward and carved his sword through the demon's tail at the thinnest end. The breath whooshed out of Eldrick as gravity took hold, and he fell. He collided with the grounded quicker than anticipated, his lungs aching.

But with each wince, Tovi's face painted the back of his eyelids.

Save her.

Eldrick didn't care for the angry demon at his back. He faced where Tovi stood. The god raised his sword. She'd fallen to one knee, bracing. Eldrick gripped his axe with two hands. He inhaled and readied to through it.

He released.

His axe spun and spun—

Until the blade *crunched* into the god's face.

Tovi didn't miss a breath. She whirled, sword angled waist height. Her blade sliced through the god's arms and torso. Eldrick's mate stepped back, and the god fell, the many pieces slipping apart in a horrific heap.

She turned to face him. Their stares connected through the chaos. Eldrick witnessed spring in her jade eyes. The future. A reminder of what they fought for—

"Eldrick!"

A pincer knocked him off his feet. The demon raced after him, spiny legs trudging through the mud. Eldrick scrambled back as the demon used its injured tail like a whip. It cracked through the air, slamming into the ground. Rain pelted his face, and his slims slipped through the bloody mud.

He halted against something—

A pile of bodies. The demon had cornered Eldrick. It released an ear-splitting screech. Rain pelted his face. Exhaustion gripped him so tightly, he couldn't rally his inner wolf. Far away, Tovi screamed his name.

Live, he wished to tell her. *Live.*

Eldrick braced as the demon raised its two pincers overhead.

The onslaught never came.

A horn blared in the distance, the kind werewolves used. Eldrick fisted his hands and peeled his eyes open. The demon shuddered and collapsed. *Dead.* A dozen arrows stuck from the monster's head. The kind whittled in the Vadon Mountains. Through the sounds of battle, he'd not heard their descent.

"Eldrick!" Tovi leaped over the demon's body and rushed to him. "Look!"

He rose on unsteady legs, following his mate's line of sight. To the west, an army of werewolves lined the horizon.

Thorn, Drabek, Alland, and Lindström.

Their colors bled one after the other. Banners and flags flapped in the wind. The alphas stood at the front, thrusting their shields into the air. The howls of a thousand thundered across the land. At the sight, Eldrick's breath bottled up in his chest. His inner beast howled in his blood, celebrating in his kind's arrival.

"Vampyrs!"

"Eyes ahead!"

Warriors on the battlefield shouted warnings to their comrades, snapping Eldrick's and Tovi's their attention north.

Another army had arrived.

Black armor. Bloodstone welded into their breast plates. Dread pooled in Eldrick's belly.

Tovi stumbled back, like someone had punched her in the gut. "Lord's Oziel's army."

Yet, their banners said otherwise. Eldrick stepped closer, trying to get a better look at the color flapping in the wind. He refused to snuff out the hope blooming in his chest.

"Tovi," he whispered.

Those on horseback stepped further through the fog. One in particular—a female—rode atop a white horse, her red hair twirling in the wind.

"Wait," Tovi said. "That's Lady Anastasia."

As if hearing her name on the wind, she rose the banner she carried high in the air. The original forces Eldrick had brought raised their shields, hollering.

For they shared the same lilac color.

Eldrick dared to smile, and his limbs tingled with the words of the prophecy.

Those of these lands will unite.

"I believe they're here to fight for you, my queen."

Chapter Ninety-Three

Rain drenched Evelyn and Kade as they sprinted across the Void. They leapt over demons, averted their course to avoid gods, and weaved through blood thirsty scáths. Kade cut down whoever and whatever grew too close.

Distance, Evelyn chanted to herself. *Get away from the fighting.*

She needed space. A place to plant the ever seed. Somewhere far from the Sun Goddess.

But the cruel deity chased after them, flames streaking across the battlefield in her wake. Shadows swirled ahead of her, settling into a feminine silhouette. The shadows sharpened into the Mother of Darkness, and she whirled towards Evelyn.

"Now!" Badb said. "Break the curse!"

Evelyn drove her staff into the earth, piercing the ever seed. Silver cascaded down her weapon, flaring out in a luminescent boom. From head to toe, she tingled as she channeled her magic into the seed. She breathed *life* into it. The magnificent power coursing through her veins chanted *light, light, light.*

It leaked and overflowed from her soul, and the earth trembled under the force.

Through the dirt, the ever seed began to glow like a star that had fallen from the midnight sky. Its skin cracked. The ground trembled again, but Evelyn kept her stance steady.

Suddenly, roots burst free and snaked outward, diving deep into the soil.

Wherever the start of the ever tree traveled, it brought Evelyn's magic with it. Light corroded any darkness it touched. Around her, frost-burnt grass grew verdant green, and purple flowers sprouted, overtaking the once rotting wasteland. The curse's hold on Drystan faltered, and loosening its claws, one by one.

Evelyn's silver flame shot upward, a beam of blinding light reaching the gray. The clouds retreated, revealing the first hint of blue. Shock rippled across the battlefield, and the fighting slowed as Evelyn's power gained the attention of a thousand.

"No!" the Sun Goddess screeched.

Her gold-plated armor swam on her bony, gaunt frame. Blood splattered across her face, her rose-colored hair disheveled. She bared needlelike fangs, fury blazing in her eyes. Before them, the strong, once all-mighty goddess unraveled.

Her aflame blade collided into the Mother of Darkness's sword, wisping with shadows. Black and red tangled together, and the soul sisters glared at one another. Macha bared her teeth. Badb furrowed her brow.

"I am the One true goddess," the Sun Goddess roared. "For a millennium, it is I who has ruled this world. Worshipped, feared, loved, revered. All of it is *mine*. You'll not take that away from me!"

The Mother of Darkness struck, movements swift and deliberate compared to the Sun Goddess's fit of rage. Color leached from Macha's face and hair, leaving her bleak and old, while the Mother of Darkness thrived in the fight. Muscles strong, shoulders set back, and hair sleek and neat. She brimmed with centuries' worth of waiting and preparation, and Evelyn admired the goddess's resolve.

She tightened the hold on her staff, holding true with her magic.

"You've already lost!" Badb said. "The world knows who and what you are, and I'll not let them suffer under your lies any longer. Today is the end for us both."

The Mother of Darkness roared with vengeance, and the Sun Goddess met her head-on, her own battle cry echoing across the lands like rumbling thunder.

Evelyn's legs tremored, and she faltered a step, but she didn't dare let go of her staff. The likeness of the wood's origin met Evelyn's power of life, fueling her magic. Alive and with a mind of their own, the roots grew wider and dove deeper into the earth. The force of her power whipped her obsidian hair from her bun, and her arms shook with exertion.

But Evelyn held on.

Ahead, Kade fought demons answering the beck and call of the Sun Goddess. She whispered in an ancient tongue through gritted teeth, and the madras came in waves.

Power incarnate, he slaughtered the demons with a swift glide of his sword and bursts of his power. The demons' inky fur turned bright, its misty darkness dissipating in the air as Kade's light overtook it.

He peered over his shoulder and roared, "Keep going!"

Life zapped through Evelyn as the seed crumbled completely to make way for a sapling to emerge. It grew and grew, green and fluorescent, but like a beacon, more demons, scáths, and gods broke away from the main fight. They abandoned their foes and charged in Evelyn's direction.

"Gah!" Evelyn cried out, peeling one hand away from her staff and flinging a ball of flame towards ravenous scáths.

The sapling wavered, its first few leaves coming to a halt as Evelyn lost focus.

"Kade!" she called out.

But her fated wrestled a *béar* demon. It latched onto his shoulder with a large teeth, and it's jagged, blood-soaked claws swiped across his back. Fresh blood slicked his armor.

"No!"

Evelyn flared her silver flames wider, creating a barrier of power to protect her from the demons and scáths nearing too close. They bit, nipped, and swiped at her flames, stalling their hunt.

Yet, one madras leveled its fathomless gaze on her, the black emptiness full of malice. It stepped through her flames, not caring as the silver burnt its paws.

Evelyn's instinct reared to life too late. The demon pounced and landed on her with a harsh thud. Her staff slipped from her one-handed grip and clattered to the ground. Her flame around the wood extinguished, the beam of light descended from the sky, and the ever tree stopped glowing.

Gray prowled back into place, and the Blood Curse hissed across the lands in a humid, prickling wind.

Evelyn scrambled to reach for her staff, but the madras clamped its jaw onto her ankle. She screamed as canines sank past muscle and pierced bone. Blinding pain rippled through her, and Evelyn writhed under the demon's treacherous hold.

"Evelyn!" Kade growled.

Her own power ate its darkness, but the wolflike demon shook its head wildly, growling through her attempts. Evelyn clutched the beast's neck, sending another shock of light through it, yet the demon sank its hold deeper. Any more and it'd tear through her ankle completely. Panic zapped down Evelyn's spine.

Life, her power sang.

Evelyn's heart thumped. Once, twice, a third time. The realization dawned on her as alignment bloomed in her soul.

She inhaled, exhaled.

But this wasn't the same as the night she'd ripped her magic out of her soul, brought Aster back to life, or risked Mirella's life. This was intentional. It wasn't desperation driving her forward but *hope.*

Evelyn blinked past the blinding pain and harrowing chaos. She was light and life, not destruction. She moved her hand into the madras's sleek, oily fur and laid a hand under where the tremoring demon's heart should reside and sent her power there.

To heal it, not kill it.

Silver shot from her fingertips, and the madras released her with a whimper. It backed away, shaking its head as if trying to flick some assailant out of its mind. It bowed, shivering as ripples of light shot through it. The demon's fur shifted from an oily black to a thick coat. Its snout receded to a smaller one, its blood-drenched canines shrank, and its eyes grew smaller and more alight, transforming into a slate color filled with bewilderment, not emptiness.

For a madras no longer stood ahead of Evelyn, but a newly made, black-furred wolf healed from darkness.

Evelyn heaved, chest rising and falling rapidly, the sensation she sat on the edge of something gripped her legs as she stood. She held her hands out, stunned at what she'd accomplished. Her silver flames snaked around her feet, and her injury healed itself, the pain dulling to a days-old bruise.

The wolf huffed and bared its teeth. More madras stalked behind Evelyn. She darted to her staff and grasped hold of it again. She whirled, falling into a defensive stance, readying to fight again, but the newly made wolf charged.

And *fucking flames,* it defended her.

Evelyn's mind reeled, and as she repositioned her staff over the ever seed, she sent her flames out differently this time. The beam of silver shot back into the sky. The Void quaked from her power. Wind and debris blew in the air, but it was not just life and light she sent to the seed but outward, too.

Like an army made of silver flame, it marched across the cursed land and washed over the demons and scáths. It lapsed back and forth, revealing beasts no longer touched by darkness, but animals restored to their true forms.

The *béar* shook its head, blinking into its new, russet-colored form. The scáths ahead of Kade dropped to the ground and writhed. Their talons retracted, the spidery veins around their eyes faded, and the hunger-crazed stare faded to shock.

Kade backed up a step. His stare snapped to Evelyn and back to the vampyrs again.

One opened and closed his hands. The other patted her limbs.

"The curse . . ." she whispered. "It's gone."

"I don't hear it," the male sobbed. "I don't hear the curse telling me to feed."

The Sun Goddess screamed and thrust the Mother of Darkness yards away. She strode towards Evelyn.

"*How dare you?*" Spittle dripped down her chin, and she dragged her sword through the dirt, flame following in its wake.

Once, Evelyn had thought the power beautiful and magnificent, but it wasn't the magic itself that possessed that characteristic but the wielder. For her flame was horrifying and brutal, *destroying* with each step as Macha marched towards her.

"You think yourself a goddess?" she whispered. "You think yourself *worthy* of creating life? You are nothing—"

"I am Evelyn Carson," she said through gritted teeth. "No one defines me—not you, not this realm. I've fought and bled to defeat the darkness, and the power weaved into my soul, *that* is the essence that has broken your curse. It is you, Macha, that is nothing now."

Underneath Evelyn's skin, veins grew alight, brimming with silver magic as she drove life one last time into the earth. She pulled her staff from the dirt, and the light continued. She'd planted enough of her life magic, now it grew without her.

Silver flame wove across the battlefield, healing anything and everything touched by darkness. Vampyrs, demons, trees, the hills. The more life that peppered the air, the more Evelyn's power glowed at her fingertips.

Ahead of her, the ever tree grew taller, its leaves silver and full, reflecting her triumphant expression. Soon, its shadow cast behind Evelyn and loomed taller than Kade, its promise reaching far below and high above the Void.

The Sun Goddess faltered a step, eyes narrowing. Metal swished in the air, and the Sun Goddess dodged Kade's blade almost a moment too late. She stumbled back into the Mother of Darkness's reach and became encircled by all three of them.

"Your hold on this world ends today," Kade said, even and calm.

The blue sky and the green hills painted Drystan in a new era. Like a dark blanket being tugged, the curse receded off the land. Wonder rippled across the battlefield, and the fighting slowed. Vampyrs stopped and basked in the rays of sunlight beaming through the parting clouds.

"No . . ." the Sun Goddess breathed, spinning in circles.

Kade held out his sword, and it flared blue. The Mother of Darkness crouched, planting a hand into the soil, a triumphant smile curving across her lips. Evelyn swallowed, gripped her staff tighter, and released the first attack.

She veered left and slammed her staff into the earth, pushing flames toward the Sun Goddess. Silver and gold burst as they collided.

At the epicenter of the battle, the four most powerful beings in the world clashed. Light and darkness fought as one. Kade's light of the moon weaved with the uniqueness of his wolf and soul, offering balance to Evelyn's light and the Mother of the Darkness's shadows.

Kade's sword clanged against the Sun Goddess's, blue sparks igniting upon impact. The goddess thrashed, yanking her sword across Kade's. Metal grated against metal, piercing Evelyn's ears. Her bones rattled with the goddess's next scream, and it reminded her all those years ago, the distinct, dark howl on the Callum wind.

The years and months stained by the Sun Goddess's touch reeled through Evelyn's mind, but instead of losing her balance or wit, she harnessed the memories and manipulation as fuel to feed her flames. She was Evelyn Carson, third born and protector thick and through, and this silver flame, grit, and determination belong to no one but her. Evelyn had written her own path, and with it, Sorin's freedom from a goddess's tyranny.

Silver flames surged higher on her left hand and flared at the tip of her staff. With a loud cry, Evelyn spun and released it all from her staff and hand.

Both bursts hit true, barreling into the Sun Goddess's belly. The goddess rocked back, her own flame sucking inward and extinguishing. She dropped her sword, and time slowed as she collapsed to her knees. She gulped, and the stench of burning flesh hung on the wind. A large, darkened hole sat in her metal armor, steam rising from the injury.

A breath whooshed out of Evelyn, and she stumbled back, unable to believe her eyes. She blinked, swallowed.

"Evelyn . . ." Across the way, pride glistened in Kade's eyes along with the reflection of shimmering silver.

Look.

Kade's voice inside her mind was the gentlest caress. Evelyn turned, and one tree rooted in the Drystan soil continued to grow, it's mighty branches full of silver leaves. The ever tree's magic pulsed back and forth over the land, and blue painted the sky more than the eclipsing gray.

You did it, love.

We *did it*, Evelyn corrected.

She swallowed and met her fated's stare again. He straightened to his full height and lowered his sword. The power of a thousand words brimmed in their locked gaze.

The truest of unions will defeat the darkness.

The line of prophecy rooted itself in Evelyn's heart. Tears stung at the edge of her eyes.

Fucking flames, they'd done it.

Between them, the Sun Goddess's life drained from her like ash twisting into the wind. Her skin peeled back, revealing a molten layer of flesh, red and angry like lava.

The battle around them stilled and stopped. Swords ceased to clang. Werewolves shifted from their beast forms. Demons retreated. Evelyn couldn't decide where to rest her sights, to find her friends and loved ones or focus on her enemy's final moments.

The Mother of Darkness prowled closer to her soul sister, blade at the ready. Her mouth fell into a thin line, her beautiful, sharp face void of any emotion. Shadows leaked from eyes, as if she released tears from the past, present, and future.

For Morrígna had created the Mother of Darkness and banished her into Hel, and now she stood, forcing her hand to end a soul sister, and ultimately end her existence, too, sending them both into oblivion.

Metal sang as it cut through the air, and Badb positioned the blade at Macha's neck. Evelyn braced for the brutal blow.

Waited, waited, and waited—

Pink darted across Evelyn's peripherals.

"Linx!" Kade's voice boomed with confusion. "What are you doing?"

The Sun Goddess's eyes widened. "*Betrayer!*" she hissed.

The Mother of Darkness recoiled back. "*No*—"

A loud boom swallowed her outcry. The force knocked Evelyn off her feet. She flew through the air, spinning and falling—

Evelyn landed yards away with a harsh thud. Her ears rang, and the world around her blurred to the colors of smoke and battle. She fought to stand, a harsh pain radiating down her right side. Fucking flames, she'd broken something. Her rib? An arm? Both?

"Fuck," Evelyn hissed.

Gritting her teeth through the aching, she crawled to the ever tree. It still stood, untouched by the explosion. Above her, the sky still bled blue, and no remnants of the curse filtered on the wind.

But where were the goddesses?

Evelyn rose, grasping hold of the ever tree's birch-like trunk and using it to keep her steady. Behind her, a crater now sat, but through the billowing smoke, Evelyn couldn't make out anyone. Not the Mother of Darkness, Linx or—

Where was her mate?

"No, no, no," Evelyn whimpered.

Kade! Evelyn shouted down their mating bond. Yet, she couldn't feel him at the other end. Their thread brimmed with love and light, but *he* was—

Gone.

"KADE!" she roared his name again, this time through the chaos.

But he didn't answer, didn't appear out of the smoke rising over the hills.

But there was *nothing*. No remnants of his soul. Not kindness. Not goodness. Not even the presence of his beastly energy. The other end of their bond pulsed with emptiness.

My love for you spans wider than the realms, and it'll burn longer than existence. No matter what world or lifetime, my soul will always belong to you.

She cried out, *screamed* an animalistic sound, like she'd been ripped open from the inside.

"EVELYN!"

Hope flitted through her. She whirled at the sound of her name, but that voice . . . It belonging to the most beautiful witch.

"Belle?" Evelyn breathed.

Her friend, awake and *running*, barreled into her. She fell to her knees and grasped hold of Evelyn's hands as she caught her breath. Behind her, Todd sprinted to them, shifting out of his werewolf form.

Matted with sweat, his dark gaze drilled into Evelyn. "I'm so sorry, Evelyn. Forgive me."

Evelyn's ears rang. "What is it? What is he talking about?"

"It's Linx. S-s-she fooled . . . us all. She's . . ."

"Breathe," Evelyn said. *"Breathe."*

Belle gulped for air. "Linx is Matilda Moore."

Evelyn's blood ran as cold as ice. In her peripherals, the battlefield spun.

"I don't understand." She shook her head, trying and failing to grasp what Belle was telling her. "Odin said Matilda died—"

"He was wrong. *We were all wrong.*"

Evelyn gripped her friend tighter. "How do you know this? Why are you so certain?"

"Because it wasn't the Sun Goddess who put me in a trance, Evelyn. It was Linx. She did it for *her*. Linx connected them all—Riven, Circe, Claus, Ingrid. . . She's been working with Macha the entire time."

Evelyn's mind reeled. "If Matilda Moore had never truly died like Odin or Badb suspected, that would make her one of the Three."

Belle nodded. "Linx is Nemain. She is the missing third soul-sister, and she just made Morrígna whole again."

Chapter Ninety-Four

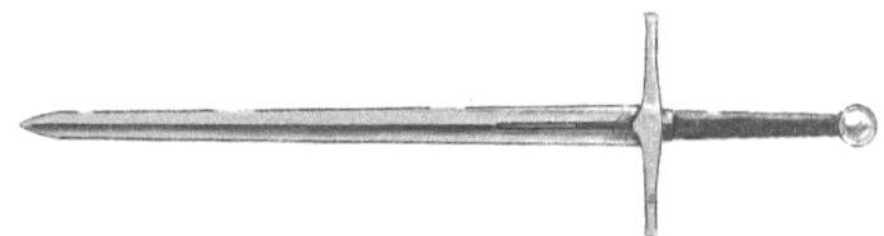

A GENTLE BREEZE ROUSED Kade from slumber. White bled ahead of him, and as he blinked, he found himself in a tent. An enchanted lantern rested on a small bedside table, lighting the space in a heady light. On the outside, someone neared, their boots crunching under rock. Kade's wolf rose to the surface, growling in his blood. The tent's entrance burst open, and he readied—

"You're awake!" Linx exclaimed.

"*Moons.*" Kade released his grip on the sheets and sat up. "What happened?"

With no shirt on and bandages around his waist, Kade occupied a tent that seemed more like an infirmary than the one he'd shared with Evelyn. He tried to rack his mind for the last moments before he'd lost conscious. Most was a blur, but he distinctly remembered Evelyn's ever tree, growing and sending its life and light across the Void. Beautiful, magnificent silver.

The color that had shined in her eyes since the day he met her.

"Where's Evelyn?"

Linx's smile tightened as she saddled herself on the nearest stool. "She's resting. You both fought hard. Now drink this—"

"Linx—"

"*Drink.*" She pushed a steaming cup of tea into his hand. "*Stars above,* Kade we, won. The curse is broken, the Sun Goddess is gone. Now rest for one damn minute. I'll take you to Evelyn after I inspect your wounds. You're no use to me if you bleed out on the way there."

Kade took the mug she offered. Its herbal remedies were floral and spicy on the nose. His inner wolf wrestled inside his blood, but he ignored the restless feeling—blaming the lingering battle gripping his bones—and sipped the tea.

"What of the others? My brothers and parents? The Gray Fenris?"

Linx smiled, releasing a small giggle. "I always forget how deeply you care for others, Kade."

She peeled back that bandage on his arm without any finesse, and Kade grimaced as the cheesecloth tugged his stitches. Linx busied herself with adding more ointment to a gash running across his bicep, and he drank the less-than-pleasant tea. It tasted similar and as foul as the one she'd made him on Captain Flynn's ship. At least, a hint of honey helped.

And *stars above*, he and Evelyn had broken the curse.

A breeze blew into the tent. Kade couldn't detect where on the battlefield they sat. He spied the darkness of night, that was all. The camp remained eerily quiet, too. No celebratory songs. No moans of the injured. No crackling fires either. Were they on the Drystan or Sorin side of the Void? Could he even refer to that landmark anymore if it no longer existed?

"How long have I been out?" he asked.

Linx ignored his question and moved on to the bandage wrapped around his middle. "Your god-like making is so impressive."

Kade fidgeted in his seat, Linx's tone sending unease through him. Her fingers grazed up his abdominal muscles, her thumb brushing underneath the cheesecloth. Fascination gripped the mage healer, her eyes wide—

Kade blinked. *No.* Linx's eyes had shifted from yellow to a deep blue. Linx peered up at him, and the color vanished, as if he'd imagined the change. Of course, the mage healer changed her hair color weekly, but he'd never known her to change her *eye* color. *Moons*, was he that tired after the battle?

As if he craved the taste, and he downed the rest of the tea.

A wave of energy flushed through Kade, and he rose from bed. An odd sensation gripped him, like he walked without the gravity weighing down his limbs. He searched for a pair of boots, a tunic, anything to wear as he went to sought out Evelyn.

"Where are you going?" Linx hissed, her words cutting through the un-natural silence with a level of venom Kade had never heard before.

He stiffened, fisting his hands at his sides. "To see Evelyn."

"I never permitted—"

"I don't need anything of the sort to seek out my mate," Kade growled.

His instinct screamed. What in the *fuck* what gotten into his teammate?

Linx didn't flinch. She narrowed her eyes, and Kade found the patience he'd had for Linx lately vanish. His legs moved of their own accord, and he sprinted from the tent, desperate to reach Evelyn because something was very, very wrong.

Outside, the desolate wasteland Kade had dreamed of many times sprawled across Sorin, and he came to a bone-chilling halt. It wasn't the loss of gravity he felt, but the empty otherness of dark magic gripping his mind.

The aftershocks of an explosion clung to his legs. Rang in his ears. Evelyn's fear-filled scream ripping through the air. Kade stared at his unmarked hands, the phantom feeling blood coated them wet and slick.

Stars above, what had he done?

"It's beautiful, isn't it?" Linx appeared at his side out of thin air, like she had so many times before.

Yet, Kade had never questioned it. Why hadn't he? Why had he let Linx join the Gray Fenris? He barely recalled meeting the mage for the first time. She'd always just...*been there*. Yet, who *was* she, really?

His mind reeled, and as desperation coursed through his blood like acid, he reached down the mating bond. He met *nothingness*. The worst possibility rooted him in place, and he replayed the last events over and over. Mere fragments flashed across his mind.

Evelyn had planted the ever seed. A magnificent tree had grown. Darkness had left the lands of Drystan, and the Mother of Darkness had almost ended the Sun Goddess. And then—

"It was you." Kade whirled to face Linx. "*You* caused the explosion—"

The mage next to of him wasn't the Gray Fenris's healer. In fact, she wasn't a mage at all.

The two females shared a likeness, but small features had changed. First, she'd grown taller, no longer hitting above his waist but at his shoulder. Her eyes shimmered a blue gray, distant yellow flecks lingering. Her pink hair, twisted into her usual buns, shined more rose gold then magenta. Her nose had shrunk to a narrower bridge and petite point. But most notable of all were the gold-like fangs peeking out of her parted lips.

One became Three.

Kade stumbled back. "You're... *You're* the third? But Matilda Moore *died*—"

"My name is Morrígna, and I am the triple goddess remade," she seethed.

Kade reared closer, his demand echoing across the wasteland. "How? *Why?* We were winning, Linx. We were ridding Sorin of darkness."

"My name is Morrígna!" she screamed.

Kade's mind trembled at the baritone.

He shook his head, disbelief chilling him to the bone. The Linx he knew. The friend he had. The teammate he'd fought with. She was *gone*. He had a thousand questions and more worries, yet he could only manage one.

"Why?" he asked again.

Morrígna paced. "Because a millennium ago, I was jilted. After the One split us into Three, I was born the measly, insignificant witch, Matilda Moore with no memories of being a goddess, no powers aside from watered-down magic in my coven, while Macha had the Otherworld and the love of witches and Badb had demons, darkness, and Hel. But what did I, have? *Nothing!*

"When the curse fell, I discovered what I was while searching for Odin. I felt him die and our fated bond fractured, and yet, I lived. Lost and broken, I found the same altar the Verena's discovered. I'd read about their bargain with the Blood Goddess and demanded the same. *Bring him back.*"

Emotions twisted Linx's features. Rage warred in her eyes while tears welled within them. Her body shook, and yet she remained in place, like her tale had put her in trance.

"Yet, Macha recognized me for who I truly was. *Nemain*, she'd said, *it is you*. Then, she offered me something greater than love."

A chill ran down Kade's spin. "What was that?"

Linx's lips split into a sinister smile. "Power."

The earth trembled under Kade's boots, and thunder rumbled above.

"If I helped Macha ruin Badb's reputation, she'd restore me to a god-like being. Though, she underestimated me. She thought I was a naïve and obedient follower to her cause. Of course, I made sure I appeared as so. I helped plant seeds of doubt in this world. As Matilda Moore, I had access to research regarding the vampyrs before the curse and burned it all. It was I who made sure only a single stanza lived on from the prophecy, enough to keep hope and chaos in balance. I weaseled my way into witch politics and influenced the use of birth order and duty. I orchestrated Riven's alliance with the Sun Goddess, manipulated Circe to darkness so she'd abuse Evelyn."

Kade's hackles rose.

"I whispered the date of your wedding to Riven, even sparked the idea about walking in the sunlight. It is *I* who funneled information who connected the prince to Claus and Circe in the first place. I *tried* to kill your mother, and at least successfully killed Evelyn's parents..." She shrugged. "I did everything in my power to make sure the third borns never succeeded."

"But you failed," Kade whispered. "Evelyn broke the curse."

Linx—no, *Morrígna*—cackled. "No, I've been remade. I didn't trust Macha to truly restore me and knew the only way to regain what I'd been robbed was bringing our souls back together and recreating the One. I almost wouldn't have succeeded if it weren't for your obstreperous and vexing witch, but then Macha's own pride got her in the end—she emerged from the Otherworld, giving me the perfect moment to draw us all back together. The curse may be broken, but the prophecy is not fulfilled. Darkness remains."

"Evelyn and I—"

Morrígna screeched. "Stop saying her name! She is not here at your side, *I* am! You might not see it now, but in time, I hope one day you will, Kade Drengr. The power in your soul was once intertwined with mine—"

"I am mated to Evelyn Carson, and nothing will break that bond or my love for her," Kade growled.

The deranged goddess blinked. Stared at him. Assessed the hills in the distance, gaze churning with calculation. "Time, all he needs is time, Morrígna. And—" Her eyes grew wide, snapping back to Kade. She smiled, the glee sending an eerie chill into the air. "You're the only one who can make her bend the knee, because she'd rather die than hurt you."

Kade gabbed Morrígna by the throat. "I'll not harm her. *Ever.*"

Morrígna laughed. "Oh, but you won't have a choice. You drank the tea."

As he had all the weeks ago.

"It was never Circe in my mind," he said, loosening his hold on her throat. "It was you."

She laughed and flicked her wrist. Immense power knocked Kade in the gut, and he let Morrígna go, dropping to his knees. She thrust her hand up, and the force had him sliding in the wasteland's muck.

"It was impressive when you removed me from your mind, but patience has been a dear friend for all these years." She slunk towards him, her shawl like a breathing, billowing cloud of black mists. Morrígna squatted ahead of him "All I had to do was wait and fool you again, as I have for many, many, many years."

"*No*—"

As if invisible shackles wrapped around Kade's wrists ankles, he couldn't move. He fought against the phantom restraints, but it was no use. His muscles and resolve quivered under the triple goddess's power.

"You will do as I command. Of course, I can't let you kill her thanks to that rather inconvenient mating bond, seeing as I need you. Instead, you'll bring Evelyn Carson to her knees so I may bind her magic. Then" —Morrígna smoothed her hand down his cheek, and Kade recoiled— "you'll rule by my side for the rest of eternity."

Morrígna planted her finger onto Kade's forehead, and pain sliced through his mind like she'd pierced him with a dagger.

He fought, pushed and raged against the darkness.

No. No. No, he chanted to himself.

Obey me, obey me, obey me, Morrígna's voice hissed inside his mind.

Kade growled. He had to fight. But she was stronger. More powerful.

A pulse down the mating bond had him falter forward. It was beautiful and magnificent and precious. Just like his mate.

Kade roared. The goddess's darkness dug deep into the fleshy surface of his mind like talons. He didn't fight the sensation, he inhaled it. Leaned into the pain. For there was only way to endure this.

He let the goddess in.

Morrígna shuddered, her eyes rolling in the back of her head. "Aye, yes, there you are."

She released him, and Kade stood on steady legs. The tent, wasteland, his wound, all of it vanished. Both him and Morrígna returned to the battlefield. Smoke blew to the east.

Kade almost lost his knees at the sight of Evelyn. Tears or nothing of the sort, marred her beautiful face. But he didn't need to see her pain to know. It burned down their bond like acid. Yet, his brave mate didn't falter. She marched towards them with her staff in hand, steely gaze as sharp as any blade.

"Bring her to me!" Morrígna said.

Kade unsheathed his sword and charged.

Evelyn met Kade's blow in a swift, effortless movement. His blue power ignited down his blade and danced with her silver flame. In her eyes, he witnessed the reflection his own.

Glowing and fathomless, it didn't appear like any true part of him remained.

But he was there, fully present despite Morrígna invading his mind. He simply needed to show Evelyn that.

Kade, she whispered down the bond.

He attacked, striking from overhead. Evelyn veered left, his blade running inches from her arm. He growled, but she didn't draw up flame. Kade tried again, bringing his blade down. His mates eyes widened.

Kade backed her closer to Morrígna. He needed her in striking distance.

Please! Evelyn screamed into his mind.

He tried a third time, his next advance the exact same as earlier. Evelyn pivoted and swiped downward, catching his blade with her staff. She paused. Blinked. Recognition rippled across her face. She swept her left foot outward. Kade mirrored the stance.

And his mate smiled.

For they'd practiced this sequence so many, many times during their training.

I'm here, love, Kade said. *I'm here.*

"NO!" Morrígna's cry shook the sky and earth.

"Now!" he shouted.

Evelyn spun, and cast her silver flame towards the goddess. Magic hit her square in the chest, and she stumbled.

She pointed finger at Kade, steam rising from her festering wound. "How dare you disobey me?"

Kade cracked his neck, tilting his head side to side. Morrígna's presence in his mind was like thorny vines that attached to stone. There, but barely. All Kade had to do was *yank*.

Sweat matted at Kade's brow as he grasped hold of the slick power. His muscles quivered as he pressed and push and *crushed* it with his own.

Morrígna crumbled and writhed in pain. Her veins glowed blue as if Kade's power burned her from the inside out.

"What is this?" she cried out. "Your mind belongs to me!"

Kade breathed through his nose, fisting his hand as he continued to push Morrígna out of his mind, destroying her essence in the process.

"I may have let you in," he seethed. "But I never *accepted* darkness."

A snap echoed between his ears as she left his mind completely. Morrígna grew ashen, frantic, scrambling away from Evelyn as she readied her flame engulfed staff.

For Kade believed both light and dark lived in his soul. Neither eclipsed the other, and like the moon shining brightest at night, he'd held onto hope and love.

Evelyn positioned her staff over the goddess's chest, and with the blunt end, pierced her heart. She drove the Gray Wood's bones further and further until she reached the soil underneath, pinning the Morrígna in place.

Kade lay a hand on her shoulder, and he channeled his power *into* his mate. Evelyn cried out as she mustered more magic.

Morrígna's flesh tore away. Her muscles corroded to nothing, revealing her bones. The skeleton splintered and burst, crumbling to ash. Sorin's winds whipped her remains into the air, and Evelyn's flame reached out, scorching the dust until not a spec of the goddess remained.

Evelyn continued to channel her power. Her dark hair twisted in the wind while her eyes glowed. Like she'd fallen into some trance of light and life. Yet, Kade felt her pure heart.

Silver burst in infinite directions. Near the first ever tree, more sprouted. Their white stalks rose to the sky. Branches burst free, splitting their barky exterior. Silver dotted for miles, and the power of light pulsed from them. Wherever it cast its light, demons shifted out of their dark forms. Animals roamed the Void, while the battle continued between mortals and gods.

A forest of ever trees overtook the Void, and Kade's chest expanded at the sight.

Underneath his boots, roots crawled near Evelyn's staff. They dug and parted the earth, ripping a seam into their realm.

Revealing oblivion.

But it was not the Otherworld, Hel or the expanse in between.

Evelyn's had *created* a new realm.

Her intentions filtered down their bond. She needed his power too in order for this to work. Kade rallied it forth and used the natural tug of the moon to grasp the lasting darkness from their realm.

On the battlefield, gods stumbled as Kade pulled them away. They flew through the air, funneling into the opening between worlds Evelyn had forged. For ridding their world of Morrígna wasn't enough. The gods themselves couldn't be trusted.

Together, Kade and Evelyn finally defeated the darkness.

CHAPTER NINETY-FIVE

FOR THE FIRST TIME in centuries, Tovi moved without the curse coursing through her veins.

Blood splattered across her face as she sliced her sword against a god's throat. Droplets landed on her lips and sweetness bloomed on her tongue. An irony tang wafted under her nose, but nothing hissed in the back of her mind. The urge to feed didn't creep up her spine, and Tovi killed another god without conjuring the red haze that had once plagued her vision.

Death hung in the air, and yet, it did *nothing* to her.

Her friends had broken the curse, and Tovi let the tears fall.

She yanked her bloodstone necklace off and thrust it into the mud. The sun kissed her skin, and *bloody hel*, despite the filth coating her, she welcomed its warmth. Tovi had fought for freedom, and now it flushed through her like she had a magic all her own.

Tovi glided across the battlefield with newfound weightlessness. She danced, *Saoirse* her partner, and she chased the tune of the blade as it sang with every kill. She plunged it into an unsuspecting god's heart. Severed a demon's head with it. Struck down vampyrs who—despite *everything*—still fought under Riven's banner.

Coated in the blood of her enemies, *Saoirse* gleamed in the sunlight.

The *sunlight*.

Its rays reflected off the numerous trees sprouting from the once cursed ground. Magnificent. Silver. Tovi's heart pounded with the familiarity of her friend's magic flowing across the battlefield. Trees grew so rapidly, they shot through the fray. Gods snarled as they weaved between them. Demons avoided them as if poison dripped from the luminescent leaves. Nearby scáths crumbled and writhed as the curse left them.

Tovi and her friends had almost won. Yet, one foe remained.

Riven.

"*ARGH!*" a god—Nótt, if Tovi recalled correctly—dug his hands into the dirt.

He clawed his way across the battlefield, fighting the insatiable pull of Kade's power as it *tugged*. Other gods flew through the air and were sucked through a seam of blinding light. Evelyn stood above it, as if she held it open.

The makeup lining his eyes smeared down his cheeks, and blood stained his fangs. "Help me, mortal! I am the God of Night, and I command you!"

The authority in his voice grated against Tovi's resolve. It echoed in her ears, joining the voices of the other males that had tried to command her over the centuries. She reared closer, fisting her hands at her sides. Tovi raised her foot in the air, readying to stomp on his hands with her boot, but halted.

Her heart pounded inside her chest. The anger in the god's gaze mirrored her own, but she refused to also embody the same cruelty the gods possessed. It *was* a thread of darkness, and she'd not let it weave into her soul.

Tovi lowered her foot, inch by inch. She inhaled, exhaled, and decided she'd let fate handle him instead. She turned on her heel and marched away, not daring to look back as he was sucked into the air and torn from this realm.

"No!" Yards away, Riven raged. He jumped into the air, trying to grasp hold of the gods as they tumbled past. "Bring back my wife and child! I demand what was promised!"

Tovi's chest tinged with pain. She hated this end. *Loathed* it. Her brother's rationale crumbled before her. She tried to recall the brother who'd left worms in her boots and whispered about faeries. Tried to envision Riven with a sketchbook, admiring the wonder of Drystan before the curse.

But that version of him no longer existed. Perhaps it had died with Iona and Oli.

His chest heaved. Madness churned in his eyes. He searched and searched the battlefield, Tovi fell flush behind a tree, hiding from sight.

"Where are you, dear sister?" Riven's voice cracked as he shouted over the chaos. "I have something of yours."

The warmth Tovi had relished in vanished. She peeked behind the tree, assessing Riven. Her heart skipped a beat. She didn't move, didn't breathe.

Eldrick fought—*hard*—against a unit of vampyrs. Four against one. They had him surrounded, and for every blow he blocked, another cut him down from behind. Tovi's heart swelled at the sight of Eldrick's unbending resolve. Despite the wounds streaking across his body, calm etched into his determined expression. Axe in hand, jaw tight, that was the male she'd fallen in love with. The one who held her heart.

Yet, Riven knew it. He watched Eldrick fight like he witnessed entertainment. He laughed and searched the battlefield again.

"You took Iona and Oliver away from me and *kept them away!*" Her brother shook. Angry tears streamed down his face. "If I can't have happiness, sister, neither can you."

Riven turned, chest heaving. He held out his sword and stalked closer, intent gleaming like his sword.

"Eldrick!" Tovi shouted his name, her throat turning raw. "*Eldrick!*"

But he didn't hear her at this distance, nor did Riven as he fell into a trance of vengeance.

Live, Eldrick had said.

But there was no breathing in this world without him. Tovi refused to shed a curse only to accept another.

Tovi stifled a broken cry. Her healed homeland seeped into her leathers, the new soil crusted her under nails. Feathers brushed against her fingers, and Tovi froze. A bow and arrow rested by her hand. She'd been running and *fighting* for so long, but the weapon abandoned by another warrior reminded her of whom she'd first been in this land.

A *survivor*.

Not a vampyr, princess, or queen.

The winds shifted, as if Drystan sang, *yes, yes, yes*.

An idea formed. In the past, Tovi had tried to reason with Riven. Met him in battle. *Fought* him countless times. Perhaps Tovi had held onto hope that he'd find a different light than foretold in the prophecy. Hope nor fate were to blame, for Riven had made his choice. Because, Tovi realized, they were nothing alike. Love, regardless of the curse and everything she'd endured, lived in her heart. It didn't poison. It didn't fester. It bloomed. Beautiful and vibrant and *pure*. Like the forest flourishing around her, Eldrick had planted the ever lasting seed in her soul, and she'd not lied all those weeks ago—she'd kill for him.

Even if it was her twin brother.

"Come out, Tovi!" Riven said. "Show yourself! I want to see the look in your eyes when I spill his blood!"

Tovi grasped hold of the bow and arrow and fell back into the fighting. She used others to hide behind, dashing from one warrior to the other. She didn't let Riven find her. *See her.*

For she hunted, and he was her prey.

She darted behind another tree. She had to get closer, at better shooting range.

For Tovi'd not kill him as a queen or an angry sister, blade against blade. She'd end him in the way she began in this land.

Tovi nocked an arrow. She had *one* shot.

A stillness entered the air. The world around her changed to the winter months seven hundred years ago. Snow kissed her cheeks. Her mark stood thirty yards away. He and Eldrick fought, *moving.* Riven seethed. Eldrick bared his teeth. Tovi waited. For the right moment, the perfect shot—

Tovi inhaled.

Exhaled.

Her breath plumed in the air as she released the arrow. The bow string echoed, and time slowed as the arrow flew through the air. It whizzed past fighters, the shaft flexing side to side. Beyond the iron head, Riven searched and searched and searched—

The arrow shot through his throat. Riven rocked back, stunned. He dropped his sword, reaching for the intrusion lodged into his neck.

Tovi's eyes stung with tears. Pain lanced through her heart. Her brother, her twin, someone she'd once loved, fell to his knees.

As she approached, Riven stared at her in disbelief.

Apologies sat on her tongue, but she muttered none of them. They'd been destined for this moment. Riven *had* hurt countless. The woman he murdered in Callum. Evelyn's parents. Lou. The curse was broken, but Tovi had slayed the last shred of darkness still left in Sorin.

"Do you think I'll see them again?" he said, words wet with blood.

Tovi swallowed. She gave him one last piece of love, choosing grace. "Yes, brother, I do."

He shuddered with her words and slacked.

Eldrick laced his fingers into hers. Tovi leaned into his touch, *needed* it. They fell forehead to forehead, breathing the same air.

A chant rippled across the battlefield.

"Queen Tovi!"

"Queen Tovi!"

"Queen Tovi!"

The war was won. No curse. No demons. No gods. No angry corrupt tyrants. It was over. The prophecy was fulfilled.

EPILOGUES

THE SCHOLARS

ONE WEEK LATER

A WARM BREEZE BLEW through Drystan's valley, the first blades of wheat shimmering in waves. Evelyn and Kade had broken the curse seven days ago, and already, Sorin flourished. No Void stood to the north, and Lorkan swore he spied the glinting ever trees and their silver leaves.

Above, the sky bled a bright blue, and late spring storms rumbled closer to the mountain peaks. Birds bobbed in the air, their song as joyous as the celebrations overtaking the continent.

Nothing compared to the occasion of witnessing Fjall Pack return to their family and loved ones, though. Lorkan had accompanied most of his pack members to their respective villages, saying his goodbyes as they started a new chapter themselves, where everyone called all of Sorin home.

One of the last of his pack stood at his side, glacier-blue eyes focused on Thorn Village, situated straight ahead.

"You're usually the one with words, Alvin," Lorkan said.

The edges of his friend's lips twitched. "Just soaking in the sun is all."

But Lorkan detected the uncharacteristic apprehension in Alvin's tone. "It'll be alright, you know?"

Alvin released a large huff. "If it's not?"

"There will always be a home somewhere in the Vadon Mountains for you. As your best friend, I'll make sure of it."

"Best?" Alvin snorted. "Can't wait to tell Mya. She'll be so jealous."

Lorkan rolled his eyes. Their vampyr-witch friend had decided to remain in Nūa and help with efforts deconstructing the Wall. Lorkan had also heard rumblings she might act as an ambassador for witch and vampyr relations, and his heart swelled at the prospect.

"Thank you." Alvin tore his gaze away from the village. "For everything you did for me and the others."

"I should be thanking you," Lorkan said. "Your friendship kept me going, and also," he grasped his friend's shoulder, "don't sound as though this is goodbye. I expect you to visit Fika."

Alvin smiled. "So, you asked her?"

"Not yet."

"Aye, but she'll say yes." His friend winked.

Lorkan was counting on it.

The village gates ground as a grove of werewolves left before sunset.

"There she is," Alvin whispered.

Ahead, a female werewolf with the same light hair and piercing eyes emerged from the walls of the village. She led a mule as it pulled a cart full of supplies. As if sensing Alvin and Lorkan, she peered east and halted on the path.

Alvin took a step forward, and after a tentative and cautious reunion, love and time brought the brother and sister together in a tight, endearing hug.

Lorkan left his friend with a broad smile on his face. Thanks to recent events, Lorkan shifted into his werewolf form. Under the sun. In front of others. And traveled back to Fika, where he was to meet his mate.

Snow didn't cover the rooftops of the quaint town anymore. Colors ranging from plum to crimson to evergreen painted the rooftops. Festive wreaths had been swapped for ones bursting with spring flowers. Lorkan inhaled the place's charm and rallied his nerves.

Blair stood outside Sages and Spines, inspecting the intricate window display. Lorkan paused, taking in her breathtaking beauty for a moment.

With her curls free, she wore a relaxed chestnut-colored button-down shirt tucked into a crimson skirt, held in place by a thick belt. More relaxed, more her than ever before. Too, she'd not stopped wearing the crimson lacquer on her lips, and thank the stars above, because it suited her.

Rook announced his arrival, snapping Blair from her perusing. She smiled at Lorkan, and he couldn't believe how much light had truly surfaced with darkness now defeated. His mate's smile was certainly one of the things that shone brighter.

"Good evening," she said in greeting.

Lorkan planted a kiss on her lips, savoring the taste of her, no matter how quick. Dust clung to her skirt's hem and dotted her shirt.

"How was your day?" he asked.

Blair shrugged. "We're on schedule to remove the last stone tomorrow."

Efforts to restore and rebuild after the war had rushed across the continent, but Nūa was actually endeavoring the opposite. Thanks to Blair's suggestion and leading charge, witches had started tearing down the Wall separating the city from the rest of Sorin. Of course, with no threat to darkness, demons or scáths, the practicality of the structure no longer existed.

But Lorkan understood Blair's true intentions. The witches would enter this new chapter open, not hiding behind stone.

Blair sighed, straightening the collar of his enchanted tunic. "Why are we in Fika exactly?"

Lorkan swallowed, taking her hand. "There's something I'd like to show you."

Amidst the evening bustle, they moved northbound through the current. Restaurants opened their doors, the scent of frying river fish traveled on the wind, and the string lights between buildings twinkled on.

At the end of the street, a small cottage, no longer covered in overgrown vegetation, awaited them. Marigolds overflowed from window boxes, and the sage-painted door didn't match a single one on the street or the next block, complementing the copper details running against the whitewashed stone. He'd spent the last seven nights restoring it, thanks to some help from Mya and Evelyn. The assistance of magic had done wonders.

"It's . . ." Blair trailed off.

Through the window, shelves lined the first room, bursting with books. She turned to him, expectant, and curiosity rushed down their bond.

"What exactly is this place?" she whispered.

"Well, it's mine. I bought it ten years ago." Emotions grew thick in his throat.

Her eyes widened. "How'd you manage that?"

"Endless shifts at the Sheild-maiden," he laughed.

Lorkan stared back at the cottage, soaking in their reflection in the window. "It was meant to be ours, though. A place we could come together as we pursued our work in our own cities."

"And now?" Blair studied him with her fathomless midnight stare.

"It can become our home. You're now a member of the Nūa council, and I'm focused on opening Vísdómr to not just werewolves, but witches and vampyrs. Though our callings are across the continent, it doesn't mean we need to be."

Blair stepped closer. "I see."

Lorkan's heart raced inside his chest. "I can understand if, giving the timing and what it once represented, you'd like nothing to do with it but . . ."

Lorkan dared a glance in Blair's direction. He didn't cheat and check her emotions down the bond. He wished to see them rippling across her face, good or bad.

Tears glistened in her eyes, and she stood on her tiptoes and gave him a kiss. Light and sweet. A warm breeze snaked down the street, tingling with her magic.

"Are you asking me to move in with you?" Blair asked, a smile playing on her lips.

"Yes, I am." He kissed her chin. "What do you say, Blair Carson?"

She shrugged, taking his hand and dragging him closer to the door. "It is perfect, but I'm not sure. Perhaps I need a proper tour inside. Convince me, Lorkan Drengr."

His wolf awakened in his blood, and he smiled, not hiding the fangs that unsheathed after the haughty promise in her tone.

THE LEADERS

ONE MONTH LATER

TOVI AND ELDRICK RACED through the hills of Drystan, their smiles as bright as the sun that shone overhead.

Four weeks had passed since they'd fulfilled the prophecy, and cold hadn't ventured through Tovi's homeland since. Summer lingered in the air, warm and spicy as wildflowers dotted the verdant grass.

Behind them, Drystan Castle stood tall and proud against the mountain it'd been built into. Flecks inside the dark stone glistened. Amethyst banners lined the watchtowers, and dozens of twin flags flapped in the wind. Wagons filled with rubble traveled from the top down the windy road to the village, construction on adding more windows for light well underway.

Tovi had promised the last time she stood in Drystan Village, the castle would be hers. She'd fulfilled that oath, along with so much more.

She'd abolished arranged marriages, naming the act after Lady Anastasia and her bravery. Families who continued the archaic practice faced prison time. Lords had grumbled when they'd heard the news, but no one seemed inclined to vex the queen when she'd helped break the curse, leading Drystan into a new era. Female vampyrs arrived daily to Drystan Village, intent on finding their freedom. Cas and Bran also reported many venturing to Sorin, excited to explore the continent.

Tovi dismounted from her horse near a gathering of trees. Ahead, the river roared to life as mountain snow melted, filling its banks with a chilly current.

"Where should we ride to next, my king?"

Eldrick snatched her waterskin, rolling his eyes. "I still haven't agreed to the title, dove."

"I didn't ask, I bestowed." She raised a brow.

Sweaty from an hour of riding, Eldrick's fresh and spicy scent lingered heavier in the air. Tovi inhaled it as he stepped closer.

It'd been only four weeks, yet her mate thrived here. He'd fallen into his duties with ease. Rebuilding the village. Managing repairs and supplies needed throughout the kingdom. He even met with those demanding an audience. Sven, who'd moved back into the castle with Opal and the littles, had also commented on Eldrick's naturalness amongst their kind. The castle had warmed to him, and he'd become a whispered name amongst vampyrs. To Tovi's delight, Drystan's silk suited his muscular frame, too.

"Must I heed to all my queens commands?" Eldrick asked, delight gleaming in his eyes.

Tovi reached out and traced his sharp jaw. "Not all of them, but this one . . ."

". . . really means something to you," he finished with a sigh. "I could simply be your consort or a prince even. I don't need a title, Tovi."

"You deserve it, Eldrick," she said, counting the rivets in his eyes. She placed a hand on his chest. "We're equals in this."

Eldrick softened at her words. "I know, dove."

Tovi's heart skipped a beat at the nickname. She wasn't sure she'd ever tire of hearing it, not when fate and the prophecy had brought them together. Restoring her kingdom was one thing, but having Eldrick at her side made it all the more magnificent.

Eldrick stepped closer, thrusting the waterskin into the grass. He threaded loose strands of Tovi's hair through his fingers, studying her lips. "You look happy."

"I am," she whispered.

Eldrick placed two fingers under her chin and tilted her head up. He placed his lips against hers, and soon their sweet sighs turned into hunger. Their hands explored. A grumble rumbled through Eldrick's chest. Tovi released a satisfied hiss. Clothes came off. Their boots thudded to the ground.

Tucked behind a tree, Tovi and Eldrick fell to the soft plush grass and entangled their naked limbs as they enjoyed one another. The sun beat across Tovi's back, ignited the spark in Eldrick's gem eyes, and warmed them both.

Eldrick's kiss screamed his devotion. His fingers found her pleasure, drawing unabashed gasps from Tovi that rang with the songbirds.

Warm and ready, Tovi straddled Eldrick and sank onto his length in one swift motion, and Eldrick groaned as he stared up at her. Tovi rocked her hips, relishing the feel of him inside her and chasing the glorious friction. Their bodies buzzed as the thread between their souls awakened.

Eldrick peppered kisses across her collarbone and up the slope of her neck. His hold on her waist tightened, and he encouraged her to quicken her speed. One hand dipped where their bodies joined, finding Tovi's bundle of nerves.

Her breaths came out more like whimpers. She whispered his name. Lay her forehead against his. The surrounding land flourished like their love, and Tovi's fangs released.

They'd not yet completed their bond, and Eldrick's eyes widened. She felt his length twitch. The tightening of his hands, and the scent of need perfuming the air.

This, in the land they saved. Under the sun. Without a worry clinging to either of them.

Tovi lowered closer to his throat, running her fangs up the slope of his neck. Eldrick entangled his fingers in her hair, encouraging her descent. Tovi's baser instinct to feed rose in one mighty wave.

She lapped her tongue over the perfect spot and sank her fangs into Eldrick.

Euphoria rushed to her core. Sweet basil and spearmint coated her tongue. Tovi rocked her hips as she drank, feeding from her mate. Eldrick growled, and his wolfish claws sprouted from his fingertips and dug into her flesh.

"I love you," he whispered into her ear, words ragged.

A sacred rawness pulsed between them, tugging the thread between their hearts closer and closer—

Tovi burst into a thousand pieces. Eldrick unraveled beneath her.

Their mating bond pulled insatiably taut, weaving with their past, present and future. The thread burned a magnificent green, pulsing with everything they'd endured together. It vibrated with strength, enough to withstand the test of time.

Entangled in one another's arms, Tovi and Eldrick didn't move from their spot in the hills. Fireflies dotted the grass, and the peaceful evening descended across the land.

Tovi traced her fingers across Eldrick's chest. "We'll need to discuss tonics now. Conceiving is far more likely between a mated couple."

He stared down at her. "I'm already taking a tonic."

She reared up, resting on her forearms. "For how long?"

Eldrick shrugged. "Since I was fourteen or fifteen. Its custom for werewolves to start taking one during their teens. It's a daily practice."

"Females *and* males? Can you somehow bring that custom into Drystan?"

Eldrick snorted. "If my queen commands it. Do you still want children?"

After everything, the bond seemed to buzz with.

Tovi nodded. "I want to build a family, with you."

"Then why the discussions of tonics?" A wry smile played on his lips.

"Because all of this is new, even us." Tovi shook her head. "You are also very young compared to me."

"We don't need to wait on my account." Eldrick tucked hair behind her ear. "If you're ready, I'm ready. I swear, Tovi, we can venture any journey together."

Tovi's heart hammered in her chest. She'd come so far, and the future before held so much promise, she refused to hold back on the possibilities. "No tonics then?"

Eldrick's face split into a wide-brimmed smile. "No tonics."

Tovi and Eldrick returned to the castle and enjoyed dinner with their family. Sven and Opal pried on where they'd disappeared to. Brynn and Juni giggled as servants tried to serve them. Cas and Bran arrived late, per usual, but with the best wine. A warm breeze escaped through the open windows of the dining room, snaking around Tovi's ankles.

It was like the land gave her a parting hug, reminding her of what she'd achieved.

THE PROTECTORS

ONE YEAR LATER

LAUGHTER AND LIGHT, DESPITE the late hour, seeped through the Shield-maiden.

Four seasons had passed since Evelyn and Kade had defeated the darkness. In the last few days, the heat of summer had begun to eclipse the crisp spring, leaving Evelyn and company sweaty and triumphantly spent after hours working to rebuild Sorin.

With the help of Blair's *danu*, they'd traveled farthest west of the Vadon Mountains, east in Nūa, and to the uncharted territories of Drystan to assist Tovi and Eldrick in rebuilding the land hit most by the Blood Curse.

No matter the miles trekked or the homes they reconstructed, one mighty truth remained absolute: Evelyn and Kade had vanished demons, darkness, the curse, and even the gods from their realm.

Darkness and light existed in balance once again. Where the Void had stood, a silvery forest now flourished between Sorin and Drystan.

The Forest of Ev.

Evelyn rolled her eyes at the name. That was all Kade, who'd coined the name in meetings with other alphas and newly appointed Elders. Tovi, too, boasted about "the forest her best friend had created," only reinforcing the name amongst vampyrs.

Evelyn had worked hard at outrunning titles, but this one she'd have to accept, for she'd already spied it on newly rendered maps. Renderings depicted the tree's silver leaves, too, reminiscent to the color of her flame, a power that still remained in her blood, as powerful as ever, but far less eager.

Not only had the life of new light driven out the darkness, but it also created a beacon for a promising, brighter future. Witches, werewolves and vampyrs now traveled through the forest, and it stood less so as a divide, but a stretch of land that brought Sorin and Drystan together—two neighbors entering a new chapter as a united continent.

Delightful music started in Shield-maiden. Evelyn smiled to herself as Todd teased Belle endlessly, earning a chorus of laughter from their friends. She peered over at Kade, finding his kind, amber eyes already on her.

Marry me, he said down the bond.

Without a moment's hesitation, Evelyn said, *Yes.*

Kade smiled. He practically beamed in the tavern as he rose from his seat. "If you'll all excuse me, I have to get ready for a wedding."

"A wedding?" Bétar asked. "Moons, who's getting married?"

"Kade and I are," Evelyn said, not breaking eye contact with him.

Their table of friends, new and old, stilled. They blinked, attention jumping between Evelyn and Kade.

"When exactly *is* this wedding?" Todd asked.

"Tonight," Evelyn said, unable to hide her smile. "At midnight."

Her cheeks ached, and Kade didn't object. He kissed her cheek in farewell and left her with a stunned table.

The next two hours became a frenzy of excitement and preparation. From chatter, Evelyn learned Kade got ready inside Lār, allowing her to use their cottage.

It all passed in a fantastical rush. The place. Her dress. Evelyn refused to make too much of a fuss. She simply wished to call Kade her husband and hear him say the word *wife*.

Belle helped with her hair. They kept it simple. Evelyn's dark waves cascaded over her shoulders while the sides were brushed back and tucked behind her ears.

Blair secured the dress.

It was more a silk slip than gown, something one usually wore *under* their attire. Yet, with a touch of magic, Blair shifted its darker color to an ivory, leaving Evelyn draped in a soft, romantic fabric.

The sheer sleeves were slightly ballooned, airy, and clasped at her wrists with three dainty buttons. Her bodice was loose, too, and the neckline plunged to the center of her breastbone. Buttons lined the tighter waistband and continued down the center of her dress until they reached her thighs.

There, they stopped and the slit started, allowing Evelyn to walk with ease as the dress trailed behind her.

In a blink, Evelyn stood at the end of the start of her next chapter. Her heart raced inside her chest—not in fear, but eagerness.

Ahead, a mossy path snaked through the trees. Fireflies dotted in the air, and candles, lit with Kade's blue power, lined the path. Amongst the branches of pine and evergreens, the different colored lights illuminated the jeweled tones of the forest.

It smelled, looked, *felt* like home.

Like not only the right choice, but *theirs*. No prophecy. No arranged union. No Elders or alphas pushing them together. Tonight, and henceforth, belonged to Evelyn and Kade.

A gentle coolness overtook the forest of the Vadon Mountains, as if it heard Evelyn's thoughts.

"Are you ready?" Blair on her left.

"More than anything," Evelyn whispered, giving her sister a reassuring smile.

Blair and Belle took turns giving her fierce, tight hugs and then continued up the path without her.

Moments later, the steady beat of drums boomed in the distance. Slow, methodical. The moss turned a brighter shade of green, the trees turning towards Evelyn, and Kade's magic grew brighter, as if beckoning her closer.

Evelyn planted a bare foot on the moss and white-belled flowers began blooming wherever her toes touched.

As she climbed the path, Kade's magic tickled her ankles and kissed her cheeks. She smiled, unable to hold back the flaring happiness scorching through her being.

Her fated. Her love. Her soon-to-be husband.

I'd do it all again, Kade said down the bond, long before she saw him.

Everything? Evelyn challenged.

All of it. There's nothing I'd change of our story, love.

Evelyn laughed, shutting her eyes as Kade's nickname caressed her entire being. It was one word, but the gravity of it was true and unbending.

Running. Crossing paths in Callum. Falling for one another as Saige and Cyrus. Fighting to be together again. Rebelling against their homelands' expectations.

Evelyn, too, wouldn't have it any other way. Everything they'd been through had strengthened their love for one another. Just like this night, they'd weaved their own story, their own path.

Evelyn continued to climb, and around a cluster of redwoods, she reached the cusp of the hill, she spotted him.

I'd have it no other way, too. I love you, you Kade Drengr.

He smiled, wide and beaming, and the glimmer in his golden eyes outshone the stars.

Evelyn couldn't fight the stinging in the corner of her eyes—Kade was a beautiful, handsome male. He wore an all-black tunic and trouser set, leather sleeves snug against his broad chest. His golden hair, completely let down, framed his face. Evelyn twitched to run her hands through his beard.

Still beastly. Still roguish. Still *him*.

Only their friends and family stood in attendance—Todd, Belle, Lorkan, Blair, Kade's parents, Bétar, Yen, Eldrick, and Tovi. The eldest Drengr brother stood at Kade's side while Drystan's queen stood at the center with her swollen belly, ready to marry Evelyn and Kade.

Evelyn had to focus on her steps—they were hurried, *eager.*

Fucking flames, who cared.

Everyone giggled as she rushed to Kade. He outstretched his hand, and when their skin touched, something zapped between them.

Power, love, and *promise*.

Tovi recited words, but Evelyn registered few. She was lost to Kade's stare. The trees, stars, and their family faded. The two of them stood alone in vast light of their realm, two beings who'd found the truest of unions—*love*—and defeated the darkness.

Tovi took their clasped hands and wrapped a braided cord around them. "Above you are the stars, and below you is the earth . . ."

"Like the stars, I vow to love you and provide a constant source of light," Evelyn whispered.

"And like the earth, I vow to love you and provide a firm foundation for us to grow," Kade said, stepping closer.

He didn't wait for Tovi's permission or some great declaration they were husband and wife, for their mating bond flared to life, an indication enough they were tied together in all ways.

Kade grasped hold of Evelyn's face, and his lips crashed to hers. They kissed.

For their days past and the future they'd created together.

THE END

ACKNOWLEDGEMENTS

I'd first like to thank my husband, Drew. Thank you for supporting me while I wrote this series. The third and final book challenged me unlike the others, and yet you kept encouraging me each step of the way. You gave me grace when I needed it, took over cooking duties too many times, and didn't bat an eye as I continued to work at night. This series would not exist without your continued love and support. Thank you, love.

I'd also like to thank N. Patel Baxi. You've been with this series since the beginning, read all the many drafts, answered all my plot-related questions and listened to way too many crazy ideas. I truly believe *To Rise & Rebel* would not exist without your writerly input and author friendship. Thank you!

As always, my family and friends remain supportive. Thank you for checking in on me and dragging me out of the house when I needed to leave the writing cave.

To my editors, Mallori and Krista. Thank you Mallori for bearing with me during the early stages of this horrendous monster of a novel. I appreciate your time and discussion. Krista, I truly can't thank you enough for your patience while editing this book. You stuck with me until the very last chapter, and I'll be forever grateful. Thank you!

Perhaps I'm biased, but my Street Team rocks. Thank you for being the champions of this series and double thanks for being excited, not frightened, when I teased about how long the trilogy's conclusion would be.

Last but not least, thank you to *you*, dear reader. Thank you for giving not only this book a chance, but the entire series. It means more than you know.

ABOUT THE AUTHOR

A lover of fantasy since childhood, C.C. discovered her passion for storytelling during high school. With a bachelor's in creative writing and psychology plus a master's in mental health counseling, she likes to blend romantic fantasy elements with an understanding of the human psyche. Beyond writing, she's obsessed with a good latte, and can often be found enjoying one with her husband as they set out on adventures of their own, traveling to various places fit for a fantasy-novel backdrop.

If you want to stay up to date on C.C.'s book news, updates, and bonus content, sign up for her newsletter at authorcctyler.com or follow her on Instagram.

instagram.com/authorcctyler